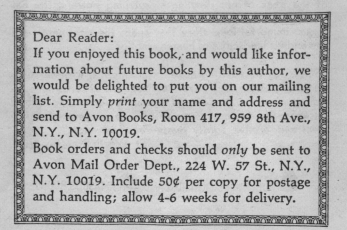

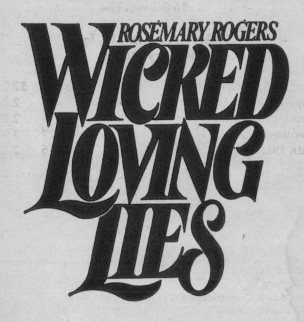

ROSEMARY ROGERS

WICKED LOVING LIES

AVON
PUBLISHERS OF BARD, CAMELOT AND DISCUS BOOKS

To Bet with love

AVON BOOKS
A division of
The Hearst Corporation
959 Eighth Avenue
New York, New York 10019

Copyright © 1976 by Rosemary Rogers
Library of Congress Catalog Card Number: 76-41555.
ISBN: 380-00776-2

First Avon Printing, October, 1976
Twelfth Printing

AVON TRADEMARK REG. U.S. PAT. OFF. AND IN
OTHER COUNTRIES, MARCA REGISTRADA,
HECHO EN U.S.A.

Printed in the U.S.A.

PROLOGUE

The Rebels

As soon as the light began to fade, the mist crept in from the forest that bounded the far end of the great park. It was just as if it had lain hidden there crouched among the densely growing trees until the approach of nightfall sent it moving towards the huge house that dominated a rise in the gently sloping ground—sending long, exploratory grey streamers out at first to curl insidiously around the stone walls; and then, growing bolder, advancing like a gauzy cloud until soon the forest was quite cut off from view, and there was only the grey-white mass pressing against the windowpanes. It almost seemed to be waiting—angry because it could not penetrate stone and glass and wood, but patient, too. . . .

Mrs. Sitwell hurried to pull the heavy velvet drapes together, shivering as she did so despite a roaring fire in the fireplace.

"Never did like the country very much! It's almost like it was *too* quiet, you know? And then the fogs here—ain't like the London fogs—at least you can see the street lights shining, all yellow and cheerfullike. But out here—" She lowered her voice as she glanced towards the vast, canopied bed that stood in one corner of the room. "Tell me, Mrs. Parsons, how is it that *he*—" a jerk of her head, "His Grace, I mean—well, it just don't seem natural for him to be down there in his study, writing letters, with his own wife dying up here."

Mrs. Parsons's thin lips seemed to disappear into her seamed face as she pursed them. "His Grace has his own ways—and his own reasons. *You* couldn't know, of course, you've only been here three weeks. But I could tell you—"

3

The woman hesitated for a moment, her fingers tightening over themselves; but then, as the desire to talk to someone after all the lonely months proved too much for her, she burst out, "I could tell you—it's a great deal stranger, all this, than anyone could guess! And of course I've been with the family—His Grace's family that is—for years. I was here when he brought her here as his bride, and I was still here when he brought her back from the Americas. *I* could have told, even when I was a mere slip of a girl myself, that there was something wrong. . . ."

The woman who lay so still in the depths of the big, dark bed heard them whispering by the fire. Over the sound of her own breathing—each breath more difficult to draw than the last—she heard words:

"Brought her here from Ireland, he did. He was only Lord Leo then, and no one ever dreaming he'd ever come into the title like he did. . . ."

She was in that half-world that lies between coma and reality, and when she heard the woman say something about Ireland, her mind slipped back easily through time; reliving the beginning was so much more pleasant than waiting for the end. Whirling pictures slid through her mind, some of them all too clear, others seeming to curl and blur about the edges like old letters.

Ireland, and her girlhood, when no one had called her Lady Margaret or Your Grace. It had been Peggy or Peg then. Pretty Peggy, the young men had named her, bringing blushes to her cheeks. And after all, in spite of what all Irishmen referred to as "the troubles," life had not been too unpleasant.

What did anything matter as long as she was young and pretty with all of her life still stretching endlessly and excitingly ahead of her? Even her brother Conal's frowns and carping didn't matter *too* much as long as she could escape from him to go down to the village for her stolen, secret confessions to Father MacManus or to visit some of her father's old tenants. Things were different since her father, the earl of Morey, had taken sick and finally died—without, thankfully, knowing what Conal had done to keep the lands

4

for himself. Turned Protestant, renouncing his own true faith—how could he?

"I have to think of myself now—don't you see that? And of you too, sister, although you do not seem to appreciate that fact. Catholics cannot inherit land. Would you rather see all that is ours and has been ours for generations pass to the English Crown? Someone has to be sensible!"

And she tried not to dwell on the fact that Conal took to going up to Dublin Castle, the seat of the English Government in Ireland, spending far too much time with the English officers who were their age-old enemies and oppressors. She hated the English! They were cold, cruel and arrogant, and they acted as if they owned even the lush green Irish earth they walked on. Conal's mother had been English, which perhaps accounted for his predilection for that hated race, but *her* mother had been French—a pretty, small, dark-haired woman who had always smelled faintly of lavender or verbena water.

Peggy had been thinking of her mother that afternoon when Conal surprised her crossing the brook barefoot, her faded skirts kilted up around her calves.

Why couldn't maman have lived? It was lonely, sometimes, without another woman to talk to, with only the sound of the chill wind blowing like a banshee around the crumbling walls to keep her company at night. If only—

Conal's harsh, angry voice had cut rudely across her thoughts then.

"It seems I must forever be apologizing for my little sister! You see, my lord, she lacks not only discipline but also the care of a gently bred woman to instruct her in the manners and deportment of a lady."

And looking up, with her face flushed with embarrassment, she had encountered those pale blue eyes for the first time. Eyes set deeply under blond brows in a face of chiseled perfection that was almost too beautiful to belong to a man.

"No use trying to run off like some startled wood-nymph, sister. We've caught you."

The young Englishman's arm, thrown in comradely fash-

5

ion about her brother's broad shoulders, dropped as he stared at her measuringly.

"Leo, may I present my sister, Lady Margaret Galvan? Lord Leofric Sinclair."

Two months later, she and Leo had been married. And within three months, she had left Ireland, never to return to it again.

Her shallow breathing quickened as the shell of the woman who had once been "pretty Peggy" moved one thin, bloodless hand as if to ward off memories that now came thick and fast, flooding her tired mind with scenes that, like watercolors, ran one into the other: Conal's loud, blustering voice, shouting at her, threatening her; the feel of his heavy hands as he beat her into shivering, resigned submission; Leo's white, soft hands, the heavy rings glinting on long fingers—his voice thick with the liquor he had consumed so heavily before he could bring himself to come to her; she herself lying trembling in bed, her thin lawn nightshift feeling clammy against her perspiring, shrinking flesh.

How long—how many months (or had it been years?)—before she was woman enough to understand that their relationship was not a normal one?

Fashionable husbands and wives did not seek each other's company too much. And if she slept alone more often than not, this, too, was nothing out of the ordinary.

She had no one to talk to—no older woman to warn her or give her advice as to what she should expect from marriage. All Conal had said, gruffly, was, "You remember your promise to obey your husband and to submit to him in everything. That's all you need to know, little sister." And he and Leo had exchanged a look over her head that she hadn't understood—not then.

After they had left Ireland, Peggy's life was too full of new things, and far too confusing, for her to want to think too closely about her sudden marriage and the cold, remote man who was her husband.

There was the big house in the country near Cornwall where Leo took her first, to meet his family. His father, the duke of Royse, was an ailing, irascible old man, who had merely raised one bushy eyebrow as he nodded and growled,

"That's right—and high time, too! Told you marriage was the only thing."

Leo's older brother, the Viscount Stanbury, was off in Europe somewhere, but his younger brother, Anthony, was kind to her, shaking her hand vigorously as he stammered his good wishes.

After Cornwall, they traveled about a great deal so that she was always tired. Visits to relatives and friends and Leo leaving her alone with them most of the time. Finally, the months in London—a giddy whirl of fittings for dazzling new gowns and one activity after another until she felt that she never got enough sleep and was relieved that Leo left her alone so much. Leo's sister, Lady Hester Beaumont, took her everywhere and saw that she met everyone and wore exactly the right clothes and jewels for every occasion. They had the use of the duke's magnificent house in London, and Peggy learned to keep household accounts and manage a large staff of servants.

But she had barely had time to become used to the routine of life in London when they were on the move again, this time a journey that meant crossing the ocean, for Leo's father had deeded him a large plantation in the colony of North Carolina, in America.

Leo was handsomer than ever in those days despite the faint lines of dissipation that were beginning to show in his face. Peggy had grown used to the fact that he was always cold and punctiliously formal to her. She was aware that there were other women who looked at her enviously and whispered that she had one of the few faithful husbands in town. But they could not know that her husband found her so unattractive that he seldom came to her, and then only when he was very drunk; or that he had never once undressed her completely, but fumbled clumsily and hurtfully for her body in the dark as if he could not bear to look upon her face or her nakedness. She had no idea what was supposed to take place between a man and a woman; and when he cursed and swore and hurt her with his groping fumblings, she blamed herself for being inexperienced. Leo was such a perfect, beautiful specimen of a man that the fault had to lie with her. The fact that he preferred the com-

Rosemary Rogers

pany of his cronies she also accepted passively. It was not until much, much later that she really understood what kind of devils drove her husband and the kind of debauchery his twisted nature craved. . . .

In Carolina, Leo had his duties with the army that kept him away for weeks and months at a time. There was an overseer to tend the crops, and slaves to perform every task that needed doing, even to the brushing of Peggy's long, dark hair. She began to read, from sheer loneliness and boredom at first, choosing books at random and with a kind of diffidence (how limited her formal education had been) from the enormous library. And then, caught up and taken beyond herself by the sudden treasure-trove of knowledge that lay at her fingertips, she began to read quite avidly. Books on art, on history, on philosophy and even music opened a whole new world to her starved, seeking mind. She was never lonely now, with her secret world to retire to; and with some of her earlier agonizing shyness and anxiety disappearing, she began to make friends with the families of neighboring plantation owners, finding that making conversation was not so difficult after all if one had something to talk about.

Leo, when he was home, expressed himself pleased at her emergence from her "dull little shell," and Peggy herself, as she became used to the lazy, leisurely life, was almost content.

Until . . .

She was to agonize over it later. To ask herself over and over if it had been worth it, being brought to sudden awareness of her womanhood and deeply hidden passions only to have everything taken away from her again. She could never even regain that fleeting sense of contentment that had come with her very ignorance of what living meant.

But at first, when it happened, she felt only stark, unreasoning terror, and a sense of unreality that kept her alive for she did not fall into screaming hysterics or try to flee in useless panic as some of the other women did, to be brought down bleeding and staring-eyed, her skull split open by a tomahawk.

To be taken by Indians! Such a thing only happened to

other people—to the wives and families of small settlers—not to her, not to the Lady Margaret Sinclair, chatelaine of one of the largest plantations in the Carolinas.

"Leo will tell me it was all my own fault," she caught herself thinking stupidly once during the long, forced march that led her and the other captives deeper and deeper into impenetrable forest and swamps. "If I had not felt it my duty to visit that poor little Mrs. Rutherford because she was having her first child and I thought there was no other woman for miles around. And then, after all, there *were*, and I need not have—"

But what was the point of thinking? After a while she concentrated only upon keeping on her feet, for if she fell she would be killed, and she had found, already, that she did not want to die.

Thankfully, her memory blurred—a series of pictures moving faster and faster in her tired mind until abruptly they stopped, focusing on one particular scene, growing brighter and larger, until all she could see was Jean's face, as she had seen it first.

Dark-haired like herself, his eyes were a strange green-grey, like the surface of a lake on a cloudy day. Surprisingly, he had spoken to her first in French.

"Sacre—" And then, biting the next word off with an effort, "What were *you* doing among those unfortunate wretches? Had no one warned you of the dangers you might encounter?"

She was too tired, too numb to respond to his anger, except to wonder dully why he seemed so angry. She said the very first thing that came into her mind.

"You—you are not one of them! But who are you?"

"Nom de Dieu! Questions! And it is I who should be asking them. Do you realize in what kind of position you are, madame?"

"I am safe *now*, though, am I not?" Again she spoke without conscious thought, mesmerized by the angry, intent look in those ice-bright eyes.

Even as she spoke his eyes seemed to change, and something made her start to blush, even though she still could not tear her gaze from his sun-dark face.

9

"I am blood brother to the Iroquois," he said. And then, more softly, almost to himself, he added, "Safe? My soul is as wild as theirs. I would not be too sure of it, madame."

She found out later that she had been a gift from the Shoshone to their Iroquois brother. But by then it did not matter, for he had made her his, in more ways than one.

The women whispered by the fire, never noticing when the shallow breathing came faster, and more convulsively and finally stopped. Their conversation had followed the same pattern as Lady Margaret's thoughts.

"But what happened *then?* I mean, it wasn't hardly the poor creature's fault, was it? Being carried off by savages and all—"

"It wasn't *that!* And mind you, you promised not to tell another living soul! No, he took her back, all right, my lord did—paid a princely sum of money for her return, too. And *then,* just nine months later, the boy was born. You mind how my lord must have felt? Never being quite certain. . . ." But the boy had his name, and *she* had the bringing up of him. Let him run wild, too, going off to hunt with the Indians and even live with them for weeks on end."

"But Lord Leo? His Grace, I mean. Surely he—"

"Ah, but he had his duties with the army, you see. And surely you can understand his feelings about the lad? Those were trying times there with riots, and hotheads preaching all kinds of crazy ideas about self-government and all. And you know what it all came to in the end! Revolution. And Lady Margaret, a British Tory's wife, entertaining the army officers and their Tory friends in their home—when all the time, she was a spy for *them,* for those rebels! Yes, and her son, too—for all that he was a mere lad at the time. Only ten or eleven he was, but he would carry them messages. It all came out in the end, of course."

"I never!" Nurse Sitwell breathed the words, licking her lips almost hungrily.

"Oh, it would have been a rare scandal, I assure you, if Lord Leo's father—my lord was the Viscount Stanbury by then for his older brother died in Italy of some fever—well, the duke hushed it all up, and only the family knew the whole story."

"The Frenchman. He—?"

"Ah, that one! It's my guess she'd have stayed with him or run off with him after he'd got the ransom money if he hadn't had a wife and family of his own somewhere. But he came back when they had the revolution. I heard them say she hid him when he was wounded and the soldiers were looking for him everywhere. And that was how it started up again. Him and her and the spying. But Lord Leo caught on when the boy was captured along with some other rebels. And then, of course, to save him, she came back to England, meek as you please; and the family put it about she was suffering from some nervous disorder."

"But you mean she *wasn't* really touched in the head then? She—"

As if suddenly aware that she had said too much, Mrs. Parsons pursed her thin lips.

"Don't you be saying anything like that. She couldn't have been right in the head at the beginning to do what she done, and well you know it! Those Irish. They say she was a papist, too, and never really changed, although she pretended to, just to get herself married to a catch like Lord Leo." She added darkly, "And I've no doubt that son of hers is going the same way, living up in Ireland all these years! He was incorrigible like one of them savages, and well I remember! They wouldn't keep him in Eton, and when my lord found him a tutor here for him and Mr. Philip, his nephew, why—one day he almost killed Mr. Philip with his bare hands! And only because Mr. Philip teased him about being a colonial. It took Mr. Grimes and two of the footmen to drag him off. And after *that* my lord sent him off to live with his uncle in Ireland. Said he didn't want to set eyes on Master Dominic again, and I can't blame him! It's been years now, and no one's seen or heard of him—and a good thing, too, if you want my opinion. I doubt that he's changed, and I used to be frightened to be around him even when he wasn't no more than a boy. Those eyes of his, like grey ice, fair startling they were, taken with his black hair—"

Mrs. Sitwell said suddenly and surprisingly, "Well, but all the same I cannot help feeling sorry for the poor lady. Fancy not setting eyes on your own flesh and blood for years and years, and not knowing what kind of a man he's grown into! *He'd* be the Viscount Stanbury now, I take it?"

Mrs. Parsons frowned.

"That's right. And the more's the pity, for the title ought to be Mr. Philip's by rights. And I've heard even His Grace say so! Ah, now *there's* a handsome, charming young gentleman if there ever was one. You'll see for yourself, I'm sure. But mind you—not a word of what I've been telling you. Family secrets—"

"Ah well, I've heard a great deal of those in all the years I've been a nurse," Mrs. Sitwell said comfortably. "And the reason Dr. Elphinstone recommends me to all the lords and ladies that are his patients is that he knows I can hold my tongue."

Settling deeper into her chair, she encouraged Mrs. Parsons to go on with her reminiscing.

*   *   *   *   *

The duke of Royse was also remembering, the old, implacable rage hardening his still handsome features.

Damn it, why did the bitch take so long to die? Why had he let his passing lust for Conal make him choose his sister for a bride? Shy, innocent Peggy, with her great, wondering eyes. Demure Lady Margaret, who would never question nor make any demands of him. And to think that for years he had congratulated himself on his choice of a wife. She was stupid and country-bred, and slim-flanked and small-bosomed enough so as not to disgust him too much when he forced himself to go to her.

"Take a wife, dammit! I'll not have any ugly scandal attached to our name!" his father had warned him after the episode with a certain young groom. And so he had gone to Ireland and met Conal, and through Conal, his black-haired sister.

"If I had not let her taunt me—if I had not been so damned blind drunk and angry that night. . . ."

But he'd had to teach her a lesson, to make her remember who she was and who he was. That bold-faced little strumpet sitting up in bed without a stitch to cover her as she said

12

softly and innocently, "But Leo, I've become used to sleeping naked. The Indians wear very little, you know."

Instead of being grateful and relieved that he had ransomed her and taken her back, she had spent most of her time crying or mooning around with swollen eyes. She'd tricked him, curse her, damn her! And all the punishment he'd inflicted on her since then could not wipe that out.

After he'd left her that night, bruised and bleeding from the force of his assault on her body, he thought he had cowed her forever. And then, a scant month later, she had announced to him quite calmly across the breakfast table, "I think you'll be happy to know, my lord, that I am expecting a child." Then, as he half rose, she must have read the ugly resolve in his eyes for she continued in the same even voice, "I could not *bear* not to confide our happy news to Mrs. Gordon and some of the other ladies whose husbands are your closest friends. They all wish us well, of course."

At least the child she bore was no progeny of an Indian savage—but he could not be thankful for that; for if it had been, he would have had the excuse and a reason to strangle it. No, she had produced a grey-eyed, black-haired brat who looked like her and might, by the slimmest margin of possibility, be his. And she had never, no matter how he threatened or bullied her, confessed to having been the mistress of that half-French American, even after he came back into her life.

"Why does she cling to her miserable existence? By God, that fool of a doctor said it would be only a matter of hours." And then on the heels of his wish he received its fulfillment with the panted cries of the women upstairs and the scurrying of feet.

For the first time that evening the duke smiled and leaned back in his padded velvet chair. So it was over at last! He had everything prepared—all the necessary papers drawn up and signed and the doctor on his way. If all went well, he would be back in London by morning—no need to spend another night in the country with a corpse and whispering servants for company.

* * * * *

"Well, Leo? 'Pon my soul! I'd hardly expected to find you back in town so soon, after—" Lord Anthony Sinclair, Baron Lydon, let his words trail away into an awkward cough as he lowered his ponderous bulk into the padded leather chair next to his brother in the Select Room at Whites Club.

The duke raised an eyebrow as he studied Lord Anthony's red, perspiring face.

"Indeed, Tony? I would have thought that you of all people would be the least surprised to find me back in town." A certain dryness crept into his voice. "Well? Did you tear yourself away from Prinny's company merely to offer me your condolences?"

Lord Anthony cleared his throat, shifting uncomfortably in his chair.

"Dammit, Leo! Why will you always put a man so deucedly ill at ease? To tell the truth, I *had* half-expected to discover you here tonight. Saves me a trip into the country, y'know, although I daresay, with the funeral—"

"The funeral, my dear brother, took place very quietly this morning as you very well know. And, to forestall any further questions on the matter, I did not feel the need to be present. So, now that *that* is out of the way perhaps you will put me out of my suspense and tell me why you found it necessary to come looking for me."

"Last thing I wanted to do, actually!" Lord Anthony confessed with a sudden burst of frankness. "Why does everything have to happen all at once, eh? But dash it, there was no one else to be the one to tell you, and you know the Prince of Wales thinks a great deal of you—reminded me that you have Chatham's ear—"

Languidly, the duke raised one white, be-ringed hand, causing his brother's words to stumble into silence.

"Peace, my dear brother, peace! I am afraid that I can make no sense at all of whatever you're trying to convey to me. I presume you *did* come here to bring me bad news of some kind? Well, I have found that news of any sort is best delivered quite directly without any frills or evasions." He paused deliberately to take a pinch of snuff and heard his brother sigh heavily.

"You're a devilish cold fish, Leo. Damned if you aren't. Never quite understood—but very well then, no need to give me that cold-eyed stare, I'll come directly to the point. It's your—it's Dominic."

This time he thought he saw a reaction in the duke's cold, composed face, a certain strange gleam in his eyes, making them grow suddenly more brilliant for an instant. But the next moment, the duke had raised one eyebrow as he said calmly, "Indeed? But now you have truly surprised me, Tony. I was told some months ago that that young man had suddenly decided to take off for France in spite of the somewhat turbulent turn of events there. So? What of him?"

This time Lord Anthony was quite blunt, his face flushing.

"He's here. In England. In Newgate Prison, to be exact, facing a charge of treason along with five other Irish rebels. And if you can't do something about it, Leo, there's going to be the very devil of an ugly scandal when he comes up for trial within the next fortnight."

The duke's snuffbox closed with a snap—his only show of emotion. He said softly, "So? And do they know who he is? Has anything been noised abroad yet?"

"He would have been summarily executed after a public flogging, along with some ten or fifteen others, if not for the intervention of a certain Lord Edward Fitzgerald, who informed the major in charge that the man known as 'Captain Challenger' was none other than the Viscount Stanbury and the heir to an English dukedom. Damn it, Leo—no need to look at me that way, *I* can't help the way matters turned out! Fortunately, this Major Sirr proved to be an exceptionally intelligent and discreet man. He had five of the rebel leaders sent here to Newgate, under heavy guard, of course. And they've been permitted to speak to no one, not even to the prison doctor. No exercising in the prison yard, and their meals are pushed in to them through a grating under the door—"

"You may spare me the trivial details, Tony, and relate to me only the facts, if you please."

The duke's voice remained unaccented by any overt feeling, but his fingers had clenched themselves over the

15

head of the slim sword cane he habitually carried. "How many persons, outside of yourself and the Prince of Wales, and this major fellow in Ireland, of course—how many others know?"

Lord Anthony, feeling himself reprimanded as if he had been a schoolboy, sounded a trifle sullen. "I told you—no one. Not even the warden of the prison himself. They are being kept incommunicado; that's not unusual, you know, for those accused of treasonable acts! But the question is, dammit, for how long can the secret be kept? There will have to be a trial, and then—can't you see what the results would be? *I*'m known to be one of Prinny's closest intimates and you—I've heard rumors you're likely to follow Chatham as prime minister if he ever decides to step down. I tell you Leo, you cannot—"

"And I *will* not, my brother. But this, you must admit, is too public a place to discuss such matters. I will order my carriage, and we will go together to the earl of Chatham's house. I think he will still be up. And then, on our—unnoticed, I hope!—way to Newgate Prison we will talk further."

"You are going to tell Chatham then? But—"

Lord Anthony was forced to cut short his expostulation as his brother, summoning a servant, gave the man instructions to have his carriage brought around to the door.

"With a personally signed order from the prime minister himself, I think we will be allowed access to these treasonable Irishmen. And then—we will see."

The duke smoothed one long finger against the line of his jaw, and his voice grew thoughtful. "It will be interesting to see if the young savage I remember has changed very much since he's grown into a man."

*   *   *   *   *

In the beginning the duke, his fastidious senses already offended by the prison stench and the tiny, windowless cell to which he had been escorted, found it hard to recognize any resemblance to a man at all in the emaciated, heavily

16

chained wretch who was half-pushed, half-carried through the iron-studded door.

The light shed by a single, flickering lantern was dim, and it took His Grace some moments to realize that the scarecrowlike, raggedly clad creature who fell back against the door as soon as it had closed was not only manacled hand and foot so that he could hardly stand, let alone move, but gagged as well. So the warden was following his strict instructions to the letter, it seemed! A conscientious man.

The duke had preferred to stand rather than take the single rush-bottomed chair that had been hastily brought in for his comfort. And now, moving leisurely, he permitted himself to take a small pinch of snuff before he reached with his other hand, still gloved, for the lantern.

Still moving slowly and deliberately, he crossed the small space between them, his polished boots rustling the dirty straw. There was no sign of movement, not even a flinching away, from the chained man, even when the duke suddenly held the lantern high, barely inches away from the bearded, bruised face. Or what he could see of a face behind leather straps that held the gag in place.

Was it possible that they had made a mistake, after all? That this was some other rascally rebel who hoped to save his own skin by pretending to be an English viscount?

The duke's thin nostrils wrinkled with distaste. They should have thrown a few buckets of cold water over him before bringing him in here! His eyes, moving over the ragged figure, noticed without surprise the collection of cuts and weals that decorated both his torso and arms.

He said aloud, letting a sneer creep into his voice, "I see that our soldiers are as efficient as usual when it comes to putting down rebellions against the crown! I take it you were persuaded to confess to your part in it?"

There was no answer, nor had he expected any, but the man's head went up at last, and slitted eyes that reflected the lantern light like silver looked into the duke's appraising ones.

"So it *is* you, after all. You should have stayed in France, after all—or did you go there to drum up help for your ridiculous cause?"

The eyes were the same, although the boy of sixteen he remembered had grown taller. They glared defiance and hate at him, precisely as they had done so many years ago when Dominic had said, his voice flat and hard, "And someday I will come back here and kill you, for what you have done to my mother and to me."

But as long as his mother lived, and the threat remained that the duke her husband might send her to Bedlam, Dominic had not dared to return to England.

The duke saw the corded muscles stand out in the young man's throat as if he ached to speak—to cry his defiance aloud, perhaps? Or to beg for mercy? But there would be time enough to remove the gag if he wished it; and for the moment there were things he wished to say first.

"Your mother died last night—a pity there was no time to send for you or that I had no idea you were already on your way here. You'll agree with me that it was a merciful release?"

This time there was a sound from behind the gag that sounded like an animal growl, and the duke smiled.

"Ah yes. I had forgotten how attached you used to be to the poor, unfortunate woman. But time, as you know, has a way of changing most things, and even the strongest bonds must break someday. You should be thankful for *her* sake that she died before she heard what you have been up to." He shook his head, still with the thin smile curving his lips. "No, no, I would not attempt to spring at me if I were you! For chained as you are you would only suffer the further humiliation of falling flat on your face at my feet. As I recall I once had my grooms hold you while they administered the beating you richly deserved for attacking my nephew. I am afraid, Dominic, that your unstable temper comes to you from your mother—and with such a poor inheritance, who knows? For your own sake and the sake of others you might injure, it might be that I could have you committed to Bedlam—"

His eyes studied carefully the effect of his words, but apart from that first instinctive, abortive tensing of his muscles Dominic seemed not to hear him, his eyes now staring stonily over the duke's shoulder.

Royse now lowered his voice slightly and his tone became almost insinuating.

"Come now, I have only tried to make it plain to you what I could and would do as a last resort! But if you are prepared to be reasonable and to curb your animal rages, why—we might talk." He watched the silver-grey eyes that seemed to reflect back the flickering of the lantern without revealing anything that was in their depths, and he continued in the same studiedly reasonable tone, "You can nod, can't you? Well then, if you wish me to remove your gag and promise that you will not subject me to any bursts of your usual insolence, I will do so. You see? I am prepared to be reasonable. You have only to move your head."

There was a long moment when it seemed as if Dominic was determined to be stubborn, and the duke cast about in his mind for other methods. But his face showed nothing of his thoughts, and at last he caught the grudging, almost imperceptible movement he looked for and permitted himself to smile again.

"There, you see? That was not too difficult, was it? It has been a long time since we have had a conversation, you and I. And believe me, we would have done so much earlier if I'd had any notion that your Uncle Conal was letting you run wild and associate with the scum who call themselves the United Irishmen."

Placing the lantern on the chair, the duke went behind Dominic and deftly began to unfasten the leather straps, noticing as he did so that the young man's back was also a mass of cuts and festering wounds. They had really done a good job on him with the "cat"—a pity in so many ways that that meddling Lord Fitzgerald had seen fit to interfere before they finished him off.

There was a certain tenseness in the figure before him that prompted the duke, as the gag loosened and came off, to give him a quick shove with his gloved hand, sending him staggering forward onto his knees.

"There is no need for you to attempt to get up, for with the weight of those chains, you cannot. And I must admit I feel safer this way. Besides—," he walked a little distance away and picked up the lantern once more—"it will do you

19

good to do some penance. I take it that you have gone back to being a papist as your mother was?"

The voice that finally answered him was a husky whisper as Dominic forced movement into his aching jaws and swollen tongue.

"Did you want to speak to me, Your Grace? Or merely to force me into just such ungovernable outbursts of rage as you accuse me of?"

The duke of Royse arched one slim blond brow. "It seems that you have actually managed to acquire some polish, after all! Did your uncle find you tutors in Ireland?"

Dominic's voice was carefully controlled. "My uncle tried to teach me many things, as I think you would know. But in the end I found my own tutors. Is this what you have waited to ask me?"

The duke's face had tightened and his eyes flickered, but he managed to control his rage within him. "My time is short, Captain Rebel. Tell me—why do you Irishmen who call yourself leaders always choose such overly dramatic names? Captain this and Captain that. But in the end you will all be brought to the same state—condemned felons, on their knees to English justice!"

"But an *English* rebel is entitled to stand before a judge, is he not, Your Grace? And before a jury of his peers. I had not thought I would sometime find a use for the grand title that my accident of birth bestowed upon me!"

"I had thought you had some such plan in mind! But be careful. I do not take my name or my titles lightly!"

"What will you do with me then? Have me killed before I can stand trial? Or committed to Bedlam as you threatened? Will you make arrangements to send me gagged into the court? I do not think your English justice, of which we've seen so little in Ireland, will tolerate it."

"You're still defiant, then. I take it you mean to make some brave, impassioned speech about justice and liberty and equality for all before they pass sentence on you? Oh— very gallant! I can tell you've been absorbing all the revolutionary ideas that have unfortunately spread from America to France! But do not think that I will let you drag my name in the dust."

Dominic's voice sounded suddenly tired. "I intend to open the eyes of some of the people in England to the injustice and brutality their armies and corrupt officials practice in Ireland in the name of King George. And if that constitutes dragging *your* name in the mire, then I must tell you, Your Grace, that only the two alternatives I've mentioned before will stop me from doing so."

"I think not!" was all the duke said between his clenched teeth before he strode to the door and called for the jailers.

He waited until they had come back and refastened the gag, and then, drawing off his glove, struck the man the world knew as his son across the face.

In French he said, "If we ever meet again, you are at liberty to call me out for this. But I do not think that we shall."

Outside the night air was clean and cold as the duke of Royse climbed into his carriage where his brother sat anxiously awaiting him.

"Well, Leo? Dammit, man, you had me worried when you took so long! And it's a deucedly cold night too—a good thing I thought to bring my flask of brandy with me. Well, what happened? You look like the devil himself."

"And so I might be called, by some! But I have decided what must be done and left instructions with the warden."

Lord Anthony cast his brother a doubtful, sidelong look. "Pitt's letter helped, eh? Thought it might. *He's* the real ruler of England now the king's health is failing. But you were saying—"

"You did not let me finish, Tony. But yes, the earl of Chatham was good enough to give me carte blanche in the handling of this unfortunate affair, along with the expression of his fullest trust." He sat back, relaxing against comfortable velvet cushions as he pulled the fur lap robe up over his knees. "Tomorrow afternoon at precisely two o'clock our five rebels will be permitted to take one turn about the exercise yard, at a time when all the other prisoners are already locked back into their cells. And at about two minutes after the hour they will be taken and impressed into the Royal Navy—a not unusual happening in many of our prisons both here and in Ireland, as you know."

Rosemary Rogers

"By George!" Lord Anthony breathed admiringly. "Damn me, Leo—I always knew you had a devilish, devious mind! So there'll be no trial after all, eh? And no scandal, thank God!"

"And our young rebel," the duke added silkily, "will serve His Majesty for a change."

22

PART ONE

~⚬~

A Walled Garden

Chapter One

The small Carmelite convent, white-washed walls almost hidden by the tall trees that surrounded it, stood like a miniature oasis on the dusty, arid road to Toledo. Like the royal estate at Aranjuez, which lay nearby, it was watered by a thin artery of a stream that branched off the Rio Tajo.

Sometimes, when one of the more adventurous young females left in the care of the good sisters was daring enough to climb atop the thick stone walls, she would see around her, shimmering endlessly under the sun, the arid brown and ochre plains of the Spanish province of Castile. How hot and desolate the countryside looked! And especially from the convent walls, where one had only to turn one's head to see everything green—the shade trees, the fruit trees, and the carefully tended vegetable gardens. A peaceful place, cut off from the world where so many unpleasant things took place. And it was quiet here, too, except for the times the nuns would raise their voices in songs of praise during the mass, or when the muted bells tolled. At this time in the afternoon, it was quiet enough to hear the droning sound of the bees as they gathered honey from the profusion of flowers that grew almost wild here, in the reverend mother's own private garden. Walls within walls. . . .

The young woman who sat on a stone bench beneath the shadiest tree in the garden wore the sober garb of a postulant. Her head was bowed, and she seemed to study her clasped hands, lying in her lap. From a distance, she presented a perfect image of piety and humility, but the reverend mother herself, turning back from her window with a sigh, knew better. She had sent Marisa outdoors into her own private garden to meditate and pray for guidance, but she knew the child too well to be misled by the outward meekness of that bent head. No doubt the girl was dreaming of something else—new ways to show her rebellion, perhaps. Marisa had never learned true humility; and if she accepted discipline, it was only up to a certain point, and because she chose to for her own reasons. However, the letter that Mother Angelina had forced herself to read aloud that same morning must naturally have come as a shock. The child needed time to adjust herself to the thought that she was not to become a nun after all. Her father, it seemed had other ideas.

'She's so young yet,' mused Mother Angelina, 'she will adjust. Perhaps it will be better for her this way. I was never really certain if she had a vocation or if she chose the cloister as a form of escape from all the ugly memories. . . . It is not right that a child, gently brought up and protected for all of her young life, should have been exposed to such horror. . . .'

As the older woman's thoughts turned back, so did those of the young girl in the garden. Far from being clasped together in meek submission, her fingers twisted against each other with a passion of rage she was unable to control; and her enormous, tawny-gold eyes were stormy.

She had tried to pray, as Mother Angelina had instructed her, she had tried to cleanse her mind of rebellious thoughts. But it was no use. Perhaps, after all, the discipline of the convent had never really left its mark on her recalcitrant nature. Humility, resignation, obedience, she could feel none of these.

Unwillingly, her thoughts flashed back to the morning, the usual routine being unexpectedly broken when she was summoned to the mother superior's study.

She had hurried along the long, cold corridor in the wake of Sor Teresa, whose brown habit seemed to rustle with sour disapproval; Marisa cast back frantically in her mind for some small misdemeanor, some infraction of the strict rules.

But everything had faded away when she saw Mother

Angelina's kind, concerned face and the pinched lines around her lips.

"Sit down, my child." Papers rustled on the small wooden desk. "I have just received a letter from your father. A special messenger brought it all the way from Madrid."

"He—my uncle the monsignor has talked to him then? He's consented?"

As usual, her eagerness had carried her too far forward, and she subsided into her chair, sitting very straight as she had been taught, trying to control her excitement under the shadow of the reverend mother's frown.

The frown she was used to, but the sigh that suddenly escaped Mother Angelina's lips made her wary.

"I'm afraid—you have to understand that God tests us in many ways. Your father—"

Marisa had not been able to prevent herself from interrupting.

"But I do *not* understand! Surely my father can have no objection to my becoming a nun? Why should he? If my uncle has talked to him—"

Oh, but it had been such a shocking, unpleasant interview! Mother Angelina, as upset in her own way as Marisa was, had taken refuge in unusual sternness, reminding her of the vows of obedience she had been willing to take.

Nothing could mitigate the shock of the contents of her father's letter. For some time, Marisa could not bring herself to believe that she had heard correctly.

"Married? He—he has arranged a marriage for me with some man I have not even *seen*? Oh no. It cannot be true! I don't wish to be married. I will not be married! I only want to become a nun, just like you. I don't—"

Her defiant outburst had only brought what she thought of as "the sad look" to the reverend mother's face; and after several stern admonishments Marisa had been sent out here, to her favorite place, to consider her "duty."

Duty! It was too much to ask of her. To be married. Why couldn't she have been allowed to find peace in a convent?

The thought of marriage and everything it entailed brought all the nightmares back. That night in Paris, during the height of the "Terror" as people were beginning to call it. Fleeing through the darkness, being only half-awake and trying to make believe that it was all an unpleasant dream —and then, suddenly, the flaring torchlights and the shouts and ribald laughter.

"Well, well! And what's all this? Some more *Aristos* trying to escape Madame Guillotine? Who are, you, eh?"

One man, saner than the rest, or perhaps, only a little less drunk, had laughed contemptuously.

"Have done, citizens! Can't you see they're only a scared band of gypsies? Hey, you—why don't you show us some of your juggling tricks? Perhaps you'll tell our fortunes—"

"Fortunes, pah! There's a likely-looking wench there, with golden skin. Perhaps we should tell *her* fortune. What do you say, citizens?"

And she remembered Delphine, the woman who had taken care of her since she was a baby, thrusting herself forward, pushing Marisa away from her as she did. "You want your fortune told, handsome gentlemen? My mother is too old and sick in her head, you understand? And you have frightened my little brother with your shouting. But me, I'll tell all your fortunes for a few sous. We are poor, hungry people. No one has any money these days, and that is why we're on our way back to Spain. . . ."

After that—no, she did not want to think of what had happened after that! At the time she had not understood. She knew only that the laughter and ribald talk of the men had turned into something else, and suddenly Delphine was screaming, screaming for them to go, to run away, even while they were ripping at her clothes, pushing her down onto the dirty cobblestones. Screaming—and suddenly, there was blood everywhere, and the men, caught up by their own animal instincts, were all clustered around the prostrate form of the woman they were using so callously, like the beasts they were. And Sor Angelina, as she had been then, dressed like a gypsy herself, had forcibly pulled Marisa away, making her run, run very fast, not stopping even when she stumbled and almost fell.

"Delphine sacrificed herself for you, child. For all of us. Would you have wanted her sacrifice to be for nothing?"

Told that over and over, she had tried to accept it. Dressed as a boy for her own safety during the long months that followed, she had tried to *feel* herself as nothing more than a ragged gypsy urchin. No, she did not want to be a woman—never, never to be used and torn to pieces that way. Perhaps maman was better off going to the guillotine with her other gay, brave friends, dying quickly and cleanly under the knife. Poor, weak maman, who loved the gaiety of Paris and had so many gallant admirers she had almost forgotten her daughter, tucked safely away in a convent, with only Delphine remembering to visit every week.

The first upheaval in Marisa's life had been her removal from Martinique, where she had lived with maman's family while her father was in Cuba. He had sent for them to join him, and Marisa could still remember how her mother had cried, complaining petulantly, "It was bad enough when he dragged me away to Louisiana—I lost two children there, you remember? The heat, the swamps and the loneliness, and the fever! And now it is Cuba. Cuba! No—I won't go! He promised me Spain, and Paris—why shouldn't I visit our relatives there? Everyone is there—even Marie-Josephe de Pagerie, who swore she would never leave Martinique. I *must* see Paris just once, at least, or I will stifle and die!"

Paris had been bleak and cold and wet. And Marisa had cried for days on end, longing for her old home and her handsome golden-haired papa, who had always made such a pet of her when he was home. Paris was *not* home—she hated the convent to which she had been sent to learn to be a lady. And she hardly ever saw maman any longer—it would all have been too much to bear if it had not been for Delphine.

Why hadn't papa come after them? Why had he waited so long to acknowledge her existence?

"Your father was naturally upset when your mother ran off with you that way. And then, for so many months, he believed you were dead—killed, like so many others during the Terror. Child! You must try to understand that your father is doing what he believes best for you. He loves you—"

29

"If he really loved me, he would have taken the trouble to try and find me before. He would let me become a nun, as I wish to be." Recklessly, in spite of Mother Angelina's reproachful look, she cried out, "He doesn't wish to be bothered with me any longer. Perhaps everything maman used to say was true, after all. She said he didn't want her after a while, because she didn't give him a son. She used to cry all the time because of the other women he had, even slaves. She said he had an octoroon mistress he loved better than *her*—"

Her almost hysterical outburst checked, Marisa had been dismissed. But even now, in spite of all her efforts, she found that she could not check her own wild, resentful thoughts.

Why couldn't she have been born a boy? Why a female—slave forever to a man's whims? Ah, for the freedom of those runaway days with the gypsies when she had been dressed as a boy and felt as free as a boy. In retrospect, the vagrant, vagabond life didn't seem too unpleasant at all. She had learned to ride astride and to run barefoot over the hardest ground, and even to pick pockets without being caught. A whole year of freedom—and then another convent. But after a while, the atmosphere of peace and tranquillity had dissolved some of the tension in her thin, highly-strung body, and the nightmares from which she would wake, screaming, had grown less and less frequent. Marisa, the little gypsy rebel had changed into Marisa the postulant, desiring nothing more than to spend her life behind these quiet, safe walls, which had become her refuge.

And now, without warning, the peaceful future she had hoped for was to be snatched away from her. Without being consulted or offered a choice, she was to be sold into slavery. Yes, that was what it amounted to, after all!

A soft hiss made Marisa raise her head abruptly to meet a pair of coal-dark eyes that sparkled with mischief. Blanca! Only the gypsy girl would be so bold as to wander in *here*, of all places.

"Hah—innocent one! Are you dreaming of your handsome caballero? So you've changed your mind about becoming a sister like that sour-faced Sor Teresa, eh? But I don't blame you. Me, I would do the same thing if I was offered a novio who is both rich and handsome. Muy hombre, that one. You're lucky!"

"I don't know what you mean!" But Marisa's sharp rejoinder was almost automatic. Somehow, Blanca always contrived to know everything. Taking advantage of her privileged position as a protégée of the mother superior, she alone was free to come and go from the convent as she pleased; her father, when they were not traveling, desired that his only daughter be given an education. And since his tribe had saved the nuns' lives, guiding them safely from a turbulent France to the comparative peace of Spain, Blanca's intermittent, giggling presence within the otherwise quiet walls was tolerated—although some of the older nuns sighed over her wild ways and prayed for her soul.

There was a time when she and Marisa had been closer than sisters, and now even while she tried to frown, Marisa could not help letting her curiosity get the better of her. She repeated, with a forced air of indifference, "I don't know where you pick such wild stories up. And you know you should not be here. If the reverend mother sees us talking, she'll find all kind of penances for me to perform."

Not in the least put off, Blanca merely gave a snort, putting her hands on her hips. "Ah, bah! You speak like a child who tries too hard to be good. And as for Mother Angelina, she is far too busy entertaining two visitors to worry about us just yet! You see—you cannot hide anything from me." Her voice dropped, and she thrust her face closer to Marisa's, her black eyes narrowing slyly. "What do you want to wager that you'll be sent for again? I'm sure your fine new novio will want to take a look at his little convent bride. Didn't you hear the bell at the gate?"

"What?" Marisa's eyes had widened, and her voice sounded faint.

Blanca giggled, pleased at the effect of her words. "You look as if you are ready to faint with fear! What's the matter, little one—have you forgotten what a man looks like? But I do not think you will be too displeased with *this* one. Your padre made a good choice; you're luckier than most, you know!"

Her self-control seemed to fall away as Marisa jumped

to her feet, golden eyes narrow, hands clenched into fists at her sides.

With a pleased grin, as if her baiting had been meant to provoke just such a reaction, Blanca danced back on her bare feet, her voice still taunting. "What's the matter? Have I made you angry at last? I thought you'd be grateful to be warned beforehand that he's here—your new novio and a friend. He must have been impatient to catch his first glimpse of you, don't you think?"

"No!" And then, more strongly, "No, I tell you! I won't be married off like—like some chattel! I don't care how rich he is, or how handsome—I detest him already. I won't see him! I'd rather kill myself than—"

"And here I was wondering if they'd got to you, after all. The good sisters, with all their preaching of humility and obedience and—" Blanca made a grimace, "discipline. Look at you! Why, you had begun to look like one of them already, wearing those clothes, your hair hidden as if you'd already lopped it off. When I told Mario, you should have seen his face! 'What a waste!' he kept saying. And he was so furious that my father should have brought you here and let you leave us. 'She was born to be a gypsy,' he kept saying. But me—" Blanca gave her companion a considering look, her head on a side, and giggled again. "Me—I think you are stupid! I saw him, this novio of yours, and he's handsome. Tall, and well-dressed, for all that he has a friend who's a popinjay. Perhaps he'll wake you up, eh? I think this is what you need, to be made aware that you are a woman, and not a—a *soul!*"

"Oh! My soul is lost already. I've tried so hard to be good and to curb my temper and my wilfulness—but what good has it done me? No wonder Mother Angelina kept asking me so solemnly if I was sure I had a true vocation! Blanca, I won't be married off, do you hear me? Go back and tell them you couldn't find me anywhere—that I'm sick—or—or run off somewhere. I won't see him! I'll not be put on exhibition like a mare up for sale at a horse fair!"

Blanca's dark eyes were crinkled to avoid the sun so that it was hard to read any expression in them.

"We are leaving tomorrow, all of us, for the big *feria* in

Sevilla. You know my father is the best horse-trader in the country—everyone says so! And after that, we might travel back to France. Things are different now, so I hear. They have become gay again. That's what I really came to tell you. Perhaps, when you're married, your husband will take you there."

Gold eyes stared into black ones—the two girls were almost the same height, but Blanca's figure was more voluptuous, her simple skirt and blouse exposing bare ankles and tanned arms—the swelling curve of her well-developed breasts rising from the low-cut bodice she wore. Marisa, covered from waist to ankle, was slim enough to pass for a boy, her only redeeming feature being the dark-lashed, yellow-gold eyes that looked enormous in her pinched, taut face. Beside Blanca, whose cloud of black hair fell down past her shoulders, Marisa would always look pale and insignificant, until, as she did now, she pulled the severe white head scarf off, and her hair, the color of antique gold, reflected the sunlight.

"You're going to France? Oh, to be so free again! Whenever I see you, I start to realize that I'm like a bird in a cage."

"Poor little bird!" Blanca repeated mockingly, softly. "But I hadn't noticed that you were beating your wings against the bars of late. You seemed a happy prisoner!"

"It's different—to choose your own kind of prison. I could have given myself to the church; it's safe and comforting not to think for oneself. But I won't give myself to a man!"

"You're stupid! And besides, your father has already done so. If you won't give yourself, he'll take you, I'm sure. He looked like the kind of man who would not let anything stand in his way. Perhaps once you've seen him you'll change your mind!"

*   *   *   *   *

It was all the reverend mother could do to hide her anxiety and her vexation behind the smooth, disciplined mask of her face when Sor Teresa had returned from her errand

33

and whispered in Mother Angelina's ear. Sor Teresa rustled out again, careful to avert her eyes from the two gentlemen who lounged at one end of the small room. Mother Angelina had to draw in a deep breath before she spoke.

"I am afraid the child is—a trifle upset. As I've told you, she was hoping to join our order. You must understand— first the shock of her father's letter, and then your arrival here on its heels. If you'll give her a few days in which to compose herself?"

The men exchanged glances. One of them raised a quizzical eyebrow, and the other shrugged impatiently, brushing at an imaginary speck on the sleeve of his blue velvet jacket.

"Heavens! I'd no intention of frightening my future bride into the vapors! In fact I must admit I'm almost nervous myself. By all means let her have time. My friend and I are on our way to Seville; we dropped in because it's on the way, you know. Didn't mean to cause any confusion. There's plenty of time. I'll be back in a month or so and that'll give her time, won't it? Clothes—and all the rest of it. I understand there are some aunts in Madrid who have promised to do the right thing by her—"

In the face of Mother Angelina's disapproving look the other gentleman, who had remained silent so far, broke in suavely.

"I am sure, reverend mother, that what my friend means to say is that he had no desire to rush things. And I am sure that *you* will do whatever is necessary to prepare the young lady for the—er—change in her life. Your pardon for the unheralded intrusion—we should have known better, of course."

Don Pedro Arteaga cast his friend a look of gratitude and quickly followed his example in rising to his feet and bowing formally to the reverend mother, who announced in stilted tones that the sisters were always pleased to offer the hospitality of the convent to travelers.

Outside the grey walls, shaded by trees, the manner of both men became almost lighthearted, as if with relief to be let off so easily. They quickly mounted their horses.

"Thank God you decided to travel along with me!" Don Pedro said feelingly. He shuddered. "I cannot imagine why

I let my sister talk me into such a peculiar situation! A postulant-bride—I wonder what she looks like? If she was scared to death about meeting a man, I'm certainly glad we were able to put off meeting her! I quite dread coming back here, I tell you."

His companion laughed harshly.

"Cheer up, amigo. Think of the pleasures that lie ahead of you. The duchess of Alba seemed fascinated by your tales of New Spain last night, and since she just happens to be visiting Seville herself—"

Don Pedro gave a self-satisfied laugh. "Did you notice that she almost ignored that painter fellow who's always hanging around her? But you, my friend, had better exercise some caution where Her Majesty the Queen is concerned! I understand she goes after whatever or whoever she wants—and Godoy can be a dangerous enemy."

"Ah, well!" The other gave a careless shrug. "Manuel Godoy can hardly look on me as a rival since I'll be leaving within the next three weeks. And Maria Luisa will find another cavalier to flirt with in order to keep her lover on his toes!"

"It must be your confounded air of indifference, I swear, that attracts the ladies to you! While the rest of us play at being gallant, there you stand, your arms folded and that damned cynical smile on your face—I can't understand it! Even my practical, icy-hearted cousin Inez, whom we had nicknamed 'the cold unassailable' almost threw everything away she had so carefully planned—and *I*, who know her better than most, could swear you hardly paid her any attention." Don Pedro laughed, glancing sideways at his taller companion, who merely raised an eyebrow and made no comment. He rode his restive stallion as easily as if it had been a tame gelding, guiding it with one hand on the reins and the pressure of his knees. Like a vaquero, as Don Pedro had commented before.

Now, slightly annoyed by the lack of response in his friend, Don Pedro added slyly, "I wonder how my cousin took your sudden departure! After you'd fought a duel over her, and with her husband lying wounded in bed, I'm sure she must have expected you'd stay to console her. Don Andres—"

"Don Andres is to be your father-in-law, is he not? Perhaps you'd best not let your little bride-to-be find out you came to inspect her with the man who came close to killing her father. She might wonder!"

"I doubt if the frightened little chit is capable of wondering about anything except what it might feel like to be mounted by a man!" Don Pedro said brutally, giving vent to a burst of coarse laughter. He felt angry and frustrated that his dutiful visit to the convent, which had delayed his journey to Seville by several hours, had proved so fruitless. Trust Inez and Don Andres to saddle him with a scared nitwit who had been planning to become a nun! No doubt she was ugly. If she took after her mother's side of the family she was probably sallow complexioned and spoke with a terrible accent as well. And that stern-faced prioress had acted as if the girl needed to be protected from him. Damn! If not for the size of the dowry involved and the connections he needed to establish himself in New Spain, he'd have told them all to find another candidate.

"Be gentle with my daughter," Don Andres had said feebly from his bed. "She has been through a great deal in France during the terrible revolution. Her mother went to the guillotine, and if not for the fact that she was still no more than a child, my little Marisa, too, might easily have lost her life." His face had hardened, words trailing off. Catching the look in Doña Inez's eyes, Pedro had made haste to assure Don Andres that he need not worry about his daughter's happiness and well-being. But now—damn it all! Since he had come to Spain, he had realized how much of life he had missed being stuck away in the wilds of Louisiana, managing a run-down plantation. Right now, he didn't want to think about marriage. His mind was full of thoughts about the fascinatingly beautiful and sophisticated duchess of Alba, who, it was rumored, had allowed her latest lover to paint her in the nude. And he was to meet her again in Seville. . . .

Both men had fallen silent, wrapped in their own thoughts, as they skirted the grove of trees that shielded the convent walls and emerged at last onto the dusty ribbon of highway, beaten down by the passage of many other travelers on their way to Toledo. Neither of them noticed the two pairs of eyes that had watched them ride away.

"I hate him already! Which one of them is Don Pedro?"

Marisa had scaled the convent walls before but always furtively—and only high enough to barely peek over. Now, full of her new mood of defiance, she sat barefoot astraddle the very top of the wide stone wall, shading her eyes with her hand as she squinted after the small cloud of dust the two riders left behind them.

"The taller one, in the dark clothes. At least I am *almost* certain, for I only heard their voices through the door, you know—and Sor Teresa almost caught me listening!" Blanca, perched comfortably beside Marisa, gave a soft giggle. "He did most of the talking. When I dared peek once, the other one merely sat there chewing his nails. He looked tremendously bored!"

"Bored! They were laughing about their latest conquests just now—didn't you hear? What fine caballeros, so puffed up with conceit! The one in blue velvet mentioned the duchess of Alba, and—do you suppose they were really talking about the queen? Oh, I can't bear it!"

Marisa's small face, looking thinner than ever amid the mass of her heavy hair, was flushed with anger. "They were disgusting—both of them! How *could* my father?"

"High time you grew up, niña! Men will be men, you know! And if you really hate the thought of marriage that much, maybe you'll be lucky, and he'll spend more time with his current mistress than with you! Or—," and Blanca winked broadly and maliciously, "can it be that you are jealous already?"

"You'll find out how jealous I am! Oh, yes, and *he* will too, I swear! I'll never marry a man like that. If they won't let me become a nun then I—I'll choose my own husband, that's what I'll do. I'll teach all of them a lesson."

Blanca stared. "You're talking crazy now, like the sun has gone to your head. What do you think you can do about it? Even the reverend mother can't help you now, and in the end you'll have to give in. Maybe they'll beat you and lock you up and starve you until you're ready to agree to anything! I've heard of things like that!"

Marisa tossed her head defiantly, impatiently pushing the hair back off her forehead.

"Now you're the stupid one! Do you think I'm going to submit meekly?"

"No?"

"No, I tell you! I have relatives in France. My mother's sister, who married an English lord. And my godmother, too. If my own papa is so anxious to be rid of me, they'll take me in, I'm sure of it." She leaned forward suddenly, grasping Blanca's wrist, her voice dropping into a thoughtful whisper. "Didn't you tell me a little while ago that you were headed for France?"

Chapter Two

The air of Seville was warm and scented with the odors of cooking, the sweet smell of flowers, and the rankness of sweat as crowds of people jostled each other on the narrow streets. It was the week of the grand fair—the feria—and from all over Spain people had traveled here to take part in the festivities. It was even rumored that the queen and some of her closest intimates were here incognito. And as if to bear out the rumors, there were smartly uniformed guardsmen everywhere, keeping an eye on the crowds.

"You notice that they are all young and handsome?" Blanca whispered to Marisa. "The queen likes good-looking young men around her. Why, Manuel Godoy was nothing but a hopeful young guardsman when Maria Luisa's eye fell on him—and now, they say, *he* is the real king of Spain!" She jostled her friend with her elbow. "Hey, wake up! Don't say you are starting to suffer from pangs of conscience at this late stage!"

"Of course not. You should know better than *that!* It's just that I can hardly believe I'm free again."

"Well then, you might show it! Stop wearing that dreaming look; you're not locked up in that convent any longer. And try smiling. It's not too hard, once you get used to it, you know! Look, those two men are trying to flirt with us."

Blanca gave a high-pitched giggle and a toss of her dark head as the two girls, barefoot and brightly clad, ran past a group of men who stopped talking to stare after them, giving low, admiring whistles.

Blanca was right, Marisa told herself as, head lowered, she hurried after her friend. She had made her choice, and she was here of her own free will—in spite of the grumbling and headshaking of Blanca's father.

But why did she find it so difficult to readjust to the free and easy gypsy way of life? Without her realizing it, the years in the convent had left their mark; and she could not help feeling curiously lost and frightened without the security of those grey-white walls to enfold her and the slow, disciplined days when her every movement had been planned for her.

What must Mother Angelina be thinking now? Would they be searching for her? She had left only a short, hurriedly scribbled note to say that she was on her way to France to stay with her mother's relatives. And since Spain was allied with France now, and there were Frenchmen everywhere, she hoped the reverend mother would think she had found some French friend to escort her.

"I will be in safe hands," she had written. But would the prioress believe that? What did she think?

They had reaached the gypsy encampment on the outskirts of the city, and Mario came to meet them, his dark face sulky, his eyes burning Marisa's hot, flushed face.

"You took long enough, you two! What have you been up to?"

Leaving Blanca to shout angrily at him that it wasn't any of his business, Marisa caught back her own sigh of vexation. Mario was another of her new problems. She had been a child when she had left the gypsies, but now, he made her only too aware of the fact that she had grown into a woman. His eyes followed her constantly, and he was forever trying to catch her alone in some dark corner, caressing her bare arm with his rough hands as he whispered to her that he adored her, he always had, and would kill any other man who tried to touch her. Blanca was amused. She would laugh, shrugging casually.

"That Mario! He's a hot-blooded one, eh? Better watch out for him, my little innocent—stick close to me!"

But how long could she continue to elude Mario? France was still a long way off. In spite of the fact that she was still far too thin and deliberately rubbed grease into her hair to darken it, he wouldn't stop pursuing her.

Now, ignoring his sister's screeching, he strode up to Marisa and grabbed her wrist. "You'd better not have been flirting, little skinny one! Tonight, when we dance for all the visitors, I want you to stay in the background, remember! I don't want any other man looking at my golden beauty."

She snatched herself from his grasp, imitating Blanca's sharpness.

"I'm not yours—I'm not anyone's property! And you'd better run back to Liuba before she sticks a knife between your ribs. Go on!"

"That's right—tell him off!" Laughing, Blanca linked arms with her, sticking her tongue out at her brother as she did so. "Come on, we've got things to do."

"Oh, I'm a patient man, I can wait!" he called after them, the glowering look on his face belying his light tone.

She told herself later that Mario was the cause of her mood of depression. If only he would leave her alone. But she could look after herself—of course she could! Like Blanca, she had taken to carrying a small dagger strapped to her thigh, and Mario knew she would not hesitate to use it on him. Oh, how she hated men! Beasts, all of them, with only one thing on their minds.

The gypsies were all busy preparing for the famous horse fair, which formed a climax to the Holy Week celebrations. On a piece of flat land between the Rio Guadalquivir and the city of Seville, they had set up their tents and their wagons; and when the day's business was over, there was dancing to wild music in the flickering torchlight and the plaintive, quavering flamenco—song of love and sadness that had been bequeathed to Spain by the Moors.

At any other time, Marisa would have been caught up in the excitement of it all, just as the others were. She and Blanca had roamed freely everywhere, and they had finally slipped into the enormous cathedral to pray. Perhaps that was why she felt so strangely sad and forlorn tonight. Last year and for so many years before that, she had spent Holy Week quietly in the convent, praying in solitude. All this festivity and frantic air of gaiety seemed strange and almost sacrilegious to her.

"I'm just not used to crowds yet," she told herself; and to

please Blanca, who had been so kind to her, she forced herself to smile and laugh and even to flirt with some of the bolder young men.

"Hey, gypsy girl! Won't you tell me my fortune?" The man who called out to her was well-dressed and handsome, but, remembering Delphine and the horror of that night, she gasped fearfully and ran away from him. Running away from the lights and the music that tugged at her she almost cannoned into a group of newcomers walking from the direction of the river.

In her headlong flight she had lost her head scarf, and her hair, newly washed that evening, slipped from the careless knot at the back of her neck, to fall in curls about her shoulders. In the faint light, she looked like a wild, tawny animal, too shy to be tamed.

"Here's a piece of luck! A runaway gypsy wench with hair the color of the Castilian plains! Perhaps she'll act as our guide tonight."

There were women among them, their flimsy, high-waisted gowns only carelessly concealed by velvet cloaks. Jewels winked around white throats, and they laughed as loud as the men.

"Don't run off, little girl! We're here to watch the dancing. Don't let her run away. Look at her hair, isn't that unusual for a gypsy?"

A man caught her around the waist, holding her captive in spite of her frantic struggles.

"Hold still, you little ninny! No one's going to hurt you. Here, perhaps *this* will persuade you to calm down!"

Still laughing, he slipped a coin between her breasts. One of the women, throwing the hood back from her high-piled hair, said in a wheedling, husky voice, "Really, I assure you we don't mean you any harm. But we're all strangers here, and we'd pay you well if you'll act as our guide. We want to join in the dancing—do you think your people would mind?"

There was wine on the woman's breath as she leaned close, and Marisa tried to control the shudder that shook her whole body, feeling her breath cut off by the pressure of the arm that still held her close to a hard, masculine body. These people were obviously of the nobility, out for a good time with the common folk. And she would only provide a source of further amusement for them if she continued to struggle. From the smiling looks of the women, she could sense that she could not expect any help from them.

"Come—we'll pay you well. Very well. And if you were running from a too-ardent lover, we'll protect you!"

The man who spoke gave a laugh that sounded strangely familiar. He added petulantly, "Por Dios, amigo, don't be so selfish! You've done nothing but drink and look sullen all evening, and now you won't share the spoils! Perhaps our little gypsy will give us a private performance later—what do you say?"

Marisa felt, rather than heard, their inane talk and laughter pass over and around her. Without quite realizing what was happening, she found herself dragged along with them, as if she had been a rag doll with no feelings and no understanding—a new toy to amuse themselves with. She felt as dazed as if she had actually turned into wood; and at the same time some deep-rooted instinct of pride held her silent. She wouldn't cry and plead with them to let her go! At least they were moving towards the lights and the music, and sooner or later, when they tired of their sport, she would escape. Suddenly she thought of Mario, and for once felt relieved that he was so jealous. *He'd* rescue her! She stopped resisting and tried to ignore the laughing comments of her tormentors.

"You see? She's quite resigned now—quite tame. It must be your charm. . . ."

"I wonder if she's a deaf-mute? Really—she hasn't said one single word!"

"Don't be afraid. You'll find us generous—and especially if you'll dance for us."

"The poor child looks as if she could use a good meal!"

"Child? She must be fifteen or sixteen at least! And among the gypsies, that's almost old! Are you married yet, menina?"

The man whose steely arm still encircled her waist said suddenly, "I think she's frightened half to death. Perhaps she'll learn to talk back to us after she's had some wine."

He spoke with a strange, drawling accent she could not place. Was he a foreigner, then?

They came at last into the flickering circle of lights, and while everyone's attention was caught by the sudden burst of handclapping as the guitars strummed wildly bringing a dance to its climax, Marisa dared a nervous upward glance.

Her breath caught in her throat when she encountered his eyes. They were like shards of splintered, glittering glass, piercing her, and she could not prevent her instinctive, shrinking movement.

His arm tightened, and he gave a soft, mocking laugh.

"Not trying to run away again are you, golden eyes? It's too late now that you've come this far with us. My companions find you fascinating, you know."

One of the other men chuckled, overhearing. "And so do you, obviously! I vow, amigo, that I have never seen you exert yourself before to catch a woman. Perhaps it is only the thrill of a chase and a capture that you enjoy?"

Held forcibly close to him, Marisa could feel the man who held her shrug.

"You know I'm a hunter. And this one, with her golden mane and the half-shy, half-wicked look in her eyes, reminds me of a mountain lion. Would you enjoy using your claws on me, menina?"

Taunted into a fury, Marisa tilted her head to glare at him.

"I would like to do worse! To stick a knife between your ribs and watch you bleed—"

"Dios! She is a wildcat after all!"

"I don't think so," the other drawled infuriatingly, and through her rage-slitted eyes Marisa could see one corner of his mouth twitch in a grin. "I think she means to challenge me."

"Ohh! You—you—" Catching the sarcastically expectant look on his dark face Marisa bit her words off short. She would not give him the satisfaction of hearing her swear at him. She would merely bide her time and run away to lose herself in the crowd that now milled around them— some still watching the dancers and others glancing curious- ly at the new arrivals. Ignoring her captor, she began to search frantically for the sight of a familiar face. Where was Blanca? And above all, where was Mario? The music was so loud that even if she screamed aloud no one would hear her! How dare these people treat her as if she were a new plaything to amuse their jaded appetites?

She noticed for the first time, with a sense of fearful foreboding, that their small group was far too well escorted. In the light, it became apparent that the men were all well-armed, forming a kind of phalanx about the bright-eyed, jeweled women.

One of the women, wearing a deep purple velvet cloak trimmed with fur, had kept glancing in their direction, ignoring her attentive escort; and now as they came to a stop she said in a rather petulant voice, "Surely you don't need to hold on so tightly to our little gypsy? Give her some more money and ask her if she'll go back with us tonight, to dance for us. But for the moment, I thought we came here to enjoy ourselves." And now the dark-haired woman addressed Marisa directly in patronizing tone. "Do you have any suggestions, girl? We are here to have fun. What do *you* do to amuse yourself when you are not running away?"

A tall man with a deep voice said smoothly, "Ah, but these gypsies never like to stay in the same place for too long, mi reina. They are a restless, free people always craving to move along—like our friend here, who plans to leave us soon."

Had there been something significant in his tone? In spite of her own anger and discomfort, Marisa could not help giving him a puzzled look.

"My Queen," he had said. Merely a flowery compliment or—was it possible? She, had heard tales of the wild, licentious royal court of Queen Maria Luisa. And suddenly, like a blow to her midriff, she recalled the careless, laughing words that had floated to her as she sat astride the convent wall on that fateful day not long ago. The nagging familiarity of a laugh—a drawling voice—oh, no! Surely not! Fate could not play such an unpleasant trick on her as to deliver her into the hands of the very man she was running away from!

Marisa became aware that the woman, refusing to be

45

diverted, was speaking to her again—this time impatiently.

"Surely you can speak? Where are your friends? Perhaps they can join us, too. The music makes me want to dance. Do you think we could join in?"

They had somehow pressed forward to the very fringes of the crowd that had formed around the dancers and the musicians.

Sheer desperation made speech return to her paralyzed tongue.

"I see some of my friends now. There—that is my sister who is dancing in the center now—the one with the long black hair. Her name is Blanca. And that is my novio over there, playing the guitar with the red ribbons. Alas, we had a quarrel, and that is why I ran, hoping he would follow." Again, irresistibly, she slanted an upward look at the man who held her so firmly. What strange, frightening eyes he had! They were truly like glass, reflecting every shade of the fires and smoldering torches while revealing nothing. The black cloak he wore, gave him an alarmingly sinister appearance, as did the bulge of the weapon he wore, which was pressing into her hip. "If the señor would let me go, I will dance for you kind ladies and gentlemen. And perhaps later, if you will, Blanca will tell your fortunes. She is very good."

"See? She can talk after all! And prettily too. Do let her dance—she's lost her fear of us now, haven't you my dear?"

"Oh, I was only startled," Marisa said demurely. She let her eyes drop shyly as she shrugged. "And a little bit afraid —because my novio is very jealous, you see!"

She felt a warm hand slide up over her breast, and she squirmed away angrily.

"Little liar!" he whispered. "I've a good mind to see how jealous this lover of yours is."

But the others were calling to him to let her dance for them, and he had to release her. With a mocking half-curtsy she whirled away from them, clicking her fingers in rhythm to the frenetic music.

"Aren't you afraid she'll get away from you?" Pedro Arteaga whispered maliciously in his friend's ear. "She seemed only too anxious to get back to that black-browed lout there—and I've heard these gypsy wenches like to choose their own lovers."

"I've yet to lose a prize I've captured. And I think she's only playing hard to get—perhaps to put her price up!"

"My God, what a cynic you are! I'm beginning to believe you really don't like women at all."

"I've loved my share of them. Why does liking have to come into it? They're all the same—sly, teasing bitches without an intelligent thought in their heads."

"Well, don't let our beautiful sovereign hear you speak that way! She's made it very clear she's taken a liking to you, hasn't she? You'd better take care, my friend!"

Pedro Arteaga's friend had folded his arms, his steely grey eyes following the gypsy girl as she made her way to the center of the crowd of dancers.

"Oh, I expect to have Señor Godoy's aid in recapturing that elusive yellow-eyed witch if she's really bent on escape. He's got two of his guardsmen keeping an eye on her already, or hadn't you noticed?"

Manuel Godoy had bent his head to whisper in the queen's ear, and now the voluptuous duchess of Alba, sulky at being ignored, leaned against Don Pedro's shoulder.

"What are you men whispering about? I thought we traveled all this way to have some fun and mingle with the peasants. Don't you dance in New Spain?"

Marisa had danced her way to Blanca's side; and now, ignoring her friend's surprised look, she began, in a breathless, angry voice, to pour out her story, keeping a fixed smile on her face all the while.

"You cannot imagine how—how arrogantly nasty they all were! Talking about me as if I was nothing more than a block of wood, without feelings. Taking all kinds of familiarities with me!" She shuddered, recalling a warm hand cupping her breast so intimately. "And to make matters worse, I think he's the one—look, over there. That crowd of strangers—you'd recognize him, wouldn't you? And his friend—"

"I think you have a crazy imagination," Blanca murmured. But her voice was doubtful, and she added, in the next breath, "Well—it might be! It's hard to see from here. But listen, if you're so scared, why don't you slip away to the wagons? I'll go up to them myself and tell them you sent me. *I'm* not afraid, and if they're throwing around gold coins, I could use a few."

"Blanca!"

"Little innocent," Blanca mocked, showing white teeth, "when will you learn that you cannot hide yourself away from men forever? You're not in a convent any longer you know! And the trick is to use them while letting them think they are using you. You'd better learn—"

"Blanca, let's both go back to the wagons. Now, when they can't see us. I don't trust them—and besides—"

Blanca turned her head, black eyes laughing. "And besides what? I've already told you that *I* know how to look after myself. And that handsome caballero you ran away from might need some consolation—even if he does happen to be your novio!"

"Oh, stop!" Marisa, suddenly frantic, clutched at the other girl's bare arm. "We'd better hide somewhere before they—before he—. You see, he made me so angry, the way he was pulling me about, that I—I picked his pocket!"

For a moment, in the midst of all the noise, the clapping and the gaiety that surrounded them, they seemed to be enclosed in stillness.

"You did *what?*" Blanca threw back her head with a wild, admiring laugh. "Oh, but you are priceless! No—you are crazy!" She grabbed Marisa's wrist, starting to pull her away into the shadows. "What on earth possessed you? Under the very eyes of the queen herself and her chief minister. Don't you realize what could happen to you? To them, you are nothing but a little gypsy. You could be arrested, thrown into a cell, even executed. Don't you understand? Picking the pocket of some stranger on the street is one thing, but a friend of the queen! They'd recognize you in an instant if they come looking for you! Quick, you must throw it away. Wait—does it contain a lot of gold, this wallet you stole?"

Blanca's eyes gleamed with a mixture of avarice and fear. In the torchlight they seemed to glow as red as coals.

"How would I know? I didn't think about the money—I just wanted to teach him a lesson. And since you're not afraid, why don't *you* take it back to him? Tell him you found it—"

"I might do just that! What a little fool you are! Where's that wallet?"

Already beginning to regret her defiant gesture, Marisa handed it to her friend without a word—glad to be rid of it. If only she could be rid of the memory of those bold, rude caresses as well! And if *that* was the man her father wanted to marry her off to, she was fortunate in having escaped such a fate.

"So, now you are taking money for your favors, eh? Is that why you kept me at arm's length, because I was not rich enough to buy you?"

Mario had materialized out of nowhere, his dark face glowering with rage. "I saw you!" he growled. "Leaning up against that stranger, his arm about your waist. Where did you meet him? Ah, you should not have brought him here, to flaunt your unfaithfulness before my face, for I shall kill him for it!"

"Here's another stupid one! Well, I shall leave you to explain to my dull-witted brother while I see what I can do to prevent trouble. Don't forget to tell him you picked the pocket of your own novio because he got too fresh with you!"

Blanca danced off, and Mario, his frown growing even blacker, caught Marisa's arm in a grip that made her wince.

"Yes. Tell me what you have been up to! What was my sister talking about just now?"

49

Chapter Three

There was the moonlight and the firelight and the torches that flickered like live tongues; and Marisa was no longer herself but someone else. A bold-eyed, bold-tongued creature like Blanca who was afraid of nothing and no one. She had tied a brightly colored scarf over her head again; but it did not disguise the gold hair that rippled almost to her waist.

"If you are innocent still, then prove it!" Mario had hissed. "If he has not had you yet then he will be eager for you, sí? Lead him away from the others; flirt with him if you must. No more than that—I will see to the rest!"

Mario had made it sound so easy! But here he was offering to protect her when not too long ago she had felt she needed protection from *him*.

What did it matter? She knew Mario and felt sure of her power over him. The other man was a different proposition. Far too insolent, far too sure of himself—and her. The last man on earth she wished to marry, if he was the one.

Facing him again was harder than she had thought it might be, even though he was alone at the moment. He had been lifting a wineskin to his mouth, and when he lowered it and saw her, one black eyebrow shot up in mock surprise.

"Oh, so you're back. I must say you put a high price on yourself, yellow-eyes. Are you worth it?"

She saw no sign of Blanca. Had she told him, or had he discovered his loss for himself?

Still acting the way Blanca would, Marisa lifted her shoulders.

51

"Why not find out? I wanted you to notice me for myself. I do not like crowds. They make me feel stifled, and —and trapped. And I do not like being made fun of, either."

"Should I apologize for my friends and myself?" He swept her a mocking bow, offering her the half-empty wineskin. "Here, now that we are alone, shall we drink to an understanding? I didn't expect to see you back of your own accord, but here you are, which proves that I am as ignorant as the next man when it comes to understanding the whims of women." His strangely light eyes crinkled at the corners, catching her attention in spite of herself. What a time to start wondering about him—what kind of man was he?

She shook her head, refusing the wine. "No, I am not used to drinking, señor."

"But an expert at picking pockets? You continue to surprise me, little gypsy."

Marisa felt the hot blood rush into her face, but she refused to give ground. "Yes, certainly. But isn't that only what you would expect from a gypsy wench? The very worst. You made that clear, all of you, when you kept talking of me as if I had no ears."

A sudden brightness leaped into his eyes, stabbing into hers like a flash of lightning. "Olé!" He said it softly, tilting the wineskin to this lips again and then lowering it slowly. "So you are a creature of emotion after all. You breathe, you feel, and you even think, it seems. Good. We have established that much, at least. Also your price— which is high. I warn you, I shall expect a great deal in return. . . ."

Without warning, Marisa found her waist encircled by a steely arm again. Before she could protest, she was drawn against him tasting, unwillingly, the wine on his breath as he forced her head back with his brutal kiss.

Instinctively, she struggled against him, hands pushing futilely against his shoulders. Horrible! To be kissed like any common slut, without consideration of her feelings. First he insulted her and then he kissed her.

Marisa kept her teeth tightly clenched together and kept twisting her head from side to side, trying to avoid the bruising pressure of his mouth on hers. In spite of her frantic struggles she felt herself drawn against his body. His cloak was open down the front, and she felt stifled in its folds; she was terrified by the pressure of his lean, masculine body all the way down hers. Her neck would surely break in another minute, and she could not breathe. There was a buzzing in her ears and she was no longer capable of the effort of resisting him, even when some faraway part of her mind realized that he had slipped her thin blouse off one shoulder and was fondling her breasts. Her body lay limply against his, still shivering with revulsion; and when she opened her mouth to gasp for breath his tongue forced its way between her lips, bringing a renewal of her feeble attempts to turn her face away.

Did he actually intend to force himself on her here, with everyone looking on? What a callous, unfeeling brute this man was to use her this way as if she had been some whore he had picked up for the night.

Just when she felt that she was about to faint, he lifted his head slightly, and Marisa saw that his eyes looked like silver now, like polished mirrors in which she could see her own flushed, terrified reflection. Remembering old stories about the devil coming to earth in human disguise in order to seduce women, she felt an overwhelming desire to cross herself.

She half gasped and half moaned and saw the cynical, almost sneering smile that flickered across his clean-shaven face.

"Be assured, little picarona, that you need not play the innocent virgin for my benefit. Tonight I do not feel inclined for the usual tussle—nor for the usual preliminaries. Come along now, and let's have no more games, eh?" Her knees were so weak with shock and terror that she would have fallen if he had not seized her by the wrist. He was taking her back to his friends, and she would never escape if she did not use her wits as she had meant to do in the beginning.

"No!" She pulled back, not having to feign the breathlessness of her tone. "Please, señor, not back to those friends of yours who laugh and make fun of me because I'm only a poor gypsy girl. My wagon is not far away, and it is empty—"

"What a changeable, surprising creature you are," he said softly, slipping his arm about her waist again. "One moment you act as if my kisses disgust you, and the next —you are as hot as fire!"

She said quickly, "Gypsy women are very independent. We like to choose our own lovers." She prayed that her voice sounded flirtatious enough as she allowed herself to sway against him. "At least, you are not a brightly dressed parrot like the other men in your party."

She dared not look into his eyes again as they strolled towards the outskirts of the crowd that now pressed more and more closely about the whirling dancers.

"Please—act casual. I do not want my novio to notice," she murmured. The conceited boor! He actually believed himself irresistible. How easy it had been to trick him after all! Viciously, Marisa hoped that Mario and his friends would teach this particular caballero a lesson he would never forget.

They were being jostled by people who were eager to see what was going on. The rumors had already begun to fly around that the queen herself was here in disguise, along with the notorious duchess of Alba, who was fond of masquerading as a maja in order to pick up commoner-lovers.

Marisa's lips felt bruised and swollen, and her breasts seemed to burn from the casual, all-too-knowing caresses she had been forced to endure. It was all she could do to lean docilely in this man's hard embrace and pretend that he had subdued her spirit. Angry thoughts whirled around in her brain. Where was Mario? Pray God he'd rescue her soon.

No one took any notice of them, not even when Mario himself, as if conjured up by her thoughtfs, appeared suddenly to bar their way. His dark features were suffused with fury, and his hand lay threateningly on the dagger in his waistband. Behind him, Marisa noticed two of his cronies, carrying heavy cudgels.

"So! This is what you've been doing behind my back! I should not have expected a woman like you to be satisfied with just one lover. Or was it his money and fine clothes that attracted you? Bitch. I saw you kissing him as if you could not bear to tear yourself away. And as for you, señor, I think that after tonight you'll think twice before you attempt to meddle with one of our gypsy women. . . ."

His tirade and his rage seemed all too real, and Marisa could not help shrinking involuntarily. Through widening eyes she saw the other two men move silently to either side of Mario as he drew his dagger.

"I think I will mark up your face first," he snarled, "before I allow my friends to beat you within an inch of your life. You aristocrats should learn to stick to your own kind!"

"I wondered when you would appear on the scene." Marisa heard the drawling, dryly sarcastic voice and tried to tear herself away, but with a quick jerk of his arm he held her before him, and she felt something cold against her side. She thought she heard a clicking sound. She saw the gypsies freeze as the drawling voice continued in a conversational manner, "This pistol is made to fire two shots without reloading—which one of you wants to get it first? And of course there's always the chance that your little friend here might get nicked in the process. Well?"

Marisa felt the hair at the back of her neck prickle, and she stood rigidly, hardly daring to breathe. He meant it! There had been a steely undertone to his voice that made her certain he would have no compunction about shooting, as he had promised.

"You had no right to walk off with my woman," Mario blustered uneasily, his eyes darting this way and that; and at almost the same moment a voice behind them made him jump.

"What is going on there?" Two uniformed guardsmen had come up, their sternly frowning faces taking in the whole picture. "Were these gypsy devils attempting to rob you, señor? A good thing Don Manuel ordered us to keep an eye on this little wench here. It's a favorite trick among these people—"

"But one I had half-expected already. No, I don't think there's any need to arrest them. I don't think they'll be in a hurry to pull this kind of stunt again."

"Get going, you three! And if you're still around when the sun comes up, we'll find a nice cold cell to throw you in!"

Mario's friends had already taken to their heels, and now, with a last, frustrated backward glance, the young man himself disappeared into the crowd.

With a desperation born of sheer terror, Marisa tried to twist away.

"Let me go! You have no right to keep me here!" She raised imploring eyes to the suddenly impassive faces of the two guardsmen. "Please, señores! They were only trying to save me from the unwelcome advances of this—this lecher! And he threatened to shoot me with his pistol if I did not go with him!"

"What an accomplished little liar she is! Listen, young woman, picking pockets could get you in a lot of trouble! A public flogging, and all your pretty long hair cut off. We've been watching you."

"Here—and you'd better keep a closer eye on her this time. I've no mind to spend the rest of the evening dodging her jealous lovers—and her nimble fingers." Marisa felt herself shoved forward, only to have her arms grasped roughly and twisted behind her.

"Better search her for a knife, too—she threatened once to stick me with it."

"Shall we bring her along to the boat?"

Straightening out his clothes, the gentleman shrugged, but his silver-grey eyes had gone narrow.

"Why not? I hate being made to pay in advance for favors I haven't received yet. Maybe she'll be more tractable in a few hours' time."

With a dazed feeling of disbelief, Marisa watched him walk away leaving her to these rough men, to be treated like a common prisoner. No, it could not be happening, not to her! Perhaps if she closed her eyes she would wake to find herself in her little grey cell in the convent, safe behind its strong, wide walls.

As she felt one of the men adroitly tie her wrists behind her, she began to sob helplessly.

The voice that spoke to her wasn't too unkind. "Now, now! There's no point in shedding tears at *this* point, you know! Count yourself lucky you aren't to be marched right off to jail. You might spend the next few years of your life picking hemp, and what a waste that would be! A pity you weren't given a different sort of upbringing—all you gypsies are thieves and sluts. I suppose it's in your blood and you can't help it! But if you behave yourself and do as you're told, you might come out the richer for this evening. Now—where's that knife hidden? Better tell us, or we'll have to strip you."

She had to bite her lip to keep from crying out with revulsion when a rough hand groped up her thigh.

"What a dangerous little weapon! You could kill someone with this, and then you'd hang. You ever seen a hanging? Come along now. A good thing you have enough sense not to scream, or we'd have to gag you. That's right. And just think, you'll have a nice boat ride—it's a perfect night for it, too."

*　　*　　*　　*　　*

The lopsided moon dropped lower and lower and the rocking motion of the pleasure barge made her feel sick. Almost as sick as the conversation of her captors, as they discussed the rest of the night that lay ahead.

"They're really having fun this evening. It was all the duchess's idea, you know. A pity we're on duty, eh, Jorge?"

"Ah well, you know they're generous with the spoils after they've tired of their sport. We'll get our share later." One of the men gave a ribald chuckle and when Marisa shuddered, he flung a blanket over her shoulders. "Here. It wouldn't do to have you catch a chill. And you might as well stretch out against those cushions and get comfortable while you're at it. You'll have plenty of exercise later on."

She closed her eyes against the cold silver stars. Their brilliance reminded her of cruel, mocking eyes. 'Delphine!' she thought suddenly. But Delphine was gone a long time ago, offering herself to that pack of raving beasts to save her—and for what? "I've sinned," she thought dully. "I've sinned, and this is my punishment. Mother Angelina was right. She used to tell me I was wayward and headstrong and that I lacked the proper humility to become a nun. If only I'd paid attention, if only . . ."

She had found her own personal hell—flickering torchlights and gay, wine-slurred voices, the sound of oars swishing through moving water, the sour-sweet taste of wine forced between her lips, and the devil's eyes which were not as red as coals after all but like silvered glass.

Her limbs were numb and aching and her wrists and arms had no more feeling than her horror-soaked mind.,

"If I stood up now and shouted who I was, they wouldn't believe me, she thought, or they'd think it was very funny. Oh God, help me!"

Marisa hardly heard the voices that continued to discuss her as if she weren't present.

"The foolish little creature! What did she hope to gain?"

The sulky voice that she now knew belonged to the queen of Spain said sharply, "I can't understand why you bothered with her! After all, one gypsy wench is very much like another, and if this little wretch is a thief into the bargain—"

"Ah, but she isn't quite like the others. Her father must have been a Castilian—look at that hair! And she's obviously still quite young."

"What difference does that make? Her kind are all quite hardened by the time thay are fourteen or so!"

"At any rate, our guest seems to find her intriguing, and something of a challenge, is not that so, señor? Since we're all paired off, it's only fair to provide him with a wench of his own choosing."

"I would think you'd have had your fill of *her* kind in the New World," Maria Luisa snapped. "Or is it the pirate in you that always looks for a capture instead of a prize that's willingly given?"

"Alas, I'm nothing so romantic as a pirate! Merely an honest privateer—and I know better than to sail too close to an impregnable, jeweled citadel. No, I've learned to be satisfied with more modest prizes."

"Like that English ship you took on your way here? I declare, captain, it is *you* who are too modest!" But the queen had begun to smile again. Marisa wondered dazedly, what they were talking about and whether that man was really some kind of pirate.

She could believe it. He had cast aside his heavy dark cloak and unbuttoned his jacket to reveal a ruffled white shirt front. More plainly dressed than the rest of the men present, his clothes were nevertheless well-cut and form fitting. When he crossed his long legs, Marisa could see the shine of Hessian boots.

He hadn't touched her since he had climbed easily into the boat to sit beside her, but she was all too aware of his closeness and the warmth of his body. What did he intend to do with her? No, she mustn't think about it—not yet. She found herself wishing that the boat would somehow spring a leak and sink, drowning them all. Such an end would be infinitely preferable to what might lie ahead.

More wine was being passed around, this time in jewel-encrusted glasses, each one tinted a different color. Rather than have it forced down her throat, Marisa sipped obediently, sitting huddled in her corner. The wine made her dizzy at first and then tremendously drowsy. Her hands had been untied, and she kept chafing her sore wrists with icy-cold fingers. She had the feeling that something terrible was about to happen, but at the moment she was too tired and too overwrought to think. Like a child worn out by tears and emotion, she curled her bare feet under her and fell asleep, only half-waking when a warm cloak was wrapped around her and she was lifted up in strong arms that held her far too closely in spite of her drowsy protests.

Chapter Four

Ridiculous! She was dreaming that she had been carried off by a dangerous-looking pirate, a scarf tied over his head and a black patch covering one eye. He was going to make her walk the plank, but instead of the icy shock of sea-water closing over her head she fell onto something soft. So comfortable, and she was so sleepy! She thought she could hear voices somewhere over her head, but the words slid across the fringes of her mind without really registering.

"And what is the meaning of this, if I may ask?"

"What the hell does it look like? She ran right into my arms tonight, and quite providentially as it turned out. I've no desire to make an enemy of the prime minister. Look after her for me, would you? They've got the gaming tables set up downstairs, and I don't want her jumping out of the window before I get back."

"So now ye've taken to drugging your females before ye take them?"

"Don't come all Calvinist over me, Donald! And she's drunk, not drugged. Give her something to eat if she wakes up, will you? And help me off with this damned coat!"

"Royalty or not, it's no decent company that you've taken to keeping since we've been in this godforsaken hot country. And that's no more than a wee bit of a girl you've brought to your bed. What's wrong with all those other fast females who've been makin' eyes at you?"

"For God's sake, stop your preaching and leave me to my own kind of damnation!"

The door slammed, and Marisa shivered in her sleep, murmuring incoherently. Everything that had happened during the past few weeks to change her whole life had caught up with her like a cloudburst, and now, limp with exhaustion and the effects of wine, she was dead to the world.

The pale dawn light was filtering through the windows when she woke up, feeling the chilly air on her body as the covers were pulled aside. Her eyelids were still so heavy they seemed stuck together, and her limbs felt cramped. But when she tried to move, a heavy weight pressed her down.

"So you're still here, after all. You might at least have undressed while you were waiting. Damn. I'm too drunk and too tired to have patience with clothes, little golden butterfly."

She heard a tearing sound, and was too paralyzed to either move or cry out. Far easier to pretend that she was still asleep, that this was not happening to her. A hand passed over her shrinking bare flesh, and she heard him say in a husky voice, "At least your skin is soft, and you're yielding for a change."

Her dazed, half-open eyes stared into desire-narrowed, flinty grey ones without any real comprehension of what was happening, until with a feeling of shock she found her thighs nudged apart. She writhed, gasping, as his fingers touched her intimately, exploringly; and for a moment, as his body was poised over hers, she thought he would let her go. Her lips parted, only to be covered by his hard, demanding mouth, tasting of wine and tobacco. And at the same moment there was a stabbing shaft of agony between her thighs that seemed to tear all the way into her belly, causing her body to arch up against his with shocked surprise.

She came close to fainting, feeling sure that he was killing her, that like Delphine, she was about to be ripped to pieces.

Marisa heard a whimpering, moaning sound, like that of an animal in pain, and it took her some time to realize that the sounds she heard were coming from her own throat. She fought to be free, but her movements only seemed to incite him to a further attack on her helpless flesh; he drove himself deeper and deeper inside her, holding her wrists over her head when she attempted to push him away.

It was no use. She was helpless—in the grip of a madman bent on hurting her, an animal.

And at last, surprisingly, the stabbing pain gave way to mild discomfort, and then to a kind of lethargy as she lay with her limbs sprawled out and let him have his way.

Her last thought, as she slipped into a state halfway between sleep and unconsciousness was, 'And I don't even know his name—nor he mine . . . how strange . . .' And further than that, she did not care to think just yet, for her head ached as badly as her bruised and violated body; closing her eyes against reality was much easier than being forced to face it.

"So now ye've taken to raping helpless virgins, have ye? And handing them over to your fine aristocratic friends after, for their sport. Well, it may be that ye're my captain, when we're at sea, that is, but I've known you too many years to keep silent, and I'll be speaking my mind, whether ye'd be liking it or not!"

"I don't recall that you've ever hesitated before, you old croaker! And as for the wench turning out to be a maid—how in hell was I to know? She played the tease very well, and there was talk of a lover. Curse your long face, anyhow, and her, too! Do you think I've a taste for virgins? If I had not been drunk, and in a bad mood into the bargain . . ."

"They want her downstairs. You heard them. And the poor wee creature still in a faint, or maybe bleeding to death from the way you used her. It's wondering, I am, what you intend to do now. And I might add—"

The harsh voice of the younger man turned into a snarl. "Spare me, Donald! I'm in no mood to listen to more! I'll leave it to your ingenuity to get rid of the gypsy wench. You can take her back to their encampment outside Seville and give her as much money as you think it would take to soothe her wounded sensibilities. The stupid slut! All she had to do was to tell me she hadn't been with a man before, and I'd have let her run away. But she seemed anxious to find the kind of fate she met with. Well—get her away. I'll tell my friends she escaped out of the window. And mind you," still adjusting his hastily tied cravat, the captain paused to let his grey eyes bore into his manservant's doleful brown ones—"I expect to see you aboard ship and ready to sail when I reach Cadiz three days from now. Better not let those damned gypsies spirit you away—or let *her* lead you into a clever little ambush!"

The voices and harsh sounds of arguing had roused Marisa out of an uneasy doze, but she was afriad to open her eyes until she heard the door slam behind *him*. Then, cautiously, she peeked from behind her long eyelashes, trying not to blink at the harsh sunlight that filtered through. She was lying in an enormous canopied bed, the curtains drawn back far enough to let her catch a glimpse of a large and luxuriously furnished room, its walls hung with tapestries and paintings that made her want to blush. There was a fireplace in one corner; coals still smoldered hotly in spite of the heat of the day. Beyond the widely opened windows she caught a glimpse of a stone terrace and a fountain that cast a shower of silvery droplets into the sunlit air.

She stirred uneasily, suddenly becoming aware of her nakedness under a thin sheet that felt like silk against her tingling flesh. And with that first tentative movement all the horrifying memories she had been trying to hold away rushed back. She sat up abruptly, gave a smothered gasp, and then snatched the sheet up to cover her naked breasts as the man who had been standing in the middle of the room turned to gaze at her with a worried, frowning look.

He spoke English, but with a strange, burring accent that made his words difficult to understand.

"So you're awake, puir lassie! Now, now, there's no need to look at me like *that*, I'm not out to harm you, you know. And if I'd had a true understanding of how it was, I'd not have permitted what took place. But I suppose ye don't even understand what I'm saying, poor child, do you?"

The kind, even pitying, note in his voice, coupled with what she had overheard earlier, made Marisa want to trust him, this stocky man with short-cropped reddish-grey hair, and brown eyes that reminded her of a spaniel's.

Mother Angelina had personally seen to her education—and the reverend mother had, at one time, been a noblewoman. "You have to know *of* the world, my dear child, before you can truly renounce it," she had told Marisa, so the young woman's knowledge of languages included English and German, as well as Spanish, Italian, and French.

She began to talk haltingly in English to this man with the kind eyes. While she was talking, she felt something hardening inside her, just like the little boy in a fairy story whose heart had turned to ice. Why, a few days before she would have been terrified at the sight of her own blood sticking to her thighs and staining these fine sheets. But last night had taught her something: she had survived the very fate she had been running away from, and she had learned to hate—both at the same time, it seemed.

Donald McGuire made clicking noises with his tongue and shook his head. Yes, *he* at least was sympathetic. He sounded almost like a father as he turned his head away after pointing to a door which disclosed a luxurious bathroom, the first that Marisa had ever seen.

"It's a heathenish invention," he warned in a grumbling voice. "Sunken tub made out of marble—just like the old Romans used to have, the captain says. But there. Ye'll want to soak your poor bruised body in hot water, and there's plenty of that, at least. Warmed by the sun in a cistern on the roof, so they tell me. And while you're in there, I'll see what I can do about finding you some garments to cover yourself with. Don't you worry now, little girl. You won't be molested again—I'll see to that meself."

Once the door had closed behind him, Marisa cast aside the sheet with which she had covered herself and gazed curiously about her, managing, for a few moments at least, to forget her unpleasant predicament. She was in a blue-tiled, Moorish-style room, which was lit from above by a skylight set in the roof. Varying shades of tile, ranging from deep blue to turquoise, gave the impression that she was underwater. Steps led down into the sunken bath that Donald had talked of, and there was the golden pump-handle he had described, which would bring heated water pouring into the tub. All the appointments were made of gold, and in shelves set into the wall there were crystal bottles, stoppered with gold, which held an assortment of oils and perfumes. A wet towel, flung carelessly to one side gave mute evidence that someone else had used this chamber a short time before. Had it been Donald's mysterious captain—the same man who had captured her last night and had, just as heartlessly, deprived her of her virtue this morning?

She remembered his irritable, brutal words before he had left. Her face flushed, and her whole body became hot with humiliation and anger. How lightly he took what he had done! He had actually blamed *her* for everything—and now he was only anxious to be rid of her.

Marisa became conscious for the first time of the gold-streaked mirrors that reflected her body from all angles. Averting her eyes, she began frantically to pump the gold lever and watched the streaming water gushing into the bath. As it filled, she wondered with a kind of detachment whether she would have the courage to drown herself. That was what she should do—she did not want to go back to the gypsies, to face Blanca's knowing, malicious grin or Mario's jealous rage. And now she could not possibly go back to the convent. No, she was cut off from everything and everyone familiar, and all because of her own foolishness.

Steam filled the room, clouding the mirrors, and with a sigh Marisa let herself sink into the water. Almost immediately, her tense muscles began to relax, freeing her mind; opening it to all kinds of thoughts that began to weave in and out of her consciousness. She was her practical father's daughter, and her sensuous mother's child. What was there left to lose that she had not lost already?

But Marisa didn't drown herself, and three days later she had her first view of the ancient port of Cadiz.

Whitewashed houses and old fortresses, meant to keep off pirate attacks, leaned towards the sea. A sharp breeze had come up, and the ships lying anchored in the great harbor seemed to dance in a stately fashion over the heaving swell of the waves.

A tiny cockleshell of a boat took them to a long, sleek-hulled schooner that lay close to the harbor entrance.

"She's sharp-ended, instead of square," Donald explained proudly. "Baltimore Clipper type. Takes very little rigging and a small crew, but she's fast!"

Looking up curiously, Marisa almost expected to see the vessel flying the skull and crossbones flag of a pirate, but the flag that fluttered from one mast was one she had never seen before—bold red stripes against a white background, and in one corner a blue square, clustered with silver stars. The flag of the young Republic of the United States of America.

"Captain's not back on board yet." There was a relieved note in Donald's voice as he hustled her up the rope ladder that someone slung over the side. "Now, mind you lie low like I told you; and try to remember you're a young lad now—I'll tell the boys you don't speak nothing but Spanish, so you'll be spared the questions they'd ask otherwise."

He hurried her below to a tiny cabin containing only two bunks and a tiny porthold. He told her, in a harassed tone, to stay there until he sent for her. He was obviously having second thoughts about bringing her aboard, the poor man, and Marisa told herself penitently that she should be ashamed of herself for taking advantage of his kindness to her. She had practically blackmailed him into it, ever since he had mentioned that they would be sailing for France.

To France! But she had relatives there—she had run away from the convent with the gypsies only because she wanted to get to France. Oh, if she could only go there, she wouldn't be a trouble to anyone. . . .

The gypsies had already left Seville, and in any case Donald had had reservations about delivering her back to them. Unlike his captain, he was a man possessed of a conscience. He couldn't very well abandon her—the "puir lassie" needed protection. And when, in a fit of temper and contrition, Marisa had sheared off her long hair, he had reluctantly given in. Very well then. Since she was small enough and slim enough to pass off as a youth, he'd smuggle her on board the *Challenger* as the new cabin boy. The short voyage to France would take less than a week, and if during that time she followed orders and kept to herself, perhaps they'd both get away with the deception.

Now, remembering a pair of steely grey eyes, Marisa shivered preferring not to think of the consequences if they were discovered. If only she could contrive to stay out of his way! She could pretend to be seasick as Donald had suggested. She suddenly recalled her dream of being made to walk the plank, and she shivered again.

She heard the sound of raised voices and activity on deck

and tried to control the dangerous direction her thoughts were taking. What kind of man was he, the cold-eyed stranger who had taken his brutal pleasure of her unwilling body and then promptly wanted to be rid of her?

His name was Dominic Challenger. What conceit, to name his ship after himself! Or was it the other way around? Donald had been mysterious on that point, although he had talked freely of some of the adventures they'd shared. They had been common sailors on an English man-of-war at one time, and had deserted, sailing off with a French ship that had been taken as a prize. No doubt the English themselves would have called it mutiny! But now "the captain" as Donald called him, commanded an American privateer, a fast schooner with rakish masts, meant for preying on other vessels. A pirate ship, no matter what kind of flag she flew and in spite of the fact that this same ship had brought the new American ambassador to Spain.

"Ah, something's up, but it's not my place to ask," Donald had admitted. "We've had conferences in Washington—once with the president himself! But now don't you be repeating anything I've told you, mind, for the captain doesn't take kindly to other folks prying into his affairs."

Well! As if she cared for anything except getting safely to France and finding her aunt again, or maybe her godmother. France was different now under the consulate, and she'd learned that they'd just signed a peace treaty with England—the Treaty of Amiens. Paris must be as gay again as it had been before the revolution. Gay enough for her to lose herself—or find herself—if this Captain Challenger didn't find her out first.

The thought that he might discover her made Marisa remember her instructions, and with a hurried glance around the tiny cabin, she heaved herself onto one of the narrow, uncomfortable bunks, and pulled a dirty brown blanket over herself. Her head felt light, without the heavy, familiar weight of her hair. A few moments earlier, the reflection of her own face in the porthole had given her a start. She *did* look like a boy, after all; her face was all eyes and her figure far too slender, without the well-defined curves that Blanca had been so proud of possessing. In the loosely fitting, raggedy garments of a peasant lad, no one would take her for a young woman unless they looked very closely.

The ship began to sway quite alarmingly, and the shouting and movement on deck seemed to have intensified. Remembering that all she'd had to eat that day was a piece of hard bread and a slice of goat cheese, Marisa swallowed convulsively and closed her eyes very tightly. Perhaps it would not be necessary to pretend that she was seasick. Already, she had begun to feel slightly nauseated and quite dizzy; and a cold sweat broke out all over her body, in spite of the hot, close atmosphere inside the cabin. Oh, she must have been mad to have forced poor Donald into agreeing to this crazy plan! She wondered vaguely if she would ever live to feel dry land beneath her feet again and drew her knees up under her chin, like a small, frightened child, willing the discomfort in her belly to go away

Chapter Five

The schooner *Challenger* put out to sea under full sail, with a crew of forty-eight men, instead of the fifty she was supposed to carry. Her captain, coming on board late, was in an exceptionally unpleasant mood, a thunderous frown drawing his black brows together as the first mate, Mr. Benson, bellowed orders and the men scurried to obey them without the usual joking and ribald banter.

Waiting only until she had cleared the harbor and was ploughing her way through the first rolling breakers of the Atlantic Ocean, Dominic Challenger turned and made his way to his cabin, throwing a curt word of command over his shoulder as he went that caused Mr. Benson and Donald McGuire to exchange guilty, conspiratorial looks as they followed him.

"Well?" The captain seated himself in a chair behind a desk that held an untidy collection of maps, charts, and other papers, all of which were held in place by a collection of pistols of varying sizes and shapes. "Perhaps you'll explain why we're short two hands—and why discipline always seems to go to hell when I'm not aboard this ship! You were to be prepared and in readiness to sail at precisely four this afternoon. Those were my orders four weeks ago." He stared at Donald, and his grey eyes turned to a metallic steely color in the light that poured in through a large porthole.

"And you—can it be that you found some reason to dally along the way you took in getting here? I understand that I arrived in port hard on your heels."

As his eyes went from one red face to the other, Dominic found himself wondering casually how it was that these two, who had always been each other's enemy, had suddenly turned into allies. Or so it seemed. . .

Benson was a Methodist, a follower of the fiery and controversial preacher John Wesley. And Donald, as he well knew, was an uncompromising Calvinist. Usually the two men argued for hours, almost coming to blows, over various points of doctrine. Today they both seemed filled with brotherhood. He wondered if his own escapades during the time he had spent ashore had united them in the common bonds of disapproval. If so, be damned to them both, with their long faces!

He waited for them to speak, and seniority took precedence.

"Sir!" Mr. Benson said gruffly, his Adam's apple bobbing in his scrawny neck. "You did not give me time to explain the situation—sir. Begging to report that Parrish went on shore without leave a week ago, and, being in a disgustingly drunken state when he attempted to return, he fell into the water off a pier, and was discovered drowned. And as for young Ames—" here Benson's face reddened, and he appeared on the verge of apoplexy—"he—ran away, captain. With a woman old enough to be his mother, too! She used to sell fish and fresh fruit in the market place. And then one day she wasn't there. I sent Jenkins on shore to look for Ames, and he came back with a garbled message. . . ."

Benson regarded fornication as a crime only slightly less serious than murder and drunkenness. For himself, he never drank and was not interested in shore leave or gambling or any of the other vices that sailors were wont to indulge in. He had planned, at one time, to become a fire-and-brimstone preacher himself, until one day a press gang had caught him. Now, he was just as single-minded in his hatred of the English Navy as he was in his attempts to convert the men under his command.

Dominic had caught himself wondering more than once if perhaps Benson did not secretly cherish a fondness for young men, but if he did, he was not overt about it, and all that mattered was that he was a good sailor and an excellent mate —cool-headed in times of danger. Young Ames had been something of a protégé of Benson's—no wonder he was upset.

Captain Challenger had had far to much wine to drink

the previous night, which had something to do with his bad mood. He had literally lost his shirt at cards and had ended up, in spite of all his stern resolutions, in the queen's own bed. Just as well he had planned to leave Spain today! She was a savage, insatiable lover, and his back still bore the marks of her long, sharp nails.

There was a dull pounding in his temples, and he craved sleep; and so when Benson began to explain that he had personally hired a new cabin boy, a Spanish orphan who had relatives in France who would be glad to take him in, Dominic merely waved an impatient hand.

Dry-voiced, he asked, "I suppose the brat doesn't even speak English! And why wasn't he on deck when we sailed?"

"Well—" Looking embarrassed, Benson shuffled his feet. "To tell the truth, the lad's seasick, sir. But he'll be useful once he gets over it, I'll see to that. I gave him the extra bunk in my cabin. I wouldn't want a lad as young as he is corrupted by the dirty talk and gambling in the fo'c's'le."

Hell—maybe Benson *was* that kind after all! But as long as he did his job and the new cabin boy knew what was expected of him, what the devil did it matter?

There was still Donald to be coped with, and Dominic said harshly, "Since we're short a man, and I don't have to impress people on shore with the fact that I, too, have my own valet, you can go back to your usual duties, my old friend! I'm sure you'll be relieved."

Catching the fleeting impression of thankfulness on Donald's face as he and Benson turned to leave, he held up one hand, staying him after the door had closed behind the first mate.

"Wait a minute. Why are you in such a deuced hurry? I haven't heard a word out of you yet, and you must admit that's unusual. Well? Aren't you going to tell me I'm headed for perdition?"

Donald sounded unusually solemn.

"It's not for me to say, as ye've reminded me often, captain. I reckon ye'll be after finding your own kind of damnation, at that."

"I reckon I will!" Dominic Challenger gave a harsh laugh that seemed torn from his throat. The thin white scar that stretched from his temple and across one cheekbone like a crescent gave him a look of the devil—or so Donald always said to himself, seeing the captain in this kind of mood.

He hoped there would be no more questions, but on the heels of that hope came the curt command to fetch a decanter of wine—since there was no cabin boy in a fit state to perform such small duties.

"By the way—how did you manage to be rid of the gypsy wench? Were the gold coins I gave you sufficient to compensate for the loss of her virginity and provide her with a dowry?"

Halfway out of the door already, Donald's back stiffened, but he did not turn his head.

"She asked only to be taken to some distant relatives, captain, and it was the least I could promise, wasn't it, now? She returned your gold to you, too—said she didn't want payment for what she hadn't sold."

With a look of dour satisfaction on his face, Donald closed the door behind him, ignoring the angrily muttered, explosive curse that was hurled at his heels. Let Benson say what he would—*he* knew best how to handle the captain in one of his black moods.

The mood lasted for the whole of the week that followed, along with a spell of bad weather that was almost as ugly.

It appeared they were carrying secret dispatches to the newly arrived American minister in Paris, and so instead of looking for likely prizes, they were to avoid running into any other ships if they could help it—a highly unusual situation for a notorious privateer. All the same, there were the usual duties to be performed, just in case; the decks had to be kept clean and clear and the guns polished and cleaned for action. The *Challenger*'s slim, rakish lines were too well known to King George's Navy to permit any relaxing of their vigilance; and it was well known that in spite of the so-called Peace of Amiens, there were British war frigates skulking off the coast of Portugal and in the Bay of Biscay itself. And so the *Challenger* kept to a slow zigzag course heading well out to sea before she turned back again to head for the French harbor of Nantes.

A series of storms plagued them after they had rounded

Cape Finisterre—both sea and sky as grey as the captain's cold eyes. At first Marisa was far too sick and miserable to care if they broke into pieces and sank to the bottom of the ocean, in fact, in her lucid moments, between spasms of sickness, she almost welcomed the thought of an end—any end —to her misery.

Except for Donald, who looked in occasionally, bringing her food she refused, and shaking his head in a helpless fashion, no one had time to wonder about her, not even Mr. Benson, whom she hardly saw.

Marisa had lost all idea of time, and when the day came that she was actually able to sit up in her bunk, craving food in spite of the constant pitching motion of the ship, she had no notion how long she had lain there.

"Ah, looks like you've found your sea legs at last my girl!" Donald said with an attempt at cheerfulness as he brought her a watery broth which she gulped down voraciously. "I canna' stay for long," he added with a backward glance over his shoulder. *"He's* in a worse mood than ever because of all the delays and having to run from a damned Britisher of only sixteen guns yesterday. Lost her in the fog, but it's a shame we could not have stayed to fight her."

Marisa shuddered weakly, and he gave her thin shoulder a clumsy, comforting pat.

"Ah, weel! Ye won't be seeing any action, an' that's a relief. We'll fetch into Nantes in a few days now, and I'll get you off the ship with none being the wiser. You just stay below now and try not to worry. The captain's an excellent good sailor, for all his hard ways—and its a powerful hard life he's had, to make him that way, too. *You* couldna' care for that though, could you, puir little lass? It's like a little drowned mouse ye look now, with no one ever suspecting ye're a lass after all. You'll need a lot of feeding up once you're safe with your relatives."

When Donald had left, Marisa managed to wriggle out of her bunk and found her knees too weak to hold her. Just then the ship dipped into a deep wave-trough and rose up again, almost on its end, and she slammed against the bulk-head with a force that almost stunned her.

'I'm surely going to die,' she thought as she crawled across the floor. And the thought alarmed her only faintly, for she felt more than half-dead already. Tears of sheer weakness and exhaustion slipped unheeded down her pale, hollowed cheeks without her being aware of them. It didn't matter; nothing mattered too much at this point. She could not even remember what she was doing here, being tossed from side to side like a tiny cork while she waited for the wave that would surely smash in the side of the ship and sweep her with it to oblivion.

Somehow, miraculously, it didn't happen. Mr. Benson came back to the cabin, smothered in oilskins, and lifted her back into her bunk, ordering her gruffly to stay there, for they expected the storm to last all night. He gave her a large, worn volume of the Protestant Bible to hold onto, and told her she should pray that she'd be saved. Still, he was as kind in his own gruff way as Donald had been, and Marisa nodded solemnly before he left her again.

Huge, foamy waves smashed against the side of the ship. The porthole had been closed with a heavy wooden shutter, and Marisa had no idea whether it was night or day. As the storm gathered in intensity the timbers began to creak alarmingly, and she had to clutch desperately to the side of the bunk to prevent herself from being thrown out.

Suddenly she began to fancy that they were about to go down—that everyone else must surely have been swept overboard leaving her alone, trapped in this cramped space like the little mouse Donald had called her. Had she really heard a cry, "Abandon ship! Abandon ship!" above the thunderous roaring of the wind-torn waves?

Without quite knowing how, Marisa found herself clawing desperately at the door. She wrenched it open at last and was soaking wet in a second, buffeted by the fury of the storm that was raging all around. The door slammed shut behind her, and she slid along the suddenly sloping deck. A wall of pale-green water came to meet her, pushing her backwards, drenching her eyes and hair and face; her mouth was filled with salty water when she opened it to scream. So this was what it felt like to drown. . . . Her mind registered the thought in a detached fashion, even while her arms flailed desperately seeking some kind of handhold. And then, just as her feet slipped from under her, she was brought up short—an arm encircled her waist, holding her firmly as the water receded, and she heard the man she had cannoned into swear in exasperation.

"What the hell! . . ."

Choking and gasping, she was dragged roughly to the comparative shelter of a bulkhead on the lee side of the still-pitching vessel and shoved roughly against the wet wooden planking.

"I thought I gave orders—," a voice she recognized only too well began, and then, still holding her pinned against the wall, he lowered his head, peering furiously into her averted face. "Who in hell are you? A stowaway?"

Her wits coming at long last to her rescue, Marisa tried to wriggle away. "The cabin boy, señor. I—I was afraid—" After the quantities of seawater she had swallowed, her voice came out as a choked whisper.

"Goddamit! Don't you have sense enough to follow orders? You were to stay below because you were too sick to perform your duties!" He gave a harsh bark of laughter. "Well, now that you're recovered enough to be up and about, you can get below to the galley and fetch up some hot grog. And look lively, muchacho, or I'll throw you overboard myself!"

He was capable of it. Oh, he mustn't recognize her!

"Get going," he said grimly, and Marisa ducked under his arm, not knowing in what direction she should flee. The deck tilted alarmingly again at that moment, and once more he grabbed at her, to keep her from sliding against the rail. This time, though, his arm caught her under her breasts, their slight curve unmistakable through her sopping wet shirt.

"Diablos!" He swore furiously in Spanish, and the next moment she felt herself dragged backwards, struggling helplessly against his strength until he kicked open a door and flung her bodily through it.

"You'll stay here until I have the time to get to the bottom of this whole affair," he snarled ominously. "Fortunately for you, I have other things to see to right now!"

The heavy door thudded shut, leaving her sprawled ignominiously on a luxurious rug. Marisa realized that she was locked in the captain's own cabin.

She lay there for a long time, wet and trembling, partly with cold and partly from sheer terror which seemed to numb all of her senses. Finally the sound of her own teeth chattering aroused her somewhat, and she lifted her head to discover she was lying in a puddle of water, which had soaked through the rug. A furiously swaying lantern overhead cast a dim orange light that flickered like the fires of hell, casting long, leaping shadows into the corners of the room.

What would he do with her? Marisa glanced fearfully at the door, expecting him to burst through it at any moment. A pirate, a deserter from the English navy who had used a stolen ship to turn robber, a man without scruple or conscience—a completely amoral rogue!

The abuse she heaped on him mentally gave Marisa the strength to sit up. She moaned. She must be bruised all over, after being flung this way and that. And he would probably kill her for ruining his fine Persian carpet, if she didn't save him the trouble by perishing with a chill. Some kind of practicality oozed back into her mind, giving her the strength she needed to pull herself slowly and painfully to her feet. Turning her head, she saw a pale, frightening face staring at her. She let out a small shriek, which was fortunately drowned out by the sounds of the storm that still raged outside.

It was hard to keep her balance, as weak and unnerved as she was, but she realized it was her own face that had scared her so! Reflected in a small mirror hung on one of the walls she could hardly recognize herself. Short, straggly hair turned dark by seawater hung about a small, gaunt face that was pinched and blue with cold. She looked like a half-drowned rat—hardly the kind of appealing prey that a pirate captain might wish to gobble up! And in any case, she had never possessed any vanity about her appearance—her nose was too short, her eyes too large for her small, high-cheekboned face, and her forehead not high enough. She had always been thin, and now after a week or more of virtual starvation, she was skinnier than ever.

'Perhaps he won't want to—to do *that* with me again after

all!' Marisa reflected hopefully. 'After all, it was only because he was drunk and angry and wanted to punish me in some way.' But in spite of all her brave efforts to comfort herself she could not escape the unpleasant thought that she was at the mercy of a man who had thought it a joke to carry off a gypsy wench for his use for the night and had taken her without a thought for her feelings or for anything but the sating of his own lust. He had wanted to be rid of her soon after—what would his reactions be now?

At that moment there was a crashing noise overhead, and the ship tossed more violently than before, pitching Marisa against a bed that was anchored to the floor.

It was just as well she had not become a nun, for she had no moral fiber at all. She had been raped and had not had the courage to kill herself afterwards. Instead, she had taken a bath! And now, almost petrified by fear, she found herself thinking that perhaps rape was preferable to death by drowning after all.

Clutching a trailing blanket around her shivering, icy body, Marisa stayed crouched where she was, one arm wrapped around a bedpost. She tried to pray, but the humble, gentle prayers of praise and invocation she had recited so glibly in the convent chapel became all garbled in her mind. She had sinned deliberately, she had no right to ask for mercy. Instead of the vision of the Virgin's gentle face bringing her comfort, she saw another face bending over her, dark and angry looking, with a white scar and eyes like daggers, cutting her to pieces, impaling her body and battering it helplessly while she lacked even the strength to cry out.

Chapter Six

Strangely enough, it was the sudden cessation of noise that woke her. That, and the pleasant feeling of warmth penetrating her chilled flesh. She must have lost consciousness during the worst of the storm, Marisa thought dazedly. At least she was still alive.

As circulation crept back into her cramped and aching limbs, the pain was almost unbearable, making her afraid to move.

Her eyes opened a fraction, and she realized that she was lying in a bed, the covers drawn over her. In front of a glowing brazier which had been set in the center of the floor, a man stood stripping off his sopping wet clothing, flinging everything aside in an untidy, dripping heap. The ruddy light played over his tall, lean body and the movement of muscles beneath the skin of his shoulders and narrow flanks. His back was to her, its symmetry broken by a crisscrossed pattern of scars. Only a criminal would carry the marks of the lash. Marisa's golden eyes widened and then squeezed shut quickly as he reached for a bottle that stood on the desk and raised it to his lips.

A few moments later she could not help cringing as the covers were rudely snatched off her cowering form.

"Whose wench are you? Donald's? Isaac Benson's? I can hardly believe it of the old hypocrite!" She felt his body drop over hers, taking her breath away, and then he had rolled to the other side of the bed.

"Don't get your hopes up, scrawny one. I'm too damned tired to find out tonight. And if you want to stay in this bed you had better shed those wet clothes; you're as clammy as a corpse!"

Numb with fear, she had obeyed him, reacting like a puppet. She fell asleep and when she next awoke, the events of the previous night seemed all jumbled up. She had half-expected to wake up in the same narrow bunk she had occupied for the last week or so, and when her senses swam back to dull awareness of the present, she felt a heavy weight over the lower half of her body and found her face pressed against a masculine shoulder smelling faintly of sweat and tasting like salt. She tried to move away but an arm scooped her closer.

"No you don't! You were content enough to keep me warm all night—what's your hurry now?"

Her golden eyes stared mesmerized into his sleepy grey ones with dark pupils that seemed to contract as recognition flared into them.

"You!" Suddenly he held her pinned down by the shoulders, his face staring down into her. "How did you contrive it? Did you put one of your gypsy spells on poor Donald and on my ship as well? No wonder we've had such a bad voyage—a woman aboard ship always brings bad luck! What are you doing here?"

There was a cruel, dangerous look on his face, and sheer desperation made Marisa shout back at him.

"You—you threw me in here last night! And if I'm such bad luck, why don't you just throw me overboard and have done with it? You're such a rotten bully, no wonder all your men are so afraid of you! Well, I'm not. You can't do anything worse to me than you have already—"

She was appalled at her own boldness.

He shook her, his fingers digging into her bare shoulders.

"Don't be too sure of that," he muttered threateningly between clenched teeth. "This is my ship. What are you doing aboard her? Did you offer yourself to Donald in order to persuade him to bring you here? Cabin boy—hah! I suppose you've been spreading yourself thin—distributing your doubtful favors to every man on board this ship. No wonder you were supposedly too sick to show your face on deck! What's your game?"

Too overwrought by now to care about the pain he was inflicting on her, Marisa screamed, "Nothing, nothing! I have

82

not done anything, and I'm not what you accuse me of being —*you* ought to know that! I only wanted to get to France, and if I hadn't been so—so sick I would have worked my passage there! I'm not a gypsy, and I'm not a whore, although you tried to make me one! And I wish you'd have let me be swept overboard last night. That would have been best, I'm sure for all concerned!"

"What a virago! I can feel you shaking like a trapped rabbit under my hands, and yet you dare shout back at me. I'll say this much for you—whatever you are, you've got courage."

"Courage is something one finds easily enough when there's nothing left to fear," Marisa shot back wearily.

It came to her with a sudden shock, when she saw his eyes harden, that he had made his last statement in English, and she had answered in the same language.

"How did you discover such a cynical truth so young in life? Well, well. Maybe there's more to you than I imagined at first. You're beginning to intrigue me all over again, little one."

She had no idea what he might have done next for a rapping at the cabin door made him stiffen and swear under his breath.

Suddenly embarrassed, Marisa dived under the covers like a guilty child. A wooden-faced Donald entered, bearing dry clothes over his arm.

"Beg pardon, captain. I thought you'd be needing these. And Mr. Benson has a jury mast up, all right and tight. If the wind and weather hold, we ought to fetch port with no more trouble." In the face of an ominous silence he cleared his throat and went on awkwardly, "Thought—you dinna' gave me a chance to explain matters last night, and—"

"If we hadn't been shorthanded you'd be clapped in irons and making your explanations to the rats in the hold. No, I'll have my explanations from the right party, and hear *your* side later, if my temper holds out! Here. You can take our erstwhile cabin boy's clothes and have them dried. And fetch me some breakfast, while I decide what to do with her."

"Captain, you don't understand. The puir lassie has no

friends or family to protect her in Spain, and those gypsies had vanished like the wind——"

"You'd be wise to vanish yourself, you sneaking old reprobate, before I change my mind and have you flogged for insubordination!"

With a last worried glance at the mound of covers on the bed, Donald decided on discretion instead of valor and fled, hearing the door kicked shut behind him.

Marisa could hear her own heart thudding, and the next moment the covers were yanked off her curled-up body, and, crying in pain, she found herself dragged upright by her hair.

"What the hell do you think you're hiding from? And just a moment ago, you were so brave!"

In spite of the tears that sprang to her eyes she noticed with relief that he had pulled on a pair of closely fitting breeches, with a wide belt that snugged his flat stomach.

"Here. You might as well put this on." A ruffled linen shirt hit her in the face. "I'll have some answers to my questions now," Captain Challenger's voice continued harshly.

She blushed all over under the cold scrutiny of his eyes as she forced herself to pull on the garment he had thrown at her; but for once he seemed not so much interested in the sight of her body as in studying her face.

"I've told you everything——"

"Only that you're not a gypsy and not a whore. You'll excuse me if I reserve judgment on the last! But I must admit it's not usual to come across a gypsy wench who speaks Castilian Spanish and English as well! Who are you?"

Marisa tried not to shrink under his look, gathering her confused, scattered thoughts together. She told him the same story she had told Donald—which was not too far from the whole truth, after all!

"My father was Spanish and my mother French. They put me in a school and forgot about me. And when I learned that they were both—gone—I ran off with the gypsies. Blanca told me they would take me to France. My mother's sister used to live there——"

"Where?"

"In Paris. She married, and I don't remember her last

name, but she used to enjoy going to the theater, and I know that if I saw her again I would recognize her. And I'd heard that Paris is gay, and all the ladies wear pretty clothes, and I had no one in Spain—"

"I see." His voice had become dry. "So you thought you'd sell your virginity to the highest bidder—or maybe your gypsy friends had such a plan. A pity I had to arrive on the scene and spoil everything! But then, you should not have been running off alone on a dark night unless you were hoping that young man would come after you!" His tone turned harsh. "All women are whores at heart, and for all your look of childish innocence, I'm sure you're no different. It's a pity you went so far as to cut off your hair. It was quite pretty as I recall."

"I don't care what you think about me, I could never become a whore. I'd rather be dead!"

"Spare me your theatrics, wench!" he sneered. "Once you've filled out a little and let your hair grow back, you might be passable—and in a better position to bargain. For now, like it or not, you've thrown yourself on my hands, and as little as I like it I suppose I'm stuck with you until we reach France. You could cause trouble, if the crew knew there was a female on board. I'd hate to have to hand you over to them to keep them mollified! So," he rose, stretching, "if you know what's good for you you'll keep your mouth shut and do as you're told. Who knows? You might learn a few things to prepare you for your future profession in case you don't happen to run into this pleasure-loving aunt of yours!"

He seemed to have accepted her story, at least; but obviously her defiance had put him in a black mood again, prompting him to insult and vilify her.

When he left the cabin, he locked the door behind him, and Marisa found herself a prisoner. She did not know what passed between Donald and his captain, but when the Scotsman brought her food and dry clothing he seemed ill at ease and almost afraid to talk to her, except to warn her not to cross the captain when he was in a temper. He shook his head and murmured "Puir lassie—puir little creature," until she thought she would go mad and was almost glad when he left her alone with her thoughts.

The rest of the voyage lasted five days, with the weather perfect, but during that time Marisa was never permitted to leave the cabin. She was more than just a prisoner—she was the helpless, unwilling captive of a pirate captain who treated her like a prize of war.

When she refused to undress for him he took her clothes away and kept her naked. When she attempted to claw at him he tied her wrists to the bedposts. Once, she tried to brain him with the heavy, double-branched candelabra that stood on his desk; he snatched it easily out of her grasp and turned her, squirming and whimpering, over his knee smacking her bare rump until all her pride and defiance left her and she screamed for mercy.

After that, she was tame—in a fashion. When he felt inclined to take her she submitted limply, without showing any reaction, keeping her eyes tightly closed and her teeth clenched against his kisses. And in this way, by her very passivity, she defeated him and gained her own small victory when, swearing, he rolled off her body.

She resisted him by not resisting, and Dominic found himself staying away from his own cabin, scowling and watching the cloudless blue skies while his crew kept their distance, eying him and shaking their heads. Even Donald had nothing to say out loud, although his reproachful eyes spoke volumes. Mr. Benson muttered under his breath and quoted passages from the Bible. Damn her! Dominic mused. A cold, unresponsive child-woman—he must have been out of his mind or blind drunk to have felt himself attracted by her in the first place.

If he'd had any sense he would have allowed her to continue her masquerade as a cabin boy, made her work until she dropped from weariness, and let her bunk with Mr. Benson and listen to his Bible-reading all night. *That* would have taught her a lesson!

She was the first woman he'd had to rape—and she'd been a virgin. She had seemed acquiescent enough, curse her! And then she'd turned up again, after he'd put her out of his mind as an unpleasant memory. What a bedraggled little scarecrow she'd looked that first night when he'd discovered her stumbling across the deck, all wet and sticky with salt water. But since then he'd made her wash her hair, and, although it was still far too short, it had begun to curl in ringlets all over her head in a style that ladies of fashion were beginning to emulate all over Europe. She was a mixture of defiance and surrender, naivete and cynicism. And someone, somewhere, had given her an education, so that she spoke like a lady. No doubt that would prove useful to her later, when they got to France. She was hardly inexperienced any longer—he had seen to that; and with the right clothes she should have no difficulty finding herself a rich lover—or more than one. The best whores were women who didn't permit themselves to feel. . . .

And he must be out of his mind to wonder what her future might be once he was rid of her. He had never given any woman a second thought, nor exerted himself to conquer one, since Lizette. Lovely, false Lizette, who had betrayed not only him but also his friends to the cursed British one long-ago night in Ireland.

"I'll be glad when we sail into Nantes harbor," Donald McGuire muttered from the side of his mouth to the long-faced Isaac Benson. "Captain's not been hisself since—"

He did not have to complete his sentence. Mr. Benson, who had thought the same, merely grunted.

"Women!" he said succinctly. Then hastily drew himself up and began bellowing unnecessary orders as their captain strode by, his face like a thundercloud.

"He'll be wanting his dinner, I don't doubt," Donald muttered hastily. "I'd best see to it, or he'll be in a worse mood than this."

When the cabin door banged open, Marisa was sitting up in his chair, reading a battered volume of Shakespeare he'd picked up somewhere on one of his voyages. Fascinated, she hardly looked up, and her voice held more animation than he'd heard in it for a long time.

"I had no idea *you* would be interested in reading. And you know, I wasn't allowed to read anything but religious literature—or geography, which I hated!"

"Get up!"

She looked up then, sighed, and rose obediently to her feet, putting the book down reluctantly. What was the matter *now?* He was so moody and bad-tempered!

She was naked, her small crimson-tipped breasts teasing him in the half-light. And in spite of the fact that she had not been out in the sun, her body retained a faint golden tint all over—a legacy, no doubt, of a Moorish ancestor.

She had given up trying to hide her body from him; in fact, she seemed quite unconcerned as she gazed curiously at him. How dared she?

"You look like a strumpet waiting for her first customer," he snarled cruelly. "For God's sake put something on or get into bed. Donald will be bringing dinner in soon—or did you hope to seduce him as well?"

"But I thought that's what you were training me to be—a strumpet. But must I lie on my back all day just in case you might come in and want me?"

Her words acted like a glass of cold water thrown in his face. It was only when she spoke in such cynical fashion that he realized how naive and innocent she had really been at first. Until *he* had changed her. Controlling himself with an effort he walked behind the desk, turning up the lamp.

"Such a painful sacrifice on your part isn't necessary, mademoiselle. Please wrap a sheet around yourself at least—improvise a Roman toga, if you can. I can assure you that a little modesty and even coyness at times can be much more appealing to a man than such a blatant display of nudity."

"Oh!" He had managed to make her angry at last. "And what makes you think that I am interested in making myself appealing to a man? If I am to judge all men by you, it wouldn't matter; all you think of is your own selfish pleasure even if it has to be forced on an unwilling victim!"

He looked at her consideringly, the reflection of the lamp's light in his eyes making them appear as golden as hers for an instant.

"Am I really that selfish? Poor little victim! But then, you see, I've been used to taking women as they come—and go. Do you want me to make you an exception?"

"I want nothing from you except my freedom!"

Sullenly Marisa turned her back on him, snatching a sheet

off the unmade bed to wrap around herself. How she detested him! And what subtle new form of torment did he plan to use on her this time? What she had flung at him was true. She only longed to be free, and especially of him!

Chapter Seven

An obviously disapproving Donald brought dinner, sniffing loudly as he laid the table and setting down steaming covered dishes with an unnecessary clatter that caused his captain to raise an eyebrow and inquire politely if perhaps he was getting too old for life at sea.

Marisa sulked in the farthest corner of the big bed, keeping her back stubbornly turned; but she could not help overhearing the conversation. She could almost imagine Donald's long face, and the way his lips must be pursed. Well, at least Donald was on her side, and as soon as they reached France she'd beg him to help her. . . .

"And why would ye be wanting both wine *and* champagne?" Donald was asking in a gruff voice. "I can't recall as ye've ever displayed much liking for the vile, wicked stuff before. All bubbles, it is, and only meant for—"

He cast a pitying glance towards Marisa who was smothered under the bedcovers, and he was angry enough to glower at the captain. He had no right to treat a young, unprotected child as if she were some dockside trollop picked up for his pleasure!

Dominic Challenger, reading what was in the older man's mind, gave him a sarcastic smile. "Why should I need to seduce her when both you and she keep reminding me that she's ruined already? And I happen to have a taste for champagne tonight—and none at all for your preaching, you old reprobate!"

Donald opened his mouth to speak again and found his speech cut off by a steely, threatening look. He left without speaking again.

Rosemary Rogers

Suddenly a spicy aromatic scent filled the cabin, making Marisa's mouth water in spite of all her resolutions. Dominic had taken the covers off the silver dishes that Donald had brought in, and the delicious smell was almost too much for her to bear! Marisa bit her lip, her back stiffening, and the next moment she jumped as a cork popped loudly.

'So that's his game. I'm supposed to crawl and beg for my food now. . . . Well, we'll see!'

The odor of seafood and spices and saffron-flavored rice took her suddenly back to Martinique. Oh, why hadn't maman left her behind on that warm, happy island with her grandparents instead of dragging her off to France?

She was so hungry that even *his* presence could not stop the involuntary growling of her empty stomach, and Marisa blushed with shame.

"If you're not hungry, petite, perhaps a glass of champagne will help you cheer up. We'll soon be in France, and you might want to celebrate the parting of our ways!"

Lately he had taken to speaking to her in French; and as usual, his sarcastic tone of voice made her grit her teeth with anger. If she didn't eat he was just as likely to have the meal cleared away as soon as his own appetite was satisfied.

Wrapping a sheet loosely around her, she finally sat down opposite him. Captain Challenger's shirt was open to his waist, and she could not help noticing, all over again, the strangely wrought medal he wore on a silver chain around his neck. She had asked him about it before, and he'd only shrugged, telling her it was a good-luck charm given him by an old friend.

"It looks like a heathen thing to me!" she'd said primly and saw his lip curl ironically.

"*You* would appear the heathen to the man who gave me this, little wildcat. Stop acting so curious."

Well, she would not ask him any more questions. She knew all she wanted to know about him, although his behavior tonight puzzled her. He had made Donald lay the table as if for a formal dinner party; and now he instructed her on the correct implements to use, all the while keeping her glass full to the brim with champagne.

"You might as well learn to eat like a lady instead of a hun-

92

gry savage! Do you want this aunt of yours to feel ashamed of you? Or your lovers—"

"I would not take any lovers! Now that you've taught me what men really want from a woman I think I would much rather be a nun, after all!"

"Just think what you would have missed—immured in a Spanish convent!"

His eyes crinkled at the corners—why did she have to notice *that?* And when she would have answered him loftily, Marisa choked on her champagne instead. She spluttered, breathing up bubbles of champagne that seemed to penetrate her very brain, making it float away from her body.

"I think it's time for your next lesson, ma fille."

The sheet she had wrapped herself with had somehow vanished, and she was lying backward on the bed, her head spinning alarmingly.

"Since you are so determined to become a nun, you had better learn the ways in which men can take advantage of you."

Had she dreamed the husky whisper? Marisa gasped with shock as something cold and wet trickled over her breasts and down her belly. Her body jerked, arching, involuntarily, and her eyes, as she tried to focus them, held a puzzled, confused look.

"You are pouring champagne all over me! Are you mad? Stop—"

Marisa began to giggle helplessly the next moment when Dominic, bending his dark head to hers, said severely,

"Will you hold still, vixen? It would be a shame to waste all that champagne."

Neither of them had eaten very much, being far too occupied in arguing, and she thought for a moment that he was as drunk as she. She became aware, all of a sudden, of a strange sensation. His lips and tongue were tracing the path of the champagne, and going even further, in fact . . .

Marisa tried to wriggle away, but he held her pinioned, concentrating first on one quivering breast and then the other until she felt her whole body burning with embarrassment. And—and—oh, it was the strangest feeling, but although she struggled and moaned, she did not really want him to stop, not even when her nipples were achingly sensitive under his hands, and his seeking mouth moved much lower—across her taut, shrinking belly—lower still, until—

Until frightened both of herself and him, she began to fight against him in earnest, her breath sobbing in her throat, limbs writhing as she fought to close her thighs against this different kind of encroachment.

Forgetting her pride in her fear, Marisa began to plead with him, although somewhere in the back of her mind a small demon sat grinning and damned her for being a hypocrite. She had come closer than she ever had before to understanding desire—so close that when with a muttered expletive he slid himself up her body and kissed her mouth instead, she was almost sorry. She felt as if she had been on the brink of some strange and new experience, and now she had lost it.

Still, when he parted her thighs with his hands she made none of her usual protest, but let him, quivering again only very slightly when his fingers touched her. There, where his lips had brushed only moments ago.

"My poor jeune fille. Is the thought of seduction so frightening to you that you have to fight me tooth and nail?"

She realized then that she had actually clawed at his shoulders. When he leaned over her, penetrating her quickly and deeply, she tasted his blood against her lips and wondered in the back of her mind what had made him so patient with her tonight. Any other man she might have called kind, but she had learned that Dominic Challenger wasn't. He was a man who took what he wanted, and women were a convenience, no more—she remembered that he had snarled that at her one night.

She would never understand him, why even try. It was the champagne that made this time different from all those others and made her head whirl and her breasts ache against his chest where the funny foreign medal he wore pressed into her flesh, warm from his body, like a brand.

He held her against him all night, his flesh still part of hers. And he took her again in the morning when she was still half-asleep, quickly and impatiently this time, without a kiss or a caress. But at least he pulled the covers back over her when he left; and turning over with a sigh, Marisa slept again.

When she woke it was well past noon. Donald, his eyes carefully averted, brought her a tray and informed her that they were approaching the coast of France. They should be safely berthed in the harbor of Nantes by nightfall.

When he had gone, Marisa jumped quickly out of bed, grimacing slightly at the bad taste the champagne had left in her mouth. She could see nothing out of the porthole, for the captain's cabin was at deck level and not high enough for her to catch a glimpse of anything but the same blue, heaving ocean. Turning back with a sigh of disappointment, she discovered her "clothes"—the same patched-up garments she had worn during her short masquerade as a cabin boy. They were folded and lying neatly on a small chest at the foot of the bed.

A tacit reminder that the captain now desired her dressed for a change? Biting her lower lip, Marisa stared at the dirty-white shirt and breeches with distaste. During the time she had spent at sea, she had managed, somehow, to detach herself from reality. A ship was a world within itself, and since *he* had elected to keep her for his use, she had not come in contact with a single other human except Donald. She found herself wondering now if the rest of the crew even knew of her existence. The ambiguity of the situation she was placed in suddenly struck her with the force of a blow, and she flinched, snatching up the garments she had despised a moment ago.

France! But they were still quite some distance from Paris. What did he intend to do with her once they had disembarked? Surely he would allow her off the ship; he had said that women were considered bad luck. And if he did, then what?

She was given no chance to ask any questions. Some time much later in the afternoon Dominic came striding into the cabin, giving her only a cursory glance, and collected a sheaf of papers off his desk before leaving again. She heard voices, running feet on the deck, the shrill whistle of the boatswain's pipe, and the creaking of timbers. Mr. Benson's voice shouted orders that were unintelligible, and she guessed they were hauling down sail, for the normally swift passage of the ship seemed to have slowed so that now she could actually hear the lapping of water against her sides instead of the hiss as the sharp prow cut through the waves. It was intolerable that she should have to stay cooped up here, and especially *now;* but she dared not show herself on deck, either.

The rough cotton garments, washed in sea water with strong soap, chafed her skin, especially at the neck and waist. For a time Marisa paced angrily about the cabin, and then, flinging herself into a chair, she picked up the shabby, leather-bound volume of Shakespeare's plays that had so fascinated her before. As she turned the pages, trying to find the place where she had stopped, Marisa wondered how it was that the bad-tempered Captain Challenger should come to have such a book in his possession. She could not imagine him taking the time to sit down and read, and yet it appeared well worn, like a book of poetry by someone called Donne that she had also discovered on his desk.

Suddenly she found herself staring down at the frontis-piece—why hadn't she noticed it before? There was a scrawled Latin inscription, *Inopem me copia fecit,* 'Plenty makes me poor'—not *his* writing, surely? The hand was feminine, the ink faded. And below it, simply a name. 'Peggy.' Who was Peggy? What had she been to him?

It was the first question she asked him when he finally returned to the cabin, once the ship was safely at anchor.

He looked tired and irritable and didn't bother to speak one word to her; he merely sat on the end of the bed to take off his boots.

"Who is Peggy? Your wife?" Until the words slipped out she had not considered the possibility that he might, indeed, have a wife tucked away somewhere. She didn't know why the thought should disturb her—except that it made her own position so much the worse. His mistress!

Still occupied in tugging off his wet boots he looked up uncomprehendingly at first; then he frowned.

"What?"

"I asked you if your wife's name is Peggy. Or was she merely one of your mistresses?"

His face whitened, and then a look of such fury came over it that Marisa shrank back against the bulkhead.

"You damned, prying little bitch!" He said it softly, between his teeth. "What in hell do you mean by that? Where did you—"

The book she had been holding dropped from her suddenly nerveless fingers, catching his eye.

There was a silence that stretched unendingly, while Marisa stayed flattened against the wall, not daring to look at him. Oh, God. Why had she spoken? He'd looked furious enough to kill her with his bare hands!

And then he said in a surprisingly quiet, controlled voice, "Peggy was my mother. And I have no wife—nor do I intend ever to saddle myself with one. Do you understand?"

At last she managed to raise her eyes to his face, and he gave a harsh, ugly laugh. "Your eyes are as big as saucers. Did I really succeed in frightening you at last?" Before she could find her voice to respond, he stood up and crossed the room with two long strides and caught her shoulders. "Don't ever ask me questions about myself, menina. You might not like the answers you receive!"

"I—I didn't mean—" She didn't mean to stutter either, but she could not help it.

He pulled her against his chest and held her there as if to comfort her for having scared her half out of her wits. "Never mind. It's not your fault, and I'm a moody devil at the best of times. It's a good thing for you we'll soon be going our separate ways."

Marisa didn't dare question him again as he swept her up into his arms and carried her over to the bed. Not then, while he undressed her with surprising gentleness and then lay beside her, his hands moving over her trembling, acquiescent body as if he wished to memorize it.

"You haven't learned passion yet, have you?" he said softly once. "And I'm too damned impatient and selfish to be your instructor, although sometimes, when you lie here like a shivering trapped animal I find myself wondering—"

He was talking more to himself than to her, and she wondered at this different mood and its cause. Perhaps he'd be relieved to be rid of her; she knew *she* would be relieved to have her body belong to herself again.

Now, recognizing the signs of his desire as he pressed his lips against the vein that throbbed in her neck, Marisa expected him to take her without any further preliminaries. For the last time, perhaps. Tomorrow—hadn't he talked of their going separate ways? But instead, he cursed softly under his breath and rolled away from her.

With disbelieving eyes she watched him get up and begin to dress.

"Where are you going?" And then she bit her lip. Hadn't he just warned her not to question him?

He answered her in the old, hard voice she was used to.

"On deck—for some air. I let most of the crew go ashore tonight; they haven't had the kind of sweet consolation you've provided me with for the past weeks, my sweet. It's time I relieved Mr. Benson and took my turn at watch." Pulling a heavy coat over his shoulders he turned to look at her with unreadable, slaty eyes. "Go back to sleep. You ought to rest well tonight."

She raised herself on one elbow, puzzled by his sudden change of mood, and half-afraid too.

"And—and tomorrow?" she faltered, to be answered by his sarcastic, cutting laugh.

"Why, tomorrow I'll smuggle you ashore, and you'll be free of me, as you long to be. It won't take you much time to find another protector—perhaps a kinder and more patient one. Good night, little gypsy!"

Chapter Eight

The next day was all bustle and confusion, and Marisa felt like a sleepwalker moving in a kind of daze.

She had hardly slept—her mind a welter of jumbled, unpleasant thoughts. She missed the usual motion of the ship riding through the ocean swells, and the bed seemed suddenly cold and far too large.

When Donald came for her, she felt as if she had barely fallen asleep, and he clucked impatiently, keeping his back turned while she bathed her swollen eyes with cold water and slipped, shivering into the only garments she possessed. The captain had tired of his mistress, and she was the cabin boy again. In fact he had not even troubled himself enough to wish her a good-bye, and she could catch no glimpse of him when she followed Donald on deck, blinking in the sudden rush of sunlight.

Donald kept hurrying her, warning her to keep the woolen cap he had handed her pulled well down over her head. Too weary and confused to ask him any questions, she went with him unquestioningly, hardly caring where he was taking her. It could not matter; she was in France at last, safe and well, if a trifle shopworn. A slight, bitter smile that she was not aware of touched her soft mouth for an instant, causing Donald to give her a sharp look and then shake his head. Poor child, poor wronged creature! What will become of her now? he wondered. It was not right that the captain should have treated her so harshly, unless it was to teach them all a lesson for deceiving him. 'I should not have brought her aboard *The Challenger*,' Donald reflected gloomily now. 'The lass would have been better off in a Spanish orphanage, or even one of them papist convents.'

He blamed himself, the poor man, but he blamed his captain more and had spoken his mind frankly, risking both the black rage and the punishment that might follow.

"You should not have brought her aboard my ship, old man, if you meant to save her from me!" Dominic Challenger had said harshly. And then shrugging, as if to temper his previous outburst of anger he said, "Besides, the chit is not important; and if it had not been me the first time it would have been someone else. Do you think she was in such a passion to get to France merely so that she could keep her virtue?"

Even Mr. Benson, after he had received his dressing down, had gone back to reading his Bible and quoting it to all. "If she was not lost before, she is now. Fallen by the wayside . . ."

Marisa was unaware of the thoughts in Donald's head. Gradually she had begun to feel as if she were waking up from a dream to realize where she was and what had brought her here. France—her mother's country. No longer living in terror and torn apart by bloody revolution, but gay and vital and bursting with all the energy of change and progress. She had been a little girl when she had fled, her mind clouded by memories of horror, but she still remembered some of the towns where the gypsies had stopped to give exhibitions of juggling and dancing—and to pick the pockets of unwary citizens. But that had been long ago, and she was back. Oh, surely there would still be some of her mother's friends alive and still living in Paris who would remember her! Perhaps, by some lucky chance she would be able to find her Aunt Edmée. In France, where all the fashionable ladies took lovers, the little matter of her lost virginity would not brand her disgraced and unfit for marriage.

Yes, what a long way she had come, the young girl who had wanted to stay hidden behind the walls of a convent for the rest of her life! She had learned that to be raped by a man did not necessarily mean being ripped to pieces inside, and that to submit passively made it easier, if no less unpleasant. If *that* was all that marriage entailed, then she would much rather be a wife than a mistress, who could be too easily discarded.

With a curiously defiant gesture of pride, Marisa lifted her head, staring about her. They had left the noise and bustle of the harbor front and were now walking down a narrow street in the older part of town. Unused to walking on dry land, Marisa's legs had already begun to ache, and the rough cobblestones stung her bare feet.

Where was Donald taking her? He turned his head to give her a worried look.

"I'm sorry to have made ye walk such a distance, lassie, but folks would think it strange to see the likes of what you look like now to be riding in a carriage. It's no' far now."

He led her through a narrow, dirty alleyway where the sun seemed cut off by the buildings on either side of it, and then through a small gate into the back courtyard of what appeared to be a small inn, or posting house. There was no one about, although a few scrawny looking chickens ran squawking out of their way. Up a rickety wooden stairway that seemed to lean against a wall for support and then from a tiny balcony into a small but clean and pleasant looking room.

To cover his own embarrassment, Donald's manner had become gruffly businesslike. "There's a change of clothes for ye laid out on the bed and water in the pitcher there if you'd care for a wash. It's a good thing they were all so busy out in front with a party of damned English stopping to change horses. They're all over France now, I hear, since the peace was signed these few months ago. But ye'll not be concerned with that. I'll be going down now to find you something to eat, for you must be starved. Best lock the door behind me—you never know in these foreign places."

Clothes, female clothes at last! How had Donald procured them for her? But before she could ask, he had disappeared, tactfully closing the door behind him, and Marisa could not bear to wait another instant before she stripped off her scratchy, disgusting boy's garments, to try on her new attire.

How the fashions had changed! She remembered that the queen of Spain and the duquesa de Alba had worn such high-waisted, flimsy gowns, although theirs had been of expensive, transparent material covered with embroidery in silver and gold. *This* gown was of cloth, a dark brown color that reminded her for an instant of the Carmelite habit. But there the resemblance ended for it was bound just under the breasts with yellow-gold ribbons that fell fluttering almost to the hem, following the straight lines of the narrow skirt. The high neck and long sleeves, puffed in tiers, were also trimmed with the same color ribbon, and so was the straw bonnet which was lined with brown.

A plain dress, obviously made by a provincial dressmaker and meant for traveling, but it was still the prettiest that Marisa had owned since her childhood. She decided critically that although a trifle loose it fit her passably well, as did the kid half boots that laced with ribbon.

Peering into the small mirror, Marisa pulled at her short curls trying to make them lie in place around her face. There. That was better! And now she almost looked like a woman, or would have if her figure had been a trifle fuller.

A knock at the door made her whirl about, and when she heard Donald's voice she ran to open it, almost throwing her arms about him in gratitude for his thoughtfulness.

While she wolfed down a slice of cold mutton pie she listened as he explained that the captain had given him orders to see that she got safely to Paris. If she had no objections, they would tell anyone that asked she was his French niece whom he had not seen since she was a baby, and that they were on their way to Paris from the province of Toulouse.

Marisa gave him a suspicious look.

"How do you know so much about France?"

"I don't, lassie! Only some of the ports. But the captain told me what I was to say."

She sniffed. "How considerate of him! I'm sure he's good at making up lies."

"Ah, well." He shook his head at her. "He's a hard man to understand, sometimes, an' there's a devil riding his shoulder that makes him the way he is. You wouldna' understand."

Marisa bit her lip to stop herself from asking the questions she longed to, and she told herself that she had already put him out of her mind. Once she arrived in Paris she would never see him again. No doubt he'd go back to his pirating after the broken mast was fixed and Donald had returned to Nantes, his errand completed.

And in the end, it was easy enough to occupy her mind with other things, once their journey had begun.

The crowded diligence followed the meandering course of the Loire River for a while, and, although their progress was slow and they stopped frequently to rest or change the horses, Marisa did not really mind. Donald pretended to sleep for the most part, and she was free to gaze out of the window, reacquainting herself with the familiar landscape. Her fellow passengers were peasants or minor clerks, and once she had told them she was taking her Scottish uncle to visit some friends of the family in Paris, they did not question her further. Even during *these* changed times there were refugees everywhere trying to find the families they had been separated from during the revolution. And spies as well, if the rumors were true. It was best not to ask too many questions.

It took them several days to reach the outskirts of Paris, and by this time Marisa felt tired and wilted. She had watched smart carriages, sometimes escorted by dashingly uniformed soldiers, rattle by them in a cloud of dust and had noticed with a pang of envy the women who rode in them. What a peasant she looked like after all!

Suddenly the whole notion of her traveling all the way to Paris on the off-chance of finding some member of her mother's family seemed utter madness. Look at the trouble it had already brought her! She should have stayed in the convent and obediently married that detestable Don Pedro Arteaga. She should have. . . .

But she had to collect her wandering thoughts quickly when the diligence pulled to a halt with a squeaking of wooden brakes and the passengers began to clamber over each other in their eagerness to alight.

They had stopped before an inn, but on what street and in what part of the city she had no idea. She had no bundle of clothes to cling to; she had nothing, in fact but the garments on her back and the small purse Donald had thrust awkwardly at her before they set out. Payment for her services, she had thought, blushing angrily, but she had taken it so she wouldn't hurt Donald's feelings, and now she was glad she had, for the few coins gave her a feeling of independence.

She had begun to glance around, confused, almost forgetting Donald until he touched her arm gently.

"It'll be dark soon—and a rainy night into the bargain, to judge from the looks of the sky." He was looking around him anxiously as he spoke, as if he, too, were at a loss now that they had finally arrived. "Perhaps we'd best—," he had begun when suddenly he gave a grunt of relief as a man, unobtrusively dressed, who had been studying the faces of the passengers, came forward and spoke in English.

"You're Donald McGuire? I'm Silas Winters, late of the brig *Stella Maris* out of the Carolinas. Captain Challenger sent me to look for you."

Apart from a slight, polite inclination of his head in her direction Silas Winters, a quiet young man, was tactful enough to leave Marisa to her own confused thoughts. He helped her into the small closed carriage, but he seemed more at ease talking to Donald, explaining that his ship had been taken by a Frenchman, and he had recently been released in exchange for a French prisoner.

"I've signed up with Captain Challenger. It was a stroke of luck running into him at the ambassador's house just two nights ago. It seems that we've settled our difference with France—for the time being, anyhow!"

All during this time, Marisa felt herself incapable of uttering a word. If she opened her mouth she might very well shriek with sheer rage and frustration. How dare he? She wouldn't become his prisoner again! If he thought he could treat her as he had done, abandon her without a word, and then have her picked up and brought to him on some whim —what did he want with her this time?

The answer, springing into her mind, made her blush and clasp her hands tightly together in the darkness of the carriage. Oh no, she wouldn't! They were no longer on his ship, where as captain he had the power of life and death over everyone on board. She was free, and in Paris, and if he attempted to molest her she would not hesitate to scream as loudly as she could, to bring the gendarmes running. He'd find out. . . .

It began to drizzle as the carriage bowled along the darkening streets, some of them already lit with sputtering oil lanterns, but Marisa was too agitated to notice anything, not even when the two men who sat opposite her fell into a low-voiced conversation that excluded her.

'He cannot do this to me. Only a few days ago he was telling me how glad he would be when we could go our separate ways. And now, oh! It's too much to bear.'

She gritted her teeth as the carriage came to a sudden halt before a tall, narrow house in a quiet street, and it was all she could do to murmur a few polite words of thanks to Mr. Winters, who bowed solemnly over her hand. What did *he* think of her being here? How would he react if she suddenly jumped back into the carriage and demanded to be taken away—taken back to the inn they had just left?

But he had turned away to unlock an iron gate set into the wall and now stood aside to allow her to precede him up a flight of steps lit by a lantern over the door that now loomed up in front of her.

An elderly servant answered a tug on the bell cord, and Marisa found herself within—looking about a small, rather shabby looking hallway leading to a thinly carpeted stairway at one end and some closed doors to the left and right.

"Guillaume will show you to your room, miss," Silas Winters said behind her. He coughed apologetically. "I am afraid there are no other servants, not yet. Accommodations are difficult to find in Paris at this time with the English swarming across the channel in droves trying to satisfy their curiosity." He added quickly, as if he had said too much, "The captain will be staying over at the ambassador's house tonight —there's a reception there. But I was to tell you he hopes you'll find everything you need. Guillaume has already prepared a light supper, and—" he said giving her a sudden, shy smile, "you must be very tired, I'm sure."

He was quite young, Marisa noticed with surprise. Probably no more than twenty-two or -three at the most. And at least he had the manners of a gentleman. She gave him a tentative smile in return, uncertain now what she would do, and heard Donald say briskly, "That's right, lass. You go upstairs and rest. And if someone would just show me to the kitchen, now, it's something I'm needing to eat!"

Once again Marisa felt matters taken out of her hands.

Mixed with a feeling of relief that *he* was not here she could feel her keyed-up mood vanish to be replaced by exhaustion. It wouldn't hurt, after all, to spend one night here, and in the morning, when she felt rested, she could leave. Somehow, she didn't feel that this polite young Mr. Winters would feign ignorance at her being kept locked up like a prisoner. Yes, there was always the morning.

How soundly she slept that night! Waking, she did not at first realize where she was. A strange room, like so many others she'd slept in as they had traveled the long road to Paris. The bed was more comfortable than most, and the room quite large but cold, for the small fire that had been lit last night had gone out.

Marisa stretched, blinking her eyes, and noticed that faint sunlight filtered through a crack in the worn velvet draperies covering the window. Somewhere in the room a clock ticked, and she remembered seeing one on the mantelpiece last night, just before she had locked the door.

Memory came flooding back, and she sat up, alarmed, but the door was still closed, and she was alone, shivering with cold and apprehension, in a sparsely furnished room. What time was it? Had he returned yet? She must get away!

Marisa leaped out of bed and ran to the door, testing it to make sure it was locked. A glance at the ormolu clock told her it was already past twelve—she had slept far too long!

Her teeth chattering now, she quickly splashed icy cold water over her face and arms, performing her ablutions as quickly and as best she could. Her crumpled clothes still lay carelessly slung over the chair she had thrown them on last night, and now she began to dress hastily, one eye on the door.

The remorseless ticking of the clock hurried her shaking, numb fingers as she fastened her gown, trying to smooth some of the wrinkles out of it by running her hands down the skirt. Now her stockings and shoes. She pushed the little purse as far down the bosom of her dress as it would go, snatched up her straw bonnet, and with a last glance around the room crept to the door and drew back the bolt, praying it would not make too much noise. Had someone locked it from the outside? No, thank God. It opened without too much squeaking, and she tiptoed out onto the narrow landing she remembered from last night, still without seeing another soul.

Marisa did not quite understand why she suddenly felt so panic-stricken. But she did not want to see him again, her instincts told her that much, and she was following them blindly, intent only upon escape.

Cautiously, she started down the worn stairs, clinging to the thin railing. One careful step at a time, testing each one to make sure it would not creak. There was still no one to be seen, but halfway down she heard the murmur of voices and froze, until she realized that they came through the half-open door of a room to the left of the stairwell.

Her heart began to pound suddenly when she recognized Dominic Challenger's harsh, exasperated voice.

"Dammit! She's worth a lot more than that, and you know it! If I didn't need the money right now I'd keep her for a while longer; she's trim and easy to handle once you've mastered her, but I'm in a hurry to get back home and must be rid of her."

Still clutching at the stair rail, Marisa felt sick with horror and humiliation. She swayed, her heartbeats sounding like pounding drums in her ears, and hardly heard the other man reply. "You drive a hard bargain, my friend, but I'll consider meeting your price after I've seen her and decide if she's worth what you're asking."

Without waiting to hear more, she began to run, as silently as she could. No and no and no! He would not sell her off so callously as if she were a piece of merchandise to be bargained for! How could even *he* be so heartless and depraved? Had he planned to send the man into her bedroom while she still slept to take her by force as he had? No wonder all her instincts had warned her!

She ran down the hallway, past the room where the two men still argued, and tugged desperately at the front door. To her surprised relief, it opened without a struggle. Obviously he had forgotten to lock it behind his visitor.

In a flash, she was outside. Running down the steps, through the open iron gate, and out into the street at last where she continued to run and run until she was out of breath.

Chapter Nine

Philip Sinclair, trying out his new pair of matched bays behind a smart racing curricle, had to swerve sharply to avoid the young woman who came running around the corner into the street. He swore angrily as he barely managed to avert being overturned or losing a wheel. Damn the female! What was the matter with her? She had been fleeing as if pursued by all the demons of hell, and now she lay in a sobbing, crumpled heap on the cobblestones. Surely she wasn't hurt? Although if she was, it was her own fault. Damned French! He supposed, however, that he'd better go and make sure she was all right. The Peace of Amiens was an uneasy one, and he was a visitor in Paris. He didn't want any trouble. . . .

Marisa was not sobbing with fear—she was past that—but with sheer exhaustion. It had not yet occurred to her how narrowly she had escaped death.

She lay there unable to move, and suddenly there was a pair of highly polished, tasseled boots standing before her eyes, and she heard a voice inquiring in stilted, accented French if she were hurt or needed any assistance.

"I must say, mademoiselle," he continued severely, "that you should take more care to look where you are going! I almost ran you over."

She looked up slowly, first seeing fashionable nankeen breeches of pale yellow, then a gold watch fob dangling from a striped silk waistcoat, and finally a high white cravat, intricately tied. Marisa blinked, hardly able to believe that such a handsome young man could exist. His blond hair, cut à la Brutus, fell over his forehead which was creased at the moment by a worried frown.

"Mademoiselle?" He repeated inquiringly, and when she

struggled to rise, he automatically put out his gloved hand to help her up.

Philip Sinclair saw a flushed tear-stained face framed by dark gold curls that clung damply to her temples. He could feel her trembling, whether from shock or fear he could not tell, and his voice sharpened with concern. "I say—are you sure you're all right? Can you stand?" She looked like a child, her thin figure encased in a poorly cut gown of a most unbecoming shade of brown, and he took her for some poor shopkeeper's daughter until she spoke to him in perfect English, her voice husky with emotion.

"You—you are English, sir? Oh, then would you please, please be good enough to take me with you? You need not take me far—but I—I *must* leave this street before they discover me gone and come after me! Oh, please, I beg you!"

He stared at her in dismay, obviously hesitant, and then when fresh tears sprang into her eyes and began to trickle forlornly down her face he decided that a scene was to be avoided at all costs. Besides, there *was* something deucedly intriguing about her and the way she spoke such flawless English. What on earth could a young woman of obvious education be doing here, shabbily dressed, all alone and terrified out of her wits?

"Come on then," he said shortly, and to her relief he asked no more questions but bundled her up beside him, driving off at a fast clip that delighted her and brought a flush to her cheeks.

Mr. Sinclair, already regretting his impulsive decision, could not help glancing doubtfully at the girl—she could really be no more than a child!—who sat beside him, leaning slightly forward. She had a delightful little profile, with a slightly retroussé nose and tiny chin, but, my God, suppose some of his friends were to see him now! He would become a laughingstock. Then a rather unpleasant thought came into his mind, causing him to frown slightly. Suppose she was not what she seemed, but a little adventuress who had deliberately run out into the street before a smart curricle so that her family could blackmail him? He had been warned to be careful in Paris, and especially now, when all Englishmen were held in suspicion. Dash it! What should he do now?

He had been driving aimlessly, still wondering what his next course of action should be when his companion, who had been silent hitherto as if trying to compose herself, suddenly clutched his arm.

"Oh, stop!" He gave her a look of surprise, and the next minute she blushed at her own boldness, saying in a softer, apologetic voice, "That is—if you would please stop for just a moment, sir? That building there, you see, I recognize it."

The building stretched for half the length of the street. It was huge and forbidding looking, with grey turrets and a bell tower; high walls surrounded it.

Philip, obediently reining up his spirited horses, looked puzzled. What the devil did she mean? He had heard that this building had been used as a prison during the revolution, but surely she was too young to remember that?

"It—it was once a Carmelite convent," she said softly in a strained voice, and she began again to twist her hands together in her lap. "Then, you see, not everyone believed in the danger, and those who did not flee, including 115 priests and the archbishop himself, were all hacked to death. I remember that we prayed for their souls after we had reached Spain safely."

She gave a convulsive shudder, the thought recalling her to the present and her reason for being here, perched up beside a strange young man with bright blue eyes who had rescued her just like a knight-errant in the early days of chivalry!

"Do you really remember all that? I say, it must have been terrible for you, and of course none of us in England realized just how badly things were going until they murdered the king himself. . . ."

She must be a royalist then, Philip was thinking. He heard that some of the former aristocrats had lost everything, and those who had survived were still forced to live in hiding, and were under constant suspicion ever since the royalist plots against Bonaparte.

The girl had turned to look up at him, and he noticed for the first time that she had really beautiful eyes, amber-gold in color, shaded by long, dark lashes that looked spiky from tears.

111

"Who are you?" The words slipped out without his own volition.

"Maria Antonia Catalina de Castellanos y Gallardo." She said it all in one breath, adding simply, "But everyone calls me Marisa. It was my maman's name for me, for *she* was French. They put her in prison, and she went to the guillotine with the others. She died very bravely, Delphine said."

"Oh, God!" Philip ejaculated, quite forgetting himself.

His concern, and the sympathy in his handsome face, made Marisa want to confide everything to him—or *almost* everything.

Her words began to tumble over each other.

"I was in a convent in Spain, but they wanted me to marry a man I had never seen—a—a libertine! And so I ran away. I thought that if I could get to France, to Paris, then perhaps I could find my Aunt Edmée again. *She* was married to an Englishman, Lord—Lord—oh, I cannot remember his name!" she cried out with exasperation. "Perhaps *you* would know him and I should be safe again."

"But—"

She was too overwrought to let him interrupt. "There is also my godmother. They sent her husband, the viscount Beauharnais to the guillotine, but I heard from someone that it was only a few days afterwards that the Citoyen Robespierre was executed, and they stopped sending everyone to the guillotine, so . . . She was very pretty and so kind! And I am quite sure that if only I could . . ."

Philip Sinclair's head reeled. The girl's story sounded too improbable to be true. And yet, could it be possible that she was talking of the same Josephine de Beauharnais who had married the upstart Corsican and was now first lady of France?

"This—this godmother of yours. Perhaps you can remember her whole name?"

"Marie-Josephe-Rose de la Pagerie—before she married the viscount, of course! And she was a Creole, from Martinique, like my maman and my Aunt Edmée. Oh, monsieur!" Excited, she had slipped back into French. "Do you think you may know her? Does she still live in Paris?"

The rest of the afternoon, which had started out so badly,

112

turned into a kind of dream, and Marisa felt that fate, which had been so unkind to her before, had surely relented at last.

Within the next four hours she had been reunited not only with her godmother, but her aunt as well. And her happiness was all due to the good offices of the handsome Englishman, Philip Sinclair, who, on hearing her story, had not wasted a moment in driving her all the way to Malmaison, where the wife of the first consul of France was in residence at the moment.

There was a long time that passed before Marisa, still slightly dazed, became aware of the full extent of her good fortune. Perhaps God had forgiven her after all!

Her godmother, her mother's childhood friend, was married to none other than Napoleon Bonaparte, the man who had conquered more than half of Europe. And her aunt, the Countess Landrey, had taken advantage of the uneasy peace to visit France. She was, in fact, staying at Malmaison with her friend when the young Englishman, whom she remembered meeting in London, had all but forced his way past the enormous, gilded gates.

From then on, Marisa's whole life changed. So drastically she could hardly believe it was all true and happening to her. Suddenly she was no longer a poor orphan but a young lady of fashion, her gowns designed and tailored by the great couturier Leroy and her hair arranged and styled by her own maid. Josephine's daughter Hortense, whom she had known as a child was her friend; and Napoleon himself had noticed her, ruffling her curls as he passed.

What a transformation! Her mirror told her so, when the others did not. Why, she was no longer as ugly as she had thought herself, after all. When her hair was dressed à la Tite, a jeweled headband showing off its burnished gold splendor, and she wore a diaphanous muslin gown embroidered with gold or silver, she was the equal of any other young woman and the target for flirtatious glances and comments. Only her aunt and godmother knew the whole story behind her sudden appearance in Paris, and not even to them had she divulged the name of the man who had shamed her.

They did not press her, and Marisa, feeling petted and protected and safe, spent the next few weeks reveling in the luxury and attention that suddenly surrounded her. Her sudden arrival in France was not questioned; since she was under the protection of the chief consul himself, who would dare? Her godmother Josephine and her aunt had let only small, casual hints drop, so that soon it was generally understood she had spent most of her life in a Spanish convent and had traveled here to be reunited with her mother's family.

She stayed at Malmaison, which had become like a home to her, and her Aunt Edmée, still beautiful and young-looking, made an amusing game of instructing her in the ways of the fashionable world.

Her time passed in a whirl of activities—flirting and dancing lessons and riding lessons, and even instructions in geography and history and philosophy. Women like Madame de Staël had made it fashionable for the feminine sex to be intelligent —at least in France. In England a woman who dared to express an opinion of her own, or to argue, would be labeled a bluestocking. So her aunt told her, grimacing slightly as she said it.

"I can imagine how it must have been for you, my pet, tucked away in that convent surrounded by nuns! No wonder you wanted to run away! But there—we will not speak of that yet, not until you are ready. I myself felt that England was like another kind of prison, where women are expected to keep their place and do nothing but simper and make inane conversation. How I've yearned for Paris!"

Obviously Aunt Edmée was not happy in her marriage. Her husband was an old man surrounded by doctors, and there had been no children.

"Still," Edmée admitted with a laugh, "I suppose I should count myself lucky! He allows me to go my own way, as long as I am discreet. I don't shock you, I hope? And he's rich. . . ."

Marisa had already begun to learn that there was hardly a married woman among those elegantly gowned indolent ladies who frequented the highest circles, who did not have lovers —or had not had in the past. Even Josephine herself had been the mistress of Paul Barras when Napoleon had met her.

These were the people she was surrounded by, and how naive she must seem in comparison! Not at all experienced, in spite of the unpleasant past she tried to put out of her mind.

Marisa had not been formally presented in Paris yet, but she was happy in the relative seclusion of Malmaison; and there was Philip, who in spite of the fact that he was an Englishman, was permitted to visit her and came almost every day.

The recent peace notwithstanding, it was well known the first consul had no love for the English. "A nation of shopkeepers," he called them scornfully. And already Marisa had heard whispers of countless royalist plots against the Republic, financed by the English. Their nobility flocked across the channel to visit France and sample the pleasures of the Continent again, and their spies were everywhere.

So it was surprising that Philip Sinclair was allowed beyond the golden gates of the château, with its tricolor sentry boxes outside and handsomely uniformed hussars who stood watchful guard. Marisa suspected that this concession was only due to the pleading of her godmother Josephine, who had been so kind to her since her unexpected arrival and had all but adopted her as another daughter.

Her first impression of Monsieur Sinclair had not changed since she had begun to see him so often. He was still the handsomest man she had ever set eyes on, and his manners matched his appearance. They strolled in the gardens together, down the ornamental flower-lined walks that Josephine had laid out everywhere, and sometimes paused to sit and rest by cool, tinkling fountains.

He talked to her of London and answered her questions about how ladies dressed and acted there; and he related witty anecdotes that made her laugh. They were never entirely alone together, for there was always a group of young people, including Hortense, Josephine's daughter, who accompanied them on their walks. But all the same, they had opportunities to talk together; and if she had far more freedom than a young English gentlewoman her age, Philip never mentioned it or acted any differently.

He was intrigued by her. Not only because of the faint air of mystery that clung to her, but also because of her transformation from timid, trembling street waif to budding beauty.

115

With her burnished, dark gold curls arranged in the Greek fashion and her clinging, fashionable muslin gowns she looked like a wood-nymph, still slightly shy and ready to run if frightened, but already showing promise of beauty.

At first it had been curiosity and an almost protective sense of responsibility that had taken Philip back to see her. But now, he admitted to himself ruefully, he was on the way to becoming completely bewitched. Who was she? The long name that she had repeated so solemnly to him on the occasion of their first meeting meant nothing to him; the fact that she was Madame Bonaparte's goddaughter and the niece of Countess Landrey established her as wellborn, at least. But how had she turned up in Paris so suddenly, without her relatives' knowledge? And who or what had she been running from that day? He did not dare press her for details, and her small face always clouded when he ventured a casual question.

Not wanting to frighten her off or destroy her growing trust in him, Philip let it be, hoping that one day she might confide in him. In the meantime, there were other matters that needed his attention, among these being the reasons he had traveled to France in such uneasy times. He said nothing of these to Marisa, leaving her to conclude that he, like all the other English aristocrats, was merely here on an extension of his grand tour. She was always transparently happy to see him, and admitted, without guile, that indeed she *did* miss him when he had to stay away for a few days.

It was left to the Countess Landrey, returning from a week of whirlwind activities in Paris, to warn her young niece to caution before she gave her heart away to Philip Sinclair.

Chapter Ten

"But why should I be, as you say, 'careful' with Philip? Why? What is wrong with him? He is a gentleman, you have said so yourself!"

Turning away from the window, Edmée-Amélie made a moue that was half-playful, half-dismayed.

"Ah no, chérie! I did not mean to say that there is anything *wrong* with this excellent young man, far from it. But you see—," she looked into her niece's rebellious golden eyes and sighed, choosing her words carefully this time— "it is you that I worry about, Marisa. Looking at you now, so chic, so pretty, it has been difficult to remember what a sheltered life you have led all these years. This Philip is the first young man you have flirted with, is he not? Yes, he is very handsome, his manners very charming, and you look upon him as the gallant chevalier who rescued you, oui? But you must not begin to mistake gratitude for—for something else. Soon you will be meeting other young men, all just as handsome and dashing and—more suitable."

"Suitable!" Marisa burst in, her eyes flashing, but her aunt only shook her head warningly.

"You do not like this word? Ah, I remember when I was told of this English earl, what we would call a count here, and was told how rich and suitable a match he would make for me, I, too, shook my head. However, if I had stayed in France and married the penniless young man I thought I loved, I would have gone to the guillotine. Philip Sinclair is a pleasant young man, but his father is only a baron and a gambler—a member of the Carleton House set. There is not much money there, only wildness. In fact one of the reasons Mr. Sinclair is in Paris at the moment *was* to pay court to a certain heiress, also English. Lady Arabella Marlowe is here with her formidable mama to see Paris and improve her French. And tout de suite, Lord Anthony scraped up the money to dispatch his son here, also. He is expected to make a rich marriage, to please not only his father but his uncle as well. You comprehend?"

Marisa's eyes, beginning to shine with tears, looked stormy. "No! How could you expect me to? If Philip was in love with another woman, he would have told me so—he is honest and kind! And—and he spends almost all of his time here, because he wishes to see *me*. I cannot believe that he would be so cold-blooded as to allow himself to be forced into a loveless alliance merely because his family wants such a match. He—"

"Ah, yes, he is bedazzled by you, ma petite. That much is easy to see. But for how long? Soon he will begin to think guiltily of his duty—and you may be sure that if his uncle who is the head of the family hears what's been going on, he will waste no time calling for his return to England, and *then* what? Do you think he will be brave enough to take you with him? What will he live on? Be sensible, my love; that is all I am asking of you. Flirt, yes and enjoy yourself! But don't be foolish enough to lose your heart."

Later, when she had retired to her room to fight back the treacherous gale of weeping that threatened to engulf her, Marisa could not help feeling as if a heavy stone had been placed over her heart.

Her aunt had meant well, she was sure of that. But oh, the humiliation of realizing that she had let her growing feelings for Philip, and her delight in his company, show so obviously! It was true; she had not learned to flirt or to hide her emotions. Did she love Philip? She didn't know. And certainly *he* had never overstepped the bounds of convention in their talks together. But he did like her, he did! And it wasn't fair that his father and this powerful uncle of his should be allowed to plan and order his whole life. As for this English heiress, this Lady Arabella. . . .

Marisa's hands clenched into small fists at her sides as she began to pace angrily about her room. Did *she* not have enough spirit to refuse a suitor who did not love her and was forced to pay his addresses to her for the dowry she would bring him?

'*I* would not do it,' Marisa thought, and then the recollection of her reckless flight and its consequences made her face burn hotly with shame and anger. Suddenly, unbidden, the image of Dominic Challenger's dark, mocking face rose up to haunt her, and she remembered without wanting to the feeling of his hands on her body and his body driving into hers. Hateful! Philip would never treat her like that: he was gentle and tender and respectful.

But if Philip knew—would he still respect her? He was English, not French, and everyone knew the English were rigidly conventional when it came to women. She could not bear the thought of telling him and watching his face change.

Her thoughts went round and round. 'But if he found out that *I* was an heiress?' Then perhaps, if he loved her enough, it would not matter. But by now her father might be so angry that he had disowned her; her Aunt Edmée had suggested she should write to him and tell him she was safe, but guilt had made her put it off. She must do so. Perhaps he would understand and forgive her after all.

Fortunately she had no more time to think just then. Napoleon himself was expected to arrive that evening, and there would be a crowd of notables for dinner. She had to bathe and dress extra carefully, and she did not dare be late for it was well known he could not bear unpunctuality.

Trying to distract herself while her maid fussed around her, clucking impatiently, Marisa went over the guest list in her mind: The other two consuls—Sieyès and Ducos, who of course were now merely figureheads since Bonaparte had just been appointed consul for life; his foreign minister Talleyrand, prince of Benevento; Joseph Fouché, minister of police; and generals, admirals—and a sprinkling of foreign diplomats as well. It had even been whispered that the new tsar of Russia, Alexander I, might be present.

It was to be a glittering, grand assembly, and in spite of herself Marisa began to feel a nervous fluttering in her stomach as she fervently hoped she would not disgrace herself.

Thank goodness for the current simplicity in fashion! Her

sheer white muslin gown was embroidered with tiny gold flowers and ended in a train. A crisscrossed gold velvet sash was belted under her breasts and matched her velvet slippers, and her hair was caught up in a mass of curls, artful tendrils falling over her forehead and temples.

"Ravissante!" her maid sighed, quickly twisting a gold chain several times around Marisa's neck then standing back to admire the effect before handing Marisa a fine silk fan, spangled with gold, that matched her shawl. A touch of rouge next on her lips and high on her cheekbones.

'Is that really me?' she wondered, staring at her reflection in the long mirror.

Her aunt came quickly into the room, smiling with satisfaction.

"You look quite charming, my love! But come along now, we must hurry. They are starting to receive already."

"I feel half-naked!" Marisa whispered, feeling sure that everyone could see right through her thin taffeta petticoat.

Edmée, resplendently dressed in silver-spangled gauze, gave a gurgle of laughter.

"Wait till you see Pauline! She *is* naked under her silk gown, I'd swear! She doesn't look at all like a mourning widow, and *he* will be furious with her, but then, Pauline doesn't care for anything but her own pleasure."

Neither do I! Marisa thought recklessly as she went downstairs with her aunt.

Usually, she never touched champagne, for its taste reminded her unpleasantly of the first time she had tried it. But tonight she consumed several glasses of it, and that and the knowledge that she looked as beautiful and sophisticated as any of the women present gave her the courage that she needed to go through the evening.

The rooms were overheated for Napoleon, who felt the cold, always ordered fires lit, even on the hottest summer days. A film of perspiration beaded her face, giving it a glow, and her thin gown clung to her figure, outlining her small breasts and slim thighs.

The château gleamed brilliantly; even the gardens were lit up, to accommodate the overflow of guests who wished to stroll outside in the cool air and engage in whispered flirtations in dark corners.

Only the most important guests had been asked to come earlier, for dinner; the others would arrive later for the dancing and a late supper served buffet style. Princes, dukes, and the highest ranking diplomats. Even the blond, handsome Tsar Alexander himself, who was given the place of honor beside Josephine.

Following the example of the other women present, Marisa found that flirting was not too hard after all, if one used one's fan and one's eyelashes to advantage. She was seated next to a Russian prince, one of the tsar's entourage, and in spite of his outrageous compliments in a heavy accent that made them difficult to understand, she managed to keep him at bay. On her other side, Joseph Fouché, the minister of police, who had recently been appointed the duke of Otranto, smiled his thin-lipped smile and toyed with the stem of his wineglass, drinking only sparingly and seeming to observe everything through his dark, heavy-lidded eyes. Marisa decided that she did not like him very much. And how was it that he had not brought his wife?

The Russian begged her to show him the gardens when dinner was over, and Marisa lowered her lashes demurely, neither refusing nor agreeing. Under the tablecloth, he put his hand on her thigh, and she tapped it with her fan, as she had seen her aunt do.

"You are far too bold, monsieur!"

"And you—can you possibly be as innocent as you seem, my golden beauty? I would like to find out."

"And if I let you, I would no longer be innocent, would I?"

She wanted to giggle then, delighted with herself for being so quick to answer him. Flirting was easy, after all, and especially in the midst of a crowd like this where she felt quite safe. All the same, she must try to avoid this persistent Russian after dinner, she thought, picking at her food as course after course was served and then whisked away. If only she didn't have the uncomfortable feeling

121

that Fouché was listening to every single word that was said! But then, why should she care?

All the same, Marisa was relieved when Josephine gave the signal that the ladies should retire. "I will see you later," the prince whispered when she rose with a polite, murmured excuse. Fouché said nothing, but she thought she could feel his eyes following her, and the thought made her strangely uneasy.

Listening to the high-pitched babbling that went on all around her, she managed to put him out of her mind.

"You are quite a success tonight, my love!" Aunt Edmée whispered to her. "And when we all return to Paris tomorrow, you are to go with us. You cannot imagine how exciting it is—but then, you will quite soon grow as blasé as the rest of us!"

Would she? Glancing around her, Marisa did not think it possible. But then look at Hortense—so recently married to Louis Bonaparte and looking pale and withdrawn instead of radiant as a new bride should be. And Pauline le Clerc, so recently widowed and excitedly talking of her latest lovers. Even Aunt Edmée had a dreamy look in her eyes when one of the other women teased her about a certain dark-haired man who had paid her so much attention at the last ball they had attended. Marisa thought perhaps what she, too, needed was a lover, to make her one of them, and wipe away all the unpleasant memories. Even the memory of Philip. . . . And then she thought boldly, her mind overexcited and floating with the effects of too much champagne, why not him? If I can't have him as a husband, then perhaps I should give him something to regret! Yes—and I'd like *her*, that Lady Arabella, to know, too, that she was only his second choice!

Gleaming with mischief and defiance, her golden eyes seemed larger than ever. And when the ladies emerged from the drawing room, the first person she set eyes on was Philip!

In formal evening dress, he looked more handsome than ever. His high-collared blue velvet coat, worn with a white silk cravat matched his eyes; the frilled ruffles of his shirt showed at the wrists, and he wore black satin knee breeches and a sword with a ribbon rosette at its hilt. Even the powdered tie wig that went with full dress could not detract from his good looks, and the smile he gave her, lighting up his whole face, made her heart begin to pound.

He came forward to meet her, and she offered him both her hands without thinking to control her emotions. Nothing could spoil her happiness at this moment, not even the fact that out of the corner of her eye she had noticed the duke of Otranto, in his dark coat, leaning up against a wall and watching them with a guarded, sardonic expression.

"Philip!"

He bowed to her in a ridiculously formal fashion, responding in French, "A votre service, mademoiselle!" And then, in a husky undertone, "You are so beautiful tonight! I can hardly believe that I am lucky enough to be here and to see you smiling at me."

"I am glad that you are here, too! Will you not ask me to dance, and quickly, before that fierce Russian approaches too near?"

The dance happened to be a waltz, newly imported from Vienna, and by the time they had made a few turns about the floor Marisa had recovered enough control over her senses to remember her resolution of a few moments before. It helped her to realize that Philip appeared suddenly to have become tongue-tied, gazing down into her flushed, smiling face as if he could not tear his eyes away.

"Is it true that in this club they call Almacks, in London, a young woman is not permitted to dance the waltz without permission?"

"The patronesses are very strict," he murmured in a bemused fashion, watching her mouth—the arched upper lip and softly curved lower lip. Why hadn't he noticed what a red, kissable mouth she had before?

"Then perhaps it is not proper that I should dance the waltz with you?"

"This is France, and it is quite all right. And you—you are so light in my arms, like a feather. I could dance with you forever."

"I have been taking lessons," she said demurely, enjoying the slight trembling of the arms that held her. Oh, yes, he

123

wanted her—and she was surprised at herself for thinking
in such a fashion.

The rest of the evening seemed to pass far too quickly.
She drank more champagne, and it seemed to impart a
golden glow to everything.

Marisa had chosen to forget her aunt's warnings of the
afternoon; she was a night-blooming flower, coming into her
own in the glow of the chandeliers and the flame in Philip's
eyes. Duty and obligation were words tossed in the teeth of
the wind, to be blown away like all her old fears and self-
doubts. Tonight she was beautiful and just as sure of herself
as any of the other lovely, bejeweled women who flirted
behind their ivory fans.

Philip was falling in love with her; she knew it, sensed it,
and hugged the thought to her as a talisman against the past.
There was nothing violent about him, nothing fierce or savage that would turn on her to use her and hurt her. Tonight
she found it easy to banish the memory of storm-grey eyes
alternately mocking and angry, bending her to their will in
spite of herself.

The first subtle beginnings of dawn had begun to silver
the sky before Marisa found herself in her bedroom again,
hardly able to stand for weariness. Her maid, grumbling her
disapproval all the while, helped her undress. Her last
conscious thought before she slept was of Philip—his golden
hair shining in the lantern light as he bent his head to kiss
her very gently and tenderly on the lips. . . .

She was far too tired to dream, and waking was an effort
for she had an unpleasant throbbing in her temples.

"Come on, sleepy head! This is no time to lie abed
dreaming of your handsome Englishman! Wake up. Arlene
is already packing for you, and we are to leave for Paris
this very afternoon!" Edmée's voice held soft gurgles of
amusement as she watched Marisa struggle to sit upright,
pressing her fingers against the forehead as she did.

"That's better! There's a lot to be done, you know. Some
coffee with your breakfast will send away the headache.
You drank far too much champagne, petite, but you will
have to get accustomed to it, if you are to be introduced to
society. And you shall be. Even *he* was impressed by the

way our little sparrow has turned into a bird of paradise. So you are to go to Paris with us and meet everybody. But only if you hurry up and are ready in time!"

Like everything that had happened to her since she had arrived here at Malmaison to be enfolded in affectionate, warmly comforting arms, this, too, seemed like a dream, a rainbow-colored, fragile bubble that might burst at any time, dragging her back to reality. But here was Aunt Edmée reminding her that it was actually happening after all and that she would be staying at the palace of the Tuileries, former home of the kings of France and now the official state apartments of the first consul of France.

Marisa was far too dazed to question anything, and even the wan-faced Hortense smiled to see her pent-up excitement.

She whispered when they were finally in one of the carriages together, "I'm sure you'll see your Englishman again. Do you think you really love him? He did not look at any other woman all evening. Perhaps, oh, perhaps you'll be allowed to be happy and choose for yourself!"

Remembering her companion's own forced marriage, Marisa felt almost guilty at her own feeling of happiness, which threatened to overwhelm her. She gave Hortense's cold hand a little squeeze.

"Of course I will be! After all, I am no one important so they won't care!"

And at that moment, with the past behind her and the future stretching out ahead, she believed her own confident words.

Chapter Eleven

Paris—the new side of Paris that she was seeing now was everything she had once dreamed it would be. Escorted by magnificently uniformed hussars, the entourage of carriages with gold-crested doors swept through the broad avenues, while people thronged the streets to stare and cheer.

Marisa became aware of the power that Napoleon Bonaparte wielded, and his tremendous popularity with the people. She almost felt herself part of a royal party, and her feeling was heightened when she noticed the obsequious ceremony with which they were greeted when they arrived at the palace.

Uniformed footmen took care of everything, and rooms had already been prepared with fires burning and fresh-cut flowers to perfume them. There was nothing to do except rest and recover from the effects of their journey here, and Marisa did so obediently for that very evening they were to visit the theater—the famous Comédie Française. And after that there was to be a late supper at the hotel of the Russian ambassador. She would just have to get used to late nights, that was all! She fell unexpectedly asleep then, while thinking blissfully of the crowded days and nights that lay so excitingly ahead.

"Tomorrow, we'll have Leroy, the great couturier, come by and measure you for all the new gowns you'll be needing," the Countess Landrey announced when she swept into Marisa's room later that evening. She added, with a twinkle, "And there's no need to look so worried, love! You are my niece—and Landrey gives me an enormous allowance that I may do with as I wish. Later on, after we have written to your papa and he has forgiven you, and I am positive he

127

will when he understands everything—don't look afraid— well, then you will have your own pin money. But for tonight, you will wear one of my gowns. See. It is what they call here à l'anglais, very plain but cut by an expert, and it is the color that is everything. It was always a trifle too tight on me, but I have had Arlene alter it for you. Do put it on quickly; I feel sure it will suit you."

Still protesting weakly, Marisa allowed herself to be dressed and turned this way and that as if she were a doll. She was still drowsy and far too dazed to do more than gasp when she saw herself reflected in the mirror.

Cut very low, and tightly banded beneath her breasts, the shimmering thin silk seemed to cling like a second skin as it fell in artful folds to her ankles. She looked like a golden statue, from her flat-heeled gold slippers to the crown of her high-piled hair.

Crimson rose petals, ruthlessly rubbed on her cheekbones and lips gave her pointed face the color it needed; and at last her aunt stepped back with a sigh of satisfaction.

"There! And now you will catch all the eyes tonight. They will all be asking who you are, and there will be many handsome young men begging for the honor of an introduction. And you must try and remember, petite, *not* to show a decided preference for any one of them. All men like the excitement of the chase—la poursuit, tu comprends?"

She was talking of Philip, of course. Had he thought her too forward, her feelings far too transparent?

'But I don't care—and Philip is not at all like that!' Marisa thought mutinously. And once they had arrived at the theater and were seated in their magnificent box, she could not help letting her eyes wander over the throng in search of him.

She sat back almost immediately, realizing with an uncomfortable feeling that *she* was being stared at. Ever since the first consul had made his entrance, seating himself to the front of the box next to a magnificently attired Josephine, there had been more eyes on them than on the stage.

The play was an ancient Greek comedy by Aristophanes, one of those she had dutifully read during the past few weeks, but Marisa found it hard to concentrate. Wait until the intermission, she told herself. Surely if he's here he's seen us and will come to our box then. She noticed almost absently that her aunt, too, seemed restless, playing with her fan and letting her attention wander from the stage far too often. So she, too, was looking for someone. A new lover? Marisa's mind went back to the teasing conversation she had overheard the night of the ball at Malmaison, and she wondered casually who her aunt's latest lover was. Por, lovely, gay Aunt Edmée—married so young to a man so much older than she was! In an age where marriages were arranged with no thought for the feelings of the woman involved, Marisa suddenly realized how lucky she was to have escaped such a fate. No matter what it had cost. . . .

She had been dreaming, paying scarcely any attention to the play they had come to watch. Suddenly the lights seemed to have become brighter. She realized with a start that the heavy velvet and damask curtains had closed for the end of the first act.

The slight buzz of talk which had been going on all through the performance now seemed to intensify in volume. Heads were turned and lorgnettes raised as the occupants of the various boxes scanned each other. Now was the time for visiting back and forth, but if Philip were here would he dare, with Bonaparte himself present? Bonaparte was scowling in the direction of his sister Pauline, who, as usual, did not lack for male attention. But unlike Josephine, who had begun to chew at her lip nervously, Pauline paid no attention whatsoever to her brother's displeasure.

Seated towards the rear of the box, Marisa began to look around again, trying not to make herself conspicuous. Perhaps Philip was not at the theater tonight. She had not known yesterday that she would be here herself.

There was a slight flurry as Napoleon Bonaparte, accompanied by his brother Louis, left the box. Josephine had a fixed smile on her face, but her fingers were pressed against her temples. Marisa felt sorry for her as she remembered the gossip she had heard that the first consul was enamored of a certain actress who was in this very play.

She heard Pauline's shrill laughter as one of her ad-

mirers put his hand on her bare shoulder, and she leaned
forward a little so that she could see better. Doing so, she
encountered, with a disagreeable shock, the enigmatic eyes
of Joseph Fouché, duke of Otranto. He bowed and his thin
lips curled slightly in what passed for a smile. Marisa
looked hastily to the next box, and her own smile froze on
her face.

She recognized Philip at last; he looked just as handsome
and magnificently clad as ever, but ill at ease for all that.
He was flanked by two women, one much older than the
other, wearing a flowered turban and holding up a diamond-
encrusted lorgnette. The younger one, an insipid, mousy-
haired young miss wearing white muslin and pearls, had to
be Lady Arabella Marlowe. How dared he? After kissing
her last night, murmuring in a shaken voice the next minute that he was sorry to have been so bold but that her
eyes in the moonlight had bewitched him completely.

And then, to add to her mortification, Marisa heard her
aunt's laughing voice saying, "Darling, *do* turn around and
give us some of your attention! Here's the Prince Benevento
come to pay us his respects, and you're wrapped up in
some girlish dream!"

Flushing hotly, Marisa turned her head, and the shock she
received rendered her speechless.

Her eyes, widening involuntarily, met and clashed with a
pair of furious, steely grey eyes; and over the buzzing in
her ears Talleyrand murmured urbanely, "May I present an
American friend of mine, who is, I believe, already acquainted with the Countess Landrey? Captain Dominic Challenger—and this, of course, monsieur, is the pretty young
niece of our lovely countess. . . ."

Marisa hardly heard what he said. *He* bowed, without a
word, his mouth hard and contemptuous. And *she* barely
retained the presence of mind to incline her head stiffly.

Marisa felt as if she had been turned to stone. It was
her aunt who saved the situation by putting her hand up to
touch Captain Challenger's sleeve as she murmured teasingly, "Shame on you, sir! After all your avowals last week,
I had expected you to join us earlier."

So *he* was the new admirer her aunt's friends had referred

to as her "dark-haired cavalier." The last man on earth she had expected to turn up here—and just when she had begun to forget and feel secure.

Her knees had begun to tremble and turn weak, but thank heaven his eyes had transferred themselves from her to her aunt, who was smiling at something he had just said.

Marisa felt that she was not capable of coherent thought, and she felt vaguely grateful to the limping Talleyrand, prince of Benevento, who was tactful enough to engage her in casual conversation while the other two carried on their blatant flirtation.

"And how are you enjoying your first evening in Paris, mademoiselle? Or do you still miss the quietness of Malmaison?"

She answered mechanically, wondering all the while when the painful, angry thudding of her heart would grow less violent, allowing her to think.

Why was he still in Paris? She had wished—hoped—him halfway across the seas by now! And was it possible that he was actually her aunt's lover? What a strange, situation she found herself thrown into! She daren't say anything—but then, neither did he.

Their box was suddenly crowded with people who came to pay their respects to the wife of the first consul and her friend, the vivacious, sparkling Countess Landrey. Marisa watched Dominic Challenger leave, without so much as a polite bow in her direction, with mixed feelings. She was relieved that everything had passed off so easily—and filled with rage at the same time, because she could not have denounced him in front of them all.

'I acted like a frightened ninny! After all, *I* have nothing to be ashamed of. I should have been able to show him that his sudden appearance meant less than nothing to me, that *he* is the one who should be afraid in case I tell them all what really happened!' Where had he gone? Would he be back?

Marisa's thoughts were still confused when the next act began and all the visitors had left their box. She was still slightly stunned and quite unable to take any interest in what was happening on the stage.

"Darling, whatever is the matter? You haven't been paying attention to anyone or anything! It wasn't seeing your young Englishman with his bride-to-be, was it? If you remember, I tried to warn you. . . ."

Edmée seemed unusually flushed as she leaned over to whisper to Marisa, and an unreasoning wave of hostility stiffened Marisa's spine, forcing an unconcerned smile to her lips.

"You must remember that this is all so new to me! And as for Philip, he is merely fulfilling his obligations. Why should *that* matter to me?"

Edmée's eyes widened at hearing her niece almost snap back in such a cynical, offhand tone. But she caught a frowning glance from the first consul and subsided into silence, her mind soon filled with other thoughts. The American—Dominic Challenger. It had been a long time since a man had intrigued and provoked her so. What had started out as a game to alleviate her boredom at the dull soirée where she had first been introduced to him had turned into something else since.

He had been plainly dressed and aloof, and it had amused her to flirt with him deliberately; she expected him to be dazzled—an easy, casual conquest. Instead, he had managed to turn the tables on her by living up to his name and remaining detached, even while he responded to her show of interest with all the proper gallantries. She had almost despaired of bringing him to heel until tonight when he had abruptly and almost bluntly asked her for an assignation.

Perhaps she should not have acceded so eagerly? Edmée's fan fluttered vigorously, cooling her hot cheeks. There was something primitively male about him that made her shiver at the thought of having him make love to her. Those diamond-hard, silver-grey eyes that seemed to see right through her defenses, sensing her surrender before she had realized it herself. And that wicked-looking scar that added to the illusion of savagery barely held in check. She was almost frightened—but pleasurably so. She must remember to ask Talleyrand about him since the prince had introduced Monsieur Challenger as a friend.

132

Fortunately unaware of her aunt's thoughts, Marisa was trying to compose her own emotions. She did not want to remember—anything! All those unpleasant events of the past had happened to someone else, not to her. Without quite realizing it, she kept her eyes on Philip. Had he seen her yet? Surely he must have! He looked awkward and ill at ease—in fact his face wore a strangely hard expression she had never seen on it before.

The plain young woman at Philip's side kept fidgeting in her seat, fingers playing with her fan as she now and then cast shy, wondering glances at him. On his other side, the forbidding-looking dowager leaned over to say something—and to *her* he listened with every appearance of attentiveness.

Marisa found herself biting her lip. Oh, if only Philip had been sitting here, beside her! She would have liked to show Dominic Challenger that she had a young and handsome escort of her own. At least now that he knew she wasn't the gypsy wench he'd thought her, and now that she was under the protection of the first consul himself, he would surely take pains to stay out of her way! 'For all he knows, I could have told them everything—the way he treated me and then planned to sell me off to another man. Oh, but I would like to see him punished!'

Marisa's cheeks were flushed, and her golden eyes held a brilliance they usually lacked, making them appear larger than ever in her small face. Had she but known it, she herself was the target for many admiring glances that evening. There were many questions asked. Who was she? Where did she appear from? And some of the glances shot her by other women were far from friendly. Her aunt's gown, so daringly cut, gave her an appearance of sophistication. Tonight she was undeniably a woman, a very attractive woman.

Making his way to the American ambassador's box, Dominic Challenger, his face a hard, cold mask that hid his fury and his feeling of being somehow made a fool of, heard comments that made his lips tighten.

"She's probably Bonaparte's latest flirt. Poor Josephine,

133

no wonder she's wearing a sad look of late. They say he forces her to keep his mistresses about her. . . ."

What a transformation she had undergone! From gypsy pickpocket to drenched cabin boy, and now, in the space of the few weeks that had elapsed since she had run away without a word of explanation, Bonaparte's mistress. Was she really the lovely Edmée's niece?

Mr. Livingston, United States Ambassador to France, cast a quizzical glance at the scowling face of his fellow American, who lowered himself into his seat without a word. Captain Dominic Challenger was something of a mystery, and in spite of his preoccupation with other affairs, the American minister could not help but wonder, as he had done before, how many of the stories about this particular man were true. Less than a hundred years ago, he would have been labeled a pirate and would probably have been hanged for his crimes. Today he was a privateer—when it suited his inclinations, and when he needed the money. Livingston had heard the tale of how Captain Challenger had sailed into the port of Charleston in a captured English ship—renamed and flying the American flag. He'd stirred up a lot of old scandals since then, besides creating new ones of his own. Was it really true, for instance, that he had arrived uninvited at Monticello when Mr. Jefferson was entertaining certain prominent gentlemen from the state of Tennessee, to ascertain, he'd said quite bluntly, whether one of them happened to be his real father?

Challenger wasn't his real name of course. His legal father had been an Englishman, a Tory whose estates had been confiscated after the Revolutionary War. But whoever or whatever he was, Captain Challenger had the advantage of friends and unofficial backers in high places. Hard faced and closemouthed, he had the look and manner of a born adventurer—not the kind of man that Robert Livingston would normally have cultivated, but in this case—

Livingston sighed to himself, recalling the subtle and not so subtle diplomatic negotiations that were taking place at that very time. They involved the question of the possible purchase from France of the port of New Orleans since it had been confirmed that Spain had indeed ceded the whole territory of Louisiana back to France. After the scandal of the X-Y-Z Affair and the ensuing strained relations between France and the United States of America, it seemed as if at last Bonaparte seemed willing to negotiate. Thank goodness the sole responsibility would no longer be his for he'd learned that the president was sending one of his most trusted advisors, Mr. Monroe, to help finalize matters.

Dominic Challenger had delivered certain secret dispatches from President Jefferson himself, along with others from Mr. Pinckney in Spain. Obviously, the president trusted him, and he also had contacts in the territory of Louisiana itself, not to mention New Spain, which made him knowledgeable enough to help in the negotiations that were going on. It was for this reason that Captain Challenger stayed on in France.

He'd managed to find himself certain sweet forms of consolation, however. The American minister let his hooded eyes wander from the stage to the first consul's box, where the vivacious Countess Landrey sat leaning forward slightly, her full lips curved in an enigmatic smile. Was *she* the reason for the angry scowl that still darkened his companion's features?

The drama that was being enacted on the brightly lighted stage went unremarked by far too many people although at its end there would be the usual storm of enthusiastic applause.

Marisa, trying to curb her disturbing thoughts, kept her eyes fixed on Philip Sinclair, willing him to look in her direction. She did not notice, as her aunt and godmother belatedly did, that Napoleon, who had returned to them in an angry mood, had begun to glance at her far too often, a thoughtful look on his face.

Philip Sinclair, for his part, made a conscious attempt to keep his eyes from straying towards a certain other box and its occupants. He realized that he still held his shoulders far too rigidly, but he could do nothing about it. The shock he had received upon recognizing a certain tall figure had made him go white, and even Lady Marlowe had remarked on it. Still stunned, almost disbelieving his own eyes, he had said more than he should, to be bombarded with eager questions from the old gossip.

God! He should have had more control over himself. But the sight of the last man in the world he had expected or wanted to see again, and here, of all places, had almost numbed his mind. Dominic—who should have been dead, or rotting away in a Spanish prison in Santo Domingo. Did his uncle know he was still alive, and not only that but on apparently good terms with the American ambassador in Paris as well? What was he up to? And—although he told himself grimly that he must not let the thought frighten him—had Dominic seen *him?* It was all he could do to remain seated, pretending that nothing was wrong and that his whole future and prospects hadn't begun to crumble around him. A few more years—with his uncle's legal heir presumed dead, *he* would have inherited everything. Damn those lazy, lethargic Spaniards anyhow! They had been paid enough, through obscure, secret sources, to make sure he died, working alongside their black slaves under the broiling Caribbean sun. And then, a few years later, when the proof was delivered—what had gone wrong?

Philip waited impatiently for the performance to be over; he wished he could have been seated in a less conspicuous place. He must see Whitworth, the British minister, and ask him to deliver a message to his father, who would know what to do. Thank God Whitworth was an old family friend! And he must see Marisa. Why hadn't she mentioned she was coming to Paris? He had not seen her until the intermission and then, soon after, he'd received his second shock of the evening when Dominic had followed Talleyrand into Napoloen Bonaparte's box. 'Perhaps Marisa will be able to tell me what he's doing here, and what name he is using,' Philip thought feverishly. God, but she looked lovely tonight! If things had been different, he would have thought of nothing else.

Joseph Fouché, duke of Otranto, had also been watching but for different reasons. It was his duty to watch all that was going on, and make his own deductions— helped, in part, by the efforts of his agents. Tonight had proved exceptionally interesting, and a chilling smile curled his thin lips as in his mind he began painstakingly to fit tiny pieces together that would eventually form a whole picture. All visitors to France during these tense times came under the surveillance of his men, and especially since there were more rumors of royalist plots in the offing.

Loyal to no one but the first consul himself, he trusted no one, not even Napoleon's own wife and her friends—especially those out of the past. Now he allowed his eyes to rest again on the young girl in the golden gown who sat just behind her aunt. Such a strange reappearance, that! Her mother had been executed as an enemy of the Republic, and the girl had fled France as a child, only to return unexpectedly and mysteriously as a young woman. But how had she got here? With whom—and why? He had burned to question her from the beginning and had been put off; but now, at last, he had been given his instructions. Napoleon, his master, was inexplicably interested in the chit, and like any one of his prospective mistresses, her background was open to investigation.

He would enjoy questioning her, Fouché thought slyly. Was she really as innocent as she seemed or merely a pawn in someone else's game? He would find out.

Chapter Twelve

Unaware of all the intrigue swirling around her, Marisa tried to force some semblance of gaiety into her manner when at last they left the theater to drive to the magnificent hotel of the Russian ambassador. Far from being ended, the evening was only just beginning!

Josephine was silent, suffering from one of the migraines that made her husband so impatient with her of late, and Hortense was her usual quiet self. But the Countess Landrey seemed exhilarated as she teased her niece softly, "You seem very quiet, all of a sudden, my love. Surely one night in Paris cannot have left you bored? That dull performance at the theater tonight was only a prelude—I've heard that the Russians are lavish entertainers!"

Edmée's high-strung mood drove Marisa to ask herself whether perhaps her aunt was expecting to meet her latest lover again here. Marisa drew in her breath sharply, in order to dispel the angry thoughts that flooded her mind. No, she couldn't tell her aunt, not yet. And having seen her and learned of her true status, she hoped that Captain Challenger would not dare intrude his presence upon her again. If only she could forget and force herself to act as if nothing had ever happened between them! If only . . .

Her preoccupation with her own problems led Marisa, who was usually sensitive to the moods of those about her, to be impervious to the subtle difference in the atmosphere since they had left the theater. She was not to know that Napoleon had had a quarrel with his latest mistress, the actress in the play they had seen, and that when he had returned to their box in a rage, he had suddenly noticed *her*, as if for the first time.

It took her some time to realize that she was being singled out—and even that realization came only when the dark-visaged Lucien Bonaparte, the one brother-in-law whom Josephine disliked excessively, had drawn her away from under the very nose of the Russian prince who had paid her so much attention at Malmaison.

"The Russians are our allies for the moment, but there's no reason why they should be allowed to get *too* friendly! Do you regret losing such a determined admirer, mademoiselle?"

Both relieved and puzzled at the same time, Marisa held herself stiffly in his arms, finding herself unable to either trust or like him. However, she shook her head as she answered mechanically, "No. As a matter of fact I don't like the prince at all. He's far too bold."

"And you don't like boldness in a man?"

While she sought for a light answer to his forward question, she wondered why he suddenly spoke to her so familiarly.

"I don't like men who presume too much on the strength of a slight acquaintance. I suppose I am not worldly enough by your standards!"

He gave her a rather cynical smile. "Why, *my* standards are broad enough to embrace the whole world, mademoiselle! However, my brother is surprisingly old-fashioned, and—shall we say conventional? Especially when it comes to women—of late, that is."

'What is he talking about?' Marisa wondered, while at the same time she decided she did not blame her godmother for disliking this particular Bonaparte.

She was even more confused when, after a few turns across the crowded ballroom floor, Lucien brought her to a halt before his brother, who had been engaged in a low-voiced conversation with Tsar Alexander.

Not knowing what to do or how to act, Marisa dropped into a low curtsy, hoping that the embarrassed flush that had spread across her face would go unnoticed. She kept her head bent, wishing that she did not have to rise, and it was Napoleon whose extended hand helped her erect again.

"And this is my charming little guest, the Señorita de

140

Castellanos, who is goddaughter to my wife. You see, she is still young enough not to have forgotten how to blush!"

Finding herself presented to the tsar, Marisa's tongue stumbled over her words, but he seemed flattered at her obvious confusion and gave her a gracious smile. She was all too conscious of Lucien Bonaparte's dark, enigmatic presence at her side, and the fact that the eyes of all the gathering must be fixed on her at this moment. What did it all mean? Why had Lucien suddenly asked her to dance with him and then brought her *here?*

Napoleon Bonaparte's blue, deep-set eyes seemed to hold her gaze against her will as he said softly in his accented French, "You are looking exceptionally lovely tonight, señorita." Did she only imagine that his hand squeezed her nerveless fingers slightly before he released them? In his resplendent white full-dress uniform, laced with gold and decorated with glittering decorations, he seemed so imposing and quite frightening as well! It was hard to believe he was the same man who at Malmaison, would join the younger set in their games and had treated her as if he were a fond, but absentminded uncle. Why was he looking at her so strangely and consideringly tonight?

"You little innocent!" the countess of Landrey scolded Marisa some twenty minutes later when they had retired to one of the smaller salons leading out into the magnificent gardens. "Don't you understand that he's quite taken with you? Cherie, you are a success! And even more so than I had hoped. And now, you understand, you must be very discreet—never more than two dances with the same man. And do *not* flirt too obviously, he can be jealous once he's fixed his interest on a particular woman. We must—"

"Stop, please! I do not understand." Marisa pressed her fingers to her temples, staring at her aunt as if she had taken leave of her senses. She said, "What are you trying to say? That General Bonaparte—that he—but no, you are mistaken. You know he's always been kind to me and my godmother. . . ."

Edmée sighed, one small silk-sandaled foot tapping impatiently on the carpet. Why must Marisa be so deliberately obtuse? After all, for all her youth and rather touching na-

Rosemary Rogers

ïveté, the child *had* been through certain experiences that should have made a woman of her. And, as a result, she had made sure with the broths and bitter tisanes her niece had swallowed so obediently that there were to be no unpleasant reminders of the past. And she had hoped—but *this* was even more fortunate, if only Marisa could be made to see reason and to think practically.

She said, in a coaxing voice, "Haven't you seen for yourself that Josephine is used to his occasional straying? She understands him—and besides, she's had lovers of her own; there almost was a terrible scandal over that young Lieutenant Denis, not too many months ago! She won't blame you, you may be sure of that. Just as long as you are discreet—and of course, you mustn't give in too easily, either! All you have to do is blush the way you are doing now and open those innocent eyes very wide as if you don't quite understand. . . ."

Edmée went on talking quickly and excitedly, giving her bewildered niece no more chances to protest. It was high time the girl awakened to the realities of life as she herself had been forced to do at about the same age. Usually marriage came first and then lovers, discreetly taken. But in this case—why, there was talk that Bonaparte would soon make himself an emperor! And it was well known, besides, that he always provided generously for his mistresses usually marrying them off to his generals or newly created nobility. Marisa must be made to see how foolish she was being, and what advantages there were to be had for all of them.

"Surely, darling, you don't want to be packed off to the wilds of New Spain, to your papa who might be extremely angry with you? And this Pedro Arteaga from whom you ran away—he'd hardly want to marry you now, you know! Nor, I'm afraid and I hate to be so blunt, would any other Spaniard offer you *marriage;* you know how stuffy and conventional they are! You could be rich and independent —how I envy you! And when you *do* marry. . . . You know that I am speaking so sternly to you for your own good, don't you petite? I only want your happiness, as your dear maman would have wanted if she had lived. Come," Edmée continued with an appealing smile, "don't look so wan-faced! You are a woman now, and you must learn to act like one instead of a frightened child who can only think of running away and hiding. Pinch your cheeks, love, you need some color in them. And now we must return to the dancing and all your eager partners before *he* starts to wonder where you are!"

Unbelievable. As she followed her aunt, Marisa's head was whirling with thoughts she did not want to face. She felt like a snared rabbit awaiting the hunter. She might not be worldly wise, but she was not stupid, and her innocence, if such a thing really existed, had been taken away from her by a steely-eyed corsair. She was just as helpless and just as much a pawn now as she had been then. And now that she had been catapulted into the limelight, there could be no escape for her unless. . . . She thought suddenly of Philip, and resolve stiffened her spine. If only Philip would understand and help her again! Somehow she must contrive to meet him.

The rest of the night passed in a kind of haze as Marisa danced and smiled and even managed to respond intelligently to the brilliant conversation that swirled about her. She knew now why she had suddenly become so popular and sought after, and she was all too aware of how often the first consul's eyes rested on her, although he did not ask her to dance. Now that she understood, there was surely something she could do. But there was no point in worrying about it tonight.

Marisa was fortunately too tired to think by the time she had stumbled upstairs to her room, allowing her maid to undress her as if she had been a doll. She slept heavily and woke late to find that breakfast was to be served to her in bed since she had a busy afternoon ahead of her.

Through all of the fittings for the new gowns she must have, she tried to keep her mind a careful blank. There was to be a reception at the prince of Benevento's palace that very evening, and *everyone* would be there. She must look her best.

Consoling her, flowers were delivered to her with a card from Philip, telling her how much he looked forward to seeing her again. She felt consoled by the flowers. But she felt

143

frightened when she opened a flat box containing an exquisite shawl, all shimmering colors, accompanied only by the boldly scrawled signature, "Napoleon."

"You see?" her aunt said triumphantly as she draped the shawl about Marisa's stiff shoulders. "It wasn't all a dream, my little Cinderella! And now you must hurry, for Monsieur Leroy is here already, and we must persuade him that your new ball gown positively has to be delivered this very evening!"

Marisa felt herself pushed this way and that, hardly realizing what was happening. Under any other circumstances she would have been beside herself with excitement, but now she was unusually quiet and docile, and the designer, who had already heard the latest gossip, wondered rather contemptuously what Bonaparte had found so intriguing about this silent slip of a girl who had only her great golden eyes and her hair to commend her. Tiens! She was so thin! And one wondered whether she had any conversation to offer. He decided that she must be dressed in white—a simple muslin with, perhaps, some artful Grecian drapery to hide the lack of curves, and a small ruff, which he had made so fashionable, around her neck, to hide her collarbones and heighten the illusion of a child playing at being a woman. Or was it really an illusion?

The high, tightly cut bodice of her gown was embroidered with tiny seed pearls, and a rope of pearls bound her hair, its dark gold ringlets escaping to lie riotously against her forehead and temples.

"I shall call this creation 'Andromeda,'" Leroy had said proudly, and Marisa wondered if she were meant to recreate the ancient Greek legend of the maiden sacrifice, for that was exactly how she felt tonight.

Josephine's dark eyes rested on her sadly, but her manner was just as affectionate as it had always been. Was it *really* true that she didn't *mind?* To make his gift to Marisa less obvious, Napoleon had also presented gifts to his wife and stepdaughter: a ruby necklace for Josephine and a pretty ivory fan to Hortense. He was nowhere in evidence when they left for the reception; affairs of state kept him busy, but he would arrive later as was his usual custom.

Marisa's hands were cold in spite of her silk gloves. She almost dreaded the thought of appearing in public again, knowing how people would be speculating about her.

Almost unconsciously, she squared her shoulders. There had to be a way out of her present dilemma, and she would find it. Philip would help her—she felt it. And in the meantime, she must pretend to her aunt that she accepted everything she had been told and that she was quite resigned.

Had Marisa but known it, Edmée was not even thinking about her niece just then. She had other things to think about. In the darkness of the carriage, Edmée bit her full lower lip, feeling the blood start to course faster in her veins. Tonight—after the reception—but how was she going to manage it? Dominic had told her that he would somehow contrive everything; he was so masterful and so—so arrogantly sure of himself! She ought to have refused him, but there was something about him. . . . Even the lightest brush of his fingers on her bare arm made her weak when he touched her. He was an American savage—the kind of man who had no time for whispered flattery and flirtation, preferring to seize what he wanted by force if he had to. It had been a long time since any man had excited her so, and she felt like a fluttering moth drawn to the flame of a candle, knowing the danger but unable to resist it. If he got her alone, there would be no opportunity allowed her for coyness or holding back—she was sure of it. He was capable of raping her without a qualm, of tearing the clothes off her body if she resisted him.

Edmée's tongue moistened her lips as she tried to suppress a shudder of pleasure mixed with fear. But could she resist? Did she want to? He was a primitive jungle animal among the civilized men she was accustomed to, and like any woman she wondered if perhaps *she* could be the one to tame him. Her heart was still beating quickly as their carriage stopped at last before the imposing marble steps that led up to Talleyrand's palace.

Thousands of candles, illuminated the crystal and silver and gold surroundings and enhanced the equally brilliant gathering that thronged the many rooms of the palace. Jeweled decorations glittered on almost every male jacket, while the women sought to outshine each other with their magnificent ball gowns and sparkling gems.

Marisa was dazzled. To think that she was here and actually a part of such a grand assembly! There were diplomats and noblemen from all over the world; she had never heard so many foreign languages spoken under one roof. The walls were hung with silk in the colors of the Republic and interspersed with garlands of freshly cut flowers whose cloying scent mingled with the odors of food and the perfume worn by the women. It was a warm night and an enormous pavilion had been set up in the magnificent walled garden for dancing. The musicians were playing already. The crush was so great that Marisa began to wonder despairingly if she would ever catch sight of Philip. In the meantime Edmée kept her close to her side even though *her* eyes too seemed to wander sharply from one face to another.

They had passed through the reception line at last. As honored guests they were escorted by Talleyrand himself, dressed in his usual somber black, to a group of gilt chairs placed a little apart from the others on the terrace.

Immediately Josephine and Edmée were surrounded by friends and admirers, leaving Marisa a little space to look around. She saw a few faces that were familiar to *her,* and she bowed and smiled politely. But heavens, how conspicuous she felt! 'It's almost as if we were royalty,' she thought wryly. At least Philip surely could not fail to notice her.

She was so occupied studying the crowd that she could not help the start she gave when a soft voice addressed her.

"Ah, mademoiselle, what good fortune to see you here. You look charming, as usual, and I'm your servant."

Joseph Fouché, duke of Otranto, bowed over her unwillingly extended hand, his cold lips brushing it lightly.

Fouché. She did not, could not like him, Marisa had already decided. He reminded her of an ugly black bird of prey, hovering lazily before it struck. Always present—watching—his cold eyes hooded and unreadable. And she remembered that he was one of the original revolutionaries, a friend of Robespierre and one of those who had voted to guillotine all the "aristos" who could be rounded up. Why did she have the impression that he was always watching her? Even when he paid her meaningless compliments his cold eyes remained remote, almost assessing.

'The Terror is over—and in any case there's no reason why I should fear him,' Marisa reminded herself.

Marisa wished he would leave, but he surprised and angered her by lingering, his urbane voice murmuring polite civilities all the while. She must try to remember that he was here tonight as the duke of Otranto and not in his capacity as chief of police. What a ridiculous thought; what did she have to feel guilty about? Funny—now she almost found herself wishing that Napoleon would arrive and "rescue" her!

"I wonder, mademoiselle, if I might have the honor of taking you in to supper? If you have not already promised it to someone else, that is."

Taken aback, she could not find anything to say. Looking at her aunt for support she found that Edmée's attention was elsewhere. Her heart sinking, Marisa saw a satisfied smile cross Fouché's thin lips as he drew up a chair to seat himself beside her.

"I am excessively flattered and grateful that you should be kind enough to spare me a little of your time. Do you know, mademoiselle, that you are a fascinating enigma? I am sure I cannot be the only admirer to be curious about you! Yes, I must confess that I am intrigued. . . ."

Growing hot and cold by turns, Marisa was forced to listen as his soft voice went on and on, his eyes holding her pinned in place like a helpless butterfly against a wall.

~∞~

Chapter Thirteen

~∞~

A series of shocks, delivered one after the other, had rendered Marisa almost numb by the time they sat down to a late supper.

First there had been Fouché with his probing, relentless questions that seemed to want to rip away all the veils she had thrown up between herself and the past. He had acted as if she were a criminal with something to hide!

"Come, mademoiselle, I know how painful it must be for you to recall certain unpleasant happenings, but I assure you that I shall be discreet. Surely you realize it's better this way, under the cover of a gathering such as this? Do continue to smile, I beg you. I am merely fulfilling my duty and attempting to spare you the embarrassment of formal questioning in my office. Please trust me. I am a father, and I understand something of your scruples."

He wanted to know how she had arrived in France, when, and with whom. And her relationship with Philip—how she had met him and how well did they know each other?

Angrily she tried to evade him, but he had merely smiled.

"If you are sensible, mademoiselle, you will tell me everything. Be assured it will not go further."

It sounded as if he were threatening her—his manner fatherly and bullying by turns. And then, like a fisherman content to play out his line for the sport of reeling in a spent quarry afterwards, he let her go with the promise that he would speak to her later, after she had had time to think.

Soon afterwards she saw Philip making his way to her side through the crowd. An unwonted frown creased his forehead. She was reminded suddenly and forcibly of the fact that Philip was English. Dear God, did Fouché think she was a spy? Part of some royalist plot?

This evening even Philip seemed changed in some way, his manner almost abrupt. "Marisa, I have to speak to you. Forgive me, but if there's some chance that we could converse alone—"

Marisa forced a smile as she tried to warn Philip with her eyes. "Later, perhaps. I hope you will ask me to dance."

"It seems as if you are always surrounded by chaperones now—and admirers!" His voice sounded almost bitter, and she longed to be able to put her hand in his and run away with him, away from all the gossip and the speculation and the staring eyes that watched her, she was sure, even now.

"Philip—," she began pleadingly. She noticed how his face seemed to close up, becoming a polite, handsome mask as her aunt came fluttering up, a teasing smile on her full red lips.

"Monsieur Sinclair! But how nice to see you again. Did your friends come with you this evening? I have been wishing to meet Lady Marlowe again ever since I learned she was in Paris with her dear little Arabella. Marisa, you must meet her—such a sweet, typical young English lady, and you must be almost of the same age, too. You must be introduced, and especially if you are to go back to England with me. Lady Marlowe knows all the patronesses of Almacks, isn't that so monsieur?"

"Lady Marlowe knows everybody," Philip said in a low, controlled tone as he bowed over Edmée's white fingers. "I will be sure to tell her that you were asking about her, of course."

"Please do!" Edmee responded sweetly, sinking into the vacant chair by Marisa's side; and after a few murmured polite remarks Philip was forced to leave.

"How could you!" Marisa burst out in a low, suppressed voice as soon as he was out of earshot. Her aunt raised one arched brow.

"How could I—what? Chérie, you ought to be grateful that I rescued you from being far too indiscreet. It's an open secret that his engagement to Arabella Marlowe will be announced as soon as they return to London; and yet, the look on your face as you gazed up at him! You really must learn to mask your feelings, darling child, for your own sake!"

Too angry to control herself Marisa burst out, "And for whose sake, I wonder, has the odious duke of Otranto been plaguing me with questions? While you were occupied with your friends he hardly left my side; he wants to know everything about my past, every sordid detail! What am I to tell him?"

"Oh—Fouché!" Edmée gave a shrug, but her brilliant eyes seemed to avoid her niece's for a moment. "It's his business to know everything about everybody, but he's closemouthed, at least. And better to have as a friend than an enemy, believe me. Why don't you tell him what he wants to know, and then he'll leave you alone! Really, my pet, there's no point in being so mysterious, although I do understand how you must feel. Tell him the truth and then forget about it. He can't hurt you, not *now*."

At that moment the whole gathering seemed galvanized to attention as Napoleon Bonaparte, surrounded by his aides, made his late entrance.

It was almost as if he were an emperor already. There was a sudden hush; the men bowed, and the women curtsied low. He walked across the room with Talleyrand at his side, his pale-complexioned face remote and unsmiling unless he recognized someone he knew, and then he would stop to speak for a few moments.

He was dressed, as usual, in his general's uniform, and in spite of his slight stature there was something dynamic and powerful about him. Even Marisa, as overwrought as she was, could not help noticing it. He approached their small group—and, oh, God, why did Josephine happen to be dancing at that moment with a young Polish officer?

Marisa had dropped into a curtsy with the others, but suddenly she felt a hand on her wrist, drawing her upward. Napoleon said, "Come—let us dance, señorita. It's a pleasure I have long looked forward to."

There was nothing to do but to obey what amounted to a royal command even though Marisa realized, with a sinking heart, what this unprecedented honor meant. Like any good

151

general, Napoleon never wasted his time, believing in making straight for his objective. How in the world was she to deny him?

They waltzed, and he was surprisingly light on his feet. She noticed that and was relieved that he did not try to engage her in conversation. Marisa tried to keep her mind on the music but could not. 'He is only being kind—no more than that. They cannot force me into being his mistress. With all the women of Paris, of all France for that matter, at his feet, he could not possibly want *me!* It's only a game, to make Josephine jealous. . . .'

They circled the floor once, twice, and then he led her back to the gilt chairs. He smiled and there was a searching look in his deep blue eyes.

"You dance very well, little Marisa. And I enjoyed the fact that you do not chatter while you dance."

Bowing stiffly, he left her and went to Josephine; but by then there was not a single person in the whole brilliant assembly who had not noticed her. The whispers of those who had attended the Russian ambassador's reception the previous night had swelled into outright gossip by now.

"They say, my dear, that he's actually installed her under his very roof! *And* passes her off as his poor wife's goddaughter."

"Who *is* she? A Spanish last name, I've heard, but is it really true her mother was French? Where does she come from?"

"I cannot remember that the Countess Landrey ever mentioned a *niece* before," Lady Marlowe sniffed. "And I really cannot say that the girl has much to recommend her! I noticed her at the theater last night—such a very *unsuitable* gown for a child her age!" She lowered her voice so that her daughter could not hear. Tapping the British minister's arm with her folded fan, she said, "Fast! But then what can one expect . . ."

Whitworth, who had noticed young Sinclair go up to speak to the same young woman earlier, merely frowned and held his peace. Strange that he hadn't mentioned being acquainted in those circles. And yet, understandably, he'd had other things on his mind last night. While Whitworth pretended to pay polite attention to Lady Marlowe's chatter, his rather protuberant eyes were searching the room for his American counterpart. Livingston was a civilized fellow, for all that he *was* an American. Perhaps, if he were approached in a casual, roundabout fashion he might shed some light on the mystery that had Philip Sinclair so perturbed. A damnably awkward thing, if Sinclair were right and this American privateer with the improbable name was really an English viscount, long presumed dead. Royse's heir? It did not seem possible! He would have spoken to Talleyrand, but it really wasn't advisable to let that wily statesman suspect the reasons for his sudden interest in an obscure American captain. Being a diplomat was by no means easy when one had to cope with so many sly intrigues! And speaking of intrigues—where the devil was Sinclair? High time he asked Arabella Marlowe to dance.

Philip Sinclair, rendered bold by the unusual amounts of wine he had consumed, and in despair by what he had just witnessed, had just bowed before a still-flushed Marisa, asking her to dance with him. At this point he didn't care if Arabella, her formidable mother, or even Napoleon himself were watching. Damn it, she didn't belong here! She was too innocent to realize what was happening—what people were whispering about her! It was all the fault of that accursed aunt of hers, a married woman notorious for her many and varied lovers. He had almost forgotten his original purpose in coming here and his intention to ask her questions.

Everyone else was dancing, even the pregnant Hortense, and Marisa had begun to feel herself isolated when thankfully, Philip appeared out of nowhere. She had just glimpsed the duke of Otranto begin to make his way towards her, and her Aunt Edmée was nowhere in sight, so it was with an unfeigned exclamation of gladness that she smiled up at Philip and took his hand without hesitation. He had sensed her distress and had come to her. Here at last was someone she could trust!

Unfortunately, the musicians had just begun to play a quadrille, and the dancers formed sets and faced each other, giving them hardly any opportunity to talk privately.

"I must speak to you!" Philip said again, doggedly, and Marisa gave him a worried inclination of her head. The dance led them apart and then together again, and in response to the pleading in his eyes she murmured breathlessly, "Soon—I shall contrive to be very tired and in need of a drink and some fresh air. On the terrace outside?"

"I'll look for you there. I'll wait, if I have to."

The urgency in his voice and the almost desperate pleading in his eyes made Marisa's pulses begin to race. Philip was in love with her! He was jealous, of course, but tonight he meant to ask her to elope with him, and she would— she would!

What did it matter if he had little money of his own? They would be happy. Perhaps her papa would relent and give her a dowry, and Philip would go to New Spain with her, and there would be a touching reconciliation with papa, and everything would end happily. They would make it so!

Lost in her suddenly happy visions of the future, Marisa did not notice that her manner had regained the sparkle and vivacity it had lacked earlier, and that she was actually smiling in a dreamy fashion. But there were others who noticed—and reacted according to their respective natures.

Joseph Fouché grinned in a ugly, narrow-lipped way, and the prince of Benevento raised an eyebrow in mock dismay, even while his cunning mind raced. Napoleon's face grew cold and forbidding, and Edmée, stepping in breathless and flushed from the coolness of the gardens, gave a smothered exclamation of annoyance.

"Oh, no! How could she—the very minute my back was turned. The little fool, what does she think she's about?"

In her anger and irritation she had said more than she would have wished to, but the tall man who stood beside her merely gave a sardonic grunt.

"So, chère amie, your so-called 'little' niece has more than one admirer?" His voice was a hard drawl, but his face, if Edmée could only have seen it then, had become a mask carved out of granite, betraying no emotion save contempt.

"Don't talk that way!" Edmee responded distractedly. "The young Englishman is merely a friend, of course, but she should not be so indiscreet as to dance with him, and especially not *now!*"

"So Caesar's mistress is very much in the same position as Caesar's wife? You ought to have schooled her not to wear her feelings so openly."

Dominic Challenger's voice was lazily indolent, but there was a certain tone underlying his sarcastically uttered words that made Edmée cast him a reproachful look over one white shoulder.

"You don't understand—"

"Is it necessary that I do?"

In that instant when they dueled with words she almost forgot about Marisa. Her lips still felt bruised from the force of his brutal kisses, and her skin burned from the roughness of his caresses. Had they not been interrupted a moment ago by some other strolling couple seeking seclusion, she had the feeling that he might have taken her right there in the moonlit garden, exactly as if she had been some trollop he'd picked up in the streets. The thought, coupled with the memory of her own uncaring yielding, was frightening. A practiced flirt, sure of herself and her attraction for the opposite sex, Edmée did not like to admit that she was capable of being swept out of her senses by pure sensuality, and especially in the arms of a man who did not waste time on the usual gallant preliminaries. Her instincts told her that this was a male animal who would treat her in exactly the same way he'd treat any other woman; and yet, inexplicably, she continued to feel attracted to him.

The music came to a stop, and relieved in more ways than one, Edmée sighed, not realizing until then that she had been holding her breath.

"I have to go," she murmured almost too quickly. She saw one black eyebrow shoot up.

"To censure your indiscreet niece? Somehow, chérie, I cannot see you in the role of a chaperone! May I walk with you?"

Taking her by surprise, he held out his arm leaving her no recourse but to take it. What did he mean by his sudden show of courtesy?

Their progress across the crowded room was slow since

Edmée knew so many people to whom she had to bow or smile. She noticed how the eyes of the women lingered on her tall, impassive escort, and again she felt a pleasurable thrill pass through her body. He was a challenge—they had not finished with each other yet.

And then they came face to face with Philip Sinclair who had just escorted Marisa back to her seat.

He stiffened. His handsome features seemed to harden and then dissolve into indecision as his face went white. He had stopped dead in his tracks, and Edmée had opened her mouth to say something when he suddenly swerved away without a word or a gesture of recognition, just as if he had been sleepwalking.

"I wonder what on earth has got into him? He's usually such a polite young man. . . ." Edmée's fair brow had puckered and her voice sounded querulous.

"Perhaps he has a guilty conscience."

She had felt the muscles of her companion's arm tense under her clutching fingers, but his voice remained uninflected. By then, she had caught a glimpse of Marisa's vivid face framed by an aureole of dark-gold curls, and she had begun to remember her duty.

Chapter Fourteen

For Marisa it was the final, crowning injustice to top off an evening that had been nothing but a tense, humiliating experience for her. She promised to meet Philip later, but then her aunt had come up with Captain Challenger in tow and had, in *his* odious presence, added to her humiliation by giving her a whispered dressing down—just as if she had been a thoughtless child!

She bit her lips sulkily, longing to burst out with angry explanations and to face her aunt with the truth about this latest lover of hers who stood there with one eyebrow raised and a smile curling one corner of his mouth.

Everything that had happened to her was his fault, after all. Her eyes had begun to sparkle defiantly as planning exactly what words she would use, she looked back at her aunt. And *then* perhaps Dominic Challenger would lose his smile! Yes, she would positively enjoy watching and listening as he tried to explain! And that would end his affair with Aunt Edmée as well.

Unaware of the direction of her niece's thoughts, Edmée finished up her little lecture with the injunction that Marisa must herself tell Philip Sinclair, if he were so bold as to ask her to dance with him again, that he should pay more attention to his own partner.

"Remind him, my love, that you are here with your own party. It was really too bad of him to act as if you were not even chaperoned! And now I shall have to contrive, somehow, to patch things up. It is really too aggravating!"

"My dear countess, if you continue to speak in such a cross tone I shall begin to think that you are not enjoying the evening I planned so carefully!"

None of them had noticed the prince of Benevento come up. He stood there smiling urbanely, his deep-set eyes slightly hooded.

Edmée had given a small start of surprise, but now she flashed him her most brilliant smile. Talleyrand had been one of her old lovers, and she thought they still understood each other well enough. *He* would help her put things right; why had she not thought right away of asking his advice?

"Your entertainments, Your Highness are unsurpassed, as usual! I have been enjoying myself enormously, I vow!"

Frustrated, Marisa was forced into temporary silence while the others made brief, polite small talk. She was being treated like a child, she thought again, and then, to her utter dismay, she heard Talleyrand murmur in his silken voice that really, his friend Challenger must not monopolize one of the most beautiful women in the room. He had been waiting for an opportunity to talk with his old friend, and indeed, even the general had been looking for her, desiring the pleasure of dancing the waltz with her.

"You must allow me to take you to him. And in the meantime, perhaps Captain Challenger might be persuaded to tell the lovely señorita something about New Spain and the territory of Louisiana. Your father owns considerable property in both places, does he not, señorita?"

Marisa was left speechless until Edmée, looking rather distracted, put her hand on Dominic's sleeve.

"Dominic? You will not mind entertaining my niece for a little while? I know you two have been presented to each other—"

It was obvious she did not want to let him go with so many things left unsaid and unfinished between them. It was positively sickening, Marisa thought viciously, not quite realizing her predicament until her aunt had walked off on Talleyrand's arm, leaving her alone with *him* of all people.

In fact when the realization hit her she made a movement to rise thinking only of flight. With deceptive negligence his arm shot out, and she felt the all-too-well-remembered strength of his steely fingers about her wrist, halting her. Forcibly he drew her to her feet so that she was facing him.

"How remiss of me not to have asked you to dance before—señorita! You enjoy the waltz, I understand?"

He drawled the words out hatefully, giving each one an unpleasant emphasis. How dared he?

"Let me go!" Marisa hissed, trying to pull free; but his grasp tightened until she gave an exclamation of pain.

"Oh, no. Didn't you hear my instructions? I am supposed to entertain you -and keep the other wolves away until your lover sends someone to reclaim you."

Tears of pain and frustration that filled her eyes. Short of screaming for help or creating a public scene that would bring even more censure down on her head, there was nothing she could do but allow herself to be led forward to join the other dancers.

Marisa felt one hard, muscular arm go around her waist, holding her firmly. His other hand grasped hers, not giving her any chance for escape.

"I must say you've done very well for yourself since you ran away so precipitately -although if I were you I'd not look around for other lovers while you're under General Bonaparte's protection. Especially not to Philip Sinclair!" There was a sudden harsh note in his voice that made her shiver in spite of her fury at his high-handedness.

Before Marisa could say a word, he continued in the same lazily contemptuous manner, "I wonder why you didn't tell me who you were. You let me go on thinking you were nothing more than a little gypsy pickpocket. And you might have spared yourself a great deal of unpleasantness if you had been honest. Or did you want to spare yourself? Were you perhaps looking for some excitement—and experience to prepare you for your present circumstances?"

Marisa's feet stumbled. Not permitting her to pull away, he almost lifted her off the floor.

Driven beyond endurance she whispered raggedly, "What did you expect, once you had—had raped me? You're the kind of man who would think it amusing, no doubt, and by then I was too ashamed. I did not want you to know anything about me, I only wanted to escape—"

159

"Is that why you followed me on board my ship? You should really try to think up a better story, little one!"

He was deliberately taunting her, goading her. With all her heart Marisa wanted to strike out at his mocking, harsh-featured face.

"Stop it! I don't owe you any explanations—anything! And if I tell them all I know about you, the way you treated me and meant to sell me off like a—a—"

"Sell you off? What the devil do you mean by that? And, my dear, if you think to blackmail me, let me tell you that it won't work! I don't give a damn what people may say about me, but in *your* case. . . . If the truth were known I doubt that you'd find life as pleasant for you as it seems to be now. Shall I tell them you were once my little plaything and that I kept you for my use while it suited me? I wonder what worth General Bonaparte would put on you *then!*"

His words were calculatedly cruel, each one like a slap in the face. Marisa went white under the savagery of his attack, and her golden eyes gleamed luminously with unshed tears. Something almost pathetically defenseless in her expression made Dominic regret his harshness.

Oh, Christ! She was no more than a child, after all, for all her defiant masquerading as a woman of the world. And he *had* been the first—although why in hell hadn't she said something? Even afterwards?

She looked quite alarmingly as if she were about to go into a swoon, he cursed under his breath and began to lead her off the floor. *That* would make a fine topic of speculation for the gossips!

"Perhaps you'd better sit down." Marisa hardly heard his voice—it seemed to come from far away—or recognized its suddenly different tone; it had veered from cruelty to exasperation. She only knew, thankfully, that she was sitting down at last and that he was holding a glass of champagne, procured from a passing waiter, to her lips.

It was all done quite impersonally. Even his sudden show of consideration was quite false, she was sure. It was put on to prevent her from making a scene.

Longing for something cool to refresh her suddenly

parched throat, she drank the champagne and was reminded forcibly and unpleasantly of the first time she had tasted it.

The little tête-à-tête between the American and the pretty Señorita de Castellanos who was the subject of so much gossip had not gone unnoticed.

Philip Sinclair, dancing dutifully if rather stiffly with Arabella Marlowe, found himself gritting his teeth. Damn it—what were they talking about? What was he saying to Marisa that made her look as if she had gone into a state of shock? He hardly paid any attention to his own partner, his mind feverishly busy with a confused jumble of thoughts, of plans. . . . He must do something! And especially *now*, when Dominic had seen him and recognized him.

The duke of Otranto, on the other hand, continued to smile even while he observed through narrowed eyes. By pure, fortunate coincidence he had just learned several interesting facts. Now his mind began to correlate them, fitting pieces together to fill in what had once been blanks.

Ah, yes. The American privateer captain, whose ship had put in at Nantes not too many weeks ago with a broken mast had come from Spain. He had moved in the highest circles there, so his spies had informed him. So had the señorita. In fact, they had both appeared in Paris at just about the same time. Coincidence?

Fouché did not believe in so many coincidences. They knew each other, he was sure of it having watched them closely while they were dancing. In fact they had seemed to be well enough acquainted to quarrel. . . .

His mind sifted pieces of information, including a report from one of his agents who worked at the British embassy. It seemed that Monsieur Philip Sinclair had reason to dislike as well as fear this Dominic Challenger—which of course was not the captain's real name. And Philip Sinclair was an admirer—the "rescuer" in fact—of the Señorita de Castellanos. It was all extremely interesting, and Fouché, who loved intrigue, almost purred with satisfaction. The evening was still comparatively young, and there was time for the messenger he had just sent off to reach his destination and return before it ended.

Fouché, who fancied himself an admirer of the theater,

thought smugly to himself that even the great playwright Molière could not have done better. To bring certain characters together and watch them act out a drama, a play within a play so to speak, why, in his way he was a genius! A detached observer of human weakness. Fouché enjoyed being minister of police. Yes, he decided. This evening was going to prove every interesting, indeed!

Unaware of anything but her own despicable weakness and her hatred of the man who now sat beside her regarding her so coldly, Marisa wished frantically for the evening to be over. He acted as if he were her jailer. Now that he had said what he had to say and made his threats, why couldn't he leave her in peace?

The champagne she had swallowed so fast had acted like a jolt, rousing her out of her fit of dizziness. How dared he presume to judge her? How could she have permitted him to do so without retaliation? And yet, she was shamefully afraid to start another argument; she longed only for him to go away.

"Do you feel better?"

Sullenly she nodded and bit back the angry retort that trembled on the tip of her tongue.

"Good." Did he have to sound so smugly self-satisfied? "And I hope we understand each other now. You'll go your way, and I'll go mine. And it might relieve your mind to know that I don't intend to remain in Paris for very much longer!"

"Oh, I assure you that is the best news I've heard for a long time!" Marisa spat, unable to control herself. "I would be even happier to learn I did not have to meet you again, ever!"

Not in the least perturbed, he stretched his long legs before him and said lazily, "The feeling is mutual, little spitfire. But for now, you'd best try to wipe that sullen look off your face. I believe the general has decided to forgive your indiscretion." His voice hardened then, as it had before when he alluded to Philip. "If you'll take my advice, stay away from Sinclair. He has nothing to offer you but the prospect of an early widowhood, if you can persuade him to go so far as to offer you marriage."

Rising politely to his feet in the next instant, he gave Marisa no chance to retort, although rage at his presumption almost choked her.

Just then the Countess Landrey came up, all smiles, followed by the dark-visaged Lucien Bonaparte.

"Captain Challenger, how kind of you to keep my little Marisa company. And darling, Lucien has been begging for a chance to dance with you. Perhaps you might prefer to go outside to the terrace. It's much cooler there, and you *do* look a little wan. It's this heat, I'm sure—so many people!"

There was no help for it. Ignoring Dominic Challenger, who had slipped his arm about her aunt's waist in a disgustingly familiar fashion, Marisa rose stiffly to her feet and took Lucien's outstretched hand. Anything was better than having to endure another moment of *his* company, she thought. She could more easily bare Lucien's strange, secretive smile and his few caustic comments.

"So you don't like your aunt's American friend? They are a rather crude and uncouth breed, are they not?" And then a few moments later while they were dancing he said abruptly, "You should avoid the company of the English, too, ma petite. It's an open secret this peace with them is not destined to last very long."

"If you refer to Philip Sinclair," Marisa said coldly, "I'm sure you already know very well that he is merely a friend, someone who helped me when I most needed help. He's been allowed to visit me without hindrance—must I cut him suddenly?"

Lucien grinned suddenly, white teeth flashing in his face.

"You had me wondering if you had claws or not. Good. My brother prefers women who show a little spirit—on occasion, that is."

She gasped at his unexpected boldness.

"Your brother, sir? All your brothers are married if I recall correctly. My spirit, or lack of it, can surely be of no interest—"

His voice grew suddenly bored. "My dear, you have proved unique so far. Don't spoil it by playing games. My brother, as you very well know, has developed a—certain tenderness for you. *I* am merely his messenger. To be blunt

—he wants you. There is a certain air of childlike innocence about you that appeals to him, I suspect, and like my dear sister-in-law, you, too, are a Creole, are you not? Yes—well, he's sent me to arrange matters. You understand that he must be discreet? And so must you, from now on. Perhaps it might be best to find you a complaisant husband who's aware of the situation—or an ostensible lover. It will be easier that way, as I'm sure you'll understand. But he's impatient. You ought to be flattered, señorita. It's not often my brother forgets himself enough to show publicly where his interests lie—"

With growing horror, Marisa listened to everything he said. She was unable to find a single word with which to respond to his startling disclosures. That she should be approached so boldly and bluntly, with the cool assumption that of course she would be willing—and flattered, no doubt —to become the first consul's mistress! Dominic Challenger had treated her like a dockside trollop, but with some reason—she had to admit that now. This—this was different! A cold-blooded proposition she was expected to jump at—and even her aunt was willing to push her into it, with no regard for her feelings.

It was with relief that Marisa realized Lucien did not expect her to answer. He took it for granted that she must accede and probably thought she was too overawed to find words.

He was smiling down at her sardonically. "You're a lucky young woman, but I'm sure you realize that, don't you? Come. I'll take you back inside now; its growing damnably cold out here!"

"I—I don't—"

He gave an impatient shrug. "I'm sure you don't know what to say, petite. But your aunt will help you find the right words later on. And the rest will come naturally, n'est-ce pas?"

After that, Marisa was very quiet, even when Lucien had taken her back to her gilt chair. Hortense was there, fanning herself; her poor godmother, for all her surface vivacity, looked as if she were about to develop one of her migraines.

Of the Countess Landrey there was no sign, and it was with *her* that Marisa had to speak, quite urgently.

She couldn't go through with it. Anything—even going back ignominiously to her convent in Spain, would be preferable to this bartering of her body. If she could only think of some way out of her predicament. . . . And then, quite suddenly, she thought again of Philip and her promise to meet him. All her earlier resolve came back to stiffen her spine. When she told Philip he would naturally offer to marry her, and as a British citizen she could go back with him to England. She could feel safe and cherished with Philip—Marisa was suddenly quite sure of it.

Chapter Fifteen

The enormous ballroom seemed to glow with light and color and careless gaiety, and the musicians continued to play without pause. It had grown noticeably warmer, and a faint sheen of perspiration seemed to add a glowing, almost transparent quality to Marisa's golden Creole skin. Color flushed her cheekbones, and her great golden eyes seemed to have become almost luminous. But it was not the heat but rather the tamped-down uneasiness and tension within herself that was responsible. But no one else could know that, and even those people who had whispered earlier that she was really nothing out of the ordinary had to admit that tonight at least, she was looking beautiful.

She had no lack of partners, although she wondered bitterly if *that* hadn't all been arranged, merely to see that she wasn't "indiscreet" again. She heard compliments, but there were no attempts at flirtation even when some of Napoleon's younger officers danced with her. Had everyone been subtly warned that she was now to be considered the first consul's property?

'Intolerable, intolerable!' her mind kept repeating, even while she kept a fixed smile on her face. And where was Philip? She had not caught a glimpse of him for a while, and she had begun to wonder if he, too, had been warned off. She preferred not to think about Dominic Challenger. The memory of his sneering, ugly threats and his unpleasant insinuations made her almost tremble with frustrated rage. Now that he had disappeared somewhere with her flighty aunt she had thought of so many things she would have enjoyed saying—comments as barbed and as cutting as *his* had been. How dared he of all people presume to criticize

167

her? And what had he meant when he talked about the prospects of her early widowhood if she married Philip?

Philip, meanwhile, had been closeted in close conversation with the English ambassador, Whitworth, in one of the small rooms Talleyrand had reserved for the use of those of his guests who wished to be private. Whitworth was uneasy, and it made his manner more than usually brusque. "Damn it, Sinclair—I don't know what to tell you! And after all, what's there to do? This is France, you know, and in any case we're at peace with America as well. He *seems* to be known to their ambassador and to the prince, our host, as well. However," Whitworth added thoughtfully, rubbing the side of his jaw, "I must admit that I'm curious. What's he doing here, I wonder?"

The last comment was made almost to himself. Philip Sinclair discovered that there was nothing more to be obtained from Mr. Whitworth except his gruffly offered advice to "wait and see."

But what should he wait for? A challenge to a duel—a bullet or blade in his heart? He had no illusions with regard to the character of the man he both hated and feared. Dominic was a savage, dangerous animal who had managed to survive in spite of everything, and even now he was probably planning what form his revenge would take. For all Philip knew, he might have come to France at this particular time for that very purpose. Somehow, he had to be gotten rid of—there had to be *something* that could be done!

Squaring his shoulders almost unconsciously, Philip walked back into the enormous room where all was glitter and sound. His blue eyes, usually bright and amiable, bore an almost glazed look. Lady Marlowe and her plain, rich daughter would be waiting for him to rejoin them. He had escorted them here, and of course they expected him to escort them back to their hotel. Lady Marlowe had mentioned several times that she did not care for her dear Arabella staying up too late and that the French kept deplorable hours.

It was a pity that Arabella was not prettier and that her mother insisted upon dressing her in colors that did not suit her rather sallow complexion. . . . Without volition, Philip's eyes had begun to search the throng—sliding past the glowering Lady Marlowe without noticing her at all and coming to rest on the slim figure he had been unconsciously looking for. Like Arabella, she was dressed in white —but what a contrast! White muslin cunningly embroidered with seed pearls made her skin seem more golden and formed a contrast to her hair that was a darker burnished shade of gold. God, what a stroke of luck that *he* should have been the one to find her running alone and terrified through the shabby side streets of Paris. And what a change had taken place since then!

Across the room, her golden eyes met his—and surely he didn't imagine the look of relief, even of pleading, that entered them? She had been standing talking to Bonaparte's sister-in-law, Hortense, and seemed on the verge of crossing the room when a man clad in black stepped forward and put his hand on her arm.

Fouché! Why couldn't he leave her alone?

"Ah, señorita. I had been hoping to have a word with you in private. You are not engaged at the moment? Good. Then perhaps you will honor me by taking a turn about the gardens. You will find it cooler outside, and the fountains, when they are all lighted up, are truly magnificent!"

Marisa did not have a chance to refuse. Taken by surprise while her attention was fixed on Philip and wondering at the rather haggard expression on his face, she found herself drawn through one of the open glass doors that led out onto the brightly lit gardens.

"My lord—surely—"

Fouché smiled wolfishly. "As I said, only a few words! You see, I am a curious man—it is my job to be curious— and with so many unanswered questions. . . . Of course I am in no doubt of *your* loyalty to the Republic, señorita, and that is why I thought you would not mind sitting me straight on a few points. We both have the same loyalty, do we not?"

Anger made Marisa tip up her head to stare back at him rebelliously.

"Why do you ask? Have I given you any reason to think otherwise? I beg you to come to the point, my lord!"

He seemed undisturbed. "Yes, I had intended to do so. And certain—uh—delicate matters are best gotten out of the way at the very beginning, don't you agree? You may trust in my discretion, I assure you. In fact we might be of mutual help to each other."

What on earth was he getting at? They were alone now, on a tree-shaded walk, and Marisa refused to go any further, her disturbed emotions making her blunt.

"How? I cannot see—"

"How did you arrive in France, señorita? And with whom? That will do for a start."

Marisa stared at him, feeling her heart beginning to beat thickly in her throat. How much did he know already? Was he trying to trip her up? She heard her own voice emerge, sounding low and strangely husky.

"Am I under suspicion? Why is it you ask me all these questions? If I am supposed to have done something wrong, then I demand that you ask your questions in front of others. My aunt—or—or the first consul. Yes, I'm sure he'd like to know what it is I'm supposed to be guilty of!"

He hadn't expected her to react so defiantly, throwing his own words back at him. Fouché felt his whole face grow tight, and he longed to be able to put his hands on her slim shoulders and shake the truth out of her. She was hiding a great deal, and he was sure of it. But he was a man who preferred extracting confessions from those he had already rendered fearful and uneasy with his hints and with his threats. It was so much easier that way! And now this little chit of a girl dared prove recalcitrant when he had expected no opposition from her.

"Excuse me—"

They both started, Marisa with surprise and relief and the duke of Otranto with annoyance that was soon replaced by calculation. So the Englishman grew bold, did he? Interesting, to see what lengths his obvious desperation might drive him to!

Philip Sinclair's face was white and set as he bowed

before Marisa, ignoring the taciturn and suddenly smiling Fouché.

"I hope I do not interrupt? But I believe you had promised this waltz to me."

Such a lame excuse, Fouché thought scornfully. But the reason for it? Ah, *that* was what might prove most interesting of all!

Before Marisa could frame an answer, Fouché was bowing low. And if there were a lingering trace of irony in his voice, only *she* would recognize it.

"Far be it from me to intrude on you young lovers with your quarrels! Señorita, I shall busy myself finding some champagne for you—you said you were extremely thirsty, did you not? Perhaps we shall have the opportunity to continue our conversation later—what do you think? Monsieur—"

Philip returned the sweeping generous gesture stiffly, wondering why the man was content to surrender the field so easily. He recognized him vaguely and thought they might have met before—but why was Marisa so stiff and silent?

No sooner had Fouché disappeared from view beyond the shrubbery than Philip seized her hands.

"Marisa—"

Her hands were cold. For a moment in the diffused moonlight, she seemed turned into an icy, gold-and-silver statue. And then she almost flew at him with what sounded suspiciously like a sob in her voice.

"Philip—oh, Philip! If you only knew how much I have been longing to talk with you! Oh, at least *you* do not think the worst of me. I cannot begin to tell you how horrible—how very confused and upset I've been and how much I've needed a real friend." She began to tug at him, pulling him along the barely defined path. "Quickly. I don't trust *him* one inch, and he has his reasons for leaving us alone. But I must speak with you!"

Puzzled and taken aback he suffered himself to be led by her—plunging, it seemed, into the very midst of the tall, ornamental shrubbery that grew so thickly on either side of the narrow pathway. It seemed like a kind of maze, and, although Marisa did not know her way, sheer instinct seemed to guide her wild flight until they came out at last in a small clearing with an ornamental summerhouse at one end.

Philip at least had become aware of the impropriety of their actions. This was a place for lovers hiding from the lights and music and everyone else. What if someone found them together here?

He drew her to a halt, feeling her panting like a wild thing, and then, without conscious volition, drew her against himself. She came, quickly and easily, and he could feel her trembling—from fright or exertion he had no way of knowing. It seemed the easiest and most natural thing in the world to bend his head—and her lips were waiting. . . .

Philip's kiss was sweet, undemanding, comforting. All the things that *he* was. He had come to her in spite of everything. He loved her!

It was Philip who broke away first; he made what sounded like a groan. All his reasons for following her outside had disappeared, and yet he retained enough sanity to realize that this was madness. He wanted her, but it was too risky. She kissed so innocently, her lips barely parted, and even if she had been the one to bring him here surely she did not realize what she was doing! He remembered what Whitworth had said, the latest salacious rumors, and could not believe that there was any truth in them. She was a frightened child looking for comfort, and he must retain his self-control or all would be lost. He must try to remember the reasons he had wanted to meet alone with her in the first place—the questions he had to ask her.

With a sense of shock he realized that Marisa had been talking, the words almost spilling out.

"You must help me—you *will*, won't you? I won't be bargained off. He's been nice enough to me, but I don't want to be his mistress. Or any man's mistress, for that matter. Oh, I should never have run away from the convent. Even the man my papa picked out for me might not have been so bad after all, or I could have refused to marry him— I realize that now. But I was so frightened. I thought that by running away I could save myself, only—"

He didn't know what she was talking about. Suddenly

172

aware of the passing of time and his own reasons for being here, Philip grasped her hands with a fierceness that made Marisa wince.

"What do you know of this man they call Dominic Challenger? I saw you dancing with him."

"I hate him!" The words burst from her, and she didn't try to stop them. Was Philip jealous? How much could she confide in him of *that* part of her past? Marisa forced herself to look up into Philip's face, and something in its almost tortured expression made her draw in her breath sharply. "*Why*, Philip? Do you know him?"

The sound he made was half laugh, half curse. "Do I know him? God, I wish I did not! You mean he has not boasted of the connection? He is my cousin—legally, that is. His mother was an openly unfaithful wife, and my uncle would like to disown him, but our name is old and respected in England, and any scandal—don't you see? Haven't you recognized the kind of man he is? He thrives on violence and intrigue and would do anything to destroy us all. My uncle saved him from the gallows when he was mixed up in one of the rebellions in Ireland. He hoped, I think, that his wild, savage nature would be changed. But instead—" Philip's voice, which had grown unrecognizably hoarse, seemed to change and grow harsh. "I think he would kill me if he could. I think he plans it, even now. Out of some idea of being revenged. I've seen the way he looked at me—"

"But why? Philip—why?"

He had forgotten himself now, driven by his own demons.

"Because he has always hated me! From the time we were both boys. Perhaps he resented the fact that my uncle always showed a preference for me. And later I was second officer aboard the *Dauntless*, and he was a common seaman. There was discipline to be upheld, and yet he constantly provoked me, jeered at me, taunted me! I had no choice but to—to—"

"No choice but to—what? Tell me, Philip, I want to understand!"

"But to see that he was punished for his insolence." It was a half-whisper, growing stronger as he continued, "It was a matter of discipline, don't you see? On board a man-of-war I could not afford to be weak or to let myself be intimidated. He knew it, and yet he continued to—challenge me! And in the end, when we were in port in the Indies, there was a mutiny. They stole a ship—he and some others. It was Santo Domingo, where there was that slave uprising—they took off for the Spanish part of the island. They were all taken prisoner, we learned later. But the Spaniards wouldn't return the ship, and my career was ruined. I should have had him hanged, and then none of it would have happened, but I was too weak. And *now*, to have him turn up here, of all places. What is he doing here? What does he want? He wouldn't be above blackmail, *I* should know that!"

He was still holding her hands in a grip that was unconsciously hurtful, but Marisa, her mind stunned by Philip's revelations, did not try to draw away. How taut and strained his face looked in the moonlight! Poor Philip! And now that he had confided in her, how could she possibly tell him the truth about *her* connection with Dominic Challenger? Philip would despise her; he would not trust her. And yet—they were cousins! Her thoughts whirled round and round as she wondered what she should say to wipe that tormented look from his handsome face. Should she warn him? Dominic's carelessly uttered words about her possible widowhood took on a new, frightening meaning as she searched her mind for words that would reassure Philip without giving herself away.

'I'm a coward, after all,' Marisa thought despairingly. At that moment her nerves received an unpleasant jolt.

It was the kind of scene Joseph Fouché loved to stage manage. He had gathered everyone here, and now all he had to do was to observe their reactions while his mind made notes. His voice sounded almost playful, as he said, "Ah, señorita, so here you are! I have brought the champagne you were so thirsty for a little while ago, and a gentleman who is desirous of making your acquaintance. Perhaps you'll recognize his name? Señor Pedro Arteaga—"

Marisa felt herself rooted to the spot as she looked into a sullen, dark-featured visage. Behind him, hard grey eyes looking dark as smoke from hell, Dominic Challenger stood with his arms folded, her aunt clung to his sleeve. And next to her, still wearing his cynical, drooping smile, was their host, the prince of Benevento.

It was he who drawled, breaking the silence that seemed to stretch interminably, "My dear Fouché, I hope you have some reason for this—er—dramatic confrontation? If not, you're being extremely tactless, I think!"

Philip Sinclair's profile looked like that of a statue carved out of moonlight, and his arms had dropped to his sides, fists clenched.

"Oh, Marisa!" Edmée breathed reproachfully, and Pedro Arteaga made a stiff, angry inclination of his head.

"My regrets, señorita, that you should have seen fit to run away from me. Had I known my suit was so distasteful to you, I would have withdrawn it."

Marisa found her voice at last, feeling herself driven into a corner like a hunted animal.

"Your regrets come too late, señor! I think you looked for a simple-minded child-wife with a large dowry—and I was fortunate enough to overhear some of your comments to your *friend* here. But I'm surprised to find you can face me now after certain events that *you* were a part of!"

He had the grace to flush, his speech growing clumsy.

"Dios mio! But how was I to know? We all thought you were nothing but a gypsy wench—"

"How interesting," Talleyrand drawled, his eyes narrowing. "But where is all of this leading us? I cannot imagine that this young lady's past should be a threat to the national security, friend Fouché, nor why you should have summoned us all here to witness what should surely have been a private discussion."

To Marisa's utter surprise it was Dominic Challenger who put an end to the tense scene that was building up. Shaking off her aunt's clinging fingers, he suddenly strode forward and caught her wrists in his steely grasp, pulling her against him.

"There's no need for any more discussion, nor for secrecy, since the duke of Otranto's capable spies seem to have ferreted out the truth of the matter. Marisa was masquerading as a gypsy, as Pedro has just admitted, and I made her my mistress. She came to France with me." His voice became heavy with sarcasm. "Do I hear any challenges from any of the gentlemen here? And you, my lord duke—have I admitted to a crime against the Republic?"

Edmée gasped as if she had been stabbed; Pedro Arteaga scowled, but said nothing; and Philip Sinclair made an unintelligible sound at the back of his throat.

Only Talleyrand laughed—and that mostly at Fouché's obvious discomfiture.

"Ah! L'amour! And what did *you* imagine, my friend? A royalist plot? Some dark conspiracy? It seems we have only uncovered some embarrassing facts that were none of our business in the beginning. My very deep apologies, señorita —and to all the rest of you."

Feeling the ground cut away from under him, Fouché lost his head. Angrily he burst out, "I beg your pardon, sir, but that is not all! Monsieur Sinclair is an Englishman related to the duke of Royse, and his father is a member of the English cabinet. The señorita, who is an intimate of those in the highest circles of *our* government, has shown a decided preference for his company. And there is also the strangely hidden relationship between Monsieur Sinclair and this other gentleman here who calls himself an American—"

"I do not *call* myself an American, my lord—I am a citizen of the United States. Do you wish for proof? You may call on Mr. Livingston if you wish. And as for this relationship to Sinclair that you mention—I assure you it's nothing that he nor I cares to acknowledge. Frankly, sir, I am a legitimate bastard!"

Shocked in spite of her own tumultuous emotions, Marisa made a movement to free herself and found herself held even more closely against the hard length of Dominic Challenger's body; one of his arms was clamped closely around her waist now.

"That—that you should dare—you admit it then—," Philip Sinclair stuttered.

"What does all this talk of legitimate or illegitimate matter?" Fouché growled, his face no longer the composed mask it had been earlier. "The fact is no matter what his real parentage, Monsieur Challenger here is not Monsieur Challenger at all, but the Viscount Stanbury and perhaps the next duke of Royse? An Englishman masquerading as an American—how intriguing!" His voice dropped to an almost threatening murmur. "And what of your relationship with this young lady here? A citizen of France through her mother and a lady whose virtue you admit violating?"

Even Talleyrand winced at his crudity and abrupt about-face, and he seemed about to interject some dry reproof when Dominic Challenger gave a harsh laugh.

"The lady's virtue would have remained intact had she seen fit to tell me who she was! But in view of these very public disclosures and my regard for her—reputation—I am willing to make honorable amends. Pedro—you may call me out later, if you wish—but you *did* say there was a sizable dowry involved? Edmée, my love, are you the chit's guardian?" Still holding a squirming, furious Marisa in an inescapable grip, Dominic, a strange, caustic smile touching his lips, looked around at the stunned, disbelieving faces that gazed blankly back at him. Looking directly at Edmée he said in a soft, signficant voice, "I promise you, my dear, that I will not prove a *difficult* husband—with your permission?"

Chapter Sixteen

He had only done it to spite Philip, of course. And to protect himself from the consequences of his actions once he was faced with them! But whatever his reasons for that sudden, surprising announcement made with no regard for her feelings, *he* was committed, and *she* was compromised.

There was no way out of it, Marisa found to her growing horror as the next few days passed. She was to marry Dominic Challenger, no matter what her real feelings for him were, and no matter that she continued to yearn for Philip and for a chance to explain to him. . . .

She was a prisoner of time and of circumstances, and there was no avenue of escape. She was always surrounded by people, all of whom paid no attention to her protests and her tears of rage. Her aunt continued to be reproachful and told her only, in a colorless voice, that she should consider herself lucky. How *could* she countenance marrying her niece to her lover? But Marisa did not dare put her thought into words although she felt sure that Edmée and Dominic continued to see each other—ostensibly to discuss arrangements for the forthcoming wedding, of course! She gritted her teeth whenever she thought of it.

Even Napoleon, suddenly cold and unapproachable, had given his formal consent, and her godmother cried, wishing her happiness. Was she relieved for herself?

Right up until the very day and hour of her wedding, Marisa could not let herself believe that it would really take place. She tried to pretend that her being forced to marry the one man she most loathed and despised was all an ugly nightmare. And she had not once seen Philip—not since that terrible, fateful night when he had turned on his heel to walk away, the duke of Otranto choosing to accompany him.

Quite suddenly, without quite knowing how, here she was dressed in a creation of white silk and lace that had been whipped up by a grumbling Leroy; she had diamonds in her hair and around her throat; and the prince of Benevento himself was to give her away.

Hortense Bonaparte had spent the last two hours with Marisa helping her dress and whispering words of consolation to her. Hortense's soft hazel eyes, so much like her mother's, seemed to brim with tears of sympathy that she tried to hold back for her young friend's sake. Of them all, only Hortense understood what it was to be forced into a loveless marriage when one's heart was elsewhere.

Several times, ignoring the clucking protests of her maid, Marisa had stormed, "I won't! I will not go through with it! Of all the men in the world, he's the last one I'd wish to marry! How could I let myself be forced into such a thing? I shall refuse to give my responses—I shall let everyone know how disgusting I find such a match!"

The face that looked back at her in the pier-glass was hardly recognizable as her own. A white-faced, terrified-looking stranger stared back at her—bright spots of color on high cheekbones, mouth reddened with lip rouge—a pathetic imitation of a Columbine puppet, with only the huge, staring golden eyes giving some life to her expression.

"I cannot!" Marisa whispered again, and Hortense caught her hands, gripping hard with an unfamiliar sternness.

"You *must* and you will!" Her voice dropped to a whisper. "How do you think *I* felt when my mother told me who I should marry? There was never any love on either side—there is not now. Only jealousy and mistrust and—and—oh, forgive me! I had not meant to say too much although my feelings must be apparent. But you see, you, too, will manage to survive just as I have! Perhaps it's even better this way, for us both. It's—easy to put up with certain things when the heart is not involved. . . ."

She carried the memory of Hortense's bitter words as she slowly walked down the wide staircase at Malmaison. The wedding was to take place here—a simple civil ceremony

with a small reception to follow. Better that way . . . Marisa
wondered how many people knew the real story behind her
sudden, hurried marriage to an American privateer captain.
She had been the subject of gossip and speculation ever since
she had emerged on the public scene, and now—oh, yes now
—the gossips would really enjoy a field day! But what did it
signify after all? She was past the point of caring what anyone
said or thought by now. And the sooner this mockery of a
ceremony was over, the better. She refused to think of what
might come afterwards, relying only on Hortense's hint,
whispered at the last moment, that she must not worry, she
would continue to be protected.

What Hortense had meant by her mysterious words Marisa
did not want to think about, but she could not help wondering, with a hardness that was new and unfamiliar, whether
it meant she was to be handed over to Napoleon as soon as
she had been safely and respectably married off. He was,
after all, a man used to taking what he wanted!

The Gold Salon seemed to contain far too many people.
Marisa, followed by Hortense and now joined by Edmée
and Josephine, hesitated at the arched, flower-festooned doorway, and Talleyrand, prince of Benevento stepped quickly to
her side, drawing her arm through his. He gave her his rather
tired, cynical smile as he murmured in a low voice, "There's
no need to be nervous, my child. Just think about all the
women who have been through this ceremony not once but
several times! It will all be over before you know it."

She had to grit her teeth together to stop them from chattering with the sudden waves of cold dizziness that seemed
to wash through her. Oh, God! Was this really happening?

Musicians were playing softly from some hidden alcove;
it was a haunting melody written by Mozart. There was a
rustling of gowns and a turning of heads as every eye in the
room was fixed upon her. She saw Napoleon, resplendent in
his glittering uniform, his face set and rather pale, by his
side, like a dark shadow, his brother Lucien smiled twistedly.

Marisa's eyes blurred as she averted them quickly. Why
did the room suddenly seem so large, the distance from one
end to the other so interminable? Her steps faltered, but
Talleyrand led her firmly on, and at last, unwillingly, she was

forced to look directly at the man she was to marry. Marry! It still seemed impossible. Cold grey eyes that silvered when the light touched them, dark, dangerous, predator's face— the face of a terrifying stranger. Why couldn't it have been Philip instead? *He* would be looking at her lovingly and eagerly, the lights shining on his bright gold hair. And then, perhaps, she could have smiled back, just as lovingly and trustingly.

The perfume of flowers was heady, becoming almost too cloying in the hot room where, as usual, Bonaparte had ordered fires lighted. Her mind blank, Marisa managed to make her dutiful responses in a voice that was barely above a whisper. The grey-haired, black-browed magistrate made a short, laconic business of the ceremony, and Marisa could be thankful that in the republic of France only civil ceremonies were permitted. She could not have endured such a mockery of a marriage in a church! This way it did not seem quite real.

Nothing seemed real—not even afterwards. Dominic had not kissed her when it was all over, merely taking her hand in a hard grip that made her new ring dig into her fingers. And then there was the reception, with mountains of food that she could not touch and the interminable bowing and smiling as her voice, seemingly disembodied, repeated the same polite acknowledgements over and over. The women kissed her cold cheeks, the men her equally cold hands. They danced out on the terrace where, as daylight faded, hundreds of lamps and torches were lit. Marisa drank champagne until her head ached; her mouth was stiff from smiling. When would it all be over? But could she face what lay ahead afterwards?

She had danced with her silent, saturnine husband, with the prince of Benevento, with Lucien, and even with Napoleon, who squeezed her hand slightly as he reproached her, in a hard and almost stilted voice for not having confided in him at the very beginning. She didn't know what she said in reply. By then she was feeling faint and dizzy with exhaustion and too much champagne.

"You look like a little ghost!" he said in his abrupt fashion, but at least there was some concern in his voice. "Perhaps it's time you retired with the ladies; I'll send them to you, and you can escape." He added in a lower tone, "You have nothing to worry about. I have arranged that you are to spend the night here, after a formal leave-taking, of course."

What did he mean? She had no time to think about that either, as she was led away surrounded by smiling, chattering women. They kept turning her around undressing her as if she were a doll, and suddenly all she wanted was to be sick. It was her aunt who took her away, holding her clammy forehead while she heaved and wished she might die right then.

"Darling, you're not?" And then, in an impatient voice, "but I made sure, with all those tisanes I had you drink—and you did bleed, didn't you? Oh, but it would never do, if you were. . . . Never mind, I'm sure it's only the excitement. And believe me, all this was only for your own good; *don't* look that way! You're the viscountess Stanbury now, and someday soon you might even be a duchess! Don't you realize what it all means?"

She had been undressed to her shift before, and now she was dressed again. A crimson velvet traveling gown, a matching, gold-frogged spencer, and gold kid half boots. Her hair was arranged again, and a becoming tucked silk bonnet trimmed with gold lace framed her face. Edmée tucked a lacy handkerchief into her hand.

"There's no need to wear a coat for you will be returning soon. And then we will have a nice long talk, my love, and you will understand everything."

Anger penetrated even through the fog in her brain. They were *still* treating her like a child—arranging everything for her without troubling to consult her inclinations.

In much the same frame of mind she was hustled downstairs again. She paused to drink yet another toast, this time something stronger than champagne that made her cough and brought tears to her eyes. "A stirrup cup," she was told. There was much giggling and conspiratorial whispering before she was led to a small side door where Dominic stood waiting, a caped greatcoat swinging from his shoulders to give him an even more forbidding look.

He seized her hand with a growl that at least sounded

familiar. "What the devil took you so long? Those horses are fresh—"

Small pellets hit her in the face making her close her eyes and gasp before she realized that they were throwing rice —an irony to cap all ironies! And then she was being handed up into a small, closed carriage, and her new husband leaned inside to say in a sarcastic voice, "You won't mind if I take the reins for a while? I'm used to driving myself." And the next moment she fell back against the velvet-covered squabs as the carriage took off with a leap.

They were traveling so fast that Marisa was forced to take hold of the strap; she closed her eyes as she was jounced and jolted about. What was he trying to do? Overturn the carriage so that she would be conveniently killed? She didn't know what had put such a thought in her mind, but it lingered as she was flung this way and that, and she began to moan aloud with a mixture of fear and rage.

They continued to travel forward at a breakneck speed, and by this time Marisa had given up caring what happened to her. The horses' hoofs sounded suddenly muffled, and peering through a crack in one of the blinds she realized that they were traveling through a forest. St. Germain? But he was supposed to turn right around and take her back. What was he about?

Totally concerned with keeping herself from being thrown off the seat, she lost count of time. And by now her whole body ached as badly as her head. On and on they went, as though all the hounds of hell had been loosed after them; at any moment Marisa expected that they would lose a wheel or not be able to negotiate a sharp curve. Then it would all be ended. He would leap from the seat and leave her to die in the splintered wreckage.

When the carriage suddenly jolted to an abrupt stop, Maria continued to cling to her handhold, too dazed to wonder what had happened.

The door was suddenly wrenched open, and she was dragged outside, hardly able to keep to her feet.

"Hurry, damn you! I don't want them to catch up yet."

She was being dragged off the road into some dense underbrush that tore at her skirts. No sooner had they alighted than the carriage had started up again, flying round a bend in the road to be lost to sight.

There were soon no sounds but those of the forest that pressed in darkly on all sides. The creaking of heavy branches, the crackling of dry leaves underfoot, and her own ragged breathing. An owl hooted somewhere nearby and Marisa was startled into a frightened cry.

Dominic did not pause, but she sensed, rather than saw, the glance he threw over his shoulder.

"You've done all right so far. Stay quiet, or I'll gag you if I must!"

Sheer lack of breath and trying to keep her footing kept her obediently silent. Even when she stumbled she was dragged mercilessly forward, and she had the feeling that had she fallen he would continue to drag on onward—on her face, if need be.

Suddenly, and just when she had begun to feel that she could not take another step, they emerged into a small moon-lit clearing.

There was a horse tethered here, and it lifted its head nervously at their approach.

He mounted easily, and without effort, slinging Marisa—there was no other word for it—across the saddle in front of him. The horse took off, and Marisa closed her eyes as the animal plunged between the trees following a path that was no path at all. She would have cried out protesting, questioning, but the arm that was clamped around her waist was like an iron band cutting off her breath; she could only gasp like a mortally wounded animal.

On and on they went, light and shadow making patterns that seemed to whirl like a kaleidoscope and melt together....

She must have fainted, Marisa thought dazedly later. Or perhaps she had imagined it all.

They were cantering quite decorously up a graveled driveway, and a small house, a villa of some kind, loomed up ahead of them, dim lights shining in a few of the windows.

There were shallow marble steps leading upward to a great wooden door that seemed to swing open as if by some secret signal. And she was being carried across the threshold like any new bride, hiding her face shyly against her husband's shoulder.

It was *that* thought which made Marisa stiffen, suddenly struggling against encroaching arms that held her far too closely.

"So you've decided to wake up and take notice? Good. You're heavier than you look, and I'm no gallant Sir Walter Raleigh."

She was deposited, almost dropped, onto a satin-covered sofa with a curved back. The shock made her bolt upright.

"You—what—"

"Save your recriminations for later, my lady! After the servants have left. And in the meantime, let me bid you welcome to our honeymoon retreat. It's only a small villa, I'm afraid, nothing like Malmaison, but at least we shall be able to spend some hours here in *privacy*."

White teeth showed against his tanned face in the travesty of a grin, and then, slinging the heavy greatcoat carelessly off his shoulders, Dominic Challenger turned to greet the man who had just entered bearing a tray.

"Donald, you're a sight for sore eyes, you old scoundrel. And a drink is just what I've been needing."

"Donald!"

Marisa almost croaked the words, her eyes widening with surprise and relief, and the man made a short, awkward inclination of his head in her direction as he set the tray down.

"Miss—I should be saying ma'am—or is it m'lady now? I keep forgetting." His usually crusty tone took her back in time as she gazed at him. At any moment she expected him to start calling her a "puir lass" again, putting aside his rather stilted manners. In fact an unwilling smile had started to tug at the corners of his dour, down-turned mouth when Dominic interrupted.

"Thank you, Donald. That will be enough. I'm sure you've seen to the rooms, and now you can take yourself off to bed —and take everyone else off with you. My little bride and I would like to be alone. Wouldn't we, chérie?"

The look in his eyes gave the lie to his deceptively soft voice, and Marisa felt a long shudder go through her tired body as she gazed imploringly at the older man.

"Please don't go yet! I had no opportunity to thank you—"

"Donald!" Dominic said ominously, and the man shrugged his shoulders with an apologetic, half-ashamed glance at the young woman who looked so wan and so frightened.

"Ah, well, I only did what I could, and there's no thanks necessary. But—," shooting a sharp glance at his captain who stood frowning at him blackly—"if ye'll be needing anything else later, I'll be waiting up."

He made his escape from the room quickly enough then, slamming the door behind him with more than necessary force.

Chapter Seventeen

A clock ticked somewhere, but Marisa had no idea of what time it might be. She had forced herself to eat a slice of cold meat and to swallow a glass of dry sherry, but that was only because she felt both the food and drink might be forced down her throat otherwise.

They had hardly spoken more than two words to each other since Donald had left so reluctantly, and Dominic Challenger seemed wrapped in a black mood that Marisa was afraid to interrupt. Questions clogged in her throat, and she did not dare ask them. Why had he brought her here to this lonely, isolated place, practically abducting her in the process? They were married—what did he mean to do with her? She realized that this was the first time they had been alone since the night they had become "engaged." Always before, there had been someone else present, making her feel safe. And even at those times she had tried to ignore him, wanting to show him how much she hated him. Was it revenge he was looking for now? And if so, what form would it take?

She sat huddled on the uncomfortably slippery sofa, trying to pretend that nothing was amiss, and all the time she was conscious that he drank much more than he ate, his face closed and darkly forbidding.

He had ignored her presence so far except to press more food and drink upon her, and at one point when he stared narrowly into the fire she had made a motion to leave, thinking him asleep.

"Sit down!" His voice grated harshly, and she subsided again, glancing at him fearfully. What did he intend to do with her? What was he waiting for?

He came around to her in his own time, waiting, it seemed,

189

until she was so stiff that she felt her body might fold up and collapse at any moment. The silence stretched interminably, and her nerves along with it, until she felt she might easily scream out loud.

At last in a low voice she said, "I—if you'll forgive me, I'm so tired! I should like to retire now, if I may—"

"If you may! My God, how meek you sound now that you have achieved your object, my dear viscountess! Have you been waiting for me to apologize for spoiling the rest of your clever plan? Was the first consul keeping his bed warm for you tonight?"

She gasped with shock at the sudden savagery of his attack.

"*My* object? *My* plans? You are mistaken my lord—the planning was all on your side! *You* forced me into this—this unpleasant mockery of a marriage, and you brought me here—for God knows what object! I must put up with your presence, it seems. Must I also put up with your insults?"

Marisa was too weary and too numb to care for the consequences of her words. Her violent rebuttal of his studiedly cruel speech surprised even herself, but now, suddenly, she was determined not to give in.

He leaned back in his chair, arms folded, studying her with an almost malicious satisfaction. So she had decided to show some fight, had she? It only served to make the game they both played more interesting.

"Why, madame, I think you'll put up with whatever I decide to inflict upon you! Did you imagine you'd have everything your own way?"

"I don't know what you're talking about!" Marisa responded wildly. "I never wanted to marry you—you forced it upon me. I had much rather—"

"You had much rather what? What a little hypocrite you are, in spite of your girlish ways! Although I'm sure you'd much rather it was Philip Sinclair than I and failing that, your powerful lover. Why did he decide to marry you off, I wonder? Was it only to make you seem more respectable and to have easier access to your bed? You've learned fast, I must say!"

"Oh! You're intolerable! Does it make you feel more of a man to try and browbeat me in this way?" Sheer rage brought

Marisa to her feet, hands clenched at her side. There was a pounding in her head that made her careless of everything, even the consequences of her rash words.

"Well, you won't succeed, not even if you kill me! You're not a man, but a rutting beast—an animal! I'm surprised that my aunt, who is usually discriminating should have accepted you as a lover. But then perhaps that's why she decided to palm you off onto *me!* You are nothing more than a brutal animal! You should have stuck to whores who ask nothing more than that they be paid. Have you ever satisfied a woman, I wonder? Have you ever thought of anything beside your own satisfaction? I think all the women you've had were either bought or forced, as I was. You're not capable of anything more. And yes, I would rather have anyone else as a lover— even Napoleon, who is capable, I'm told, of making a woman want him!" In the face of his stunned, furious silence, she had begun to sob, but the words kept spilling out. "You—you can do what you please with me because you're stronger than I, as you've shown me before. You can rape me or murder me—I know I can't stop you. But you will never make me feel any more than loathing for you—"

"By God, madame," he interrupted at last between clenched jaws, "if I didn't know better, I'd think you were trying to instruct me in the arts of lovemaking!"

"Lovemaking? You're not capable of anything so refined. You—merely fornicate, my lord!"

She had gone too far at last. She realized it when she saw his face looking as black as thunder, the brows drawn together over icy eyes.

"So it's 'my lord' this and 'my lord' that, now that you think you've got yourself a title, eh? I don't like having anything forced on me, my dear, not even the mistress of the most powerful man in France—or the whole of Europe, for that matter! That's why I brought you here—to teach you a lesson."

"You cannot teach me any lesson that you have not forced me to learn before—my lord," she responded between stiff lips and saw him scowl.

"Then damn you, why do you continue to stand there as stiff as a marble statue? Take your clothes off—and quickly.

There's not too much difference between a wife that's forced on a man and a whore, and there's no need to stand on ceremony between ourselves, is there?"

"*You* were forced upon me, not the other way around. And if you want me, you'll have to take me for I'm not your whore, and I won't strip for you."

How dare she stand there so defiantly, daring him to tear the clothes off her back? Was that what she wanted?

Their eyes locked—gold and silver, neither giving ground. With a sudden, calculatedly violent gesture Dominic put his hand on the front of her velvet gown, ripping it down to the navel.

She winced, swaying slightly, but refused to give ground. He caught at the fraying material with both hands, completing the business, so that she stood naked in the firelight.

"You seem more familiar this way," he drawled wickedly, watching narrowly for any signs of her breaking. He thought she shuddered, but she only said in a whisper, "*You* should know, my lord!"

What kind of game was she playing this time? Frustrated and furious, he gazed at her, letting his eyes travel slowly and deliberately over her slim, gold-tinted body. He waited for her to flinch and try to cover herself, but she did nothing. Had she had enough opportunities to grow used to the sight of her own nudity? Who were the other men who had seen her like this? He remembered her contemptuous, cutting words of a few moments before and wanted to strike her and bring her to her knees. But something held him back—her stiff, waiting attitude, perhaps?

Surprising himself, Dominic put his hands on her shoulders instead of around her slim, stemlike throat. He could feel her flesh quiver and flinch under his touch.

"Christ! Do you really expect me to murder you? Feeling the way you do, why did you pick on me for a husband?"

"I didn't. It was *you!*"

"Are you trying to tell me you didn't know about my talk with Talleyrand earlier? He told me Fouché had found out everything, and he hinted in his sly, diplomatic fashion that if I didn't do the right thing by you my ship would be confiscated." He shook her angrily. "Do you dare pretend you didn't know? There you were, flirting guilelessly under the moon with Philip Sinclair. Had you planned everything between yourselves already? You little bitch."

Marisa flinched from the note in his voice, but sudden realization made her throw her head back to meet his eyes.

"I didn't know anything! Except that he—that Bonaparte had suddenly developed a fondness for me, and they were all pushing me at him. I thought—I thought Philip might help me—"

Why had she blurted out so much? Her shoulders felt bruised already from the force of his grip, and his eyes seemed to stab into hers like silver daggers.

"Either you're a consummate liar, or I'm a fool." His voice was harsh. "I brought you here to hurt you—you know that, don't you?"

She nodded, not being capable of anything more at the moment, and closed her eyes against the blaze in his.

"Marisa." She kept her eyes tightly shut, her body taut, not wanting to acknowledge the sudden softness of his voice. He continued in the same oddly withdrawn voice. "We're married to each other with neither of us wanting it. It's done. What's left but to make the best of it?"

"No!" she whispered sharply, but he suddenly swung her body up in his arms, and carried her upstairs in spite of her choked, halfhearted protests.

This was what she had expected in the beginning when he had dragged her here. It was what she had been expecting and dreading, and yet it was different.

He put her down on a bed, with moonlight from an open window falling across it, and undressed, taking his time, before an orange-embered fire. She watched without being able to help it, remembering other times and telling herself that a few muttered words by a self-important magistrate did not make any difference.

She had steeled herself not to make any protest regardless of what he did with her, but now with the moonlight silvering her flesh and his, she wanted it to end quickly like all the other times.

She was naked, and he was naked. She hated him, but his

flesh was warm against hers, and she could not stop his hands from roving.

Her body was uncharted territory, and her taunting words had awakened him to that fact. Not once before in his life had Dominic thought about a woman as anything except an instrument of passion, there to give him satisfaction. But now, against his will, he found himself stung into a sudden awareness of something different. He knew she hated him—she had made no bones about it. And yet she belonged to him. He had not taken the time nor the trouble to notice before how satiny-soft her flesh was, nor how her skin seemed to quiver under his inquisitive touch.

He brushed his fingers across her small, taut breasts and felt the tiny engorged nipples spring to prominence under his hands. Now at last she moaned softly and struggled against him, whispering "No!" But he ignored her protests, swinging his body over hers to hold her still while he continued with his searching. He kissed her soft mouth feeling her lips tremble and then finally part helplessly, allowing him full rein, making the most of his plunder until he felt her yielding as she kissed him back. And then he wanted more. He tangled his fingers in her curls, keeping her head still while his lips explored lower—first her breasts and the taste and feel of her nipples, and then, when she was almost mindless, his mouth moved even lower, passing over her taut, quivering belly and the deep surprise of her navel to that other secret place she tried to keep hidden by crossing her legs.

He pulled her thighs apart roughly, taking perverse pleasure in her resistance and pressed his mouth against her moist softness, feeling her tense hips arching before she yielded at last, crying out incoherently until his lips stopped her mouth again and the throbbing ache in his groin found its solace in the pulsating softness of her body.

Marisa had never dreamed she could feel this way. She had tried to fight against him at first, and then her body had taken over from her mind, rendering her helpless to combat the strange, unusual feelings that made her tingle from head to curling toes.

His tongue ravished her mouth, and she wanted it. Just as

he made her want the hardness of his flesh inside her, forcing an unfamiliar response from her that made her forget everything but assuagement—her legs twined around his, her hands clutching at his muscled flesh, relishing every driving motion of his body against hers, bringing her to peak after peak of emotion she had never known existed before.

It had all taken place without a single word, and she fell asleep with his flesh still a part of her, waking drowsily when she felt him swell inside her. This time, too, he held back, kissing and caressing her until every inch of her flesh tingled and she cried out for the fulfillment of the promise his poised, hard-muscled body offered her. She slept again, to wake cradled in his arms, the sunlight, warm and gold, falling across them.

Everything that had happened last night seemed like an odd, not-too-unpleasant dream; and for a few moments Marisa could not remember where she was or what she was doing here, lying naked and uncovered in a strange bed with a stranger beside her, and the light streaming in from open windows throwing every detail into relief.

Dominic had kept his arms and one leg thrown over her to keep her possessively close to him, and in that first moment of realization when all the memories of what had taken place last night came flooding back, she was unable to move, feeling the heat of her blushes cover her whole body. Slightly and almost fearfully she turned her head, studying his sleeping profile, hardly able to believe even now that this was the same man who had taken her so quickly and brutally so many times before. Now he was her husband and her lover—and still a stranger to her. She almost felt a stranger to herself, a woman sated by lovemaking—a woman at last. How peculiar that *he* should have been the one to teach her what it meant!

She must have moved, or perhaps it was only her suddenly quickened breathing that had aroused him. She felt his arms tighten and his lips brush her forehead, and slanting her eyes upward met his silver-grey, thoughtful gaze.

"Good morning, viscountess! Did you sleep well?"

The guarded, cynical look she remembered too well seemed to have been erased from his face; and the sun-wrinkles by his mouth and eyes sprang into prominence as he gave her a lazy grin. Marisa found herself smiling back.

"Well enough, my lord," she responded demurely, dropping her eyelashes. "Considering how little sleep you allowed me."

He laughed, and she realized with a sense of shock that she had never heard him laugh before.

"As I recall, you gave me little chance of falling asleep myself, you unexpected little vixen! Not that I'm complaining." His voice roughened slightly before his lips swooped down to claim hers in a kiss that was both searching and hard and tender, leaving Marisa breathless.

This was a side to his nature that she had not dreamed existed. And yet she was almost afraid to give way, still unable to trust either him or herself.

Was he playing some subtle game with her? Had he decided to add refinement to his cruelty so that he would catch her off guard? What had made him change so suddenly from ravenous wolf to considerate lover? And yet, lying here in the warm sunlight, her body open to his eyes and his touch, Marisa did not want to think. Her body craved the new and unusual sensations he had aroused in her last night. Having only just learned the meaning of desire and fulfillment, she wanted to be carried out of herself again, to reassure herself that such sensations actually existed.

That it should be Dominic Challenger of all men who should teach her! Keeping her eyes tightly closed at first, Marisa let her hands, shy and curious at the same time, explore the length of his hard body. She had seen him naked before, but this was different. He had learned the secrets of her body intimately, and she knew nothing of his. What kind of caresses did a man enjoy? The thought was wicked, taking her by surprise. She peeped at him at length through the shadow of her lashes and found him grinning down at her.

"Don't stop now! Or are you disappointed that my body isn't as smooth and as pretty as yours is?"

She blushed, pulling her hands away as if they had been stung.

"My lord—"

This time he frowned, his voice becoming harsh in the old

way. "Damn it! Don't call me that! I'm an American. The title your friends set such store by is meaningless to me, and I'll never claim it. Do you understand?"

"But—"

"And I'm not your lord and master either, although it might have been my intention to make myself so—earlier." He gathered her more closely to him when she stiffened, lips brushing against her averted cheek. "For God's sake, don't start pretending, Marisa. Gypsy vixen or hoyden—stay yourself. I've no desire to change you. You've never been exactly conventional since I've known you, my love, so don't start now!"

Chapter Eighteen

What would have happened between them if Donald had not chosen that particular moment to knock at the door?

They might have come to a better understanding of each other, and she was unconscionably disappointed when Dominic decided to let her breakfast in bed alone while he pulled on his clothes and went below with his grumbling man.

The small bathroom that adjoined their bedchamber was purely functional, containing only a washstand with a pitcher of icy cold water and an oval shaped, claw-footed tub which had, however, been thoughtfully half-filled with tepid water.

Marisa spent as short a time as possible over her ablutions, emerging to find a low-cut peasant blouse and full, flower-patterned skirt thrown carelessly on the bed.

"I had to borrow those from one of the kitchen maids. I hope you don't mind?"

The kitchen maid was obviously buxom. Well, the clothes were clean, at least. She looked a fright and thought longingly of her rows upon rows of new gowns hanging up so neatly for her to choose from. But *that* thought reminded her of how she had arrived here and the reasons for her being here, and on a green and gold afternoon like this she did not really want to think—either of the past or of the future.

It seemed as if Dominic felt the same way, for he took her walking with him across an overgrown garden that led out onto wild parkland bordered by the forest. Surprisingly, delightfully, the lands that the borrowed villa stood on ran alongside a brook, a small tributary of the Seine. And here was an old wooden bridge, rather shaky, that crossed the stream at its narrowest point, leading to an old stone summerhouse, open on all four sides.

They walked holding hands like lovers, making only occasional casual conversation. Dominic with his white ruffled shirt open at the throat, looked almost as much a peasant as she did in her borrowed clothes. The sun was hot on their shoulders, and bees droned sleepily in the warmth, making time unimportant.

'I am happy at this moment,' Marisa thought contentedly. And then, without wanting to, she wondered, 'Will I always feel so with him?'

No matter what events had led up to this moment she was married to Dominic, and everything seemed changed between them; the old antagonism and mistrust vanished like mist clearing before the onslaught of the sun.

A grinning Donald had thoughtfully provided crusty, fresh-baked bread and great hunks of yellow cheese, and they ate with their shoes pulled off, dangling bare feet in the languidly running water. Once a small fish nibbled inquisitively at her toe, and Marisa fell back with a shriek, to find her body suddenly covered by his.

"I was wondering when you'd decide to lie down," Dominic murmured wickedly, pulling down the shoulder of her blouse to press his mouth against her shoulder, then pulling it down even further to kiss her breasts in spite of her halfhearted struggles.

The blouse came off and then her skirt. The afternoon sun moved lower as they lay together on the grass making love first, and then, when the urgency of passion had left them both, merely lying there together. "To think I wanted to become a nun!" Marisa said suddenly, and he chuckled deep in his throat.

"I'm glad you changed your mind. The role of a half-tamed little gypsy suits you better."

"I hated you! You were so callous and so brutal."

"I know," he said drily. "Last night you told me very explicitly what you thought of me. You looked like a bedraggled little sparrow masquerading as a gamecock! I had intended to be an ogre and make you suffer, but somehow you managed to drive all other considerations from my mind except possessing you." With one finger he traced the outline of her small, upturned nose making her wrinkle it. "You're such a strange mixture of defiant child and mysterious woman. I find myself at a loss how to deal with you!"

"Must you *'deal'* with me, as you put it? You have done very well so far."

"And so have you," he replied with a certain note of grimness underlying his voice. "You've managed to make me forget everything that brought us here together, and even the business I'm supposed to be engaged upon. Certain other matters as well. Did the gypsies teach you any spells? Have you asked yourself what you are doing here with me, seducing me with the artless movements of your body, when not too long ago you ran away from me as if I was the devil himself?"

Forgetting the mood of pleasant lassitude that had seized her Marisa struggled up on one elbow.

"You were going to sell me to that horrible man—some acquaintance of yours! I heard you talking together, discussing me as coldly and heartlessly as if I had been a—a—oh, I heard you haggling! You said I needed to be mastered, and *he* said he could not decide until he had—inspected me. How *could* you have done so?"

"What in hell are you talking about? *Sell* you? I had intended to set you free and forget about you once we had landed in France, but damn you, I couldn't get you out of my mind. Why do you think I had Donald bring you to Paris? I had some urgent business to take care of, or I would have taken you myself, but *you* it seemed, were in a hurry to be reunited with your long-lost friends! Oh, I'll admit I did not believe any part of your story, but—"

"I *heard* you, I tell you!" Marisa hissed furiously, glaring down at his set, equally angry face. "I came downstairs that morning, and you were in the room off the hallway with a man talking about me and the price you hoped to get—"

She was stunned when the tension left his face and he suddenly burst into laughter.

"My God! That ought to teach you not to listen into private conversations! You little imbecile. I was talking about my *ship*. Yes, damn it, I intended to sell her and buy another one, but it didn't cost as much as I thought to get another mast rigged up, and I decided to keep her after all. Is *that* what sent you fleeing so precipitately?"

She wouldn't let herself be mollified now that he had goaded her into losing her temper and had laughed at her into the bargain.

"You meant only to set me up as your mistress then—until you tired of me," she muttered sullenly. "And you had not shown me the slightest consideration before then, as you very well know! Why should I let myself be *used*—"

The laughter gone from his face he scowled back at her.

"What do you think Bonaparte had in mind? Marriage, when he has a wife already? Or was it my cousin Philip you'd set your cap at, hoping to play both ends against the middle?"

The beautiful sunny afternoon seemed suddenly clouded, and Marisa gave a sudden, involuntary shiver. Why had she started such a discussion?

"Oh—don't!" she whispered remembering Philip and his bitter, angry words and even recalling that she had wished it was he she was marrying. Her face mirrored her conflicting emotions, and Dominic knocked her supporting elbow from under her, pinioning her against the crushed grass with hands that were suddenly cruel and merciless.

"How your face changed when I said his name! You should really learn to set a better guard on your far too transparent emotions, madame! Has he been your lover, too? Is that how you learned enough about me to set Fouché on my trail?"

"No, no!" She moved her head helplessly from side to side, closing her eyes to shut out the image of his dark, angry face. How could he change so fast?

"Oh—you're really a consummate actress!" he said between gritted teeth, and his fingers seemed to sink like claws into her soft, shrinking flesh. How could he have forgotten that only a few moments ago he had accused her of not being able to hide her feelings!

"How well you've played your role so far. I'm almost sorry the game has ended, for I must say your show of passion, your clever pretense at resistance before yielding was really mag-

nificent. Whoever taught you, taught you well. My congratulations! You almost had me fooled, you know."

She began to sob hopelessly, tasting bitterness like bile in
her throat, and with a smothered oath he almost flung her
away from him, rising lithely to his feet to stand looking
down at her.

"The play's over, my love. Get up and get dressed. It's time
we were returning."

Pride alone kept her from begging him to understand, from
trying to explain everything to his set, unyielding face.

At least he turned his back on her while with fumbling fingers she struggled into her crumpled clothes. And on their
walk back to the house he neither looked at her nor touched
her.

By this, Marisa was so drained emotionally that she felt
physically sick. There were no feelings left in her—not the
hate she tried to recapture, not even despair.

She went up to the bedroom they had shared last night
and flung herself uncaringly across the freshly made bed,
while Dominic stayed downstairs with a decanter of brandy
at his side.

The servants, well-trained, pretended to notice nothing,
and even Donald dared not say a word, recognizing what he
referred to as one of his captain's "black, murderous moods."

As the evening changed into night and the captain stayed
closeted in the study, Donald prepared a tray and went upstairs, tapping hesitantly at the closed foor to the bedroom.
He was shocked at the sight of Marisa's white, strained face,
and he tried in his own clumsy fashion to find words that
would comfort her, but she only shook her head, refusing
comfort as well as food. She had vomited and blamed it on
the sour red wine with which they had washed down their
bread and cheese. The door clicked shut behind him as he
went dejectedly back down the stairs, shaking his head.

They had seemed so happy this morning, and he had never
seen Captain Challenger look so lighthearted and at peace
with himself. What had happened between them to change
everything so drastically?

It was a question that Marisa, still lying inertly across the
bed, asked herself, too. And she was not yet able to sort out

her real feelings. Dominic had made her want him when he taught her lust. That was all it had been—that had to be all! She had taunted him, and he'd thrown her challenge back in her teeth. Was it possible that she still loved Philip? Was that what her face had shown when he mentioned Philip's name? She *had* loved Philip, who was honest and open and wore his emotions on his sleeve. Dominic was too complex, too changeable, too cruel.

She began to sob again and cried herself to sleep not waking until he came to her, breaking open the lock on the door. He reeked with the fumes of liquor. He took her savagely and painfully and without a single caress just as he had been used to doing before on the ship. Then he left her, still without a word.

Worn out, aching and degraded in both body and spirit, Marisa managed to fall off to sleep just before dawn. She woke to an ominous stillness.

She had no idea what time it was. She had pulled the heavy drapes together last evening and hardly any light filtered into the room. Her head felt heavy, and her eyes ached from tears. There was a soreness between her thighs that remindedly her vividly of the previous night. The pain forced her upright against the feather pillows; then she dropped back with a moan. Oh God, she felt so ill! And what new form of torture and humiliation had he planned for today?

The house was so silent--where was Donald? Surely he at least should have been up by now, trying to tempt her with another tray. Poor Donald!

She felt hungry; a cramp doubled her over the next moment and she gasped weakly. 'I have to find something to eat. Why should I give him the satisfaction of starving myself to death?'

She had no clothes left to wear. Her borrowed skirt and blouse had been torn brutally off her back last night. Wrapping a sheet around her and gritting her teeth to fight off the waves of dizziness that threatened to overcome her, Marisa made her stumbling way to the door.

Clinging with one hand to the polished mahogany stair rail, she managed to walk downstairs; she gasped with shock and fright when a man with a round face and rather vacant-looking eyes came out of one of the rooms to gape at her stupidly.

She had never seen him before—who was he? And where was Donald? For the moment, Marisa had forgotten her own state of deshabille.

She forced herself to speak, trying to put some semblance of authority into her voice.

"Where is everybody? And what time is it? I am hungry."

He grinned suddenly, frightening her.

"All gone· ─mistress. Nobody here but poor Jean." She stared at him, trying to focus her thoughts.

"What do you mean?" she cried sharply, and he seemed to cringe.

"Don't be angry with Jean! He's done nothing bad! Stay here, the new master said, and Jean stayed. Yes!"

He was an idiot. Oh, God. To be left all alone here with a grinning, vacant-faced madman! Another cramp knotted her belly, and Marisa grimaced, hanging onto the railing. She forced her voice to sound calm.

"Jean, it was good of you to stay. But you must tell me where they have all gone. And, you see, I need something to eat. I'm very hungry—"

At least he understood that much. His face seemed to brighten.

"Hungry? Food—in the kitchen. Jean will bring bread. Jean is good."

"Of course you're good. And they must trust you, or you wouldn't be here to look after me, would you?"

Diverted, he nodded his head solemnly.

"Jean good. Jean look after mistress. You keep Jean as servant?"

This was worse than trying to communicate with a four-year-old child! If only she didn't feel so dizzy and sick and if only those cramps would leave her!

"Of course you may stay on. You'll make a good servant if you'll remember everything that you're told. *Can* you remember, do you think? Was there any message for me? Please try to remember, Jean!"

His face clouded, but now he grinned suddenly.

"Jean remembers! The men came, many of them, and the

new master and the other one who spoke so strangely went with them. The master said—he said—" He frowned, while Marisa held her breath, and then suddenly gabbled as if by rote, "Said tell her the game is all over-played-to-a-finish— and she can go back to her friends now!" He ended triumphantly, looking at her as if he hoped for some reward.

"Oh!" Marisa swayed. Her head ached, and then another worse cramp came to join the pain in her head, and she crumpled, moaning, into a heap at the foot of the stairs. She was vaguely aware that Jean was bending over her, his round face creased with anxiety.

"Jean say wrong? Jean good—"

"Jean—I'm sick—very ill—do you think you can remember *that?* You must bring help—do you understand? Bring someone—a doctor—someone!"

The words ended in a muffled scream of anguish as an even worse pain shot through her making her writhe.

"Jean—please! Help—"

There was a gush of warm stickiness between her thighs, and then, thankfully, everything went black.

PART TWO

Dark Night of the Soul

Chapter Nineteen

Voices—there were voices all around her, some of them strange and some of them familiar, and they were all talking about her. But why did she find it so difficult to open her eyes?

"I thought—I truly thought that she was all right! There were no symptoms. I gave her all those strong tisanes that always worked so well for *me*, and—" *That* voice belonged to her aunt, but whose was the other?

"All women are different, my dear countess! Now if I had been called in earlier, I would have been able to tell! However, she's lost the child she was expecting, poor young woman, and I must advise . . ." There was a buzz of voices then, making her move her head fretfully against something soft. Disjointed words penetrated the fog in her brain.

"Some women are not meant for childbearing. The width of the pelvis is important, you see— *Hips*, madame, hips! And the fashions of today be damned! She's far too slim— needs feeding up. Better tell her husband to stay away from her bed for awhile—it's not likely—" What were they talking about?

"Her—husband has gone away. I shall be taking her abroad with me, doctor, as soon as she's strong enough. You're sure she's going to recover? My poor darling—"

It was far easier to subside into blackness again than to try to make sense of what they were talking about. And somewhere, deep in the hidden recesses of her brain, there was the knowledge that waking up might bring even more pain than that which had already racked her body.

After what seemed to be a long time, Marisa opened her

209

eyes and found herself lying on a day bed before an open window. She felt very weak and very tired, but at least the pain she remembered was gone, and someone had made an effort to make her comfortable!

Soft pillows propped her up into a semireclining position, and she was swathed in a warm, lacy shawl.

"Dearest! Oh, thank *heaven* you decided to wake up! If you only *knew* what a terrible fright you've given us all! Oh, I never *would* have forgiven myself if you had . . . Thank God that—that village idiot had *enough* sense to run for help!" Edmée, in a plain muslin morning gown, kept dabbing at her eyes with a lacy handkerchief.

Marisa frowned with the effort to remember and then wished she had not tried for the memories that came flooding back were far too ugly and painful to be faced yet. She said in a small whisper, "Dominic? He—he—"

Shaking her head, Edmée made a rush to her side.

"Chérie, don't! Please don't upset yourself. The doctor said . . . Oh, you told us everything while you were delirious, and you mustn't think about it now! Only of getting well, and the fine time we'll have together in London, you and I! And just think, love, Philip Sinclair has called every single day just to find out how you are. I vow that I have never seen a more infatuated young man! And you *do* like him, don't you? Forgive me, my love. I should never have—"

Edmée's warm hands caught Marisa's cold ones, and her eyes swam with contrite tears.

Even Josephine and Hortense cried when they came to visit her. Only Marisa herself had no more tears left to shed. They told her she had wept constantly during her delirium, but now she felt empty and drained of all emotion.

Later on, though, as she began to recover her strength, she found room in her mind for a single emotion. Hate. Whenever she thought of all that had taken place—the callous way in which Dominic had tricked her and used her, the way he had played upon her emotions with consummate skill, waiting for the moment when she had completely dropped her reserve to pick a quarrel with her and do what he must have intended to do from the beginning—she could feel herself grow hot with almost murderous rage.

210

His ship had sailed that very morning he had abandoned her—she had Fouché to thank for *that* piece of information —and she wished savagely that the ship would sink to the bottom of the sea!

But it was strange that even the unctuous Fouché had called to pay his respects, especially since *he* had had a great deal to do with the matter of her unfortunate marriage. Marisa had to grit her teeth in order to force herself to be polite each time one of his visits were announced, and he bowed over her hand, calling her "my lady" and the viscountess. Oh, God! Why did he have to remind her of a sham of a marriage that had left her with nothing but an empty title and a feeling of coldness inside?

But Fouché had his reasons—and these Marisa were to learn of later after she had been adjudged well enough to go about again.

Leaving the comparative seclusion of Malmaison, she had spent a day in Paris, and outside the dressmaker Leroy's establishment she ran into the duke of Otranto.

Smiling his thin smile, he bowed over her hand. "Viscountess Stanbury! What a fortunate coincidence, madame! I had been meaning to call upon you before you leave for England —a small matter on which you might be of some help to France, if you would. May I?"

He climbed into the coach with her, not waiting for the grudging inclination of her head. He settled himself beside her comfortably while he regarded her out of his hooded, curiously cold eyes.

"Well, my lord duke?"

But he seemed determined to pursue his own oblique course. "Ah, yes! Paris will be sorry to lose you, madame. Even the first consul was expressing his regrets to me the other day. But with an *English* title, and, I fear, the clouds of war gathering on the horizon again, I suppose after all that your departure is for the best. A change of scene, eh? And, of course there is the chance you will soon become the duchess of Royse!"

"What?"

Fouché lifted an eyebrow and shook his head in mock commiseration. "But surely you were told? I had believed your estimable aunt—or perhaps Monsieur Sinclair, before he sailed last month—it's really too bad that *I* should be the one to deal you such a shock, madame! But *this* one surely, might come as a *pleasant* surprise—eh?" He showed his teeth in what was supposed to be a grin; Marisa drew in a deep, shaky breath. "Come—would you not like to be a duchess? The old duke has been ill for some time, I've been informed. And more recently, he's been ordered confined to his bed. The reason, no doubt, for his nephew's hasty departure before you were up and about." He sighed unctuously, adding before Marisa could interject angrily, "I suppose it is sad—death is sad, reminding us all of our mortality! But in this case—an old man who has lived his life—I'm sure you're enough of a Frenchwoman to think as practically as I do about such matters, madame. To be a duchess and in control of a vast fortune! How does it strike you? Especially since it is—um—unlikely that the *future* duke, your husband, would dare to show his face in England. . . ."

Fouché's quiet, almost silky voice went on and on, and Marisa listened. What the man suggested was preposterous, of course, as was the chance that *she* would ever be acknowledged as the duchess of Royse and allowed to control a fortune. And as for his hints that she should use her position to become friendly with the émigrés that thronged England, that she should *spy!* . . .

"*Spying,* madame?" Fouché gave her a reproachful look. "Come, come. You are intelligent enough to realize that I suggested no such thing! I have my own well-trained and efficient men to ferret out their military secrets. Bah! These stupid, meddling Englishmen! But in your case, madame, knowing your great loyalty and sense of *gratitude* towards the Bonaparte family, I was only suggesting. . . . You've heard, surely, of several murderous plots by these same émigrés who skulk across the water hoping and planning to bring their Bourbon king back to the throne of France? Their aim is to kill the first consul, to bring chaos and tyranny back to France. And they are financed with curst English gold!" His voice had grown surprisingly impassioned.

Marisa stammered, "But—I fail to understand what *I* can do! Surely I'll be considered suspect, and especially by those

English visitors who *knew,* that is . . ." She flushed with embarrassment, wondering what, indeed, English society would think of her. And particularly what opinion *Philip* held of her. He had sent her flowers daily during her illness and then a short, rather stilted little note informing her that he was forced to leave at once for England and that he hoped to renew their acquaintance there. But . . .

Fouché brushed aside all her objections, pointing out heavily where her real *loyalty* must lie. As for the English—pah! They would see a pretty face and a title—her aunt was accepted by the ton, after all, and there was no reason why she should not be. It was all arranged then? *He* would see to everything—the story given out officially would be that she had fallen from favor since her marriage. . . .

In spite of everything she said and all her protests, there were many more meetings with Fouché; and Josephine herself, with tears in her lovely eyes, begged Marisa to help them.

"All we wish is to—to prevent them from harming my husband! He—he refuses to take sufficient precautions, and the émigrés have spies everywhere. If there is a chance that by becoming friendly with some of them while you are in London you might be able to—"

Even Hortense added her pleas, and finally Marisa acceded wearily. It was not quite *spying* after all! There would be no military secrets involved, no betrayal of the English themselves. Merely a matter of becoming friendly with the exiled French émigrés and gleaning whatever bits of information she could. Why not? She *did* owe something to the people who had been so good to her and had taken her in without question.

Marisa moved into a small apartment with her aunt and remained there in virtual seclusion until the day came that they were due to sail for England. She left France on a cold, gloomy day—the same day, as it happened, that a certain Mr. Monroe from the United States of America arrived in France to be met by a worried-looking Mr. Livingston.

Talleyrand had mentioned Mr. Monroe's impending arrival when he had called to say his farewells. "An American. A special ambassador sent by their president, Mr. Thomas Jefferson—an extremely erudite and able man I've had the pleasure of meeting—is arriving. I will have to meet him, or I would come to see you off, my dear."

His penetrating, heavy-lidded eyes narrowed the merest fraction as he took in the young woman's rather listless air of apathy. However, all he said was, "I do hope you will be sensible and contrive to dress as warmly as possible while you're in England. They have a truly atrocious climate there, I'm told!"

"It was so kind of the prince to have come!" Edmée gushed afterwards, but Marisa had already put him out of her mind. She had trained herself of late to make her mind a blank when she chose to, cutting out thoughts from her mind yet still being able, quite mechanically, to smile at the right times and even to make polite little exclamations that gave the impression she was paying attention.

The Countess Landrey actually shed a few tears as they pulled away from the shores of France. She was going back to her old husband who would, no doubt, insist that she spend some time with him in the country, if only for appearances' sake. The country! She shuddered and thought dolefully that even London would be a dead bore after the glittering night life of Paris.

Marisa, on the other hand, had no real feelings in the matter. She did not know what to expect in London, but did that matter? At least, she thought a trifle grimly, her sojourn in France had taught her that she could face almost anything!

They had chosen to take an English ship, and in spite of the bleak weather their crossing of the channel was uneventful. The countess, once her fit of the blue devils had lifted, proved an experienced traveler, surprisingly efficient at arranging everything for their comfort.

Her own magnificent coach awaited them when they dropped anchor. Following a cold repast at a local inn while their baggage was being bestowed in the boot, they set off immediately for London.

Quite worn out, Marisa slept almost all the way, hardly managing to rouse herself when they stopped to change horses. She had no idea how long the journey took them, but at last she was forced to sit up and take notice of her surroundings for her aunt began to shake her insistently to inform her that they had already reached the outskirts of London.

Speaking in English, as they had agreed upon at the outset, Edmée said laughingly, "Come, my love. I know it is considered quite fashionable to appear bored, but *not* when we are alone together, I implore you! Tell me, what do you think?"

It was dusk, and lights glowed in windows as the well-sprung coach rattled along a wide, tolerably well maintained road.

"The *roads* at least are better than some of those in France!" Marisa ventured, and her aunt gave a crow of laughter.

"You are so droll, sometimes, chérie! But of course you cannot see too much, can you? Wait until tomorrow morning! Then, ah then, we shall have such a lot to do!"

The earl of Landrey was in the country at one of his larger estates somewhere in Somerset, but his large and imposing town house had been thrown open in expectation of the countess's return, and lights gleamed welcomingly from every window as the carriage drew up with a flourish.

"I shall have to greet all the servants," Edmée whispered to Marisa with a grimace. "they'll be all lined up in the hall— and most of them dying with curiosity for their first sight of you!"

It all passed off quite easily in the end, Edmée smoothing everything for Marisa who did not need to do anything but smile and incline her head. Her aunt had taken her own maid with her to France, but a young woman who was being trained as an abigail by the housekeeper was assigned to Marisa for the time being.

And then, within the space of a few hours, she was able to tumble into a wide, comfortable bed that had been warmed —letting her half-closed eyes gaze drowsily into the fire for a while until they closed all the way and she fell asleep.

Chapter Twenty

It seemed that all of London buzzed with rumors and speculation about the Countess Landrey's lovely niece who was seen everywhere with her.

Dowagers put their heads together and whispered, bringing up old scandals. The Prince of Wales professed himself charmed, and young men flocked to receptions where they might be expected to run into the young viscountess. Bets were taken at White's and the other gambling clubs, and even the "bow-window" set unbent enough to discuss among themselves what the outcome of *this* would be. What would Royse do about the chit who claimed to be his daughter-in-law? Would he acknowledge her or ignore her?

Edmée herself had something to do with the story that went the rounds. The girl was the daughter of a Spanish nobleman—her own sister's child, who had escaped the Terror after her mother had died so bravely. She had returned to France hoping to find her relatives, and. . . .

But the questions remained. Was it true that she had caught the eye of Napoleon—or Boney, as he was sometimes called? And had hastily married this mysterious son of Royse's whom no one could remember seeing, in order to escape Napoleon's advances? But then—where was her husband? Dominic—everyone had thought him dead, all these years!

Lord Anthony Sinclair, forewarned by his son, who had been annoyingly reticent about the whole strange affair, posted down to his brother's estate—almost dreading his errand. To have the whole ugly business stirred up again after all these years of thinking themselves safe—of thinking of himself as Leo's heir and the next duke—how was it possible that Dominic should suddenly turn up, quite alive, and still calling himself by that ridiculous last name he had adopted during the Irish rebellion? And, above all—where was he now?

Having disdained his doctor's orders to keep to his bed, Leofric Sinclair, fifth duke of Royse, was seated in a comfortable velvet-covered chair with a high back and padded arms. The back of his chair was to the window so that Lord Anthony, walking in from the sunshine to the comparative gloominess of the firelit room, could not at first read the expression on his brother's face.

Leo's voice was deceptively soft. "My dear Tony! Knowing that the smell of sickness is not to your taste I had quite given up the idea of seeing you here. Or is it, perhaps, some legal matter that has dragged you down from London at the very height of the season?"

"You are not in bed!"

Confused and ill at ease, as he usually was in Leo's presence, Lord Anthony blurted out the first thing that came to his mind and heard the duke's whispery, acid chuckle.

"How observant, Tony! And yet, I would not have you worry yourself. I *am* dying, or so that fool of a doctor who was recently knighted has informed me. There are some things that even wealth and influence cannot prevent, eh, Tony? But in my case, it is not carelessness but—the excesses of my younger days, I'm told. We must all die, eventually. And speaking of that, you really ought to take more care of yourself if you wish to enjoy being a duke. You have put on a great deal of weight, I notice. Along with a predisposition towards apoplexy, to judge from the color of your face! Come sit down, man, and don't stand there with your eyes popping. You remember the excellence of my Madeira? Or would you prefer some brandy?"

"Leo! I—"

"Do sit down, Tony. You only remind me of my own—er—unpleasant infirmity when you continue to stand there."

The duke made an almost imperceptible motion of his head, and a young man whose presence Lord Anthony had not noticed, detached himself from his rather brooding stance by the fireplace to come forward, politely proffering a chair.

"The Chevalier Durand. And this, Meurice, as you will have guessed, is my brother Lord Anthony Sinclair. Will you be kind enough to fetch the brandy from that sideboard, mon ami? I do not, I think, wish Simms to hear the news my brother is so obviously bursting with."

Even though he bowed rather stiffly and begrudgingly, Lord Anthony raised a mental eyebrow. The Chevalier Durand? An émigré, he supposed, judging from the name. And the latest of his brother's "friends."

His mind shied away from the thought almost immediately. Dammit, it was none of his business! And this other affair was.

The chevalier bowed deeply, being revealed in the light from the window as a man in his late twenties, slim and rather dandyishly dressed. His curly chestnut hair, à la Brutus, framed a handsome, rather sulky face with full lips.

"A votre service," he said politely, in a rather lisping voice.

"The chevalier is of the old nobility and the last of his line," Leo murmured in his drawling, world-weary accent. "He is also an excellent swordsman and a crack shot with the pistol. I was thinking, in fact, that when young Philip can spare the time he might be well-advised to spend some time here. Meurice is a good instructor, and with duels becoming so common these days. . . . Well, Tony? You can speak freely, I assure you."

Lord Anthony sank thankfully into a chair, accepting with a gruff murmur of thanks the crystal goblet that was offered to him.

"Damn me, Leo, you *know* then! Although how you contrive to learn everything—"

"I have my ways, my dear brother. Surely you should be aware of it by now? I had been expecting you sooner, as a matter of fact."

The baron's face reddened.

"I—well, I waited to—to be sure of the facts before I came posting down here."

He pretended not to notice that the chevalier had gone to stand beside his brother's chair and rested one slim white hand on the chair's back. Who was he? Damn, dying or not, Leo really ought to be more careful.

"And the facts are? Come, Tony, you didn't ride all the way here to stutter and beat around the bush, did you? This

219

young female who calls herself the Viscountess Stanbury
—she *is* young, I take it? And the long-lost niece of the
notorious Countess Landrey. Well, what have you learned?"

"Oh—ah—as to *that* part of it, it's true enough that she *is*
the fair Edmée's niece. Granddaughter of the last count of
Aymar—went to make the family fortune in Martinique but
only produced the two daughters. Well," he added hastily,
noting the slight, impatient narrowing of his brother's eyes,
"her *mother* was a friend of the late queen of France. Died
under the guillotine. Daughter was very young at the time
—escaped with some nuns to Spain, I understand—convent
and all that! The chit's *young,* Leo! Couldn't be more than
seventeen or eighteen at the most—good manners, and all
that! Her father's governor of some province in New Spain,
I understand, well off, making her an heiress of sorts. But—"

"*But!* Ah yes, now we come to the *real* point, do we not,
brother? Tell me the rest of it. I grow tired far too easily
these days, to my shame. And *you* have a stake in this business, too, do you not? I am sure your enquiries have been
as efficient as mine would have been."

Refusing to let himself be daunted by the chevalier's
slightly frowning presence, Lord Anthony plunged into his
story, laying out what facts he had been able to ascertain and
glossing over Philip's part in the whole bizarre drama.

The duke listened silently, his long white fingers now and
then drumming absently on the arm of the velvet chair.

He did not *look* so very ill, Lord Anthony found himself
thinking as he continued to talk. Could it all be some kind
of a hoax on Leo's part? Some devious scheme. He would
not put such a thing past Leo. But the chevalier's awkward
presence made it deucedly difficult for him to speak his
mind!

His speech stumbled into silence at last, and the duke said
thoughtfully, "So he's decided to vanish again? Do you know,
Tony, I find myself wondering why! And what made the
young woman decide to come here, of all places, to flaunt
her newly acquired title in the face of English society?
Wouldn't you have thought she would have preferred to
return to her father? Or stay in France?"

"Madame Bonaparte is her godmother, I understand.

And Philip tells me it made it awkward for—for the young woman when Boney showed too obviously that he'd like to make her his mistress."

"So—*Dominic* rescued her? My dear Tony! . . . No—I think you had better send Philip down here to me. After all *he* has a great deal at stake, too, does he not? Or—is it true that he can hardly tear himself away from the side of the lovely young viscountess?"

The suddenness of this last statement gave the effect of a hawk pouncing, catching Lord Anthony so unprepared that he almost choked on his brandy and began to stutter.

Smiling thinly, the duke pressed home his advantage.

"I understand that Lady Marlowe is quite upset with him, and that Lord Ormsby is now the favorite to win her daughter's hand—and fortune! My dear Tony—must a dying man take a hand in mending your own affairs?"

At that moment the chevalier leaned boldly down to whisper something in the duke's ear—in the "frog's language" that Lord Anthony so despised.

Royse, instead of stiffening icily at such familiarity, merely lifted an eyebrow, the action bringing out all the lines in his dissipated, age-ravaged face.

"C'est vrai? Ah well, brother, perhaps there's no need to be too hard on my nephew. Have you met her? No? Well, we cannot have a scandal after all the trouble we have taken these many years, can we? Do, I beg you, send Philip down to me—and—I will give you a letter of invitation. Perhaps he'll be obliging enough to escort my new daughter-in-law down to Cliff Park on a visit? It's high time we became acquainted, don't you think?"

If Lord Anthony was flabbergasted and indeed almost stunned by his brother's almost pleasant reaction, so—and much more so—was Philip Sinclair. Upon receiving his uncle's somewhat peremptory summons and the sealed note he was to deliver to Grosvenor Square, he did not know what to think. What the devil was Uncle Leo up to? Such meek capitulation wasn't like him at all, and yet, on the surface, what could be more proper? The duke's acknowledgment of his daughter-in-law was all that was needed to ensure

Marisa's acceptance by society—the one thing that could put a stop to the whispers that were going the rounds.

And yet he knew his uncle's utter ruthlessness and lack of scruples. Who could know better? He had meant to go down to Cornwall and explain it all himself, but like a coward, he had left it to his father instead. And now he was in the very devil of a fix! Should he warn Marisa? But of what? They had not had the opportunity to talk intimately since she had arrived in London—a sense of delicacy having kept him silent on the subject of her sudden, forced marriage and subsequent illness that had almost cost her her life. Not even to his father had he mentioned anything of *this* part of her background. But he was curious, all the same, and angry when he thought of all that she must have had to go through. The question was—how much had his uncle learned?

Philip Sinclair's valet found his usually amiable young master difficult to please that morning; and by the time he had left the house in Portland Place more than a dozen discarded neckcloths littered the bed.

Lord Anthony, waking late and inquiring for his son, was informed that Mr. Philip had taken out his curricle to go riding in Hyde Park. A scrawled note left for him informed him that his son would be calling at Grosvenor Square first and expected to be engaged for the rest of the afternoon, although he expected to see his esteemed father at the theater tonight, where the incomparable Mrs. Siddons was expected to give one of her performances.

Lord Anthony was left with his headache and his questions while Philip, at that very moment, was being announced by the butler at Landrey House.

"Mr. Sinclair, my lady."

He had been shown into the morning room where the countess was taking tea. She was dressed in a becoming gown of sea-green India muslin, adorned with ribbons of the same color. She looked up with a somewhat abstracted smile from the letter she had been frowning over.

"Oh, Philip! You had promised to take Marisa riding, had you not? But I fear she is not down yet. She had a shockingly late night, and so I gave instructions that she was to be allowed to sleep longer than usual. You won't mind keeping me company for a while? I'm sure she's almost dressed."

Edmée noticed that Philip's face looked white and set, his chiseled mouth almost hard, and she dropped her husband's letter onto the small table at her side.

"Is there something wrong? You look—"

When Marisa came downstairs more than a half hour later, she found them still talking and was unaccountably piqued that Philip did not pay her his usual extravagant compliments on her appearance. He rose to his feet—almost reluctantly, she thought—and merely bowed over her hand. Her mind raced. Had he found out about her surreptitious visit to Mrs. Butler's gaming house in Bruton Street last night? Was *that* why he looked so grim? But then, Philip did not *own* her!

Her aunt broke the rather constrained silence that had fallen between them following her entrance.

"Just think, chérie! Did I not tell you that everything would work out? You have been invited to visit the duke of Royse next week. It's rather in the nature of a royal command, is it not, Philip? And Philip is to escort you there!" She went on quickly before Marisa could utter a word, "It will just fit in with my plans, too, for Landrey has tiresomely ordered me down to Somerset. He is entertaining some cronies and says he needs me to act as hostess. I have been wondering what to do—you know I cannot leave you here *alone*, my love! But everything has worked itself out, and we will not be away from London for too long, I promise you that. A week or two, at the most. But don't you see what this means? With the duke's backing we can get you vouchers for Almacks—"

Marisa said in a dry voice, "But we do not yet know if I have the duke's backing, as you call it, or not—do we, chère tante? And I am not at all sure if I *want* to have the entree to Almacks. It sounds like such a dull, stuffy place!"

"Marisa!"

"Well, it's true! I am not considered quite—respectable, as you know, and of all the patronesses only Lady Jersey has been kind enough to acknowledge my presence in London! Well, I don't care! And I think—I'm sorry, Philip—but I think my lord duke only wishes to—to inspect me. He

223

sounds a frightening kind of person, even if he is old and so very sick, and I—I do not know if I want to be *inspected*, and questioned, and. . . . Oh, I am quite sure he will not like me in any case! And why should I care if I have his approval or not? I have made enough friends of my own to get on quite happily—"

"The Lades and the Manvells merely inhabit the fringes of the ton, Marisa! And although I know you have much in common with the émigrés, still, you cannot move forever only in *their* circles! And it is not enough to have taken the *gentlemen* by storm—how many *ladies* have come calling? My dear—"

They had both forgotten Philip, who now cleared his throat awkwardly.

"Marisa, please! I believe my uncle sincerely wishes to see you. Unless you are frightened—"

He had said exactly the right thing for her chin lifted slightly.

"Why should I be afraid? Of what? He cannot harm me, and I'm sure he cannot *blame* me for—for—"

Oh, why was it still so hard for her to think about Dominic? Her marriage, that seemed like a distant, unpleasant dream, those cold grey eyes that had seemed to grow warm for a time—but it had all been pretense! But Philip at least was honest and sincere. *He* had neither abandoned nor betrayed her in spite of everything he knew about her. For Philip's sake at least, she must make an effort. And, truthfully she was curious about the duke of Royse. The strange mystery that made father and son strangers to each other, and two cousins hate each other. What had Dominic said once? "A legitimate bastard." Yes, that was it. What had he meant? He did not even use the family name. Well, perhaps this was *her* chance for revenge.

Both Edmée and Philip were happy that she had changed her mind, and Marisa went along meekly enough with their plans for departure from London next week. In the meantime, the countess was more than usually complacent about Marisa's new friends and allowed her a great deal of freedom, as well as a generous allowance, not even questioning how she spent it. Which was just as well, Marisa reflected ruefully, for she had developed quite a passion for gambling of late.

It was exciting to stake one's fortunes on the turn of a card or a little wheel. And even more exciting, as she had learned, was the intrigue. For it was here, at the gaming houses, that she met the French royalists she was supposed to discover more about. The houses were select, private places where, in addition to gambling, rooms could be hired for private discussions and even more private tête-à-têtes. Her aunt, she thought amusedly, would be surprised if she knew how many members of the ton frequented such places! And surprisingly, Philip often accompanied her—for her own safety he said, and she had to admit she did feel safer with an escort. Frequently, when she had been losing, Philip would stake her, and yet, he never made any demands on her apart from an occasional, gentle kiss. Yes, she was fond of Philip, and she had begun to trust him. When they returned to London, he had at last promised to take her to the most select and secret of all the clubs—the Damnation Club, run by a Frenchwoman of the old nobility and frequented by the Count D'Artois himself.

Her old relationship with Philip restored and with her aunt in a good mood, Marisa was therefore able to prepare with comparative equanimity for her forthcoming visit to Cornwall and the duke of Royse.

Chapter Twenty-one

The earl of Landrey's properties in Somerset being on the way, so to speak, to Cornwall, Edmée, Marisa and Philip traveled together for part of the way, spending a night at Greythorpe, where Marisa found the earl to be an amiable, nearsighted old man, still spry and active for his age.

He seemed delighted to meet his "niece" and took her to the window where he could peer more closely at her, pronouncing her to be almost the exact image of his dearest Edmée.

"You'll allow me to look on you as a daughter?" he asked abruptly after supper. "Always did wish I had one—only I did not decide to marry until it was too late. Spent too much time jauntering about the continent—and fighting wars. Spent some time in India and that was in the old days, when the company was just carving itself out a portion. . . ."

Edmée smiled politely, if a trifle fixedly, and hid her delicate yawns behind her fan. Marisa listened to the earl's rather rambling discourses, quite fascinated. She recognized in him some resemblance to her father and men who had gone before him seeking to find a new empire for Spain. She said so, and the old man chuckled, quite delighted with the compliment.

"So you compare me to the conquistadores? Ah, child, I wish it were so! I should have been born a century or two earlier—and *then*, you may be sure, I would have made some account of myself! Ancestor of mine served with Drake and Hawkins, though. Plundered some of those rich galleons that *your* ancestors tried to get safely back to Spain!"

They both laughed, but Edmée wrinkled her brow, and Philip stared down into his glass of wine.

Marisa was sorry to leave Greythorpe the next day, for she had taken quite a liking to her new uncle—and he to her, for he made a point of waking up early enough to see her off, pressing a fat purse (which he said in a gruff whisper was a small recompense for what *his* ancestors had stolen from *hers*) into her cold hands while he adjured her that she must not hesitate to consider Greythorpe her home. He cast a rather fierce look at his sleepy, yawning wife and added that Marisa must not feel herself constrained to remain anywhere she did not *wish* to remain—not for a moment! Not only Greythorpe, but his home in London would be at her disposal, and he *hoped* she would not hesitate to turn to him *in loco parentis*, if ever she felt she needed help or advice. Finishing this unusually long speech, he waved his hand and stumped back into the house, leaving Edmée with her eyebrows lifted.

Marisa had felt tears spring into her eyes, and it was with an effort that she held them back, not wanting Philip to notice. She had already schooled herself carefully to present a cool, insouciant exterior from now on; she resolved that no one was going to browbeat her, not even this uncle that Philip was so much in awe of, and who happened to be, by the merest coincidence, her father-in-law.

All the same, as their journey progressed and Philip had sunk into silence, Marisa found herself wishing that they might have remained at Greythorpe. She *liked* the country, and the English countryside seemed so orderly and green and neat compared to that of Spain!

She found, however, as they approached Cornwall, that here was a part of England that seemed almost foreign. Even the people were different, dark-haired and dark-eyed, with a strange accent. She could believe now in the joking conversation she had had with the earl of Landrey when he had said, with a defiant glance at his wife, that the Cornish people were mixed with the Spaniards who had been washed ashore after the sinking of the great Spanish Armada.

"Aye, and with the French as well. The Cornishmen have always been great smugglers, you see," he had added with flattering frankness.

Edmée had fluttered her fan, looking bored and slightly

embarrassed, and Marisa had actually found herself wishing that she had met this particular old man in his youth. He had been, as he confessed to her, a "rounder"—far too busy adventuring to settle down. Well, *there* was one old man who was quite different from her earlier expectations. She could only hope that the duke of Royse might prove to be the same.

Marisa was accompanied by her maid, an uncompromising middle-aged woman by the name of Simmons, and Philip by his valet. Thus even when they were obliged to stop and spend the night the respectabilities were strictly adhered to. In fact Philip had actually grown so conscious of propriety that he had actually engaged a separate parlor for her so that they hardly had a chance to exchange more than a few words together before their journeying commenced again.

The country they had begun to travel through became bleak and forbidding; lush green valleys were overset by frowning black mountains. And now, as they neared Cliff Park, Marisa could almost smell the sea, sucking greedily at the foot of the enormous craggy cliffs that must have given the duke's estate its name.

They arrived at the great stone house at night, which did not add anything to Marisa's depressed frame of mind. She was aware that they drove up a broad avenue that was shaded by trees and stretched, it seemed, for miles. A creeping mist shrouded everything, giving the sound of the horses hoofs a kind of ghostly echo. And even when they came out of the trees and the road wound across a vast extent of grassy parkland, the mist seemed to follow them stealthily all the way to the crouching house that looked like a miniature castle.

Marisa had to scold herself, angry that she had let her imagination run away with her. They had arrived at a bad time; no doubt tomorrow when everything was bathed in sunlight she would be able to laugh at her childish apprehensions!

Philip leaped down first and helped her out as soon as the groom had let down the steps of the large, old-fashioned traveling carriage. On either side of a massive wooden door, lanterns hung from ornate wrought-iron holders driving back the mist. They were only halfway up the broad steps when the door swung open, and more light streamed out to welcome them.

An elderly, stiff-looking butler stood there, and, behind him, a much younger man with chestnut curls and the look of a dandy. He also had the assured air of a man who was very much at home here—but who was he?

He bowed very deeply as Philip made the introduction with what seemed to Marisa an unusual stiffness in his usually easy manner.

She recognized the name, having heard it before in London. The Chevalier Durand—renowned duelist who had, for a while made his living as a fencing master. But what was he doing *here,* and why had not Philip mentioned his presence?

The chevalier greeted her in French, apologizing that the duke, by order of his doctor, was forced to retire early and could not stay up to greet them. But everything had been prepared, including a light supper, and he was *charmed* to meet her, he had heard so much from his friends. . . .

'I wonder what he has heard?' Marisa thought, but she was too tired from traveling to care. She was *here,* and thank God Philip was with her even if he had become so silent. And tomorrow would be another day when, hopefully, all her questions would be answered.

The rest of the evening passed quietly. Marisa had been shown to her chamber and could find no fault with its magnificent appointments, from the enormous four-poster bed mounted on a wooden platform to the equally large fireplace and the silken hangings on the wall. She had pleaded tiredness, and a tray had been sent up to her room from which she had picked a few morsels of excellent food which had obviously been prepared by the master hand of a French chef. And then with Simmons's efficient aid she undressed and fell into bed, to sleep dreamlessly until some time in the morning when she was awakened and offered yet another carefully arranged tray.

By the time she was seated in front of a mirror, having her hair curled and held back from her forehead with a bandeau, Marisa had time to think about the incongruity of it all. That she should be *here* of all places, to be looked over by the duke as if she had been some poor governess aspiring for a position! When after all she didn't need his approval at all. What did it matter if he liked her or not?

Fortified by that thought, Marisa left her room to go downstairs, becomingly attired in a high-necked gown that clung to her slight figure.

She was shown into a large room on the east side of the house. Expecting to find Philip there, she was taken aback at the sight of what she thought at first to be an empty, overly warm room. She heard the butler close the double doors behind her, and then, as she hesitated, a dry, almost whispering voice greeted her.

"You don't mind that I wanted to meet you alone for the first time? Come—I am confined to my chair and cannot leap up to attack you. I wish that you would come closer to the window so that I can get a good look at you—or are you not as curious as I am?"

"I suppose so," she found the presence of mind to murmur, moving forward as she had been instructed so that at last she had her first full view of the duke of Royse seated in his velvet chair before the window. Her first fleeting thought was that he himself was steel under velvet.

Marisa saw a man who must have once been very handsome—a great deal like Philip in some ways—but now the skin hung upon the bones of his face giving him a ravaged and somehow dissipated look, although his pale blue eyes were nevertheless penetrating in their regard of her. His lips were thin under a high-bridged nose. Cruel, Marisa thought instantly, without knowing why. For those very same lips were turned slightly upward at the corners in what could have passed for a smile except that it did not reach those cold, weighing blue eyes.

He seemed to take pleasure in studying her—every inch of her, as she stiffened involuntarily—although there was no lechery in his gaze, only a kind of measuring. He was a cold man, and somehow she could sense that he expected her to be frightened and to fidget nervously under his stare. It was for that very reason that Marisa stood still, forcing herself to look directly back at him, giving him stare for stare.

It was the duke who broke the silence between them.

"So you're the one. And, I'll admit, not quite what I had

expected. Are you as young as you look?" He gave a soft laugh, and not waiting for an answer went on, "Tell me, child, did he choose you, or was it the other way around? What brought such an unexpected and ill-assorted union about? I hope you will not disappoint me by shrinking away or playing coy. I think we have both something to gain if you'll be honest with me."

Marisa stared back at him, disliking him, and not knowing what to say. So this was Dominic's father—no, better to think of him as Philip's uncle. Dominic had given her nothing but the capacity to hate—and the name that he, in turn, apparently hated. All the more reason why she should not let the duke set her down.

She said in a deliberately colorless voice, "You have me at a disadvantage, your grace. For I cannot know what you expected. And it is not in me to be as *honest* as you demand with someone I do not know." She took a deep breath and added, "You must take me at face value, your grace, or not at all."

"Gad—do you actually show some spirit?" Long, clawlike fingers tightened on the arms of the velvet chair. "Good. Then you're not looking for a blessing from me—or are you? Did you come here for the money? Or in the hope that I would accept you as a daughter-in-law. Is this some plan that you and *he* cooked up? I refer to your *husband,* madame!"

It seemed to Marisa that she had been trying for far too long to keep her temper at bay. And for what reason? If anyone was the injured party, *she* was! Angry color stained her cheeks.

"I am here at *your* invitation, my lord duke! *I* did not seek this meeting. And there is nothing I desire from you, except perhaps"—she bit her lips—"the leave to take my leave!"

She had turned on her heel and had halfway crossed the room when his voice stopped her; she remained poised for flight.

"How do you know that I was not testing you? Come back here, madame. If you seek nothing from me, then I'll admit there's something I seek from you. Would you deny a dying man?"

Wicked Loving Lies

"I think you use that fact, your grace, to bend others to your will. You do not frighten me."

"Good!" The suddenly agreeable note in his voice made her pause at the door. "Then we do not need to fence any longer. Or has your curiosity deserted you? I can engage to offer you a great deal, including the protection of my name, in return for—nothing but the truth, I assure you!"

There was a note in his voice that brought her back, her feet dragging. That, and her own curiosity. What did he want? What was all the mystery?

"Sit down," the duke said, still in the same softly agreeable voice, and Marisa sat obediently in a small straight-backed chair that was placed just across from his; there was a table between them. She folded her hands in her lap while she strove to compose her face so that it showed as little emotion as his; but all the time she was conscious of his cold, milky-blue eyes watching her.

"Well," he said at last, having deliberately allowed the silence between them to lengthen. "So now we'll dispense with the fencing play of words back and forth and have some honesty between us, eh? I have not much time left, whether I use this fact to bend others my way or not. That is not important. What is, to me, is the disposition of my name—my title if you will—and my possessions. The lands, most of them, are entailed, although I have managed to accumulate some properties and wealth of my own. However, the bulk of the estate, such as it is now, has belonged to the Sinclairs for generations. I wonder if you begin to take my point, madame? I would have it remain so for many more generations. And so, as you might be aware, I have looked upon my nephew Philip as my heir."

Marisa had been regarding her clasped hands, wondering why her fingers had begun to tighten upon each other. Now she raised her head, wondering how she contrived to sound so cool. "I beg that you will be even more direct, my lord. Why do you tell me this?"

He gave way to a sudden fit of what was almost passion, his whispery voice sharpening. "Damn—you are European are you not? French and Spanish. You should understand. Tell me now, how much do you know of the true story? And

233

your marriage—was it contracted out of love and wanting or forced upon you, as Philip has given me to understand?"

Dark lashes tipped up to reveal golden eyes that seemed to glow hotly.

"The marriage was forced upon us both, my lord. As you have said, I'm European bred, and such things happen. But there was no love, as you call it, on either side. I know nothing of the man I married except that he is a privateer—a pirate would be more like it—and proud to call himself an American. And that I have reason to hate him. This title he bestowed upon me means nothing. *He* did not wish to acknowledge it, and I do so only because—because it seemed as good a way as any of obtaining some small part of revenge upon him for the way he mistreated me."

She had said more than she meant to, and yet the duke seemed pleased, his lips thinning and curling.

"So you understand revenge? It's more than I had hoped for in one so young. Ah, yes—revenge! It has a sweet taste on the tongue, where there has been only bitterness and hate before, eh?" He added, almost to himself, but with a kind of chuckle underlying his voice that sent a cold, involuntary shiver up Marisa's spine, "I have known revenge—and hate and frustration and even love, of a kind you would not understand, young woman. I think you have not yet had the opportunity to relish the satisfaction of wreaking vengeance upon defiant wrongdoers, and yet you are half-Spanish. *That* part of your blood must brood and cry out to be revenged—am I right? Perhaps we can help each other if you will not weaken like the majority of your sex. Do you have the stomach for what I might propose? Or the same single-minded purpose that I have had? I wonder—and yet perhaps during the time that you are to spend here we will both find out. You will have the freedom to talk with Philip—I will not bind you with convention while you are under my roof. And in the end I think that you will understand something of my mind —and I of yours."

What had happened? The duke had done most of the talking, and yet it almost seemed as if there had been a bargain struck between them, and Marisa said nothing to deny it, not even when he pulled a velvet cord that hung on the wall beside his chair and asked the silent-footed butler to fetch the sherry—and, as an afterthought, Mister Philip and the chevalier.

* * * * *

The Chevalier Durand stayed close to the duke at most times as Marisa was to notice. And the rest of the time he seemed happy to remain in the bleak, vaulted chamber that had been set up as a fencing room where he practiced hour after hour with swords or with pistols. On several occasions, instructed by his uncle, Philip went to join him, and sometimes Marisa herself went to watch—drawn in spite of herself.

The chevalier was always politeness itself, once or twice pausing to explain this pass or the other, by name. She found the swordplay graceful and somewhat like a ballet to watch, but she did not like the pistols, which after they had been discharged at targets set along the walls, smelled as deadly as they looked.

For the rest of the time Marisa rode with Philip about the vast estate and sometimes down a steep path that led to the ocean, where he pointed out several small coves and rocky inlets that he said had been used by smugglers in the past.

"They're still at work now, I suppose, but even the revenuers in this area turn their eyes the other way. You know the Peace has ended? They say that Boney—I'm sorry, Marisa—has assembled an armada at Boulogne—and it's not only brandy and silks but spies as well that are smuggled back and forth. Our people can learn a lot under the cover of smuggling, although it's the brave French royalists who take most of the risks."

"And aren't you taking a risk telling *me* all this? After all—"

"Do you forget that I know everything? I trust you, Marisa. I know what you were forced to go through. You came to England to escape from it all, didn't you?"

She whispered, "Oh, Philip!" And turned her face slightly away, not knowing why she did so, so that his lips only grazed her cheek. "Philip, I—"

"Do you think I mean to press you? I love you, Marisa, and I think you know it already. That is why I can be endlessly patient until you are ready. You're like a little wounded bird, and I've no desire to cage you. Only to have you start trusting in me."

She put her hand out impulsively, touching his; she felt the salt air sting her face.

"But I do trust you. More than anyone else. It's only that —you know the truth of it as well as I do! Here, we can be free with each other, but in London—in London I am the Viscountess Stanbury, and you are my cousin. I am a married woman, Philip, like it or not. And—"

He said in a muffled tone that was unlike any he had used before, "Do you think I'm not constantly aware of that? And yet you're married to a man who vanished like a puff of smoke—have you thought that someday you might find yourself a widow? And then—I care nothing for the scandal that might ensue or the wagging tongues! Or for anything else— you must believe me. I would be proud to be your husband, without any question of *force*—"

She was caught by that word, her mind going back unwillingly to the first time she had been taken—by *force,* certainly—and by a stranger whose name she did not know. And those other occasions afterwards; when he had continued to take her forcefully and last of all to that shameful time when there had been no force necessary and she had been willing. A "game" he had called it afterwards, leaving her on that mocking, hateful note with nothing more than his name and an unwanted intrusion in her womb which she had thankfully lost. Yes, thankfully! For now she was free, and she had begun to understand part of the duke's purpose in bringing her here and keeping her here to be thrown constantly in Philip's company—unchaperoned even by her maid.

She was being given free license to take Philip as her lover, and if there were a child, a son, he would fall heir to the dukedom of Royse and be a true Sinclair. Did Philip himself know what was afoot? And if he did—how much of the feeling he professed arose from a desire to be revenged upon the cousin he hated and how much from love of her? She could at least say this much for him—that he never tried to force his attentions upon her, although he might read her poetry and talk softly to her, hold her hand and even kiss her. Never once did he attempt to go further than that; and she admired him the more for it.

He was not quite his uncle's pawn, then—any more than she was. And yet there was the element of time, which hung over both their heads. And the secret knowledge, masked behind smiles and the slowly growing awareness of each other as male and female, that sooner or later, it was bound to happen. When they were both ready, they would become lovers. It seemed almost inevitable.

Chapter Twenty-two

The day before they were to leave for London the duke talked to Marisa in private again. The lines in his face seemed more pronounced than they had been on the first occasion when she had talked with him alone, and there was an ashy grey pallor to his face that she dared not mention. Still, his wits seemed to be unimpaired as he said without preamble, "Well? Are you merely shy or is my nephew not to your liking? You've been away from France for over two months, madame, and there will be a counting of fingers among the old biddies if you delay much longer. What's amiss? Hasn't Philip been forward enough for your taste?"

By this time, Marisa was not afraid of him. He was merely an old, wicked-natured man with a penchant for younger men —the chevalier, whom he had taken up with as a mere boy seemed devoted to him—but she had heard enough of the story of his marriage to almost feel sorry for the woman who had died in this very house. Dominic's mother—the mysterious Peggy she had once imagined a mistress of his.

No, she could not like the duke of Royse, but they had at least one thing in common—hate. And so she was able to answer him composedly,

"Neither Philip nor I are barnyard animals, my lord, to be mated at your will. If I'm to be seduced, then I beg your leave to choose my own time and place. And as for the *counting* of months—there is always the country to retire to, is there not?"

He gave a sudden cough of laughter that surprised her.

"So you'll have it on your own terms, would you? Very well—I'll let it pass. Although if I was stronger I'd make my own arrangements to be sure. Philip needs to be led, or *guided,* if you prefer. And my brother is far too weak. So I am forced to look to you, young miss. And your practical common sense. My faithful Meurice will be visiting London shortly. Did you know he is an ardent royalist? Perhaps he'll bring good news back with him."

Marisa did not know if that last statement was supposed to be a veiled threat or not, and she told herself that she did not care. London would be like a breath of fresh air after *this!* Philip seemed to share her views, for away from his uncle he seemed more like the carefree young man she had known when they had first met. She wondered if the duke had made the same infamous suggestion to *him* that he had made to her and what Philip's reactions might have been..

The next day as the carriage took her further away from the bleak, craggy cliffs of Cornwall that looked like blackened, jagged teeth, and away from the constant, creeping mists, it seemed impossible that she had even listened to such a thing. Well, she decided, she would try to forget about it and enjoy herself. 'I am tired of being used by other people for their own ends,' she thought, leaning her head back against the squabs of the luxuriously sprung carriage that was taking her back to Somerset and from there to London again. 'I am going to belong only to myself, from now on.'

This resolution, however, was more easily thought than effected for upon their arrival in London Marisa found several surprises awaiting her.

The first was Philip's father, the Baron Lydon, who had so far ignored her existence. *He* made a formal call the morning after they had returned and set himself out to be thoroughly agreeable as he informed Marisa that his brother, the duke, had instructed that his magnificent town house be thrown open for her use while she was in London. There was also a draft upon his bank in London made out in her name, making her the mistress of what seemed to be an enormous sum of money. No need for her to impose upon her aunt any longer—the Viscountess Stanbury was to maintain her own household from now on, with a Mrs. Willoughby, a gentlewoman fallen on hard times, as her chaperone.

And while she was still in a state of shock, Lady Hester Beaumont, Royse's sister and Philip's aunt, came calling also and graciously offered her assistance in helping Marisa set up house.

So much for her thinking that she could belong to herself! Marisa had guessed already that she could not look to her aunt for help—Edmée was thoroughly bedazzled by the extent of the good fortune that had befallen her niece and urged her to make the most of it.

"After all, love, it's not as if it wasn't yours by *right!* You *are* the Viscountess Stanbury, and I understand—Landrey was telling me—that there are certain jointures that come with the title. But as for Royse being obliging enough to publicly acknowledge you and give his stamp of approval —that, my love, is almost beyond all I'd hoped for! Your position in society is quite assured now, and you will have an entree everywhere! Oh, if you only knew how happy I am for you! Even your father cannot object to *this,* and now we can write to him without feeling that he might reproach us both. Oh, chérie," Edmée went on, dabbing at her eyes, "don't look so forlorn—there's no need to! We will not be lodged too far from each other after all, and just think of what this means!"

Marisa realized very well what the duke's sudden, unexpected gesture meant, although she could not bring herself to confide in her aunt. He was binding her to an unspoken agreement and to a promise that had not been given—showering her with luxuries he hoped she'd grow too used to to want to give up. And yet, even while she realized all this, she was helpless to stem the tide of events that seemed to sweep her along.

Royse's name and influence were sufficient to ensure her acceptance by even the most conservative circles. In spite of his enforced retirement from politics, he was still a powerful figure; if not for his sudden illness he, and not Addington, would have been the prime minister.

As it was, Philip's father, the Baron Lydon, acted as her unofficial sponsor—and it seemed sufficient to have *his* stamp of approval for her to be accepted everywhere.

Even Mr. Brummell had grudgingly admitted that she was passable, and once he had stood up with her on a few occasions at Almacks, there was no longer any question of the Viscountess Stanbury's acceptance by the ton.

Once again, and in spite of her resolve, Marisa found herself being manipulated. *She*, at least, had no illusions concerning the duke's sudden generosity. and neither did Philip for his manner, since she had set up house on her own, had grown almost unbearably constrained. So Philip did not care to be treated like a puppet any more than she did! The thought actually made her respect him more. And to feel more than usually relaxed in her manner towards him on the night when he came to call for her—to introduce her to the Damnation Club.

By this time Marisa had been longing for some end to the formal boredom of her existence. Being accepted by the ton was one thing, but to be bound by convention was another, and she had been growing heartily tired of the restraints that being a lady of fashion put on her when Philip had made the almost apologetic suggestion—reminding her of something she had had her mind fixed upon before she had left London.

She almost fell upon his neck with excitement when he mentioned it on one of their rides in Hyde Park, this being one of the few occasions when they could be seen out together without a chaperone in public.

"Oh, Philip! Do you mean it? But how—"

He gave her a reluctantly conspiratorial grin. "To be alone with you again, without that well-meaning Mrs. Willoughby breathing down both our necks, I could contrive anything! But listen—I've taken Sally Repton into my confidence, and *she's* to arrange it all. She'll call for you tomorrow night, and I will meet you at her house. We'll go there together, as a party. It's better that way. If you're still sure—"

"Of course I'm sure! How could you doubt it? I've been so bored!"

It was all settled then. And this time she had enough money with which to play as much as she pleased without having to worry how she would redeem her losses—*if* she lost! Marisa felt sure that she would win. And if she did not, there would still be the thrill of the forbidden, the excitement that came with the feeling of having been daring.

Pleading a sick headache, she cried off from an engagement to visit the theater in Drury Lane with her aunt. And Mrs. Willoughby, she was sure, seeing the company she was in, would make further excuses for her if need be. She felt a sensation of freedom as she left the house—a feeling that was all the more exciting for being unusual. Not for anything would she have cancelled at this late stage, even though Philip offered her the chance when they were in his carriage, later on—the ladies trying on their masks with cries of delight.

"Marisa, you haven't changed your mind? This is no ordinary gaming club, you know. Certain things might take place that would shock you—"

"And do you think I'm still capable of feeling shocked? There are times when I wish I might be, but I've progressed beyond that. And who should know better than you, dear Philip?"

"I only know that I do not like to hear you speak in such a way. I shall stay close to you all evening, Marisa. And afterwards. And forever, if you will let me!"

Before she had time to do more than cast him a look of surprise, the carriage had stopped, and they were all alighting. They were in a quiet side street on the outskirts of London—in front of what seemed to be a respectable house, with no lights showing at its windows.

Lord Drummond, who was with them, knocked at the door, and immediately a kind of peephole was slid open, revealing no more than a sliver of light and an eye.

"Who is it?"

"Drummond and his friends. We are expected, so let us in. 'Tis plaguy cold out here!"

Marisa barely had time to think how dramatic it all was and how mysterious—and then the heavy wooden door opened just wide enough to let them in.

She had not known what to expect, but it looked like any other gambling hall if a trifle more luxuriously furnished than most.

She saw a great many familiar faces—several of her émigré friends, as well as a sprinkling of foreign diplomats, among others.

Almost all of the ladies were masked and quite a few of

the men as well. In spite of his disguise, Marisa recognized
at least one of the royal dukes and was glad of the feeling
of protection her own mask gave her in such an assembly.
However, she had to admit she was disappointed by her first
impression of the notorious reception. Only the card tables
that had been set up in the elegantly furnished rooms they
now strolled through made the difference.

"Come along. Madame la Marquise will want to meet you,"
Lord Drummond urged. "She's very particular about greeting each one of her guests personally."

"Madame la Marquise?"

He grinned. "Oh, everyone calls her that for she has such
an air—still dresses in the old way and wears an elaborate
powdered wig! She goes by the name of Madame De L'Aigle,
but *that*, I'm told is to protect the name of a very old and
respected family."

Intrigued, Marisa allowed herself to be guided into one of
the smaller rooms on the ground floor of the house, where
Madame De L'Aigle normally held court. Here everything
was furnished in crimson and gold, the rich colors throwing
her white wig and even more pallid complexion into relief.
She was the rare kind of woman who appeared ageless. Under her elaborate makeup her face seemed remarkably smooth
and unlined, and her eyes were greenish blue and penetrating.

She held out a hand that was weighted down with rings,
and her voice had a husky timbre as she murmured, "So *you*
are the pretty young viscountess that they are all talking about?
You'll forgive my habit of always being direct. It is better so,
I have found. I have been told you have remarkable eyes—
ah, yes. In this case rumor has not exaggerated! I am glad you
decided to visit my house this evening, viscountess, and you
will return again, I hope."

Marisa restrained her absurd impulse to curtsy and instead
took the hand that was offered to her and made a polite rejoinder. And then Philip was being greeted with a smile and
some half-whispered, teasing remark that made him flush
boyishly. Marisa found herself wondering, as they moved
away, how often he came to this place, and why he had not
mentioned it to her earlier. As far as she could discern, there

was nothing so very shocking going on to have earned this house its name!

They had become separated from the others of their party as Philip took Marisa from room to room, but it did not seem to matter, for everyone who was not playing seemed to be wandering around; even the ladies carried glasses of wine or champagne which were replaced by quietly unobtrusive butlers as quickly as they were consumed. There was music that drifted down a double stairway from a screened gallery, and in one room Marisa actually saw couples dancing with each other under rose-shaded lights; they were clasped so closely that they seemed oblivious to all else.

They paused in the doorway and then moved on, and since Philip had grown quite silent Marisa felt bound to break into his thoughts by inquiring with a small laugh, "Is *that* what gives the Damnation Club its reputation for wickedness? Why, I've heard that the Vauxhall Gardens—"

"Are not nearly as private!" Philip broke in with a note of grimness that was unlike him, and with a look of surprise she turned her eyes to his face.

"What do you mean?"

"I should not have brought you here tonight," he burst out in a low voice that held some suppressed emotion. "But better that you should come with *me* than with someone else. Your friend Sally had been talking for some time of introducing you here—but *she* comes mainly because the play is so steep and the atmosphere so—easy. I—oh, God!" he said violently, his fingers suddenly tightening over her arm, bringing her to a stop before him in a small, curtained alcove. "How am I to explain without being too blunt? People come here for the gaming, as you have already seen, and for—other forms of pleasure—or excitement, if you wish! The betting book here is as large as that at White's, but it is kept secret. And there are no vows accepted here—one plays as one loses, in cash or jewelry or—any other fashion determined by the winners. And upstairs—no, don't stop me now, Marisa, or I shall not find the courage to continue!—upstairs are rooms where people can be private, without interference. God knows how many royalist plots are hatched up there—and even government strategies planned. My father is a member, and the Prince of Wales—but the membership is very select, make no mistake about that! It is a safe place, this for the very rich and the powerful to indulge their every whim and appetite with no fear of it getting about. Must I say more?" He made a sound that was almost like a groan. "You're intrigued now—I can read it in your eyes. But I beg you—to be careful! And to promise me that you will not come here again without me. Marisa—"

Her eyes had opened very wide during his stumbling recital, and he could feel her soft flesh quiver under his unknowingly hurtful grip. But now suddenly her lashes dropped, and she said in a quiet, oddly thoughtful voice, "But then—why did you really bring me here, Philip? And warn me *now?* You might easily have—"

He did not learn what she had been about to say for at that moment there was a burst of clapping and "huzzas" from one of the gaming salons directly opposite the alcove in which they stood.

They both turned to look towards the sound, and, disbelieving, Marisa saw that a tall, elegantly gowned woman she had noticed deep in play earlier had stood up in the center of the room and was removing her clothes. A domino mask covered her face and hair, but as she flung her last flimsy garment aside and stood there naked, the triangle of red-gold curls at the apex of her thighs gave away her coloring. She seemed to tremble slightly, whether from embarrassment or excitement it was hard to tell, and as one of the players got up from the table and walked towards her a flush seemed to cover her very white body.

"You've paid off the first part of your debt to me, my lady!" he said in a deep voice and deliberately passed his hand across her breasts in front of them all before he lifted her up into his arms saying triumphantly, "And now you'll pay the rest of it!"

She gave a rather high-pitched giggle as he walked out of the room carrying her and took her upstairs, past the musicians who still continued to play without interruption.

At Marisa's side Philip said in a strained, bitter voice, "And now you have seen for yourself what I meant! The one rule here is that no one ever speaks of anything they may see or

hear so that a duchess can be a strumpet for a night and go
back to being an icy cold lady the next. Or a man who is
outwardly reserved and austere can play the satyr! Marisa, for
God's sake, haven't you seen enough?"

Still hardly believing what they had witnessed, Marisa saw
that everyone else in the room had gone back to their cards,
some of them shrugging amusedly. A bet. She felt herself
caught up in some strange spell—half-shocked and half-
fascinated and, yes, a little bit afraid as well! But it couldn't
happen to her. She would never let herself get so carried
away that she would wager herself.

"Marisa!" Philip repeated, giving her a little shake to bring
her out of the trance she appeared to have fallen into. "I'm
sorry that you had to witness such a scene. But perhaps it was
for the best. I know you will not want to come here again.
Let me take you home now."

She was glad that the mask she still wore hid the color that
suddenly flamed in her cheeks.

Had Philip brought her here intending to seduce her and
then changed his mind? How far would his obedience to his
uncle's wishes take him? As for herself and her own wishes—
she needed time to think! Was her acceptance of the duke of
Royse's sudden and surprising generosity to be construed as
a tacit acceptance of his terms as well? What did Philip himself think about such a cold-blooded arrangement? He said
he cared for her, and surely he had shown it! But—did he respect her? Could he?

They sat opposite each other in the carriage that was taking
them back, for the others had elected to stay on longer. A
few times Marisa was positive that Philip would burst into
speech, but he seemed to control himself with an effort, and
most of their ride back to Duke Street was accomplished in
silence.

Chapter Twenty-three

In spite of all her serious resolutions, Marisa found that she had very little time in which to think during the days that followed.

Her hours seemed crammed with activities, and every day there were more invitations lying piled up on her desk; there were so many that she was forced to think of hiring a secretary to deal with them. She did not get to bed until the early hours and slept until past noon whenever she could. Suddenly time seemed to whirl by much too quickly, and she had hardly any moments to herself any longer.

Or moments of peace, for that matter, for she had suddenly found herself involved, without quite realizing it, in a deadly dangerous game of intrigue and politics. And now she was frightened, but she was too deeply involved to dare show it. She was forced to go on as if everything were quite normal and she did not have a thought in her head besides a life of pleasure as a young lady of fashion who was now accepted everywhere.

Sometimes Marisa thought tiredly that she deliberately ran herself ragged in order *not* to have time to think and wonder where it would all lead her. She had almost forgotten about Philip and her dilemma there. And neither Philip nor the duke of Royse himself could help her if *they* found out what she had been up to. And she was being watched and tested—she was sure of it and helpless to do anything about it at the same time. At all costs, she must go about just as usual—not showing any change in her way of life and her friends even though she had learned that what had started out to be merely a small adventure—an act of loyalty to her old friends—was no amusing, easy game after all.

The French royalists who had escaped from the Terror in most cases with nothing but their names and their ancient titles, were not merely the gay, amusing and effete group that she had thought them to be, after all. Now, it was easier to believe in all the stories that circulated in France about their plots and their continued, stubborn efforts to regain what they had lost during the Revolution. They were desperate men who had lost everything and thus had everything to gain. And the English government supported and helped them for their own ends. She could look for no help *there*. Why hadn't she realized the danger at the beginning? Or how flimsy the story of her own sudden decision to come to London, just before the renewal of hostilities, must seem to some people?

She hadn't thought of any of this, especially since no one had appeared to question her. Some of the aristocratic émigrés had been her mother's friends, and they had accepted her—or had they only seemed to? It was hard to tell.

Passing on the stray bits of information she happened to pick up every now and then to a self-effacing little French clerk at the circulating library had been an amusing little adventure until the afternoon following her first visit to the Damnation Club. . . .

Marisa had stopped in to return a book on her way to visit her aunt and had inquired about a volume he had promised to reserve for her. The proprietor himself had come up, looking unusually pale and upset. He apologized —but hadn't she heard? The poor little Monsieur Beltran had been found dead in his room—murdered! And—the man had lowered his voice—tortured as well before he was finished off, probably to try and make him reveal the existence of a secret hoard of money which of course he didn't possess! Poor man! They said it was the work of the Assassin—some fanatic who went around killing Frenchmen who were suspected of being sympathetic towards the new government. Such an unfortunate affair—such unpleasantness! He hoped he had not upset Lady Stanbury, and he himself would attempt to find the book she particularly wanted.

Marisa could not remember afterwards how she had managed to leave the book shop and circulating library without showing what a frightening shock she had received.

She felt numb, at first, managing to express no more—she hoped—than ordinary concern. But afterwards—afterwards she had begun to feel quite terrified as she remembered other stories she had not paid too much attention to.

There had been that young opera dancer who had been found strangled in her small apartment less than two weeks ago. Rumor had it that she had been the mistress of a high-ranking official in the French ministry before the Peace of Amiens had ended. And soon after he had departed she had found a new protector, an English colonel who served directly under Wellington himself.

And before that another Frenchman who had called himself a chevalier had been found in an alley. . . . All coincidences? But then why had people begun to whisper about the man they called the Assassin? He always left a certain mark on his victims—Marisa had not heard exactly what it was, such subjects not being considered fit for female ears. She didn't want to know! In fact soon after she had reentered her carriage she had begun to shiver as if she had taken a chill, and her aunt had remarked disapprovingly that she looked far too peaked and pale and should get more rest.

She could not rest until she was literally so tired that she almost fell into bed. And in spite of all her brittle surface gaiety, Marisa continued to be afraid. Her background, her connection with the Bonapartes, her mysterious, hurried marriage, and even her present circle of acquaintances all put her in a precarious, vulnerable position. Now she would have gladly foregone the company of the charming French émigrés that she had so eagerly sought before, but it was too late to back off without appearing guilty or afraid. She had to go on just as usual, although there were a hundred or more times she wished herself back in France or even on her way to New Spain.

Philip had left London for a few days to go hunting with

some of his friends in Lichfield where his father had a shooting box. And in spite of the rather strained and ambiguous relationship that now existed between them, Marisa found herself longing for his return. When her aunt teased her about pining for her handsome and devoted lover, she did not deny it. For when Philip came back, she had decided to make the rumors a fact. She would let him become her lover and beg him to take her away somewhere. No doubt the duke of Royse would be happy to help them make some discreet arrangement.

And then, when a week had passed and she was still safe, the natural resiliency of her youth began to assert itself, and she began to think she had been jumping at shadows. Perhaps Fouché's agent had not incriminated her before he died—and why should he have? She had not been able to tell him anything important, after all, and he must have had other sources of information. At least it was all over now, and she would never be so foolish again!

Philip was expected back in London in two more days, and Marisa felt more like her usual self than she had for a long time when her maid awakened her on a sunny morning.

"Your ladyship is engaged to go driving in the park this morning with Lady Repton. And a fine day it's turned out to be too, for a change."

So even the impassive Simmons could be influenced by the change in the weather, which had been gloomy and overcast for these past few days! Marisa gave her a smile as she sipped her hot chocolate. She wrinkled her short nose as she decided what she would wear.

She was to try out the new light curricle she had ordered, which was drawn by matched chestnuts. It was all the rage these days that a lady of fashion should drive herself, and since a friend had been kind enough to give her some instructions in handling the ribbons, she thought she would do quite well. Sally, at any rate, had laughingly professed herself to be all agog with curiosity to see how Marisa would manage.

Both ladies were in high spirits as they set out. Madame Rose had outdone herself in creating Marisa's new riding costume made of yellow-gold cloth with rich brown velvet lapels on the short, tightly fitting jacket. Under the jacket she wore a striped silk waistcoat which was the latest affectation; her white muslin cravat with a topaz stickpin showed off her slender neck to advantage. Under the wide brim of her gold-corded felt bonnet, Marisa's eyes sparkled.

Her friend Sally pouted. "How very fetching you look this morning! Madame Rose, of course? Oh, the annoying creature. She has never done so well for *me,* and I vow I feel positively dowdyish perched up beside you!"

"I've never noticed that you lack for admirers, though," Marisa retorted. "In my case, it's my clothes they notice first, but in yours. . . . Why, how many sonnets have you had written to your eyes and your lips?"

Sally burst out giggling, quite mollified. Well, it was true that *she* was an acknowledged beauty, while her friend was known for her *smartness.* Marisa still had too much of a childish, rather immature quality about her for the more experienced rakes to pay her more than passing attention, and Mr. Brummell had only pronounced, in a grudging way, that she was "quite passable."

They were well matched—both members of the younger set that the old dowagers called "fast," but who cared? They said the same of the Prince of Wales himself, and with position and enough money one could get away with practically anything.

The two young women had driven through the gates by now and were bowling along the promenade. Lady Repton had observed that her friend had learned to handle the ribbons quite capably so that she was able to sit back and relax while she bowed and smiled to several of her acquaintances, keeping up an amusing running commentary all the while that made Marisa smile.

"Why, there's Clarence and York—*together,* who would have thought to see it? And Alvanley—what is *he* doing out so early? Oh! And Mrs. Wilson—that woman! How dare she parade herself so publicly? She has young Scunthorpe with her—the poor young man is hardly out of leading strings!"

Marisa was inexperienced enough to keep her mind severely on the task of driving. In any case, how could she look in so many directions at once? But then Sally gave a squeal that almost unseated them both, making the horses snort and toss their heads nervously.

"It's Tom Drummond—and that devastatingly handsome Italian count—di Chiara or some such name. Don't you remember how hard he stared at you when we were at the opera two nights ago? They are both in Tom's new high-perch phaeton. You know he's been elected a member of the Four-horse Club? Do draw up, Marisa, ma chère. He's signaling to us."

Rather unwillingly (remembering her introduction to the Damnation Club) but knowing that Lord Drummond was her friend's latest lover, Marisa managed to manoeuver her curricle onto one side of the wide promenade—taking heart from the observation of her groom, who had accompanied them, that she had done "a very good job of it." Leaving the horses to be walked by him, she allowed herself to be helped down and introduced to the count, whose coal-dark eyes stared searingly into hers for a moment before he bowed very low, kissing her hand lingeringly.

"We're well met!" Lord Drummond said in his bluff, laughing fashion. "We were only just speaking of you two lovely ladies, in fact—trying to think up some occasion when we could meet." He turned to Marisa with a twinkling smile and said in a stage whisper, "Di Chiara has been plaguing me for an introduction, you know! I had been almost forced to plan an expedition to Raneleigh—have you been there yet? It's nothing to compare with the Vaux-hall Gardens, but the rotunda is very pretty, and you ought to see it."

Having dispensed with the formalities, he now took Sally's arm and began to stroll with her down a narrow, tree-hung path—leaving Marisa no alternative but to accept the count's gallantly proffered arm and to follow them. It was not the thought that they were acting unconventionally by strolling unchaperoned with two young men that worried her—she was used to being unconventional—but the laughing comment Tom Drummond had thrown over his shoulder that she really must go back to the Club again with them, for Madame la Marquise had been asking after her.

His teasing statement made the day seem suddenly chilly so that she shivered slightly, and all the fears that she had so resolutely put to the back of her mind came back to spoil the day. Why should they have been asking about her? What did they want from her?

"Are you cold?" di Chiara asked solicitously, and she shook her head at once trying to shake off with the same gesture her frightening thoughts.

"Oh, no! How could I be on a day like this? The weather, until today, has been so. . . ."

She had noticed, with a shred of uneasiness, that Sally and Lord Drummond had disappeared around a bend in the secluded path. She would have hastened her steps to catch up with them if the count had not, suddenly and inexplicably, drawn her to a halt.

"But why should we waste time talking about the weather, most beautiful lady? Let us talk instead of your Uncle Joseph. Was he well the last time you saw him?"

Marisa almost fainted with shock, hearing him give, so abruptly and unexpectedly, the password that Fouché had arranged with her. She swayed, shock and terror mingling in her mind, and she might have fallen if he had not hurriedly caught her about the waist.

"This is no time for hysterics!" he hissed sharply, his gallant manner quite falling away. "Come, stand up straight and lift your head! What are you frightened of? Surely you expected that since the unfortunate Beltran was murdered someone else would get in touch with you? Any information you can give us is needed now, more than ever. We know several royalist spies have crossed the channel, but where they'll decide to strike—"

Marisa made an effort to control her agitation although the whole world seemed to spin before her eyes.

"Are you mad? You're asking me to—to—"

"To risk your life? Yes, perhaps. Just as I am risking mine," he observed dispassionately. "But *you* bellissima, have the entree to certain places that I have not. And who would suspect you?"

Fiercely blinking her eyes to clear them, she tried to pull away from him.

"I am already suspected, and I've been living in terror, can't you understand that? I'm not made of the stuff that spies are. I'm afraid, and I refuse to risk my life—no mention was ever made of my taking any risks—" She broke off short realizing with a new horror that this all might very well be a test, and the count not one of Fouché's agents after all. In which case she had betrayed herself. Her face whitened, and her eyes became enormous in her suddenly pinched face. Reading something of her thoughts the count gave a short laugh.

"No, no! I am not one of them sent to trap you, I assure you! But it is true that you should learn to be more careful and to guard your tongue, just in case. So you are afraid of this Assassin? Pah! He's taught our agents to be more careful, at least, and sooner or later, when we find out who he is, he, too, will be eliminated in his turn." He added mockingly. "But perhaps we had better resume our walk? A stroll should give you time in which to compose yourself by the time we catch up with the others. I see I've quite terrified you so I won't pursue our conversation today. But—as an ardent admirer, may I not pay you my compliments along with your other admirers? Just think about what I have said, and if you hear anything, you have only to whisper it in my ear while we are dancing or when I am bending over your little hand—thus!"

He bent suddenly and kissed her hand, squeezing her fingers, and she looked up with a flushed face to see that Tom Drummond and Sally had retraced their steps and were now standing smiling conspiratorially at them.

"Aha!" Drummond murmured knowingly, and then with a wink, "But I haven't seen anything—did *you*, Sal? Always did say, though, that persistence wins out, what?"

"I should assuredly hope so," the count said smoothly, with a languishing glance at Marisa. "For I am a very persistent man. . . ."

He did not release her hand until he had kissed it again. Tom and Sally laughed.

"You needn't worry that Tom will say anything to Philip," Sally assured Marisa when they had started back again. "He knows how to hold his tongue. But *do* tell me, my dear, what did you think of the handsome count? He's not married, you know, and I've heard he's enormously rich, beside being a relative of the queen of Naples."

"He was far too bold on such a short acquaintance," Marisa found the strength to answer, still trying to still the whirling thoughts in her brain. Lady Repton gave a tinkling laugh.

"Oh, my dear, but what does that signify if he has fallen madly in love with you? And all Italians are impetuous, you know, as well as being gallant lovers. You did like him though, didn't you? You were so flushed. . . . Well, I won't tease you about it any longer for you are blushing again. And we will contrive to keep your new admirer a secret from Philip, shan't we? Unless you would like to bring him up to scratch! It really *is* rather a pity that you're married, you know, but at least you don't have a husband breathing down your neck, and you're independent."

Once again driving the carriage, Marisa was relieved that Sally's endless stream of chatter gave her hardly any reason to respond. And yet her friend complained that she was growing absentminded—or was it that she was thinking of the count—when she did not answer a question she had been asked at *least* twice.

"I'm sorry. You see the streets are so crowded today, and I did not want to overturn us both and become a laughingstock! What was the question?"

"Why, it was about visiting the—the *Club* tonight!" Sally's voice was belatedly lowered as she remembered the presence of the impassive groom behind them. "Don't you remember what Tom said? It's obvious that the marquise has taken a liking to you, and *that's* not usual, I assure you. And if you are worried that your persistent count will be along, well, don't! He is engaged this evening with the Prince of Wales, I understand, and so the three of us might go together. Oh!" she exclaimed as the curricle swerved sharply, "only *do* be careful, my love! I don't mean about tonight, of course. It will be quite proper, for women often go there alone, and if you feel awkward about it I promise to stay with you unless you find some reason to want to go off on your own. You are not *afraid,* are you?"

"Of course I am not!" Marisa said sharply (Would *they* think that and take it to mean she was guilty?). "But I did promise Philip that I would not go there without him, you know."

"Oh—Philip grows far too protective! You should show him that you are quite able to look after yourself and that you are not ruled by him, or you will find yourself quite hedged in, you know. Besides," Sally added reasonably, "he need not know! Pray *don't* cry off or it will quite spoil my evening."

Marisa felt herself caught between two fires and quite unable to think rationally. What on earth was she to do?

In the end, as Sally continued to tease and to cajole, she gave her an evasive answer, promising that she would go if she had no previous engagement for that evening. She would send word.

"But you *don't!* I remember that you told me only yesterday that tonight was the only night you had free, and you were quite sure you wouldn't know what to do with yourself! I'll call for you soon after an early supper, and we can tell your Mrs. Willoughby that we are going to Lady Cowpers—she is giving a musical evening, can you imagine?"

By the time Marisa walked up the steps to her own house she was quite wrung out, both physically and mentally. And then, as she was about to go upstairs, Danvers, the austere butler, handed her a folded card on a silver tray.

"The Chevalier Durand called while you were out, my lady."

She did not need to be told. She had recognized his name beneath his family crest, and she could not repress a small shudder of distaste as she unfolded the card to read what he had written inside.

Only a few laconic words, penned in a surprisingly neat and legible hand.

"I am desolate at having missed you but will see you tonight at the 'D' Club. There is a message from the duke that I was instructed to deliver."

Chapter Twenty-four

She did not want to go to the Damnation Club that night and would have given anything to cry off, but suddenly it seemed as if matters were being taken out of her hands—even if she had not been curious as to how the chevalier knew she was to be there tonight.

When Marisa tried to sort it all out and make sense of it she became so frightened that she could hardly breathe, and her fingers fumbled at the clasp of her ruby and amethyst necklace so that her maid had to do it up for her. In spite of the warm, scented bath she had had, her body felt cold —cold with fear and apprehension although she tried to tell herself that if she were suspected, if they wanted to kill her off, they would hardly do so in a place as public as the "D" Club, as it was familiarly known.

So she managed to make herself talk and smile and even laugh as Sally asked her teasingly whether she had been sure to bring enough money with her, for otherwise. . . .

"Oh, I know what that otherwise means, and tonight I mean to be careful."

"Oh, be careful by all means, love, but pray, do not be *tame!* For ordinary play, one can always go to Bruton Street!" Sally's eyes were sparkling, and once or twice, in the darkness of the carriage, Marisa saw her lean against Tom Drummond, allowing his fingers to dip into her low-cut bodice to caress her breasts. It was obvious that Sally enjoyed the excitement of being daring—but how far would she go? And as for herself, she had no inkling of how the evening would turn out. Without Philip to protect and advise her, how would it all end? She had to fight off the feeling that she was in a tumbril headed for the guillotine and unable to do anything to prevent her fate.

On the surface everything seemed the same as it had been on her first visit, and Sally kept her promise not to desert her. They wore masks, as usual, and wandered through the various rooms while Tom Drummond, his manner much more familiar since the afternoon, kept his arms around the waists of both women. Sally looked longingly towards a faro bank, and he reminded her laughingly that they had their duty to fulfill first.

Marisa's attention was caught by a woman dressed in black and silver, with hair of a distinctive red-gold color which she wore in coils at the back of her head in defiance of the current fashion for cropped hair. She wore a black and silver half-mask, under which a red mouth parted provocatively to show pearly white teeth.

"The duchess of Farnsworth," Sally whispered, catching the direction of her gaze. "She is known as one of the loveliest, coldest women in all of London. Her father was a duke, too, and it's rumored her own husband has to knock at her bedroom door to beg for entrance. She's a devout Whig. I'm always surprised when I see her here, but then, I've heard that gambling is the one vice she cannot control."

"Dash it, Sal! No gossiping. You know the rules!" Lord Drummond broke in in a warning whisper, and Sally Repton shrugged. But Marisa thought she recognized the duchess and flushed under her mask, remembering that degrading and yet strangely erotic scene she had witnessed before.

It was almost with relief that she found herself led into Madame De L'Aigle's crimson and gold receiving chamber, to meet her. Her green-blue eyes had the same piercing look. Her painted lips turned slightly upward in a smile that moved not a muscle in her white, curiously still face.

"What an exquisite gown, viscountess." With her spangled fan she tapped Marisa lightly over the knuckles. "For shame. Does it take an invitation to bring you back to my house?"

Sally came to her rescue saying laughingly, "You mustn't blame Marisa, madame. I vow, she's been positively moping since Mr. Sinclair left London! He made her promise—"

"Sally!" Lord Drummond interjected, but madame gave an unexpected, husky laugh.

"So! It is Philip Sinclair I must take to task. You're forgiven, my dear child, and I will make it right with him myself. But," she went on archly, "you must have an escort tonight then, so that you will feel quite safe. You are already acquainted with the Chevalier Durand so I'm sure you'll feel quite comfortable with him."

The chevalier himself came forward from the group of young men who clustered around Madame la Marquise. Removing his mask, he bowed politely.

"I'm honored."

His chestnut curls were burnished by the golden lamp light, and his full, rather sulky mouth smiled. He held out his arm to Marisa, and she had no choice but to take it.

The introductions performed, they all went out together, but soon Sally and Tom Drummond, feeling Marisa taken care of, wandered off to try their luck at the tables, and the chevalier, in his politely distant voice, asked Marisa if she had been upstairs yet. Hardly waiting for her reply, he began to lead her up one flight of heavily carpeted stairs, past the musicians' box and along a dimly lit corridor of sorts, with rooms leading off it.

Acting like a guide he said, "These are some of the private rooms that may be reserved by persons who wish to speak together or play cards together undisturbed. On the third floor, above this one, there are other rooms, each differently furnished and equipped for—other purposes." Feeling her start to draw back, he went on, still in the same even, expressionless tones, "I have reserved a room where we may talk in private, but you must not imagine that I mean to seduce you, for my tastes lie in a different direction from that which you are used to."

Marisa gasped with shock at the bluntness of his speech, but he had already drawn a key out of his pocket as he was talking and used it to unlock one of the doors. Ushered in politely, she found herself in a small but exquisitely furnished room, decorated in the style of Louis Quinze, with a small fire blazing cheerily in the grate. Still bereft of words, Marisa saw herself reflected in an ornate mirror, her mask of violet silk matching her gown, which clung closely to her slim figure. When she moved, as she did now, swinging around to face him, deep blue threads cunningly woven into the silk made a shimmering effect. But the chevalier seemed unconscious of the entrancing picture she made, her wide amber-gold eyes staring inquiringly and a trifle fearfully into his.

"Monsieur."

His lips curved in a smile which did not reach his cold, weighing eyes.

"Your pardon, madame, for my abruptness. But you must have received my card? I cannot remain for long in London for the duke needs me, and so it was essential that I see you tonight. Will you be seated? I shall endeavor to be brief."

As if to give her time to compose herself he turned away and poured two glasses of wine from a decanter which had been left on a table, and now, without asking if she cared to drink or not, he handed her one.

"I have news of an unpleasant nature to give you, so perhaps it might help you to drink first."

Marisa's hand shook with a strange mixture of shock and numbness, and she continued to stare at him uncomprehendingly until he gave an impatient shrug.

"No? Well perhaps you are stronger than you look. You will understand why I chose to talk with you alone when I have told you. Your father, madame, is dead. I am sorry that you have to be informed of it by a stranger, but on the other hand, perhaps it is better so. He died some three or four months ago following a lingering illness—which in turn was caused by injuries he sustained in a duel fought over his wife—you were not aware that he had married again?"

Still stunned, Marisa must have made some faint motion of her head for the chevalier went on in the same impassive tones, "I believe his wife came of a very old Spanish family who had settled in the Louisiana Territory a long time ago. It was her half brother you were supposed to marry—and the man who in effect killed your father was, I'm afraid to say, your husband."

Some of the wine spilled, and the chevalier sprang forward to rescue the glass from her shaking fingers. He held it impersonally to her lips.

"You had better drink it, madame, and I will give you more. I am not used to dealing with female hysterics."

She drank, hardly knowing what she did, her mind like a whirling kaleidoscope that made her feel she was becoming unhinged

"But—how? Why?"

Pedro and Dominic, laughing together outside the convent walls. . . . Inez. . . . Had the name really sprung back into her memory or was it only because the chevalier mentioned it.

"I believe Doña Inez is a very lovely woman—and I am sure she expected to inherit everything. But it seems your father did not think to change his will and so you are his heiress after all and Doña Inez merely the caretaker of his estates."

Marisa's teeth chattered against the rim of the glass as she drank again, unthinkingly.

"I didn't know—oh, God! Do you think I *care* about being an heiress? But how did you—"

"The duke has his own ways of finding out things. And in this case, he wished me to tell you that *your* interests are his. You comprehend, madame?" The chevalier's voice suddenly hardened as if the real mask had dropped away from his handsome, boyish features. "And the duke's interests are *mine*. That is why I take it upon myself to advise you to stop playing at silly games that might jeopardize your future. There are persons around you who would stop at nothing, and even the merest suspicion of betrayal would be sufficient. Be careful of the company you keep, viscountess, and think carefully of where your real loyalties lie."

First he had dealt her a numbing shock, and then, while she was still stunned, he *warned* her! Of what? Could it be? . . . Although she could not stop trembling, some instinct of self-preservation came to Marisa's rescue, and she gave way to tears. *That* was a natural enough reaction—he must not on any account know that she was choked with such stark terror that even the news of her father's death and its circumstances had not really touched her yet. *That* reaction, with hate and fury and humiliation all mixed together, would come later. For now, the fit of weeping she let herself indulge in afforded her both protection and assuagement.

After she had sufficiently recovered to go downstairs again, thankful for the mask she wore which disguised her tear-ravaged features, the chevalier took her home. He said very little on the way there except to remind her obliquely of her "obligation" and what was expected of her.

And it was not until she had safely regained the sanctuary of her own room and her maid had left her that Marisa began to cry again, this time truly for her father, remembering him as a young man and the occasions when he had taken her in his arms and tossed her up on his shoulders calling her his little princess and his treasure. So many years had passed since then, and they had turned into strangers. She had thought he'd forgotten her and cared nothing for her except to marry her off. But he must have loved her! And then she tried to picture the Doña Inez, and thought of a woman who looked something like the queen of Spain, black-haired and hungry-eyed, with a ripe red mouth. Over such a woman Dominic had fought her father and married his daughter! Yes, he had known very well who she was when he had suddenly offered to wed her. He and Pedro and Inez—had they planned it all between them. Even now, did he gloat over what he had achieved?

Marisa slept only when she was too exhausted from weeping to stay awake All of the next day she stayed in her room refusing to see any visitors. Count di Chiara sent his card up, among others, and she tore it in two. Was he deliberately trying to compromise her? Oh, if only Philip would come! With him, at least, she would be safe—and he, of all people, would understand!

But Philip sent her a message the next morning that he was delayed by bad weather and that same afternoon her Aunt Edmée came calling, accompanied by the charming Count De Brasselle whom she had met a few times before. While her aunt chattered to Mrs. Willoughby, the count, his charm in no whit impaired by the black of the mourning dress Marisa had put on, proceeded to question her deli-

Wicked Loving Lies

cately on the state of affairs in France when she had left it and the habits of the first consul and his wife. Was it true they stayed at Malmaison for most of the time? How often did Napoleon go to St. Cloud? She answered evasively that indeed she could not remember very well following the news of her bereavement, and her aunt was just as well qualified as she was to answer such inquiries. He looked disappointed, but did not press her, and soon after that he and her aunt took their leave, Edmée promising to come back and keep her company that evening for it would not do for her to become too melancholy.

Marisa did not know what to think or where to turn. When the Count di Chiara called again that evening she pleaded a sick headache and her state of mourning and would not see him.

Her aunt arrived soon after, and found Marisa lying in her bed, a cold compress on her forehead. Her lips compressed, Edmée dismissed both Simmons and Mrs. Willoughby, who had been fluttering about ineffectually, and then she leaned over her niece, speaking angrily and not at all sympathetically.

"And what do you think to achieve by going into a decline. It is sad and very unhappy for you, I agree, to hear that your papa has passed away, but it is done! It happened some months ago! Do you think he would want to see you as you are? Ah, I must say I am disappointed in you— to see you turn into a coward! Yes, it's true! What are you hiding from? Have you considered that if *you* should pine away and die, your *husband* will inherit everything that is yours. That will be a fine piece of news for this Doña Inez, I'm sure! And for him, too. Perhaps they'll marry, in the end, and live contentedly on *your* inheritance!"

"No!" Marisa sat bolt upright, her eyes glaring into her aunt's. "Do you think I would let—that I would stand— how could you talk so when *you* were once his lover? Are you jealous of this Inez creature, who was my stepmother? Oh—and it was you who made me marry him, too! Have you forgotten that?"

Edmée paled slightly, but her eyes refused to drop.

"It's true—that part of it. It was the unleashed savage,

the danger in him, that drew me, I suppose. And then when I realized that he was the one who—don't you realize that I, that we all, did only what we thought was best for you? Just as what I said to you just now was, too. I know what a lot you've been through, but you're still young and have so much to gain. I hate to see you give in so meekly!"

In the face of Marisa's stony silence, Edmée continued quickly, "Well, I suppose I cannot help what you think, but if I did not care for you I would not trouble myself! I really came here to tell you that I am thinking of removing to Bath for a few weeks—you know how fashionable it has become recently since Mr. Brummell set his seal of approval upon it! The air is bracing, besides, and the waters beneficial. *I* need a change from London, and since I have already taken a house there for the season I thought that you might like to come down—if you can tear yourself away from your new friends, that is. Perhaps Philip will come, too, if he knows that *you* are going. But heavens, I don't need to be reminded that you are now a rich and independent young woman and can do as you please!"

Marisa had had almost too much time in which to think and to brood, and her aunt's sudden attack on her weakness acted like a glass of cold water thrown in her face. Yes, her aunt was right, after all! Why should she lie back meekly and allow herself to be terrified and used without making any attempt to fight back? She had been made a fool of and tricked far too often. Suddenly she remembered her talks with the duke of Royse and the way he had talked about *revenge*, dwelling on the word. The Italians had a word for the kind of revenge she thought of now, letting it fill her mind and her veins where her pulse began to race furiously with a mixture of anguish and anger. Vendetta.

From this moment on, that would be her sworn course, blinding her to anything else—to see the man who had given her so much cause to hate him brought to her feet to die, knowing that it had been she who had caused it. And she would do anything, use anyone, to gain her objective. She closed her eyes and repeated the gypsy blood curse in her mind not questioning how she remembered the ancient Romany words.

"Marisa!" Edmée said suddenly and sharply, thinking that her niece had fallen into some kind of a trance.

"I shall be all right now." Marisa opened her eyes and smiled, and Edmée noticed that her face had suddenly become flushed. Before Edmée could utter another word, she said thoughtfully, "I suppose I had better get dressed and have something to eat. I have starved all day! Will you join me in a light supper? Perhaps we can discuss the journey to Bath and what kind of clothes I would need."

Chapter Twenty-five

It was settled, in the end, that Marisa should follow the Countess Landrey to Bath within a week, as soon as she had made all the necessary arrangements. There was the house to be closed up, and the duke of Royse to be informed. And of course there was Philip. . . .

Her aunt, glad to see her out of her depressed mood, did not question her too much but said only, in a troubled voice, "You *will* travel chaperoned, won't you, my love? It would not do to set people talking!"

"Oh, I've no doubt Mrs. Willoughby will be glad of a chance to visit Bath," Marisa answered carelessly, although her mind was already made up, and she intended to send Mrs. Willoughby down with Simmons and a quantity of baggage by coach.

Once her aunt had left London, she told Mrs. Willoughby that she would be driving down in her own curricle with her friend Lady Repton—it was a bet they had taken; and although that lady protested weakly she did not persist, knowing on which side her bread was buttered. At least Mr. Sinclair was to be one of the party, and *that* was all the more reason why she should not make more than a token objection to the Viscountess Stanbury's traveling to Bath under his protection. The viscountess was, in any case, used to doing just as she pleased!

"So you are going to let Philip become your lover?" Sally Repton said directly, her brown eyes sparkling. "But what about your poor count? I vow he has been at my heels these past few days, begging that I should arrange another meeting. Are you running away? And what of that handsome chevalier with whom you left the Club so hastily the other night?"

Being of an excitable, adventurous nature herself, Sally loved scandal and boldness above all things. Only her title and her wealth saved her from more censure than she already incurred for her madcap ways.

Marisa, in her new, hard mood, found it easy to fob off her friend with smiles that admitted everything while aloud she admitted to nothing.

"Please don't tell the count where I have gone! If he's as madly enamored of me as he says, it will do him good to cool his heels for a while. And as for the chevalier, he was merely a messenger from my father-in-law, bearing unpleasant news."

Sally's face clouded as she gave Marisa's hand a squeeze.

"How could I have forgotten. Your father—but still, my dear, I do wish you would give off wearing *black*. It's too, too depressing, and if you don't intend to remain in seclusion, where's the point?" As if she had suddenly thought of something, Sally's fair brow wrinkled. "My love, speaking of *seclusion*—you are not yet a widow, are you? I haven't wanted to pry before, but goodness, you've been so closemouthed about your—your *husband!* You can't imagine the stories that have been going the rounds. He's not a cripple, is he? Nor horribly disfigured? And after all Royse seems perfectly happy to accept you as his daughter-in-law—have I said too much? It's just that I am simply *dying* of curiosity! How is it he's never set foot in England?"

Marisa had been expecting to be questioned before and had prepared what she would say so that she was able to look back at Sally as she answered in a rather pensive manner, "He—he prefers to live abroad where he has his own interests. And an English title means nothing to him, or so he has said. I—our marriage was arranged by others, you see, and then having done his duty we were both free. I hardly feel as if I were married at all—and I don't wish to think of it."

"Oh!" Sally exclaimed, her eyes becoming enormous; and although it was clear she longed to ask more questions, she made a noble attempt at forbearance. There must be a strong reason why Marisa did not care to discuss her husband—and indeed seemed happiest to forget she had one! Sally had heard some of the old stories since Marisa had suddenly burst upon London society calling herself the Viscountess Stanbury; there were some persons who, until the duke of Royse had given her his official approval, had not wanted to believe she was any such thing.

Perhaps, Sally thought, it was true that he was an idiot. After all, his mother had been deranged and kept at Cliff Park with keepers to look after her until the day of her death! Perhaps the son, too, was tainted and that was why he had been sent off abroad at an early age. Poor Marisa! What a terrible fate, and how lucky for her there had been no *results* to be seen from her unfortunate marriage!

Satisfied at having enlisted Sally's connivance and not knowing what direction her friend's thoughts had taken, Marisa stayed quite cool as she continued to make their arrangements. *Theirs*. Hers and Philip's. For since his return to London from Lichfield, matters had been settled between them—almost without words. Now it only remained for the physical act to consummate their strange agreement and make them lovers in fact.

Her baggage and her chaperone having been sent off ahead, Marisa left London in the company not only of Philip but of Sally and Lord Drummond as well for those two were determined to see them on the first part of their journey at least. They had left late in the afternoon, however, and since they had packed a picnic lunch which they stopped to eat along the way, the first part of their traveling did not take them beyond the borders of London itself.

Here Sally and Tom left them discreetly and where before they had all been almost too gay, a sudden, almost constrained silence seemed to fall between Philip and Marisa. The sun had begun to dip behind a heavy bank of clouds to the west, and it was growing cold enough for Marisa to pull her heavy cloth redingote more closely about her shoulders.

Philip glanced towards her as he said with an air of awkwardness, "Are you cold? We are not far away now from—the cottage I told you of that belongs to my father.

271

And we will travel across the heath by coach until we reach the Journeyman on the new Bath road, where we will again transfer to a curricle. You're sure? . . ." He did not have the courage to put the rest of his question into words, and Marisa herself, finding her nervousness grow now that they were alone, merely nodded her head.

For all of her earlier determination and cold resolve, she found herself almost afraid now that the moment was almost upon her. Tonight she would become Philip's mistress. Oh, God—how would she know how to act? Did he realize that such an adventure was new to her? And above all— what would he think of her afterwards? Better that it should have happened unplanned than like this. . . .

But there was no point in worrying about it, and Marisa was relieved to find that there was only one old man, stupid looking and half-deaf into the bargain, there to greet them. He led the horses away, and Philip took her inside the cottage, which although small was comfortably furnished and warm, with fires lit in every room. A cold supper was laid out on the table.

She drank more than she ate, and so did Philip; and all the time that they were alone, sitting across the table from each other, they could hardly find two words to say. It was with a feeling of relief that Marisa saw Philip push his chair back suddenly, holding his hand out to her as he said gruffly, "Shall we go upstairs? You must be tired."

Upstairs there was only one bedroom. It was very large, taking up almost the whole of the floor, with a dressing room and bath adjoining it. Sir Anthony had built this hideaway for his mistresses. It was all very cosy and warm, and the big four-poster bed looked comfortable, its covers drawn back invitingly. Here, too, a fire had been lit, and when Philip had left her with a tactful, murmured excuse, Marisa found herself thinking giddily that this should have been her wedding night. How shy they had both become of each other! And Philip at least, would not insult her and ravish her. . . .

Hastily she turned her mind away from those dangerous memories and began to undress· before the fire, gritting her teeth as she did so. She decided against wearing her long, frilly nightshift, thinking it would seem too coy and kept on her sheer silk shift. She glanced apprehensively towards the closed door as she hastily brushed her curling, unruly hair. Just a few strokes—and then she got hastily into bed, blowing out the candle that stood beside it before she pulled the covers up to her neck.

Now! Now she had crossed the threshold and made up her mind, and it remained only for Philip to come in and put an end to all her fears and uncertainty. 'I love him,' she thought experimentally, and another part of her mind laughed mockingly and told her that she could not love anyone because the hate in her was too strong. The wine in her belly made her face hot, even while her hands and feet stayed cold, and she wished now that she had drunk more. Pray God that Philip, being a man, would know how to go about easing her fears and her discomfort and that he would be kind and gentle, as the *other* had not been. But she was committed.

It seemed an age before Marisa heard the door creak and saw the outline of Philip's figure as he entered quietly and almost hesitantly. He crossed in front of the fire and she saw that he was wearing a dressing gown, and she could smell the fumes of wine on him as he said softly, "Marisa! Are you asleep?" His voice shook slightly, and she realized with a shock that he was as nervous as she, and the knowledge gave her the courage to respond in an unintelligible murmur that he could interpret as he chose. She saw him hesitate, and then he came quickly towards her, taking off the dressing gown and flinging it away just before he climbed into the bed with her.

She had just time to see how fair his body was and how blond hair gleamed on his chest, and then he pulled the covers up again over them both and put his arms around her, and she felt the length of him against the length of her and his trembling, and he buried his face against her shoulder, still saying nothing and doing nothing else.

There was no clock in this bedroom, and yet she could almost hear the ticking away of time in their heartbeats. And still all he did was to hold her tightly, and she knew that he was not yet aroused, and at last she made her fingers stroke the smooth skin of his back tentatively as she murmured, "Philip? Philip, dear, it's all right—"

"Is it?" he said, his voice sounding like a soft groan, and then he kissed her desperately and stroked her shoulders and her back, his fingers slipping over the thin silk of her shift. Marisa let her lips part under his, but still he did nothing more than caress her gently and almost impersonally; although his thighs lay against hers, she could feel no signs of desire in him.

He raised his head at last, and said, "Oh, God! I cannot —Marisa, I am spoiled. I want you—I've wanted you for so long and dreamed of this moment, and now that you are here in my arms—I cannot!"

She tried to hush him, not quite comprehending what he was saying, but he rolled away from her and held her shoulders while he looked into her face.

"You don't know what I'm trying to say, do you? And how could you? But—you see—I must be blunt or I will not be able to say it. I am—not used to being so intimate with ladies. I can perform very well with whores—and now you will hate me, but it's the truth! I was only sixteen when my father introduced me to his current mistress, to 'initiate me' as he put it. And since then I've had my share of the birds of paradise, as I'm sure you've heard them called! They've known what to do, you see, and I've needed only to be a—male! But you are different, and although I want you as I've never wanted any of *those*, yet I cannot —and now you will despise me."

"No, Philip, no!" Moved beyond herself by the agony of his recital, Marisa put her arms about him, trying to draw him closer. "Philip, I'm not so very experienced, and I, too, have been afraid, but isn't it possible that we can learn together?" More boldly she added, with the breath catching in her throat, "Do you want me to play the whore for you? Then you will have to teach me, for I don't know how."

She wished now that she had not kept on her shift, and she forced her hand to move down his rigid body, touching him where she had never willingly touched a man before, to find him limp.

"Philip?"

He shuddered and caught her hand, drawing it up to his lips.

"I'm—not ready yet. And yet I want to hold you in my arms and feel your body next to mine. Can you understand? Let me hold you, my love. . . ."

And so they fell asleep clasping each other, and Marisa did not know if she was glad or sorry for what had not happened between them.

At least she felt safe and comfortable, and when in what seemed less than an hour or so there was a discreet knocking at the bedroom door, she felt like giggling hysterically at the speed with which Philip got up and wrapped his dressing gown around himself.

"You asked for the horses to be ready by four, my lord." It was not quite that time yet, but she realized there was no point in remaining here, for if they started early enough they would reach Bath by evening.

The carriage was small, and since Marisa had only a small portmanteau with her, that was easily bestowed within. Philip got up on the box to take the reins of the two restive horses.

It was still dark, and the sky was heavy with clouds that seemed to press down upon them, but Philip said that driving across the notorious Hounslow Heath would be safest at this time in the morning when no one would be expected to be abroad. He seemed to know the way even though they drove through patches of dense fog. Marisa, her teeth chattering with cold in spite of the thick redingote she wore and the lap robe of fur tucked about her, tried to fall asleep again so that she would not have to think of the night. Time enough to think later. . . . and then she dozed off for the carriage was well sprung and Philip was careful to avoid the worst of the ruts in the road.

She was dreaming of Philip and wondering why his eyes had changed from blue to slate-grey when a sudden shout and a shot aroused her.

All of a sudden the coach seemed to leave the road and was jouncing horribly, flinging her from side to side, while she heard more shouts. She had no time in which to think; when she tried to look outside everything was shrouded in a thick fog. And then the coach came to a sudden halt, and she distinctly heard a cry, which was quickly muffled, a sound of scuffling, and then the door was wrenched open and the orange light of a lantern glared at her like a fiery eye. She heard a groan, and as the lantern was brought closer, she saw, through widening eyes, Philip's limp body thrown inside, to slide across the seat opposite her. There was a gag in his mouth, the side of his face was bloodied and his arms were bound behind him. And then she heard a rough, jeering voice.

"Well, and just look at what we 'ave 'ere. A bleedin' beauty, me buckos! And a bit o' luck fer us, eh?"

Marisa tried to scream, but the scream was locked in her throat as a long, brawny arm reached out to push her backward.

"No, no!" his voice crooned deeply in his throat, "no use to try an' scream, for there's nobody would hear you, my fine gentlewoman!" One hand caught her about the throat, almost strangling her; and even though she tried to flail at him with her fisted hands, she felt, with a sickening sensation, the front of her gown ripped open.

In the cramped space of the carriage Marisa felt herself smothered and rendered completely helpless, as helpless as Philip, who lay groaning only a few inches away from her. Robbers—highwaymen! Her dazed mind registered that much as she felt her reticule snatched away; and then, much worse than that, rough hands fondling her exposed breasts while she writhed and tried to cry out and felt her wrists grabbed and held while coarse laughter rang in her ears.

Her body was wrenched forward and then flipped around, and she felt the bite of cords about her wrists as they were pulled behind her back. And then, while she still struggled, she felt the rings yanked off her fingers, bruising her knuckles, before she was turned about again, to look with glazed, desperate eyes into the yellow light of the lantern and the masked faces that leaned over her.

"Do ye think she's the one?"

She tried to kick out and was impeded by her skirts, and then she heard ribald laughter and a ripping sound. A foul-tasting gag was thrust into her mouth as she opened it to scream, and there was cold air on her thighs for a moment before their hot hands pawed at her, squeezing her breasts and exploring brutally between her squirming, bared thighs.

"Do you think she'd fight as hard if it were *him?*" one of the men said with a coarse chuckle.

"If we had enough time, perhaps she'd not fight at all," said a voice with an Irish accent, speaking softly. "For faith, it's true that there are whores who are ladies and ladies who are whores."

It was true that she had expended almost all her strength in struggling, and now, when rough hands dragged her legs apart, holding fast to her ankles, and the remnants of her gown were pushed aside, Marisa could do nothing, even when she was pulled to the edge of the seat and the lantern light fell fully upon her exposed, contorting body.

"We'd best hurry and do what has to be done," someone said, his voice coming from a distance, almost shrouded by the drumming of blood in her head. And someone else muttered, "Hold her steady then." And more loudly, "You'll take this as a warning, madam, and count yourself lucky to stay alive. So they branded whores in the times when kings ruled France. . . ."

Her eyes half-blinded with tears, Marisa had hardly noticed what was happening until one of them, the Irishman, as her mind had dubbed him, moved his hand from over the lantern, and she felt a sharp, searing pain on the soft inner flesh of her thigh. It jolted her with agony, sending her body arching convulsively against restraining hands.

Half-fainting, she had no more energy left to struggle when the same man who had branded her so brutally now put his body over hers and raped her, quickly and efficiently, so that it was thankfully over almost before she had realized it was happening.

The worst part of it was when he stood up and rearranged his clothing, and then, with his knife, he slit open the front of Philip's breeches, exposing his swollen member. He gave an ugly laugh.

"Mayhap ye'd best stick to what you're best at, madam whore—and leave politics alone," he said softly. With a shudder, wishing she had lost consciousness altogether, Marisa felt him raise her up quickly and cut her aching wrists loose.

The next moment they were all gone, and the lantern that had seen so much was extinguished before it was flung away to smash against the ground.

It was suddenly dark, and the soft thudding of horses hoofs gave way to a thick silence in which Marisa continued to writhe with pain and shame and revulsion at what had been done to her within such a short space of time. She could hear her own heartbeats and the sobbing, moaning sounds she made that seemed to come from beyond herself. After she had snatched the gag from her mouth she started to sob wrenchingly.

It was some time before she became aware of other sounds and movement as the horses, which had been tethered, moved restively, jolting her about. Unconsciously, hands fumbling, she tried to straighten her torn clothing, and then she heard a groan from Philip and remembered with a fresh wave of loathing and sickness that he had been forced to watch and listen to everything. He groaned again, and she forced herself to grope towards his dim, stiff form, trying to push aside the pain that stabbed through her with every movement.

It took what seemed like aeons to loosen the knots that held his wrists together, and all the while she could not stop the sobs that shook her body.

"Oh Philip! Philip, they—they—"

"I saw," he said at last when he was able to get rid of his gag. His voice sounded strange and muffled as if the gag he had worn had swollen his tongue so that he no longer sounded like himself but a hoarse-voiced stranger. "Dear God! Do you think I could help seeing? And hearing the way they talked to you, as if—oh, *God!*" he said again, and this time it sounded like a groan of anguish as he made a clumsy attempt to put his arms about her trembling, tear-wracked body. And all the time he was unconscious of the uncalled for, unwanted swelling of himself protruding beyond his ripped breeches.

"Philip—Philip!" she kept saying as he took her outside the carriage, her redingote hanging about her shoulders and her dress all torn so that she might as well have been naked.

The fog had turned milky with the approach of dawn, and as she clung to his shoulders; he could see the gleaming of her flesh and the swelling of her exposed breasts with their darker, swollen nipples. And he remembered again, without wanting to, the way she had touched him, so gently and so intimately, during the night.

The horses moved sharply and impatiently and made snorting noises as they tossed their heads. Philip lowered Marisa to the ground, her heavy cloth coat under her as he leaned over her.

She shivered and still continued to clutch his shoulders while she kept repeating his name between sobs. Whatever light there was seemed concentrated on the golden patch of hair between her legs where that man had gone before, and before him the rough, calloused fingers of the others as they had explored her softness that he had not yet known.

There were faint bruises like shadows lying across her breasts from other hands rougher than his—common hands —used to handling whores that walked the streets. They had called her so, along with other things he did not understand. But now as Marisa stirred and shivered under the onslaught of cold, damp air, crying out almost incoherently, Philip covered her body with his. It was nothing he could help; indeed, he had almost ceased to think coherently, conscious only of the enormous throbbing in his groin and the exposed, limply sprawled body beneath his that he had just seen handled and used so casually and lewdly. No—he could not help himself nor prevent what happened next. He put his lips over her open mouth, tasting the salt of her tears, and his hands touched her breasts and then moved lower to push her trembling thighs apart. She screamed under his lips as his fingers brushed over the spot where they had burned her, and he felt the convulsive movements of her body as he touched her where she was still damp and sticky from the leavings of the last man who had used her. There was no need to adjust his clothing, for the job had

279

already been done for him, and still groaning, begging her pardon against her crushed mouth, he thrust himself inside her and took her just as she was, a half-naked, straining body under his.

Chapter Twenty-six

It seemed a long time later when Marisa opened her eyes and found herself gazing up at some ornate, unfamiliar silk curtains. It took her some time to realize that she was lying in a canopied bed, with the sheets as soft as silk against her feverish skin. So comfortable—and yet when she moved she could feel the constriction of a bandage around her thigh and a throbbing pain that brought everything back.

"Philip brought you here to me. Oh, my love, he did not stop except to change horses and he had drawn the blinds in the coach so that no one knew. . . . I vow he has not had a moment's sleep, poor young man! He's been waiting outside. What a swoon you've been in—and the things you muttered when you were in a fever—I have been at my wit's end wondering what to do, and yet I dared not call in a doctor to see you after what Philip told me. Marisa! Are you sure you are feeling better?"

The Countess Landrey's face hung over her and was replaced by Philip's. When Marisa flinched he dropped to his knees beside the bed, pressing one of her cold hands to his lips.

"Can you ever forgive me? I felt as if I was possessed! All I could think of was wiping out what they had done to you—to set *my* seal upon you! It was inexcusable. You cannot think worse of me than I do of myself. It all seems like a nightmare—"

"To me, too," she managed to say wearily, wondering why it hurt her so to move until she remembered. She found that she could not hate Philip, who had been used as much as she had, in a way. At least he was faithful enough and honest enough to stand by her! But now, as the first shock wore off, Marisa began to recall, unwillingly, the things that had been said to her between the crude insults and the more cruel use they had made of her body. It had been meant to be some kind of a warning. She wondered, shudderingly, if the brand they had put on her was the mark of the Assassin—left hitherto only upon his dead victims.

Her body healed, and so did the brand, a miniature fleur-de-lis, they had put on her shrinking flesh. It could not be seen unless she spread her legs apart; it was a tiny purple scar no larger than a large birthmark. Only a lover, if she took one, would discover it and question its origin. And the thought made Marisa weep again with shame and anger. Someone had set those horrible men upon her, and she knew now that it was not only in her imagination that she had thought herself watched. Someone knew, or suspected —but who? She thought of the chevalier's handsome, sulky face and *his* warning—and the faces of all the other men she had met. The Count di Chiara, angry because she had refused to do as he had demanded? Or the other side, suspecting her affiliations? Oh, she would drive herself mad if she tried to think—and her aunt kept begging her to try and forget, trying to assure her that she would always be well-protected from now on.

Tears expend their own force—and when Marisa had finished with the convulsive fits of weeping that seized her from time to time, she felt a cold emptiness inside her that defied any emotion, even fear, to penetrate it.

She was supposed to have contracted a chill on her way to Bath, and when the blistered burn on her thigh had healed, she got up and took an interest in the clothes she had sent ahead of her, and the arrangement of her hair and the jewels she would wear on different occasions.

What had really happened to her remained a secret that was shared by her aunt in part and by Philip wholly. She found, once she was able to think clearly and rationally, that she could not blame him for what he had done. At least he had been honest in admitting his weakness and his guilt, and he did not try to evade her afterwards but played the part of her admiring cavalier to the hilt.

He swore that it was no game he played and that he was

in earnest, but even *that* no longer mattered. He had been the third man to take her, following her husband and the lilting-voiced, coldly callous Irishman—and in doing so he had only taken what she had decided to offer in the first place. The duke should be pleased, and with Philip, at least, there was no need to explain the small, ugly scar that marred the symmetry of her golden thighs.

Marisa's stay in Bath was marked only by the number of assemblies and routs she attended with Philip as her escort and the one occasion when she took the waters with her aunt.

The Prince of Wales had come down there, too, but he was very much taken up with Mrs. Fitzherbert at the time, and Marisa was not the only one to hear the rumors that he had secretly married her according to the rites of the Catholic Church. They all attended a late supper party given by him, and then, since her aunt was occupied with an old admirer, Marisa let Philip take her home, stopping at his lodgings first, where she undressed before a roaring fire, making her mind a blank, and he took her with no signs of his earlier difficulties.

He delivered her back home before her aunt had returned, and Marisa slept late the next day, to be greeted by her sour-faced maid with a note in her hand from Philip, explaining that he had been urgently summoned to Cornwall because his uncle had suffered a turn for the worse.

"We might as well go back to London ourselves, my pet," Edmée grumbled later, pressing white, tapered fingers against her temples. "*Everyone* is going back since the prince decided he needs seclusion—and you know what *that* means!"

This time they were well escorted, and even that portion of their journey which lay across Hounslow Heath was accomplished in the daytime, with the sun shining brightly all the while. The Countess Landrey, who had a practical turn of mind, whispered to Marisa before the carriage dropped her off, "Just think, petite. It's not impossible that you might soon be a duchess! And *then* how those old cats will squall!"

Marisa could not summon up more than a half smile to

greet this sally for she was deathly tired. Even Simmons was trying to hide her yawns, and Mrs. Willoughby was fast asleep already, her mouth slightly open as she snored delicately. She could think of nothing beyond the comfort of her own warm bed and a cup of steaming hot chocolate to sustain her before she fell asleep.

The torches on either side of the massive door had been lit, and lights shone welcomingly in almost every window. So her last-moment message had been received, after all, and they were expecting her. But why was everything so lit up? The doors were flung open after Simmons, muttering, had tugged violently on the bell rope, and Danvers stood there frowning coldly until with a start he recognized who stood there.

"My lady! I beg your pardon, but we had no idea—"

Mrs. Willoughby, yawning behind her hand, had followed Marisa and her maid into the brightly lighted hallway, and now she took it upon herself to say reprovingly, "What is the meaning of all these lights? I'm sure you must have received the message we sent, but—"

The butler's face seemed to close upon itself leaving nothing more than an impassive mask as he stuttered, "My lady —we had not expected you yet—"

And Marisa, light-headed from tiredness, had begun to wonder if she had come to the wrong house or was quite mad, when she heard a familiar voice as a young woman dressed *en grande toilette,* came bursting out from one of the rooms that opened onto the entrance hall.

"Marisa! Oh, my dear! I declare this is such a wonderful surprise! And to think we all thought you were rusticating in Bath for the next fortnight at least! But why didn't you tell anyone you were arriving? You cannot imagine how we've all missed you—and oh, you naughty, secretive creature, not to have told even *me* the truth! I suppose I should be sorry that you have returned—"

Confused, dizzy, Marisa's eyes blinked as she wondered if she were dreaming. And yet she could distinctly hear music coming from somewhere and the sounds of laughter and loud chatter. What was happening? And why was Sally here, so much at home that she welcomed her into her own house? Even Mrs. Willoughby gaped and sought for words, and Simmons, carrying a bandbox in either hand, snapped at Mr. Danvers as she inquired where all the footmen were.

"Oh, goodness," Sally said quickly and penitently as she caught sight of Marisa's white, troubled face. "You mean that you didn't know? . . ."

Danvers, seeming to recover from his trance, had snapped his fingers, and two uniformed footmen suddenly appeared. It all seemed very much like some kind of play!

And as if to heighten the effect, one of the doors opened silhouetting a tall figure against the light for a moment before he came forward, taking her nerveless hand and bowing formally over it.

"If you sent a message, I'm sorry I did not receive it, my love. But now that you are here at last—must I admit before so many others how much I've missed you?"

She thought her eyes and her tired mind were playing tricks on her. It could not be! Not—Dominic, of all people, in a wine-red velvet coat, white ruffles showing at the wrist and neck, a black pearl stickpin nestled in the folds of his cravat.

There were other voices in the background—Danvers talking softly to Simmons and Mrs. Willoughby, and Sally having a fit of the giggles as she looked from one face to the other, enjoying the drama.

The blood rushed into Marisa's head, warming her face and throbbing in her temples so that his hateful, mocking face seemed to swim before her through a red mist.

"You! How dare—" Without giving her time to complete her stuttered sentence, he seized her hand.

"Danvers, you can see to my lady's companions and her baggage. Sally, ma chère, will you make my excuses for a while? My wife and I need a few moments alone together."

As dazed with shock as she was, Marisa could hardly wait until he had taken her into the library and closed the door before she tugged herself away from him and spat, "How dare you? What are you doing here in *my* house, ordering around *my* servants and entertaining your—your—"

He made no attempt to retrieve her hand but leaned

against the mantelpiece instead, the leaping fire striking silver sparks in his eyes.

"*Dare,* madam? *Your* house and *your* servants? I think you forget how matters really stand, as well as your position in this house. For I am the Viscount Stanbury, and you are —yes, of course. I had almost forgotten. You are my wife, are you not? And if I discern in those golden eyes of yours a design to fly at me—have a care, my love. For this is England, and the law places you beneath me," he went on unpleasantly, watching her widening eyes, "under my rule, that is—did you think I meant otherwise? You're my wife, and I own you, if you'll forgive my bluntness. Not only you, but everything you possess—or thought you possessed. Have I made matters clear?" She was still silent, dumbfounded, feeling rooted to the spot until he straightened from his comfortably leaning stance and came towards her, putting a long brown finger under her chin to tilt her white, staring face up to his.

"I'm glad to find you so sensible, my dear. It will make for an easier relationship between us." And then he shrugged, as if he were bored with her already and turned away, straightening the ruffles at his wrists.

Over his shoulder he said, "I'll give you time to refresh yourself after your journey and to change into something more suitable before you come down to help me entertain our guests."

As if some invisible cord that had held her still had been cut, Marisa sprang forward, her fingers curved into claws that sought to tear at his sneering face.

"Never! I won't—you treacherous murderer! Do you think I'll submit so easily to your threats? I'll denounce you before them all for what you are—I'll—I'll see you dead before I—"

He had swung round on his heel, catching her hands with no visible effort so that she was helpless.

"Will you indeed, madam? You tried before and failed, and this time I'm forewarned. We're in England, and you don't have Fouché's secret police to turn to for protection. In fact, as I understand it, you've put yourself in a very dangerous spot with your playing at being a spy!"

She had been struggling against him, and now she suddenly hung limply in his grasp, staring up at his hard, merciless face with horror in her eyes.

"You! Oh, God—it was *you!* There is something about the way you speak and the cruel way your hands hold me—"

With a harsh laugh, he flung her away from him.

"Are you comparing me with one of your lovers, madam? One who was rougher than your delicate appearance would dictate? I must tell you that I don't like comparisons. If you interest me enough so that I decide to have you again, you'll know me for what I am, and this time I'll give you reason not to forget!"

She continued to look back at him with glazed, dilating eyes as she repeated again in a whisper, "It was *you!*"

And now he crossed the room to her and shook her roughly, swinging her head back and forth.

"You can explain to me later what you mean by that! But for now—you might try remembering that we have guests, and since you're here you can help me entertain them. You've learned that much during your stay in London, I'm sure!"

Marisa felt turned to stone, both from tiredness and from shock, and as if he had discerned her sudden weakness and meant to make full use of it, Dominic dropped his hands from her shoulders and took her arm, tucking it beneath his in a semblance of politeness and devotion for those that might see as he took her to the door and through it to the foot of the wide staircase.

He released her here, and the inclination of his head was a mockery in itself as he murmured softly, "I shall expect you downstairs again in—say forty-five minutes? That should give you sufficient time in which to refresh yourself after your tiring journey and dress more suitably. This is a formal affair tonight, although I'm sure most of our guests are here out of curiosity more than anything else. I shall expect you to act the part of a devoted wife—as practiced as you are at acting a part. I think you will contrive to acquit yourself tolerably. And," his voice hardened as he gave her arm a last, warning squeeze, "you had better appear— or I shall be forced to come looking for you."

There were too many questions churning around in her mind for her to be able to think coherently. It seemed like a bad dream—a nightmare! And yet Marisa's feet climbed the stairs, taking them one by one, while her hands clutched at the curving, polished rail. He was here! From where had he come and for what? So much for all his hypocritical talk of being an American and disdaining his English title!

Marisa had merely stepped into the copper bath, filled with scented water on which a thin film of attar of roses floated, and then out again. Turning down her maid's offer of help, she dried herself quickly, scrubbing viciously at her own skin until it was all reddened and glowing with warmth.

She seemed lost in some kind of trance. Simmons and Mrs. Willoughby, exchanged glances. Neither of the two women knew quite how to react to the presence of the viscountess' missing husband in the house; he was very much at home, it seemed, from the way he had ordered things around.

Marisa seemed oblivious to what they were thinking, but her mind raced under her silent exterior. She allowed herself to be dressed in a gold satin sheath of a dress, very low cut, its stark lines modified by a gold-spangled tunic of transparent gauze that was caught up just below the bust by three tiny diamond buttons and fell open all the rest of the way. While Simmons swiftly arranged her hair into shining ringlets, she kept thinking, 'What is his motive for coming here? Does the duke know, I wonder?' The hate for him she had felt and fed had intensified, and she felt sure now that it had been he who had branded her and then raped her so brutally—but for what reason? *She* had reason enough to hate him, God knew, but why had he begun to hate *her* so?

Whatever kind of game he was playing at this time was a dangerous one, she felt sure of it. And she would not betray herself again; she would play along with him and destroy him in the end, as she had vowed to do. Before she went downstairs, Marisa handed Mrs. Willoughby a sealed note, addressed to her aunt. It had to be delivered— privately, and tonight, if possible. She could not quite *bribe* a faded gentlewoman, but she gave the lady a generous present of a pair of diamond eardrops and hinted at an annuity. Seeing Willoughby's eyes gleam with sudden avarice, Marisa gave her a hug and murmured that she was the dearest creature and that she was positive the duke of Royse would be overjoyed to find out how well they got on together.

That done, she felt more capable of facing Dominic and the crush downstairs. Sounds of music and laughter and a subdued buzz of conversation assailed Marisa's ears as she slowly began to descend the staircase, wondering as she did why her knees felt so weak. No sooner had she thought it then her back stiffened, and she drew in a deep breath. No! He would not see her cowed and beaten and afraid, no matter what she might feel inside. She was no longer a gypsy wench, nor the naive child he had taken as a bride only to discard publicly a few days later. Dominic Challenger, or the Viscount Stanbury, as he had unaccountably chosen to call himself now, would soon discover that he had a woman to match wits with this time.

Chapter Twenty-seven

The magnificent London mansion of the duke of Royse, which Marisa had once thought far too large and imposing, was crammed almost to bursting tonight. Although it was close to midnight, it was still considered early by those accustomed to keeping town hours.

The Viscount Stanbury, it seemed, was determined to make sure all the ton knew of his return to England. There could be no question of his sudden, enforced disappearance *now* without creating quite a furor, as he was very well aware.

With one arm thrown casually about the waist of the lovely, laughing Sally, Dominic surveyed the crowded ballroom with a kind of grim satisfaction. Even the old dowagers were represented tonight in force, and it was not hard to imagine what they whispered behind their fans. Royse's scapegrace son was back to claim his inheritance—and he was neither crippled nor disfigured if one did not count the small scar on his face, which only lent his rather harsh features a more interesting, dangerous look.

"I told them all you'd been adventuring all your life, and that you made your fortune in the Indies as a pirate!" Sally gave her gurgling, irrepressible laugh. "You do not mind, do you? After all, if you won't even tell *me* what you've been up to all these years, I felt bound to give the gossips *some* story that will keep them busy for weeks to come! I vow they've been able to talk of nothing else since you appeared on the scene so unexpectedly! I know that *I* came near to fainting when Madame de L'Aigle introduced us that night. But why didn't you tell Marisa that you were coming? It wasn't fair of you, you know!"

"Wasn't it? Perhaps I wanted to surprise her. But then, my sweet, I'm neither *fair,* as you call it, nor honorable. So be warned!"

Marisa, walking into the room with her head held high, had not missed the way Dominic's dark head bent to Sally's fair one as he said something to her that made her laugh provocatively. Sally was an inveterate flirt, of course. But did they have to make their apparent closeness so public? She fought back an unaccountable wave of fury, and the next moment she found herself surrounded by people, a veritable horde of friends and acquaintances who vowed they had missed her and asked her archly why she had not told anyone her husband had been expected to join her so soon.

"Why, because I did not know it myself!" Marisa answered lightly. "My—husband is a very unpredictable man."

He had not left Sally's side yet to greet her, and she gritted her teeth, even while she continued to smile fixedly. And then, out of nowhere, it seemed, the Count di Chiara was bowing before her, lifting her nerveless hand to his lips.

"London has been a desolate place without your lovely presence, madame," he murmured in a low, significant voice, his eyes fixed on her set face. "But I had hoped you would return tonight, and so, you see, I am here! May I congratulate you on your happy reunion with your husband?"

His presence here reminded her of all the unpleasant, frightening events she had been trying to put out of her mind. How had *he* managed an invitation here? She was fortunately spared the prospect of a more intimate conversation with him as she murmured something stilted and meaningless and moved on to greet more of "her" guests. Even Lady Jersey was here, her lively eyes agog with curiosity, and the smiling, urbane Count De Brasselle who had questioned her so closely about the Bonapartes. Which of these smiling, civilized men was the Assassin? Was it Dominic himself?

Suddenly the tiny scar on the inside of her thigh seemed

to tingle and throb, and if she had not been surrounded by people she would have fled in horror and blind panic. Even the dark streets outside seemed safer and more friendly than this glittering mob of fashionable people. But she was given no chance to do so for suddenly Dominic sauntered up, taking her hand and squeezing it intimately as he carried her off from under the noses of three determined dowagers, one of whom professed to have met the Viscount Stanbury's mother and thought that that gave her the right to ask far too many blunt questions.

"I thought you needed rescuing, my love!" Coldly he smiled down at her. "May I get you something to drink? Some champagne, perhaps, to put the sparkle back in your eyes?"

She was sickened by his duplicity and the touch of his fingers as they slid up her arm to hold it possessively—and tightly enough so that she could not break away.

"You will pardon me, my lord, if I prefer not to drink with my father's murderer!"

The grip of his fingers grew painful, and she thought she heard him draw in a long breath.

"So you know?"

"Is that all you have to say?" she hissed furiously, suddenly oblivious of the roomful of people around them. "Yes —I know everything! Did you think I would not find out? This farce between us will not last long, I can promise you that!"

"Keep your voice down!" he said in a harsh, deadly whisper between gritted teeth. "Because if you do not I'll find ways of silencing you, my dear, scheming little wife! You have as much to gain as I have for continuing with this *farce,* as you call it, and you'd best remember that."

He halted a passing footman and took a brimming glass of champagne from the tray he carried—toasting her with it in what must have appeared to be a loving gesture to everyone who watched them. Still holding her arm, he touched the glass to his lips and then held it against hers.

"Why not drink to a new arrangement between us? This time, at least, we both have our eyes open. And if you do not drink," he muttered savagely under his breath, "I'll be forced to pour the contents of this glass down your throat!"

She drank and forced herself to smile as she whispered back into his coldly watching face, "I drink to your death, you despicable, murdering *assassin!*" She was rewarded by the sudden narrowing of his eyes as the muscles in his face seemed to tauten.

"So now we know how we stand," he said quietly the next instant and took her off with him to meet more people.

They knew where they stood—and played the game of keeping up appearances for the rest of the night and into the early hours of the morning, when the last yawning guest had left.

By this time Marisa was almost too weary to be able to keep on her feet. She had expected and dreaded this moment, but now she was too dizzy from too much champagne and too little sleep to be able to face another confrontation.

Dominic was yawning, too, and the first thing he did when Danvers began to lock the massive front door was to grimace and shrug his shoulders out of his tightly fitting coat.

Marisa started to turn away, hoping he would let her alone, but his hand closed over hers as she touched the stair rail.

"You did well tonight," he drawled, his eyes heavy-lidded. "But then you always were a good little actress."

She shook her head tiredly and, starting to climb the stairs, she pulled her hand from under his.

"And you did as well as usual, too, sir. But there's no reason to keep up a pretense any longer, is there? If you'll excuse me, I should like to seek my bed."

He climbed the stairs beside her, and in spite of her exhausted state of mind and body Marisa felt herself grow tense inside. Surely he would not—*she* could not bear it!

Looking almost pathetically defiant, although she could not know it, she turned to face him at the door to her room. And he made her an elaborate, mocking bow.

"You need not fear that I'll break down your door, my dear. *My* rooms are across the hall from yours—although we must have that remedied tomorrow. It would not do to have the servants wonder why we sleep so far apart." And then, turning on his heel he left her, and relief mingled with surprise in her mind at his having let her off so easily.

Marisa was far too worn out to try and think further just then, and in spite of all that she had been through, she slept soundly. But her waking, at an hour long past noon, was far from pleasant, for instead of Simmons's familiar face leaning over her with her tray, she found herself looking into a pair of coolly appraising grey eyes, giving her back her own sleep-ruffled appearance and no more.

He waited until he was sure she was awake and then, with a contemptuous flick of his fingers, sent a folded sheet of notepaper fluttering down to land on the sheets she had quickly and instinctively pulled up to her neck.

"You don't need to send any private notes to your aunt, my love, since we'll be calling on her this evening—if *she* does not come posting over here first. And as for warning the noble duke, your sponsor—you should have asked me first, and I would have told you that I came up here after seeing him."

Marisa did not stop to wonder how he had intercepted the note she had given to Mrs. Willoughby. He might have done *that,* but his last, casually thrown out statement had to be a lie!

The drowsiness she had felt upon first opening her eyes was banished by the rage that now swept through her, and she sat up, eyes glinting stormily as they clashed with his.

"And now I know for sure what a—"

"Be careful what you say," he reminded her harshly, dropping his sarcastic pretense at affection. "I didn't say we fell on each other's necks, he and I. But I was fortunate enough to meet with him alone for his latest friend, this chevalier, was unaccountably away. It was a more equal meeting than our last—did he tell you of it, I wonder?"

There was a strange note in Dominic's voice that sent a shiver up her spine, bringing back forcibly into her mind all that she knew and had heard about him. And guessed. . . . She was alone with him and suddenly afraid, neither knowing nor understanding what he was about this time. Marisa remembered that Philip had been suddenly summoned to Cornwall, and she thought of the bad blood between them.

The direction her thoughts had begun to take made her face go pale.

"You are a monster!" she whispered, and he laughed as if she had said something to amuse him.

"We monsters are created—by other men, madam! But I think you exaggerate, as you are prone to do." His eyes raked coldly over her, taking in every detail. The thin shift she had worn to bed because she was too tired to change into her pretty lawn nightgown and the sheet which she had unconsciously let drop so that she was almost naked from the waist up. "You have been quite practical up to this point, if a trifle foolhardy at times. But now that we are thrown into this situation together, there's no reason why we should not rub along together quite tolerably, until the need for pretense is over. If you will forgo your sense of the dramatic, we might even reach some temporary truce. You see, you need my protection as much as I need the façade that you will help me present."

She did not—would not ever—unnderstand him! And even while Marisa's confused thoughts chased themselves around her brain, he rose from the foot of her bed, his face a guarded mask.

"Think about what I have said. And please. No more notes begging to be rescued! They will only embarrass us both. I will expect you downstairs in about an hour. That will give you sufficient time, I hope? Au revoir, my dear viscountess!"

There were many times during the days that followed when Marisa longed for Philip's comforting presence. She did not know why he stayed away so long or even if he were sick or wounded. She felt isolated and friendless, in spite of the large horde of acquaintances that always seemed to surround her now. And there was Dominic, the American privateer captain who had first ravished and then even worse seduced her, transformed suddenly into an English lord. An unwanted and unlooked-for husband who did not, fortunately, force his attentions upon her in private, although she was forced to endure them in public.

She hated him—and her hate grew and fed upon itself. She would have liked to see a sword thrust through his body many times, until he dropped dead at her feet, but they were bound together, in one way or another, by the forced ceremony that had taken place so many months ago in France. Until she heard from the duke or from Philip, she had no choice but to submit.

Marisa's Aunt Edmée, as much dismayed as she, had not much to say when she was confronted by her former lover. She was an eminently practical woman and enjoyed her position in London society—certainly she did not want some of her behaviors, while she had been in France, made public. And since Dominic had threatened just that, in a terse and extremely unpleasant interview that they had together, she held her peace and advised Marisa to do the same.

"Until," she said when her niece stormed and wept with frustration, "something happens to release us all from this predicament." But Edmée herself did not know what aid they could expect, or where it would come from. There was the duke of Royse, of course, but *he* had not sent them any word nor shown his hand yet, and Philip had still not come back to London, while his father was supposedly in Bath with the Prince of Wales.

And in the meantime they had some function to attend every evening, and Marisa watched Tom Drummond sulk while Sally made it clear that *she* was Dominic's mistress. It had already become known that Marisa and Dominic had a "fashionable" marriage, with each of them going their own way when they were not appearing together in public. And yet Marisa was more than ever sure she was being watched, by whom or for what reason she did not know, and the thought only made her more frightened so that she began to feel she was existing in a trance.

Then, when things started to happen, they happened all at once. The first inkling that Marisa had that something might actually happen to change her tense existence was when her aunt whispered to her one day that she had heard from Philip. He and his father would both be returning to London within the week, and Philip had implied that he must see her and talk with her.

"I'll arrange it. I don't know how, yet, but we will contrive something," Edmée said consolingly.

Marisa's heart had already begun to beat furiously with a mixture of excitement and apprehension. Dominic could not stop her from meeting Philip! During the past two or three days, he had hardly appeared in the house, and when he did and she happened to see him, he seemed preoccupied, forgetting even to bait her. She heard from Sally that the two of them went often to the Damnation Club. 'He is gambling away all *my* money,' Marisa thought angrily. He had no *real* right to either the money that the duke had deposited in her name nor to the title he had denied all these years and now carried off so casually. But what was he doing here? What was his real motive in coming to England?

She might never have found out, Marisa was to reflect bitterly later, if not for the Count di Chiara, who almost forced himself upon her one day when she had gone riding in the park with Sally, who insisted that there was no reason after all that they could not remain friends, was there?

"After all, dearest, you had already told me your marriage was arranged for your protection from that horrible Boney!" Lady Repton shuddered delicately but continued to turn her saucy, amused eyes upon her friend. "And since *you* are madly in love with Philip Sinclair—what difference does it make? We are all quite *modern* these days, I hope! And I find your Dominic quite fascinating. I'll be obliging and keep him busy enough so that *you* can go your way!"

Sally's directness left Marisa with a confused mixture of emotions that she had not time to begin to sort out. Just then a dashing phaeton was brought alongside Sally's new curricle, and the handsome count begged the honor of being able to converse with the viscountess. But it was at Sally that he looked, his eyes imploring, and despite Marisa's protests she whispered with a twinkle, "Why not? The poor man is positively dying from love of you! I vow that's all I hear when I happen to meet him. Better to talk with him, my love, and set him straight—if that is really what you *want* to do! I will set you down here, where there is no one about, and you can stroll with him in private—and then I will come back for you again in, say, a half hour?"

Marisa was not given time for more objections, and before she quite realized what had happened she was walking alongside the persistent count, whose face, once they were alone, had turned hard and urgent.

"You have been avoiding me." It was not a question but an abrupt statement. And before Marisa could speak, he went on in a low, furious tone, "I have asked myself why? Why? Is it because your husband showed up so unexpectedly? But that is not reason enough—for he allows you a great deal of freedom, does he not? And now that you have a foot in the other camp, so to speak, I have been wondering—"

"You have no right to wonder! I told you the last time we met that I was not prepared to risk my life for some silly game of politics. I said I would try to find out what I could, but it's become too dangerous. I've been warned, even threatened—and worse! They suspect me. I tell you! And I will not be this Assassin's next victim, no matter where my loyalties may lie—no one can expect it of me!"

"By whom, madame? Who has warned you and threatened you? Even that much might prove useful—among your gay émigré friends, which ones? Or was it your husband himself?"

Marisa gave a sudden gasp and stared at him, while the count nodded in a satisfied fashion. "Ah yes, it stands to reason! He frequents the same places that *they* do, and when he broke out of the prison at Brest, it was with two royalist spies. He is working with them, then—for reasons of revenge, perhaps, or for money while he plays at being an English viscount. Do you pretend that you did not know— or at least suspect? Why do you think that even those here in England who are his sworn enemies have not touched him yet? Honor among thieves, eh?" Question after question shot at her, some of them hardly needing an answer, all of them combining to make her head reel with their implications.

At last Marisa recovered enough of her usual spirit to say quietly, "You need not act like an—interrogator, count!

And in any case, if you did not need something from me, you would not be here. So you need not try to bully me because you will only make me stubborn if you do! And you must make yourself clearer, first, before I can understand what it is you want from me *now*."

He swore under his breath and stopped upon the path, suddenly closing his hands over her arms. "My God! Is it possible that you do not yet understand? The royalists keep plotting, and they have tried before. But this time we have reason to believe that they are going all out. A Bourbon prince will lead them, *we've heard*, and they plan to infiltrate into France on all sides—many of them have done so already! Do you realize what it means? Murder—chaos! A return to the Terror while everyone suspects the other. Bonaparte is France's hero, its only hope for stability and glory. And not only France's, but the rest of Europe, too. We've had the cursed English walk over us and sneer at us calling us 'foreigners' in our own countries for far too long! Will you sit back and let him be assassinated? *Will* you? And especially after he's protected you? The regard he has for you?"

Marisa almost winced as the count bent his inflamed face towards her. It was true that she had almost forgotten— had tried to forget, in fact, being far too concerned with her own problems. The Count di Chiara reminded her too much of his master, the duke of Otranto, and yet, among all the things he had said there were some that puzzled her and some that needed answering. And in spite of her stay in England and the friends she had made here, she had to admit to a sneaking, covert loyalty to France as it was now under the first consul. She could not help admiring him as a general, as a diplomat, and even as a ruler, which he was, in fact. He had abolished the dreaded "émigré list," permitting those French aristocrats who wished to return to France without fear of reprisals. He had tried to be fair. She remembered Napoleon the family man, ruffling her hair in the gardens of Malmaison where he had joined the younger children in their games—and even Napoleon the would-be lover, whose gifts and attention had flattered her at first. Even on the occasion of her marriage he had thought of trying to protect her. . . .

Di Chiara must have seen the changing play of expressions on her face for his grip on her arms slackened, and he said in a softer voice, "I don't try to blame you! You are only a woman, after all, and I can understand why you must be frightened. After our last conversation, I would have left you in peace if not for what I have learned since then. Anything you can tell me without betraying yourself —that's all I ask! The smallest detail might help. You see I have reason to believe that some of them, a picked group of men, plan to return to France soon—to set their diabolical plot in motion. And your husband has a ship—you comprehend? All I need to know is when he plans to leave— and the names of those who—shall we say—disappear at the same time that he does?"

Chapter Twenty-eight

"Philip, for God's sake be careful!" Lord Anthony Sinclair's usually cheerful voice sounded strained as he watched his son pace up and down before the fire, his long shadow leaping against the far wall of the comfortably furnished room. It could be seen that young Mr. Sinclair gritted his teeth, the muscles along his jaw jumping, whereupon his father added with unwonted seriousness, "Be sensible, my boy! You know there's nothing can be done at the moment, especially with your uncle lying so sick—"

Philip swung around from his contemplation of the flames and said in a stifled voice, "Yes—and you know that *he* caused it! And now he parades himself through London playing the popinjay and bringing all the old mystery and gossip to the forefront in order to humiliate *us* and cover up his own activities! Must I stay hidden from him? I tell you, sir—"

"And I tell you again to have care! If it's your light of love you're thinking of, she'll keep. I understand Dominic's openly keeping Sally Repton as his mistress, and he's been careful enough to let everyone know of his presence in London. It will not be so easy to get rid of him as it was before, and especially not *now!* Dammit—you know very well what the doctor said! Another unpleasant shock to Leo's diseased heart, and there'll be a new duke of Royse —and it won't be *me*, nor will you have a chance then of becoming the Viscount Stanbury! I tell you, we'll let the chevalier take care of him in a duel, all right and tight and in the open. That's what your uncle said, and you were beside me to hear it."

Philip made an effort to control himself.

"The chevalier, for all his show of devotion, is very slow! Must I—"

"Durand has his reasons, as you know. And dammit, for your own sake and mine, you *must*, as you put it!"

Philip Sinclair's handsome face seemed to contort with hatred for an instant and then became smooth again.

"You will not, at least, tell me I must not go about in London merely because *he* is here? I will promise you not to put myself in his way on purpose, but beyond that I will not go!" He gave a short, bitter laugh as he added in a harder voice, "But if our paths should happen to cross I have the feeling that my bastard 'cousin' will not be too anxious to make an issue of it. I have been practicing daily with Durand, as you know, and fighting a duel with a gentleman's weapons is a different matter, you'll agree, from swinging a cutlass or a tomahawk!"

Lord Anthony, realizing he dared put no further restrictions upon his son, merely shrugged helplessly as he repeated in a heavy voice, "At least be careful! And do not make the mistake of underestimating him, for he seems to make a habit of surviving even the worst of circumstances."

But Philip, sulky and burning with humiliation, made his own plans, and in these he had the secret connivance of the Chevalier Durand, who came up to London the very next day on some mysterious "business."

Marisa knew nothing of these undercurrents. She had been shaken and puzzled by some of the things the Count di Chiara had told her, and yet when she tried to press him with questions he had given her a strange look and shrugged, reminding her they had not much time, and he must have an answer from her at once.

"If I agree—if I *try*, that is—without arousing their suspicions, can you arrange for me to be taken back to France?" She shivered in the bright sunshine. "I've had enough of England—and only if you give me your word will I agree to help you."

They had started to stroll back along the path to the edge of the promenade. Seeing Lady Repton's curricle approaching at a distance and seeing the stubborn set of his companion's mouth, the count acceded quickly. "You have my word. It will be difficult, of course, but it can be arranged. We'll help each other then, and I will contrive a meeting with you before the week is out."

There was no time for more. He bowed languishingly over her hand and had thanked Sally profusely before the two young women drove off.

Marisa had a great deal to think about during the rest of the afternoon and the day following. Sally had teased her about being absentminded and unusually flushed ever since she had her short rendezvous with di Chiara, and knowing that her friend would only keep prying if she denied it, Marisa had made some only vaguely evasive answer, while admitting that she did indeed find the count quite charming after all, but to take him as a lover was another matter.

"But why ever not, dearest?" was Sally's sly parting shot. "I have always thought that we women need variety just as men do!"

The count one day—and Philip the next. They met at her aunt's house, where everything was all a-bustle for the earl was expected up on one of his rare visits to London. It seemed so strange! After all that had taken place since that first time when Philip had picked her up, literally, off the street, and after all that had bound them together since, she felt, almost, as if they were strangers meeting.

Philip's manner was more tense and strained than usual, perhaps, but when they had been left alone in the small morning room, he came forward and took Marisa's hands, bending his head down to kiss her possessively. "My love, if you only knew how much it goes against the grain to be forced to meet you like this, in secret! Are you really well? He has not hurt you too much, has he?"

Something made her throw her head back to look directly into Philip's bright blue eyes.

"Hurt me? Not at all. He has not touched me, for we have separate rooms, and in fact, we hardly see each other except in public!" Marisa realized, with a faint sense of surprise, that she had seen nothing of her stranger-husband for two days.

"If you only knew how—tormented I've been!" he whispered against her soft curls. "I've begun to think of you as *mine* now, and I could hardly bear the thought. . . . Well, it will not matter now!" His eyes seemed to suddenly burn into hers. "Marisa, will you trust me? *Do* you trust me? I would put an end to stolen meetings between us and claim you for all the world to see as my own—*my* wife someday. We can go away together. . . ,"

Marisa blamed the sleepless night she had spent for the lack of a leaping in her pulses. How often she had imagined that Philip would say just these words to her and dreamed of her own wild response. But now she had committed herself to the Count di Chiara and *he* in his turn had promised to send her back to France. Yet here was Philip actually suggesting that they should run off somewhere. Where could they go? And how would they manage it?

Philip's hands—she had not noticed before how large and strong they were—suddenly stroked her shoulders, while his tongue sought the recesses of her mouth in a wild, passionate kiss. She remembered that he had been kind and then remembered, contrarily, how he had taken her body with none of the inhibitions he had confessed to some hours earlier; he had taken her on the very heels of that other. What did Philip *really* want of her?

And yet she yielded to his kiss until his fingers reached her breasts under her thin muslin gown, and then some instinct made her twist away.

"Someone might come in!" Her voice sounded breathless and uncertain, and Philip, too, was breathing heavily although he managed to control himself after a moment.

"It will not matter, soon, who might enter a room when we are together!"

"Philip—"

"My darling," he said triumphantly, "I have everything arranged. We will only have to play our respective parts for a few days or a few hours longer. Do you hear me? You will be free—we will both be free."

Almost everything about her meeting with Philip seemed rather blurred and not quite real afterwards. Was it possible that it had really taken place? Marisa felt quite frighteningly as if she were suspended in some kind of a vacuum with all her thoughts and emotions turned upside down. First the count—and now Philip. Both of them offering her escape for something she must perform in return. Which way to go? There was only one thing in her mind that remained unchanged, and that was her hate and her desire for revenge against the man whose borrowed name she bore and who had both ruined her and changed her whole life by his selfish intervention.

She was to have gone to the theater that night, with a party of casual acquaintances, but she cried off, using the excuse of a headache; having dismissed the sober-faced Simmons she waited a while until the house seemed quiet and then went downstairs to the room that was known as "the study." It was a rather dark and severely furnished chamber with books lining one wall and an extra-large fireplace on another. In between was a wall of windows that were always kept darkly curtained.

There was a high-backed settle in one corner of the room, set at an angle to the fireplace in which the logs had been allowed to burn low until they only glowed redly in the gloom. Marisa curled herself there, with her bare feet tucked under her, feeling almost as she had felt in the Spanish convent when she had escaped from the nuns to sneak outside into the prioress' garden just to be by herself. It was strange that she should suddenly remember that quiet and innocent part of her life, which was so far behind her now. Had she ever been a postulant, with no other thought in her mind but that of joining the sequestered order of the Carmelites? Even then, there had been that reckless disobedient side of her nature which she, and the good nuns too, had tried to curb. And this was where it had brought her—with all her illusions lost along the way!

At first, Marisa tried to read by the light of a small lamp, but the words blurred before her eyes, and she set the book aside and turned down the wick, leaving the room in semidarkness while she gazed into the red coals and tried to sort out the thoughts that whirled around in her brain.

She had almost dozed off when she heard the door open and voices speaking. Then the door closed with a thud. And while she hardly dared to breathe, trying to make herself

as small and unobtrusive as possible in her corner, she saw
Dominic walk across the room stripping off heavy riding
gloves as he did, to stand directly before the smoldering
fire as if he craved its warmth. He tossed his gloves on top
of the mantel and stood there with both hands braced
against it, his head slightly bent as he contemplated the
red-hot embers, just as Marisa herself had done a short
while ago.

There was a tautness about him that made her taut, too,
and she sat very still as she watched him while he thought
himself unobserved—the tallness of him and the width of
his shoulders, the way he stood with his legs braced apart
as if he were still on the deck of a ship. His profile was
thrown into relief by the dim, ruddy light, and it might have
been carved out of some reddish rock; it was harsh and
strong and arrogant. He might have been accounted handsome if he permitted his features to relax and smiled more
often instead of scowling or sneering—but why should such
a thought have come into her mind at all?

'We're enemies,' Marisa reminded herself and continued
to watch him even while she tried to still the forbidden
memories that his presence had suddenly set free to run
riot in her mind.

A sudden knock at the door made Marisa press the back
of her hand against her mouth. Not knowing why, she
crouched lower still in her concealed seat.

"The whiskey you asked for, my lord," Danvers pronounced in a disapproving, slightly stifled voice and
Dominic swung around from his brooding contemplation
of the fire.

"Thank you. You may set it down. No, you may give me
the tray and take yourself off to bed. I'll see myself upstairs
when I'm ready."

There was a silence after the door had closed again, and
Marisa had time to wonder why she stayed where she was,
frozen like a rabbit in a snare. Dominic walked back to the
fireplace holding a bottle in his hand. She saw him tilt it
and drink deeply, and then, without warning, his whole body
seemed to go stiff, and he wheeled around, suddenly staring
directly at her.

Marisa felt her heart start thudding uncomfortably, and she could find no words to utter as she looked back at him. With the fire's glow reflected redly in the silver mirrors of his eyes and his poised, almost waiting stance, he reminded her of a wild animal taken unawares—a dangerous predator who might too easily turn on her.

More frightening still was the fact that *he* had not spoken either. She thought he expelled his breath slowly after he had seen who it was who sat curled up in one corner of the settle, but he merely stood where he was and let his eyes travel over her, with no expression that she could read on his face except a strange kind of tiredness.

At last, no longer able to bear the suspended stillness between them, Marisa said hesitantly, "I had not—that is, I did not mean to disturb you. Only I must have fallen asleep—"

He gave a short, harsh laugh. "I must confess it surprises me to find you home this early of an evening, madam. Or were you expecting to receive a visitor? A messenger bearing good news, perhaps?"

Marisa sat up straight, and then gave a cry of pain when she discovered that one foot had gone to sleep under her. She began to rub it fiercely as a vent for her frustrated feelings. He was always sneering at her, always accusing her of something, when it was *he* who was the cause of all the pain and unhappiness in her life. And he continued to punish her and to humiliate her, but for what reason she did not know. Well, this time at least she would keep her head, and soon it would be *her* turn!

"You don't have a quick answer ready?"

"I don't choose to dignify your silly accusations with a reply, sir."

In spite of her ridiculously disheveled state and the voluminous wrapper she had huddled herself in, her words had been given with a stiff pride that took him unwillingly aback for he had fully expected her to storm and rage at him. She kept her dark gold head bent as she continued to rub her ankle, and Dominic found himself noticing that her hair had grown long enough to have a ribbon laced through it, allowing artless curls to escape to her shoulders. She looked like a child, her long, slender neck held just so and her face turned away from him sulkily. And yet he knew how much she must have learned during the past few months. And could guess at some of her instructors. She was obviously the kind of woman who had been born with the instinctive knowledge of every trick, every bit of artifice and guile she could use to gain her own ends. He remembered that she had picked his pocket on the first occasion they had met even while she had pretended to be terrified out of her wits and a few moments after that she had attempted to lead him into an ambush! And now she was playing a game of evasion, and he was sorely tempted to go to her and take her by the shoulders and shake the truth from her, shake her until her robe fell away and she lay sprawled and naked under him, the way he remembered her best. He had never met a woman yet who did not hide a whore's heart behind the most seemingly innocent smile.

He had to thrust his hands into the pockets of his buckskin breeches to prevent himself from touching her even while a jeering devil at the back of his mind urged him to take what was his and test her powers of resistance. And then he winced slightly as a jarring pain shot through his arm, and he swore under his breath. No, he didn't want her. And she had no business to be here, cozily ensconced in the room he had taken to using as his private retreat unless she had been waiting. But Christ, waiting for what? Had they meant to kill him, those unseen assailants outside the dock-front tavern, or only to wound him as they had done? What had she been expecting, his lady-wife? How much did she know?

As if she had sensed his brooding, ugly thoughts, Marisa suddenly raised her head, and he noticed detachedly that her eyes still retained their limpid golden glow. What a little hypocrite she was! And it infuriated him to remember that once, for a short while, he had thought differently.

Not knowing his thoughts, Marisa saw only the hard, forbidding look on his face. She had felt his eyes on her and had been almost afraid to lift her face to them, but now she told herself angrily that she no longer feared him for what could he do to her that he had not done already?

She put her memories behind her and thought only of what she must do to fulfill her promises to herself and to be free. She wondered at his sudden, ominous silence and the reason for the barbed, sarcastic accusations he had flung at her earlier. Mixed in with those thoughts were some of the things the Count di Chiara had said which had puzzled her and still continued to puzzle her. But she remembered now, as she forced her eyes to meet his, that they were antagonists, and he was the one man in the world she had reason to hate.

"I think my presence makes you angry and vicious," she said in a purposefully distant voice, resenting the way his eyes stripped her. "My foot had become cramped, but I think I can stand now; so, if you don't mind, I will go up to my own rooms and leave you alone."

He put his hand out, and she flinched instinctively. She heard him laugh shortly as he grasped her wrist and almost dragged her to her feet.

"I'm vicious, am I? I wonder why you would say so, little Jezebel, when I've been careful to leave you as much alone as possible. In fact, this is almost the first time when we have been entirely alone for a long time, is it not? The last time, it was 'my lord' this, and 'my lord' that, and you were just as cold and just as angry. But you yielded easily enough in the end. Is it a habit with you now, I wonder?"

She gasped as if he had struck her, and her head went back in a gesture of fierce defiance.

"The last time I did not fully know you for what you are my lord! And I was more naive in those days. You will not now find me so easily gulled as I was then by your —your clever, cruel *game* as you called it!"

"As *I* called it? By God, madam, you spread your hypocrisy too thin! You planned the little game we indulged in and thought yourself a winner at the finish, I'm sure!" She tried to break away from his grasp, and he deliberately tightened it, feeling the thin bones of her wrist almost crushed under his fingers. And at the same time his other arm, his right, had begun to throb damnably, sending shooting waves of pain all the way up into his brain, like the beginnings of a fever. He should let her go, but she had provoked him, and now he was determined to have it out with her, the little two-faced bitch! For how long did she think she could continue to play the innocent?

She had clamped her lips against the pain he was inflicting, but he saw her face go white as she stopped her struggles, swaying obligingly against him. Why was she so stubborn? Why was she *here?*

"I would have despised you less if you had been honest," he growled furiously. "I had almost become resigned to being forced into marrying, but I had time to think otherwise in that prison where your friend Fouché's men threw me. You should have told me, petite, that I was supposed to be a bridegroom in name only!"

The pain in her wrist became so intolerable that Marisa almost fainted from it. She heard his words come from a long, buzzing distance, and she struck out wildly at him with her free hand, feeling her nails draw blood.

"Stop! You're mad! I didn't—" She beat against him again, angrily and desperately, and wondered vaguely why he made no attempt to imprison her other hand as well. And then, the very next moment, she found herself free and stumbling backwards to fetch up short against the side of a table. Her bruised wrist was already aching and throbbing.

She saw him through a film of tears. *His* face, too, had paled so that the red nail-tracks she had left on him were red and bloody against his skin. He leaned with one shoulder against the wall by the fireplace and said not another word until she had, in part, begun to recover herself and her panting, sobbing breaths had slowed.

And then he said in a soft, jeering voice, "Why don't you go? Run away. A cold compress will take care of your wrist, and you may add that to the list of wrongs I've done you. The next time be more careful where you fall asleep, madame viscountess."

He could feel a slow trickle of blood down his arm, where her flailing blows had broken open the ugly knife gash he had bandaged; and now he was only anxious for her to leave him so that he could lie down and fight off the despicable weakness that threatened to overcome him.

He closed his eyes and opened them to find her still there, staring at him, one hand holding her wrist, and her eyes wide. Damn her! What did it take to drive her away? She should have fled by now.

He reached for the bottle he had left on the mantelpiece and took a drink from it, swallowing more than half its contents before he put it back. The liquor jolted through his veins, and Dominic said with deliberate crudity, "If you stay here, I will strip you naked and take you on the floor by the fire, like a whore. There will be no love in it."

"There never was, between us," she whispered back at him. "Only your lust and my ignorance. And now there's hate, and I don't care what you think of me for you know what I think of *you!* And I can thank God now that I lost the child you gave me because I would not have cared for any reminders of you and what you are!"

Whatever shock her words might have dealt him was far too quickly masked, except for a brief, sudden flare of white light in his eyes. Then it was gone, and he said indifferently, "Feeling as you do, you won't want any more such reminders of me, will you? Unless one of your lovers has already taken care of *that.* So what do you want from me now, madam? More fuel for your hate?"

"I have all I need already!" she spat back at him, as she gathered the trailing skirts of her robe up in one hand and whirled about to make for the door.

His mocking voice halted her momentarily on the threshold.

"You have left both of your slippers behind, Cinderella!"

Chapter Twenty-nine

The slippers were dropped on her, one by one. One on her face and the other on her breast, rousing her from a laudanum-induced sleep filled with dreams of writhing monsters and assassins who chased her down dark, echoing corridors that gave back her screams.

She had no strength left to scream now or even to wonder how he had got here or why he had come after all that had passed between them. A fire had been lit in her room, making it seem so warm and close that she had kicked off her coverings; and her nightrobe lay twisted about her thighs, impeding her feeble struggles which soon gave way to limp passivity.

The flimsy material of her nightrobe ripped, leaving her body bare and vulnerable and he lay between her thighs, with his weight holding her down.

"There's no love in this," he whispered against her neck in a slurred, husky voice, repeating what he had said before. "And I do not even know why I feel the need for your body, you fickle gypsy wench."

Marisa's eyelids felt as heavy as her limbs, but she half-opened them and saw how the firelight turned his skin to bronze. She saw also the stark white of a blood-stained bandage wrapped around his upper arm. She moved then, instinctively, and his body moved with hers, poising and penetrating, while his mouth abruptly covered her parted lips, stifling her half-formed question.

Her mind was too tired and too drowsy to continue to have any control over her body and soon stopped asking any questions as he moved slowly against her and inside her. She began to feel as if she were still dreaming as his mouth

315

moved across her soft cheek and down the side of her neck, to stop there, kissing the pulse that beat madly under his lips.

"There's no love in this," Marisa heard herself whispering back into the stillness that was broken only by his breathing and hers. "I hate you, Dominic Challenger!"

He slipped his hand between their bodies and caressed her breasts and then kissed them as she arched up against him. Between kisses he said softly, "Hate's as strong an emotion as love, my sweet gypsy bitch. Show me how much you hate me."

And even while her mind rebelled, her body had gone beyond its control and showed him, in a language all its own, drowning reason and memory as wave after wave washed over her and she felt herself sucked under, not wanting to surface to reality until fulfillment brought her there at last, and she lay limp and shuddering and weak and from there drifted almost naturally into sleep.

This time there were no dreams to disturb her, and Marisa slept until afternoon, waking with a strange ache and emptiness between her thighs. And then her returning memory brought revulsion and shame and a renewal of her hatred.

At least he had had the decency to leave before she woke. Oh, God, why had she taken those laudanum drops to help her sleep?

Simmons came, wooden-faced, in response to her tug on the bell cord, and murmured, "My lord gave orders that you were to be allowed to sleep as long as you wished. And Mrs. Willoughby took the liberty of canceling your morning appointments, my lady. On his lordship's orders, I believe."

So all the servants knew—and even her companion. He had made sure of it, of course! Did he also think to make sure of her? Marisa gritted her teeth but said nothing to satisfy the curiosity she sensed lurking behind her maid's expressionless façade. In as ordinary a tone as she could manage, she ordered her bath—no, she would not care for breakfast, only a cup of chocolate—and her curricle for an hour later. His lordship, she discovered without asking, had already left the house, and he hadn't said when they could expect him back.

All the better, for she did not want to set eyes on him again, and she no longer cared to look for explanations for certain statements made by the Count Di Chiara and by Dominic himself. She did not *want* to know more about him —what she knew already was enough.

Recklessly, ignoring the distraught Mrs. Willoughby's tearful objections and the wringing of her hands, Marisa insisted upon driving herself to her destination. And no, she would *not* take a groom with her. She did not care what people thought! Over her shoulder, as she walked down the stairs trailed by the openmouthed Simmons and her companion, she ordered her abigail to pack some clothes for her—two or three bandboxes would be sufficient, and she needed only those garments that were suitable for traveling in—and her jewel case.

"But—oh my goodness. My dearest child, surely you do not know what you are saying! Traveling? But where will you be going? You—"

Mrs. Willoughby had followed her outside, her voice querulously raised as Marisa thanked the pop-eyed groom who had been holding the restive horses for her and sprang into the seat, taking the ribbons in her gloved hands.

She leaned over then and smiled as she said sweetly, "Why, I am going to run away with Mr. Sinclair! Shouldn't you have been expecting it?"

And before either one of the flustered women could say another word, she dramatically cracked the whip that was looped over her wrist, and the curricle went bowling down the street, sending several urchins scattering before it.

Marisa drove directly to Lord Anthony's house on Portland Place, still buoyed up by her angry, uncaring mood. One of the footmen, polishing the brass railing outside, was called upon imperiously to hold her matched bays and walk them up and down if they seemed restive. He obeyed as if thunderstruck, and she walked up the steps and rang the bell.

If the stately butler who answered its summons was just as surprised and stunned as the footman in the street, he showed no signs of it as he informed the young lady that Mr. Philip was not in, but his lordship was just up and taking breakfast. He seemed uncertain as to whether he should let her in or not, but when she said impatiently that he should tell Lord Anthony that the Viscountess Stanbury was here and wished to see him most urgently, he opened the door wider and bowed her inside, giving a quelling glance to the footman who had stopped walking the horses to stare.

His eyes still bloodshot, the Baron Lydon, attired in his dressing gown for what he had thought to be a breakfast taken by himself, was both taken aback and intrigued when his visitor was announced. He saw from the expression on his butler's face that the poor man had not known what else to do—and waved him out impatiently while at the same time rising with as much dignity as his informal attire would permit.

"My dear—er—child! 'Pon my word, if I'd had any idea—"

"But you could not have had, for I only made up my mind to come here less than a half hour ago," Marisa responded composedly. Only the sparkling of her golden eyes and the high flush on her cheeks betrayed her inner agitation.

Lord Anthony—she must get used to thinking of him as Philip's *father*—offered her a chair, but she shook her head and burst out, before her resolution deserted her, "I beg your pardon, my lord, for this—unwarranted intrusion, but I must find Philip, and—give him an answer to something he asked me. I—it has become impossible for me to spend another night *there,* under the same roof with *him*. And I cannot go to my aunt for she's afraid of him, so—oh, I've no doubt this is very shocking to you, but I have the feeling that the duke would not be so very displeased with the step I have taken."

"Yu've left him? Egad! Does he know? Well, I don't suppose so, or you wouldn't be here, eh?" Trying to collect his wits, Lord Anthony, caught between several fires, could think of nothing else to say except to blurt out the truth.

"Damn. I don't know what to say, but—but Philip isn't

here! Went out last night with the chevalier, who arrived at
a devilishly late hour. Said they were going to the Club—er
—you'll know which one I mean, I'm sure. He's probably
there still, and if you have the entrée. . . ." His words
trailed off, and he offered belatedly, "I'll escort you there,
m'dear, if you'll give me a few moments."

But Marisa, in her tensed up mood, did not want to wait;
nor did she really want Lord Anthony to accompany her.
She wanted to see Philip—and if he were still at the Damnation Club, well, she would beard the lions in their den—
and be damned to them!

And so, still driving herself, Marisa managed to negotiate her way through the busy streets, not caring a whit for
the glances that were thrown at her or even some of the
comments made by would-be gallants who saw a well-
dressed young woman driving a curricle unchaperoned.

She tried not to spring her horses, keeping to a comparatively sedate pace until she had reached the quiet street
where the club was situated. And only then, when she
caught sight of its innocuous facade, for all the world like
a discreet town house set among others of its kind, did she
start to wonder at her own urgency and what she was
doing here. Perhaps they were closed during the day—and
how could she be certain that Philip was still here? If he
wasn't—what would she do next?

She could not give herself time to think. Flinging the
reins and a silver coin to a wise-eyed street urchin who
seemed to have sprung up from nowhere, Marisa marched
up the shallow steps and used the grotesquely shaped
knocker. There was almost too slight a pause before an
invisible, oiled panel set in its upper half slid open, and
she felt herself being regarded.

"I've been here before," she blurted out before she lost
her courage. "I must see Madame De L'Aigle. You may
tell her—" But before she had time to finish, the door had
already swung open on well-oiled hinges, and Marisa
stepped inside, blinking her eyes to get them used to the
dimness of the small hallway.

"This way, Madame Viscountess," a soft voice said, and
she followed the tall shape of the man who seemed to

recognize her without an effort. She thought wryly, 'So much for our disguises!'

She was led into the small crimson and gold parlor where madame usually held court, and it did not look so very different in the daytime with a fire leaping in the grate and all the lamps lit—except that it was empty.

Marisa turned around, and the man who had brought her here bowed and murmured in French that madame would be with her shortly. She didn't remember seeing him before, but then how should she? Who looked at servants? He was tall and largely made and wore unrelieved black except for a plain white shirt, and his face had a strange pallor to it. . . . But Marisa had time to notice nothing else for he left, closing the door behind him; and *she* was left quite alone with her thoughts and her doubts.

She was still staring at the door, frowning with indecision, when a slight sound behind her made her whirl about, to confront "la Marquise" herself, Madame De L'Aigle without her elaborately powdered wig—hair drawn up under a pretty lace and ribboned cap. Even without the makeup she affected for the evenings the woman's face was still curiously smooth and unlined. Her dress was of silk, in the shepherdess style that Marie-Antoinette had made so popular, and her eyes glittered with the same penetrating look Marisa remembered from other occasions.

"So you came by yourself. I had begun to wonder if you would." And then, catching sight of Marisa's startled face Madame laughed—a curiously harsh sound when taken with the soft huskiness of her voice. "La, child! Don't look so frightened! I came through a sliding door that's concealed behind the wall hangings. It is always useful to have more than one mode of exit when one runs the kind of establishment that I do!" Before Marisa had the chance to say a word, madame laughed again, but more softly this time. "Well—which one of them have you come seeking? They are both here, but I have kept them separated. Have you made your choice yet?"

Marisa paled. "I was told that Philip had spent the night here—"

"And so he did. Quite alone, too. Your husband came

this morning—and in a very ill humor, too. Ah!" Madame De L'Aigle suddenly stiffened and held a finger to her lips, although Marısa had heard nothing. With a strange undercurrent to her husky voice the Frenchwoman continued in a whisper, "Would you like to make sure that you'll be safe? They are about to leave, I think, for the coast. Be very quiet now, and you shall see for yourself."

This room must be full of hidden doors and sliding panels! Madame grasped Marisa's wrist in a surprisingly strong grip and drew her along to the door where she pushed aside a portion of the velvet wall hangings to display a long and very narrow slit set into the wall alongside the door itself, permitting one to see out into the passageway.

Marisa kept very quiet as she had been asked to—partly from surprise and shock and partly because she recognized at least two of the men who now walked down the stairway, talking among themselves. They were all unmasked at this hour of the afternoon. The Breton, George Caduodal, had an air of suppressed excitement and anticipation about him. He talked quickly, almost stammering his words, but she caught the names "Moreau" and "Pichegru," remembering both as trusted generals on Napoleon's staff. "You're sure about the ship?" The Breton paused to turn his head upward towards his companion, and Dominic, looking grim and not at all excited as the others were, inclined his head. "If I weren't, gentlemen, I would not be here. But there's no time to waste if you want to catch the evening tide tomorrow."

"And our friend Durand will be there to see us off. You're sure you won't come with us, Meurice?"

She hadn't noticed the chevalier among them, but there he was as the group paused for an instant.

"Not yet—I do not think so. But who knows? At any rate, I am with you in spirit, my friends, as I'm sure you all know. And I shall be with you at least as far as the coast. . . ."

They passed out of view then, and somewhere in the distance there came the sound of a door opening and then closing with a thud.

The wall hanging was dropped back into place, and

Marisa turned to face Madame De L'Aigle, who stood regarding her with an enigmatic smile upon her smooth, unlined face.

"So now you're sure of what you were uncertain of before. And I think you have chosen wisely. You may look like your mother, but you are not as—romantic and impractical as she was, are you, my dear?"

Marisa felt as if she were floundering in a morass, as her eyes opened widely.

"My mother?"

"Ah yes—I keep forgetting you were only a child at the time. I knew her. We were friends until she decided to take my husband as her lover. And in the end they went bravely to the guillotine together—so I was told. For you see, I was fortunate enough to have escaped by then."

The ageless face seemed to crumble for an instant, and Marisa was taken aback by the look of hate and destruction that suddenly showed through. She did not know what instinct made her whisper, "Was it *you* who set them on me? Because of—my mother?"

Madam De L'Aigle faced her closely, and wrinkles showed for the first time around her eyes as she laughed.

"You're more clever than your mother was—but you possess the same easy nature, I think. If she had been born into different circumstances she would have been a whore—and so would you. But then perhaps the upstart Corsican who treats France as if it were his kingdom would not have noticed you. Did you think no one knew? Or wondered? Yes—I thought it was a fine piece of irony to set your own husband on you—and you should be grateful to me that you were let off so lightly. If it had been—the other one—you might not be standing here before me today. But I think you have enough of your father in you to be sensible—and that is why you came here today, is it not? It's just as well for your sake. And if you're wise, you'll get away quickly—do you understand? You have been fishing in waters too deep for you, little one, and you're lucky that you got off with a warning. You'll be safe when you're far away!"

Marisa had begun to back off, terrified in spite of herself

by the almost toneless voice that dripped venom, scalding her every nerve. And then the door was flung open, and Philip stood there, and she flew to him while behind her the woman laughed again as she said in her husky voice, "Take her away with you, mon cher. I think she has no stomach for all this intrigue!"

It seemed like a miracle when she was out in the sunshine again, Philip's arm still around her, and his voice murmuring soothingly that she must no longer be afraid, that he would look after her from now on, and soon she would be free of both fear and entanglement.

"But she—you don't know what she said! What she—"

"Shh, my love, it doesn't matter! She's a half-crazy fanatic with a grudge against everyone else—forget her! Now that you have come to me of your own accord, we can start our life together, and be damned to everyone else! We'll go away to the Indies for a while, until the talk dies down. And then when we return to England, you'll be my wife."

Her earlier mood of bravado mixed with anger was now submerged by fear, and Marisa did not argue, not even when Philip dropped her off at the house in Grosvenor Square, promising to call for her within the hour.

Dominic would not be here—that much knowledge was enough—and she tried to blot all the other thoughts out of her mind as she made sure that her earlier orders had been followed and her bags were packed for traveling.

There was one more thing. Recklessly, she sat down and wrote a letter to the Count di Chiara telling him everything she had learned. She sent the sealed letter off by a puzzled but well-bribed groom who swore to deliver it to the count himself.

After that she had only to wait for Philip and the freedom he offered her.

Chapter Thirty

"We're going to Cornwall," Philip said, making the announcement with an assuredness that was new to his normally easygoing manner. He squeezed Marisa's hand as she turned to look inquiringly at him. "I have to see my uncle, dearest. And he wants to see you. To see *us*, together. He owns a vast estate in Jamaica, and he's offered to deed it to us both—don't you see what that will mean? A few years in exile, perhaps, but we'll live in luxury and will have slaves to wait on you. And then when you're free, we'll be married and return to England as man and wife. As far as any of the other planters *there* are concerned, we'll be married already! So you see, there's no need for you to worry at all. I'll look after you, and I'll make you happy, I swear I will!"

She had lapsed into a strange, almost dazed mood ever since she had made up her mind to take this step and run away with Philip. To be free, finally, of fear and intrigue—to be free of the shadow of the mysterious Assassin and even the Count di Chiara—to be free . . . but was she? What would Dominic do when he returned to London from his mysterious errand to the coast and found her gone?

Philip seemed jubilant and not at all afraid of consequences. Their journey was accomplished at almost breakneck speed, with only a few stops to change horses and one night spent at a posting inn. Here he obtained a separate room for her, announcing casually that her abigail had met with an accident along the way. *She* was the Viscountess Stanbury, and he was her cousin. They traveled in a crested coach with armed outriders to guard them, and neither the innkeeper nor his wife made any demur, but sent their own daughter up to act as maid to the viscountess.

325

Marisa slept uneasily, for all that she was completely tired out and drained of all energy after the mental and physical strain she had been through during the past twenty-four hours. And all too soon it was morning and time to set out again with Philip sitting beside her, his mood of suppressed excitement making her wonder. . . . However, she did not question him again, and apart from a few solicitous comments about her comfort, he seemed satisfied to remain silent, wrapped in his own thoughts.

Why did she suddenly feel so emptied of all emotion? She was escaping—and with Philip. She ought to feel elated! 'I really don't know what I want,' Marisa thought tiredly and leaned her head back against the squabs, closing her eyes so that Philip would think she was sleeping. Suddenly Madame De L'Aigle's face swam before her eyes. It was contorted with the vicious expression she had seen on it that last time when she had talked about her mother. Could Madame herself be the Assassin? She knew everyone, and she had reason to hate. . . . And then suddenly she saw Dominic's face and heard his harsh laugh in her ears. Unconsciously, she stiffened. Was it *he?* The same man who had branded her and then ravished her body so cruelly—but why? She was sure in her own mind, and the thought only made her feel revulsion at herself for having let him take her that night when he had mockingly called her Cinderella and brought himself to her bed along with her dropped slippers. But then who was "the other" that Madame had talked about? Oh—it was all too much for her, and she didn't really want to think. Better keep her mind firmly fixed upon the future and Philip.

She must have slept after all, for the next thing she knew was that he was shaking her shoulder lightly.

"We're almost there now. Can't you smell the sea?"

And it was only then, with an unpleasant shock, that Marisa remembered Cornwall, too, was on the coast.

There was an air of waiting about the old stone house with its blind, mullioned windows turned towards the mist that even now came creeping up about it like an old friend. She could not like it nor this part of the country with its ancient, cruel history and its tales of witches and goblins. The mist came up from the sea and spilled over craggy cliffs; it flowed across moors and filtered between old, lichened trees until it reached the parkland that surrounded the crouching house; it flowed across it eagerly as if with a rush. And it followed their coach and overtook it, like a milky white river that deadened even the sound of the horses' hoofs.

Marisa was glad all over again of the four surly-looking, taciturn men who had escorted them all this way and now took charge of the horses while Philip sprang down and came to help her alight.

How still and silent it all seemed! Even the old butler who opened the front door spoke in a subdued voice, and there were no bright lights to welcome them, only a dim lamp to light up the gloom of the hallway. It was dusk. Perhaps they lit the lamps late here.

Tired, confused thoughts spun around in her brain, and she clung tightly to Philip's arm as they went inside.

"My uncle? . . ." Philip said quickly, and Simms shook his head in a somber way.

"The doctor left only about an hour ago, Mr. Philip. Sent away, he was. Like most of the new servants. My lord duke's orders. And half the house is closed up, but there are rooms kept ready for you, sir, and for my lady, in case you came."

A very old woman, her grey, shapeless skirts rustling with starch, had come soundlessly up behind the butler as he spoke, and Marisa could not help starting. From under her white cap a pair of button-bright eyes stared with the unabashed curiosity of old age, and when she actually seemed to smile, her thin lips seemed to disappear among the seams and wrinkles of her face.

"So Mr. Philip's back home at last! You'll remember me, Mr. Philip? 'Find me Parsons,' you used to say when you was hurt. 'She'll know what to do.' And I always did, didn't I? I mind me the time when *he,* that young savage from the colonies, near killed you, and it was Parsons who bandaged up all your cuts and took care of your bruises—"

"Parsons! Of course!" Philip broke in with a forced tone of lightness while his eyes sought Simms's inquiringly.

Simms permitted himself the slightest shrug. "My lord duke's orders, sir. He didn't want any of those young, flighty maids from the village waiting on the Viscountess Stanbury.

'Parsons is loyal to the Sinclairs,' he said. 'Bring her back.' And so I did, sir."

"Yes—yes—my lord duke knows how loyal I am." The old woman nodded in a satisfied manner. "And glad I was to come back, too, not that my lord didn't see to it I had a nice fat pension—"

"Yes, yes," Simms said in a harried fashion. He looked apologetically at Marisa, who stood still and wide-eyed. "Parsons was lady's maid to—hrmph—the late duchess, my lady. And housekeeper after that. She knows her way around and has kept your chamber aired and the bed freshly made. If you wouldn't mind—"

"Of course she wouldn't mind! Would you, love?" Seeming to recover his composure, Philip gave Marisa's arm a slight, reassuring squeeze. "Look here," he said in a lower voice, "I'd best find out how my uncle is, and what has been going on these past few days. I'll have your bags taken up directly, and after you've refreshed yourself, we'll meet in the small salon, shall we? Parsons will see you have everything you need and show you the way, won't you, Parsons?"

The woman smiled again and bobbed in a rather stiff curtsy, and Marisa had no alternative but to follow her upstairs, while Philip was immediately engaged in a low-voiced conversation with Simms.

Why had Philip abandoned her to the care of this old crone? Marisa tried to smile and be pleasant to the woman who kept eying her in such a strange, almost sly fashion, but Parsons seemed determined to dwell on the past as she walked about the enormous room, lighting a fire and pulling aside the curtains of the old-fashioned four-poster bed as she explained almost ghoulishly that this was the very room where the late duchess had spent her last years dying in that same bed while the duke sat downstairs waiting.

Marisa shuddered and tried to turn her conversation away to other, lighter channels, but when her bags were brought up the old woman insisted on unpacking them and putting everything away, while she continued to talk in her cracked voice.

What a lot she knew about the whole family! All their secrets—so much about the past that she might never have learned, for Philip was always reticent and Dominic silent on the subject.

In the end, fascinated in spite of her initial repugnance, Marisa sat brushing her hair at the massive dressing table and listening to the story of the Irish lady who had been the duke's wife, and who, on her return from America with her mind unhinged, had been condemned to spend her last years locked up in her room with the duke her only visitor.

"And he always sent me out when he came in, of course," Parsons said with something of the old resentment creeping into her voice to be replaced by an almost salacious note when she added, "She always took a turn for the worse after, although I'm sure Mr. Leo—the duke, that is—tried to talk her out of it. Or into telling the truth—who knows? After her son was sent away, she was easier to manage—became real quiet and cried a lot. But she hadn't brought him up proper, and that was a fact! I remember when my lord duke and Sir Anthony came back here from London. It was right after *she* died, and *he'd* been put in jail for getting mixed up in that nasty rebellion they had in Ireland in '97—or was it '98? They should have let him hang along with some of the others, but he was a Sinclair by name, at least, and in spite of all the threats he made they arranged for him to be pressed into the navy. And ay, that was a mistake, that was, for he didn't die, did he? Only showed up again to make more trouble and put my lord on his deathbed. But the French gentleman will see to *him*, won't he? Will you be marrying Master Philip then or living *here* like she did? I'd look after you, you know. They always call for Parsons when there's trouble in the family!"

Suddenly, the room seemed far too stifling. A large black cave, with the fire throwing grotesque shadows on the wall and the single lamp on the dressing table far too dim. Marisa's silver-backed brush fell to the dresser top with a clatter that made her own nerves jump, and she had to fight to appear calm as she rose to her feet.

"I think I'm ready to go downstairs, now. Philip—Mr. Sinclair is expecting me."

For one frightening moment she thought that the old woman might actually refuse and lock her into the room. She pursed her mouth and she cocked her head to one side as she regarded Marisa suspiciously.

"They wouldn't have served dinner yet, and if you're tired I could bring yours up on a tray. My lady never went downstairs—he didn't want her to."

"But I am not the late duchess. I am—Mr. Philip's lady," Marisa said with a desperate burst of inspiration. "And he's waiting for me. He would be angry if you made me late."

At that, grumbling under her breath, Parsons stood aside from the door and let her go. And Marisa, groping her way down the dimly lit staircase, had to control the nervous shivers that chased themselves down her spine while she managed to walk slowly instead of running panic-stricken.

'I will *not* spend a night in that room nor another minute with *her!*' she vowed silently. 'I'll share Philip's room if I have to—and be damned to gossip! The Duke won't mind—he'd only chuckle—if he isn't too ill to know what's going on. I must tell Philip so and be firm even if he laughs at me for being afraid of an old woman's tales of the past. . . .'

Why had she ever agreed to come here? To this crouching, ugly house surrounded by fog and to a dying old man who continued to plot and plan all their lives for them, even from his bed. And where was the ubiquitous chevalier who was not supposed to join his friends when they secretly crossed to France? 'And I betrayed them. Suppose they find out before I can leave here?' She was seized with a mad impulse to run, to lose herself in the blank whiteness outside, and then, as if in answer to the frightening turn her thoughts had taken, there came a shout followed by a cry so bloodcurdling that Marisa's knees almost buckled under her.

She had fortunately reached the bottom of the staircase, and she stayed there clutching at the rail so tightly that she thought her fingers might snap from the strain.

Someone rushed past her—she felt the wind of his passage without knowing who he was—and sheer terror at being left alone here in the dark hallway made her follow, running blindly and holding her trailing skirts with shaking fingers.

The duke's rooms were downstairs. He had had them moved while she was on her last visit here because he did not relish being carried up and down the stairs like a cripple or a senile old man. The door stood open, and as she followed Simms in—only now realizing that it was he—she heard Philip say in a choked voice,

"Oh, my God! This is murder!"

Marisa almost fell over the threshold, only to be brought up short by the sight that met her eyes.

The duke's chair had fallen on its side, and he lay half in and half out of it, his face turned blue and contorted, his sightless eyes staring up at the ornately carved ceiling. Sprawled half over his body lay the body of the chevalier, still bleeding from a deep wound in his chest—a sword clenched in the slowly relaxing fingers of one hand.

"Murder!" Philip said again, and this time his voice cracked from emotion. "You murdered them both, and you'll pay for it!"

"My mother was murdered by slow, painful degrees. *This* was merely retribution. Your uncle's cher ami killed him, if anyone did, when he staggered back against him in his dying throes. And you should remember, my dear *cousin*, that when you planned this duel between the late chevalier and me, that you also arranged for witnesses."

Dominic! Dear heaven, what was Dominic doing here? He was in his shirt sleeves. Blood trickled down his arm, and he held a bloody sword in his fist.

Disbelieving, thinking that she had waked from sleep to be precipitated into some horrible nightmare, Marisa saw his silver-grey eyes strike into her like twin daggers for an instant before he looked away from her and turned his gaze upon the soberly clad man who had been kneeling over the bodies sprawled on the floor.

The man straightened up, sighed, and said in an incongruously soft voice, "It's true that we were summoned here, my companion and I, to witness a duel. And we were not entirely willing either, except that Sir Robert gave us orders. But a duel it was, Mr. Sinclair, in spite of a sorrier ending than any of us had expected. These gentlemen fought with their swords, and His Grace sat in his chair, talking all the while. I'll have to give the gist of what he said when I make my deposition, and maybe it'll make a difference to you, sir, and maybe not. I'm only a runner, and it's my business to

331

know criminal law, not the other kind. However, I was a witness to the fight being a fair one—and His Grace's death an unfortunate accident." He sighed as if he had not relished what he had said. "Mr. Sinclair—"

"Philip, dammit, Benson is right! I'm chief constable of this county, and I swear I don't know why I let Leo talk me into being here tonight to witness such a—a nasty piece of work! Poor Leo! I didn't know . . . I'll make my deposition before a lawyer, too, but I have my sworn obligations to uphold, and I can't say it wasn't a fair match. If anything, the chevalier had the advantage, and I had to point that out, too, before they began. . . ."

The second speaker was a well-dressed gentleman with a ruddy face, wearing an old-fashioned bagwig. And there was another man in the room looking just as nondescript and inconspicuously dressed as the man Benson, who had spoken first. Marisa's mind noticed all these details, including the muscle that jumped nervously in Philip's clenched jaw and the piercing, almost wild brightness of his blue eyes.

"I don't care what anyone says! This was murder—and I won't acknowledge this bastard upstart as duke of Royse! He's a deserter from the Royal Navy and a rebel who should have been hung! An American pirate, too. Let's see you face the charges my father and I bring against you, damn you!"

"But until you make those charges formal and they're proven, I am, ironically enough, the sixth duke of Royse. And this is my house—and here is my wife, whom you so obligingly brought here. I'm surprised you're not wearing mourning clothes, my love. Didn't you expect to find yourself a widow?"

Marisa could neither move nor speak, but suddenly she felt the bile rush up to her throat and had to press both her hands against her mouth with a choking sound that made one corner of Dominic's mouth twist up in an ugly grin. She shivered. He looked at her, his eyes impaling her, and said slowly and distinctly, "You treacherous, adulterous bitch!"

She heard someone gasp and did not know if it was her own voice or someone else's.

And then Philip flung out, hate and triumph mixed in his

voice, "Marisa is my mistress. We are going away together, and you will not stop us, you know. You may think about that while you are rotting in jail waiting for the hangman's noose."

She had turned her head to look towards him, wondering dazedly why he had chosen this moment to announce such a thing, and an involuntary cry tore itself from her constricting throat when she saw him snatch a pistol from the case that lay on the table and level it.

"Or just before you die—" Philip whispered then, and there was a blinding flash and an explosion that seemed to fill the room and reverberate against Marisa's ears. She felt herself slump to the floor onto her knees.

The room seemed filled with smoke, and there had been an anguished scream and a thud—or had she fainted? She heard voices that seemed to waver coming closer and then receding.

"God! What happened? It must have misfired."

"No—no, sir, it did not. You see—it was planned that way. Both pistols. Monsieur Durand did it himself at His Grace's suggestion. Just in case—in case the—other gentleman chose pistols instead of swords." Simms's voice sounded tired and old and quite unlike itself.

"And so all the chevalier had to do was stand there with a pistol in his hand and watch his opponent blow hisself to smithereens—my God! I've seen a lot of nasty things but never anything like *this*, not in all my born days!"

Someone helped Marisa to a chair and held a glass of wine to her lips. And she couldn't look at what had been Philip— she *wouldn't*—not even if he tried to force her to. She gagged on the wine, and he put his hand in her hair forcing her head back and making her swallow some of it while the other half trickled down the corners of her mouth and dripped onto her —like blood.

"I don't know what to do! Before heaven I don't. Three of them dead. What a bloody piece of business. How am I going to explain all this and my being right here when it all happened?" The chief constable's voice sounded querulous. "I'm going to be ruined—"

"And Sir Robert's going to bite *our* heads off, too, for sure!" one of the Bow Street runners said sourly.

Marisa felt a viselike grip that was all too familiar close over her arm as she was dragged up and out of the chair.

"While you're all wondering what to do, you'll excuse me if I take my wife away for some air? And you don't have to look so alarmed, gentlemen. I have no intention of murdering her—at least, not tonight!"

She went with him, sleepwalking, passing through the small group of servants who were huddled in the doorway with Parsons rocking and crooning to herself in their midst. Walking without pause or hesitation, Dominic took her down the silent passageway and out of the front door into the mist with its cold streamers that seemed to lick coldly against her face. She didn't care—better to imagine for a short while longer that she was dreaming; and it really seemed so as he continued to lead her inexorably onward down the graveled path and then swerving sharply into a dense patch of shrubbery with bushes that clawed at her out of the dark.

She did not even ask him where he was taking her or why. It seemed natural and inevitable that they should come out into a clearing bounded by the woods and that there should be horses waiting here held by an impatient and obviously nervous man whose face was concealed by some kind of a rough hat such as peasants wore.

"Cor! You took a long time coming, guvnor! Almost decided to take off by meself, I did. This ain't no fit night to be standin' out here—"

"Well, your waiting's done." Money exchanged hands, and the man gave a low chuckle as he knuckled his forehead. "You're a right one, guv. Knew it the minute I clapped eyes on you. I'll lead you to where the boat's waitin' now, you an' your lady—an' then you can give me the rest of what we agreed on an' be on your way."

The man mounted his horse quickly. Still unresisting and silent, Marisa felt herself hoisted sideways onto a saddle as Dominic held her before him with one arm tight around her waist.

He did not say a word either, and yet as they started off into the dampness of the all-enveloping mist, Marisa felt wearily as if all this had happened before and she was going backward into time. Further and further back until reality dropped away, blotted up by the fog, and there was only the motion of the horse under her and the beating of a heart against her shoulder and an arm holding her, an arm that was wet and sticky with blood that slowly dripped down the side of her gown, staining it.

Chapter Thirty-one

'Where am I? What am I doing here?' Marisa's tired mind asked, but the blackened, oak-beamed ceiling and paneled walls of the room gave back no reply except for an occasional creak as the fire began to heat the small space.

Oh, she felt so exhausted! Her gown was still damp from sea spray, and there was a sour taste in her mouth. She had been sick, she remembered, on the tossing boat ride that had brought her from a secluded beach on the Cornwall coast to the much larger harbor of Plymouth. She remembered seeing what seemed like a forest of masts as tall ships from all over the world swayed at anchor with only their dim riding lights to guide the small boat she was on, as it slipped between them, silently cutting through the night-black water. By the time they had reached land and some rough stone steps at the end of a crumbling dock, Marisa had been almost insensible, she felt as if she had been turned inside out and didn't care if she dropped dead the very next moment.

There had been voices. A cloak was wrapped around her limp body, and hard hands dragged her up the steps. And then, suddenly, warmth and loud, raucous laughter and the smell of sour wine and ale and greasy food. And she had been carried upstairs and left here in a narrow, not-too-comfortable bed; she was still fully dressed even down to her ruined slippers.

So much for remembering. In spite of it, her mood of apathy persisted. Further thinking seemed too much effort, and after all, what was the point? She didn't want to remember anything unpleasant; and at the same time she had the feeling that she had come such a long way—turning in a

337

circle to where her real experience of living had begun. From fine lady to homeless waif again.

The door opened, and the heady aroma of food made her stomach cramp with hunger. A round-faced, harried-looking serving wench with straggly brown hair escaping from under a dirty cap set a tray down on the only table in the small room.

"It's only boiled beef and potatoes, with some fried fish on the side. It's all we got. And a bottle of wine, because the water here ain't fit fer drinking. It's been paid fer, so you kin eat as much as ye want. An' I can't stay, because they're all hollering and cussing downstairs for me already."

In spite of her tiredness, Marisa sat up. And a minute later, she was wolfing down the food which was already growing cold—the fat congealing on the edges of the thin, watery gravy. It didn't matter. When had she last eaten? The food went down, filling her empty belly, and the tepid, sour tasting wine sent streamers of warmth along her chilled limbs.

With some food inside her, she began to feel human again, but she was more tired than ever. Grimacing with defiance, Marisa finished what was left of the wine and staggered back to the bed where she threw herself on her side before drawing the covers up to her chin. She gazed into the sputtering fire and wondered again how she had gotten here and why she stayed instead of throwing herself out of the small, uncurtained window. She had lived through a horrible nightmare, and she still wasn't quite certain how she had managed to survive. There had been those grotesque dead bodies sprawled one atop the other—and then Philip, his handsome face blown into bloody tatters by the pistol he held in his hand. And Dominic—walking her calmly and surely through the crowd of frightened servants. Dominic! Why had he brought her here?

As if in answer to her thoughts, the door thudded open and then closed, and he stood there with the dark cloak he had lent her earlier swinging about his shoulders and then tossed it aside.

His shirt sleeve had been ripped up to the shoulder, and his upper arm was encircled by a grubby, stained bandage. She remembered then, vaguely, that someone had applied the bandage on the boat while she had leaned over the side, being violently sick. A bandage soaked with salt water, and he had said in a dry voice, "That's all they used on board His Majesty's ships after a man had his back torn to bits by the 'cat.'"

But he seemed none the worse now for the opening of his old wound or the loss of blood, and without more than a silent, raking glance at her huddled figure, he walked close to the fire and warmed himself before it.

Marisa found herself wondering what he had been through to make him as hard and self-sufficient as he was now. Against her will, snatches of the monologue that the woman Parsons had poured into her ears came back to make her shiver under the covers she had pulled up over her shrinking body. Dominic the man, who had been a rebellious, half-savage boy, seemed more of a mystery than ever now that she knew more than she cared to about his past

Marisa stared at him through wide, frightened eyes and saw a tall, harsh-featured stranger who had turned to look at her measuringly and impersonally.

It was she, almost compulsively, who broke the silence that stretched between them. "Why did you bring me here? Was it to kill me where no one would find out about it?"

His eyes were silver mirrors under lifted black brows, giving away nothing.

"Why, if that was all there was to it, I could have left you behind—and the Assassin would have taken care of you. Or I could have thrown you overboard a few hours ago. But don't ask me why I brought you here with me because I don't know myself. That wound must have made me light-headed!"

"The Assassin!" A sudden jolt of anger made Marisa sit bolt upright. *"You* are the Assassin, aren't you? I saw Madame De L'Aigle before—before I left London, and she told me—"

His mouth thinned, curling downward in a disgusted expression.

"That old witch! I'm sure it suited her to tell you whatever she did. Don't you have any sense? *She's* the Assassin—or the brains and the will behind the instrument who dealt out punishment. It was the chevalier at first, but as *you* know, he was not often in London, and his visits could not always coincide with violence. So it became a custom for certain trusted gentlemen to dice or draw lots for the privilege and the risk of being this Assassin."

He caught the look on her face and the unspoken cry formed by her parted lips and he gave a short, ugly laugh. "Oh yes—your Philip, too. How else do you think he found the money with which to pay his gambling debts? The last one he killed was a woman, and I understand he enjoyed it."

"No!" Marisa managed that one choked word before he interrupted her cruelly.

"How else do you think we knew exactly where and at what time to intercept your carriage? Philip knew, but he did not know that it was I who won the toss of the dice that night, nor what la Marquise had planned. As far as he knew, you were only to be frightened—and warned. And then you would fall into his arms. . . . Madame made sure that *he* was not to be injured in any way; but if it had been the chevalier or one of the others who had thrown high, it would have been much worse for you, my sweet. The brand would have been put on you in any case. As it was, you were only raped by your own husband and not by a multitude of others, nor were you used by the late chevalier in his own peculiar fashion—can you not guess at it? I must admit that at the time I, too, thought that you needed punishment, but I've come to the conclusion that you cannot help being what you are, a treacherous, hot-blooded little bitch! When Philip Sinclair wasn't available, it was that well-known rake, di Chiara. Did you think your meetings with him were a secret? It's a pity the convent walls weren't high enough to hold you, for if they had been, neither you nor I would be in such an awkward position right now!"

He had dealt her shock after shock, and now, capable only of thinking how to strike back at him, Marisa stammered, "How dare you condemn me? *You*—who caused my father's death because you lusted after his wife! Would you punish me for the same crime your own mother committed? That of loving a man other than the one she was forced to marry?"

His face grew white and taut. Seeing it, Marisa pressed home the slight advantage she had gained.

"You've warned me to give up meddling in politics when that is what *you* are doing and have always done. I would not have been involved in anything; I would not even be here if you had not forcibly meddled in my life and—and—"

"That's enough!" Jaws clenched, he cut through her frenzied speech. "You've said enough. Say one more word and I'll stuff a gag in your mouth before I strangle you!"

She gasped but fell silent, still staring at him resentfully while he seemed to make a conscious effort to hold back his temper, expelling his breath so that it whistled between his teeth.

"You had better try to get some sleep for we sail with the morning tide. I've booked our passages on an American merchantman that sails first to Spain. From there you can make up your mind what you wish to do. In the meantime, I'll attempt to find you some clothes—they'd hardly accept you on board without baggage."

He left her after a few moments, leaving the door unlocked as if he dared her to try and make her escape. But escape to what? She probably would get no further than the common room of this cheap tavern—to judge from the bawdy songs and shouting that filtered all too clearly up the stairs. Perhaps that was all he was waiting for—before he handed her over to them. No! She would not give him the satisfaction! At least, as he had reminded her, they were wedded; and if he meant to take her as far as Spain, she could find her way from there.

There were still portions of the night before that Marisa's weary, confused mind blanked out, and she was content to let it be so. *He* had gone, leaving her alone for the time being. And like an exhausted animal, she seized her moment of respite to stretch out and sleep.

Morning came all too soon, and Marisa's state of apathy persisted even as a woolen cloak with a hood that covered her hair and most of her face was wrapped around her, and she was dragged to her feet to go where she was taken.

Marisa was vaguely aware of a cold, stinging salt breeze whipping against her cheeks as she walked down a stone pier. And then she was put into a small boat which delivered her to a square-rigged brig. She was hustled inside a small cabin and left there. Lying alone across the narrow bunk that had been allotted her, and hearing all the noises and motions of a vessel about to weigh anchor, she seemed hurtled back in time. Presently, when she had heard the sails crack before the gust of fresh wind that took them and knew they were finally out into the Sound, *he* came back to lie beside her, fully clad except for his boots; and somehow, impossibly, she fell asleep again.

From that time onward an uneasy truce developed between them. Husband and wife when they emerged from the cabin, they were still antagonists in private. Not even lovers now, in spite of what had taken place between them in London before she had embarked on her precarious journey with Philip. Not even bondage of the flesh held them together now, only the vast, rolling emptiness of the ocean about them and the cramped space of the cabin they were forced to share at night.

There were only two other women on board the *Marie-Clair*: the captain's wife, a thin, angular woman of middle age, who was given to quoting from the Bible, and Tessa Purvis, a sleepy-eyed, gardenia-skinned woman who was younger and quite attractive. She had her own small cabin where she stayed most of the time, seemingly wrapped in her own secret thoughts.

All in all, the first few days they spent at sea were strange and strained, with odd undercurrents—a time during which the three women conversed very little among themselves. It was clear that Mrs. Meeker, the captain's wife, approved of neither of the younger women, and she ignored them by either reading aloud from the Bible or bending her head over her embroidery. She was not used to other women on board this ship, and she made that clear, too. Tessa Purvis remained silent for the most part although her full lips seemed always curved in an inward, secretive smile. Marisa retreated into haughtiness and a strong French accent which made both women eye her strangely and a trifle curiously although there were no blunt, outright questions asked.

Marisa hardly ever saw Dominic except at meal times or late at night. He had taken to frequenting the bridge with the taciturn captain, who seemed to welcome his presence there, or to dicing with those of the crew who were not on duty.

The second night, when he entered their small, cramped cabin reeking of liquor, Marisa made an attempt at recrimination—after having stripped to his breeches, he lay beside her and forced her against the wall. Her vehement whispered words of abuse and anger were directed at his back which he had turned on her. After a few moments, during which she could feel his body stiffen, he whispered back at her in a pleasant, silky-steel voice that if she continued to keep him awake he would be forced either to beat her or to gag and bind her.

Sensing the very real threat beneath his conversationally offered alternatives, she fell silent, biting her lip. Huddled as far away from him as the cramped space would allow, she heard his even breathing for a long time. She stared into the darkness, and her memory conjured up frightening images. In the end, she fell asleep from sheer exhaustion.

After that Marisa retreated into icy silence as cold as the storm-grey of his eyes when they happened to encounter hers. One morning very early, she saw him lean toward Tessa Purvis as she looked over the ship's polished railing, and she could have sworn she saw the white flash of his teeth as he smiled at the woman. Did they know each other? *Had* they known each other before? Marisa felt her mind almost bursting from the weight of the anger she was forced to hold back. Why had he really brought her here? Why was he a passenger on this ship when he had a vessel of his own? And above all, what did her aunt, and everyone else in England, think of their sudden flight together after the bloody events of that night that she still could not bear to remember too closely? 'He's made me a fugitive, too,' she thought tormentedly, furiously. But for what ends? For what devious, twisted reasons of his own? Oh, she thought she might go mad from thinking, and she knew more strongly than ever that she mistrusted and hated this man, her husband, more than anyone else on the world. But fate kept throwing them together. How would *this* journey end?

By the afternoon of their sixth day at sea, the answer to this question was thrust upon her with frightening force.

Rosemary Rogers

With a strong wind behind them and every available bit of canvas spread, they had been making excellent time, and even the usually silent Captain Meeker was heard to remark with an air of satisfaction that it shouldn't be long now before they came in sight of the coast of Portugal. The *Marie-Clair* hoped to beat her sister ship *Ruth* into the Mediterranean, and Marisa could sense the growing jubilation among the crew. The *Ruth* was well behind them, and so was the usually stormy Bay of Biscay. From here on it would be a clear, straight run, and to hell with the fog banks that had begun to gather in the distance.

"We'll make landfall within the next two days, maybe sooner, if this wind keeps up," Marisa heard a man chuckle to his mate as she passed by on her way to her cabin. And then a shout from the lookout stationed in his lonely crow's-nest made her stop and turn. "Sail!"

From the corner of her eye she caught sight of Captain Meeker standing on the bridge with a brassbound telescope to his eye. Curiosity drove her to the rail. They had passed very few other ships on their voyage so far for the British and French were playing hide and seek with each other; and although Marisa understood that the American navy had a small squadron patrolling the Mediterranean, they had seen only one other ship flying the United States flag so far. She drew her shawl more closely about her shoulders and stared towards the horizon that was faintly shrouded by mist.

"She looks to be a foreigner, although I could swear from the sleek lines of her that she's a Salem-built schooner. Can't make out her flag yet, though."

Whoever she was, she came flying towards them so that now even Marisa could make out a vague outline taking shape as she squinted her eyes to see better.

The next moment, as the captain cried out in a puzzled fashion, "That's the Moroccan flag," there was a white puff of smoke and a distant booming sound from the other vessel, and the *Marie-Clair* rocked, sprays of water drenching her decks. Marisa tightened her grip on the rail.

Suddenly, everything was commotion. There was a tumult of angry, shouting voices as men came running past her.

344

"By God—she fired on us, the dirty pirate! What's a Moroccan ship doing in the Atlantic?"

"Mebbe our new president forgot to pay them their tribute an' they chopped down our flagpole—I've heard as how that's the way they declare war, those heathen dogs!"

The voices made no sense. What did they mean? Why had they been fired upon? Marisa clung to the railing as if she had been frozen to it until her arm was seized in a grip that made her cry out with pain, and she was dragged across the deck to the comparative shelter of her cabin.

Dominic released her so suddenly she fell back, but he remained standing with his back to the door. His face had gone white under its tan, the scar he carried and the lines of strain standing out clearly. He no longer wore a mask over his emotions.

She stared at him in puzzled wonderment, and then he shouted, "What the hell were you doing out on deck? Don't you have any sense?" And then, before she could frame an angry reply, "Christ, don't start to argue with me now. Listen, because we don't have much time before they board us. Try to remember not to show too much fear. Tell them you're French. It won't hurt to mention your connection with Bonaparte. They won't harm you as long as they think there'll be a fat ransom to be gained." He smiled at the stricken, uncomprehending look on her face. "Now's your chance to escape me once and for all, kmenina. For your own sake—better take it. You can tell them I abducted you for your fortune. Don't admit we're married or they might consider you an American citizen, and things might not go as well for you."

He frowned, then, at her continuing silence and cleared the small space between them. Shaking her, he growled desperately, "Do you understand anything I've been saying? If this was *my* ship we'd stand and fight, but Meeker doesn't have the guns to fight off a Barbary gunboat, and he says he has a responsibility for everyone on board. He's going to surrender. Do you understand *now* what that means?"

She had started to shake under his hands, but the golden eyes that were finally raised to his were steady, with a strange, startled flame in their centers.

"And *you* are going to surrender, too?" They both felt

Rosemary Rogers

the ship slacken pace as the sails were unwillingly hauled down. The next moment the whole vessel seemed to shudder from stem to stern.

Marisa was looking at Dominic, her eyes still unwavering; she thought she read regret in his eyes before he dropped his hands from her shoulders and said harshly, "Do you think I'm of a mind to commit suicide? I've been in prison and been little more than a slave before. I've lived to remember because I've always been practical enough to bow my head when I had to. It's a lesson that you might keep in mind, too. At least they no longer sell the women they take on the auction block. Not usually, that is. Remember, if you stick to your story and keep your courage, they'll probably keep you unharmed for the ransom you'd bring."

"I would think," she said in a whisper, "that you'd be glad to see me hurt and shamed. *You* have done both, have you not? Then why, now, do you warn me?"

For a moment, she thought he flinched from the bitter question in her eyes and her voice. But there were the sounds of grappling irons thrown hard against the side of the *Marie-Clair* and running feet and voices everywhere. Dominic had no time to let the mask drop back over his face before he answered her with a twisted smile curling up one side of his mouth.

"When it was I who hurt you, it didn't seem so bad. But I've had time to recall, perhaps, that you were no more than a child playing at being gypsy when I met you, and since then —you've shown you have strength of character at least! You remind me—" He bit the words off short and instead took her lifeless hand and raised it, palm up, to his lips. "I think we are both survivors, my love," he said in a voice so soft she thought she must have mistaken his words. And then, laughing, he again surprised her by kissing her on the lips before he turned and left the cabin, letting the door slam behind him.

346

PART THREE

The Perfumed Days

Chapter Thirty-two

Kamil Hasan Rais, captain of the Turkish Janissaries, was, for all his youth, second only in importance to the bashaw himself, and there were some who whispered that Kamil, owing his first allegiance to the sultan of Turkey, was the real ruler of the Mediterranean fortress of Tripoli.

At the moment, although none but his sister Zuleika would have known it, he was in a towering rage as he paced about the luxurious, many-windowed room, tugging at his short beard.

"So Morad Rais wishes to see me. Does he think that I do not know of his latest exploit? It's bad enough that he goes skulking out into the Atlantic Ocean hiding behind the flag of Morocco, but now we have these bold Americans patrolling our very shores and blockading our waters for just such exploits as he boasts of! They took the *Mirboka*—did I tell you so before? And the faction in Morocco that might have supported us is stifled while its petty sultan cries peace with the American dogs! Are we to fight alone, then?"

"You should let His Eminence the bashaw worry about that," Zuleika murmured in a deliberately pacific voice, fanning herself while she watched her brother. "Mustn't we fight back, after all? Not only have they refused to pay us tribute according to the treaty their last president signed, but they continue to harass us. Don't you remember the uproar when they took the *Tripoli*, firing upon her without warning? If Morad Rais has used guile, so much the better! And you, my brother, should be the first to applaud him."

He swung round from his pacing, one hand still on his beard; she gazed at him placidly until an unwilling smile twisted his lips.

"Now, as usual, I realize all over again why I sent for you to rule over my household, dearest sister. It was not for nothing that mother said you should have been born a man. So I should see him then? And accept his tribute in the name of the bashaw? Yes—I suppose so! He was clever to have gotten so far, in the teeth of the blockade! And he's brought us a ship—and more slaves. Since he's the bashaw's son-in-law, I suppose I would have seen him anyway!"

Half smiling, deliberately calm, Zuleika studied this brother that she loved. He was slim, tense, and handsome, the handsomest of her father's sons. Because of the vows he had taken when he became a Janissary—to abstain from women until his three-year term of duty was over—he turned to young men—but why not? That, too, was normal in their society. He was a powerful man, her brother, and he was rich. No doubt he would sign up for another three years soon, and she would continue to run his household until he was appointed to even higher honors.

"I will see him," Kamil pronounced. And then, affectionately, "Would you like to watch from behind the screen?" He turned to leave her, his mind made up, and he shot at her teasingly from the arched doorway, "You had better hurry then, because you know how impatient Morad Rais is!"

Morad Rais, a Scottish renegade who had been known once as Peter Lisle, was not only impatient to have the formal audience over with but annoyed as well. Following his latest daring exploit, he had sailed into the harbor of Tripoli in triumph in his captured American vessel and had fully expected his appointment as admiral of the Tripolitan fleet announced forthwith by his father-in-law, the bashaw. Instead, he had learned that the bashaw had gone hunting in the desert, and would not be back for a whole week. In his place sat the cold young Turk, Kamil, to whom Morad was forced to pay token obeisance.

However, Morad had lived among the Arabs and the Turks long enough to start thinking as they did, and as he strode into the vast chamber his face showed no signs of his inner rage. Richly attired, his ceremonial robes sparkling with jewels, he even managed a flashing smile as Kamil gave him the punctilious honor of stepping from the raised dais to greet him.

The two men embraced as if they had been brothers, each one thinking his own cynical thoughts. Then, the usual formalities over, Morad Rais accepted a seat beside Kamil and began to describe his voyage into the Atlantic in a captured American-built vessel, which had resulted in his easy capture of the merchantman *Marie-Clair*.

"And your own vessel?"

Morad laughed. "Abdul Mousafer is sailing her in, with some of the more recalcitrant prisoners we took. Those who were frightened or easily threatened, sailed *my* ship in here for me with my men covering them with their weapons every minute of the time. We actually passed an American gunboat —and when the American captain heard his wife screeching, he obligingly ran up the correct signals!"

Kamil raised one slim eyebrow in question.

"His wife? There was a woman on board the ship, then?"

Rather nervously, Morad Rais tugged at his brown beard.

"As a matter of fact, there were three of them. The captain's wife is old and ugly and spends her time screaming or wailing. But there were also two younger women, one of them looking to be no more than a thin slip of a girl, although she seems to have more spirit than the other two. She says she is of Spanish and French extraction, and," he leaned forward, lowering his voice slightly, "the goddaughter of the woman known as Josephine Bonaparte. She told me quite boldly that there would be a large ransom paid for her safe return, that, in fact, she was not sailing on the American ship of her own accord but because she had been forcibly abducted by a man she termed an adventurer who hoped to lay his hands on a part of the fortune she is heir to. It *sounded* like a rather farfetched tale at first, but the man actually corroborated it."

"I see." Kamil's long, slender fingers touched his beard thoughtfully.

"The other woman, who is American, said also that she has a rich cousin who would ransom her. As for the old woman, she would not talk, except to screech and pray aloud to her infidel God." Morad spat and then grinned wickedly. "I had all three of them stripped and locked into one of the cabins, mainly to frighten them and discourage any thoughts of escape. One of my eunuchs examined the younger women—they are neither of them virgins." He did not add that he had taken pleasure in watching, and that after lusting after the voluptuously shaped woman who said her name was Tessa, he had taken her the next night. He said aloud, though, his voice querulous; "The question is, what am I to do with them? I am ready to go back to sea within three days, and my wife—well, she's inclined to be jealous, especially of foreign women. I could leave them in the bashaw's harem, I suppose, but, to tell you the truth, my friend, I need my share of that ransom money! I was thinking that if they could be lodged in the care of your sister until the negotiations are all completed, I would give you a tenth of my share. How does that sound?"

It was Zuleika, curious about these Western women and intrigued by the thought of using them as slaves, who persuaded her brother to agree to Morad Rais's proposal. And there was the ransom money to be considered, too, of course —why not?

Kamil reminded her sternly that the women, if he agreed, were to be treated as guests. Zuleika shrugged, saying airily that perhaps she could make companions of them. The presence of other women, educated women, would help to allay the loneliness she felt sometimes.

*   *   *   *   *

Marisa had been frightened, humiliated, confused, and angry during the weeks that followed the capture of the unfortunate *Marie-Clair*. Now, by the time that she and her two companions had been hustled from the small closed carriage in which they'd ridden after disembarking from the ship, she felt merely drained of all energy—although some of her anger remained to save her from complete collapse. What now? It had been miserable on board the ship, cooped inside a tiny airless cabin, and she had been as naked as an odalisque. What had followed the forcible stripping off of her clothes by a black eunuch had been much worse. But she had survived even that, feeling thankful that Morad Rais's lascivious eyes had lusted after Tessa and not *her*. She had tried as best as she was able to show no embarrassment when she reminded him that his master the bashaw was at peace with France, and its ruler, Napoleon, would be concerned for her safe return

"Only if he knows you are here," the renegade Scotsman had reminded her smoothly, and now she wondered what her fate would be. Did he care about a ransom or would she be auctioned off as a slave to some fat Turk?

All three women had been heavily veiled before they left the ship. Now they were all silent, even Mrs. Meeker who had subsided into a state of staring-eyed, silent hysteria. They were taken to a thick walled, whitewashed house with small barred windows set into the wall where it overlooked the street and a heavily barred gate guarded by two Turkish Janissaries.

The women were hurried through a dark, cool passageway which led, surprisingly, into a magnificent courtyard where fountains played, spraying water into an enormous, blue tiled bathing pool. This had been part of the harem of the former owner of the house, and it was still guarded by eunuchs carrying curved scimitars. And here the lady Zuleika, attended by her female slaves, greeted her three foreign "guests."

It was plain to see that she was curious, and her gaze lingered longer on Tessa than it did on Marisa. Mrs. Meeker she ignored altogether.

"So you are the female captives of Morad Rais? I bid you welcome to the house of my brother Kamil Hasan, captain of the Janissaries. You will be lodged here under his protection until the matter of your ransom has been arranged. And in the meantime," she added with a touch of arrogance, "you will be my companions and entertain me—and perhaps we will teach each other many things."

Zuleika spoke in Spanish, a language she had learned from one of her father's captive wives, and Marisa found herself in the unwilling position of interpreter. Zuleika did not like the language, and so, as the days progressed, Marisa found herself being instructed in Turkish and Arabic—this instruction being carried out by a very old man wearing the green turban of a *hadji*—one who had made the long pilgrimage to Mecca. He was a priest, an imam, and, along with his instructions in languages, he insisted that his pupils be also taught the tenets of Islam.

"So they're trying to convert us?" Tessa said with a lift of one slim, plucked eyebrow. She did not seem concerned, having taken to life in what was more or less a harem with lazy, shrugging indifference. She enjoyed the long, perfumed baths and the anointing of the body with scented oils afterwards, as well as the plucking of her brows, and the instructions on the use of henna on the nails and hands and kohl to outline her eyes. She admitted to Marisa that she almost enjoyed this lazy, pampered life.

"It'll be something to tell the folks back home, won't it?" she said in her drawling, sleepy voice. "At least you and I have friends who will ransom us. I could almost feel sorry for poor Selma Meeker—if she hadn't always been such a straitlaced holier-than-thou snob! And look at her now. As long as she can keep her clothes on and there's no man to bother her, she works harder than any of the other slaves around this place. I wonder if they had to beat her?"

"I do not think it's fair," Marisa said, tight-lipped. "And I do feel sorry for her. If they'd only allow me to write a letter, I'd see that she's ransomed, too."

"Don't get soft," Tessa warned her. "Why should you bother about the old witch after all the nasty names she screamed at us? You should think about yourself, just as I do. And learn to adapt, if you haven't learned to do so already. I mean, if Dominic Challenger carried you off with him. . . . And even *I* could not have suspected you were not really married! I met him in the Carolinas— he's always been such an *elusive* man! I know a lot of women who would sigh and say you're lucky."

"So lucky that I ended up *here?*" Marisa said bitterly. But she had learned to listen to Tessa without really paying too much attention. Except when she talked about Dominic. Then, against her will, she would find herself wondering what had happened to him and the other men aboard their ship.

'It's his fault I'm here!' she would reflect stormily. 'How I hate him! And I hope he's suffering. They'll make him a slave, and he'll find out what it's like!'

She wondered—and did not dare ask Zuleika. And the hours and the days dragged by in almost interminable boredom so that she welcomed the classes with the old imam and quickly picked up both languages he taught them.

Marisa refused to have her eyebrows plucked, and she refused to dust her face with rice powder and paint it, or to have henna dye put on her nails and the palms of her hands. Sheer vanity, she decided after she had studied herself in a polished silver mirror after the women had put kohl around her eyes, made her submit to *that* at least. But she would not let herself be turned into an odalisque, painted and perfumed for her master's pleasure. For what reason? The master of *this* household, fortunately, was vowed to continence, and so there was no danger that she would be summoned to his bed. In fact, she had never even seen him. . . .

Kamil Hasan Rais had been kept far too busy managing the affairs of Tripoli during the bashaw's absence to do more than ask his sister casually how her three women guests were adapting themselves to their enforced captivity. Moreover, he was still angry at the way Morad had practically trapped him into agreeing to take the women into his own household. Morad was a crafty devil, and he would probably regret having given his consent so easily.

But Zuleika, on the other hand, seemed happier and more animated than she had been for a long time. She enjoyed having female companions of her own rank to talk to, she told him. And she was even learning some French. The woman who had been called Tessa and was now renamed Amineh was most interesting to talk to, and she actually seemed to enjoy her life here. As for the old, ugly one—pah! She had no breeding, she was a staunch Christian, and it was obvious she enjoyed being a servant—just as if she had been born to it!

"And the other one?" Kamil questioned amusedly, "The one even Morad said had spirit? She's the one we think will bring the largest ransom—I hope you haven't made a servant out of her!"

Zuleika grimaced and looked sulky for a moment.

"Ah, that one! To tell you the truth, I do not know what to make of *her*, although the imam Ibrahim says she has a quick mind and learns fast. She is not rebellious, exactly, but she is stubborn. And," with a trace of complacence, "she is as skinny and slightly formed as a youth. I, for one, cannot imagine why any man would want to carry her off. She does not seem interested in men at all. In fact she was bold enough to announce in my presence that she despises men."

"Perhaps she prefers her own sex," Kamil said drily, but his curiosity had been piqued, and the very next day he made a point of returning to the house early, without being announced.

From a stone-grilled window within the house he watched the women of his household, naked and half-naked, beside the pool—and wondered which was the one his sister had renamed Lelia.

Zuleika, her hair still damp, was having it combed by one of her black slave women. She had been dressed, and as she leaned back against a pile of brightly colored cushions, two other women were busy adorning her hands and feet with henna. The woman beside her, who stood allowing herself to be dried by one of the eunuchs, must be Amineh. Her black hair contrasted strangely with her milky-white skin. Yes, it was clear to his dispassionate eyes why Morad Rais might find this woman attractive, with her heavy breasts and voluptuously curved hips. He was almost ready to turn away when he saw *her*, rising dripping wet and naked from the pool like a Greek Diana—slim-flanked and slender-waisted, with small breasts that did not sag pendulously with their own weight. Her skin had a golden shade to it that matched her short, dark gold hair that curled close to her head and about her neck, and she carried herself erect and proudly. Viewed from the back she might easily have been taken for a boy, small, taut buttocks tapering into slender, muscled flanks and calves that were neither too thin nor too well-developed.

As he watched, spellbound, she snatched the cloth held out to her by one of the slave women and insisted on drying herself before she lay down on the raised marble slab by the pool and let herself be massaged by a eunuch. After he had finished massaging her, she rolled over, and the sun struck off dull gold glints from the sparse triangle of damply curling hair between her thighs. In that moment, Kamil, for the first time in many years, felt an almost overwhelming desire for a woman.

A boy-woman. He had long ago lost his taste for the plump, fat-ridged women considered beautiful in this part of the world. And yet, apparently, not for all women.

Against his sister's grumbling, direful warnings, he gave his orders that night. The woman they had re-named Lelia, her wine at dinner drugged with a secret aphrodisiac, was brought to his chamber. Hamid, his chief eunuch, gently undressed her, slipping the baggy harem trousers and the thin tunic from her body; then he left her on his master's bed.

All the lamps in the curtained chamber had been turned out save one which hung from the ceiling over the bed giving only enough light to turn her body to pale gold.

They were alone. And Kamil came to sit beside her, taking oil from a narrow-necked flagon to rub into her burning flesh while she bit her lip in an effort to control the tremors that shook her unfamiliarly from head to foot. He was very gentle as he massaged her. He spoke to her softly in Turkish and Arabic, and by now she understood enough of both languages to know he was praising her body and calling her flattering love names. He quoted from the Song of Solomon or Suleiman, as the Moslems called him, and he told her that her body was like that of a young gazelle—a perfumed garden of delight that lay sleeping, waiting for the touch of the sun to bring it to life.

His hands were soft and gentle on her fevered body, assuaging some of its tight-coiled tension and the strange itching feeling that made every muscle writhe. He massaged the perfumed oil into her flesh, lingering over her breasts until she was gasping, each brush of finger over her nipples making her cry out aloud. And then his hands moved lower, still gentle, until they were between her thighs which she spread helplessly and without conscious volition, craving only release now from unbearable tension. And he brought her release and made her crave it again, turning her over this time and finding, cunningly, where she was still virginal, his oiled fingers making it easy when he finally entered her there where she would not have imagined any man would take her. Putting one hand under her writhing, straining body, he brought her to climax after climax of unwilling, shameful ecstasy until she was incapable of anything more and either fainted or slept.

The next day—it was afternoon when she woke—Marisa would have preferred to believe she had dreamt everything, but Zuleika's malicious smile and her acid, unsparing words told her everything. Zuleika was, however, careful to say nothing that might make her brother angry with her, and her manner told Marisa that she should consider herself lucky—and flattered.

"My brother does not give his affection easily, nor is he given to desiring women. You're more fortunate than you know for he is an honorable man and considers his vows seriously. He's treated you as our Turkish men treat a virgin they desire. From now on you will have your own slaves and freedom to go riding, if you so desire, just like one of those Bedouin women!"

Marisa still felt drowsy and strangely languorous. There was only a slight stinging between her thighs—and elsewhere—to remind her of the lamp-lit night she had spent with a stranger named Kamil who had sworn he loved her.

Nighttime came again, and again she was given wine to drink. She lay back against soft cushions while her own slaves made her ready, drawing thin black lines on her eyelids and beneath her lower lashes, reddening her nails and cheeks and lips, and brushing her short curls until they gleamed like gold.

That night was a repetition of the last, and Kamil, enamored, swore he could never grow tired of her. Within another year, his term of service would be over, and he would take her to Turkey with him as his wife. He would make up the amount set as her ransom from his own coffers and would not take any other wives as long as she remained his.

In the meantime, Marisa had her own suite of rooms, her own servants, and even Zuleika had no jurisdiction over her.

She did not quite understand what had happened to her, but a feeling of sensuous languour and well-being filled her. There was a man, a powerful, rich man, who desired her above all others. Much easier to forget the past and everything in it and live only in the luxurious present where her every wish was law and she had slaves to wait upon her.

There were still the lessons with the imam, who was pleased with her progress and talked of her formal conversion to Islam. And, dressed as a young man, her golden hair covered by a burnoose, Marisa had taken to going riding beside Kamil; she managed a spirited Arab stallion with an easy manner that pleased him.

Marisa began to look forward to the days, when, disguised as a young Janissary, she could ride everywhere at Kamil's side and feel free. The nights were different. Then, when she was perfumed and painted and satiated with wine, he made her aware of her body in ways she had not dreamed were possible, the unnatural method of his taking her becoming almost natural when he, and the sharp-tasting wine, had made her blind to everything but fulfillment.

Kamil worshipped her. He would kiss every inch of her body, starting from her toes and going up to her eyelids. Marisa felt cherished and pampered for the first time in her life. Kamil was both companion in the daytime and lover at night. He invariably aroused her with his aphrodisiac wines and his caresses to the point where the unusual way he chose to penetrate her no longer mattered. It was because of the vows he had taken when he became a Janissary, she reasoned. Later, when he married her, it would be different. And even Zuleika, as resentful as she had become, dared not say a word that might indicate her disapproval, for if she did, she had the feeling that her brother would have no qualms in sending her back to their parents in Turkey.

So Zuleika sulked discreetly, and Tessa, growing bored, languished while she longed for a man, even such a one as Morad Rais, who had used her without a thought for her own pleasure. And Selma Meeker, not wanting to believe she was where she was, worked harder than ever at the tasks the head eunuch contemptuously assigned to her. Marisa had become suddenly aware of the pleasure of all things purely sensual, like the wind against her face when she was riding and the heat of the sun and the perfume of flowers and of the excitement of market places they passed when she rode beside Kamil, a scimitar lying coldly against her thigh. Having learned to live only in the present, she had no cares. Even the thought of turning Moslem no longer alarmed her. Moslem or Christian—what did it matter? It was the same God they worshipped, calling Him by different names. And as for *her* position as a woman, it all depended on the man who was her protector! She needed only to know what Kamil whispered to her every night when they lay together afterwards, his hands continuing to stroke her body gently and almost worshipfully. He loved her. He desired no other woman above her, nor the young men he had been fond of before. He would give his life to protect her. . . .

Chapter Thirty-three

Amid much formal celebrating, the bashaw returned from the desert. Kamil was away for over a day, and when he came back he was smiling. Morad Rais came back from his latest pirating adventure with a new prize, and he also was in a good mood. Kamil returned from that interview with a set look on his face.

"It has all been arranged," he said to Marisa, who sat cross-legged, in a fashion she had learned and now came easily to her, on the cushions before him. "The letters demanding ransom have already been sent. When they offer ransom for you, I will meet their offer or increase upon it if I have to. Then we will tell them that you died of a fever. Within the year, when my present term of duty is completed, we will be married. By Allah, my little slim gazelle, I will take no other wife but you even though the Koran allows it. And then, at last, I will be able to give you children."

Her head stayed down as if she were pensive, and he wondered with a pang of worry why she did not lift it and look him straight in the eyes as she usually did. Was she angry because he had stayed away from her for a night?

Cajolingly he said, "My little golden one, my life's desire, why do you look away from me? Have I done something to offend you? Has anyone else in my household? If so, you have only to tell me, and I will—"

She cut across his soft speech with the gasp of an indrawn breath, and then she said in a dull, even voice, "Perhaps you will change your mind about me now. No—don't say anything, *please*, until I have finished! You see—oh, but they *told* you, did they not, that I was no longer a virgin. And how I came to be aboard the American ship? Well, it seems as if

361

that journey is to have its results. I am—almost sure that I am to have a child." She raised her head at last, and he saw that her face had gone white with strain, and her golden eyes seemed more enormous than usual. "Oh! Don't you see? I had to tell you, to be the first to tell you. And there is more that nobody else knows, but I must tell you anyway. The man —the man who—"

"No!" he said with a controlled violence that was new in her experience of him. He had been sitting across from her, smoking, but now he cast the thin stem of the water pipe aside and reached her with a bound, pushing her back among the profusion of silken cushions and tearing aside her flimsy garments to bare her body to his eyes. His hands touched her slightly rounded belly, and she flinched involuntarily; but then he slid them lower, between her thighs, and she shuddered with a strange mixture of emotions, lying there limply with only her eyes alive and unwavering on his.

"I do not wish to hear the name of this man," Kamil said quietly enough, although each word seemed bitten out. "I do not wish to remember that any other man could have known you as I have. And I tell you that it is past and forgotten! It does not matter. No one need know besides my sister and the old woman who brews herbal medicines. You will take these medicines, and they will make you cramp and bleed, but you will be carefully looked after, and then it will be over, do you understand? Over—and neither of us will remember!"

It was her turn to cry "no!" and shake her head, in spite of the intensity of his gaze upon her and the feel of his hands on her.

There had been other hands on her, before, and in spite of herself and her reluctance to think of that time in the past, she could not help it. She remembered another time, and the pain and bleeding and the sense of emptiness and loss inside her. Even now the sense of another life within herself brought forth a fiercely protective instinct that would not be denied.

"No!" she repeated, more strongly this time, her eyes continuing to hold his brown, smoky gaze. "I cannot. I wish that you would understand, but if you do not it is nothing I can help. The life inside me is a *life,* and part of myself, don't you see that? I will not commit murder. I cannot kill my own child." In the face of his silence and his sudden stillness, she drew in a deep, wavering breath and said shakily, "If you would kill me for this, then do so—but make it quickly, please. In any case, I think it is too late for herbs and medicines to work."

He leaned over her, and his hands slid up to her shoulders, holding them down against the cushions while his warm breath fanned her cheek.

"Too late? When was this child conceived? Are you only ignorant of certain facts, or was it before he took you on the ship?"

"It was before," she acquiesced tiredly. "One night, in London, when he was angry with me; and the act was done from hate and a desire to humble me. You've noticed the mark on my thigh? You never asked me about it, but he did it. To brand me as a—a whore, he said."

She whispered the last words, and Kamil let himself down beside her, holding her in his arms.

"I think you must tell me everything now. The whole of the story. And I will try to understand."

Once embarked on her tale she felt like Scheherazade spinning endless stories to keep her master from putting her to death. And yet, Kamil heard her out patiently, his arms about her neither tightening nor rejecting.

"So you are married, after all," he said at last, drily. "Even though I believe that it was forced upon you, and upon *him*, this man whose child it is you carry. I don't blame you for obedience to your relatives— don't you think it is not the same here? But why didn't you tell me all this before?"

Marisa moved her head wearily. "For what reason? It did not seem important before. I tried to put all of the past out of my mind—only it has caught up with me."

"Do you love him. Did you ever?" Suddenly he questioned her fiercely, raising his head to look into her face.

"No! I did not love him—how could you think it? I disliked him and distrusted him, and after I learned that he had been responsible for my father's death, I began to hate him. He knew it."

"And you would still bear his child?"

"*My* child! Yes, mine. *I* carry the life within me, it is *my* womb that nurtures it. If the child is born it will be mine and mine alone!"

"And mine also," Kamil said quickly and harshly, putting his face against her shoulder. "For I will still have you—and take you as my wife according to the laws of Islam."

"But—" she began protesting, and he silenced her with a long, burning kiss.

"You do not belong to an infidel dog," he muttered presently, his hands smoothing perfumed oil into every pore of her skin. "The imam tells me you are ready now, and once you are converted to Islam, there will be no obstacles in our way. Even though you may grow big with a child that is not of my loins, you will be slim again by the time we are able to marry. And I will continue to want you."

Skillfully, with the cleverness of his fingers, he brought her to the point where she no longer remembered anything or cared for anything but release from the tension he had built up in her body. And turning her over gently at the last moment, one hand cupping her breast and the other caressing her between her thighs, he took her in his own fashion, delighting in the feel of her slender, writhing young body beneath his.

It was a few days after this that Zuleika, hoping to surprise and anger her brother with her disclosure of the young woman's condition, heard the truth from him instead—and learned to her dismay that he was more determined than ever to pursue his course.

"Will you accept her as a wife after she has borne another man's child? A child who will no doubt be fair-skinned and light-haired? If you will not think of yourself and your future, think of the shame it will bring you before our parents and our relatives. And you could be a pasha—"

"And I will still be as long as the sultan continues to smile favorably upon our family." But he had begun to pace the room in the manner she knew so well, his hands clasped behind his back, and a slight, almost unnoticeable frown creasing his forehead.

"Can you not take her as a concubine if you must? And there are herbs—"

"She will not consent to destroying a life, and I have given her my word that her child will be unharmed. However—" he turned, suddenly, so that his back was to the window. His dark brown eyes burned in the dim light. "I am not so lost to pride as you think, and I have decided—yes, I have decided—that a girl child she may keep. A white-skinned female will quickly find a place in the harem of the sultan himself. But a boy—"

"Yes," Zuleika said quickly, leaning forward, "what if she bears a son? Will he be your heir and bear your name which is also your father's name? Will you—"

"No! That far I cannot and will not go. But the child will not be harmed, you understand? If Lelia should have a son, she will be told only that the infant died, and I will arrange for it to be taken to the seraglio of my friend Osman the Trader. At the right age . . . with a wet nurse."

A small, almost savagely satisfied smile played about Zuleika's full lips.

Kamil did not need to say more for she was familiar with custom and had heard of Osman. At the right age, a handsome boy child would fetch a great deal of money—either to be used for the pleasure of rich merchants or as a eunuch slave. Fortunately, her brother was not *completely* bewitched after all!

Zuleika continued to think deeply, however, and she took pains to be charming and make an especial friend of the languid, full-figured Amineh who had (or so she related) taken the fancy of Murad Rais himself. They chattered among themselves, and it was Amineh, slyly, who broached the subject of Lelia-Marisa's husband.

"Of course I could tell that all was not well between them. *She* was sulky and silent for most of the time, and he seemed to find *my* company more congenial than hers. I was surprised to discover that Dominic Challenger was to be one of the passengers on the *Marie-Clair*. He was a privateer captain and had his own ship when *I* first met him at a ball in Charleston. And even there all the women were mad for him, and the men talked in guarded whispers about him. They said he was the legal heir to an English dukedom—and the natural son of a *very* highly placed politician in my country. But nobody could ever find out for sure whose son he was. I heard that he escaped from a Spanish prison in Santo Domingo and stole an English ship, sailing her right into the harbor at Charleston. And that he went to Monticello on his own, when Mr. Jefferson was entertaining some very important men as guests, and said he was looking for his father. You can imagine what a little scandal *that* must have caused! All the same, ever since then he's seemed to have had support of the government. I wonder what he was doing in England and how he ended up with *her*?"

Zuleika waved away her two Ethiopian pages, perfectly formed identical twins. She raised her slim, plucked eyebrows as she leaned closer to her companion.

"I, too, wonder what my brother sees in her. For to look at, except for her hair and her complexion, she seems no more than a half-formed girl. But this man she calls her husband—one wonders what happened to him when our great Admiral Morad Rais captured your ship. . . ."

Zuleika let her words trail away suggestively and caught an answering gleam of awareness in her new friend's eyes.

"Dominic Challenger? I don't know. We were separated from the men, you see, and I did not set eyes upon him again. What *does* happen to the males who are captured?"

"They become slaves. Some of them are sold to different masters, and some of them are set to work building new ships or working in the stone quarries. Others? Well, there are a few who might be ransomed, and they are set the easiest tasks of all. The bashaw has many foreigner slaves, and some of them, even after they have earned their freedom, elect to stay."

"Now that you've brought the subject to my mind, I *do* wonder what happened to Dominic. Do you think *he* is curious about what happened to his wife?"

In perfect accord, Amineh and Zuleika met each other's eyes and smiled.

Zuleika, born to it, wove her own plots while her brother continued to be enamored of his young companion who was still skinny enough to ride beside him as one of the Janissaries and unwomanly enough to enjoy such excursions.

Amineh was rewarded for her friendship and her complicity by stolen meetings with Morad Rais, who was rapidly becoming infatuated with her and gave her many expensive gifts. In return for *her* aid and her silence, Zuleika asked only for a certain slave—one of the many that Morad had taken himself.

The newly appointed admiral of the Tripolitan fleet looked at her in surprise and curiosity as he grumbled, "It's going to be difficult to buy him back, you know! He's a stubborn, cunning devil and even speaks some Arabic. He's working for old Abdul the shipbuilder now—and giving no trouble, from what I understand. But I've heard he's a convert to Islam. When I first talked to him he was wearing an Islamic medal that named him an adopted son of a very powerful desert sheik. That's why I sold him to Abdul, who understands such things. You sure that's the man you mean?"

"Does he have grey eyes and black hair? If so, that *is* the man." Zuleika looked down and sighed pensively, her breath fluttering her soft half-veil. "I have heard of him, from Lelia. And we need someone to look after the horses and the stables. Besides that, you are a man of the world, effendi, and you must understand how lonely it can become. . . ."

She let her words trail off suggestively, and his blue eyes brightened, becoming thin, sly slits.

"Oho! So that's how it is? Well, you can rely on my discretion—just as I rely on yours, Lady Zuleika. I'll have him brought here, although it will cost me quite a bit to do so. But please remember that if his story of being the protégé of the Sheik Khaireddin Hadj is true—and I have sent word to the sheik himself—then you might be lacking a slave. His ridiculous story and the medal he wore are the only reasons why I did not have him sent to the stone quarries."

Zuleika bowed her head and murmured appropriate words of gratitude—and apart from that remained silent. She was glad that her brother was kept busy with the bashaw, who was upset at the renewed American blockade of the port of Tripoli that followed the capture of the United States frigate *Philadelphia*, which had run aground on fortunately uncharted reefs in the harbor itself. The *Philadelphia*'s crew of over 300 men had been taken captive and were being kept under close confinement while their ship itself was being readied for use against the Americans who had built it. It should have been a time for rejoicing, but instead, with a bad winter setting in, the American blockade made everything difficult. Even the intrepid Morad Rais thought twice about setting out again in the teeth of the patrolling American gunboats which had rendered even the navies of Morocco and Tunis half-tame and reluctant to attack American shipping.

As a result of the angry feelings that ran high, most American prisoners were treated worse than ever, and there was not a week that passed that one or two of them did not die horribly, impaled on the enormous iron hooks that were set into the harbor walls.

If Marisa was aware of these happenings, she pretended not to notice. After all, she considered herself more French than Spanish—and neither of these countries was at war with Tripoli. Neither was England, for that matter, and she wondered, secretly, if perhaps Dominic had overcome his pride enough to appeal to the British consul. She did not know why but at certain times when she was off-guard, she would suddenly think about him. He was good at surviving—hadn't he told her that, a few minutes before they had been captured? For all she knew, he might already be on his way back to England, trading on his ill-acquired title of duke of Royse.

She tried not to remember him or anything in the past. She was Lelia, which meant darkness in Arabic; while it was not a name she would have chosen for herself, she supposed it described the state of her soul, if she had one. For at Kamil's request she had embraced Islam, and was now a "true believer."

In the meantime, when she was not out riding with the Janissaries, feeling the freedom of a youth, she tended to stay in her own quarters, visiting the bathing pool at a time when Zuleika and *her* entourage did not. She had long ago sensed Zuleika's resentment of her new position and Tessa's jealousy, and she preferred to avoid them both. The only familiar face she saw was that of the former Selma Meeker, incongruously named Bab, who scuttled around with her head bowed as if she had been born a slave.

The nights passed like a sense-drugged dream, and during the days following an early morning bath and a soothing massage, she could almost forget her unfortunate condition and the fact that soon, as her belly expanded, she would become large and awkward. For now, she could still revel in the feeling of being reborn as a man and in the freedom of movement wearing male dress could bring her. To ride astride like a man, broad sash around her waist and the feel of steel weapons against her thigh, a burnoose covering her newly cropped, curling hair and partly muffling her face—she should have been born a man! And she was happy that the Janissaries commanded by Kamil did not wear the conventionally elaborate headdress but instead had adapted the garb of the desert men as their own. Under the flowing white robes, who would ever take her for a woman?

Her arrogance grew with her sense of safety and power through Kamil. She was intelligent enough to have learned that the delicate balance of power in almost all the so-called Barbary states was kept by the Janissaries, on whose loyalty deys and beys and even sultans depended. Kamil had the loyalty of his men, and he was powerful; in reality, he was the most powerful man in the kingdom, for all that he had sworn allegiance to the bashaw of Tripoli.

Kamil had ambition. He and Marisa would talk together of Napoleon and the way he had risen to power from being an obscure Corsican officer in the French army. In spite of his ill-fated Egyptian campaign, Napoleon still had many friends in the Middle East. Who knew what might happen later, after he had conquered all of Europe? She and Kamil would talk thus sometimes, until he became distracted and made love to her. And she had grown used to his way of making love, understanding his reasons for it.

hoofs on sand and a small band of desert men rode into the firelight, looking fierce in their white and gold embroidered caftans, with daggers and scimitars flashing menacingly in the wide silken sashes at their waists.

"Ah, Gott!" a German mercenary said under his breath. "And this lot has not even women,

Chapter Thirty-four

The woman Lelia who was sometimes the youth Ahmed had become both secure and sure of herself. One day she strode into the stables, frowning impatiently as she inquired why her mount was not ready for her. She carried a short, braided quirt, and she was ready to use it on the slave who had been responsible for the delay. Always more confident when she played her role as a young man, she tapped the riding quirt against her high, polished boot and frowned angrily.

Until she saw the face of the man who led her horse towards her—and then, without volition, she fell back a step, her face going paper-white.

"What—what are *you* doing here?"

Dominic Challenger, his face sunburned and unreadable, made a parody of the formal Arabic greeting, his right hand touching his head and his heart before he bowed deeply.

"I thought it was purely due to *your* good offices that I found myself here, in fact. Effendi. Or should I call you 'most illustrious lady?' You'll forgive my uncertainty as to how I should address you, I hope? At least I see that you have found your feet. Did you follow my advice or did you achieve it all on your own?"

The color rushed back into her face, making it burn.

"Do you realize what I could have done to you for speaking to me as you have? I don't know how or why you are here, but if you know what's good for you, you will show me respect—and pretend that we do not know each other!"

His grey eyes, smoky-dark in the half-light of the stables, seemed to mock her.

"Why? Because it would suit your plans for the future bet-

371

ter?" And then, without a change in tone, "I understand you are Kamil Rais's latest lover. And that, being honorable in his way, he takes you Turkish fashion—or boy fashion, as they would call it elsewhere. Is it true? Is that why you are dressed as one?"

She did not know how they suddenly happened to be quite alone, and yet she would not show her sudden fear. There was an underlying insolence in his speech that made her gasp with rage.

"How dare you talk to me so? Haven't you learned your true position yet—slave?"

"And what is *your* position—wife? Or had you conveniently forgotten?"

With a smothered cry, she struck him, the viciously wielded riding quirt drawing blood through the thin cotton shirt he wore. But as if he were used to such punishment he hardly flinched, merely catching her wrist as she raised her arm again.

"Be careful. It is written in the Koran that a husband may strike his erring wife but not the other way around. Tell me, how did you intend to marry Kamil Rais with a husband in existence already? And I hear you're with child although I see no signs of it. Whose is it? And what did you intend to do with it?"

"Let me go! I could have you killed for touching me!" she raged. With a sarcastic inclination of his head, he released her.

"A thousand pardons—effendi. But the questions I put to the woman who was, and is, until I divorce her, my wife, still remain. Well?"

She was angry and humiliated by his barbs, but it was her turn to deal out hurt and she took it, her eyes narrowing like those of an angry cat.

"You have no right to ask me questions, and you know it! But I will give you answers, as hard as they may be to swallow. Yes, I am with child—and as far as I know it may be yours. But once before, when I carried your child, you made me lose it. That time when you left me at the villa, having successfully played your game with me, as you called it! It was none of my doing then, but I tell you that this time—" her voice choked before she went on thickly—"this time it will be of *my* doing, whatever happens. Why do you think I take rides every day? Do you think that I would bear a child of yours, knowing it was yours? I would rather see it dead, along with you!"

The words she spoke appalled her even while she said them. She searched for their effect in his face.

Seeing him here so suddenly and without any warning had unnerved her, and she hardly knew what she was about, apart from the need to hurt him, just as he had hurt her.

His surface humility was just that—on the surface—while below it raged all the temper and violence she remembered too well. And perhaps that was what she had been trying to force from him, some *real*, honest reaction.

She saw the lines in his face deepen under the beard he had grown, and the scar she remembered too well grew white with tension.

"You evil, conniving bitch!" he said between his teeth, and she gave a short, hysterical laugh.

"Am I more so than you have been? You have used me and hurt me and—and marked me. And you were the cause of my father's death. Did you think I would ever forget or forgive? Now it's your turn to suffer—and I want you to!"

She raised the riding whip again, daring him to stop her, and he started to put one hand up and then let it drop to his side, taking her blow with only a slight flinching of his muscles.

What had she expected? Certainly not *this!* Only half-realizing it, she had tried to trap him into some kind of emotional reaction—she did not know what. Why didn't he react? Was he going to stand there and let her slash at him again and again without retaliation?

And then, when she had started to raise her arm again, she heard the voice behind her and grew as stiff as Dominic had become.

"What is happening here? Why are you late for our ride?" Kamil's voice from being merely angry, had taken on an overtone of coldly controlled rage. "If this infidel slave has dared to insult you, you should have left the matter of his punishment to me. Stand back, dog!"

Rosemary Rogers

Kamil had drawn his scimitar, and, without thinking, Marisa held to his arm.

"No—it's not quite as you think! I swear I don't know how he came to be here, but this man is—"

"What she is trying to tell you, effendi," Dominic said in perfect Arabic, an unpleasant smile on his face, "is that I am her husband. And, I should remind you, O mighty Rais, a Moslem like yourself."

Unbelievable—impossible—ugly!

Marisa was in her own quarters, lying across her softly cushioned bed. She was in a kind of stupor from a mixture of rage and weeping when Zuleika entered without her usual formality.

"You fool! What are you weeping for? My brother is not angry at you—far from it. He blamed *me* at first, until I had fully explained my motives in arranging a confrontation between you and that—that man who was your husband."

"Was?" Marisa raised her head, staring at the other woman through tear-swollen eyes. "Was?" she repeated on a rising note of hysteria. "He did not—it was not necessary—"

"Is it possible that you secretly nurtured some kind of affection for this slave I purchased?" Zuleika's voice, with its false note of concern, had a vicious undertone that Marisa could not miss. "Well, he's not dead yet. I fear it will be a few days before he is permitted to die, and by then he will long for death and beg for it out loud! He will be given the bastinado and then crucified in the marketplace as a warning to all other presumptuous American slaves. But, in the meantime, he has divorced you. It is easy, according to our religion. For men, that is. Had you learned that yet? You are now free to remarry."

"Ohh!" Marisa said, on an almost hysterical note. Then, controlling herself with a visible effort, "Why did *you* choose to tell me this? Why not Kamil?"

"Because I wanted to see your true reaction," Zuleika answered her coldly, her eyes like bright brown stones. And then, cunningly, "would you like to go riding with me through the marketplace? My brother is at the palace, but you could see for yourself how his orders are carried out in

374

this city. And I understand there is a matter of blood revenge—your father, was it not?"

"Yes—my father. But the fact is that this marriage of which you tell me I am freed was forced upon me. What did you hope to find in me—remorse? Pity? Yes, I feel both, but not for the reason that *you* might imagine. I will get up and look for Kamil. I think that he will understand. What happened today was neither Dominic's fault nor my own, and I would not have the guilt of his death on my conscience."

Zuleika continued to stare at her unblinkingly, although her small brown eyes had become narrow. What did she care for Zuleika?

Marisa swung her feet off the low bed and said strongly, "I will find Kamil. And if you try to stop me, I will tell him." Inside she quaked, but she deliberately kept a rein on her emotions, which she herself did not quite understand yet. And Zuleika backed off, although her voice was sullen.

"It's too late, if you hope to save him!"

"Why? Unless he has already been executed? Kamil would not order him crucified, not if he is a convert to Islam! I think you are lying to me, and I tell you again—I *will* speak to Kamil!"

She said Kamil's name, but surprisingly it was Dominic Challenger's mocking face that she saw in her mind, his slaty grey eyes fixed on hers. She hated him! But now she did not want him dead because of *her*—and she didn't know why. At least she had learned to guard her emotions, and Zuleika, for one, would never guess at the confused, jumbled thoughts that had tortured her all afternoon.

It was at this moment that Kamil himself entered and with an abrupt, angry gesture, dismissed his sister.

Still sitting upright, clad only in a thin silk shift that clung to her sweating skin, Marisa looked back at him, seeing a slim, handsome young man with a carefully trimmed black beard and brown eyes too much like his sister's.

There was a long moment of silence between them, and then he said shortly, "And what would you have spoken to me about? Was it to plead for your abductor—your former husband?"

"Yes!" she said on a sharply indrawn breath, and she

thought that he almost smiled—a twist of his full lips under his carefully trimmed black mustache.

"At least you are honest. Good. And I will be honest, too, in my turn. What did my sister tell you? I was mad with fury, I admit, and I gave certain orders, orders that I had time to regret afterwards. I should have run him through with my scimitar, but I wanted him to suffer before he died. And so he would have done, if our glorious admiral, Morad Rais, had not taken a hand—"

She stood up, without knowing that she had, and put her hands on his taut arm.

"The admiral interfered? And what happened then?"

Kamil did not remove his arm from her clutching fingers, but his eyes slashed downward into hers.

"He did not die. Does that make you glad, I wonder? Will I ever know you truly? They had him up on the platform, having used the bastinado to some effect, and were about to drive the first spike through the palm of his hand when Morad Rais saw fit to intervene with questions. In spite of his state, that devil had the wit to answer them correctly, proving his knowledge of the Koran. And then Morad took him into his own custody. He explained to me later that your—*former* husband was none other than the adopted son of a certain powerful sheik, whose alliance the bashaw needs. So you see, I have been made to look a fool. Is that what *you* think me, too?"

He raised one clenched fist as if to strike her, but when she did not flinch but turned her face upward as if to meet his blow, he gave a groan and held her closely in his arms instead.

"Oh, Lelia! Because of you I am blinded to everything else—even sense and honor! For you I would dare anything and sacrifice anything! Even the vows I made mean nothing to me now. If I would still have power, it is only so that I can set you on a throne beside me, to rule. If it means nothing to you, this failure to wreak *your* vengeance, then it means nothing to me either. As long as you are mine, and will play Roxelana to my Suleiman."

She did not quite realize what he was saying or promising her but relief and pity drove her into his arms; in a short time, locking the door of her chamber behind him, Kamil forsook all his vows and took her at last as a man takes a woman.

And in the magnificent home of Morad Rais, his newly acquired guest-slave lay naked on a soft-pillowed couch while some of Morad's female slaves gently rubbed ointments into deep weals and cuts, some of which still oozed blood.

Morad Rais, formerly Peter Lisle, still spoke English with a Scottish accent.

"Never trust a woman! That's what I've always told myself. And yet, how was I to know she had such a devious thing in her little mind? Pretty Zuleika. Always wondered why she didn't marry. But a mind as sly as a trap. A good thing I had second thoughts and made inquiries." In the face of silence he went on querulously, "Come now! You've heard that all's fair in love and war, eh? You're a renegade like meself—and the motto is 'seize the main chance.' *I* didn't know what Zuleika had in her mind! Thought I might be helping you out in arranging for a meeting with that tender young morsel who was a mite too tender and delicate for *my* taste, o'course," he added hastily. He continued, "Well, now. Haven't I stuck my neck out? And only going on your word that you know Sheik Khaireddin, and he adopted you as his son. Saved his life, did you? Well, that means he'd do anything for you, but I don't need to tell you that. Fact remains that you're here. And *I've* saved your life. Listen, we could use men like you. You could gain prizes richer than your imaginings if you'd join our navy. The Americans are going to grow tired of blockading us after a while, especially after we've refitted their own *Philadelphia* and turned it against them. And then they'll continue to pay tribute like all those bloody European kingdoms. And we'll have the run of the seas again. I tell you, man, there's plunder to be gained and riches like you've never dreamed of! Look at me! Married to the bashaw's daughter and with me own seraglio of women —aye, and boys, too, if I've a mind. You could have it all, if you're sensible. Are ye listening?"

Dominic, his head pillowed on his arms had been listening carefully, if only to keep his mind determinedly off the pain that lanced through his body every time one of the women touched it gently. It would not do to groan out loud. And he didn't want to remember that ghastly moment when a Janissary had held his head against the wooden post in the fly-ridden square, palm out, ready to drive a metal spike through it. Then, he had been glad enough to hear the voice of Morad Rais speak from the crowd, demanding what was going on. Just when he had steeled himself to endure, for as long as possible, what had to be endured and put everything else out of his mind.

Carefully, he made a noncommittal sound and heard Morad chuckle.

"Aweel! I guess ye're in no state to think straight tonight, eh? But there's no need to worry. I've talked to the bashaw and ye're safe. Good thing you had the sense to become a convert. Puts that damn Turk in the wrong, and I've been thinking for a long time he's got too much power. Now, maybe, he'll tread more lightly, if you know what I mean!"

The women had finished their annointing, and Morad Rais clapped his hands lightly to dismiss them.

"There's wine by your elbow, if you've a mind for it. Captured off a Frenchman we weren't supposed to capture! And if you want a woman, you've only to call out."

Dominic lay still, forcing himself to breathe slowly as Morad heaved himself from his pile of cushions and stood above him.

"Ah well. I suppose you haven't been here long enough to learn the other pleasures. Ye're a fine figure of a man, in spite of all the scars and the cuts, and I've grown tired of Arab boys. But maybe later, when ye've had time to grow accustomed to our ways, eh?"

And then he must have left. Or else it was just that the hold Dominic had been keeping over himself slipped. A warm body crept beside him, not touching him, and her flesh was as black and as smooth as ebony.

"I have been sent to keep you warm and comfortable. It is my pleasure to pleasure you, my lord."

Soft fingers touched his face and soft lips sought his; and as numb as his body felt, he moved onto his side, and lissome and yielding, she slipped beneath him.

He had already had wine tinctured with opium, and now,

378

only half-aware, he felt clever fingers caress him, moving over him; and then she squirmed, as agile as a cat, and it was her mouth that held him, tongue and lips working sweetly until he groaned in spite of himself and the black satin body uncoiled like a spring, lips against his again while he felt himself slide into warm, closely pulsating depths.

"I am called Narda. And I am yours, for as long as you want me," she murmured softly against his mouth. And he thought that he would surely want her forever for she was woman—giving, loving, wild, tender and satisfying all at once. A child of nature, without guile or calculation.

Chapter Thirty-five

"Morad Rais grows old before his time and frustrated like a tiger trapped in a cage since these stubborn Americans have decided to bring the war to *us!*" Kamil said, reclining against cushions. His eyes touched the woman he had chosen for himself, lingering on her golden-eyed face instead of on her body, whose growing heaviness was covered by a loose silk caftan.

She was in pain again, he could tell, in spite of the effort she made to smile and pay attention to his words.

"The burning of the *Philadelphia* inside the harbor by the Americans themselves must have been a blow to his pride," she murmured. And then, with the quickness of her mind which he still continued to admire, she said, "But everything that has happened only makes the bashaw realize how much he needs you, and your Janissaries who follow you, does it not?"

"The bashaws of Tripoli always needed us, in any case," Kamil said surely. "And all the petty lords who have set themselves up as deys and beys and pashas along the coast. They depend on the loyalty of the Janissaries to keep them in power, just as it was we who appointed them in the first place and will rule *them* in the end! And that is why Morad Rais made haste to send the slave who *was* your husband once, into the desert. From there he will either escape and find his way back to his country, or he will decide to live there, along with the black slave woman who went with him. Either way, you are free of him."

"I was never—" Marisa began, and then she gave a cry, her hands touching her swollen belly. Another cramp, this one much more painful than the last, rendering her almost insensible. She bent over, her hair falling over her eyes, her pale lips clamped together.

"I think—" she gasped painfully after a few seconds, "I think I—" But Kamil was already calling for help, and the chamber that had been so private a moment before was filled with slaves, his sister, and the half-crazed old American woman who rushed to Lelia's side and began muttering to her in English.

After that, there was only pain and helplessness as she was lifted up and carried away to the small chamber that had already been prepared. Marisa was obedient now, tolerating even Zuleika, who seemed unusually kind and concerned. No doctor here, only a bent old woman with dirty hands who called herself a midwife and had delivered the children of the bashaw's wives. Marisa had no strength left with which to protest. She drank the bitter medicine that would lessen the pain and let them strip her clothing from her. How public the process of giving birth was! Sweat pouring off her face, Marisa clung to a hand, strong and bony, and she protested when Zuleika tried to drive the woman away.

"No! No she must stay! I want her to stay."

Selma Meeker—she could not think of her by her Arabic name of Bab—was at least familiar and spoke a familiar language. They let her stay, and the woman muttered Christian prayers while she provided her own whispered instructions.

"These heathen! They don't know what to do, but I do! Watched the birthing of my own baby brother and sister— and two of my own, only they were stillborn. But your babe's a Christian, and if it's live, I'll watch out for it, don't you worry. You cling onto my hand now and disregard what *they* tell you! Push hard on top of each pain, you hear? Just take a deep breath and push hard."

Sobbing, gasping she clung to Selma's hand and pushed obediently, until everything started spinning around her and she felt herself being sucked, inexorably, into a whirling vortex of pain and wetness.

Then everything dissolved leaving only vague dreams. She was a young child again, running from some unnamed fear to be swept up in her blond-bearded father's arms. . . . Then she seemed to see the round face of simple-minded

Jean who had found her at the foot of a staircase. . . . Then she was caught and pinioned by a pair of silver grey eyes, and she saw a smiling mouth, and felt the stabbing pain of a tiny brand placed upon her thigh. . . . Then she saw Philip's face bending over her, distorted with lust—and Philip with no face at all. . . . There was a final, stabbing pain that reached through the drug she had been given, and she heard herself scream as her body arched convulsively against the hands that held her down. And after that, nothing. A vague feeling of relief, perhaps and a sense of weightlessness as something slipped wetly against her thigh. Nothing . . . relief . . .

And hours, or perhaps days later, Marisa opened her eyes and saw Zuleika bending over her.

"My poor sister! You lost the child. It could not live with the cord wrapped round its neck. But thanks be to Allah, you are well and will recover."

Slow, helpless tears drenched her eyes and slipped down her face, to be wiped away solicitously. Kamil came and held her hand for a while, whispering to her that she would soon be well and strong again and would bear many more children. "It was the will of Allah. . . ." Did *he* say it, or had it been Zuleika? It did not matter. She was empty again, and must not remember the kicking and movement in her womb that had made her almost-child seem real for a few short months.

Marisa died, and in her place Lelia survived, her will growing stronger with her body, which was massaged and pampered until a month later she was able to ride again, her bound breasts secreting no more milk, and her hips and thighs and belly as slim and flat-muscled as they had been before.

Her face and her body glowed from hours beside the bathing pool, and her eyes and hair were a darker gold. She had grown lovelier and more womanly since she had borne a child, and Kamil was more enchanted with her than ever.

Amineh and Bab had disappeared since Lelia's recovery— the latter sold to a rich merchant to care for his children, Zuleika said contemptuously. And as for Amineh, the bashaw himself had taken her into his seraglio. From there she would eventually travel to Constantinople and if she still wanted to go, would return to America when her ransom money was paid.

"The French consul displayed some interest in you, but he was told that you were very sick of the plague and would probably not recover. And the French, as you know, are very much occupied with their war with England." Zuleika's brown eyes lingered on the face of her companion. "Did you know that their leader, Napoleon has had himself crowned emperor? And I've heard that all his brothers and sisters have been made kings and queens of the provinces he has captured. I wonder how long it will all last."

So her godmother Josephine was now empress of France. But for how long? In any case, that part of her life seemed so far away that it was almost unreal. Lelia, clad as a Janissary, uncrossed her legs and rose easily to her feet to take formal leave of the plump Zuleika.

"It doesn't matter to me," she said lightly. She touched her fingers to her head and her heart before bowing elaborately in a mannish fashion that she knew Zuleika detested. "I must go now—sister. The American ships have been firing on the city, and we are to inspect the damage and make preparations to fire back the next time their gunboats dare enter our harbor."

Zuleika's teeth clenched themselves together, but she made no answer. Her brother was surely bewitched! Under any other circumstances he would have transferred *her*, his sister, to another, safer place. Even the bashaw had sent most of his wives away to his summer palace. Much worse than the almost daily bombardment by American ships was the rumor that they actually planned an overland attack next under the command of one William Eaton, a fire-eater who had been American consul in Tunis at one time. Why didn't the sultan send reinforcements? And what was her brother doing dissipating his strength every night with that foreign witch she was forced to call "sister"?

Taking her courage in her hands, Zuleika decided to visit her friends in the bashaw's harem. Among the women, gossip was rife; and it was there that most rumors had their start.

If the bashaw heard, indirectly, that a Frenchwoman, related to the now all-powerful emperor of France, was being kept here, perhaps he would do something about it. Bargain for French ships to come to his aid in return for her safe delivery back to her people, perhaps. Her plans had failed once before, but this time, they must not!

Tripoli, arrogant and invincible so far, was in a state of turmoil and unrest. A great deal of its wealthy population had moved to the small seaport of Derna. The bashaw himself stayed within the confines of his heavily fortified and guarded palace. Every day the Janissaries were called out to put a stop to some kind of trouble, and the American slaves who were left went about with secret smiles on their faces. Even Morad Rais, it was rumored, had sold his services to Algiers and was on his way there overland. How did one know what to believe and what not to? Zuleika, dogged and single-minded, went about achieving what she firmly imagined to be her duty. She had an ally in the white-skinned woman now called Amineh, to whom the bashaw had taken an inordinate fondness. She was his favorite concubine now, and some said might even become one of his wives if she were not poisoned or ransomed first.

In any case, it was to Amineh that Zuleika spoke first, phrasing her questions and suggestions in a roundabout way. She was satisfied when Amineh's languid manner was replaced first by sharp interest and then by sly thoughtfulness.

"You're right. She'd fetch a rich ransom, wouldn't she? And more than that—a possible French alliance. Perhaps her removal from *danger* might also be worth a lot. I'm sure my lord the bashaw would be very interested if I were to remind him of the bargaining power he has in his hands right now. And your brother—I'm sure you would be happier if he, too, was transferred to a safer place? To Derna, perhaps?"

Having been brought up to be patient, Zuleika bided her time and waited. And in the meantime the bombardment of Tripoli was intensified. American frigates and brigs crowded into the harbor itself, so that not a single ship of their own navy dared venture out.

Zuleika began to be anxious, wondering if her delicate

hints had borne fruit or not. In the meantime Kamil wore a perpetual frown etched between his slim brows. With the bashaw in hiding behind the walls of his palace, it was Kamil's job to keep order, and it was difficult for the population of the besieged city was likely to fly into a panic at any time.

But Kamil lost his frown at night when he lay with his gold-skinned, gold-eyed mistress and lost himself in the spell cast over him by her delicately curved, perfumed body. To her, he opened himself and talked of the time, only a few months hence, when he would be able to take her as his wife. And in the meantime, not daring to get her with child again yet, he continued to take her in the old way; while she, in her turn, had learned to pleasure him with her mouth and her supple hands.

These were the times when she closed her mind to all else and became nothing more than a body, a finely tuned instrument made only for giving and receiving the pleasures of the senses—an odalisque. And when she was not riding with the Janissaries, she learned the ancient arts of dancing from a young woman whose wide hips could vibrate with a life of their own to the sound of wailing music. It was in this way that Lelia learned to control and tighten the loosened muscles of her belly until she could move them independently while her arms and shoulders swayed in contra-time. Kamil was entranced and Zuleika envious, although she muttered contemptuously that such arts were for slaves who had no other way in which to catch their master's attention.

"But I *have* Kamil's attention." Lelia smiled with as much malice as Zuleika had shown. "I learn to dance only for his entertainment and to condition my body which has grown lazy." Her eyes flickered over Zuleika's folds of flesh, and the other's face flushed darkly under the layers of rice powder she invariably wore.

Forgetting herself, Zuleika said softly and tautly, with unmistakable hatred, "You are nothing more than a whore! A plaything whose newness will soon wear off. My brother may marry you, but he will also take other wives, remember that!

And then he will remember that you once belonged to someone else, and he will divorce you—if he doesn't make you a slave to one of his other wives! You will not always be young and slim, remember that!"

"But I am *now!*" the younger woman said, and stretched her half-clad body deliberately. She laughed when Zuleika, her brown eyes narrowing, hissed: "Bitch! She-devil!"

She did not tell Kamil of their little exchange for she almost felt sorry for Zuleika. And when she considered it, she had to admit that perhaps the other woman was right. She had become a complete hedonist, living on her nerves and controlled only by her newly-awakened senses. But then, what else was there? She had been thrown into a society where the only role of women was to bring delight and pleasure to men. And while Kamil enjoyed her intelligence and discussed affairs of state with her, the nights they spent together put her back in her proper perspective again.

The late summer days were pitilessly hot, and the sun burned out of the blue cauldron of the sky. The blind storyteller in the market place recited ancient poetry when he was thrown a coin or two, and street peddlers continued to hawk their wares as though nothing had changed and the days would go on endlessly as they had gone on since the time of the caliphs.

Within the cool-walled inner courtyards of Kamil Hasan's house, the perfume of flowers and scented oils filled the still air, and music drowned out the faint, booming sounds of desultory cannon fire. Everything was as it might have been a hundred years ago—why should it change now?

But it did—and so suddenly that not even Zuleika was prepared for it. The bashaw's palace guards came late one afternoon while Kamil was away—to take both women under his illustrious protection, they said politely. Kamil Hasan was being transferred, by order of the Turkish sultan himself, to defend Derna. In the meantime, his sister would reside within the seraglio of the bashaw himself until arrangements could be made for her to rejoin her parents' household. And as for the Frenchwoman to whom Kamil Rais had given his protection—it would no longer be needed. The French consul had become adamant about it, and the bashaw, embroiled in a war with distant America, had no desire to incur the enmity of France as well.

Dressed as a woman again and heavily veiled, Lelia found herself carried, along with all her belongings, in a litter through the crowded streets where she had once ridden freely with the Janissaries.

She was taken to the French consul's house which was safely on the outskirts of the sprawling city, and she found that arrangements had already been made for her journey overland to the nearest unblockaded port, from which she would take a ship for France.

Monsieur D'Arcy, the French consul, was a small-statured, fussy man who insisted on treating her as if she had been through a terrible experience and therefore—naturally!—could not be expected to have all her wits about her.

He would not listen to her but reiterated patiently that she mustn't worry herself any longer. Her ransom had been paid to the Turkish sultan himself, and *he* had given strict orders that she was to be returned unmolested.

"The emperor has sent a personal message stating his deepest concern. And the empress says she wept on hearing that you were still alive and safe."

Monsieur D'Arcy looked at her in the strangest fashion. He was half in awe of her and half impatient because obviously the poor young creature had undergone such strain that she did not quite realize how flattered she ought to be!

He repeated kindly in the face of her stony silence, "Do you understand, my dearest er—madame? I have here a personally written note signed by the emperor of France! No doubt you are still in a state of shock. Perhaps you had given up all hope of being rescued, no? But it is a fact that you are now saved—and safe! I dare not take any chances with your continuing safety. It has all been arranged, and you will leave tomorrow morning, with a personal escort provided by the bashaw himself, who has guaranteed your safe conduct to Tunis. From then on you will have the protection of the French navy." She wept impotently, and he patted her shoulder awkwardly.

D'Arcy made sure she was heavily guarded, and he even

provided her with some European clothes, which she refused to wear. He was relieved when the escort promised by the bashaw arrived bright and early and his sullen guest departed in their midst.

Chapter Thirty-six

News—and rumor—had a way of carrying fast across the vast desert that lay between Tripoli and Egypt. There were the endless caravans that traveled regularly, stopping at different small oases to pay tribute to the sheiks who owned them and fill their water skins. And there were the itinerant storytellers, and the dervishes, or holy men, who paid no tribute, but wandered through the desert and were accepted wherever they went with awe and respect.

Word was carried to the bashaw at Tripoli, now trapped in his small kingdom by the renewed American blockade, that a small but hard-bitten force of men under the command of William Eaton, the American navy agent for the Mediterranean, had started to march from Alexandria towards his kingdom. The motley army was composed mostly of volunteers, including some mercenaries and foreign adventurers, but they were dangerous, experienced fighting men and with them came Hamet Karamanli, brother of the deposed ex-bashaw, and pretender to the throne.

The bashaw chewed on his nails and sent messages to Constantinople, or Stamboul as it was now called, and to neighboring states like Tunis and Algiers. But they were all having their own problems, it seemed; and while Commodore Preble, in charge of the American fleet in the Mediterranean, hoped to put a quick end to the war, Eaton's small army moved slowly and determinedly towards the small seaport of Derna. And at Derna, Kamil Hasan once more lived in the barracks with his Janissaries while he organized its defense and dreamed of glory.

William Eaton, who knew the temper of his motley crew, did not try to push them on their march across the desert.

He was enough of a cynic to realize that most of them, apart from the few American volunteers, were out for plunder and position.

But by early in 1805, Eaton was growing impatient. They had hugged the coast, except for occasional forays into the desert and had taken Salum, with hardly any loss of life. However, Derna was another matter. The commander of the Janissaries there was obviously a wily man, and he was expecting them. They had already engaged in several small skirmishes with the Tripolitan army that had gained nothing except the knowledge that these men were both angry and fierce adversaries.

Deliberately, Eaton headed his force into the desert, hoping that the defenders of Derna would think they meant to attack Tripoli itself from its unprotected flank. A grizzled veteran of the Revolution, Eaton tried to curb his impatience as he sat with some of his captains around a campfire, their tents pitched on the outskirts of a small desert oasis.

There was also a small caravan camped here, escorted by some haughty-looking Bedouins who sat apart from the merchants and their servants and did not drink the raki that was freely if unobtrusively passed around. They did, however, permit some of their boldly unveiled women to dance for the entertainment of the other travelers, and they accepted the coins that were thrown when each dance was over.

Eaton himself drank only sparingly as he pretended to be fascinated watching the women dancers. Outwardly relaxed, he waited. And soon, out of the darkness beyond the fire, one of his most trusted men, a naturalized American who spoke Arabic, came to sit beside him, loosening the folds of his cloak as he did so.

"Well?"

"Well, ye say, sir! D'ye realize how full of alcohol I am now? If I hadn't been used to good Scotch whiskey, and right out o' the still at that, I wouldn't have a tongue in my head. That stuff they call raki is mighty powerful!"

William Eaton moved his shoulders impatiently under the burnoose he wore.

"But did you hear anything?"

"Sure! That this oasis, like many others like it, is owned

by the most powerful Sheik Khaireddin el Sharif el Hadj—to use just a few of his long titles. And those fierce-looking tribesmen you see there, clutching at their daggers, are of his tribe. I ran into a storyteller, whose tongue had been loosened by raki, and he told me a whole, long story about it. About how this sheik is descended from the prophet and about what a powerful, holy man he is. But that ain't what you'll want to be hearing, eh? The main thing is that this sheik controls most of the nomadic tribes in this area. Aye, and he is even connected by marriage to the Touaregs. Ye'll ken what that means? With his help—or with just his neutrality, we'll be home safe. And—" The speaker drew in a long self-satisfied breath, pausing slightly until Eaton humored him and said gruffly, "And? . . ."

"*And* it seems that one of his sons has a grudge against the Turks. Particularly their damned Janissaries. And *particularly* a certain Rais, who commands them in Derna. He wants to get in there pretty bad. And the point of it all is that with him to guide us, and the sheik playing hands off—"

"Quite so!" Eaton said drily, and then, "But how far can you trust this storyteller? How long would we have to wait? And above all, how do we know we won't be led into a trap?"

His companion sighed as he stretched. "Darned if I'll ever get used to sitting cross-legged, like these heathens do. But aye, I thought of the same objections you're thinking of—and yet, what's there to lose? This Saqr Ibn Khaireddin—they told me the name means falcon—will come along to join us, and as long as *he's* with us, as a kind of voluntary hostage, you might say, we have the help of the desert people at best—and their noninterference at worst. And if you ask me, that storyteller was sent here on purpose, just to sound us out!"

"Exactly what I've been thinking!" Eaton said, and stretched. "Well," he continued grudgingly, "I suppose we'll be here for another day or two at the very least. I'll talk to this storyteller of yours, if you think I should, but if you've already established a rapport with him, *you* can tell him I'm willing to wait for this—this desert falcon to show up. But not too long, mind you, for the men are getting restive, as you can see."

They were restless, and they were even more so by the third night they spent at the oasis, since the Bedouin caravan had gone, and they had no lovely, open-faced girls to dance for them. William Eaton, a frown on his face, had just announced that they would prepare that very night to leave in the morning when there was a whisper of camels' hoofs on sand and a small band of desert Bedouin rode into the firelight, looking fierce in their white abas and richly embroidered caftans, with daggers and scimitars stuck menacingly in the wide silken sashes at their waists.

"Ah, Gott!" a German mercenary sighed beneath his breath. "And this lot has not even women with them to keep us amused!" But he dared not say it aloud for they had all been warned against angering the Bedouins.

The minor chieftain in whose care the oasis was came out of his tent, and then made a bow before the first and the tallest of the riders to dismount from his camel.

There was a short, low-voiced conversation between them, and then while the tall man stood arrogantly still, his booted feet placed apart, the caretaker of the oasis came shuffling over to talk to the American "general."

"Wonder if that's him?"

"Well, we'll soon find out, won't we?"

And in a few minutes the tall, richly dressed sheik, his burnoose still concealing most of his face, followed the caretaker to the tent of William Eaton, who came out to greet him. Eaton, who had lived among the Arabs for long enough to learn their customs, made all the polite observances.

The black slave who was the sheik's bodyguard brought in wine and raki and fresh lamb steaks that still sizzled from the fires outside. And then he left them. With carefully guarded curiosity, Eaton waved his guest to a seat on the pile of cushions opposite him.

"If you will honor me—"

He spoke in Arabic, and the Bedouin replied in the same language. He seated himself and threw open his aba to disclose a richly embroidered caftan sashed at the waist. He also pulled aside that part of his headdress concealing the lower half of his face, revealing hawklike, sunburned features that were marred only by a small, crescent-shaped scar running down from the right temple. He had, surprisingly, light silver-grey eyes.

'So he had a Circassian mother, this particular son?' Eaton thought swiftly, even while he schooled his craggy features into studied blankness.

He became aware that he, too, was being studied just as carefully as he observed his recent guest, and not being a diplomat unless it was forced upon him, he said bluntly, "Are you here to join us? Do you know where we travel next?"

"You go to take Derna; and I shall be with you, if you will permit me." In spite of the flowery Arabic, Eaton thought he detected a note of polite irony, which made him frown slightly.

"I've heard you have your own reasons for wishing to enter Derna, but there is one thing I should make clear ahead of time, and that is that *I* have my reasons, too—and I head this army, such as it is. Are you willing to take orders from me?"

He proffered a wineskin as he spoke, as a kind of test, and released a short breath when his guest accepted it and drank deeply.

"I've followed orders before, and I can do so again. But there is one man in Derna who belongs to me—and a certain errand I must perform when we take the town. It will not interfere with your plans, I assure you."

Eaton could not help asking, "A personal revenge?" He was answered in the same drawling, ironical voice which suddenly turned hard.

"A personal quest. But once I have found what I am looking for, I will place myself and the men who accompany me at your disposal, Mr. Eaton."

"You know my name?"

The reply came smoothly, "Who does not?"

And still Eaton was nagged by a strange sense of familiarity—of—something!

"If we have to do it by surprise or trickery—you know your way around the town? Its entrances and its exits?"

"I know every street and every building and most details of the fortifications. I have not been there, but I have studied maps drawn on sand. And if I did not go there with you and your army, I would still go alone. Do you think I could pass for a wandering dervish or a storyteller in the marketplace, Mr. Eaton?"

The wineskin passed back, and William Eaton put it to his lips before he answered bluntly, "It would be easy, I suppose, except for the unusual color of your eyes. But I suppose that, too, could be accounted for."

The Bedouin laughed a trifle mockingly. "And who would ask questions in the face of a dagger or a scimitar? But that is beside the point. I am here, and I would join you if you will permit it. What is your answer?"

"I think you already know it!" Eaton grunted and reached for the wineskin again. "Will you be ready to leave in the morning?"

"I am ready now, Mr. Eaton. And I have learned not to need too many hours of sleep."

While they ate and drank, William Eaton studied his latest ally covertly, feeling slightly annoyed at himself because he could not quite understand the man, nor place him in a particular category. He ate with his fingers like any Arab, wiping them fastidiously afterwards with the napkins that were provided, and his Arabic was flawless. Still, some instinct told him that this man was no ordinary Bedouin, in spite of the religious medal that swung at his neck. That he drank wine and raki did not count—most sophisticated Arabs did, in private. But there was still something different, and therefore slightly disturbing about this one.

A trap? Eaton wondered. But the Bedouins who were caretakers of this small oasis had seemed to recognize him. On the other hand—did that mean anything? 'A whole army, marching on Derna, cannot be hidden anyway,' his mind reasoned. 'And fifteen Bedouins, even if they are traitors, can soon be wiped out, especially if I have some of my most trusted men ride alongside them. If it's a chance, it's a chance worth taking.'

Once his mind had been made up, he relaxed. And after the Arab had left him, thanking him for his hospitality, he let his mind range forward to the time they might be at the very gates of Tripoli, where so many Americans were held captive. The men of the *Philadelphia.* And the nameless others taken off merchant ships and forced to toil as slaves. Well, there was no way a two-pronged attack by "Preble's boys" at sea and by his own army on land, could fail. All the Barbary states needed a lesson, anyhow. Maybe they wouldn't be so eager to meddle with American ships after this!

Eaton's army was on the march again before six the next morning. It was still cool in the desert, and the sky showed traces of oyster-shell pink against pale blue.

The Bedouins who were to join them were already mounted on their camels, waiting impassively. Once William Eaton had emerged from his tent and mounted his camel, they started off at a slow pace which would give the others a chance to catch up with them.

Cursing and grumbling, Eaton's "army" straggled out against the burning yellow sands. They wore the costumes of half a dozen nations, these hard-faced men. They were all bristling with weapons. Most of them wore loose white burnooses over their clothes just as the Arabs did, to protect themselves against the pitiless heat that burned down from the yellow globe of the sun and reflected off the sands which became quite hot as the day advanced.

The Bedouins stayed effortlessly in the lead. They made camp for the night some fifty miles from Derna, behind banks of sand dunes. By the time Eaton and his men arrived, the Bedouins' tiny campfires were already burning, and the smell of roasting goat flesh was sweet on the night air.

"They've even set guards all around already."

William Eaton turned to the man who had spoken, his bushy brows drawing together. "And we'll set our own, too. Do I hear you volunteer, or would you rather try to strike up a conversation with our newly-found Bedouin friends?"

"I'll do the latter, if ye don't mind," Eaton's companion said with dignity. "After all, I can smell *their* dinner a-cooking, and ours ain't even started yet. Maybe the young sheikh knows something of Tripoli and the true conditions of the Christian slaves there."

"Good!" Eaton responded drily. "And maybe it will be *my* turn to be asked to dinner this time. I found this Saqr a very interesting man to talk to."

"Is that so? Well, perhaps I'll find out for meself then— ye'll remember the luck I had with that wandering story-teller?"

Donald McGuire pulled his ill-hung burnoose about his shoulders and, with what he hoped was a casual gesture, set out determinedly towards those distant fires where meat roasted on slowly turning spits, scenting the air and making his mouth water.

As he drew near, a Bedouin, scimitar drawn, seemed to rise up out of the sand, eying him impassively. Donald, smiling widely, spoke to him in Arabic, and after a few moments the man, seeming to shrug slightly, led him towards the small tent that had been erected for their leader, the mysterious Saqr.

Like the rest of Eaton's men, Donald was curious about what kind of grudge this Arab had against the Turkish defenders of Derna. And above all, it had been a long march, and he was hungry and thirsty.

His Bedouin escort muttered something in a low voice to the two men who stood guard outside the tent, and one of them, after a glance at Donald, ducked inside, to return soon after with grudgingly uttered permission for the infidel to enter. Politely, Donald left his heavy boots outside, hoping they would be safe; and for an instant, the light from two oil lamps and a small brazier made him blink.

And then a voice, all too familiar and cutting said in English, "What the hell are *you* doing here? And what did you do with my ship?"

Later, his mouth full of stringy goat's meat, Donald chewed vigorously and murmured, "And why all the mystery? I'd not be here meself if not for *you!* Ye might at least have told General Eaton who you were—he'd not tell a soul! And now that you know your ship's safe with young Silas, will you no' tell me why you keep scowling at me? Not that I ain't glad to find you alive and well, when all the while I was thinking you'd be some heathen's slave, if you hadn't got yourself killed for your recklessness. But damned if you ain't a

398

heathen yourself, just like you were born to it! I suppose you have yourself a harem of women by now—so why Derna?"

Dominic sighed, but his grey eyes, narrowing, warned Donald to caution.

"I have my own reasons for going to Derna. And as usual, you talk too much, old friend. Must I remind you that *you* are the heathen here? And no, I will not hear any sermons on the subject. You may tell Mr. Eaton who I am, if you wish, but I would prefer that it not become common knowledge. Do you understand?"

"Oh, aye!" Donald said sulkily, wiping his mouth with the back of his hand. "But there's a deal of matters I don't understand yet, and a deal of questions in my mind, too. That old Arab in a green turban we picked up more dead than alive and you risked your fool neck to save—I thought his half brother had seized his lands? So—all right! There's no need to be looking at me like that! So my tongue runs away with me! I ain't saying he wasn't a good sort—taught us both Arabic, didn't he? And I minded very well when you and he would get to talking about his religion *and* when he gave you that heathen medal you still wear around your neck. But man! Do ye intend to live among the Arabs forever? And that puir lassie who was your wife—I've had time to think that maybe it wasn't all her doing that Monsieur Fouché's men picked you up that time—"

"Donald—that's enough! Even from you, there are limits to what I will take." Uncoiling himself from his cross-legged position, Dominic suddenly stood up. In the flickering lights he seemed all Arab, his face as flinty hard as his eyes.

Realizing that his "audience" was over, Donald scrambled unwillingly to his feet also.

Switching to faultless Arabic, Dominic said evenly, "You may tell Mr. Eaton whatever you think fit—once you've had his assurance that it will not go any further. And you may also tell him that we will be ready very early in the morning. Derna is very close now, and I am anxious to arrive there."

Chapter Thirty-seven

They took Bomba early in April and soon after that, attacking at night, Derna itself. Hard pressed, the trained Janissaries fought hand-to-hand with the grinning, shouting invaders in the narrow streets, while the populace hid and waited to greet whoever turned out to be the victors.

Having found out, from a dying Janissary, the location of the dwelling of Osman the Trader, Saqr Ibn Khaireddin made his way there, trailed by two faithful Bedouins who had made their sheik an oath not to leave his side, and by the faithful Donald McGuire, who was driven by curiosity as well as concern for his reckless friend.

Derna was already a conquered city. The screams of women mingled with the loud whoops and laughter of the victors, proclaimed it, as did the flames rising high against the blue-black night sky.

Inside the tightly closed house of Osman there came a subdued noise of wailing and the high-pitched crying of young children.

Outside the heavily-shuttered wooden door, Kamil Hasan waited, and his teeth, drawing back from his lips, were a white blur against the darkness of his bearded face. The fires from the burning buildings cast a red glow everywhere, reflecting off the scimitar in Kamil's hand.

"I had the feeling that you would come here. I, too, have my sources of rumor. So, slave, will you fight me for the life of your son? *If* he still lives? Or will I have to battle against all of you?"

Dominic made a gesture with his arm, and the others fell back a few steps, Donald grumbling under his breath.

"A man is only enslaved by his senses—and I think you

were, Kamil Pasha. I will kill you unless you stand aside, but I would rather not. Derna is a captive city, as Tripoli soon will be. If you are sensible you will drop your sword and surrender."

Kamil made a lunge instead, his scimitar flashing where his mocking adversary had stood only a few seconds ago. There was a blur of white robes, and a blade met his, drawing sparks.

They fought up and down the shallow steps, and Kamil, being a man who had lost everything, showed it in the fierce desperation of his attack. He was a Janissary, one of the elite who had been trained since childhood. But in this case there were his bitter emotions that also entered into this combat which would be his final one. He would either kill or be killed—and in either case he would die, for there was nothing he had to live for any longer.

The Bedouins watched impassively, moving back slightly to give the combatants room. Donald, too, moved back, but unwillingly; he muttered words of encouragement under his breath.

The shining blades lunged and clashed together, glittering in the eerie glow. Although shouts and screams could be heard in the distance, here there was only the sound of breathing, the stamp of feet, and the sound of steel jarring against steel.

It was over very suddenly. Dominic seemed to stumble, drawing back slightly, and with a harsh cry, Kamil's scimitar slashed through the air finding only space as his opponent ducked and slid sideways, to drive his own blade upward and outward.

It was done. The bleeding, half-decapitated body rolled to lie half on and half off the steps, which were reddened with his gushing blood.

"I think he wanted to die," Dominic said to no one in particular. He wiped the stained blade of his scimitar against his white robes before banging with the flat of it against the door.

"Poor devil!" Donald said perfunctorily. And then, "But what did he mean when he talked about your *son?* Ye dinna tell me—"

"Do I have to tell you everything, you inquisitive old goat? Hold your tongue now—I don't know how we'll be greeted."

There was a sound from the other side, and one of the Bedouins raised his voice, to call harshly and threateningly in Arabic. After a short hesitation there was the sound of iron bolts being slid and the door swung open to reveal, a woman standing there—tall and angular, her sparse hair pulled back from her face. She held a child in her arms.

"I'm American—and you *are* American forces, aren't you? They've treated me quite well, all things considered— I said I'd tell you that." She was clad in black, and was unveiled, and her voice was pure New England. "Well, who are you? You all look Arab to me, except *you!*" Her eyes fixed themselves accusingly upon Donald, who had lost his headdress sometime during the fighting, and in spite of his indignation he felt his face redden.

It was Dominic, standing very still, who expelled his breath and said in a strange voice, "Oh, God! Mrs. Meeker?"

Selma Meeker had a great deal to say, but Dominic turned and left, and it was poor Donald who had to listen to most of her diatribe.

"So *he's* turned heathen, too. And I can't say that I'm *too* surprised, although there *was* a time when I almost felt sorry for him—the way that little hussy acted! Wanting to be rid of her own child so she could live with that—that— Turk! Do you have any idea what they do with boy children here? Well, I'd rather not say, myself, it's too horrible to speak of. And the only reason they let *me* alone was because I wouldn't give in. They said I was mad, you know —and crazy people are considered holy here. Hah! But I looked after the child. I lost three of my own, you see, and they're so tiny and helpless at this age! They tried to give the poor mite some heathen name, but I gave him one of my own. Christian. Yes, and no matter what his father's become, that's what the boy will be! He knows me already and holds out his arms to me. I won't let them take him from me, do you hear?" Suddenly, her strident voice became questioning and almost pathetic. "He won't be taken away from me now, will he?"

"No, no!" Donald said soothingly, wishing that Dominic would come back and rescue him. "Of course he wouldn't do that. The wee bairn needs someone to look after him, doesn't he? Captain Challenger can't do it, nor can I." He leaned forward, making clucking noises, and touched the child under the chin. He received a wide, unblinking stare from grey eyes before the child turned his face against the shoulder of the woman who held it.

No mistaking whose child this was—but where was his mother? And why in hell didn't Dominic come and rescue him from this ridiculous situation?

It was close to dawn, and the sky was growing pearly. Derna was a captive city and its inhabitants, used to the comings and goings of different masters, were beginning to creep out of their low-walled, flat-roofed dwellings like mice who sensed that the cat was sated for a time. The dead and dying had been conveniently removed from the street.

In the house of Osman the Trader, the woman who had been a slave called Bab held undisputed sway.

In yet another house, commandeered by the victorious army he had led, William Eaton sat in frowning conference with the man his followers called El Saqr'—whom he now knew to be someone else. Eaton was understandably annoyed. "You could have told me, damn you! Not that it would have made a difference, but I like to know things! So you're Dominic Challenger. I've heard of you. And *you're* the reason why Donald McGuire joined me. Well, now you've found what you came looking for, what do you intend to do?"

"Why—follow your orders, Mr. Eaton. As we agreed some days before."

Eaton's bushy brows peaked in the middle of his forehead.

"And your son? The child you came here to find?"

"I've found him, haven't I? And he has a formidable nurse. Naturally, I will make sure that they are both kept safe."

"You sound cold-blooded, sir! Although it's not my place to say so! However, I knew your—"

Dominic said smoothly, "A man has many fathers. But I wish you would not remind me! In case it worries you, however, I have the sheik's permission to leave if I see fit. The affection between us does not depend on closeness, and he has other sons of his blood."

"Then you intend, when this is over, to go back to America?"

"I think I would like to see my son brought up there, where he has a chance to be himself. And to tell you the truth, Mr. Eaton, I have been growing homesick myself!"

Blue eyes and grey met and clashed until Eaton grunted, dropping his to the brazier that flared between them.

"Well, whatever you do later is your own business, I suppose. And I've been grateful for your help here. Tomorrow, we'll fly our flag from the highest building to let Captain Barron know we're in charge here now. You know he's taken over Commodore Preble's command? The commodore was a sick man, I understand."

"And the navy hasn't changed at all," Dominic responded drily. "It's all rank and seniority now. Why do you think I elected to become a privateer?"

He was still an adventurer, Eaton thought after he had left. How long would their association continue?

As it was, Eaton's "army" kicked its heels in Derna while the bashaw of Tripoli negotiated a hasty peace with the Americans he had once despised. And Eaton, when he heard of the treaty, was furious; like Commodore Preble, he had been certain that the matter could have been settled once and for all through outright conquest. Barron had been quickly replaced by Captain John Rogers. A civilian negotiator, Tobias Lear, arranged for the peace and the release of the *Philadelphia*'s crew. The American public wanted peace, Mr. Lear explained through pursed lips, and in June of 1805, the treaty was signed.

During the same month, Donald McGuire and his former captain wearing rather awkwardly what Donald termed "civilized clothes" were granted passage to America on a naval vessel. Accompanying them was the woman Selma Meeker, whose husband, it had been discovered, had unfortunately died of a fever during his captivity and servitude. There was also the child Christian, jealously tended by Mrs. Meeker.

The captain of this particular gunboat was young and rather naive. He had heard of Captain Challenger—who had not? But to find his idol in the company of an old and ugly woman several years older than he—with a child to be accounted for between them . . . well! It was enough to make a man lose some of his ideals!

As for the widow Meeker, she was not too much disturbed by her widowhood, having long ago resigned herself to that state. All the love she had held pent up within her for all her strictly regimented life was now lavished upon the child she had named Christian. She did not quite approve of Christian's father, but as long as he allowed her to care for the child she supposed he could be tolerated.

Donald, his voice cracking, said one evening: "Do—do ye realize what they're all thinking? That *that* woman is the mother of your bairn! Captain, I've put up with much from you, but do I have to put up with such a slur? I ask you—"

"Don't!" Dominic said shortly. And then, "Do you think I care about what they say? If not for Mrs. Meeker I might not have a son—and if I find I have to marry the old witch for convention's sake, then I will."

"Oh, God!" Donald said strongly and piously and retired forthwith, to concentrate sulkily on his own thoughts and to spread subtle rumors among the crew that the child belonged to his captain's lost love who had killed herself after it was born, rather than be shamed. He felt better after that.

Dodging French and English ships, they sailed for the Carolinas. During the voyage, Dominic deliberately made himself drunk enough to propose to Mrs. Meeker—finding himself not quite drunk enough to be relieved that she turned him down bluntly.

"I won't be separated from Christian, and I tell you that right now! But I wouldn't marry the likes of you, either! I'll be his nurse and your housekeeper as long as you keep a decent house, but that's all. Do you understand?"

Apologetically, he murmured that he did understand and said he was sorry for his lack of control. As he backed out of her cabin, he ran into Donald who was bent double with the effort of holding back his ribald laughter.

Dominic's hands took him about the throat, shaking him until his laughter gave way to alarmed grunts.

"All right! So she turned me down, and I don't blame her. But how is it you've grown as old as you have without a wife? And she's a Presbyterian. You'll make a good pair, I'm sure. *I'm* a ne'er-do-well fly-by-night and a heathen into the bargain, according to the pure Selma. But she has a great deal of admiration for *you* it appears. So—"

"No!" Donald croaked; and then he saw his erstwhile captain grin, and his eyes rolled up imploringly. When he was able to speak again he gasped, "Must I? I always thought that if I settled down it would be with a nicely shaped young female—"

"Can you think of one who would have you?" Dominic said relentlessly. "No, my old friend. I'm afraid it's either propose honorably matrimony to the widow Meeker or fall overboard."

"So much for friendship and loyalty!" Donald muttered bitterly, massaging his aching throat.

He was only momentarily relieved when Selma Meeker, studying his red face and shuffling feet, decided to reserve her decision until she'd had a chance to get better acquainted with him. But for the rest of the protracted voyage, he was forced to dance attendance on her under Dominic's steely eyes, and on the few occasions that she went so far as to give him a smile, he quaked in his boots.

Chapter Thirty-eight

On another ship, a French one, Marisa leaned against the rail. She stared at the blue-green water, topped with white foam, that rushed by.

It seemed to her that she'd been on a ship for most of her life, and she should have learned her lesson by now, but here she was, one more time, this time on her way to New Spain and her uncle the bishop.

It seemed to her that she had come full circle. She was going back to her roots. And the Emperor Napoleon's France lay far behind her now, along with the high-waisted, beautiful gowns and her position, for a short while, as the emperor's mistress.

He was not as tender and devoted a lover as Kamil had been, and he had offered her nothing more than the doubtful honor of being his mistress. The emperor of France and most of Europe was a man like any other, after all, afraid that his wife might find out about his peccadilloes, on the one hand, and desirous on the other of being reassured that he was the best lover she had ever had.

After her return to France from Tripolitania, Marisa had spent a month in seclusion and then four months as Napoleon's mistress. They tired of each other almost simultaneously, and since she had been clever enough not to show him how bored she had become, he believed that it was *he* who had wisely put an end to their affair. Always generous with his ex-mistresses, Napoleon had seen to it that she was provided with plenty of money, a magnificent wardrobe, and jewels in addition to an escort as far as Cuba.

'At least he gets rid of his ex-mistresses in style,' Marisa thought cynically, as she tried not to remember Kamil and

409

wondered instead what the future, such as it was, held for her.

She was still young, and since her flesh had filled out somewhat, men had told her she was so beautiful, so lovely —all as a prelude to wanting to lie with her. And of that, too, she had grown weary! One man was very much like another—and now she had begun to even think like a whore. Was it possible that she had come so far, yet nowhere?

The water rushed past, now blue, now turquoise, and now light green. What would it be like, to go back to being a protected child again? It was what she had chosen, when she had finally received her uncle's long-delayed letter. A fresh start to a new life, and although there were some things that could not be changed and memories that could not be erased, it was what she needed.

She continued to think so even when they had landed at Havana, after having spent most of the voyage dodging British and American gunboats. It had been an exciting voyage if one considered such things exciting; and there had been times when Marisa had wondered if she would die, sinking to the bottom of the sea, or if she would be taken prisoner and be forced to use her body again for survival. She had almost agreed to the casual, persistent requests of the captain, a man of middle age who would have enjoyed being able to boast discreetly to his colleagues that he had slept with one of the emperor's mistresses. She flirted and didn't say no, but at the last moment she drew back, telling herself that she was not yet one of those women who took lovers merely to pass away the time. To save Captain De Vigny's pride she implied, with a sigh and downcast eyes that she was still trying to get over the emperor, his master.

'This way is best,' Marisa told herself firmly; and she was still repeating it to herself when, clad in a high-necked gown of black silk that nevertheless clung to her slimly curved figure, she walked down the gangplank into the heat and fly-ridden bustle of a stone dock that stretched like a finger into Havana's blue harbor.

"You're sure you are to be met, madame? Faugh!" Captain De Vigny drawled, holding a perfume-drenched lace handkerchief to his nose, "I could vow those bananas are rotting! What an insane place! I will gladly take you to Martinique if your friends are not here. This is hardly a place I'd like to leave you alone!"

"Oh, I'm sure my uncle will be here. Or that he would have sent someone, at least."

Marisa was glad of her fashionable poke bonnet which sheltered her face from the broiling sun. In spite of it, she could feel her newly cropped hair, already damp with sweat, curling against her face. It was so hot! Perhaps she should have worn something else. But then she caught sideways glances from dark-eyed Spaniards, glances that seemed to strip her of her clothing in less than a second, and she was glad she had gowned herself so conservatively.

"Some of my men are unloading your baggage," De Vigny murmured, his fingers tightening slightly over Marisa's arm. "Perhaps we had better wait here for a while until they are done—and I will protect you, chère madame, from these hot-eyed Spaniards who would like to devour your frail beauty! It's a good thing I decided to escort you to shore myself—what a place! So many blacks—I suppose they are slaves? At least the Spaniards seem to know how to keep them in their places—a shame we could not have done the same in St. Domingue, where I hear that one of them, calling himself emperor, has set himself up as ruler. The Princess Pauline's husband, General Le Clerc, died there, of the yellow fever. You will be careful, I hope?"

She was almost grateful for his stream of chatter as her eyes searched the crowds. Would her uncle be here himself? Would she recognize him? She could not remember him at all—did he look like her father?

At that moment a closed carriage drove onto the dock itself, and the crowd drew back slightly.

"It's the governor himself—the captain-general!"

Marisa heard the whispers and glanced up curiously. This was a title her father had once borne, before he took to traveling, adventuring, looking for lands for himself, and looking for other women besides her mother.

The carriage, flanked by uniformed outriders, swept to a

halt. Several black urchins, their eyes round with awe, ran to hold the horses.

"Mon Dieu! So we are to be honored!" Captain De Vigny murmured in his laziest, most sophisticated drawl. And yet he bowed deeply as the governor, alighting from his carriage with his plumed hat in his hand, looked all around him, his eyes finally alighting upon them. He turned to say something to the somberly-clad priest who had followed him out of the carriage, and the bend of his head indicated respect.

Marisa caught a glimpse of dark blue eyes, so like her father's, and a small cry was caught in her throat. She took an impulsive step forward and then stopped, fighting embarrassment and shyness. With an unconscious movement her hand brushed at the hair that curled damply on her forehead, inadvertently pushing her bonnet, off her head, and the blue eyes fixed hers with a deep, penetrating gaze.

She heard in her mind the ancient, sad, malagueña of Spain, and in spite of herself the tears started to her eyes. Her uncle? He strode forward, his walk as vital and springy as that of a young man. The cardinal archbishop of New Spain was dressed as plainly as an ordinary friar, but there was something about his manner that put him above the ordinary. And the governor of Cuba, the Conde Aguilera, followed behind him, with his armed escort.

"You are Maria? My niece? Yes—for your eyes are those of your mother."

She started to kneel, from old habit, and was swept into his embrace.

"My little niece, who wanted so much to be a nun! What shall I call you? Marisa, as your mother did? It's not a name for a nun, but I think it suits you. And you must remember that whatever has taken place and wherever your willfulness has taken you, you are here now. You will rest, my child, and try to empty your mind of those things which you find unpleasant to remember."

She had been taken in to the household of the governor of Cuba. De Vigny was gone already, having paid his formal respects, and her uncle had heard her garbled, mixed-up confession. How could he still smile at her so lovingly and touch her bent head in blessing?

"You don't understand, monsignor! I have sinned. I have been so weak, so—"

"And you are also very young! Would you argue with me? Do you seek some kind of punishment to help you throw off the burden of what you call your guilt? My niece, I am an old man, older than my brother, your father. And I have seen much. I can set you a penance, which you will perform dutifully, I'm sure, but will that help? No. The help you seek must come from within yourself. And to begin with, you must stop running away. Haven't you found that out already? There is no real escape except into worse toils than those you wished to avoid in the first place. Be at peace. That is the first step."

Would she ever find the kind of peace her uncle talked about? She had made her confession to him. Almost disappointed, she could not read any trace of shock or disapproval in his lined, sun-browned features. No doubt during his life he had seen so much—heard so many things!

At least he had agreed to take her to New Spain with him; but in the meantime there was a whole two-month period during which she lived in the governor's mansion, and found the conde's wife and daughters overwhelmingly curious about *her* life in England and in France, and most of all about the time she had spent sequestered in a Turkish seraglio. She could not possibly tell these respectable, protected women the truth; so, hating herself for being a hypocrite, Marisa hedged and told them only what they wanted to know. What the latest fashions were and what she had thought of the Spanish queen when she caught a glimpse of her. About Napoleon himself—yes, he was a handsome man and quite devoted to his Josephine! And as for her imprisonment in Tripoli—that had not been so very bad after all, and had not lasted very long; they no longer sold women on the auction block as slaves, and she herself had been well treated.

What had happened to Kamil in the end? Did he still think about her? And what had become of Dominic? Her mind still shied away from *that* memory. Did a woman ever forget the first man who took her and made her a woman? Unbelievable, to think that they had been married once. A civil marriage, her uncle had told her, could not be recognized by the church. Still, he would arrange for a formal annulment for her sake.

"He became a Moslem. He—I was told that he divorced me, Moslem fashion."

"You will be free to marry again, if that is what you wish. You may leave it to me."

"I don't wish to marry! I should have stayed in the convent and become a nun! Can't I still do that now?"

"Such matters cannot be rushed as you should have learned by now. We'll wait and see. And in the meantime, you have a duty to perform. Your father left you lands and responsibilities. We'll spend some time in New Spain first, and then, before you make up your mind, you must travel to Louisiana."

"To meet my—my stepmother? Must I? Monsignor, you know what I would much rather do!"

The archbishop's voice grew stern. "I know what you say you want to do, Marisa. But in order to renounce the world, you must know of it first. You will face what has to be faced first, and *then* you will be in a position to truly decide."

They traveled to New Spain together, first by ship and then overland. Here was where Cortez and his conquistadores had come and conquered, and here was slavery such as she had seen in the Middle East. And if women weren't locked up in harems it amounted to almost the same thing, for the well-born Spanish woman was a slave to her father first, and then to her husband. Marisa had grown beyond that, and she questioned their customs that must have been handed down from the Moors originally and caught her uncle's quizzical look.

"Yes, precisely!" he said softly and not at all condemningly. "And that is why I feel you are not ready for the veil yet, my beloved child! You have a questioning independent mind, and it must be given full rein before you make any final decision."

"And if I have done so already?" she cried out, and he

smiled at her as if she had been in truth the child he called her.

"I would still advise you that you need time. You have not found inner peace yet, and the cloister is not a refuge, but a sanctuary. Later, perhaps, you will understand what I mean."

Days turned into weeks and weeks into months; gradually, without her quite realizing it, Marisa resolved some of the conflict in her soul, and she became more peaceful within herself. She and her uncle traveled extensively and had soldiers who always escorted them. She learned of his power, despite the fact that he lived, personally, like the humblest of the peasants in the wild lands they traveled through. Her Paris gowns, her dainty, filmy underwear, and her jewels followed wherever they went, packed carefully away in iron-bound trunks. But she let her hair grow longer and become bleached in streaks by the sun, and she wore simple clothes and no longer protected her face from the glaring sunlight so that it became tanned to a deep gold.

Once, when they had left that part of New Spain which was known as Mexico and were in the vast, relatively uncharted province that some called Tejas, Marisa sat with a woman, the wife of a commander of a small Spanish fort, who had just lost her child at birth; and in the face of the woman's frenzied weeping and depression she said quietly, "I, too, have lost a child. Two, in fact, although I was only three months gone the first time."

"You?" In spite of her sense of loss and sorrow the woman turned a tear-streaked face to her. "But you are so young and so untouched by this harsh climate and the even harsher life here—I did not know you had been married."

"I have been." In spite of the composure she had learned, Marisa could feel her face become flushed. "It was not—a very happy marriage," she went on unwillingly. "I do not know if the man who was my husband is alive or dead now."

When she went back to her own small room she sat for a long time at the barred window watching the colors of sunset paint the sky in a garish assortment of crimson, red, and gold colors. She had not wanted to think of that part of her life for a long time now, and her uncle had never pressed her for details. Now, suddenly, memories filled the sparsely furnished adobe chamber and pressed against her mind. Suppose her child had lived—would things have been any different? She remembered Spain and France and London —and ocean voyages and the white-walled houses of Tunis and Kamil's face bending over hers. Kamil. Did he remember her, yearn after her? And did her Aunt Edmée ever worry, wondering what had become of her? The memory of a pair of silver-grey eyes lanced through her, and she wondered painfully, 'If he—if Dominic is still alive, does he hate me as much as he did the last time we saw each other?'

Forget, forget! That was the message that her senses drummed into her mind. She had survived, and everything was new. But what did her uncle plan for her future?

They had traveled up what was known as El Camino Real, the golden road of conquest and treasure, all the way up from Mexico City to the small, fortified township of San Antonio De Bexar. It was a small fort, like so many others she had visited or traveled through. It was a tiny patch of Hispanic civilization in the middle of nowhere, with hostile Indios and greedy Anglos, who had begun to cross the river since Napoleon had sold the vast Louisiana Territory to the Americans.

"We will stay here for a while," Marisa's uncle said gently. He seemed preoccupied, and she knew that part of the reason was because the missions had been falling into disrepair or secularized recently, and everything was in a state of confusion since the advent of Carlos IV to the throne of Spain.

Marisa stayed behind the fortified walls while her uncle rode abroad with the soldiers, often not returning for days. Sometimes, from her window, she saw the tall, proud-faced Comanche warriors come to trade with the Spanish. They brought Lipan scalps on occasion, but mostly hides and fresh meat; and sometimes they brought wretched captives they had picked up on their raids into Mexico and further north.

This was a very quiet and frustrating time for Marisa. There were times when she felt caged, and the sound of music, when the soldiers and their women danced, would make her long for everything she had known before: the balls, the bright lights, and the whirling movements of the waltz, with a man's strong hand grasping her waist; the flirtations, the intrigue, and the feeling of being taken beyond herself. . . .

It was hot, and in spite of the simple cotton garments she wore, her body would begin to glow and sweat, and she would walk angrily up and down the cramped space of her small room wondering what it was she yearned for. She would go down to talk with the nuns who ran a small convent and there would find temporary peace. But beyond that was a feeling of emptiness inside her, when she wondered what she was doing here and what her future would be like. Could she, would she, ever be completely content?

There was a young Spanish officer, a captain, who often looked at her, and seized occasions to speak to her shyly—no more than a few polite words. He had no wife, although Marisa was sure that like the other Spaniards who found themselves isolated here, he had an Indian mistress.

One night when the music sounded very loud and she could not sleep, Marisa wrapped a shawl about her head and shoulders and walked down the small, twisting stairway and out into the courtyard. There was the smell of meat roasting on slowly turning spits, the strong, flamboyant perfume of cheaply bought women, and the even stronger smell of tobacco and the oil that the Indians used to grease their hair and bodies with.

She stood in the shadow of an arched doorway and watched. The wild, bold music reminded her of the gypsy music of Spain, with its throbbing undertones that owed so much to the Moors. She knew she should not be here, but her uncle had been away for over a week, and without his soothing presence she felt so lost and so restless! 'He's right. I'm not yet ready for the cloister, not when just the sound of music can make me feel this way,' she thought feverishly. She turned to run away when a half-drunk soldier came by and squinted into the gloom, seeing her fluttering movement.

Laughing, he seized her by the wrist. "What are you hiding from, muchacha? And who are you, anyhow? Never mind! I need a partner to dance with. Come along now, don't be shy! I'll give you some aguardiente to drink and that will heat you up, eh?"

It was clear that he had no idea who she was—and she did not know him. But it had been a long time since a man had treated her so, as just another female.

Rather than pull back and make a scene, Marisa let him take her to join the others who were dancing. She thought weakly that she could always make her escape later. And, after all, what harm could it do to dance?

They had never heard of the waltz here, perhaps, but the steps of the fandango were familiar to her, and she was laughing, the music drumming in her ears, when she came face to face with the Spanish captain.

He recognized her at once, his brown eyes widening. From that moment, he kept step with her, shouldering away her original partner with a muttered, terse order that made the man stamp sullenly away. When the musicians paused to toss down the drinks that were offered to them, Captain Higuera took both her hands in his and led her away from the dancers, his face still flushed with shock and surprise.

"Señora! What are *you* doing here? Don't you know it's dangerous? These men—"

She faced them defiantly, pulling the shawl, which had slipped, more closely about her. "It was the music and the longing to dance again and to be one of a crowd of other people," she confessed recklessly, adding even more daringly, "I learned to dance from the gypsies of Seville. I only came down to watch for a little while, but—do you disapprove of me very much, señor?"

"You know I do not! I—I have the greatest admiration for you, Señora. But if your uncle were to find out or the good sisters in whose charge you are. . . . Señora, you must go back to your room. My men have been indulging too freely in aguardiente and wine; and you can—er—see for yourself the kind of women they are used to associating with! Please, I beg you to let me escort you back!"

He had dropped his hands from hers, but not before she

noticed that they had been trembling. And in the dim light his light blue eyes looked almost grey. She was suddenly seized by the strangest feeling of déjà vu. She gasped and half closed her eyes waiting for him to seize her by the waist and bend her body back against his arm for a kiss. And, shamefully, she would have yielded, but nothing happened.

"Señora ? . . ." the young man said urgently, and she opened her eyes fully to look into his worried eyes that were plainly blue again. She dropped her head with a sigh.

"Yes. I apologize, señor. I will not be so reckless again, I promise you."

He started to stammer then, "I—I wish that I—that you—"

"Were one of those mestizo women who are so free? I have wished so, too, capitan. But I suppose you are right. I should leave discreetly while there is still time for discretion."

She whirled about and escaped the way she had come, leaving him openmouthed and feeling as awkward as a schoolboy. Belatedly he wondered how she would have reacted if he had pulled her into his arms and kissed her as his senses had clamored for him to do.

Chapter Thirty-nine

It was just as well, Marisa had time to reflect later, that she had run away from that serious, calf-eyed young officer —and herself. For when her uncle returned to San Antonio three days later, he returned with a man she had forgotten about—and never thought to see again.

Don Pedro Arteaga—dark-faced, magnificently dressed. He was now a plantation owner in Louisiana, and since his return from Europe, he had been appointed commandant of the Spanish forces bordering the Mississippi, his orders signed by Manuel Godoy himself and endorsed by Queen Maria Luisa.

But for the time being, he was on official leave, having been granted several months in which to settle his affairs, one of which, apparently, was herself.

"No—no!" Marisa stormed. "Uncle—monsignor—how could you? I don't want to leave you. I've told you what he's like—I have the most unpleasant memories of him! And after that time when he turned up in Paris. . . . I *know* what my father wished, but that is all changed now, and Don Pedro knows of my—that I am hardly the innocent little virgin he was so reluctant to face at first!"

"Is it possible you might underestimate Arteaga's strength of character? And can you tell me honestly that you are content with the nomadic life you've been leading of late?" Guiltily, she dropped her eyes and felt her uncle's calloused hand touch her bent head lightly. "Marisa, child, there are things you cannot run away from forever. There is the inheritance that your father left you, and your own nature, which is still willful and still curious. I've been an old celibate for a long time, but I haven't abandoned the world yet. Do you think I cannot understand?"

"But—," she began rebelliously, and he sighed before his voice became stern.

"Must I give you orders now? Don Pedro is here to escort you to Natchez and from there to Louisiana, where you will meet your stepmother. You will mix with civilized society again, as an independent heiress, and you will see for yourself exactly what you have inherited. After that, my child, you will be able to make a true choice. And remember that if you need me, I shall be here. You have only to send me word."

"I don't wish to marry Don Pedro!"

"You do not have to marry anyone, if that is what you wish. But you must find that out for yourself."

Marisa felt, when she had to face Pedro Arteaga for the first time since he had so suddenly appeared in Paris, as if she had truly been locked up in a convent for all her life. She had come close to forgetting all the brittle, surface sophistication she had learned in the glittering courts of Europe, and his very mention reminded her too strongly of events she would much rather forget. He had been the novio she had run from in the first place, the reason for all the strange and unpleasant adventures she had been through. And that time in Paris—what could he have thought of her then? What must he think of her now? She ought to have explained things a little more bluntly to her uncle. It was impossible that Pedro, of all people, should be her escort back to civilization such as it was on this godforsaken continent.

And yet, some devil of pride or vanity made her dress up for him when they met formally for the first time at dinner that night. She opened one of the brass-bound trunks that had not been opened for months and dressed herself in a gown of embroidered muslin. And she brushed her shoulder-length hair vigorously before she pinned it atop her head and circled it with a Greek-type headband of gold and pearls.

The reward for all the trouble she had gone to came with

her uncle's raised, amused eyebrows and the sudden fire that glowed in the depths of Pedro's dark eyes.

His manner, rather stiff at first, relaxed graudally over the meal. Neither of them mentioned previous meetings. Under the benevolent chaperonage of her uncle, they conversed politely of trivialities—*her* shallow accounts of court life in Paris and London, and *his* attempts at describing cities like Natchez and New Orleans. Finally Don Pedro shrugged and smiled deprecatingly.

"But how can a mere man describe such things to a woman? My cousin will do much better, I'm sure. And she is looking forward very much to meeting you. The task of running a vast plantation is too much for a woman, as she has found. I have tried to be of some help for my plantation is close; but now that I have other duties, it is difficult to be in two places at once!"

Marisa wondered cynically what exactly he meant. A veiled, renewed offer, or a renunciation? Not that it mattered. Everything had changed since their last meeting, and, above all, she was now officially under the protection of the Monsignor De Castellanos. And her uncle was powerful in New Spain as she had already discovered.

Some of her cloak of cynicism dropped away when it was time to say farewell to the crusty, willful old man who had become more than a father to her during the past few months. She dropped quite naturally to her knees and kissed his ring as he gave her his blessing. He gathered her in his arms for a few moments as he advised her gruffly to make the most of the opportunity that had been offered her.

"No more looking backwards—you understand me? Remember who you are and be proud. I wish that I could have come with you, my dearest niece, but I have my lost flock to take care of here—and besides I think you will do better without me at your elbow! I do not need to tell you to be careful. You are an extremely rich young woman now and able to be completely independent. Remember that freedom, too, has its own responsibilities."

To Marisa's relief, Don Pedro Arteaga was respect itself, even when they had parted from her uncle. He seemed to have forgotten previous circumstances or at least, to have put them from his mind. There was no hint of presumptuousness in his manner, although there were times when he could not veil the look of desire in his brown eyes. Still, he managed to keep it from his voice when he addressed her, always formally, as señorita. She had told him shortly that her marriage had been annulled and that due to its circumstances, it had been easy for her uncle to arrange it. And thankfully, he did not try to remind her of what her father had wished.

They could have been strangers, she and this gallant Señor Arteaga who was so solicitous of her comfort at every point during their journey together. He had even found a woman of mixed Indian and Mexican descent to act as her servant and duenna; and he never once tried to force his company upon her during the time that they traveled through New Spain.

Once they had crossed the river and were in American territory, his manner became even more solicitous, and he spent more time riding at her side, talking to her, pointing out this point of interest or that, and explaining various matters to her. It was true that the Americans now owned all of this vast territory. Pedro's face darkened when he spoke of Napoleon's double-dealing.

"We let them have Natchez some time ago, thinking it would satisfy their land greediness for a while. But Louisiana! By the treaty that Bonaparte promised to recognize, he should have ceded the territory back to Spain! Instead of which he sold it to the Americans. Now they are pouring in here, and it is all we can do to keep them out of New Spain as well. Certain adventurers keep stealing across the river on various pretexts." He shot her an enigmatic glance, and she wondered why. He went on in an angry voice, "To trade with the Indians, they say. Or to capture wild horses! It is really treasure they are after—and conquest. That is why, as you might have noticed, we have had to double our border patrols."

"But the Americans still permit the Spanish and the French to hold their lands in Louisiana, do they not?"

Marisa, riding sidesaddle beside him, permitted herself

a glance at his dark, angry features and caught his annoyed frown.

"Oh yes! *That*, at least, was part of the agreement the American President Jefferson made. But after all, they could hardly have done otherwise. We've been here for generations. It was the French and the Spanish after them who colonized this country and made it safe for the Anglos! No, they haven't interfered with our landholdings. You'll discover that for yourself." His mouth twisted for an instant. "They have even gone so far as to consider those of us who own land here as American citizens! But we have to abide by *their* laws, and it is not at all the same thing!"

"There are bad feelings, then?"

Again she caught his glance; he seemed surprised that she continued to ask questions.

"Not on the surface, of course. Oh, on the surface everyone is very polite to each other. But underneath—well, naturally there cannot fail to be some resentment! You should have heard the silence when the American flag was run up in New Orleans. However, it is nothing that should make any difference to you. You'll find, I'm sure, that the Americanos are gallant towards women, and I'm sure you won't want to bother your head with politics."

His sweepingly masculine assumption made Marisa's eyes sparkle dangerously, and she had to bite her lip to fight back a retort. Pedro, after all, was a typical Spanish male, and there was no point in antagonizing him. Perhaps she would be better off if she let them all think she was the shy, brainless, and helpless female they all expected her to be.

Her thoughts turned to her stepmother. Marisa found herself wondering what kind of woman her stepmother might be. "The lovely Inez." That phrase, overheard one hot and still afternoon, kept coming back to haunt her. A woman lovely enough and clever enough to captivate her aging father. Young enough to find herself a lover. Strong enough to run a huge plantation on her own—or did she have help? How would Inez, used to power and wealth, react to having a stepdaughter foisted on her? And especially one who owned the land that by now Inez must have looked on as her own? She must keep reminding herself that Don Pedro was cousin to Doña Inez. What, then, did he really think of *her?* Certainly, he had changed in some respects from the licentious young dandy she remembered. Here, in his own territory, he seemed more mature and more sure of himself. Also, in the uniform of a Spanish colonel, he looked harder. . . .

But after they had crossed the Sabine River that formed the natural boundary of Louisiana, Pedro Arteaga stopped wearing his uniform and became an ordinary citizen again, although now he dressed more plainly than he had done in Spain.

He explained, grimacing. "After all, my rank of colonel is mostly honorary. I have lands and interests here, and our government understands that. I know I can trust in your discretion, señorita? It is hard to be torn in two directions, but I am needed here in the province of Louisiana as a go-between, a liaison, as you would say in French. Governor Wilkinson is a friend of mine, and he understands my position."

"How—nice," Marisa murmured politely. She had been going to use the word "convenient" but bit it back just in time. The truth was that she had already heard too much about this man Wilkinson—General James Wilkinson, a veteran of the Revolutionary War, who was a good friend to the Spaniards, or so Pedro said. But she said nothing, continuing to ride quietly beside him.

Pedro Arteaga stole a covert look at Marisa's delicate, cameo profile. She seemed to have matured a great deal, he thought with satisfaction, besides turning out to be quite a little beauty with her pale gold skin and dark gold hair. Perhaps this time she'd prove easier to manage, especially after the varied experiences she must have had during the past two years. He wondered about those experiences and how much she'd learned. How many lovers had there been along the way that had led her there? And what had made her turn her back on Europe? Well, he would find out soon enough. She was here, and he had promised himself to be patient. He also wondered what his lovely cousin would think when she saw this golden beauty he'd brought back with him. Her stepdaughter. How Inez would hate that!

Catching Marisa's eyes he said hastily, "We will reach Natchez before nightfall, so you will have an opportunity to see something of the city itself. It sits high on the bluffs overlooking the Mississippi River and is very old. Built by Spaniards, most of it. The Americanos, unfortunately, moved into that section they call 'Natchez-under-the-hill' where all the worst elements are gathered. It is a blot upon the city and one section that you must never visit, of course."

'What a boring, pompous man he is, after all!' Marisa thought, even while she smiled sweetly at him. And he was highhanded, too. Without consulting her, he had already made arrangements for her to spend at least two weeks in Natchez before they traveled on to New Orleans. She must meet everyone. Her father's friends and *his* friends, including the mysterious General Wilkinson. And of course—Inez.

* * * * *

"New Orleans can be *so* unhealthy at certain times of the year!" Inez said in a voice like honey. Catlike, she did not merely talk, she purred, her voice low and slightly husky. "The gutters act as sewers, and they overflow onto the street. And oh, the stench, and the *heat!* And the fever. I swear, the slaves die off like flies! That is why I persuaded Andres ,," with a sidelong glance at Marisa—"your dear father, to build me a house here in Natchez. I love it here, and of course it is more Spanish than French."

Inez had long hair like black silk. She wore it coiled on top of her head, giving her a regal effect. Her skin was as white as magnolia petals and unlined, and her mouth was full and red. It did not take Marisa long to recall who this woman reminded her of. Madame De L'Aigle. Although Madame De L'Aigle had been much older, of course, and a little more subtle than Inez, whose hazel eyes gave the lie to her small speech of welcome and her affectation of instant fondness for her stepdaughter.

Still Marisa could understand why men would invariably find Inez attractive. She was beautiful, her figure, unmarred by childbearing, was perfectly formed. And she was a man's woman, putting on a pretty air of helplessness mixed with an innate seductiveness whenever there was a member of the male sex present. Within a few hours of their meeting, she had succeeded in making Marisa feel gauche and almost unfeminine.

"Darling—you do not mind if I call you so? I know you have lived for most of your life in Europe, and no doubt you've been to all those fashionable *intellectual* salons in France. And I'm sure you must be a very intelligent young woman, as well as being quite a world traveler!" Inez gave a small, deprecating laugh as if to take the sting out of her words, but Marisa knew it was there and looked back at her without expression. "But men here are so— old-fashioned, I suppose you'd call it!" Inez went on in her husky, slightly breathless voice. "They don't *want* a woman to appear too clever even if she is. And this *is* a man's world, here. Still so new, and so wild and—almost frightening, at times. So—you don't mind that I tell you this? Even if they're *wrong*, as I'm sure Don Esteban Minor was at dinner tonight when he was discussing Bonaparte's career. Well, why not just let it be? After all, it's not so very important, is it?"

'It is to me—and you are such a hypocrite!' Marisa wanted to scream like a fishwife; but she had learned some self-control, and so she folded her hands together in her lap and looked guilelessly into Inez's narrowed, watching eyes and nodded.

"I'm sorry. Of course you are right. I really must learn to guard my tongue, mustn't I?"

She was thinking, hoping her face had not gone stiff with revulsion, 'So this is the woman Dominic loved enough to fight a duel with my father—to kill an old man who was foolish enough to marry a young and pretty wife. And my father—how *could* he have not seen through her? All that surface sweetness hiding poison. She hates me, but she wants to hide it. She wants me to be a success socially. I wonder why?'

Seemingly satisfied, Doña Inez rose gratefully to her feet and smiled.

"There! I knew we would get on well together and that

we would soon come to understand each other! I know you must be tired so I won't keep you up any longer tonight, my dear. Please sleep as long as you want to in the morning, won't you? We shall be going to a ball at the governor's house tomorrow night, and you will be meeting everyone there, so you must look your best! Good night."

It was all Marisa could do to murmur a polite good night in return before the other woman went gracefully out of the room, closing the door softly behind her.

Marisa lowered the wick of the lamp by her bed, watching it sputter and then go out, leaving a faint smoky odor on the air. She lay in the darkness waiting for her eyes to get used to it and thought with a wry smile how different this large and magnificently furnished room was compared to the miserable little chambers she had been lodged in for the past weeks. She had learned to sleep almost anywhere: on hard and lumpy mattresses with not-too-clean sheets and on mattresses filled with straw in the homes of poor Mexican or Spanish settlers. But the large and ornately carved four-poster bed she lay in now, with its frilly canopy, was almost too comfortable.

She really ought to get some sleep, but there were too many conflicting, confused thoughts to keep her awake. The undercurrents she had sensed, for instance, from the very moment she had been introduced to the sleekly beautiful Doña Inez, who played gracious hostess and apologized prettily for the fact that she had already invited guests for dinner that night, not knowing exactly when Marisa would arrive. Had she expected to find her stepdaughter some kind of a freak or too tired from her travels to appear at her best before a fashionable company? Doña Inez did not like her, but Marisa had to admit honestly that *she* had been prepared not to like Inez, either. And so here they were, thrown together for weeks, possibly months, with a charade to act out between them.

'I wonder,' Marisa thought casually and maliciously, shifting her position in the wide bed, 'if this very house belongs to me, too? If it's so, then no wonder she dislikes and resents me. She must have been furiously disappointed when she found out that my father left everything to me after all.'

Would he have changed his will if he had not been wounded in a duel and taken sick of his wounds soon after? Why had he arranged for her to marry Don Pedro? There were too many questions. Although her uncle had answered some of them, she had sensed that there was also a great deal he had deliberately not told her because he had wanted her to keep an open mind. Well, she would try. But it was impossible, she already knew, for her to like Inez!

Well, she was here. If not completely against her will, then against her inclination. But she was here. Against Marisa's closed eyelids, the night seemed to swing like the giant sweeps of a dark scythe. Back and forth—each swing bringing back vague and unrelated vignettes: the long and tiring journey with Pedro at her side; the look in his eyes negating the polite gallantry of his voice and manner; her first glimpse of the white galleried house surrounded by lush green lawns and an avenue of moss-laden trees; the cool breeze blowing up from the Bayou St. Pierre that fanned straying tendrils of hair against her hot cheeks; the black and café-au-lait faces of slaves everywhere; Doña Inez sweeping down the wide staircase to greet them, and the candle-lit dinner when she had worn one of her Paris gowns and scandalized the men by arguing politics with them.

Tomorrow when she was less tired, she would be more discreet. She would appear to be shy and demure and charmingly helpless—if only to annoy her stepmother.

'But what am I really doing here?' was Marisa's last conscious thought before sleep finally claimed her.

Chapter Forty

It must have been well past noon when Marisa awoke. She lay in the wide, unfamiliar bed trying to gather her wits together and remember where she was and why.

The room she lay in was large and gloomy looking with the heavy draperies drawn against the windows; but even through these, the sun pushed with a kind of angry glow. And beyond the thick, cool walls she could feel, like something palpable, the promise of its intense, golden heat.

It was a sound in the room that had awakened her, and her head turning on the pillow, Marisa met the frightened, curious eyes of a pale-skinned young woman who must have been younger than herself—a white scarf hiding her hair, and a white, starched apron concealing most of her somber colored gown. One of the maids? No. Suddenly Marisa remembered where she was. A slave, one of the house servants. The girl was obviously terrified at having awakened her.

Marisa smiled, feeling herself impelled to say something reassuring.

"You didn't disturb me. I'm sure that it's high time I was awake! Is it very late?"

The girl bobbed a curtsy, dropping long lashes over her liquid brown eyes. "No, ma'am. It's only just past noon. The mistress sent me to see if you was awake yet, but I wasn't to bother you if you wasn't, she said."

Her name waas Eulalie, but everyone called her Lalie, and she was being trained to be a lady's maid.

Later, Inez said carelessly, "Lalie is yours if you think she will do! But you'll have to keep her in her place, my dear. She's new. I acquired her with an old, run-down

431

estate I bought not too long ago. Her father was a Frenchman, and he taught her to speak English as well as French. I thought that perhaps she might suit you for that reason."

Horrified, Marisa looked into Inez's cool, appraising eyes. "Her father was French? But—but surely—"

"You've been brought up in Europe so you don't understand our ways. Yes, Lalie's father was French, and her mother was a mulatto slave, which makes her a slave, also. In fact, it was *his* estate I bought, and she was lucky not to end up in one of the New Orleans houses of pleasure— you'll forgive my bluntness? But you must understand that things are different here and the laws regarding color very strict. They have to be! Don't you recall what happened in St. Domingue? We have to be careful that the same thing doesn't happen here. Lalie's father could have freed her if he had thought to do so, but he was an old, drunken man who let his plantation go to seed and gave his blacks far too much freedom. I've had to sell most of them off, for they were too undisciplined. This is something you have to learn about, before we go back to Congracia."

Her father had called his Louisiana plantation Congracia —"with grace"—but it had been founded and run by slave labor, and still was. Humans were treated and sold as animals. And yet, as Inez pointed out, it was on slave labor that the economy of these rich American states and territories was based. She herself owned slaves. And Marisa remembered the blazing North African coast—and Tripoli— where captive men and women of all races were forced into slavery, and she could say nothing to Inez without making herself a hypocrite.

It was in a subdued and thoughtful frame of mind that Marisa accompanied Doña Inez on a last-minute shopping expedition.

"I must pick up the new gown I ordered from Madame Andrée. And I will introduce you to her in case you might wish to order some dresses and bonnets yourself. She keeps up with all the latest fashions."

Inez was suddenly gay, laughing, and determinedly charming, and Marisa, in spite of herself, was curious to see more of Natchez. But it was hot, and the unpaved streets were dusty and crowded; and she developed a headache that drove her out of the oppressive humidity of Madame Andrée's establishment soon after the politeness had been dispensed with.

Inez turned back to gossip with the plump, black-clad woman for a few more moments, and Marisa, excusing herself politely, climbed into the open carriage to wait for her.

Idly, to distract herself from the throbbing pain in her temples, she began to scan the street, and the passers-by. Such a collection of people from all walks of life! Merchants, planters, slaves and even a few bedraggled-looking Indians. A carriage containing two gaudily dressed women swept by, the horses rearing when a drunken man chose that moment to weave across the street. The women shrieked and shouted bawdy curses at him while he turned to make an age-old gesture of contempt at them. Behind their carriage, a small, canvas-topped buggy driven by a dignified-looking black man with grizzled hair was pulled to a halt for a few moments, and Marisa could not help noticing the small boy, jumping up and down with excitement, who almost flung himself out, only to be caught firmly about his waist by a stern-faced, angular woman who was obviously scolding him. His eyes, a limpid grey, caught Marisa's, and he grinned, making her smile back. And then her heart gave a jolt as the woman—his mother? his nurse?—glanced towards Marisa and then ahead, giving some order to the driver, who quickly maneuvered the small buggy around the carriage ahead of it and disappeared up the curving street. That face, under the black poke bonnet; those pale blue eyes that had stared into hers for just an instant—it couldn't have been Selma Meeker at all. Her imagination and the heat were playing tricks on her! Because what would Selma Meeker, who had been Bab, Zuleika's slave, be doing here? It was her headache, which seemed much worse now, and the heat. And perhaps her strange and fevered dreams of last night when she had imagined herself back in Tripoli with Kamil bending over her; only whenever she opened her eyes in her dream, he had turned into Dominic, his eyes biting into her like steel. No—she wouldn't, mustn't remember! And yet the sweat had started to trickle down from her hairline to her temples by the time Inez came out of the small shop, with madame bowing at her heels. Marisa did not have to feign her feeling of sickness nor the pallor which made Inez say crossly that she should have stayed indoors where it was cooler.

She was given a cool lime cordial to drink and made to lie down for the rest of the afternoon in her shaded room. And she slept for a little while until Lalie's soft voice roused her with the warning that it was time to start getting dressed for the ball that evening.

Ah yes, the ball! Soaking in a tub of hot, scented water, Marisa reflected on the affair. She had been to grand, glittering balls in Paris and London, but here in this far-flung frontier where she knew hardly anybody, the prospect of what *they* called a ball almost bored her.

Lalie was exclaiming over her jewelry as well as her array of gowns, which had been carefully unpacked and hung up in a cedar-scented closet. Poor Lalie, whose skin was fairer than hers and whose father had been French. She would have been considered a raving beauty in Europe; it was some monstrous ugly joke of fate that she should be condemned to such a degrading existence as a slave. 'I'll set her free as soon as I can,' Marisa thought, and in the meantime she let Lalie help her put on her dress, a deceptively simple gown of the muslin still so popular in France. The very palest shade of green, the material was spangled with gold thread in an Eastern design. Gold ribbon crisscrossed from her bared shoulders to tie just beneath her breasts in a trailing knot that reached to her knees. Based on a Grecian design, the dress was a masterpiece of simplicity and sensuality. Her hair was worn Greek-style in a coronet of burnished gold curls held back from her forehead by a gold filet studded with emeralds. Gold bracelets clasped over her upper arms formed a contrast to her slim, nymph-like appearance. Daringly, Marisa added the slightest touch of color to her lips and high cheekbones, and threw an evening cloak of emerald green velvet over her shoulders, wrapping it closely about herself. There! Now let Inez guess at what she wore. A pity, in a way, that there would be no Apollo to run teasingly away from tonight.

As it happened, Inez was waiting impatiently for her at the foot of the staircase with Pedro Arteaga, his dark head shining under the oil-lit chandelier. Inez looked very Spanish tonight, with a jeweled comb in her high-piled hair and a white mantilla trailing down just past her shoulders.

"There you are! We must hurry—it would not do to be late."

Inez was obviously confident of her own appearance in a low cut gown of turquoise silk. She wore diamonds at her throat and ears. She barely glanced at Marisa, saying over her shoulder as she led the way to where their carriage was waiting, "You need not have taken such precautions to stay warm! The nights here are never too chilly as you will soon learn."

It was Pedro who explained, once the carriage had started off, that the man they all called "the governor" was named Winthrop Sargent, and he had actually been governor of the Mississippi Territory for several years before he turned cotton planter following his marriage to a wealthy Natchez widow. His house, named *Gloucester* after his home town in Massachusetts, was a charming example of southern architecture. But she would see for herself. Their carriage joined a long line of others that moved at a sober pace up a tree-lined driveway, and Inez was grumbling that they really should have left earlier.

The house that Pedro had described was ablaze with light, and Marisa had an impression of an imposing three-story structure of red brick and white Doric columns supporting a graceful gallery. There were two large front entrances as Pedro had described and twin staircases that led onto a wide inner gallery where the musicians were stationed.

Before they walked into the brightly lighted ballroom, Marisa handed her cloak to one of the bowing, unobtrusive servants and was rewarded by Inez's narrow-eyed look as she took in her appearance.

"One of your Paris gowns? It makes you look very—lovely! But—"

"I'm glad you like it," Marisa said sweetly and ingenu-

435

ously. "As a matter of fact, it was the emperor's favorite of all my gowns."

Before Inéz could say anything else, Pedro interposed hastily that the gown was most becoming, and he was proud to be the escort of two beautiful women tonight. Marisa felt the heat of his eyes on her bared arms and shoulders, and it was all she could do not to flinch, as if he had actually touched her.

He stayed close to her while the introductions were being performed and even afterwards when Inez had let herself be drawn away by some friends.

"How very lovely you are," he whispered hoarsely as they danced the first waltz. "You make me realize what I have missed and what a blind fool I was."

He dropped some of his air of careful politeness and let her know that he wanted her. And quite soon it became apparent that quite a few of the other guests present had the impression that she and Pedro were, if not exactly affianced, on the verge of being so. No doubt Inez had something to do with that, too. Her smile had a curiously self-satisfied quality when she glanced towards them, and Marisa could almost guess what she was whispering to her friends and the men who almost fought for the privilege of partnering the lovely widow.

How cleverly she managed things! Having done her duty by making sure her stepdaughter was introduced to everyone present, she must also have dropped little hints that implied Marisa was Pedro's property. There were interested looks in her direction, but apart from her elderly host who danced with her once and inquired politely whether she was enjoying her stay in Natchez, it was Pedro who danced attendance on her, somehow managing to steer away every other man who might have wished to make her closer acquaintance.

He had just led her off the floor, following an energetic fandango, when a small flurry at one of the double doors announced the arrival of some latecomers: the hot-tempered Andrew Jackson and his plump, still pretty wife Rachel, over whose divorce (or lack of one) there had been such a scandal; General James Wilkinson, newly appointed governor of the upper Louisiana Territory, (who was here without his wife) smiling, portly John Byron, one of the richest planters in the area and his wife; and others. Marisa heard the murmured gossip and did not afterwards remember whether it was Pedro or Inez who had come up from somewhere to stand beside her, whispering all this in her ears.

She heard Mr. Sargent's Negro butler make the formal announcements and suddenly she felt herself grow as still and as cold as a statue.

"The pretty blonde is Jane Byron, their only daughter and heiress," Inez continued. "And her fiancé. They say her parents were set against the match until she threatened to elope with him. He's a man with quite a reputation, of course—and a past! Still an adventurer, isn't that so, Pedrito? But heavens! I'd almost forgotten, my dear—I'm sorry! If I'd known *he* was to be here tonight, I'd have warned you, of course. Although you need not worry. No one knows of what happened in the past except for Pedro and myself."

"And Dominic," Marisa heard herself saying in a soft, distant voice that did not seem to belong to her at all. "I wonder how *he* will react?"

Inez gave a soft, malicious gurgle of laughter. "I must say you're very calm, and I'm sure you'll carry it off beautifully. Isn't she a marvel, Pedro? But as to our friend's reaction, shall we find it out for ourselves? You two were bound to meet sometime, I suppose. Why not get it over now?"

"Of course. Attack is the best form of defense," Marisa said in the same cold, disembodied voice. Inez, disappointed at her outward poise, let the venom under the surface creep into her husky, honeyed voice.

"How true! Did the conqueror of Europe teach you that?"

"He taught me a great deal more—but so, of course, did my other lovers," Marisa said in the same kind of tone and was rewarded by the flickering look of hate that flashed over Doña Inez's usually composed features and the hissing intake of her breath.

They had both forgotten Pedro, until his fingers tightened over Marisa's arm.

"Basta!" he growled in Spanish. "Enough of such talk which I know you do not mean. My sweet cousin, I advise you to be careful!"

It was easier, Marisa found, to fix her eyes on Inez's face instead of on the laughing group of people by the doors.

"I should think so," she said sweetly in Spanish. "After all you and Dominic *do* know each other rather well, don't you?"

Marisa had the small satisfaction of hearing Inez gasp with fury before Pedro all but dragged her away, muttering under his breath that there must not be any scene, or any scandal here in front of all of their friends.

"But you knew, too, and you didn't tell me!" Marisa said furiously to Pedro.

"I knew he was here, and I did not tell you. Yes, I admit it! I will even admit that I wanted to see your re-actions—and his. Can you blame me for being human? But I am proud of the way you bested Inez, do you understand? Even if she is my cousin. You are so cool, so col-lected, so—lovely! I want you, and you know it! For yourself now, and not because of something that was ar-ranged a long time ago between your father and me."

"No—," she began to protest, but he had taken her to a far, secluded corner of the room, a kind of alcove that led out onto a tiny, enclosed balcony overlooking the gardens. He held her with both hands on her arms, and the gold bracelets bit into her flesh under his grip.

"Yes, I say! And I accept my share of the blame for what happened. I can forget it, if I can call you mine *now*. Would you not rather face that Americano who was once, for a short while, your husband, and who now has a young fiancée, with a fiancé of your own? I can protect you, and I will, if you'll let me."

Delayed reaction set in suddenly, making Marisa's body tremble and her knees grow weak. Dominic! Here! Why did he keep turning up in her life so unexpectedly? Why couldn't she be free of his taunting presence? And this time he had had the gall to get himself engaged to a young milk-sop girl with a rich father. Were there no limits to his

438

ambition and his lack of scruples? And every time he forced his presence into her otherwise peaceful existence he had brought her shame and unhappiness. Well, not this time! This time she had seen him first and was armed against him.

All the old hate flared up in her again, making her raise her head suddenly to meet Pedro's hot, searching gaze.

"Very well," she said coldly, taking him by surprise. "But please remember that if I consent to become engaged to you it will only be to still the gossip and it will be a period of trial. I have not had time to think seriously of marrying yet. Before I do, I must be very sure for you see, I have learned to be woefully independent and to think for myself. You might not want these qualities in a wife."

"I would want you under any circumstances and any conditions!" Possessively, his warm hands slid down her arms to clasp her icy fingers.

And it was at that moment that Inez's voice, filled with malicious triumph, said behind them, "What a tender scene! I do not mean to interrupt you two lovebirds, but since I have managed to detach my friend here from his fiancée, I did think you would want to become reacquainted. You all know each other, do you not?"

Chapter Forty-one

There was no help for it now. Marisa felt a chill creep all through her body. Deliberately, she did not disengage her hands from Pedro's, but turned her head instead and met the icy, furious, contemptuous gaze of the same silver-grey eyes she had tried to forget for so long.

He was deeply tanned and looked very fit, the width of his shoulders emphasized under a fashionable single-breasted claw hammer coat with pearl buttons and a velvet collar under which a richly brocaded waistcoat and frilled white shirt showed with casual grace. Yes, he had always worn his clothes with the careless, casual ease of a dandy, but always beneath lurked the impression of a sleek muscled, stalking panther.

Dominic Challenger threw no sops to convention. Marisa thought furiously an instant later that she should have known better than to expect any show of courtesy from him. He neither inclined his head nor smiled, but he let his eyes rake over her openly before he said sarcastically, "Was this supposed to be some kind of tricky surprise on your part, Inez? I should have known, I suppose. Madame." Now the angry contempt in his eyes was obvious as they swept up from her ankles to her flushed face. "You look as well as you were the last time I saw you. Was there a reason for our meeting again?"

"Be careful!" Pedro said harshly, his eyes growing narrow. "The Señorita de Castellanos has agreed to be my wife."

"I thought that matter had been agreed upon a long time ago—amigo." Dominic drawled. "Did you wish my congratulations, or my blessing? I offer both, freely."

441

Pedro made an angry movement, and Marisa moved so that she was between the two men.

There was no help to be had from Inez who stood back with a catlike, satisfied smile upon her full lips. Marisa said, forcing her voice to remain cool, "Please! There would be no point in creating a scene here for the amusement of the others in this room. As for myself, the past is dead, and I'm sure I'm not the only one who wishes it so." She addressed him directly for the first time, forcing herself to meet the hateful regard of his eyes. "You have a fiancée—why don't you go back to her? I'm sure there is nothing more that you and I have to say to each other that has not already been said before."

White lightning flared behind the silver mirrors of his eyes for the tiniest instant, and Marisa could feel herself flinch.

He said softly and conversationally as if there were only the two of them there, "You're still a cold-blooded little bitch, aren't you?" And then, very much the arrogant gentleman, as she could remember him being while he was masquerading as an English viscount, he bowed to Inez, sarcastically acclaimed her cleverness, swung around, and left them.

"I think that I am going to have to kill him after all," Pedro said in a voice that sounded heavy and muffled with rage. "And in spite of *you,* my sweet cousin!"

Inez laughed angrily and huskily. "In a duel or an ambush? But certainly not here and now, I think. You must really learn to hide your feelings, Pedrito. Sometimes you show them far too obviously."

And then without a word to Marisa, she, too, turned away and left them.

"I should never have come here," Marisa said on an expelled, shaky breath. And then, her spine stiffening, she looked up at Pedro, seeing his dark face still suffused with frustrated anger. "I do hope you are not planning a duel on my behalf? Because I won't have it, you know. I would rather go back to my uncle. And in any case, neither one of us is worth risking your life for."

"You are," Don Pedro said. And then, he went on in a strange, thoughtful voice, "But I will not challenge that

bastardo to a duel here, for your sake. However," he laughed suddenly so that she glanced at him in surprise, "he will stray across the river to *our* territory once too often to steal horses, and then I will have him, and all the scores between us will be settled."

She did not ask him then what he meant, for she did not want to pursue the subject any further. Somewhere across the room Dominic had gone back to his young, vapidly pretty fiancée, and his dark head was bent over her bright one. No doubt, to *her* he would be very charming and loverlike. She had the protection of her parents and her innocence. He would not dare carry his stupid little Jane off and take her by force! No, he was going to marry her—of his own accord and without coercion.

Marisa could hardly remember afterwards how the rest of that interminable evening passed. Thank God she managed to retain some control over herself so that no one who watched her could have guessed at the strangely warring tumult of emotions within her. She drank just enough wine to make her gay, and she smiled and laughed and flirted with Pedro, who vowed himself bewitched by her. She received the congratulations of his friends and danced with a few of them—and it did not matter to her in the least when from the corner of her eyes she saw Dominic walk out onto the small balcony accompanied by his giggling, flushed bride-to-be. Did he kiss her out there? Marisa did not care. She hated him, despised him! How and when had he arrived here, of all places? She did not care about that, either. He had no right to bring back memories that spoiled everything for her.

She sparkled, and she was introduced to the Jacksons— Andrew and his pretty Rachel whose face was sad until she smiled or looked at her husband—and to the enigmatic General Wilkinson of whom she had heard so much, and even to John Byron and his handsome, condescending wife.

One other moment stood out with almost unpleasant clarity against the whirling, confused backdrop of the night. She danced with General Wilkinson, who was agile for a man his age, and when he led her back to the group of chairs, Pedro was engaged in earnest conversation with Mr.

Byron—something about the market for cotton and indigo and the menace of outlaws along the Natchez Trace. The Jacksons were dancing together, and Inez, returning to them at last, was gossiping with Mrs. Byron. She ignored Marisa except for a subtly malicious glance that promised more mischief.

"Ah, Miss Jane!" the general said, bowing gallantly. "I was beginning to think that my possessive young friend here would hide you away for the rest of the night! You have not honored me with a dance yet. Dominic, you've met the charming Señorita de Castellanos? You've both recently returned from Europe; perhaps you might have friends in common there. You'll permit me to dance with your fiancée?"

She had been warned that he was a dangerously subtle man used to playing both ends against the middle while keeping his own position and rank intact. Now, seeing how cleverly he had maneuvered them, Marisa had time to think fleetingly that all the rumors she had heard were correct. But what was his game, and how much did he know of the truth?

Left alone with Dominic glowering at her from beneath drawn black brows, she had no more time left to wonder, for he abruptly and surprisingly asked her to stand up with him for the waltz that the musicians had just started to play. Before she could say a word, he had taken her hand, and, short of making a scene, she had no choice but to go with him.

Everything became unfocused when he put his arm about her waist. And no one but the two of them could have known that his grip on her hand was so tight she felt all her fingers being crushed.

"We had better get a few matters straight between us," he said harshly and uncompromisingly between his teeth. "I don't know why you're here or what you want this time, but I'm warning you, my sweet, that whatever your game is, I'm not playing. Do you understand? And I'm warning you to stay away from Jane. She's soft-natured and unspoiled, and I won't have her hurt."

The shocking slash of his words made Marisa almost lose

her footing so that he had to lift her off her feet for an instant to keep her from falling. Her head snapped back, and she glared into his eyes, meeting their fury head-on. If he had not held her so tightly, she would have slapped his face or clawed at his mocking eyes.

"How dare you?" Her voice shook, and the air between them seemed to vibrate with the force of clashing wills. "And since when have *you* turned into a protector of virtue? You cared not a fig for *mine,* when you—"

"You should not have gone about masquerading as a gypsy wench if you meant to preserve your virginity, menina. And if you'll recall, I paid for my sins by marrying you—unfortunately for us both! But you've come a long way since then, and so have I—no thanks to you and your scheming, conniving little mind! You'll always contrive to fall safely into some man's embrace, won't you? I'm only surprised that you left Europe and its master. Or did he tire of you and send you away?"

"Ohh! You—"

"What I am is no concern of yours any longer—Señorita de Castellanos. Don Pedro Arteaga is a far cry from Napoleon Bonaparte, but at least he seems fooled by your innocent act so I'd advise you to stay with him. And away from me and those I care for. In return, I will try to keep out of *your* way. It's the only kind of bargain we can make, you and I, at this late stage."

Her fingers felt crushed to a pulp, and only the pain kept her on her feet, matching his steps, as the room whirled around them and the musicians kept playing a waltz she remembered too well.

"I won't make any bargains with you. I don't care what you do or who you marry, do you understand? If I had known that *you* would be here, I would not have let my uncle force me into coming. And in any case, I'll be leaving for Louisiana soon, so I should be out of your life, shouldn't I? But *you* had better think carefully before you cross the river again to steal horses, or your Jane might find herself a widow, like—like Inez!"

She hardly knew what she was saying any longer. She felt half-crazed with pain and anger and humiliation.

Now that he had said what he wanted to say, why didn't he let her go?

"What did you say?" His voice was like steel, cutting through her jumbled thoughts, and the arm about her waist tightened as she stumbled. Already, she regretted her unthinking words.

"It—it was only something Pedro said. What does it matter? Please! You're hurting me, and I don't want to dance any longer. What would your Jane think if I fainted in your arms?"

He looked down at her, really seeing her for the first time through the red haze of rage that had not left him since he had first caught sight of her this evening, so cool and lovely and insouciant with Pedro Arteaga holding both her hands as she smiled up at him. Bitch! Whore! he thought furiously now, as he had thought then; but there was something about her sudden pallor that alarmed him, coupled with the way her dark lashes lay like fans against her cheeks, hiding her golden eyes, and the way her steps seemed to drag. She seemed to lean against him, unknowingly and unwillingly. Just as unwillingly he remembered the feel of her slim, naked body struggling against his in those early days before they had really known each other in any other way. He knew her capacity for hate and for easy yielding, but was she capable of loving? And why, of all things, did he have to ask himself that now, in the middle of a crowded ballroom, with God knew how many curious eyes watching them? It didn't matter to him, of course. She was a heartless little bitch, and he had evidence of it. He wondered if she knew or cared what had happened to the child and decided against telling her.

"Please!" she whispered again, and this time her voice sounded so soft and so strained that Dominic muttered an oath under his breath. He looked swiftly around. The floor was crowded with dancers. It would be just like her to create a public scene by fainting—or pretending to—and leaving him to make the inevitable awkward answers. And Inez, who had not forgiven him for his engagement to Jane Byron, would no doubt "help out" in her own, malicious way. Better *this* way. And he danced her to the edge of the room and from there out onto the small balcony.

Marisa gulped in quantities of the slightly chilled air and clasped her hands together, wondering if her fingers would ever feel the same again.

"You were crazy to bring me here!" she whispered at last, and in the comparative darkness she felt, rather than saw, the shrugging movement of his shoulders under the coat that fit him so well.

"Better than having you faint out there—or was that one of your little acts?"

"Why should I bother to act, as you put it, with *you?*" she responded bitterly. Shivering, she straightened her shoulders. "Very well. I thank you for your gallantry in bringing me out here before I disgraced us both. But you had better take me back inside now before your little fiancée begins to wonder."

"Or yours—who would like to see me killed. Thank you for the warning." His voice was dry, but at least it held none of the ugly sarcasm she had learned to dread.

◆　◆　◆　◆　◆

"Nothing happened between us, I tell you. Nothing!" Marisa repeated angrily to Pedro on their way home. "I felt faint from all the wine and the whirling about, and he took me outside for some fresh air—and that's all. You saw how eager he was to relinquish me and go back to his fiancée, to whisper in her ear. I hope she did not forgive him easily, though. The man is a savage, uncivilized brute, and I dislike him intensely. Do you think *I* can forget, even if you can, that he was responsible for my father's death?"

It came out into the open between them at last, and the sneering, insinuating smile on Inez's face was wiped away to be replaced by rage that contorted her lovely features.

"So you know about *that?* At second or third hand, I suppose! It was all so silly and so pointless! *He,* your Dominic, your former husband, tried to force his attentions on me, and your father took offense. He insisted on fighting a duel, although I begged him not to. And afterwards, when he was wounded, I nursed him for months on end. I never left the plantation—but what would you know about that? You were so busy yourself, chasing about Europe, going from one man to another! No, Pedro, do not try to stop me for I am tired of pretending, I tell you! I tried to make her welcome because she was Andres's daughter, but I tell you that her own father would have disowned her if he had known what she would become! She's like her mother, who was—" Inez suddenly seemed to recover her self-control and stopped herself, although Marisa could hear her angry breathing.

"For God's sake," Don Pedro said into the ominously weighted silence, "I think that there has been enough unpleasantness for one evening. You will both be sorry tomorrow, and as for myself, I will try to forget what happened tonight. We all need sleep."

How pedantic he sounded after it had been he, with his angry, searching questions who had started it all, Marisa thought viciously. But she could not deny her own weariness and her need to be alone with her thoughts, in order to sort them out. Let Pedro act pedantic and possessive— she had no intention of remaining engaged to him. In fact, she wanted nothing more than to run away. She did not care where, at this point.

They were all silent now, but there was an unpleasantly poised quality to Inez's surprising stillness. As for Pedro— it was difficult to tell what Pedro was thinking, even though he had tried in his clumsy fashion to act as peacemaker.

Later on, when she was in her bed and the faint light of dawn stole through a crack in the draperies, Pedro tried the handle of her door, and Marisa was glad she had locked it and gladder still that she had asked Lalie to sleep in her room.

Marisa lay still in her bed and heard the girl's frightened whisper say, "Who is it? The mistress is sleeping." And then there was silence, and she was actually able to drift off into a brief, uneasy slumber until fitful, frightening dreams woke her. She sat upright in bed. She had thought for a few moments that she was back in the white-walled house at Tunis, morning pouring in through the narrow, slitted windows.

Lalie had been bent over, rolling up her cloth pallet, and now she straightened up with a dismayed look in her soft brown eyes.

"I did not mean to wake you, ma'am. It's still very early."

Lalie's lips were trembling, and she looked as if she expected to be shrieked at or beaten. *Did* Inez beat her house slaves? Thinking of Inez made Marisa think of last night and all the ugly words that had been exchanged. Back in the present again, with so much weighing on her mind, she could not sleep. No, she needed to be alone somewhere with her thoughts.

Becoming aware that Lalie was still looking at her and was almost cringing, Marisa forced herself to smile reassuringly.

"I could not sleep very well. I suppose I am overtired. But I do not feel like staying in bed this morning. Tell me, Lalie—," a sudden thought struck her, and she looked directly and almost conspiratorially at the girl, "do you think you could bring me a cup of coffee, very strong and black, and—order a horse saddled and brought out front for me? Without disturbing anyone else, of course. I think I would like to go riding—by myself. I won't go far, only to the bluff where I can see the river."

Chapter Forty-two

The morning sun slanted up from behind the bluffs and fell warmly on her thighs. Marisa remembered, with a pang, the days when she had ridden astride instead of side-saddle, posing as a young, slim Janissary, with Kamil at her side. Why were women condemned, because of their clothes, to ride sidesaddle instead of properly astride a horse, riding it as it was meant to be ridden? Never mind. There were other questions to plague her mind this morning.

The sun gave its sly threat of the heat that was to follow later, and the river, she discovered, was concealed still by a heavy, low-lying fog that hung like a coating of yellow oil over the sluggishly moving waters.

The area known as "Natchez-under-the-hill" was just going to sleep after a bawdy, roistering night, but up here the sun shone and winked back a million times from the tiny drops of dew on wet grass and on the moss-embroidered trees that seemed as ancient as this land itself.

Lalie had been shocked and frightened by her insistence that she *would* go riding by herself; but the girl, well trained, did not dare to disobey a direct order anymore than the Negro groom who brought her a saddled horse would have questioned her. Slaves did not question or argue—but was *she* any less a slave to circumstances because she had a mind of her own and a will to go along with it?

'What am I to do?' Marisa thought. Then, more strongly, 'Why should I let *his* presence here frighten me off?' She would be going to Louisiana soon—to Congracia, the place where she had been born but did not remember. Her earliest memories were of Martinique and the house

451

of her grandparents. She did not want to go to Louisiana, but now that she was more than halfway there, why not? Her uncle expected it of her—but was that the only reason? Wasn't part of it, *now,* because she disliked Inez and wanted to thwart her?

She had let her borrowed bay horse go where it pleased while she was thinking, and now Marisa raised her head to find herself in unfamiliar territory. However, the river bluffs at her back would guide her; she had only to swing her horse around and ride to the left, through the grove of trees. Oh, *damn* this cumbersome sidesaddle!

——Her gloved hands tightened on the reins, taking control again, and just at that moment her horse raised its head and whinnied softly. Another horse and rider topped a rounded, grassy slope, full in her path, and the sunlight, behind her, shone directly on them both. Grey stallion with an arched neck, looking every bit as wild and dangerous as its grey-eyed rider.

The old imam who had instructed her in the ways of Islam had talked of kismet, and because her thoughts had already gone back to that time this morning, Marisa disdained trying to run away. Outlined against the blue, cloud-flecked sky, she sat straighter in the saddle and waited for him to come to her.

"You're trespassing. What are you doing out here so early and alone?"

She remembered then, hearing vaguely that the Byrons' lands adjoined those that her father had bought for his young bride. And what could be more natural than that he should stay with the parents of his fiancée?

She answered him tartly, her chin tilted up, "Am I trespassing on *your* land? And where is your innocent little Jane this morning? I came out here to be alone, but if I'm intruding I can easily find my way back." Some devil prompted her to add maliciously, *"I* don't have to account to anyone for my actions, you know!"

"Then its high time Pedro Arteaga put a bridle and a halter on you!" he answered her harshly, kneeing his horse closer to hers until she felt the first stirrings of uneasiness and of fear.

He hated and distrusted her. What better time and better opportunity could he have than *now* to be rid of her forever? There was no one else here beside themselves, and if she fell, or was driven, over the cliff that fell down steeply to the river, it would be termed an accident. . . .

Dominic Challenger, formerly known as the duke of Royse and privateer captain was a man who traded on a talent for violence and for survival. Why should he let *her* stand in his way?

She did not take her eyes off him, but her hands on the reins made her mount dance sideways, snorting as the big stallion approached it.

"Didn't anyone warn you that it would be dangerous out here by yourself? Those toughs from under the hill sometimes come this far away from the river fogs to sober up—and look for easy pickings." He was close enough now for her to see the contemptuous curl of his lips. "Like you, for instance. Or do you enjoy going out to look for trouble?"

He looked harder, bigger, and more menacing than any other time she could remember. He blended into this environment where savagery lurked just under an opulent surface. He wore fawn leather riding breeches that were tucked into high-topped leather boots, a silk shirt open at the neck—and he had a pistol tucked into his wide leather belt.

Marisa eyed him nervously and licked her suddenly dry lips before she retorted, "Why don't you stay out of my way so I can go back to where I *won't* be accused of trespassing? The only danger I can see here is *you!*"

Surprisingly, he grinned mockingly at her. "Were you by any chance thinking that I might be tempted to shoot you? Or throw you over that cliff? I must admit it *is* a very intriguing thought, especially as there would be no witnesses to see what happened." Without her quite realizing it, Marisa had begun to back her horse away from his, and his voice suddenly sharpened. "Careful, menina. Or had you thought of saving me the trouble?"

Intent on escaping *him*, she had forgotten the steep drop behind her, and now his sarcastic reminder made her saw sharply at the reins of her horse, making it rear.

In an instant, swearing under his breath, he had cleared the small distance between them, and she felt the steely pressure of his fingers over hers as he brought her nervous animal to a standstill.

They were so close now that his thigh brushed hers, and he swore again as instinctively she fought to be free of his grip.

"Damn you! You'd rather court death than be touched by me? Any other man, and you'd be falling into his arms!"

His eyes, a furious, icy grey, were so close to hers now that she could see their black pupils.

"How can you blame me for it?" she cried out. "You raped me and used me, and then—then all you could do was accuse me of the very thing you'd taught me to be—forced me to be! Yes, and even before there was anything you could rightly accuse me of! What do you want now—revenge? Because I preferred other men who were more gentle and understanding than *you?*"

He snatched the reins from her hands so that she was forced to cling to the mane of her horse in order to keep her balance. And she saw his arm arc against the sky in the instant before he slapped her, snapping her head sideways with the force of a blow that made her mind reel crazily and brought tears to her eyes. No one, man or woman, had ever struck her like that before. Her face felt numb for an instant. Then the bruising pain started to spread like fire across one cheek, and she tasted blood from the corner of her cut lip. She did not even have time to whimper. He dragged her off her horse and stood her, on trembling legs before him while his hands gripped her shoulders.

Unconscious, unwanted tears coursed down her face. Her one cheek was burning and already bruised and bore the imprint of his open hand like a brand. She tried to fight him off and to collect her reeling thoughts at the same time. He had struck her, half stunning her. Why, when he could have killed her instead?

She hadn't realized that she had sobbed the same words aloud, gasping for breath, until he answered her.

"I should have done that before. Someone should have,

to bring you to your senses—if you have any that are not between your legs."

Her fists came up and pounded at him angrily, but he brushed them aside and slapped her again, not as hard this time, and not with as much anger. Enough to barely sting her cheek and make her cry out.

"*Don't!* Leave me be, let me go! Animal! Savage!"

His grasp on her shoulders tightened before he threw her, with a force that left her stunned, on her back in the long, damp grass.

"You expected me to murder you. This should come easier, and be more familiar to you, my *lady*." His sneering voice mocked her coldly formal "my lord" of a night that seemed aeons ago, and through swollen, dilating eyes Marisa watched him unbuckle his belt. "This is a reckoning that's been a long time coming," he whispered harshly before he dropped his body down to lie over the the length of hers, tangling his fingers in her slipping, unbound hair while his mouth gagged her involuntary scream of pain and rage, drowning her and depriving her of breath until her hands stopped their ineffectual beating at his shoulders, and she felt him uncover her, ripping away her flimsy underclothing to enter her with a shock and force that was even worse than his slaps had been.

Like a creature caught in a snare, she fought for breath and for freedom, her slight body arching and twisting under his encroaching weight until at length she realized the uselessness of her resistance and let him have his will, her eyes closing with the heaviness of tear-drenched lashes that lay against her wet cheeks like bruises.

And contrarily, once she had stopped trying to resist the rape he inflicted on her, Marisa felt as if she had surrendered her body as well as her will. Having stopped thinking, her limpness turned gradually into response, taking him by surprise.

The dew soaked through her velvet riding habit, and his hands found her breasts under her thin lawn blouse while his mouth moved from her mouth to kiss her bruised, tear-stained cheeks.

There seemed to be an inevitability to what took place

between them now that blinded them both to everything else—even the thought that someone—anyone—might come across them lying coupled in the long grass, their two rider-less horses in plain sight.

They had gone beyond caring. The fire of the sun that rose by inches overhead joined a different kind of fire that flamed in their senses, wiping everything else out. There had been one other time like this—beside a stream in a half-wild garden of a villa on the outskirts of Paris—and that had ended in hurt and rejection. When Marisa came back to reality, memory returned, too, making her body which had been wildly yielding a few moments ago turn stiff.

And as if he, too, regretted the unexpected passion that had flared up between them, Dominic rolled away from her to lie on his back at her side. The only sign that he had been affected was in the quickened cadence of his breathing.

She should fasten the buttons of her blouse and her rid-ing skirt and step away from him with as much cool indif-ference as he displayed now, Marisa thought. But she was not yet capable of movement. No doubt she had proved, by her very weakness, everything he had said and thought about her. His lust spent, he had found it easy enough to move away from her, and now he lay on his back like a sated animal, not even bothering to look in her direction. Her body, starved for too long, had played traitor, but now that she was slowly gathering her wits together again, her mind would not deceive her.

Marisa's teeth gritted together, but she forced her voice to sound cool—lazy.

"Mmm. I could almost fall asleep right here. But it wouldn't do for your fiancée or her parents to find us, would it? Or Pedro, for that matter, if he decided to come looking for me. Would you mind doing up all these buttons and hooks for me, mon cher? I'm not used to dressing my-self again, once I've been undressed."

This time she noticed with satisfaction that it was *he* who reacted as if she'd suddenly clawed at him; his infuriating air of male complacency disappeared into narrow-eyed anger as he sat up abruptly to gaze at her as if he could not believe his ears. Well, let him! He could not do worse to her than he had done already, and the last thing on earth she wanted was for him to know what effect he had had on her already irritated senses. No, she would not let him find out, not if he killed her for it!

"Dominic?" she used his name deliberately, watching for its effect and finding it in his deeply drawn breath. Daringly, she pushed him even further. "Would you mind? I swear I couldn't move a finger, I'm so tired. Or did you plan to keep me here like this for the rest of the day?"

She had gone too far. She realized it when he leaned over her, pressing her shoulders back against the softly yielding earth.

"There are times when I almost forget what a little bitch you are at heart. But not for long." He bent his head, still holding her down, and his tongue flicked over her enlarged, pointing nipples, making her gasp and try to squirm away.

"You're easy to arouse, ma petite. And I would like to keep you here all day on your back where you belong. But it wouldn't do, would it? Neither your fiancé nor mine would understand, and so I suppose we'd better go our separate ways—for the moment. But if you should ever feel in the need for adventure again, you can always send word to me in care of the Ram's Head Tavern in Natchez —*under* the hill, naturally."

"Oh! You—you bastard!" she swore at him unthinkingly, but he cuffed her lightly into silence and began to fasten up her garments as she had directed him to do earlier, all without another word.

He even helped her onto her horse, avoiding the kick of her booted foot with a laugh.

"I hope you can think of a plausible story for Pedro on your way back, ma chère," he called, meeting her earlier sarcasm with his own. now that he had set her on her way minus her pride and self-control.

She would not look back again to where he stood, booted feet apart, one hand on the grey stallion's neck, gentling the beast just as he had gentled her a few moments ago making her forget everything but the feel of his hands and lips and body taking hers.

Explanations, if he ever made them, would be easy enough for *him,* Marisa thought bitterly when she reached the house and found them all awake and waiting for her.

Carelessly she had tossed the reins of her horse to the groom who stood waiting at the foot of the steps. Her bluff of cool indifference carried her as far as the entrance hallway. Had they been watching for her through the shuttered windows?

She was in no frame of mind to face anyone—yet face them she must. The glowering Pedro and his cool, secretly smiling cousin.

It was Pedro who caught her by the wrist and dragged her into the breakfast parlor, its table set for three.

"Where have you been? Did you arrange it all last night? You don't have to answer me. I have only to look at you to know what's been going on! Your face, your eyes, your hair. And your riding habit—all crumpled and stained. Have you no shame? Where have you been? Where did you arrange to meet?"

Marisa pulled herself free of him, her face set, and paced to the opposite end of the room where she swung around to face him.

"I think you forget yourself, señor! What I have done or might do is no concern of yours. I don't have to answer to you or to anyone else for that matter."

"Oh, bravo!" Inez said softly and surprisingly from where she had seated herself on a cushioned window seat, and Marisa could not help shooting her a look of surprise.

But Pedro, striding forward angrily, took up her attention again. "What do you mean by that? Last night, you promised to become my novia—I have every right to know what you've been up to!"

"And last night I told you it would only be a trial. I warned you, if you'll recall, that I was very independent. Well, I find that I do not like being questioned. And so, señor, you are released from your gallant offer. You are no longer responsible for me or for my actions. It ought to be a relief to you!"

Pedro Arteaga was so taken aback that he lost all power of speech for a moment. His mouth hung open like that of a beached fish while he surveyed the insolent, shameless little hussy who had dared to defy his rightful fury.

Marisa, rightly gauging his reaction, began to walk past him, her head held high. But he caught her arm and spun her about, his voice actually trembling with rage now. "Perdition take you! You will not walk out of here so easily, to parade your disgraceful behavior before all the slaves! Have you forgotten that I was made responsible for you? You owe me, and Doña Inez, some explanation for where you have been this morning and what you have been doing!"

"Let me go!" she raged, her eyes shooting fiery sparks of defiance at him. "You have no right to lay a hand on me. I am nothing to you and you are nothing to me, do you hear?"

He noticed then, for the first time, the ugly bruise along her cheekbone and shook her, growling, "But obviously someone else, has, eh? What happened? Was it possible that you put up some kind of a struggle and he had to subdue you? Is *that* the kind of treatment that you need to make you act like a real woman?" His voice had risen until he was shouting at her, and in the background Marisa could hear Inez's soft, amused laughter. It was all turning into a nightmare. First Dominic, who had treated her like one of his river sluts, and now Pedro who was belatedly trying to act the heavy-handed guardian.

Marisa said suddenly, "If you do not release me at *once*, I will begin to scream. And I will not stop screaming until you do. And *then* you will have a lot of explaining to do, won't you?"

"Why, you little—," he began, his dark face becoming suffused with blood, and Marisa thought for one second that he was going to strike her. But just then the smooth voice of Doña Inez interposed itself between them.

"Pedro—no! Por Dios, have you gone crazy? The poor child is hysterical—can't you see that?" Inez got up, and put her hand on Pedro's arm, and Marisa could see how her white-ringed fingers bit into it. The honeyed voice became sharp. "You had better leave her alone with me—do you understand, cousin? There are some things that women can only discuss freely with other women. If Marisa has been—hurt in some way, then you are not helping matters by yelling at her. Please leave us. And you'd do well to get rid of all the servants who must be listening out in the hallway at this moment—you know how slaves gossip!"

Inez made an incongruous ally, but for the moment Marisa could only feel relieved at her surprising about-face. She had been through just about all she could endure for one morning!

"Here, you look as if you could do with a glass of wine. And in case you are suspicious—I did not get rid of Pedro because I feel sorry for *you*. *I* happen to have a reputation to protect here, you know! And you have been very foolish. Now we shall have to think up some story to account for your—your bedraggled appearance."

Mechanically, Marisa took the glass of wine that the other woman handed her, and her teeth chattered against its rim. She drained the glass quickly and defiantly, and Inez refilled it from a silver encrusted decanter.

She sat down across from Marisa with the small breakfast table between them, and leaned forward. "Now. We can never be friends as I'm sure you realize by now. But this is not France nor even England. And since you are here of your own accord, you should learn to act with some discretion a, long as you are here!" Without giving Marisa a chance to reply Inez went on, in her low, purring voice. "You should not have gone, and must never again go riding by yourself! Perhaps you realize by now what risks you lay yourself open to. I heard you threaten to scream a little while ago, but you should have screamed *then* if you wished anyone to believe that you were raped. And this is a man's world here, you know. They might pretend concern, and even anger, but secretly all men believe that a woman who goes out by herself has either an assignation to keep or is inviting just the kind of attack you seem to have brought on yourself. There, you see, I am being very blunt. But we must try to hush this up, if you are to be received anywhere again. You understand?"

The wine she had taken so recklessly rushed straight to Marisa's brain, reminding her that she had had not a bite to eat since the previous night. Her limbs had begun to ache, and her jaw felt as if it had been dislocated. She had the strangest, most treacherous impulse to droop her head over her tightly clenched fists and give way to a storm of weeping. But not in front of Inez, never in front of Inez, with her all-knowing feline eyes!

Instead she compressed her lips and narrowed her eyes and stared Inez straight in the face. "I understand that I've been—incautious. It won't happen again." Inwardly, she thought furiously, 'No wonder Dominic dared to be so smugly self-assured! No doubt he makes a habit of that kind of thing and feels quite safe afterwards. I feel quite sorry for his poor little fiancée! But if he thinks that he'll get away so easily with treating me like one of the whores he's accustomed to—oh no! I'll make him sorry. . . .'

Inez had started to lift one arched eyebrow, surprised at this unexpected capitulation when Marisa said in a soft, demure voice, "I intend to follow *your* example and be very discreet and very careful the next time."

Chapter Forty-three

Marisa soaked in the big tub that Lalie had painstakingly filled for her. She was lucky, she supposed, to have a small bath chamber adjoining her room. Most houses in this part of the world, no matter how palatial, usually lacked the creature comforts she had grown used to in Europe. This wasn't a marble tub with steps leading down into it, but it was adequate, thank God; and she leaned her head back, feeling the water dripping down from her hair into her nose and mouth. She remembered the old Romans whose favorite method of suicide was to cut their wrists in a steaming hot bath. But she wasn't going to kill herself. *He* wasn't worth it.

She soaped herself languidly, all of her body. Arms and legs and breasts and belly and especially between her thighs, where she still felt sore. He hadn't been gentle. He had used her for his own ends as he had before. And partly to punish her. And then, no doubt, he'd gone back to his shy, pretty Jane, whom he wouldn't dare touch until after they were married. Hypocrite! Bastard! She regretted the fact now that she had been weak enough to try and stop Kamil from having him tortured to death. How had he managed to get back here?

Marisa felt a sudden cool draft of air against the back of her neck and turned her head quickly, glad to be free of her own vengeful thoughts for a short while.

"Lalie?"

"I told Lalie to wait outside. When you wish to dry yourself, I will hand you your towel. But in the meantime, I thought we should finish our talk. Whether you like it or not, we are to be thrown together, you and I, and there is still the matter of your father's will to be discussed."

Quite calmly, Doña Inez De Castellano drew up the small stool that stood in a corner of the room and seated herself on it, her enigmatic hazel eyes narrowed against the steam that rose from the tub. A faint, sarcastic smile twisted her full lips when Marisa instinctively slid deeper into the water.

"I thought—"

"You thought to silence me with your barbs and your insults? It's plain to me that for all your pretense at being a sophisticated woman of the world you are still a malicious little child in some ways! I don't intend to try and make you like me, any more than I can ever like you. But that is still no reason why the two of us should not come to some—settlement. Or have you changed your mind about staying? If so, I can arrange for your return to Europe if you prefer that to a convent in New Spain!" She laughed softly. "Somehow, I cannot quite picture you taking the veil. Pedro told me how you ran away from the convent in Spain—or was it from him?"

It was hard to be dignified lying naked in a tub of hot water. Marisa gave a grudging shrug of her shoulders.

"I'm not running away. Why should you and Pedro have everything your way? Since my father left everything he owned to me—"

"Almost everything," Doña Inez said smoothly. "He left me a certain allowance, of course. And my personal slaves. The rest? Yes, you are right. He left the rest to you, but it was *I*, I who saved the plantation from ruin after he died and built it up to what it is now while *you* had your fill of excitement in the capitals of Europe. It was not fair! And he was going to change his will—he told me so. Only—"

"He found you had been unfaithful to him?"

Doña Inez shot Marisa a spiteful look, but her voice remained unchanged.

"He was not as young and as strong as he thought he still was. After the duel—such a stupid pointless affair, that —which you have heard about, he was sick for a long time. I tried to persuade him to leave the plantation, for the climate of that part of Louisiana with its swamps and its mosquitoes is not healthy. But he was stubborn, your father. And so in spite of all the nursing and everything that the doctors could do, he died. Without changing his will, fortunately for you!"

The water was growing tepid, and Marisa stood up, taking the towel that Doña Inez handed her with a politeness belied by her eyes.

"And what happens if—if something should happen to *me?*"

"Then everything comes to me, of course. But I hope you don't think me so insanely foolish that I would *arrange* for an accident? There are too many people who are jealous of me and would be glad to make accusations. It's the kind of thing that any young woman who marries a man much older has to face. No, my dear. I have been patient for a long time, and I would not throw everything away by being stupid. I must admit, though, that I am hoping you will find life on an isolated planatation far too lonely and boring after you have tried it for a while. And then, perhaps, we can come to some practical agreement? In the meantime, I was hoping that we could at least pretend to get on—if only in public. For *your* sake as well as mine. You're the newcomer here, after all."

It seemed strange that they should be here together, conversing in such an oddly intimate fashion. But then Doña Inez was obviously a clever as well as practical woman, as Marisa was forced to realize. If she did not accept the truce the woman offered, it was *she* who would seem gauche and immature.

"What happens if I decide to marry?" Marisa asked abruptly, and Inez shrugged.

"You know that your father wished you to marry Pedro. We kept the news of your—escapades from him because he was so very ill. Of course he did not know of your— *former* marriage and I don't need to tell you that he would not have approved—for the obvious reasons that *you* have pointed out to me, among others."

"That's over!" Marisa said angrily and too quickly.

"Oh, of course! Dominic Challenger is far too clever a

man to have gotten himself engaged to the only daughter of the richest planter in the area if he wasn't sure his marriage to you had been annulled. Poor infatuated little creature! *His* type always attracts hers, doesn't it? Not only will he get a rich marriage settlement and an heiress, but he gets a mother for his son as well. They say Jane's very fond of the child. Of course he could hardly *hide* it, and that was one of the reasons her parents balked at first. But—"

Half-dressed, Marisa stood stock still, frozen with shock she wasn't able to hide from Inez too-knowing eyes.

"His—*son?* He has a child?"

"Oh, of course! I'm surprised that you would not have known of its existence, unless your paths didn't cross since your unfortunate marriage! A boy he calls Christian— about two years old, I suppose. And he has his father's eyes, at least! He brought him back here with him, with a fierce old woman as his nurse. There were a few whispers at first that *she* was the mother, but they were soon scotched when people got a good look at her! She's a veritable dragon, with a nasty, twanging Americano voice."

"And the child's mother?"

"Does the thought upset you after so long? No one knows who the unfortunate creature was. Jane, who *will* romanticize, told me she had died in childbirth, before they could be married. But then, he *would* think of a plausible story, wouldn't he? *You* ought to know how unscrupulous he is—"

"Yes, . ." Marisa whispered, and then, in spite of all her resolutions, she fainted.

* * * * *

"You ought've eaten breakfast, madam," Lalie said in her soft voice, spooning a hot thick soup she called gumbo into Marisa as if she had been an invalid child. "And the sun here gets very hot. If you ain't used to it, it can be dangerous, 'specially if you go out without a hat to shade your head. Please eat some more, madam. The mis-

tress said she'd whip me if I didn't see you finished every
bit. It wouldn't do for you to get sick."

"If I have any more, then I *will* be sick! No, honestly,
Lalie, I've had enough. You may empty the rest of it into
the slop pail. It was very good, and I feel much stronger already, but I cannot eat another mouthful."

Marisa felt sick every time she remembered the words
that Inez had so casually (or not so casually?) let drop.
It *had* been Selma Meeker she'd seen yesterday with a little
boy. *Whose* child? "About two years old," Inez had said
carelessly. Oh God—*whose?* Selma, whose hand she had
clung to in those hours that were filled with pain, from
which she'd wakened up to emptiness and Zuleika's falsely
consoling words. "Your daughter was born dead. . . ."
She'd believed her child had died, for she had remembered
what the doctor in France had said. And Kamil had been
kind and tender afterwards. "What had happened to Selma?
"I sold her to the trader. . . ." Oh no, it wasn't possible!
Kamil had *promised!* . . . She was letting her imagination
run wild. There must have been another woman, a fellow
slave, perhaps—a captive of the sheik he had gone off
with. Another woman who had given him a child who had
lived.

Inez came back to see her later and said lightly, "Pedro
has taken himself off to the taverns under the hill to drown
his sorrows. I told him you'd probably taken a slight sun-
stroke. That *is* all that is wrong with you, is it not?"

How much did Inez know, or guess?

Then came the attack—the first, soft, silken pounce.

"We have been invited to dinner with the Byrons tomorrow
You know their lands adjoin these? Perhaps, under the circumstances, you would have me refuse?"

"Under what circumstances?" Marisa said thinly, fighting back. "I feel fine now. All I needed was some nourish-
ment. And besides," she added boldly, seeing the gleam in
Inez's eyes that promised more, "being raped is a shock
to the system. Have *you* ever been raped?"

"Why, no," Doña Inez said silkily. "I have always been
very careful to choose my lovers—and never to promise
what I did not intend to give. Is that what happened to

you this morning? I should have warned you that our hot sun breeds hot-blooded men. Although you *did* seem composed enough when you first came in.

"Why not? It happened, and it was over. What was I supposed to do, kill myself afterwards?"

"Some women have been known to do so, of course, but you are stronger than that, aren't you? Unless, of course, you are accustomed to being—raped, as you call it."

Her claws were showing, and in spite of her incipient drowsiness, Marisa's spine stiffened.

"Only by the same man. But he did not need to rape *you*, I imagine."

"Dominic and I have always understood each other. In some ways, we are very much alike, you see. But it was something your poor father could never understand."

Unhurriedly, Doña Inez rose from her chair and smiled down at Marisa.

"You look very sleepy. I'll leave you now, and Lalie will sleep in here again tonight. I do not wish you to be disturbed in case Pedro returns very late and very drunk. Two rapes in one day might prove too much for your delicate nerves; and after all, I must look after you, mustn't I?"

But there were no more rattlings at her door in the small hours. Rising refreshed the next morning, Marisa breakfasted with Doña Inez before they drove to town.

They went to see a pompous old attorney, who gave Marisa a copy of her father's will.

"The original was filed in Louisiana, of course. But the señora insisted that a copy must be made available for you to read. You understand everything in it, I hope? I'd be glad to explain. . . ."

He made it clear that he imagined the intelligence of women to be only slightly removed from that of children and frowned with displeasure when Marisa smiled and told him coolly that she understood very well, that she had learned to read Latin as a child.

"I'm surprised that the nuns gave you such an excellent education," Doña Inez drawled.

Marisa countered with, "But *I* expected to become a teaching nun, you see."

"Like the good Ursulines in New Orleans?" Inez gave a theatrical shudder. "Somehow, I cannot imagine you as one of *them!*"

An uneasy truce between them established, they went shopping together and returned to the house with the carriage piled with bandboxes.

Pedro sulked, and Inez suggested gently that perhaps it would be just as well if he and Marisa continued with their farce of an engagement for a while—at least until they left Natchez.

"After all, he will be leaving for New Spain in a few months so what does it matter? You will be meeting Dominic Challenger everywhere while you are here; and even though I am sure your pride will not allow him the chance to *rape* you again, surely, as a female you will feel safer at facing him with a fiancé of your own? I have spoken to Pedro, and he agrees, although he says you have hurt him very much. He's really quite stupid, even if he *is* my cousin —I do believe he is still infatuated with you!"

"Only because he cannot have me!" Marisa retorted, but she made no other demur and listened thoughtfully to Inez's half-malicious gossip as they dressed for dinner.

"Challenger is not his real name, of course, but I'm sure you already know that. When he first turned up here, you should have heard the rumors that went flying around! Everyone knows his *legal* father was a Tory who went back to England, but who is his *real* father? No one knows, but I've heard several names bandied about—*not* in Dominic's hearing of course! President Jefferson himself? Colonel Daniel Morgan? Even General Wilkinson, and that is most likely for they are very close, and it was Wilkinson who arranged for him to get a passport to enter New Spain under the last Spanish governor. And then of course, there is John Sevier, who has also taken an interest in him. *He* is of French descent—of a very old and aristocratic family, they say. He was a fighter in the Revolutionary War—a blood brother to the Five Nations—and still a very important man in the State of Tennessee. But who knows? Dominic's mother is dead, I understand; and *that* is something he will not talk about to anyone."

"With such important connections, earned or otherwise, he ought to be a very rich man in his own right!" Marisa said stiffly.

Inez raised her shoulders in a graceful gesture.

"But he is a born adventurer! Such men are determined to make their own fortunes or die trying. Surely you have understood that much about him? He was a privateer when it suited him, and now his ship is an investment, and another man sails it as captain. It was Jane Byron's parents, I understand, who persuaded him to try his fortune on the land; they did not want their daughter to be left alone for long periods! But—if you talk to him alone again, and I hope you will be wise enough not to—you might warn him to stay out of New Spain! He and Pedro were good friends once, but no longer. He ought to be content with the fortune that Jane will bring him."

●   ●   ●   ●   ●

The dinner party given by the Byrons was a crowded, drawn-out affair, and Marisa agonized through it, pretending not to notice how Dominic hardly left Jane Byron's side, smiling down at the pretty blond girl with an affection and tenderness he had never shown *her*.

Knowing that Pedro and Inez watched her sharply, Marisa managed to present an appearance of gay insouciance. She was prettily and guilelessly deferent to all the older people present, flirted mildly with some of the younger, unattached men, and did not engage in any intellectual or political discussions.

After dinner, however, it was inevitable that there should be dancing; and it was just as inevitable, of course, that Dominic must ask her to dance. He could hardly *not* do so without exciting comment.

And she had been waiting for this moment, having eaten and drunk sparingly so that her mind would remain clear and unclouded.

Marisa had dressed deliberately to suit the role she in-

470

tended to play tonight. A simple white muslin gown with a high, standing collar, caught just beneath the breasts with a circlet of embroidered daisies. She wore a rope of pearls threaded through her hair, which was dressed casually, curls escaping onto her forehead and temples.

"Pearls for purity?" he said mockingly almost as soon as he had taken her unwillingly into the circle of his arm. "They're very becoming, and I must say you've managed to make an excellent impression this evening."

She smiled at him for the benefit of those that might be watching, but her voice was taut.

"I'm sorry that I am not as good at pretending as you are, Dominic Challenger. I can see that you haven't told Jane about the other morning. Does she know about us? How did you account for becoming a father when you already had a wife?"

She could feel the sudden tensing of his muscles, and she saw the first blind fury of his reaction in the icy look of his eyes and the flare of his nostrils. Oh yes, she could sense that he would have dearly loved to strangle her at this very moment; he was like a wild leopard, poised and ready to strike for her throat. And that was why she had chosen such a public place to say what she had to say.

He didn't miss a step, but she knew what an effort it must have cost him to keep his voice a casual drawl.

"Perhaps you'll tell me what you mean by that?"

"Must you continue to play the hypocrite? Very well, I'll put it more plainly then. It's obvious that you've only told your unfortunate fiancée just as much as you chose to tell her. Voilà, there are certain things you do not want her —or her parents to know. I suppose you take rape in your stride—especially if it's only your ex-wife, but *she* might not!"

His lips were a hard, straight line, white around the edges with the effort of holding his temper.

"Get to the point, madam!"

"The point is that—" she faltered for the first time, and then went on quickly, before she lost her courage—"I want to see—Christian. And talk to Selma Meeker. It *is* Selma Meeker who looks after him, isn't it? I have to—oh, never mind! But I don't care what you threaten me with or what you do. I must see this child you acknowledge as your son and talk to Bab—to Selma. I—"

"Be quiet!" he said angrily under his breath. And then, more softly still, each word uttered with the force of a mortal blow, "Damn you! I should have thrown you over the bluff yesterday. If I'd known—"

She began to tremble with an unknown, unwanted fear and forced herself to look up into a face that hated her.

"Well? You may call it blackmail if you will—it *is* that, if you force me into it. But I have a right—"

"A right?" She could feel the barely leashed fury emanating from him like a physical force almost driving her to her knees. "What makes you remember that you were a mother at this late stage? Do you think I've forgotten a single word you said to me when you swore your hate for me and for the child you carried, because it was *mine?* Did you know or care what happened to the infant you bore and abandoned without even wanting to see it? If not for Selma—"

"Oh—God!" Marisa said quietly. She had called his hand and won her answer without really expecting it.

"All right," he said suddenly, as if he could not bear to keep holding her another moment longer, "there's no need to pretend to faint again. Jane wouldn't understand if it happened a second time. I'll meet you tomorrow at three o'clock in the afternoon outside the millinery shop. You can bring Inez, if you like; I'm sure she knows the whole story already. But, by God, *then* we're going to talk this out. I don't give a damn how much you hate me, but you hurt Christian and I'll kill you with my bare hands, do you understand that clearly?"

She could only nod. Her whole attention, almost thankfully, was concentrated on *not* swooning again. There would be time in which to think about the terrible, incredible truth he'd admitted to her in his rage.

472

Chapter Forty-four

Marisa could not remember later how she had managed to walk and talk and even smile her way through the rest of the time she was forced to remain there in the same house, the same room as Dominic, who neither looked in her direction nor spoke to her again.

"You made a good impression tonight," Inez said when they were in the carriage again. "So very shy and quiet! The only derogatory remark I heard about you was from an old lady who complained of your lack of animation!" She laughed softly.

Pedro, sitting cross-armed and scowling, muttered sneeringly, "You were like a little puppet moving on strings. I wonder what it takes to bring you to life?"

He was more than half-drunk tonight, and he had held her far too closely when he danced with her, a fact which, in her agitated state, she had let pass. Now, occupied with her confused, whirling thoughts, Marisa let his insinuating remark slide past the edges of her consciousness, not bothering to answer him.

She could not believe it! It had never once entered her mind that they might have been lying to her when they told her that her child had been born dead. Kismet. The will of Allah. Was *that* what had brought her here, quite unsuspecting, to be faced with the knowledge that—that—no! She almost didn't want to believe it. Better, at this point in her life, never to have known than to feel herself suddenly torn into pieces by the twin claws of memory and conscience.

Pleading a headache, she went straight upstairs to her

bed and lay tossing and wakeful until dawn, when sheer exhaustion made her doze for a little while.

Dominic Challenger did not sleep at all. Buoyed up by anger and self-disgust, he had bid a polite and rather chaste good night to his surprised fiancée and made his excuses to her parents. He had been supported by his friend and so-called patron General James Wilkinson who said they had business to discuss.

The two men went their separate ways later, Wilkinson still smiling his enigmatic smile.

"The wedding is not to be delayed, is it? I think the little Jane is becoming eager to be finally bedded. Can it be that another heiress has caught your eye? If so, you'll have to fight my friend Arteaga for her—and he would make a bad enemy. You've heard of his new appointment?"

Dominic, who knew Wilkinson very well, gritted his teeth beneath a careless smile, and said, "It's no secret I met Marisa De Castellanos a few times in Europe. But she's more the kind I'd look for as a mistress instead of a wife."

"I understand she's secretly betrothed to Arteaga. And he's been in a strangely ugly mood of late. You *will* be careful?"

"Haven't I been so far?" Dominic retorted flippantly, and the subject was closed. Wilkinson was far too intelligent and wily to ask him more questions, and the two men parted amicably—Dominic riding directly to the elegant establishment presided over by a Madame Aivoges, who had been called "the paragon of prostitutes."

For the remainder of the night, he gambled in one of her private rooms and lay with a golden-haired octoroon who was new and spoke English with a delectable French accent. But she reminded him too much of his ex-wife, being possessed of the same qualities of pretended innocence and seductiveness, and he rose from her wide, soft bed in an unpleasant, wicked mood, his eyes bloodshot and smarting.

By the time he drove his small, rented carriage down the street where he was supposed to meet *her,* he had taken the time to bathe and shave, but his mood remained un-

changed. Dominic Challenger was not used to defeat, nor
to being forced to give in—especially to a woman he had
thought was long out of his life. What was her game this
time? Some kind of revenge for her hurt pride? He did not
want to admit to himself that it was partly his fault for
not being able to keep his hands off her. Which surprised
him, for he had already made up his mind that she was
a cold, heartless little bitch with an eye to the main chance
and a hate that was larger than his. Why then, had he
allowed her to get under his skin? Why had she looked so
whitely shocked when he admitted he had Christian? She
had known it already in spite of what he'd thought earlier;
she *must* have known. Now he was committed to meet
her, and it would be a sore trial on his self-control, which
had been already taxed by a sleepless and frustrating night.

Marisa had brought Lalie with her instead of Inez. Fortunately, she had learned when she came downstairs that
Inez had gone to visit some friends, and Pedro was nowhere to be seen.

She had already explained to the wide-eyed Lalie that
she was to wait, right here, until she returned. Apparently the small millinery shop was the rendezvous for
many such secret assignations. Lalie had admitted as much
when she asked apologetically if Marisa had given Madame her usual fee. Once that was done, Madame would
swear to the heavens that Miss or Mrs. such-and-such had
been in her shop all afternoon—hadn't her carriage been
waiting outside? No doubt that was why Dominic had
picked this place for their meeting.

She gave Lalie money to buy herself something to eat,
or even some pretty ribobns, while she waited. The girl
thanked her with downcast lashes.

"Are you happy, Lalie? That is, are you? . . ." How
could a young, educated female be happy or even content
to find herself owned body and soul by someone else? She
should not have asked.

"Oh yes, ma'am," Lalie said almost too quickly. "Why
shouldn't I be?"

A small carriage pulled to a stop beside theirs, and

Marisa's heart started to pound thickly when she saw Dominic's harsh, unsmiling face.

"Climb in. I can't leave the horses, they're too restive."

"I'll be back as soon as I can," she said to Lalie and obeyed him without argument, aware of the traffic all around them.

He reached out one hand to pull her to the seat beside him and gave the horses their heads almost before she had time to lean back. She felt the jolt all the way down her spine. And now that she was sitting here beside him, she could not think of a word to say. What *was* she to say? Launch into explanations he would not believe? Beg for his understanding? Once they had been married, but now through her doing and his, there was not even that tenuous tie between them. Only a small boy. Almost two years old, she had been told. And even the child, like its father now, was a stranger to her.

Marisa meshed her fingers together, unable to utter a single syllable. She was glad of the fashionable poke bonnet that shielded her features, not only from passers-by but from him as well. She did not trouble to ask him where he was taking her because suddenly it did not seem to matter at all.

Her sudden, passive silence forced Dominic into unwilling speech. With icily-controlled politeness he said, "My house is downriver. Quite some distance away. But I think we ought to have a talk first. If you insist upon seeing Christian, for your own damned reasons, there's also Selma Meeker to be considered. She's very—forthright, in case you'd forgotten. And she's become used to the idea that I'm to marry Jane."

"Oh!" Stung, Marisa sucked in a deep breath. "So you have to ask *her* permission first, is that it? What is *she* doing here with you? Her husband—"

"Captain Meeker died of a fever in one of those filthy dungeons they kept their slaves. But how would *you* know? *Your* position was quite different, as I recall."

She flinched. "Oh, don't! Haven't we said enough to each other? What difference does it make now? I only want—"

Seeing that he had her at a disadvantage, he cruelly pressed home his point.

"I'm damned if I know what you could want at this late stage! But I won't have Christian hurt—or Jane. And I warn you not to threaten me again, or you'll end up floating in the river." The horses went around a narrow curve so fast that the carriage seemed to balance on one wheel for an instant, and she was flung against him. "I didn't intend to kill myself, too," he said between gritted teeth. "Be quiet now, until we get to where we can talk in private. I'm sorry if it isn't the kind of place you are used to, but at least no one will recognize you in this part of town."

"This part of town" was, as she should have expected, the river front, filled with noise and litter and foul smells. And the privacy he had promised her was the small area of the room he rented over the Ram's Head Tavern.

Silent now, her head bent, Marisa allowed him to hustle her up a squalid back staircase behind the tavern. She wrapped her silk-fringed shawl closely about her shoulders as if she could feel the stares of the drunken loiterers who looked after them and made ribald, jeering comments.

His room was small and plainly furnished but clean enough. And the one small window it possessed was open. It overlooked the sluggishly flowing river, and she could smell its dank, rather fishy odor mixed with that of rotting refuse.

She had gone past caring what he might plan to do with her. Not even when she heard him lock the door behind them did she move; instead she stood like a statue in the center of the room.

"Now—," Dominic said, spinning her around with his hands on her shoulders as he ripped away her shawl. "Now perhaps you'll tell me, with no more hedging, what the hell you're up to this time?"

Everything she had planned to say dried up in her throat as she stared into his eyes, gone dark and slaty now with pent-up fury. She had been stupid to let him bring her here where she was beyond help. It was ridiculous to have imagined, even for a moment, that he might listen to her stumbling explanations, or even try to understand what had driven her away from him from the very beginning.

Now she could only look back at him, her eyes wide. In spite of herself, she was terrified.

"Have you lost your tongue now that we're alone? Not too long ago, you were making threats."

"So were you," Marisa finally managed to whisper. "If you are going to kill me, for heaven's sake, make a quick end of it! I seemed to have lost my instinct for survival."

With a smothered oath, he swung away from her, saying over his shoulder, "You seem to have done very well so far! Why act the martyr now?" His fingers itched to fasten themselves about her throat, and no doubt she sensed it. He was also all too tempted to rip her demure grey gown off her body and throw her on the bed, treating her as the slut she was. What was there about her that invited just that kind of treatment?

With his back to her, Marisa found it easier to talk. "I've had time to wonder if it's any use trying to explain anything to you. You know what I've done, but have you wondered why? Why is it you've always been ready to believe the very worst of me? But whatever I've done, or been, I can swear this much—I didn't *know* that I'd borne a live child! Even Selma Meeker can tell you that much! I don't know what they gave me—something to ease the pain, they said. But afterwards—afterwards I was told that I had given birth to a daughter, who was born dead." He stiffened but did not turn, and she cried out with a renewal of anger, "I know what I said to you! But I didn't *know!* I wanted the child because it was mine, too. I wanted it, and Kamil promised—he said. . . . For God's sake, did *he* lie to me, too? Or was it only Zuleika?"

"Does it matter?" His voice sounded so flat it was almost indifferent. And he would not turn his head to look at her. "Did you love him so much that you still care even though he's dead?"

Dominic heard her gasp behind him, and the satisfaction he expected to feel was like ashes in his throat. Still, he finished what he had started to say, his words clipped and harsh. And even when he forced himself to turn around and face her, Kamil's ghost was between them. In her huge, tear-wet eyes he saw the image of the smiling man who must have bent over her making love to her. The man who had risked everything and lost everything because of her. It was possible she was telling the truth. Kamil would have gone to any lengths to keep her, although he lost her in the end, along with his life.

"He was kind to me," Marisa whispered. "He—he made me feel. . . . How would you understand? I don't think you've ever loved or really cared for anyone in your life. I can't forgive the fact that he lied to me—but then, he's dead, isn't he? You killed him—just as you killed Philip and the chevalier and the duke. . . . Oh, I didn't really love Philip, I know that now! We used each other—but you let it happen! You—"

He crossed the room to her, shaking her, knowing she was close to hysteria, not knowing if he hated her or. . . .

Her eyes opened, and tears spilling from them, she looked into his.

"Dominic—what happened? How did it happen?" She began to laugh, the sound of her laughter startling him. "I think you will have to kill me. You see, I'm too much of a coward to do it myself. If you do not, I will spoil everything for you—why not? You did the same for me. Remember? You—"

He put his mouth over hers, stemming her rising hysteria. And at first she fought against him like a wild thing, striking at him, clawing at his shoulders, kicking and struggling when he lifted her off her feet and dumped her onto the bed.

Her gown ripped, exposing pale-gold, flailing limbs. She continued to fight him, screaming invectives at him until he flipped her over, holding her down with one hand over her mouth. She bit his fingers, and he held her face against the pillow until she was gasping for breath. She squirmed frantically under him, and brutally he grabbed one of her thrashing arms and twisted it behind her back until she screamed and finally lay still, sobbing with frustration and rage and pain. He took her, and she screamed again—once—and then all the tension seemed to leave her body and she lay under him, acquiescent until he released her aching arm and began to kiss the back of her neck while his hand under her body caressed her. And then, finally, she began to twist under him again, still sobbing, but this time with surrender and a feeling she was not able to control. Her mind went spiraling, and her body no longer belonged to her but to him until he brought them both to rest again.

Was this part of his revenge? To take her as Kamil was used to taking her, only to prove—what? Why hadn't he killed her instead? For nothing was resolved between them yet, except the fact that he could want her and she could respond.

And yet, when it was all over—her surrender and his victory (or had it been the other way around?)—he moved her limp body onto its side and held her against him with his arms tight about her, his face buried in her rumpled hair.

She remembered, half-dazed, the time he had dropped her lost slippers on her sleeping body, one by one, before he joined her in bed and exacted just such a surrender of her will and senses. And the times before that. Why couldn't she have stayed as she first had been—ignorant of this kind of pleasure? What was the strange, unnatural bond that kept bringing them together like this in spite of the hate and mistrust between them?

As if he could sense her confused thoughts, he held her even closer to him and murmured "Marisa?" against her hair, his voice sounding muffled and sleepy. What would happen if she stayed here with him? It would be a scandal that no one in Natchez would forget for years, no doubt. Why not stay? *She* could survive a scandal—but he would lose everything. The perfect revenge, if she wanted to take it.

Tentatively, her hands touched his back, feeling the scars that laced across it. Half-asleep, he seemed helpless, even with the weight of his leg flung over hers. She thought of the child he had taken and cared for which was *their* child, even though she had not known of its existence until just a day ago. She might never have known if not for him.

The strangest thing was that the tears she had started to shed for Kamil and her memories of the past had ended up being for herself and Dominic and what might have been. She remembered Donald saying, a long time ago, "There are things you don't understand. . . . There's a devil riding his shoulder that makes him the way he is. Ye wouldna' understand. . . ."

Knowing as much as she did now, she *did* understand—even if he had no understanding of her.

And so she stirred, trying to break free of his drowsy embrace. In the process, she roused him enough so that he swore and lifted his head, then squinted down into her face.

"What's the matter now? If you're waiting for me to apologize for what just happened or for what happened before, you'll wait a long time." He made his voice deliberately harsh, but this time she refused to flinch from it, her abortive movement to escape stilled as she lay trapped in his involuntarily tightening embrace.

"You have never apologized to me before—why should I expect it now? I was only thinking that Lalie will be waiting for me, and I have no clothes left that are fit to wear outside. What do you mean to do with me?"

He scowled down at her, the scar she remembered standing out against his sun-browned skin.

"Oh, damn! You have the habit of driving me past rational thinking, do you know that?"

"No," she said uncompromisingly, looking back into his eyes. "To me, you have always seemed to know exactly what you were doing. *My* impression has been only that you did not care whom you had to hurt in the process. Perhaps you've had reason to be mistrustful of people, to be hard and even cynical—a user of others. But, God, did you have to make *me* that way, too?"

She lay naked and helpless in his arms. She had begged him to kill her, instead he had used her in the most insulting, painful fashion it was possible for a man to use a woman. He had every cause, his mind told him, to hate her but in some subtle way he felt himself defeated by her very acceptance and passivity now.

Dominic was tired and still half-drunk. He looked down into her golden eyes and saw in the shape of her face and the stubborn set of her mouth something he had already discovered in Christian. Had she told the truth—at least about *that?* And why should that make any difference to either of them at this late stage? She was not the kind of woman who was cut out to be a mother; perhaps she could see that for herself now and that was why she was so anxious to be gone. He had meant to punish her, to show her up for the kind of woman she was—weak, wanton creature who gave in too easily to circumstances, flinging herself from the arms of one lover to the next like a giddy butterfly. In his own mind, Dominic was sure that Pedro Arteaga was already her lover. He frowned. Pedro was his enemy now. Had *he* sent Marisa here? Did they intend to try and use the fact that she was Christian's mother as a weapon against him?

Marisa had been watching the changing expressions on Dominic's face. So he was back to hating and distrusting her! She turned aside saying in a tight, cold little voice, "If you have—done with me, then I wish that you would let me go. Unless you do not care who knows that you brought me here this afternoon?"

He gave a short, particularly unpleasant laugh.

"Is that why you came here so readily—and alone? Are we to be discovered here by Don Pedro, who will naturally be thirsting for vengeance when he finds I've ripped the clothes off your back and ravished you?"

"Oh, God! What kind of a mind do you have? Must you twist everything I say? You know why I came here with you—and now I only want to leave. Please, I beg you! Let me go—leave me be!"

Breathlessly, Marisa attempted to roll away from him, but he pulled her back easily with one hand and rolled his body over hers to keep her still.

"Oh, please!" she whispered brokenly, no longer struggling but limp. From beneath her tightly closed eyelids, slow tears trickled forlornly down her face, giving her the appearance of a hurt child.

He was unreasonably angered. What right had she to act

482

like a martyr undergoing persecution? And the worst part of it was that in spite of everything he knew or guessed about her, there was a part of him that could not forget: the feel of her softly yielding body lying sprawled out naked beneath him; the fact that he lay between her thighs; and above all the peculiarly silken texture of her skin that had never been duplicated by any other woman he had known. Damn her! How was it possible to despise a woman and to desire her at the same time?

It was to save his own sanity that he left her abruptly, swinging himself to the side of the bed and then onto his feet.

"Get up, then, and I'll take you back to the respectable part of the town!" he growled at her. "As I'm sure you've learned by now, I'm neither respectable nor scrupulous. Here." He had crossed the room to rummage furiously in a battered, leather-bound sea chest. When he turned, he tossed a violet silk gown at her.

Marisa gasped with shock first and then surprise. "Oh! How did you—" And then she broke off, flushing when she caught the sarcastic light in his eyes.

"How did I come by such a garment? Well, I'll tell you, even if it *is* no concern of yours. I bought it at a pirate auction in Louisiana, thinking to surprise my fiancée with it. But it seems I owe you a gown, so you may have it. And now get dressed if you're still in such a hurry to leave and scuttle back to safety!"

He had already began to pull on his own clothes, and she had no choice but to take the exquisite, shimmering garment he had flung at her so carelessly; she felt herself paid off like a whore for his use of her body.

It was as if he had a compulsion to hurt her and go on hurting her. Her fingers fumbled with rows of tiny buttons, and he brushed her hands aside impatiently. He turned her around, and, as if she'd been a doll, he fastened the buttons.

'Don't!' Marisa wanted to cry out at him. 'Don't say anything more—nothing more, for pity's sake!'

But she had done enough pleading already, and she felt bruised and battered and sick inside as he said conversationally, "I hope you have enough sense to realize now that it would not be a good idea for you to see the boy. Christian's very young yet, but he's begun to call Jane mama, and she dotes on him. I don't want him confused or hurt, and if you feel anything for him at all, you ought to realize this is what's best for him. He's my son, and I've taken the responsibility for him. You'll be free to lead your own life and have more children—if you really want to be burdened with a child. Do you understand?"

"Yes," she said numbly, all the spirit gone out of her, longing only to be away from him now, never again to have to meet his familiar, hateful eyes that always seemed like daggers piercing through her.

He picked up her carelessly discarded shawl, and because she stood there in the center of the room as if her feet had taken root, he put it about her shoulders roughly.

The violet silk dress molded itself to the slim lines of her body, its high-waisted bodice outlining the slight curves of her breasts. It might have been made for her—Jane's breasts and hips were fuller, and they would have strained at the material. But Marisa. He remembered her in Paris and in London, jewels in her hair and jewels sparkling at her ears and around her throat. She ought to be wearing jewels now.

Dominic's eyes had turned smoky. Marisa saw the sudden change in them and felt his fingers brush her shoulders, almost unwillingly.

Time hung suspended for the tiniest instant as he said quietly, "You've turned into a beauty, gypsy wench."

If he had drawn her to him then and kissed her, she would have yielded. She would have let him take her back to that bed and do whatever he wanted with her. She had the absurd yearning to reach her hand up and touch again the harsh planes of his face, to make him smile at her again as he had once in the garden of the villa outside Paris, where, for a short time, they had been truly happy with each other.

But it was too late. Already, as if regretting his momentary weakness, Dominic moved away from her and was advising her brusquely to be sure and wrap the shawl closly about her head and shoulders.

"You're a far cry from the dove-grey puritan who walked in here with me," he drawled. "I don't want to have to fight off the usual crowd of loiterers outside. They're not used to seeing a fancy piece of goods like you walk the streets in broad daylight."

From somewhere, Marisa found the courage to retort, "Then you must just tell them that you have me on loan from Madame Aivoge's establishment—where I can be bought for an evening at a very high price—mustn't you?" She had the small satisfaction of seeing him scowl at her knowledge of that elegant establishment.

PART FOUR

~•~

The Surging Torrent

Chapter Forty-five

The huge, luxuriously appointed flatboat slipped down the river carried by the lazy current that would take them eventually to the city of New Orleans. Shrouded by the blackness of an almost tropical night, the muddied yellow waters of the river parted silently; and there was a feeling of being isolated in time and space. There was only the slight rocking feeling of movement below and the black outline of the river banks, here and there broken by pinpoints of light, and the timeless stars pricking the velvet darkness of the sky overhead.

One of the Negro boatmen, keeping watch for unexpected shoals or floating logs, softly sang a song in the French Créole patois that spoke of sadness and breaking hearts.

Mo pas connin queque quichause,
Qu'appe tourmentier moin la,
Mo pas connin qui la cause
Mo couer ape brule moin comme ça. . . .

Lalie translated softly when Marisa asked her to.

"He is saying, 'I do not know what is this that torments me, I do not know the cause, that makes my heart burn so much. . . .'"

'And I do not know either,' Marisa thought, leaning against a wooden railing and watching the river slip by.

She did not know what kept her awake. Was it the muted heat and stillness of the night? Or was it the sense of slipping through the darkness to something unknown and frighteningly mysterious? "Down the river to New

Orleans . . ." How often she had heard people say the words, making the fabled city sound more exciting and voluptuous than Paris itself. And now, with Natchez left far behind them, they were already in Louisiana—Orleans Territory, as President Jefferson had provisionally named this lower part of the vast territory that had been bought from France.

It was better to think of what lay ahead than to remember what was behind her, Marisa thought with wry cynicism. And yet, annoyingly, there were the unpleasant memories that kept her awake on a night like this. She should be asleep in her small cabin as Inez already was in hers, heavy netting drawn around her bed to keep off the mosquitoes. Or, on such a night, there should have been someone beside her who could share the newness of everything: the stars overhead, the silken, swishing sound of the water, the green smells of lushly growing vegetation, and even the cloying perfume of night-blooming flowers hanging heavily from wild vines. What would she find on the plantation she could imagine only vaguely as a black-lined section seen on a map? She knew it was comprised of close to a thousand acres and had been a grant made by the Spanish king to her father; it was a miniature kingdom of its own where almost everything needed for sustenance was either grown or made by slaves.

"We grow mostly sugar—and have our own refinery there, of course. But at my suggestion, your father also ordered the planting of rice in an area that was too swampy to grow anything else. Congracia is a very rich plantation, but unfortunately, it is also quite isolated because of its size and location. I hope you will not feel too much cut off from civilization. . . ." Inez had lifted one dark, arched eyebrow when she added that.

Marisa, shrugging, retorted, "If *you* did not mind it too much, then I'm sure that I will grow used to it, too."

Anything would be better than staying on for much longer in Natchez, she had thought feverishly at the time. Staying out of Pedro's scowling path and his constant trying of her door at night. Avoiding Dominic, making cowardly excuses not to attend any more evening functions where he might be present with his fiancée at his side. 'I am running away,' Marisa thought dully and wished that the words of the boatman's sad song did not keep repeating themselves in her mind. Running away from Dominic who had hurt her and would hurt her again. And—unbearable thought—even from the son she had never known and would never know now. Never. Such a cold and final word.

She thought of Dominic, his voice coldly withdrawn, saying as he led her down the dirty, uncarpeted staircase from the sordid little room where he had taught her the extent of his disgust for her, "It might be best that we do not run into each other again as long as you are here. I'll make some excuse to take a trip upriver."

Worse than his dispassionately uttered speech had been the ugly little incident that had taken place soon after, when they had gained the street.

Three drunken men lurching out of the tavern below the stairs almost barged into her. With red-rimmed, leering eyes, they looked her over.

"Will you lookit *this?* Ain't she a dee-licious morsel?"

"I could swallow her right up in one bite, I'm that hungry for some woman flesh."

"Heard the quadroons in this town were right purty—better'n those stuck-up gals in New Orleans. That true, honey gal?"

She had been aware of Dominic's stiffening behind her. Of his move to loosen the knife he wore at his belt. And yet, as wrapped up as she was in her own hurt and despair, the *words* the man had spoken had hardly registered. Not then. Only the way they looked at her, and the way they spread out as if at an unspoken signal and began again to come forward.

"You gonna be nice and share?"

"Hey gal, we can pay. Good American money." A ribald laugh.

"Three's better than one. An' we ain't as fussy about color as the folks back in New Orleans."

A short, ugly incident. She had not even protested when

Dominic thrust her back against the wall, knife out now, its blade shining.

Those other three had knives, too. She'd had time to notice that when a smooth voice had interrupted.

"Are you interfering with my friends, you three? Sinners, I'll expect you at the prayer meeting I will be holding tomorrow night—just across the river."

One of the men, blinking under shaggy eyebrows, started to growl, "Who in hell—"

But the other two paled, their drunkenness falling away. "We didn't mean any harm, Mr. Murrell," one of them whined. "Din't know—"

The man who had unexpectedly come to their rescue was not tall, perhaps five feet, eight inches. He had dark hair and a pale complexion and a pair of burning eyes that made Marisa shrink instinctively under their regard.

He sauntered forward, and the three keelboatmen seemed to disappear, their knives vanishing.

Belatedly, Marisa found herself shivering. To be taken for a quadroon whore was bad enough, but now Dominic ignored her and became engaged in a low-voiced conversation with this man who dressed like a preacher and yet wore a gun as well as a knife under his black jacket. The name John Murrell meant nothing to her; she was merely relieved that he had turned up when he did, to avert a nasty incident.

Later, when she ventured to say in a stilted voice, "He seemed very kind. I suppose I should have thanked him," she wondered at Dominic's harsh laugh.

"If I were you, I wouldn't mention his name in the circles *you* move in. Better still, if you can bribe your woman to keep silent about this afternoon, you might be lucky enough to escape Inez's questioning."

She hadn't seen him since then. That had been less than a week ago, and she and Inez were already on their way to New Orleans. She ought to feel relieved, Marisa thought, that Pedro had not elected to come with them. He had suddenly announced his intention of returning to New Spain and his duties there.

The fiery spark of a falling star arced across the blue-black blanket of the sky for an instant, tugging Marisa's mind back into the present. She became aware of Lalie's quiet presence beside her. What did the girl really think— or feel? She had had a white father who had educated her. And in spite of it, she was still a slave, with no future. Lalie's skin was fairer than her own. Did the girl never wonder what it might be like to be free? To go away somewhere to a place where no one knew of her background— or did Lalie ever think of such things? Did she accept fate?

"Lalie, what would you do if you were free?"

The girl's eyes widened slightly in the faint starlight.

"Free, madam? I—I do not know. Where would I go— what would I do?"

"But don't you ever wonder?"

Lalie's head dropped as if she did not want to answer.

"No, madam," she said softly at last. "Of what use would it be—to wonder? I am not treated badly now. I am safe, and luckier than most others in my position would have been when. . . ."

It was evident that the young woman did not wish to go on, and Marisa felt contrite immediately, for prying.

"I'm sorry, Lalie."

She saw the girl's surprised look rest on her for a moment before the dark eyes were lowered again. And for the first time in years, Marisa thought suddenly of Delphine. Had Delphine been a slave, too? Or had she been freed? Was it by choice that she had gone with her mother to France or because she had to? At any rate, she had always known that Delphine loved her. It was to Delphine that she had clung, crying, when she had hurt herself. It was Delphine who sat by her at night and soothed her when she had childish nightmares. And it had been Delphine who had come to save her when all Paris had exploded and the streets had run with the blood of innocent and guilty alike. Delphine had bled, too, screaming before she died. Oh, God! Marisa shuddered, although the air was thick and humid. Why think of that now?

Gnats stung at her face and arms, and she abruptly turned away from the wooden railing of the flatboat.

"Perhaps we should go back in. Didn't you say we should make New Orleans by nightfall tomorrow?"

It was the "bad time" in New Orleans. The late summer when the yellow fever raged, and the city lay caught in its grip—hot and sweating and suffering. This was the time of year when everyone who could afford to do so left the city for their plantations; the houses were silent and shuttered against the heat and the smells from the overflowing gutters.

Bad news was everywhere. Governor Claiborne's young wife and infant daughter had died of the fever on the same day, and the new American governor himself was slowly recovering. The slaves, of course, died like flies; and even the small apartments on Rampart Street were tightly closed against the miasmic fogs that rose from the river every night. The theater was all but deserted, and even the famous quadroon balls were held off until later when the city would be populated again.

"I would not have brought you here at *this* time of the year if I could help it," Inez said, sounding preoccupied. "But I have to pay a visit to my bankers as well as pick up some supplies. I have had the fever already, but perhaps *you* would do better to stay on board the boat. There's running water here on the river, at least."

Even her white skin seemed to be sheened with moisture, but she was used to the stagnant heat, and Marisa was not. Even Lalie looked wilted, and the colorful scarf she bound over her hair seemed limp instead of crisp and starched as it usually was.

Marisa's stiff poke bonnet seemed to constrict her head, and the soft flesh of her chin and neck became chafed and red from the velvet and silk ribbons she tied to keep her bonnet in place. The weight of her hair, curling damply over her neck and forehead, seemed almost unbearable.

"Tie a scarf about it like Lalie," Inez advised. "Or carry a parasol as I do." She alone seemed almost unaffected by the heat, and in spite of the mutual dislike for each other that stayed beneath the surface, Marisa envied her in a way. Inez was always so sure of herself! She seemed to wear, at all times, an unshakable air of arrogance.

"Well? Are you coming ashore with me or not? We should be back on board before it gets dark. There's no reason to stay here for longer than we have to."

Marisa had looked forward to seeing something of New Orleans, but from the river the city looked half-dead—stricken by the sun—lying exhausted and gasping in the grip of the humid, airless afternoon.

She would not admit it to Inez, but she felt limp and almost sick with the damp heat. Gripped by lethargy, she shook her head listlessly and said, "I'll stay here and lie down. Perhaps I'll see New Orleans another time."

Once she lay down and Lalie had drawn the heavy mosquito netting about her bed, she felt sicker and more oppressed than ever and had time only to wonder vaguely whether she was coming down with the dreaded fever after all, before she fell into an uneasy sleep.

She half-awoke from time to time, wondering uneasily where she was. But the slight rocking motion of the boat lulled her, and she drifted back into oblivion again.

Lalie had helped her undress, down to her sheer silk shift, and Marisa had removed even that, feeling stifled by the moist heat and trapped by the netting over her bed. She slept, but there were strange dreams hovering on the edge of her unconsciousness. She dreamed that Inez came back from the city with a stocky, red-faced man with a sheaf of papers in his hand, and that while they stood looking down at her and talking about her, she tried to move and protest, but she was caught in the netting that stopped up her eyes and her mouth. The netting turned into a sea of sand under which she was buried. And somewhere above her, booted feet astride her face, she knew that Dominic stood scowling, as she remembered him last.

Later, when she woke up, her head ached, and her mouth and throat felt scratchy and parched. The flatboat had begun to move again, and Lalie, looking concerned, gave her fresh lemon juice to drink while she murmured that the mistress had returned, and they were finally on their way across the river to the point where they would have to disembark and transfer everything into small pirogues which would travel up the bayous for a short distance after that.

"When we get to the landing at Congracia, it will be only a few miles overland to the house."

* * * * *

They had been met at the boat landing by the overseer, a rangy, taciturn American who addressed himself only to Inez. He rode beside her, head leaning down as he conversed with her in a low voice. Marisa and Lalie rode in the small carriage that had been waiting for them. Marisa was so weary that she leaned her head back against the rough upholstery and did not care. Let Inez think of business; all she looked forward to was a hot bath and a bed to throw herself down upon.

Lalie was very quiet, her silence leading Marisa to wonder, as tired as she was, how the girl must feel coming back to a place that must remind her of her early life and her white father who had not thought to free her before he died. Had he loved her? Hadn't he thought what might happen to her in the end?

Even Inez was strangely silent, except when she roused herself enough to point out certain landmarks. Marisa was aware of canebrakes that seemed to stretch for miles and the outlines of larger buildings—the sugar refinery and the warehouses—and smaller ones which were the slave cabins. In all these the small oil lamps or candles had already been lit.

An avenue of oak and cypress trees lined the well-maintained road that led from the landing stage to the elegant mansion. The house was built in the French-Spanish style so popular in this part of the country. The roof was tiled. Silvery-pink brick and white Doric columns supported a graceful gallery. A beautiful, gracious mansion—but her mother had turned her back on it. And this was the house to which Inez had come as a bride, to take the reins of the household into her capable hands. But then, Inez was used to this kind of life. Her father's plantation had adjoined Congracia. How long had they known each other, the lovely, strong-willed Inez and the aging Andres de Castellanos whose wife had run away from him? Had he felt his first doubts about his new young wife when she started to make excuses for visiting New Orleans more often than usual? And when he was carried back here after the duel that had taken place between them?

Marisa's first impressions were confused. The long, murky twilight made everything seem strange, Marisa thought as they rode up the avenue. And she was bone-tired. There would be time enough tomorrow and the days after that in which to adjust herself.

"This is Congracia It is beautiful, is it not?" Inez's voice held a strange note of possessiveness as she turned her horse around to stop by the carriage.

The overseer, Mr. Dekker, shouted a command; and as the carriage drew to a halt there was suddenly a flurry of activity as slaves came running to take care of the horses and the heavy boxes that had been loaded into an open wagon.

One of them, a very old man with a bent back, came hurrying out to help Inez dismount. She laughed and patted his grey head as if he had been a pet dog.

"How are you, Juan?" she said in Spanish. "Has everything been put in order since I sent a message from Natchez? The house -the linens have all been aired? The floors polished?"

"Everything you ordered, Doña Inez!" he said seriously, nodding his head several times.

Feeling herself forgotten in the melee, Marisa shrugged, and unlatching the carriage door, she stepped down herself, with Lalie following her.

Lanterns had been hung from poles to illuminate the courtyard, and the great doors leading into the house itself had been flung widely open by the servants.

Marisa looked up the white stone steps, catching a glimpse of polished wooden floors and an enormous, wrought-iron chandelier burning with candles.

So this was Congracia, which should always have been her home. A huge brick and cypress and tile edifice rising proudly and a trifle arrogantly out of the wild, fecund earth.

Built by her father for a wife who did not choose to live here and for the large family he had hoped to have. Left to *her*. Why not to Inez, who should know what to do with such an inheritance?

She heard Inez's soft, husky voice saying, "It's good to be back home!" And Marisa knew that the other woman was stretching like a cat when she said so. But would *she* ever come to think of Congracia as home?

Marisa was aware of Lalie at her elbow when the girl said softly, "Ma'am?" And then her eyes became fixed on a woman who seemed very old, who came hobbling around the side of the house leaning on a cane. For all that she was dressed like a slave, in a dark-printed calico gown and white apron, she held her head higher than the others did. Her nose was straight, and the wrinkled skin of her face was the color of pale coffee. Even the greying hair that escaped from under a carelessly tied scarf was almost straight.

"I heard the sounds of your coming. You're back, mistress?"

"Didn't I say I would be? And Tante Cecile, look who I have brought."

To Marisa, staring curiously at the old woman to whom Inez had spoken with such unusual gentleness, it seemed as if there were suddenly a moment when everything was suspended. The talk, the calling back and forth of the slaves, and even the atmosphere of busy movement.

Tante Cecile, with the familiarity of a very old and trusted servant, cocked her head at Inez, muttering querulously, "Who you brought? You brought someone new here? Someone I should know?"

Marisa became aware that two men, dressed in dark clothing, had emerged from the house. They began to walk down the steps, and then they, too, paused, watching the old woman turn her head slowly to peer curiously towards her. And Marisa herself, as if magnetized, took a step forward so that the lantern light fell directly on her face and hair. Why? She had the feeling that this was some kind of a test, that Inez—oh, ridiculous! Surely Inez could not think her to be an imposter? And how could such an old woman possibly recognize her when she had left Congracia as an infant?

Tante Cecile's face suddenly seemed to break up into a mass of wrinkles. Her mouth worked, and she seemed to sway on her feet.

"It's my baby!" she cried suddenly in a cracked voice. And surprisingly there were tears coursing down her face. "Oh, praise the Lord, it's my baby come back!"

Chapter Forty-six

"It's not true—it's not true!" It seemed as if that was all she was capable of saying now that those two men had left. The sheriff and the justice of the peace, who was also the judge. After a while the words they said to her made no sense, any more than the important looking papers they read from. All the time they were talking she could feel their eyes crawling over her curiously with a mixture of pity and condescension and contempt—and finally, anger, when she refused to accept what they were telling her.

No—it wasn't possible. It was some kind of a plot—an ugly conspiracy! And she refused to believe. . . .

She screamed as much at the judge, once she had realized that they were not joking, not trying to frighten her, but stating what they believed to be the truth.

"That gal deserves to be shown her place," Sheriff Blaisdell growled, and his pale blue eyes fixed her balefully.

It was Inez—Inez!—who smoothed things over with her husky, purring voice, biting her lip as she murmured pityingly, "But of course it's been a shock! I was not certain myself—I did not *want* this to happen. You understand? It is—oh, it is such an embarrassment! If only my husband had told me, had confided in me, I would have made sure—"

She had signaled to Cecile and Lalie, and through the daze of weeping and frustration that rendered her hysterical and hardly capable of coherent thought, Marisa had heard Inez's voice trailing away down the long hallway as she shepherded her visitors outside.

Made sure of what? But the door closed behind Inez, and

when Marisa would have started up, Cecile's hands, surprisingly strong for a woman her age, pressed her back against the cushions of the ornate chaise longue where she had flung herself defiantly.

"Lie still, child! You lie still now! Shouldn't have come here, for all that I longed and prayed to see you again. But now you're here I won't let you hurt yourself. You, girl!" This to Lalie who stood by openmouthed, "What you standin' there gaping for? Go on down to the kitchen and tell that lazy nigger bitch who calls herself a cook to send up one of them potions I taught her to make. The soothing kind. Hurry!"

"It's not true!" Marisa moaned again, wondering why she seemed to have lost the capacity to repeat anything more than those three words. "Please—why didn't you tell them it wasn't? Did she threaten you or bribe you to say what she wanted you to say? I would have known—"

"Hush, child, you hush now, hear? Know it's a shock, 'specially if you didn't know nothing. But you got to be strong now. Like me, and I've done my share of suffering. Doin' it now, seeing you this way. Strong like my Delphine, yes! Strong like your father, too, who let *her* go, and you. He was going to see that you married white—he tol' me that. 'It's our secret, Cecile,' he'd say and laugh. 'When my daughter comes back here she'll come as a married lady, with a husband and a plantation of her own.' No one was to know. But I'm an old woman, and when I saw you with the light falling on your face. . . ."

'She's old—she's rambling! She doesn't know what she's saying. It's what they told her to say!' The thoughts flew around in Marisa's mind like bird wings beating against a cage. She was living a nightmare—not *her* nightmare but someone else's. Because, of course, they were all wrong. They had her mixed up with someone else! A love-child of Don Andres by Delphine, who had been her mother's half sister—oh, God! It was all too confusing coming on top of her tiredness and the long legal documents that had been read aloud to her. Papers, they said, that her father had hidden away and had only recently been found; papers that proved Delphine had never been freed; that

Delphine had borne a daughter to Don Andres at the same time his wife had miscarried for the fourth or fifth time; that she, Marisa, was Delphine's child in reality and that she had been foisted off on the world as Don Andres's legal offspring. The only reason he had let his wife go her way. The reason he had allowed his daughter to be educated abroad. . . .

The same reasons why her "mother" had all but ignored her leaving Delphine to care for her and love her and finally die for her?

"My little Creole," Napoleon had laughingly called her because she was golden-skinned and reminded him, perhaps, of Josephine when she was younger. In France, it was fashionable to be Creole. If she were still in France, it would not have mattered even if it were true that her mother *had* been an octoroon. But she was in Louisiana now—an *American* Louisiana—with an American governor who had expressed himself shocked because the *gens de couleur*, or free people of color, were permitted to own lands and slaves themselves. But she wasn't—she wasn't! Only weeks ago, a few hours ago, she had been pitying Lalie. And now, apparently, there was not much difference in their circumstances. But it was all a trick, some kind of monstrous joke cleverly engineered by Inez. Why, only a week ago Inez would have been glad to see her safely married off to Pedro, her own cousin. How could any of this be really happening?

That Cecile was her grandmother—murmuring to her, soothing her, petting her while she muttered in jargoned patois—she could hardly believe. And—no, *that* part at least she would not believe. *Not* that she was a slave, belonging to Doña Inez. No and no! Marisa tried to say so, but Cecile, still mumbling under her breath as she massaged the shaking girl's shoulders, would not listen. And when Lalie, skirts rustling, came back with a steaming hot tisane she had no choice but to swallow it down, even though it burned the roof of her mouth and her throat.

After that, still sobbing, still whimpering her protests and disbelief, Marisa found herself sinking, against her will, into a quicksand that seemed to suck away her strength as well as her ability to think. She heard her own voice, the words slurred, coming from a long distance away.

"I—I cannot sleep! I must—"

"You needs sleep, child." A long sigh. *"Must* can come later. . . ."

Granny Cecile was right, of course. And it was just as well that she slept and was allowed to sleep through until late in the morning. Because when Marisa woke, the nightmare was only just beginning. Her free will had been taken away from her, leaving her broken and completely helpless, like a butterfly whose wings had been plucked off.

"It is too bad it had to happen this way," Doña Inez said in her honeyed voice that had not changed a bit. "You should have married Pedro when he wanted you to, and then, of course none of this would have had to be dragged out into the open. But did you really think that I would let you take Congracia from me? You, a stranger, after all these years? You should have stayed in France or even in New Spain with that uncle of yours. But I am sure you are wishing that yourself now?"

Her hazel eyes seemed more green than brown in the shaded room—narrowed like those of a cat about to pounce. As if to emphasize the difference in their positions now, Inez lounged at ease on a silk-covered divan, and she took pleasure in seeing how awkwardly the young woman who stood before her wore the light ankle and wrist irons she had ordered put on before this interview.

Inez had actually offered a light, laughing apology when they were alone together. "I know what a shock this must have been to you; but for your own sake, I did not want any attempt at escape, or even violence, for then I would be forced to punish you for the sake of discipline, if for nothing else."

Blank-looking golden eyes gazed into hers without blinking or looking away, but Marisa said nothing at all after her first, whispered, "You *know* it's not true—any of this! And sooner or later, it will be found out—whatever you did to make it appear so!"

Now, trying to force some reaction, Inez said brutally, her voice hardening, "You are a slave. *My* slave! Do you understand that? You do not wish to accept the fact, and that is natural, but I can prove it. And I have proved it to the satisfaction of the gentlemen who were here last night—or do you remember since you were hysterical? Nevertheless, when your father neglected to free this Delphine he was so fond of, although he let her go with his wife to France, that meant that you, too, were born a slave. At least, according to the law in Louisiana. Why do you think he was so anxious to get you married off before you could come back here? But I had really hoped it would not come to this. After all, you are *almost* white!" She laughed, stretching languorously. "Delphine was his wife's half sister, did you know that? A coincidence, that their girl babies were born at the same time! So you have some of the family features—your hair and your skin. I've seen lighter colored octoroons in New Orleans, though. Your father hid the iron box with his very private papers, but I found it. And of course when Tante Cecile recognized you——"

"How could she recognize me when she couldn't possibly have seen me since I was an infant?" Marisa had planned to stay silent, but she could not help herself in the face of Inez's catlike assurance. "She's old, and I think she would believe anything she was told often enough. And papers can be changed or altered. How are you paying that old man who called himself a judge to swear he witnessed such documents? Delphine was closer to me than my own mother, and she would have told me——"

Inez sat upright, her eyes starting to gleam with anger. "Told you what? Why should she have? Let me tell you that it will be *my* word and the evidence of those papers your father left, rather than your word, that would be taken here! This kind of thing has happened before—and very often. Lalie is an example. You felt sorry for her, did you not? Now you must start feeling sorry for yourself. And if there is any doubt, in anyone's mind, I have a way of putting an end to it. You will see. Even my poor, deluded cousin would not want you after *this!*"

The nightmare continued and grew worse. If not for Cecile, who might be her grandmother or might not, and for Lalie, who risked her own skin to give her whispered consolation, Marisa felt she might easily have passed the fine borderline that led from sanity to madness.

"Take her," Inez said to the black field hand recently promoted to foreman over the rice fields. "Haven't you always wanted a bright-skinned girl for your own, Paulus? This one's yours until I say so; and she needs to be shown her place."

Dekker, the lank-haired overseer scowled and muttered under his breath, and from the way his eyes lingered on her, Marisa realized through her sickness and terror that *he* had wanted her, too. Inez spoke to *him* in English, which most of the Spanish- or French-speaking slaves did not understand.

"It doesn't matter. I m selling her to Mr. Jonas in any case. He's on his way from New Orleans now. Do you think I can keep her here? But once she's lain with a field hand, or if he gets her breeding—that'll shut her mouth if anything will!"

Marisa screamed and kicked and struggled, but the chains they had put on her, hobbling her like a recalcitrant mare, rendered her impotent. She felt herself lifted and being carried away, the sound of Inez's laughter growing fainter until she could not hear it any longer. There was instead, over the noise of her own sobs and her panting, the sound of crickets and screeching birds and water flowing steadily somewhere. There was sunlight falling on her face and then suddenly darkness and the smell of smoke and cooking grease. She was put down on a thin pallet, and she screamed again. A hand covered her mouth, and she stared up, terrified almost out of her wits, into the sweat-gleaming black face that glared down into hers.

"You hush!" Paulus said in a deep voice, speaking a Spanish dialect that she knew was Cuban, although she was almost past thinking coherently. "Do you think I want you?" he went on angrily. "Think that every nigger wants a white woman just because she's bright-skinned and yellow-haired? Got me my own woman I *want—mine—* and she ain't you. You hear me?" He gave a sudden laugh that was like a rumbling in his chest. "Even if I did, that old voodoo woman already done tol' me I ain't to touch you. *No* one on this plantation goin' to harm you with her saying that. You understand?"

She forced her head to move slightly, and he looked closely into her eyes as if searching for signs of hysteria, before he took his hand away from her mouth. She sucked in long breaths of damp air and could not stop her helpless sobbing.

Paulus gave her a long, contemptuous look and stood up, flexing his muscles. Bare from the waist up, they rippled under his skin which bore the whitish streaks she knew were scars from the overseer's whip. In some way, in his animallike pride in his masculinity perhaps, he reminded her of Dominic. . . . But then she realized that her thoughts were disjointed. He walked to the door and closed it with a bang that made her jump, and then he squatted down beside the dirty hole of a fireplace.

"You don't scream how," he said in his deep voice. "Least—not until I tell you. The maîtresse, she better think I take you. An' you better let her think I do."

Paulus sat as still as a statue, not looking at her again; and gradually, Marisa was able to gather her scattered, blindly frightened thoughts together. Her breathing slowed, and she became aware again of all the sounds outside the cabin to which she had been taken, and of the smells of the river.

'Oh, God, God!' she thought. 'What will become of me now?'

Cecile had warned her to be careful of what she said to the mistress and to be patient. But she had been neither. And how could Cecile help her now or protect her from what Inez planned, even though it had become obvious that being known as some kind of a witch woman she could at least protect Marisa from the other slaves on the plantation? 'Other slaves.' It was too late to catch back the thought and her body shuddered. She didn't belong to herself any longer. She could be bought and sold and used. Nothing that had happened in her life before had prepared her for this. It did not seem real and could not be real.

It was Lalie, and not Cecile, who came slipping into the cabin later. And Paulus stood up and took her in his arms, crushing her slight figure against his broad chest as his hands ran hungrily over her body. It was Lalie, then, who was his woman. Obviously, Inez could not know.

She tried not to listen to their low-voiced conversation, turning her head away until at last, disengaging herself with a playful slap, Lalie came over and knelt beside her. The soft voice Marisa remembered was full of pity.

"They're watching Tante Cecile, so she sent me. The mistress is with that gentleman from New Orleans now, and she plans to send you away with him tonight." Lalie touched Marisa's stiff shoulder lightly. "But you're not to worry! That's what Cecile sent me to tell you. You're to go along with him without fighting so the mistress won't have you whipped. And *he* won't whip you either, 'cause he won't want you marked up before the auction."

"Auction?" Marisa could not help herself, her eyes widened with shock and horror before she remembered painfully that Lalie herself must have gone through the same degradation.

"Yes, that's what they do. Only sometimes, for light-skinned women like us, it's private. And there are private rooms—" Lalie broke off apologetically. "I'm sorry. You're not used to it yet, are you? But you don't have to worry, because—"

Paulus, standing by the door, had suddenly stiffened, and now he seemed to cover the room in one gigantic bound as he grasped Lalie's arm, pulling her up.

"Someone coming. You better git out of here quick before they find you. *I'll* tell her the rest. You go on now."

With a frightened gasp, Lalie slipped away as soundlessly as she had come, and this time the door was closed so softly that no one approaching on the beaten-down path would have known it.

It was growing very dark inside the cabin, a thin grey light that presaged twilight outside. Paulus's big body was ebony against grey as he quickly divested himself of the loose white cotton breeches that all the slaves wore.

"Ain't gonna hurt you, but it gotta look right for them. You try to understand that." His voice was almost kind, but Marisa cried out softly with shock when he came over to

508

her and ripped her gown down the front, leaving her naked.

He lay down beside her, warning her, in his sing-song Spanish to be quiet and lie still.

"You know I ain't touched you, and *I* know that. Yes, and my woman knows and your voodoo granny. But they gotta think it. They'd strip you off anyways so that Mr. Jonas could get a good look at you. But you remember, gal, that you're goin' to be free again soon. That's what my Lalie came here to tell you. We's all goin' to be free. But you keep your mouth shut about it and wait—you understand me?"

Roughly, he stilled her abortive movement to escape, and some of the meaning of his words forced themselves into her dulling mind so that when the door was kicked open and the torches shone inside, lighting everything up with an eerie orange glow, there was no need to feign her startled exclamation, nor her attempt to cover herself.

Paulus had sprung up, fumbling for his breeches, his voice changing from being that of a man who was sure of himself and becoming, instead, a parody of sheepishness.

"Didn't know you was coming, mistress! I sure is sorry I ain't in a fitten state."

Doña Inez's voice held both triumph and laughter in it as she spoke over her shoulder to the man who had followed her in.

"There! What did I tell you? Paulus likes bright-skins." And then, the purring note evident, "Did she give you much trouble?"

"No, mistress! She fought some, but I took care of that. And I didn't mark her up either, jes' like you tol' 'me. Just got her quieted down."

Marisa had rolled over onto her side, pulling her knees up in an effort to hide herself. Her movements were weak and purely involuntary. Suddenly, she could not remember when she had last eaten or had as much as a cup of water to cool her parched throat. She wished herself dead rather than have to go through the next few moments of shame and degradation, but she was trapped, inescapably, like a shy wild animal in a net.

As long as she lived, she would try to close her mind to

the rest. Evening and night merged into one prolonged horror.

"You must understand, Mr. Jonas, that she had to be made—safe! That's why I had those irons put on her. It would not normally be necessary, of course, but I have already explained the circumstances to you. She'll be more likely to accept what she is after this. And of course she's been educated in Europe and speaks French and Spanish as well as English. I believe she has other accomplishments as well. No doubt you'll find out what they are before you sell her?"

To hear Doña Inez talk about her as if she weren't present or couldn't hear was bad enough, but the brutal examination of her naked, cringing body was even worse. And when that, too, at last was over, she was tossed a cotton shift and taken to a boat—an ugly, long-hulled, black-painted craft moored at the landing stage she had arrived at only yesterday.

Mr. Jonas had a cargo of slaves on board already. She could hear the groans and the clanking of chains much heavier than those that fettered her wrists and ankles.

The man that took her on board was heavy-featured and sullen-looking, with a broad red face and small eyes that flickered over her incuriously.

"Bright-skinned, ain't you? Octoroon or sang-mêlé?" Besides that he said nothing else to her, but he brought her a bowl of some kind of soup that had been thickened with rice and stood over her while she wolfed it down hungrily. And then he took her to the cabin that was occupied by Mr. Jonas—it had to be his because all the appointments were comfortable, if not actually luxurious.

There was a bed covered with a red velvet spread and a desk fastened to one wall, the drawers left carelessly open and sheaves of paper spilling out of them. And on the wall opposite the bed were two iron rings spaced just right, and two more at floor level.

The same man who had brought her on board and fed her now pushed her up against the wall, facing it, his hand shoving at the small of her back.

Marisa had stopped fighting. Somewhere, sometime, during the horrible hours that had already passed, she had begun to feel herself almost an animal. An object that had been handled and sold and would be sold again. She tried to remember the consoling words that Paulus had whispered in her ear, but they kept slipping away from her. "Don't fight 'em. . . . We's all goin' to be free, all of us."

And then, as she felt herself spread-eagled against the wall, wrists and ankles drawn apart, she could not help beginning to whimper with pain and fear.

"You're almost white, so I'll give you a piece of advice. Don't talk back—an' take what's coming. He won't mark you up if you behave 'cause he's goin' to get the best price he can for you. You just remember that, gal."

Marisa tried to remember. That, and everything else she had been told. But after a while, all she could feel was a terrified apprehension that knotted her stomach, overlaid by the strangest sensation that none of this was really happening to her.

When Jonas finally returned to the boat, he waited until his taciturn crew had cast off and they started floating down river before he allowed himself to turn towards his cabin.

Chapter Forty-seven

General James Wilkinson had traveled down, quietly and without fanfare, from his headquarters at St. Louis. He had spent some time in Natchez, and now he was in New Orleans for a few days. For privacy, he had engaged one of the upstairs rooms at an elegant gambling establishment on Royal Street which masqueraded as a coffeehouse downstairs. While he was there he entertained several visitors, some of them stealthy, coming up the private back staircase, and some of them not. But in the end the General was obliged to go looking for the particular man he sought, and he found him, as he had half expected, in the small room reserved for those who enjoyed the dice game beginning to be known as craps which had been introduced to New Orleans by Bernard Marigny.

There were a sprinkling of Americans here, but Dominic Challenger, lounging back in his chair in his well-cut clothes, with ruffles of lace at the sleeves and neck, looked as much a Creole as any of the others there, with his dark hair and tanned complexion. Wilkinson frowned with annoyance, but since he was a man given to dissembling, he managed to cover it under a smile and polite words until Dominic, shrugging, made his apologies in perfect French, and, gathering up his winnings, followed the older man to his private room. Here he flung himself into one of the comfortable, velvet arm chairs and stretched his long legs lazily before him.

"I'm sorry. But the game had begun to be interesting. And I was winning for a change."

An unobtrusive black servant had brought in steaming hot coffee and liqueur, and Wilkinson pushed the decanter and a gold-rimmed cup towards his companion, letting his shark-toothed smile show for an instant.

"Do you waste your time gambling for pleasure or for profit? Your wedding to the heiress is still on, I take it?"

"It's still on—why shouldn't it be? As a matter of fact, Jane and I had tentatively fixed on next month. But what was it you so urgently wanted to speak with me about?"

Wilkinson sipped his coffee and smiled again, shaking his head reproachfully.

"Shall we not go about our business in the Creole way? If the coffee is not to your taste, do try some of this excellent cognac at least. They have started to name this particular vintage after Napoleon, and it is straight from Paris."

Dominic stared moodily down into the amber liquid in the glass, wondering what the devil Wilkinson was up to this time. If it was another expedition over the Spanish border, then he had his answer prepared. He was through with risking his neck, whether Wilkinson liked it or not. But then his companion's next words made him raise his head, grey eyes narrowing slightly.

"Ah, yes, Paris and Napoleon! Which brings to mind, if you do not mind some gossip, the unfortunate Señorita De Castellanos. It's not universally known, of course, but I know I can trust you to keep it in confidence."

"What are you talking about?"

It was the general's turn now to lean back in his chair, appreciatively inhaling his steaming coffee that was liberally laced with liqueur. "Ah, well. An unexpected turn of events, that. I wonder if one would call it a scandal or a tragedy? At any rate, Doña Inez has Congracia . . ." Wilkinson saw with satisfaction that he now had his companion's undivided attention. In fact, Dominic Challenger's whole body had gone taut, for all his air of indolent ease.

"What?"

"You mean that you really hadn't heard? Although it's supposed to be a secret of course. You know the saying the Creoles have, *On lave son linge sale en famille!* Or in other words, wash your dirty linen in the bosom of your own family! However, rumors *do* have a way of spreading, and naturally, in my capacity as military commander, Governor

514

Claiborne—who was as shocked as I was, I assure you—informed me of certain facts that had been brought to *his* attention by the local magistrate. Pedro Arteaga had a lucky escape, one has to suppose!"

Dominic Challenger lost his patience then. Leaning forward he slammed his glass on the table so hard that some of the liqueur spilled. He said in a suppressed, dangerous voice, "If you will kindly get to the point—*sir?*"

Wilkinson lifted one eyebrow, shrugging.

"Why then—it seems the girl was a product of Don Andres's cohabitation with an octoroon slave although it appears she did not know it herself. But trust the fair Inez to find out—*and* obtain sufficient proof! There were letters and documents that the late Don Andres was incautious or careless enough to keep, I understand. And naturally, Inez did not want to keep the girl around. The scandal, you understand. She had actually introduced her to so many people as her stepdaughter! She sold the wench in a hurry, to Seth Jonas; I'm sure you've heard of him? But Jonas met with an unfortunate accident on his way downriver to the slave market at Baratria. At about the same time, coincidentally, there was an attempted slave uprising at Congracia. You are interested to hear more? I found out just today that the story had a rather interesting denouement—"

Dominic picked up his glass and drained it, and when he looked up his eyes were hard and wary. Wilkinson saw the mask drop over the angry emotion he had showed only a few seconds earlier and was almost disappointed.

"And that is?..."

"It seems that our mutual friend Murrell was fortunate enough to pick up Jonas's cargo—papers and all! He held a private auction this afternoon at Maspero's, and a visiting Cuban sugar planter is now richer in the fact that he obtained an attractive and educated mistress—and poorer seven thousand dollars, which I am sure he will not miss. An interesting story, don't you think?"

Dominic Challenger stood up, controlled fury apparent in every move he made. The general had a strange half-smile on his lips, even while he feigned surprise.

"But you're surely not leaving yet? I had a proposition for

you that involves a great deal of money, and possibly
even—"

"I will hear your proposition, sir, after I have spoken with
my *friend*, Mr. Murrell. Maspero's, you said?"

The door slammed behind him, and James Wilkinson
leaned back in his chair, lighting a cigar with careful concen-
tration. Presently, he ordered more coffee and something to
eat. And when the waiter left, he gazed into the small fire
and smiled. He did not feel sleepy, and while he waited
for Dominic to return, his mind schemed and made plans.
He had always been clever enough to trade on the weak-
nesses of other people—even Aaron Burr, who would be
pleased at what he had to tell him. Yes, Burr was plausible
and had a following, but he was also a vain, weak man.
Sooner or later, when all their plans came to fruition, strength
would win out. And Dominic Challenger would discover
in his turn that he was merely a pawn—but not yet, of
course. Not until his usefulness was over.

Discover a man's weakness and use it. This was one of
General Wilkinson's talents.

John Murrell, who could be all things when it suited him,
had other talents. Tonight he was not the Methodist preacher who gave sermons of fire and brimstone up and down the
Natchez Trace, nor the sinister and elusive river pirate. He
was a rich gentleman planter from Tennessee, out to have
himself a good time in sinful New Orleans.

The slave auctions took place in the afternoon. By nightfall Maspero's was a coffeehouse, bar, and a place where
friends could meet to gamble. La Bourse de Maspero was a
two-story wooden building on St. Louis Street, with its main
entrance on Chartres Street, and it was this entrance that
Dominic Challenger used, brushing past the colored door-
man, and giving him a scowl instead of the carelessly tossed
coin the man was used to.

He walked into an atmosphere of noise and laughter and
excessive warmth. In a corner, three hired musicians sawed
busily away at their fiddles, but for the most part no one paid
them any attention. Murrell had to be here. If he were not,
Dominic had a good idea where he could be found. And

516

even if he had to visit every single pleasure house in the city . . .

But Murrell himself saved him the trouble when, smiling, he crossed the room.

"Dominic! I thought I recognized you when you came in here, in spite of the bad light in this place. You'll join me in a game of écarté?"

The scowl on Dominic's face had been smoothed out by his will, but Murrell caught a glimpse of his eyes and his own narrowed slightly before he lifted his shoulders and sighed.

"No écarté. But I will not go to the Oaks with you to fight a senseless duel, either. You should know that that's not my way."

Dominic was brief. "I know your ways, Murrell. Do we talk here or somewhere else?"

"Here's as good a place as any. It is so crowded that no one will pay us any attention. Follow me. I have a small table against the corner over there, where the room is darkest."

Once they were seated, he continued talking as if there had been no interruption.

"You know about the successful auction I held here this afternoon? Had I known you were in town I would have sent you a personal invitation. But, after all, from all reports I've been hearing, you're a happily engaged man. A mistress is a mistress, eh? However, when I recognized the—young female, I took pains to see she wasn't mistreated. And in fact she was even grateful to see me. You know of the unfortunate Mr. Jonas's reputation?"

"Yes," Dominic said through his clenched jaws. With one part of his mind he was able to wonder at himself and the blind rage he had felt when Wilkinson told him. He did not even know why he was here, watching John Murrell across the table, or why he longed to kill the man. He said now, with a deliberate attempt at self-control, "Go on."

Murrell shrugged. "He had not time to hurt her too much. And he did not rape her for that was never his way with the colored wenches he picked up. A few weals, a few bruises. She has a delicate skin, that one. I almost regretted the necessity of having to sell her, but then there's always a question of money and how fast it gets spent! *And* the necessity to get her out of Louisiana. You understand that, I'm sure. I went out of my way to be kind, however, realizing the circumstances, and the—er—background. I went so far as to risk the profit I made on *her* by insisting that this Señor Mendoza buy two other slaves along with her—a big black one and another pretty quadroon wench. Even a villain like myself has his weak moments!" He grinned into Dominic's tight-muscled face before going on deprecatingly. "Besides, I did not want to have to beat her and mark up that lovely gold skin before I showed her. So we —came to an agreement of a sort, and she was tame enough when the time came. She realized, too, I think from her experience with Jonas, what could happen. But why am I telling you all this? By now the Cuban has her on his ship, unless he decided to stay another night in New Orleans in order to sample the goods he bought!"

Dominic Challenger's eyes were like chips of ice, and his voice just as cold. "When did you plan to steal her back?"

He watched Murrell, knowing the man and his methods from past association. Slaves would be "stolen" or enticed away from their owners with promises of freedom—and resold with the same promise to keep them docile.,

Leaning forward, Murrell said softly, "Are you offering me a price that would make it worth my while to do so? One black slave is very much like another, but a woman like that would be remembered too well. The auction was very well attended."

"I'm sure it was," Dominic said tightly. "Your price?"

He knew as he said it and saw the black fires flare up for an instant in Murrell's eyes that he was playing into their hands. Murrell, who would sell even his best friend for money. And the smiling General Wilkinson, who needed something from him and had no doubt set the stage.

"Ten thousand," Murrell said without hesitation. And then, shrugging, "I must make some profit, after all. And there is the risk I'll be taking to be considered as well. For you, my friend, ten thousand dollars. If it had been anyone 1 else would ask at least twelve."

Ten thousand dollars came close to being the sum total of all he possessed at the present: his share in the ship and the small plantation whose acres lay unworked because he had not yet been able to afford to buy the slaves that would be needed. Of course James Wilkinson would know.

"It will have to be in cash, I'm afraid," Murrell was saying with false regret. "But I'll take your note for now—the cash when the goods are delivered. You have friends who would loan you that much, I'm sure."

Later, Dominic spoke to the general, and the general's understanding smile was just as false. "My dear boy, if I had known! It's a high price to pay for any female even if she is pretty and accomplished. But if you're sure, of course I'll advance the money. No—no! I won't take your note. How would you explain that to old Byron? He's not a fool, you know, and you don't want to jeopardize your marriage, do you? I have confidence in you; you'll make that much or more selling off the horses you could pick up in New Spain. *And* you would be doing your country a favor at the same time. That's the proposition I had for you—and I can give you my assurance that I will explain it all to Byron so that he will not mind. It's agreed then?"

Why in hell had he allowed himself to be so manipulated and trapped? Now, instead of being married within the next fortnight, he had to make plans for another furtive expedition to New Spain. The adventure appealed to him, as it always had, but not the risks. Ever since he'd had a son to think about, he had deliberately curbed the reckless side of his nature. And now he was risking everything because of —Marisa. As he thought her name, her image formed in his mind. A golden statue, with eyes to match. And he was just as much of a fool as Kamil Hasan had been. Or Philip Sinclair. Or any of the other men who had allowed themselves to become entangled and snared by her innocent appearance and wide-eyed gaze. At least *he* knew what a treacherous bitch she was underneath. She usually asked for whatever happened to her. But in this case. . . .

Dominic swore to himself, softly and profanely, in French

and then in Spanish. All right—face it! No matter what she had done or had been he could not throw her to the wolves. She was Christian's mother. She was. . . . He realized with an unpleasant shock that ever since their last meeting he had not been able to get her completely out of his mind. The memory of her tears, her wild, stumbling words, the sudden change in her from hysterical rage to passive acceptance. Even the way she had left him, without asking to see Christian again. Well, this time he would see that she was safely taken care of. Perhaps he'd arrange to have her sent back quietly to that uncle of hers. And then the sense of obligation he inexplicably felt would be fulfilled. That was all he felt, of course. But a demon voice in his mind kept whispering mockingly, 'Are you so sure of that?' And because he was alone in his rooms and could not sleep, he drank more cognac from the bottle that General Wilkinson had thoughtfully given him, and willed his mind to think instead of the general himself, and his plans.

Typically, he had not been told too much—Wilkinson trusting no man but himself. But he had been promised a valid passport. And Wilkinson had even promised that Pedro Arteaga would be transferred to Mexico—tacitly admitting, by his doing so, that he still retained his connection with the Spanish government.

"You may pick your own men for the expedition," the general had offered generously. Giving him a crocodile smile, he added, "Naturally, you need spare no expense for whatever you may need in the way of supplies. I have complete confidence in your judgment and your—discretion." There would have to be at least twenty men. And they would have to be adventurers who were not adverse to taking risks, and men who could be trusted. And he had a week —ten days at the most. He would have to make explanations to Jane, who would smile bravely and try to keep back her tears—and there was Christian, too. And Selma, who would not hesitate to show her disapproval of what she would no doubt call "a crazy, dangerous venture." And so it was and would be. Passport or no, Dominic had no illusions as to the reaction of the Spaniards who so jealously guarded their territories in New Spain if they suspected what he was up to. He would have to be very careful. . . .

And yet, even while he was thinking that, his mind suddenly freed itself from all the sober, responsible thoughts he had fastened around it and went flying ahead of him to the wild country of the Comanche and the panther and the endless sea of buffalo, the place where the birds flew up in the thousands when you startled them and where the horses ran free. He thought, 'My God! I've missed all that.' 'All that' was living off the vast and beautiful land itself, as free and as wild as any of the creatures that inhabited it; hunting when you needed to eat; and sleeping out under the stars or under a hide tepee when you needed to sleep. And the tepees themselves were made to be folded up and moved, whenever and wherever you wanted to move. No white-pillared permanent house that started to own *you* after a while. No cities with their flaring, smoking lights and all their incidentals that you began to think of as comforts, needing money to buy more. He began to think again, as he had not done for a long while, of the Moslem teachings he had absorbed because they were useful to him at the time when he needed to survive and of the old sheik whose life he had saved and who in turn had saved his, a man who lived by those teachings. Kismet. Fate. But he had always fought to make his own fate and his own future after he had won the struggle to stay alive. He had the strangest feeling that he was back at his beginning and that somehow this was the way it had to be.

Dominic stood by the small fire he had built himself and stared down into the tiny, leaping tongues of flame, remembering campfires he had built and the smell of fresh meat roasting. The taste of venison and buffalo steaks and the feel of riding bareback on a half-wild horse. And at night, the feel of a warm, willing woman's body. 'What in hell's name am I doing here?' he thought. His mind was pulled back with a jolt into the present when he heard the triple tap that he had been expecting at the door panels.

Chapter Forty-eight

Once John Murrell had collected his money and left, making his annoyed complaints before he did, an awkward and terrible silence seemed to have settled between them. Marisa, brushing past both men without a word, had gone straight to the small fire where she had crouched beside it on the floor, her legs curled under her.

She heard the door close and was aware, without having to turn around, that Dominic was leaning against it, watching her. 'Surveying his property!' she thought bitterly and refused to turn around to meet his eyes. The fire was warm on her face, and she kept her head slightly bent as she chafed almost absently at the ringed purple bruises the manacles she had worn had left on her wrists and ankles. Apart from the bitterness which was instinctive, she tried, as she had learned to do during the past week, to keep her mind blank, to detach it from her body. Her body was an object that could be bought and sold and used. She had learned to guard her mind jealously, not allowing any of her thoughts to show. But *not* thinking was even easier.

But still she was increasingly, uneasily aware of his presence behind her and of the barely leashed tautness she had sensed in him when he opened the door. His first, flickering silver glance had made her aware that she wore only a thin shift, with the dead Cuban's cloak wrapped closely around her. The señor had been impatient to try out his latest plaything. . . . She could not help the involuntary shudder that shook her whole body, and from behind her Dominic asked harshly, "Are you cold?"

The sound of his voice and the angry note in it stiffened

her will, giving her at last the strength to turn her head and face him.,

"No." She kept her voice deliberately colorless and received the reaction she looked for in the hardening of his mouth.

He sauntered forward and stood looking down at her, frowning, as if uncertain what to say or do with her next. Marisa drew a deep breath, steadying her nerves and her heart which had started to beat far too fast. She was completely defenseless against him now, and they both knew it. What *did* he plan to do with her? She was under no illusions as to why he had Murrell bring her to him. He did not want it generally known that they had once been married to each other. And most certainly, he would not want even the slightest rumor to leak out that his blond-haired son had been begotten by an octoroon slave. He had too much at stake to take the risk that she might talk. So now—how would he dispose of her?

As if he had read her thoughts, Dominic said in an ill-humored voice, "What in hell am I to do with you now? If you had any sense you would have married Arteaga and then neither of us would be in this predicament." His voice hardened, and she thought she detected a note of contempt in it. "But then, you have never shown any sense, have you? How you manage to get yourself embroiled—"

Something snapped inside her, and she sprang to her feet, careless of the cloak that slipped from her shoulders to fall about her ankles.

"Embroiled! Do you actually try to blame *me* for everything that has happened since I was unfortunate enough to set eyes on you? If *you* had been able to resist the thought of taking your pleasure with a defenseless gypsy girl, *none* of this would have taken place! And let me remind you that *you* were the one who high-handedly abducted me from England where I had friends to protect me! And if you had left me alone afterwards in Natchez, I might have married Pedro! But no. You couldn't resist the opportunity for a little rape, could you? How do you think Pedro reacted to *that?* Not that you cared. You have never cared for anything but your own pleasure and snatching what you want, no matter who might be hurt in the process. You are—"

His fingers dug into her shoulders with such fury that she cried out.

"And *you*, my fine octoroon wench, are the most ungrateful bitch it's ever been my misfortune to come across! I should have tossed you over the side of my ship when I discovered you'd stowed away on it—" he shook her until she gasped aloud—"instead of beggaring myself to rescue you from the consequences of your own stupidity!"

"I didn't ask to be rescued, did I?" she stormed at him, using every weapon left at her disposal. "And now you have three slaves for the price of one. I suppose you could get all your money back if you sold us again! You're even worse than Mr. Murrell, your *friend*, who is a thief and a liar as well! *He* made all kinds of promises and encouraged Paulus and Lalie to run away from Congracia, and he tried to make me believe that he had rescued me from—from that horrible Mr. Jonas! And then. . . . But perhaps you had all this planned between you? Perhaps you even knew what Inez planned? After all, you and she—"

"You evil-minded, vicious-tongued little bitch! You deserve everything you've asked for. And believe me, I've cause to regret that I ever meddled in your life or ever set eyes on you, for that matter!" His voice snarled at her. "You enjoy having men make fools of themselves over you, don't you? You're damn right about one thing, at least. I should have let you be! Seeing the way you're dressed or, rather, *un*dressed, I'm sure the late Señor Mendoza didn't have cause to regret his extravagant purchase! Well, by God, I intend to get you off my hands as soon as I can. But until then you'd best learn to keep your mouth shut, do you understand? I've a good mind to keep you gagged or have you whipped—and I don't know which I'd rather do first!"

The shift tore at the shoulders as he flung her away from him. She fell against the wall and then slid down it, sobbing with pain and fury. She turned her back to him, and he saw the livid weals across her shoulders. All the anger she had roused in him evaporated very suddenly and he regained some control over himself.

His long legs covered the space between them in two strides.

"Marisa."

She flinched from his touch, making him swear under his breath.

"Oh no—don't!" The words seemed wrenched out of her, and he pulled his hands away, letting her weep, the sound of her sobs like a dam bursting.

Much, much later, Marisa realized that it was Lalie and not Dominic who bent over her. In her soft French, Lalie murmured soothingly, "It is good to cry, yes? And you needed the release. But too much is bad, you will become sick. So come now and eat something, and then you will sleep."

"I will never sleep again," Marisa said dramatically, but she did, all the same, after Lalie had forced some chicken broth down her throat. And everything that had happened to her ran together, one ugly scene superimposed upon another until she had to close her eyes to shut everything out. And she and Lalie slept together on a bed which was not too comfortable but was better than a cotton pallet on the floor; and she realized, just before her mind let go, that she had not seen Dominic again since their last terrible confrontation. Her sobs had turned into hiccups, and she murmured in a sodden whisper to Lalie, "He's out finding a way to be rid of me. He hates me—do you know that?"

Just before the point when she could not fight off sleep any longer, she thought she heard Lalie chuckle.

"Oh—I do not think so! I think he is very nice, this gentleman of yours."

And then she knew nothing else as her mind and her body slipped away, down what seemed like a long, black mountaintop, all the way to the bottom where an inky cavern waited for her, swallowing her up.

In the morning, very early, there was a smell of cooking, and Lalie was shaking her.

"Never tasted food this good before! And it's right off the streets where the sellers go crying their wares. You ever eaten pralines? Better eat them while they're still warm, then. An' we got hot coffee and rice cake and fresh-caught crab, too. You sit up now and eat, yes? We're going to be leaving soon, and you and me, we have to pack everything up and have it ready.".

Lalie looked happy, and the rice cakes smelled delicious. Marisa wondered, rubbing sleep from her eyes, whether she was still dreaming.

"Packing? Leaving? But for where?" Remembering, she said suddenly, "Where is Paulus? And—" She would not say his name, as memory came back, but Lalie giggled.

"Paulus, he went out with Mr. Dominic. He gave us our free papers already, but like Paulus says, we're not going to be safe here, in New Orleans. So we're all going to New Spain with him. Maybe we'll find a place of our own there. Mr. Dominic said that any man who helped to trap those wild horses got to keep his share of the profits. He said it might be dangerous, but that's better than being taken back to Congracia and being branded, or worse, as runaways. Paulus says any man, white or otherwise, who's been whupped and knows what it's like to be a slave, he don't mind following. And I'd follow Paulus if I had to go barefoot and naked."

All the angry sarcastic words that had started to her tongue were cut off when Marisa looked into Lalie's brown eyes and saw the slight flush that had come into her face. Dominic had the knack of winning the loyalty of those he came in contact with. She remembered Donald, who had known the worst side of him and still remained faithful. Was she the only one who could see through him to the dark side of his nature? Or was it only she that brought it out?

Lalie was happy and confident. If Marisa had to bite her tongue, she would not spoil things for Lalie or for Paulus. But what did Lalie mean when she talked of New Spain?

She found out later, after she had eaten and drunk several mugs of the delicious café au lait.

Helping Lalie, Marisa discovered there was not much to pack. Dominic was obviously used to traveling light. And where was he? How dared he stay away like a coward and leave orders that she should perform this task or that, just as if. . . .

If her mind shied away at the next thought, it had to be

527

faced. Dominic *owned* her. He had freed Paulus and Lalie but not her. Of course he wouldn't! He had to make sure that she was safely out of the way before he married his shy little heiress.

Marisa had to grit her teeth before she could speak in what she hoped was an ordinary voice.

"New Spain? Why New Spain of all places, when Dom— when *he* is supposed to be married soon?"

"Don't know about that," Lalie stated. "I know for sure, though, that he's going to New Spain to trap wild horses. And we're going with him."

A spurt of defiance made Marisa raise her head, her eyes sparking.

"I won't go anywhere with him! He—"

"You don't have no choice, do you? What you want to do —stay here in New Orleans and maybe have that Mr. Murrell catch you again and sell you? Or end up in one of those places where you'd be sold over and over to whatever man will pay the price the madame asks? Don't know what's between you and *him*, but from what Paulus told me, and what he's learned from talking to some others, you're lucky. Don't you have an uncle or someone like that back in New Spain?"

'Yes—but I don't want to be grateful to *him* not for anything!' she wanted to scream back at Lalie. She kept silent because Lalie would not understand, and *she* didn't understand herself either, wondering why she was still shaking with anger inside. Was it possible he intended to hand her back to her uncle? What kind of a bargain would he strike? Immunity for himself on his secretive, nefarious trips across the Spanish border, no doubt! Oh, but she had learned, paying for her knowledge with anguish, that he was not to be trusted. He was unpredictable—completely unscrupulous! Under the cleansing force of her anger, even the events of the past ten days or so faded away, leaving only the inexplicable rage and resentment that made her hands tremble as she helped Lalie get ready for a journey he hadn't thought to tell her about.

The rented apartment was small and dark and rather rundown, in spite of its defiant air of shabby gentility. The smells and sounds of the street outside drifted up through the barred window, and the bars themselves reminded Marisa of a prison. Damn him—damn him! Why hadn't she stayed in France or gone back to England? But no. She had had to cross oceans and continents to come here and be faced with a situation far worse than the one she had run away from.

"Think we got everything ready, but I'll just make sure," Lalie called as she sped into the adjoining room.

Left alone, Marisa used the back of her hand to wipe off the stickiness of the praline she had eaten from her mouth. And Dominic, kicking the door open without warning, caught her in mid-action, freezing her.

She didn't know, now that he was here, what kind of reaction she had expected of him. For a moment he had looked as frozen and taken aback as she was, and then he began to laugh. She was used to his anger and to seeing his eyes freeze into chips of ice; the last thing she expected was laughter. She could have withstood his scorn or even his indifference without flinching, but now she was blinded by a passionate rage that made her fly at him without thinking or judging her actions, her fingers clawing for his dark, mocking face.

He had barely time to catch her wrists before she fell against him with a force that shook them both.

"Don't you—don't you *laugh* at me! I don't care what else you do, but don't you—"

Her eyes were wet with fury, and she had begun to fight and struggle against his restraining hands like a wildcat cheated of its prey, white teeth showing between her parted lips as if she would have liked to have used them to tear him into pieces. The laughter was wiped from his face as instinctively, without thinking, he set his mouth over hers, stilling her angry, disjointed cries.

He kissed her until her knees buckled and she felt like a swimmer taken with a cramp, sinking helplessly under buffeting waves, sinking deeper and deeper to the point where it no longer mattered whether she surfaced or not.

"Panther eyes!" he whispered a long while later while she was still gasping for breath and no longer capable of resistance. "I only laughed because—because I am not used to seeing you with a scarf wrapped around your head, and you had tied it crooked, like a butterfly with one broken wing!"

There was still a slight tremor in his voice that made her snap her head back to glare at him suspiciously.

"You—"

"I won't laugh at you again, menina." He had gone back to calling her "little one" in Spanish, and she wondered why her knees were still so weak that she had not the strength to pull away from his rough embrace. "But you did say you didn't care what else I did!"

"You're despicable." She was capable of no more than a whisper, and he silenced even that by kissing her again, lightly and possessively.

"Of course I am—haven't you always said so? But I do think you'd better dress as a boy again before we start out. For all your demure calico dress and crooked scarf, you still make too damned attractive a wench—and I don't want my men distracted."

Marisa started to say sullenly, "I won't—" And then, catching his eye, "I don't want—" But he merely grinned at her mockingly, whirling her away from him with a pat on the bottom that made her gasp with fury.

Paraphrasing what Lalie had said earlier, he said equably, but with one eyebrow raised as if he dared her to disagree, "It doesn't matter what you say you don't want or what you do. Until I make up mind about you, you belong to me. And you'll save us both a lot of trouble if you remember that!"

Marisa found no support from Lalie, who merely shrugged and shook her head when she tried to explain just what kind of a devious, conscienceless ruffian Dominic Challenger really was. And she clamped her lips together and would not talk to Paulus again after he had told her bluntly that she was luckier than she deserved—if it had been *he*, now, he'd have taken a hickory stick to her just to teach her she was only a woman, after all.

"He'll probably beat you every day of your life!" Marisa warned Lalie darkly, but the girl only smiled a secret, withdrawn smile.

"Oh, no, he won't because I ain't going to give him cause to! Besides, you ever heard what they say about catching more flies with honey than with vinegar? The trick is to let a man think he's boss while you go about gettin' you own way and lettin' him think that's what *he* intended in the first place!"

"That's not honest!" Marisa blurted out, and Lalie giggled.

"But it's the quickest way, honey! What difference do it make *how* you gets your way?"

"Well. . . ." She chewed on her lower lip and was silent for a long time.

* * * * *

In her guise as a boy, she was able to ride, at least, and she made a point of riding beside the wagon carrying the supplies, where Lalie rode in state. Paulus had his own horse, with so many cartridge belts wrapped around him that the other men began to tease him about being a walking arsenal who might blow them all up if one of his guns happened to go off by accident.

They had left New Orleans at last, headed north, although Marisa had heard that Dominic and Paulus, acting the stupid servant, had taken pains to spread the rumor that they were headed south towards the gulf, and Mexico.

At any rate, it was unlikely that a band of armed men, traveling cautiously at night, would be molested.

Dominic had said shortly, "Even Murrell's been warned off—by General Wilkinson. You might say we're under his august protection—at least until we cross the border!"

The harshly cynical note in his voice had warned even *her* off; and she had taken pains to stay out of his way since their last encounter, although the recollection still smarted.

However, when he rode by soon after her talk with Lalie, asking impersonally if everything was all right, she forced herself to smile sweetly at him and was rewarded by the way his horse reared as if he'd tightened his grip on the reins. He raised one black eyebrow at her but rode on without another word. Lalie, who was full of laughter these days, gave a small gurgle of amusement.

"You see?"

Already annoyed at herself, Marisa shrugged inconsequentially.

"He knows too well what I think about him to be fooled."

"Oh?" Lalie murmured, and Marisa could not help flushing as she wondered how much the other woman had seen that morning—and what conclusions she had drawn.

Chapter Forty-nine

For days, they had seemed to plunge deeper and deeper into the wilderness that was Louisiana, forsaking the more usually traveled trails. Marisa put down the fact that they were not molested by either outlaws or Indians to the villainous appearance of the men that Dominic had talked into going along with them on this expedition. Bearded, mustached, some clad in buckskins and others looking for all the world like river pirates, they were a motley and dangerous crew who persisted in referring to their leader as captain.

Her disguise as a youth had soon been seen through, but none of the ruffians made any move to molest her, although she did not escape certain leering, sidelong glances from time to time. She thought, angrily, that they all assumed she was the captain's woman, brought along to relieve the boredom of a long journey, and to save him the trouble of going hunting for some Indian woman to assuage his male needs. She would have been even more furious if she had known that he had explained to them that she was a safer passport than the one he carried to ensure their passage through Spanish territory. A valuable hostage, just in case . . . But he had also warned them that any man who touched her he would kill himself. *This* part, too, she was unaware of. She had begun to wonder, however, secretly and angrily, although she would have died rather than admit it, why he continued to leave her alone at night when they made camp.

Of course it was difficult, if not downright impossible, to obtain any privacy when they were forced to make camp in small clearings where everyone lay close to each other, wrapped in their blankets while some of them took turns standing guard, their long rifles primed and ready. And of course she was relieved that he had decided to leave her alone! But did he have to treat her with such callous indifference, snapping orders at her on occasion as if she had really been a green boy taken grudgingly along on his first adventure? He was more polite to Lalie who had adapted herself quickly to their mode of travel and their new environment.

More and more, in spite of herself, Marisa found herself watching him covertly. With the shackles of civilization cast off, Dominic seemed to belong and be at ease in this primitive, savage wilderness that was half swamp and half forest. He had let his beard grow and had taken to wearing fringed buckskin garments that made him look like a savage himself. Marisa found herself thinking how little she really knew about this man who had interfered in her life over and over, bringing her to *this*. She told herself that she hated him and must continue to be wary of him, but her eyes continued to follow him all the same. She noticed the way he rode a horse, as if he were part of the animal. Along with wearing buckskins he had taken to riding his Appaloosa pony Indian fashion, without a formal saddle. She noticed the way he walked, wearing moccasins instead of boots, like a stalking panther. And the way his eyes squinted against the sun, and his rare smile when one of the men cracked a ribald joke as they sat around a small, smokeless campfire. She had never known him! Any more than he had taken the trouble to know her, she reminded herself grimly at this point. They had always been strangers to each other, and they always would be. She prefered it that way! And yet—and yet— after the way he had kissed her that morning in New Orleans, after laughing at her, how could he act as if she had suddenly ceased to exist for him?

'You're a fool!' she chided herself angrily. 'Don't you know when you're better off?' The trouble was that she had suddenly begun to discover her ex-husband as a man instead of a hated nemesis, and she did not know how to cope with her own wayward, dangerous thoughts. When she had stopped being afraid of him, he had started to intrigue her;

and now it was her own thoughts, unbidden and unwelcome, that she had to guard against.

The days were bearable, in spite of the hard riding they had to do and the danger, when they crossed some of the bayous, of alligators and water moccasins. But the nights! They were hot and humid, and sometimes the gnats and mosquitoes made it difficult to fall asleep. On other nights there was the heavy, almost overpowering perfume of night-blooming flowers, and the moon shone so brightly it might just as well have been day. On such nights everything was silver and black, and every shadow seemed dangerous while every leaf seemed to reflect the moon in its own tiny way; there was a constant silver shimmer whenever the slightest breeze sprang up.

Something was happening to her, changing her, as they pressed closer to their destination. She had begun to see the land for what it was, vast and primeval and *real,* instead of being so much scenery seen through the window of a carriage while she was on her way somewhere else.

Suddenly, Marisa had begun to understand why her father and the men who had come here before him had wanted to stay. Oh God, the fascination of the untouched wilderness! The desire to be the first to conquer it! Had Europe ever been like this? Or such a challenge to the barbarian tribes that had swarmed through it?

Here was pre-history, still untouched and unspoiled by axes and wheels. Everything seemed as old as time—the shades of green and the gold of the sun and the blue of the sky, and the inky-black waters that hid primeval creatures with snapping jaws.

There was no lack of food, for game was abundant. Some of the men set traps; others, like Dominic, hunted Indian fashion with a bow and arrows. It came to her mind, suddenly, that she was actually happy living like an Indian squaw, and learning to clean and dress game and to cook over an open fire whatever the men brought in. The others had finally begun to take her presence among them for granted. In spite of her boyish dress she was a woman; and they began to talk to her of mothers and sisters and sweethearts. Only Dominic stayed aloof.

Marisa had stopped asking, "Where are we going?" and "When shall we get there?" She had, in fact, stopped caring. Small details that had always seemed important before had ceased to matter, like time itself. Sometimes, when she lay staring up at the stars, Marisa had visions of an enormous clock stopped in mid-motion. How long had they been there, these same stars? How much had they seen?

After a while the days and nights seemed to merge into each other, and only the appearance of the country they were traveling through changed. They had crossed the quietly flowing Mississippi River on clumsy, hastily constructed rafts at a place that was incongruously called Walnut Hills, and then traveled through miles of gloomy swampland towards the Ouachita River.

"There's some mighty fine country on the other side. Fertile soil—trees—lots of game. Belongs mostly to the Indians, if it can be said to belong to anyone, but they'll be friendly to *us*. The captain used to live with them a while back. And I learned their sign language the last trip we took over here."

Jean Trudeau was a Cajun who spoke both French and Spanish fluently. He seemed to have appointed himself as Marisa's bodyguard. It was he, grinning, who instructed her in the use of a bow and arrows, and a knife.

"Once we're in Spanish territory, we won't be firing off any rifles unless it's to defend ourselves."

"Do you think we'll need to?" Marisa asked, and he shrugged.

"Never can tell. The captain's got a pass, but ever since the Purchase the Spaniards have been afraid we're going to come over here and take their lands away from them. They don't take kindly to Americanos straying into their territory even if it's only to hunt game. It's best to be careful."

Just then Dominic passed by, lifting an eyebrow when he saw her deep in conversation with Trudeau. It was obvious he wasn't jealous, for he didn't pause in his stride. 'But why should he be?' Marisa castigated herself furiously, not realizing that her eyes continued to follow him. 'I mean nothing to him except as a hostage. The way he acts is as if he's begun to think of me as one of his men!'

536

Trudeau, following the direction of her gaze, had begun to grin. "The captain, he's one fine man, eh?" he commented slyly, and she could not control the rush of angry, embarrassed blood to her face.

"He's nothing to me. I'm only his—prisoner!" she burst out waspishly, but he continued to grin, showing white teeth under his long mustache.

"Prisoner? Me, I don't think so. But maybe, one evening, you wear woman's clothes, and you find out how *he* feels for sure, hmm?"

"Believe me, I'm much happier when he's ignoring me!" Marisa snapped, but Trudeau did not appear convinced. And neither, in the deepest recesses of her mind, was she.

The days passed, with nothing to show for their passage except the constantly changing countryside, teeming with game.

"Don't you wander too far from camp by yourself," Lalie warned Marisa. "There's panthers out there. Paulus seen one yesterday, stalking us or else the horses."

Marisa was far too busy looking at her reflection in a still pool of water to pay much attention. Heavens, what a fright she looked! Sunburned even darker than Lalie who always protected her face with a bonnet and insisted in wearing long-sleeved gowns like any Creole lady.

'I do look like a boy—and a grubby one at that!' Marisa thought resentfully. Her hair had grown longer, but it hung in straggling curls to her shoulders, and the endless days of riding and walking, combined with the hard work that setting up camp and cooking for a large number of hungry men entailed had made her lose weight. She was as thin as a rail and as slim hipped as a youth, and under the rough cotton shirt she wore with its too-long sleeves rolled up above the elbow, she probably looked as if she had no breasts at all. No wonder Dominic's villainous band treated her like a little sister! And no wonder Dominic himself continued to ignore her presence. In fact his avoidance of her was all too obvious; even Lalie had begun to look at her in a half-pitying, half-curious way, although she said nothing aloud. At least she had Paulus, and they usually contrived to slip off together to be alone at night. And Paulus himself had begun to be grudgingly accepted by the other men because of his innate pride and his strength and gigantic stature. "I ain't never again goin' to apologize to no one cause I'm black," he said to Lalie fiercely one evening when they sat by a small fire. Marisa could not help listening. "And I ain't *ever* goin' to act stupid or dumb 'cause that's the way white folks expects us niggers to be. My father was an Ashanti warrior an' the chief of his tribe until he got sold to the slave traders by his own brother. Me, I'm goin' to be proud of what I am from now on—an' that is a *man!* You hear me, woman?"

Marisa had pretended to stare concentratedly into the fire. Lalie leaned forward to run her fingers caressingly across her man's chest.

"Think I don't know that? I chose you, didn't I?"

He laughed—a deep-throated, primitive male laugh.

"You sure did, I guess! Although I'd have had you anyways—ef'n you wanted to or not. But I likes it better this way. . . ."

'They really *love* each other!' Marisa thought painfully and wondered why the thought should surprise her so. People did love, with no subterfuge or drawing back. She had thought Kamil loved her. And even Philip, in his way. But they were both dead—indirectly, because of her; and she was in the middle of a trackless wilderness and not even sure who she was or what she was. The walls of the nunnery that had cloistered her were long ago crumbled away, like the feeling she had had of living by her wits. Paulus and Lalie looked forward to a new beginning in a new land. And she—what could she look forward to? Most important—what did she *want?*

They crossed the Ouachita River at last and camped on its westerly side. They would stay here for three days or more to rest the horses and smoke or dry meat. Already the men were talking among themselves of another river—the Red. And by now Marisa had lost all sense of time and of distance. How much further? Did it matter? What *did* matter, more and more, was the feeling of uncertainty inside herself. The same question, repeating itself over and over. 'What do I want?' It seemed as if everyone else knew why they were here except her; she had come along because she had no other choice; at least none had been offered to her. The thought should have made her angry—it would have done, perhaps a few weeks ago. But now she had started searching for herself and did not recognize any of her emotions any longer.

She could not help watching Dominic Challenger when his long-legged stride took him past her; she noticed that with a beard he looked more like a stranger than ever, and only the caustic gleam of his grey eyes was familiar. She wondered if he missed Jane Byron and longed to be back with her. Was it possible that he really cared for the girl? But if he did, what was he doing here, leading this foolish, risky expedition into forbidden Spanish territory? He seemed more at home here than he had ever seemed in the drawing rooms of Natchez and New Orleans. Was it only because he was the type of man who craved adventure above all things, above even the profit that was to be gained? She had the advantage over Jane—she at least had known him in other environments. In Spain, and on his own ship, in France, and in London. And even in Tripoli, when he had been the slave and she . . . But her mind continued to shy away from that memory and all its implications. There was nothing between them now except dislike and distrust; and she would do well to remember that. And within a few months he would be back in the States, married to his faithful, unquestioning Jane, while she. . . . Why had he really brought her along with him?

It was Lalie who opened her eyes for her.

"You've not been eating enough to feed a sparrow. You sickening for something?"

"Of course I'm not sick. I'm never sick! I'm just not hungry, that's all."

The moon had come up, looking like an orange beacon until it climbed higher and turned to silver, its brightness like an assault on the senses. Why didn't Lalie leave her alone?

"If you're not sick and you're not hungry, you got to be pining for something—or someone. And I know it ain't that Trudeau, for all that he keeps hanging around you. Your granny was a voodoo woman. You going to sit back and do nothing about what you want?"

Startled out of her lethargy, Marisa turned her eyes on Lalie, meeting the girl's narrowed brown eyes.

"What do you mean?"

"You *know* what I mean!" Lalie spoke fiercely in French, her voice low-pitched. "Nothing wrong about a woman wanting a man. But sometimes you got to *show* them, 'specially if the man's plumb stubborn. You think I haven't noticed the way your eyes have been looking lately?" Lalie laughed suddenly, a soft, sympathetic chuckle. "Why don't you do somethin' about it? Take a walk in the moonlight with Trudeau—he's asked you, ain't he? And you'll see how long it takes someone else to follow!"

"I don't—" Marisa began angrily, and then her tongue stumbled over her own lying words. Her heart started beating so loudly that it almost deafened her. "Would you lend me something to wear? Even Trudeau wouldn't care to go walking in the moonlight with a boy."

Lalie's chuckle deepened. "Sure I will! You just come with me—and Trudeau won't be the only man wanting to take you for a stroll!"

She combed her hair out and using a strip of leather, tied it high at the back of her head so that the curls cascaded down her neck and about her face. And even Lalie's simple calico gown that was a size too large for her made her feel feminine again. She didn't see Dominic—she wouldn't look for him! But Jean Trudeau lifted an approving eyebrow as he offered her his arm with exaggerated formality.

"Ah, and now I can truly call you mademoiselle! Would you care to walk with an ignorant, backwards Cajun, mademoiselle? I promise you I will be most respectful."

Going along with his half-joking tone, Marisa inclined her head, a dimple showing at the corner of her mouth.,

"I would be honored, monsieur. And should you *not* show respect I will forget I am a lady and use my little knife on you."

He threw back his head, laughing. "I am assured that you would! Very well, we shall promenade, oui? And I will show you how pretty the little creek looks by moonlight, if you will permit me to kiss your hand at least?"

She took his gallantly proffered arm and went with him deliberately refusing to look across the small fire to see who watched them go beyond the small clearing into the shadow of the trees. Unused to the impediment of skirts, she stumbled, and Trudeau tightened his solicitous grip on her arm. At her involuntary stiffening, he gave a soft laugh.

"I only play my part, little one! You need not worry. Your friend was most emphatic! Besides, I do not wish the captain's knife between my ribs."

"I do not think he would care," she said childishly, trying to ignore the pounding of blood in her temples.

"You do not? But we shall find out, hein?"

Trudeau fell silent after that, his catlike tread silent in his moccasins. With his thick, drooping mustache that he was inordinately proud of and his curly hair growing down to his shoulders under his fur cap, he looked like the blackest kind of villain. And yet Marisa, who would have been terrified to be close to him three months ago, felt no fear of him at all. Fear lay in the past, in her memories of everything that had happened since she found herself on that boat spread-eagled helplessly against a splintery wooden bulkhead while she waited for Jonas to come. And what had happened afterwards, as ugly and painful as it had been, was not half as bad as the anticipation.

But tonight was not the time to remember. Tonight she had only her own feelings to be afraid of, and the strange, unwanted, unexpected yearning of her flesh. Every nerve in her body seemed tightly strung, played on by the sounds and smells of the night.

They had left the camp now, with its smoky odors of roasting meat and drying hides. And now she could smell the crushed, lush grass under her feet and hear the bubbling, liquid sound of the little creek and the croaking of bullfrogs and the occasional screech of a hunting owl. There were panthers lurking around, too, Lalie had warned her, but she was not afraid with Trudeau beside her. Trudeau carried knives and pistols on his body and also had a long rifle in one hand.

"Are you sure it's safe out here?" she said doubtfully after a while. "You look as if you are prepared for an enemy attack at any moment!"

They had stepped out of the shadow of the trees, pausing beside the high bank of the stream, and Marisa caught the white gleam of his teeth as he smiled.

"One can never tell. And the Comanches like to make their raids by moonlight. But don't worry, you are safe with me!"

"The—the Comanches? You mean—wild Indios?" She had heard of them from her uncle, and now, for a moment she was almost afraid. But Trudeau laughed softly and reassuringly.

"Wild Indios, eh? Well, yes, they are wild enough—and dangerous. But not to us. I have traded with them before, and the captain lived among them for two years. *They* are not what we have to fear when we cross into New Spain."

Suddenly, he turned to her, startling her out of the spell that the night had cast on her.

"Don't you know that we are all looking for something? And compared to a man's goals, fear is nothing. Not all of us will return alive to spend our money. This land takes its price, you know!"

"Then why—"

"Why? Why are *you* here? You run the same risks as we do, maybe more because you are a woman. Are you looking for freedom or a new kind of captivity?"

He had grasped her arm, and she pulled it away involuntarily.

"What does it matter? I'm *here*. And I'm only seeking answers. You're a man so that won't make any sense to you."

"I had a woman once. And she, too, looked for answers to God knows what questions she carried in her shallow little mind. She found them for a while—with another man. And then I killed them both. But before I silenced her she tried to tell me that it was only loneliness—a mistake. That she would have come back to me. Did she think I was totally without pride, as she was? She deserved to be killed. And yet, will you tell me this, since you are a woman yourself, why cannot I escape from her? Her laughing ghost as

542

she was when we were just married, before the child died and my hunting trips took me further and further away—but only so that I could give her something better than the small hut in the swamps. Women—bah! Do they ever know what they want? Must they go seeking their answers forever?"

She should have been afraid of him, seeing his face suddenly contorted in the moonlight and the grip of the hand she had brushed from her arm clenched about his knife. The stream was at her back now, but, somehow, she wasn't afraid.

"Women can suffer, too. Only—only it is more difficult for us to show it, except by weeping and tantrums. Women are looking for love, for a man who is not ashamed to say the words, and because of that I suppose we are too easily led astray."

This time it was she who touched his arm; and when he stiffened, there was an instant when she wasn't certain what he would do.

His dark eyes burned down into hers, and then he gave a sudden, hoarse laugh.

"*She* was afraid of me. I think that was one reason for what I did. Fear and guilt, all mixed up in her face. Why aren't you afraid?"

"Why should I be? I was never your woman, Trudeau, nor gave you the reason to think I might be. I'll find my own answers."

Trudeau sighed. "Oh, God! I thought I was over it—remembering her. And then your face in the moonlight . . . You are here with a murderer. Does not *that* thought make you frightened? I joined the preacher's band on the Trace after I had to—run away. And I have done things so terrible that your knees would buckle under you if I began to relate them. But I don't want to make you afraid. You were foolish to trust me enough to come out here alone with me, but I know why you did. Do not do so again—do you hear me? Not with any one of the others. It's not safe. *I* might have—"

"Trudeau!" Dominic's voice said softly from somewhere behind them. "Would you mind relieving me a half-hour early? I plan to head for Natchitoches in the morning, before first light, and I have some matters to take care of before then."

"Sure, captain." How ordinary Trudeau's voice sounded now; he even chuckled slyly. "Been wondering when you'd follow us. But I've been taking care of your woman just like you told me to."

Unable to help herself, Marisa leaned her back against a gnarled tree trunk. She hardly heard the rest of their casual conversation before Trudeau, kissing her hand lightly as he had promised earlier, had swaggered off between the trees, leaving her trembling with a long-delayed reaction to his strange, violent confession.

She was aware of Dominic's closeness, and the slight smell of tobacco that clung to his clothing. His buckskin shirt hung unlaced from his shoulders as if he had drawn it on swiftly; and she suddenly realized that beads of water clung to his hair and silvered his chest. She half-expected him to lash out at her, but he said instead in a quiet, deliberately controlled voice:

"You weren't to know about Trudeau. He's a good man, but the moon affects him strangely sometimes. Why did you leave the camp with him? Or at all, for that matter! When Paulus told me—"

"I didn't know!" she said in a ragged voice. "After all, he admitted you'd asked him to—to keep an eye on me! But I didn't know. That poor, tortured man!"

"Damn you!" And now, suddenly, his suppressed anger broke out from behind the iron self-discipline that had armored him all this time. "Do you realize what might have happened? Trudeau used to be one of Murrell's lieutenants until he came out of his killing daze and tried to fight what was happening to him. He's been all right for the past year or two, but sometimes, when there's a full moon like this—"

"He didn't hurt me! He—he talked to me about what had happened, and I think he was waiting for me to be afraid. But when I wasn't, he—I think he was only trying to warn me—"

"Why are you dressed like this?" Dominic's voice was harsh, like that of an inquisitor, and in reaction her shoulders stiffened.

"I'm a woman—in case you'd forgotten! Why shouldn't I dress like one? You didn't order me not to. If you had, of course I would not have dared disobey—master!"

"Massa or maître would sound more respectful since we're reduced to technicalities!" he drawled. Then, before she could try to fight back, he put his hands on either side of her as she leaned against the tree. She was trapped.

She was aware now only of his warm body far too close to hers and his eyes like silver mirrors reflecting the moon.

"Maybe I should find out just how obedient you've learned to be." Holding her silent, his lips brushed hers. "And maybe, like poor Trudeau, the moon turns me crazy. Do you know that I'd just taken a bath and was drying myself off by a fire when Paulus came to tell me what you were up to? And my first impulse was to let you be."

Somehow, her hands were on his shoulders.

"Why didn't you then?"

"Because you have the damndest habit of getting into trouble—or mischief. And I've known Trudeau longer than any of the others have. What did you think to find out here with him?"

It took all of her newly found courage to answer truthfully.

"You."

There was a short silence, during which she could sense his surprise at her short, guileless answer, and she thought she heard him expel his breath before he said quietly, "Then we're both crazy. Or else—"

"Must there always be an 'or else' between us?" She pulled away from his encroaching arms and stood before him in the moonlight. She began to unfasten her borrowed dress with fingers that shook in spite of all her bold reserve.

And if he should refuse her now—if he didn't want her—

He seemed frozen for a moment during which she had time to remember his indifference during the last few weeks and his contempt for her before that. But then he reached out to help her undress, shrugging off his shirt to fling it down on the thick grass, holding her shivering, naked body against his for a long time before he finally picked her up in his arms, kissing her throat and her breasts before he laid her down on the roughly improvised bed made of her discarded garments and his.

Chapter Fifty

Marisa was back to being dressed as a boy again, with only Jean Trudeau's sly grin, as he slouched in his saddle beside her, reminding her that only last night everything had been different. Today, the sun shone just as hot and as brightly as ever, and Dominic was on his way to Natchitoches.

His journey there had to do with his son: it was still difficult for her to think of the little boy she had caught a glimpse of one afternoon as *her* child as well. She had tried to school herself not to think of Christian at all, especially after the shocking facts she had been confronted with since she had traveled unsuspectingly with Doña Inez to Congracia. Christian was better off as he was, without the knowledge of his mother's blood that also ran in his veins.

But why had Dominic arranged for the boy and his nurse to be escorted to Natchitoches by none other than General Wilkinson himself?

He had only said shortly, "He'll be safer there with my friends. And if anything ever happens to me, you'll know where he is."

Afraid of destroying the new, still tenuous closeness between them, she had been afraid to press him further. But now she had time to think in spite of the drowsiness that made her sway in the saddle.

Safer because of Murrell, perhaps? And what part did the mysterious general with all his irons in the fire, play in all this? Was it possible that *he* was Dominic's real father? That, too, was something she had been afraid to ask him. And so the moments for questions and answers had slipped away while they had made love to each other instead, talking only desultorily, with no promises or assurances asked or given on either side. She was sure only of one thing after last night—that he wanted her. His hands and his lips had been gentle with her body, and surprisingly patient with her sudden, involuntary shrinking when his caresses grew more intimate.

Jonas had beaten her before he hurt her in other ways. Fortunately Murrell had come silently up the side of the boat, with his cutthroat followers, stopping it from being any worse. But although he had spoken softly and consolingly and appeared to be her rescuer at first, she had learned that he meant to sell her again; and the intimate examination of her body in that private room by the men who bid for her as if she had been an animal had been worse and more humiliating than anything else, even Murrell's casual mounting of her a few hours before—to make sure she understood what was expected of her, he had laughed.

She couldn't tell Dominic about any of it—and how much he had guessed was just as impossible for her to know. At least he hadn't tried to wring details from her. But he had persisted—brushing aside her wild, whispered protests by putting his mouth where his hands had been and kissing her into forgetfulness of everything but the same unvoiced desire that had brought her out into the moonlight. Her senses had been more knowledgeable than her mind which even now tried to shy away from the thought that all the years she had spent running away from him and hating him had been wasted and useless. They had brought her, in the end, to this—the final surrender of her stubborn will to the man who had first despoiled her body and stirred her senses without her realizing it. How could she have hated him without loving him? All the roads that had led them apart had also led them back and back again for one confrontation after another until now.

Unable to think, she had clung drowsily with her arms about his neck when he had carried her back to the camp and put her down on her own cold blankets.

"I have to go. I'll catch up with you all again in two weeks—maybe less."

"Dominic, you haven't had any sleep!"

"I've done without sleep before, and in this case, it was worth it. Try to behave yourself until I get back, menina."

Unable to keep him any longer, she had watched him leave, still unashamedly hungry for the feel of his flesh against hers.

"So it all turned out well, eh?" Trudeau's voice brought Marisa rudely back to the present. "You look half-asleep, and I would not want you to fall off that horse. Why don't you go back and ride in the wagon?"

"I am quite capable of staying on a horse—even if I *do* fall asleep!" Marisa answered him tartly, and he chuckled good-humoredly.

"Ah! L'amour! Go back to sleep then. I will keep my eye on you."

She was relieved to find that he was his usual self again, cynical and worldly-wise. And yet, because of what they had shared in the moonlight before Dominic had come to rescue her, she felt a kind of affection for him. Poor devil-ridden Trudeau!

And then she forgot about Trudeau and went back to thinking of last night and the strange, almost peaceful feeling in her since then. She had stopped struggling against the fate, or whatever it was that had flung her into the middle of this vast wilderness and into the arms of the one man she had hated and fought and run away from. She felt—she did not quite know *how* she felt! And she did not want to delve into her own confused emotions too deeply yet. There would be time later, when her body was not sated with lovemaking. When Dominic came back. . . .

It took him over three weeks to return; they were weeks during which everyone became edgy and short-tempered, and two of the men who had come with them ran off somewhere. "Chasing after squaws no doubt. And they'll have their hearts cut out while they're still alive for trying," Trudeau said laconically.

They were camped now only a short distance from the border; and for amusement the men either went hunting, bringing back more meat to be dried, or quarreled among themselves.

Even Trudeau had begun to grumble. "How long are we to kick up our heels here? We came to capture wild horses in New Spain, not to sit around in these swamps fighting off mosquitoes and looking over our shoulders for Indians."

Everyone seemed to have become sullen and uneasy, and there were some of the men, in fact, who had been arguing with Trudeau, trying to persuade him that they should start out on their own.

"How do we know he ain't got in some kind of trouble? Or—"

Catching their eyes and hearing the quickly broken-off sentence, Marisa had forced herself to move away, pretending she had not heard. But her own thoughts seemed to have grown heavy and sullen, like murky clouds filling up her mind. 'What now? What next?' A night of shared passion and intimacy, and then he had left her again as easily and as lightly as he had done on all those other occasions.

And then, while she was washing clothes with Lalie by the riverbank, her hands and arms moving lethargically, she looked up and saw him.

Frozen in mid-motion, still crouched down on her haunches, she thought at first that the sweat trickling into her eyes was playing tricks with her vision. She became aware, almost in the same instant, of her own bedraggled appearance. With an instinctive motion she brushed the back of one hand across her forehead.

Lalie gave a small, dismayed squeal.

"Mon Dieu! Les sauvages!"

"That's a hell of a greeting!" Dominic drawled as his horse splashed through the shallow water. He was closely followed by truly savage-looking Indians on ponies.

His voice hardening, he snapped, "Why weren't there any guards posted? Where's Trudeau?"

He was burned almost as brown as an Indian himself, and his hair had grown thick and longer than she remembered it; but he had shaved off the beard he had grown, and the tired, harsh lines about his eyes and mouth were more apparent than usual. His eyes, meeting hers for a moment, seemed wary. Silver-grey, turning to slate when they encountered her stunned-looking golden gaze.

Lalie scrambled to her feet. At the same time Trudeau came running from the camp—a makeshift wooden stockade the men had erected for safety.

In a minute, all was confusion. Only the small band of Indians who had come with Dominic sat on their horses impassively and almost sardonically as they listened to the questions and answers.

In none too good a mood ever since he had left Natchitoches, Dominic had caught himself thinking, 'She looks as if she didn't expect me to come back. Why did she look so startled?' He looked searchingly at Trudeau but could detect nothing but relief mixed with some anger on his old friend's face.

Deliberately testing her and not understanding why he had to, he flung the reins of his horse at her. She had just risen belatedly to her feet and stood there like a golden statue. The boys' clothes she wore fit her far too snugly; and too many buttons on the shirt were undone so that the curve of her breasts and the hollow between them made it obvious she was a female. Her hair clung in damp ringlets to her temples and her neck, and her mouth looked mutinous.

"You can take him and rub him down," he said carelessly, just as if she had been in fact his slave—or his squaw. "There are some more suitable clothes for you in my saddlebags."

Marisa sucked in her breath, tempted for a moment to fling the reins back at him; but then she saw one of Dominic's Indian friends look at her, his black eyes unwinking, and heard him say something in guttural-sounding speech, and her back stiffened. Compressing her lips, aware that they were all watching her now, she decided on discretion for the moment at least; and turning her back on them all, without a word, she yanked on the reins and led the sweat-lathered animal away.

How dared he? After all the agony of mind she had gone through wondering if anything had happened to him—how dared he return and pay her no attention at all except to treat her like a servant? No doubt he had expected—had hoped—that she would rebel so he would have the chance of putting her in her place publicly. But no, she wouldn't give him that satisfaction!

Tears of sheer rage and frustration wet her eyes, carrying her through the next half-hour. Lalie came to help her, chattering as if she noticed nothing.

"We'll be moving out tomorrow morning I heard them say. And those Indians—they've invited us to their camp on the other side of the river, in New Spain. For some kind of celebration they have before they hunt buffalo. Lucky for us Mr. Dominic used to live with them before and knows their language. Paulus heard some of the other men talk, and he says the Comanche Indians usually don't take kindly to anyone trespassing in their country. But it's different with us. At least we won't have to worry about *them!*"

"Oh?" Marisa said between her teeth, and Lalie gave an unsympathetic chuckle.

"You mad at him? No reason you should be. Men don't like to show their feelings in the open—'specially not in front of other men. But tonight—" She broke off, with an exclamation of dismay. "Why you doing that?"

Marisa had dumped out the contents of his saddlebags, feeling a vicious satisfaction in doing so. And the next moment she regretted her impetuosity.

A hand closed in her hair, hauling her up onto her feet. She let out a cry of outraged pain.

"You mean-tempered little hellcat! If you've broken anything, I'm going to take the skin off your back with a stick— or sell you to Running Water for the horses he offered me!"

The pain from her aching scalp made tears start in her but Marisa forced herself to glare unyieldingly into Dominic's coldly angry grey eyes. She was aware that Lalie had scampered off leaving them alone together, but she wouldn't back down before his anger this time—she wouldn't, no matter what he did!

"I thought you wanted me to unpack for you! Ooh! Let go of me, you—you— And what are you doing with a sextant, anyhow? I thought it was wild horses you were after, and not—*spying!*"

He gave her hair another tug, forcing her head back so far that she thought for a moment her neck would snap.

"I thought you might have learned by now not to meddle with things that didn't concern you," he said between his teeth. "And what the hell do you mean—*spying?*"

In order to keep her balance she had no choice but to clutch at his shoulders. He smelled of sweat and horses and leather and tobacco, and she felt her senses swim as she forced herself to answer gaspingly, "The sextant—that's for mapping. I'm not as ignorant as you'd like me to be, am I?"

"You have seldom been anything I wanted to be, you cat-eyed bitch! Trust you to know a sextant when you see one—and tumble it out carelessly as you just did! And there's a difference between making maps and spying. Marisa, you try my patience too far!"

She gave a gasp of sheer agony, and his cruel grip slackened as if he had been suddenly recalled to his senses. She felt his arm encircle her waist, holding her pressed against the length of his body.

"There are times when I ask myself why I haven't killed you! Do you realize how you've interfered in my life? And there's no need for you to remind me that it was all my fault in the beginning. Do you think I don't know that? All the same, if it hadn't been me it would have been some other man—that hot-eyed gypsy who called himself your novio or Pedro Arteaga. You conquer by surrendering, don't you?" His words flicked at her already raw nerves like whips. She was outraged even while her senses themselves were already responding to his closeness and maleness. And she was tired of fighting, tired of trying to defend herself, and tired of the conflict inside herself.

"Perhaps you're right," she murmured in a breathless, exhausted voice; and her sudden apathy, the yielding of her body against his when he had expected her to go on fighting, only made him grind his teeth together with frustration.

Damn her! It was because of her that he was here dancing docilely to General Wilkinson's tune. And yet while he held her in his arms, all he could think of was possessing her—if a woman such as she was could ever be possessed completely. She would belong, like any paid whore, only to the man who had her, and then only as long as he could keep her close to him. If another man came along, she would make some token attempt at resistance, perhaps, and then melt against him as submissively and easily as she was doing now with him. He wanted to fling her away from him, but he had thought about holding her just so for too long now. He wanted her—why not admit it? And as long as he could keep her, he would. Even if it was only for a short time, she would belong to him completely. No, he wouldn't let her go—not until he was sated and could put her out of his mind.

His hands slipped down her neck and her shoulders and down her back. He reached up under her shirt, feeling the smooth silk of her skin. Angry at her and himself and most of all at his own weakness, Dominic kissed her half-open, trembling lips, forcing his tongue brutally into her mouth. And as if he had to prove his ownership of her, started to caress her small, firm breasts, unheeding of her protesting murmurs. And then he cupped one hand about her taut rump, pushing her against himself as if he meant to take her then and there, no matter who might be watching.

She had begun to squirm and struggle and to push against his chest with her hands; but he used his superior strength ruthlessly, playing with her body until she lay limp and acquiescent against him with her eyes closed.

Good. Let her learn once and for all the future pattern of their relationship. And her role. But strangely enough, when he finally released her, the thought brought him no satisfaction, nor did the sight of her bruised and swollen mouth.

Even after he had turned and left her, Dominic found himself unwillingly carrying in his mind a picture of the way she had lifted her hands pressing them against her mouth like a child who would not let herself cry. He had to fight the stupid, crazy impulse to go back and comfort her.

He had been walking with angry, long strides that would take him outside the confines of the low-walled wooden fort they had built. Close to the entrance, he hesitated, still battling with himself. Then he saw Trudeau standing just inside with his back against one of the wooden uprights, his arms crossed.

There was a strange flicker in the Cajun's eyes which vanished as he raised his shoulders and gave his usual cynical half-smile.

"I did not mean to intrude. But you did not notice me, and I found the little scene very interesting."

"Did you?" Dominic's voice was coldly ominous, but Trudeau did not seem to notice. He followed him outside.

"Yes, you see," Trudeau went on his his soft, lazy voice, "since you asked me to look after the little one, to protect her, it has become a habit. Even from myself, I would protect her. But of course it is easy for you to hurt her, eh? Because she is in love with you, the poor girl, and has been eating her heart out. But what does that matter to you, eh? It's a pity you are used to dealing with whores; let a woman show some spirit and soul of her own and you have to make her feel like one of those. Bah!"

Dominic had stopped in mid-stride, whirling around to face him, and now Trudeau spat elaborately and contemptuously on the ground between them—a long stream of tobacco juice that splattered his high Comanche-style moccasins.

His eyes like splintered glass, Dominic asked with deceptive softness, "Are you attempting to provoke me into a fight? Because you hope to pick up the spoils afterwards if you are lucky enough to win?"

"She is not spoils, she is one damn fine woman! And I tell you that if I might have hoped to win her, I would have killed you very quietly—accidentally, hein? I know all the ways, for our friend Murrell was a good teacher. Why waste ammunition or risk your own life meeting an armed man face to face? A fall off a wounded horse, a chance arrow, or a knife in the back—these are done more easily!"

"Aren't you spoiling the element of surprise by telling me this?"

Trudeau showed his teeth in a wolfish grin.

"I have only been talking of what *might* have happened, mon ami! The little Marisa loves you. Why should I make her unhappy?"

Keeping his hand close to his knife hilt, he stared warily at Dominic while he was speaking.

There was an explosive silence between them for a few seconds; and then with a relief he didn't show, Trudeau saw Dominic's tense muscles relax.

"Thanks for the warning—and the advice," he said dryly. The rage had left his eyes, leaving them opaque. It was impossible to know what he was thinking.

Trudeau shrugged, still wary. "Sometimes it is best to be honest, especially since we are to journey a long way together and work together."

Marisa, wavering between sheer unhappiness and sullen resignation, had no idea of the incident that had taken place. It was Lalie, who seemed to notice everything and hear everything, who told her, giggling, "Do you see how the captain and that Trudeau walk around each other like strange cats? A while ago, when I saw them talking it looked like they might be quarreling. Now they're real polite to each other. I wonder—"

"We don't have time to wonder," Marisa interrupted her crossly. "Not with all this food to cook. Do you know what we are? Just a couple of squaws, that's all! Even your Paulus has gone to sit with the men. They're like little children, sitting there scratching their silly maps in the dirt and—ignoring us!"

"Well, men are just different when they're with other men, that's all! And it's something you just got to get used to. They just like to show off, that's all!"

Marisa followed Lalie's eyes to where Paulus was lifting a heavy saddle using only one hand—to the obvious admiration of their Indian guests.

"It's a man's country, this! But you know what? I ain't too unhappy that I was born a woman. Not now, anyways."

They shared a sudden, almost embarrassed look. Almost instinctively Marisa found herself looking across the fire at Dominic, his hair still wet from swimming in the stream, his shirt open down to his waist. Thinking of this afternoon made her wonder bitterly if she would not have been better off, after all, if he had remained indifferent to her. But no, she had had to go and flaunt herself at him that night, and now—now he had made it only too clear to her that his interest in her lay in one direction only. He wanted her as a man would want a whore because that was what he thought her.

Chapter Fifty-one

After the men, including the Indians (who were not nearly as silent as she had been led to believe but quite garrulous instead), had finished eating and she and Lalie had had their share, Marisa could see from the position of the moon hanging over the treetops that it must be quite late.

Her black, sullen mood had descended on her again, and she helped Lalie do the washing up of utensils in silence. No wonder he had brought women along! As servants. To cook and wash and do all the tiny, unpleasant chores that men liked to think were beneath their dignity. And because she was supposed to be "grateful" to him for "saving" her, she had only exchanged one kind of slavery for another.

She had worn, in a mood of fleeting defiance, a skirt and low-cut blouse he had brought her, thinking at the time that they made her look the part she was expected to play. Camp follower! He was punishing her for all the things she hadn't done —and for all of his own faults that had brought her here in the first place!

She remembered the song she had heard one of the boatmen sing on that strange voyage downriver from Natchez to Louisiana.

Ah, God! What torment, what pain,
It is suffering worse than fetters,
Better that I die five times than suffer like this . . .

Lalie was looking at her strangely, and she asked her without thinking, "How did the rest of that song go? The one you translated for me that night on the boat."

"I was thinking of it too," Lalie said softly, and her husky Creole voice sang very quietly in patois:

Ah, Dieu! Qui tourmen, qui peine,
C'est in souffrante passe la chaine,
Plutot mo mouri sin fois.

And then, "Why were you thinking of it? Are you unhappy?"

Marisa shook her head. "I don't know. My feelings are all mixed up inside me—pain and wanting and most of all, not knowing!"

Lalie put her arm about her shoulders and squeezed them affectionately.

"Well, like what you learn or not, I think you're going to find out. And I just hope you find what you really want. Listen, for all that men make a big noise and shout and act like they don't care for anything, what you think they'd be without us?" Then becoming practical, she added, "Let's get this stuff all packed up, hm? That way when they're all running around in the morning feeling important, we'll have everything ready to go."

Within the log walls of their makeshift stockade, Marisa laid down her bedding roll in her usual place. Not too far from where Trudeau usually lay down, but an isolated spot against the log walls where they were thickest. Let him come looking for her if he as much as remembered her tonight!

She burrowed under the blankets, covering her face. Yes, there were some occasions when it was convenient to be a woman. No one would wake her during the night to take her turn at standing guard. Caught between anger and apprehension, sleep was long in coming. She was aware of every sound, from the spitting of the breaking logs in the fire to the slight coughs and clearing of throats of the men who still sat around it. If *he* was one of them, she hoped he'd sit there all night! She felt almost stifled, but she closed her eyes stubbornly and concentrated on taking steady, even breaths, keeping her mind deliberately shuttered. The same formula that had put her to sleep all these weeks was only just beginning to work, her mind gradually giving way to the urging of her tired body, when she felt the hand on her shoulder and grew stiff.

He lay beside her, sliding under the blankets and putting his arms around her, holding her still.

"You looked like a small mound under this pile of blankets, just as if you were trying to hide yourself away. Did you think you could?" And then, with a touch of arrogance, "From tomorrow, you'll put your bedding roll down beside mine. Do you understand?"

His lips touched the back of her neck and moved along her stubborn shoulder. One hand stroked her breasts, and the other moved unerringly between her thighs; he found the most sensitive part of her and moved against her and in her until her half-formed protests turned into soft, stifled moans. The moon moved lower in the sky, tangling itself in her eyes until he closed them with surprisingly gentle kisses. Her body was the ocean and his the wild wind—turning ripples into foam-capped breakers that soared and curved translucently before they crashed into oblivion against distant shores.

Marisa slept more deeply than she had done for weeks, unpursued by mocking dream specters. It was as if she were sinking like a heavy stone from consciousness to unconsciousness. And then, just as suddenly, she was awake.

Trudeau cleared his throat before he spoke, and his voice came from somewhere above her.

"Can't think of a better way to keep a man trapped and—more or less helpless; but we were supposed to leave at first light, remember, mon capitaine?"

Marisa could feel herself blush as she reached vainly for a blanket that was tangled up somewhere about her legs.

Lifting her head, she looked down into Dominic's amused, sleepy grey eyes, and remembered belatedly that she had rolled on top of him just before they both slept, wrapping her arms about his neck.

Trudeau was still chuckling, and Dominic growled, "If you'll stop playing the voyeur and just move on—dammit, do you have to wake the whole camp?"

"Camp's been awake for the past ten minutes at least,"

Trudeau commented laconically. "Fact is, I've had a hard time trying to stop just about everybody from doing just what I'm doing now. Don't blame me!" he added hastily, backing off. "Your Indian friends are early risers, that's all!"

The rest of the day that followed was never quite clear in Marisa's memory, except that she lived through it with her face feeling on fire with embarrassment, trying to pretend she did not notice the grinning, sideways glances of every man she encountered. Even the Comanche Indians, who had seemed to be haughty and disdainful before, gave her sly and quite human looks from time to time. And the most frustrating fact of all was that Dominic, whose fault it had partly been, seemed to think it funny!

Interrupting her furious tirade later on that night, he drawled, one eyebrow wickedly lifted, "You have quite an enticing little derrière, menina. And the rest of you is just as distracting, too. I don't usually let myself sleep as heavily as I did after you—uh—wore me out with your squirmings and your—"

"Oh, stop!" Marisa put her hands over her ears and glared at him furiously. "How like a man! *You* don't care if everyone sees you naked. You strip off all your clothes to go swimming, and if you have to—you know what—when we're riding, you simply get off your horse and—but it's different for a woman!"

"Because you're brought up to feel ashamed of your body!" He had started to laugh, but now he suddenly reached out and touched her, brushing his fingers lightly across her breasts. "You have no need to be, you know. You're gold all over just like a little Indian girl."

She was suddenly blazingly, inexplicably jealous.

"How many Indian girls have you slept with?" And the next minute she could have bitten off her betraying, runaway tongue.

"I didn't keep count."

She felt cut off by his evenly uttered words and knew she deserved it. 'You're a fool!' she told herself miserably. Why couldn't she just accept what was between them now as easily and as casually as he seemed able to do? She had no right to question him, and not too long ago he had reminded her of that fact.

She couldn't unsay her words and wouldn't take them back or apologize for them, either. Instead she stared back into his eyes that looked slaty-grey in the firelight and heard him say in the same unaccented voice, "Did *you?*"

Well, she had asked for it, but she wouldn't back down, either. She had the oddest feeling in the back of her mind that they had reached the same barrier that had brought them down—on opposite sides—before.

"Not because I wanted to," she said carefully. "But I can, if I must. There was you—and you—and you with an Irish accent that time you decided I must be punished. And Philip—not before, as you thought, but *then*, that same night, just after, because he . . . And Kamil and you again, until—"

"Oh, *Christ!* That's enough. Do you hear? Do you understand that I don't want to hear?"

He took her in his arms, but it wasn't enough. There was suddenly an emptiness inside her like a great aching wound; and she didn't know if she wanted her hurt assuaged or needed to inflict just as much on him. She heard her own voice, coming from a distance away as if she stood outside herself, and didn't know whether to applaud or cry.

"Do *you* understand that I *want* you to hear? Why not? Kamil. I stopped at Kamil, didn't I? You know all about that. (She listened to the shrew that had been hidden inside herself all this time and marveled from the outside.) And Napoleon. You won't be surprised to learn that I let him conquer me, too? But why not? Did I have any reason not to? The funny thing is that I got bored—or thought I needed something different. I wanted to be a nun again, but my uncle didn't think I was ready. So he sent me to Louisiana with Pedro—and *he* didn't touch me, but you did! And then—Jonas only hurt me. Does that count? Murrell took me to calm me down, he said. And the last one, the Cuban, he spent a lot of time telling me just what he expected of me, before he—started showing me—"

She didn't know she was weeping until he put his hand up and wiped off the tears that coursed down her cheeks.

"Marisa. Poor little runaway nun!"

She pulled away from his touch as if she had been stung. "I'm not a poor little anything! Don't you dare pity me! Despise me if you want to, I don't care, but save your pity for someone else like—like yourself, for instance, and all these men who follow you so blindly! Do they know the risks they're taking? Do you care what might happen if the Spanish soldiers catch up with you? You keep risking your life as if it was some kind of a game, and for what? Do you think you'll always be lucky enough to escape?"

The words kept spilling out of her without conscious thought or volition—how long had she been keeping them stored up in her mind? She only knew it was a relief to say them, no matter what his reaction might be.

Surprisingly, he had listened to her tirade without interruption, the expression on his shadowed face impossible to read. But now when she had seemed to run out of words, her voice lost in gasping sobs, he surprised her again by taking her in his arms and holding her closely against the length of his body until her halfhearted struggles had stopped, and she lay passively, feeling strangely comforted by the fact that he continued to hold her in silence until there were no more sobs left in her.

"Feel better now?"

Her face pressed damply against his chest, Marisa moved her head slightly.

"Yes. No!" Her voice sounded muffled. He noticed that for all her earlier resentment, she didn't move.

"Well, you just be quiet now and try to get some sleep!" he said with deliberate roughness, feeling the slight tensing of her body against his as he moved them both into a more comfortable position and pulled the blankets up without giving her a chance at further argument. Unpredictably, she stayed quiet, snuggling up closer to him in a manner that challenged his self-control and even, after some moments had passed and he thought her asleep, giving a soft sigh and slipping her arms about his body.

The morning sun peered redly at her through her tear-swollen eyes. Marisa wondered resentfully how Dominic could wake so easily and quickly, putting her away from him as he stretched and then came lithely to his feet, slapping her lightly on the rump when she grumbled and tried to burrow back under the blankets.

"Up! We have to break camp in a hurry and cross the river before the sun gets up too high. You'll get your first real look at Spanish territory—or Indian land, as *they* prefer to think of it."

His voice had seemed faintly inflected with sarcasm, but he was gone before she sat up, and for most of the day that followed, Marisa saw little of him.

They crossed the Red River on hastily improvised rafts that the men had been busy building all of the previous day. Once on land, Dominic rode ahead with his Comanche friends. Suddenly they seemed to break out of the cover of the trees, facing what seemed to be a different kind of ocean —acre upon acre of undulating buffalo grass, blanketing an undulating prairie land which stretched as far as the eye could see.

A general sense of cheerfulness seemed to fill everyone. Even the dour-faced Trudeau was smiling. The Comanches used sign language, interspersed with quickly muttered words in their language which only Dominic seemed to understand.

"They are inviting us to visit their main camp, as their guests. They say that this is the season for hunting the buffalo and there are no Spanish soldiers here for they huddle in their forts and villages further south, afraid of the Snake People." Trudeau seemed to understand sign language, and Marisa was grateful for that fact that *he*, at least, had been thoughtful enough to explain to her.

"I thought we were here to find wild horses!" She could not keep the acid out of her voice, but the Cajun, who seemed to have appointed himself her guide and her guardian, only gave her a glance from his heavy-lidded eyes.

"There are mustangs here, too. But more of them to the southwest, in the lands watered by the Trinity and the Brazos Rivers. That is where we are headed, but first—the Comanche Indians make better friends than enemies, and once we've partaken of their hospitality, they'll let us alone." His voice became dry. "You wouldn't understand, of course,

563

how favored we are. The Comanches are usually everybody's
enemy, both other Indians as well as white men."

Marisa turned a puzzled, questioning gaze on him, and
the lanky man shrugged, directing a long stream of tobacco
juice with accuracy at a blade of grass.

"You should ask *him*. All I know is that he made friends
with them some years ago, the first time he ever explored
Spanish country. And at that time it was *all* Spanish, even
Louisiana. He lived with them for a while and *that's* unusual,
too."

He paused, adding expressionlessly, "I understand that
he was adopted into one of the Iroquois tribes when he
was no more than a boy. That would have been a short
while before the War of Revolution. Maybe that had something to do with it. Even the Seminoles, 'way down in the
Floridas, were allies of the Five Nations."

"The Five Nations?"

Trudeau shot her a disgusted look. "Think I've got time
to give you lessons in Indian history? You'll find out, maybe."

Pushing strands of sun-bleached hair out of her eyes,
Marisa watched him leave her. Dominic—how could any man
continue to be such a puzzle? She remembered times when
he had deliberately hurt her or used her with no thought for
her feelings at all. And yet last night he had slept holding
her cradled in his arms without making any attempt to take
her. Would she ever understand him? And yet Trudeau's
carelessly suddenly uttered words had put her in mind of
the past.

She shivered as she was transported back to Cornwall on
that frightening, fateful night when she had left it forever.
That old, witchlike woman who boasted of having served
the Sinclairs for years—what had been her name? It didn't
matter, she could still recall some of the things the woman
had muttered as she hobbled about that big, bleak room,
putting away her clothes. "That young savage from the colonies. . . . After they sent her son away to Ireland where
my lord hoped he'd be disciplined, she was easy to manage. . . . He should have been hanged with the others after
the last rebellion . . . But my lord duke had him pressed
into the navy instead. . . ."

Oh, God! What kind of a boyhood had he had?

"I'm a legal bastard," he'd once said, in Paris. And the duke of Royse, his legal father, had hated him and wanted him dead. It wasn't enough that the duke killed his wife, Lady Peggy, by slow torture; he'd tried to do the same with her son.

And Donald. Whatever had become of Donald? He had talked of there being a devil driving Dominic. . . .

Too wrapped up in her own unhappiness and armored by hate, she hadn't really listened then. But now that she understood in part, how did it help her? Or him? Dominic had been nurtured on hate. How early had he learned to trust no one but himself? And as for loving, was he capable of such an emotion? Having learned early that the only way to survive was to fight back, he had become an opportunist; and having managed to survive so far, he had become what he was—a reckless adventurer.

'You are only a hostage—and a woman to keep him warm at night,' Marisa warned herself. She thought of pretty, rich little Jane Byron who waited so confidently for his return. And he'd marry her, of course—if he returned. But would he ever stop adventuring?

Unconsciously, Marisa's eyes looked for him again, as if she needed a talisman against her own foreboding thoughts. What she saw only made her frown and press her lips tightly together. With the aid of two of the Comanches, who bent over his shoulder with obvious fascination, now and then pointing, drawing in the dust, or shaking their heads, he was making some kind of a map on paper. Spying! She remembered her own angrily flung accusation that had driven him to such a rage; but this time she felt only a deep, ominous unease. *Why* did he need to make maps if he knew this country so well? For *whom*? And why did they carry so many extra guns and such a quantity of powder and shot? Dear God, what was he *planning*? What kind of dangerous scheme was he mixed up in this time?

As if the fixed gaze of her eyes had actually touched him, he looked up at that moment, snaring her unaware, unhappy gaze with his own. And then he went back to what he was doing, leaving her strangely shaken.

Chapter Fifty-two

There was an air of suppressed excitement about everyone when they made camp that night. Cold camp. There would be no fires lit tonight because fires could be seen a long distance in this kind of country. So there was no cooking to be done, and they chewed on dried beef washed down with water.

Three of the Comanches had gone ahead, riding without stop, their spare ponies trailing behind them. They hoped to reach their main camp by daybreak, warning their people to expect guests.

It was cold, and Marisa shivered as she slipped, fully dressed, under the pile of blankets. If she were asleep by the time he decided to join her, what would he do? The memory of the afternoon was still with her, but *this* time she decided she would keep silent even if it killed her. Let him risk his life for somebody else's ambition and dreams of glory, that was all that mattered to them in the end! And she'd never again let him guess either her feelings or her fears.

She must have fallen asleep, after all, for she didn't know when he had come to lie down beside her. Leaving her with the blankets, he lay without touching her, a buffalo robe thrown over him as he stretched out on his back, his arms pillowed under his head, staring up at the stars.

The moon had already disappeared from the sky. Marisa realized when she opened her eyes that it must be close to morning. Why hadn't he wakened her?

She must have stirred or else he had sensed, catlike, her sudden wakefulness. And her thoughts, because he said softly, without turning his head, "You looked as if you needed the sleep. And there's at least another hour left before you have to crawl out from under those warm covers. Go back to your dreams."

Her contrariness took fire at that and she whispered back, "I wasn't dreaming! And I can't go back to sleep now. Why aren't *you?*"

"I never have needed too much sleep. See those stars? They were all men had to guide their ships by, not too long ago. And that's the same way caravans find their way across the deserts. Every group of those stars has a name, too. You can tell where you are, anywhere in the world, just by watching the stars."

She caught her breath, wanting him to watch her instead, but the strangeness of their conversation, lying together without touching, marked a different facet to all the other times they had been together, and she didn't want to break the tenuous thread of communication that had suddenly been spun between them.

"How did you learn about that?"

"Mostly by watching. And listening to old men talk."

"When you lived with the Indians?"

He turned his head at last.

"Did you guess that? Or did I tell you sometime before?"

"You never did much talking to me before. But I'd like to know now, please?"

"You sound like a little girl begging for a candy apple!" His voice was dry, but when she reached her hand out from under her blankets groping for his, his fingers hesitated only momentarily before closing around hers.

"What do you want to know, anyhow? A catalogue of all my past sins?"

All the same, he did begin talking to her, and after a while it was if she weren't there at all, except as a warm hand holding his in the dark; and she guessed somehow, intuitively, that he had never told anyone else all the things he was telling her, his voice quiet and deliberately expressionless. He didn't tell her everything; she sensed that, too, while she began to understand, painfully, what a priest must feel when he heard a confession. And there was nothing she dared do but cling to his hand and listen without comment.

And now, at last, she could ask him the question she had longed to ask him ever since he had returned two days ago. "And when you went to Natchitoches? You said—"

"Why did you wait so long to ask me that? Christ, you're an unpredictable woman! I went after Christian, and he's safe, he and Selma both, with friends of *my* friend General Wilkinson. But they'll stay there until the general has what he wants." His voice hardened. "At least they're heavily guarded—and Nacogdoches is right across the river—"

"But Nacogodoches is Spanish!"

"So it is," Dominic said softly, but something in his voice sent a tremor up her spine, and it was all she could do not to fling herself into his arms and beg him not to do anything else, not to take any more risks than he was taking now.

As it was, she began a blurted out protest. "Dominic—"

"That's enough for now!" His voice warned her as if he were already beginning to regret having been so frank with her, and she subsided into mutinous silence.

After a while he said, picking his words carefully, "At least, if anything *does* go wrong, you'll know where he is. Manuel Reyes and his wife are Spanish and staunch, practicing Catholics. No doubt this uncle of yours who is an archbishop will carry some influence."

At last she found the courage to kick her blankets aside and roll against him, clinging to his shoulders before he could push her away.

"Nothing is going to happen! You have me as a hostage, remember?"

"That's not what you said earlier," he reminded her drily. "And hostage or not, I'm going to find it difficult to carry out any threats I might have to make about killing you. But there's no reason why anything should go wrong, either, so stop talking like the voice of doom!"

He left her with that. He disengaged himself from her clinging arms, dropping a light kiss that was far too chaste for her liking on her forehead.

The next day was all confusion and far too much hard work. For Marisa and Lalie, anyway, pounced on by eager, curious women who were obviously unused to strange females in their camp who weren't captives.

Marisa had the opportunity to realize how lucky she was that the latter wasn't the case. Women could be much more cruel than men, and she saw examples of the fact everywhere for there were cowering, unfortunate women captives in almost every lodge; some of them were mutilated; most of them were covered with ugly bruises and burn marks. Both Dominic and Trudeau had warned her, but even so it was all she could do to keep silent and try to appear indifferent to the degrading fate of these women, each of whom under different circumstances, might have been herself.

Now she understood what Trudeau had told her about the Comanches. For the first time she found herself in a society where males were all-important and all-powerful, their women less than chattel, and their slaves even less than that.

A gaunt, hollow-eyed Spanish woman who had been lucky enough to be chosen as third wife to the chief acted as interpreter while the women, giggling, showed Marisa and Lalie how to erect a tepee and take it down in a matter of minutes. Buffalo hides lay drying in the sun everywhere, and Marisa's stomach revolted when the women demonstrated how they cured them to make robes against the winter cold. One of them described a buffalo hunt—the bravery of the men and the scramble afterwards for the raw liver and intestines. And one of the strangest things was that most of the women wore their hair cropped short, but the men grew theirs long and braided it carefully.

Half-naked children played everywhere, little boys already practicing with toy bows and blunt-tipped arrows, while girl children played more quietly with clay dolls or helped their mothers with the tasks that seemed to continuously occupy the women. The younger men strutted arrogantly like peacocks against such a background—*they* had only to see to their weapons and their horses—and the old men sat in front of their lodges teaching little boys the rudiments of hunting and warfare.

Even Lalie, usually mild-mannered, whispered angrily to

Marisa, "Makes me know how lucky I was even being born a slave. Compared to *this!* Ooh, that Paulus, look at him strut! And wait until I get him alone tonight!"

"Be careful. He might find himself a docile squaw and trade you off," Marisa responded maliciously, and Lalie shot her a half-frightened, half-reproachful look.

"You really think? . . . No, he wouldn't, that big black ox! Because he knows I'd stick a knife between his ribs if he as much as looks too hard at one of *them!* I would, too!"

"What on earth are we doing here?" Even as she said it, Marisa found her eyes looking for Dominic, sitting cross-legged and half-naked beside the chief, his dark head bent as he listened respectfully to whatever the older man was saying.

"I swear I don't know," Lalie whispered back to her, but her voice had become lighter. "At least I know this much: we're going to have some privacy with our men tonight, under a tepee!"

The buffalo steaks (or at least that was what she *hoped* they were) were burned black on the outside and half-raw close to the bone. And the women ate only after all the men had eaten their fill—and they ate with their fingers.

Catching Dominic's questioning, amused glance across the fire, Marisa chewed on her portion determinedly, trying not to think of what she ate.

Comanche women didn't believe in bathing except on ceremonious occasions. They had stared in astonishment when both Marisa and Lalie insisted on doing so. There was a stream running nearby, of course. They always made camp beside the water if they could. But. . . .

"Tell them she's a female witch doctor—a voodoo woman," Lalie said mischievously, nodding her head towards Marisa. The woman who acted as their interpreter became round-eyed, backing away almost imperceptibly.

But at least they were given their way and went bathing in the stream with some of the female slaves to watch over them.

"You didn't have to say that!" Marisa scolded, but the cool water running over her body felt so good that the next moment she began to laugh, and she sprayed Lalie with water.

571

Stepping out of the stream into the cold night air, she began to dry herself vigorously with the thin man's shirt she had been wearing earlier and became aware that half the women in the camp were watching her curiously.

"They say you are the color of the pale sun all over," the Spanish woman translated nervously. "They say you bring *puha*—good medicine—for the buffalo hunt even though you are a woman. Three moons ago our puhakut—our shaman—told of the coming of such a female who would bring to our warriors the capture of a white buffalo."

Marisa looked reproachfully at Lalie, who avoided her glance. She felt still more awkward, and almost frightened, when the chief's first wife made her a present of a pale buckskin skirt and overblouse, embroidered all over with beads and colored porcupine quills.

"And what will happen if they *don't* find a white buffalo?" she asked Dominic when he came to her that night, ducking his head to enter the tepee she had erected herself under the supervision of the laughing Comanche women.

"I don't think you'd really want to know." He answered her carelessly, and then, laughing in the face of her angry, wordless cry, "But they will, of course. You have strong *puha*, my sweet. I should have realized a long time ago that you were a witch."

"It's not a joking matter!" she cried out at him, gritting her teeth with anger. But he came to her and began unlacing her buckskin garments; and after a while she forgot both her fear and her anger and lay with him on a couch of buffalo skins, with no other concern but the feel of his hands and lips on her body and the mounting fever in her blood.

Three days later, when the hunters returned with the hide of a white buffalo, even Lalie started to look at her with something like awe.

"Don't you tell me once more that my granny was a voodoo woman!" Marisa cried out at her. "It was only luck—or maybe my prayers—not voodoo! For heaven's sake—I've been terrified!"

She was more than relieved when they started out on the final stage of their journey a few days after that; she didn't even mind that some of the men brought along bought

Comanche squaws—or unwanted captives in some cases—to help with the loneliness and hard work that lay ahead.

More than ever, they seemed like a small army with their camp followers. And she was one herself. Only she had stopped caring or thinking of anything but the present. The past was behind her, and the future didn't exist. But when she was alone, riding with the wind blowing in her face, a relentless, terrible logic tore at her mind, forcing its way into her consciousness, ripping away all the painfully thin barriers she tried to set up against such thoughts.

When he had captured and broken enough wild mustangs and made his maps, Dominic would have to return to Natchez with them. And in Natchez, Jane Byron would be waiting for him. The woman Christian had learned to call mama. Dominic might not love Jane, but he was fond of her, and he respected her. He wouldn't let her face the humiliation of being a jilted bride. Oh, and no doubt Jane would be good for him! She would make him a compliant, "suitable" wife, and run the household affairs of his plantation smoothly. Give him children and a stability he had never had before.

Oh, Marisa could see all these things with pitiless clarity. Right down to the unwanted, unadmitted fact that now, when it was too late, she had begun to love him. And where did that leave her?

It was easier, therefore, to exist wholly in the *now* of her life and to look forward only a few hours at a time, to the nights. . . .

Sometimes they would come together and make love, fiercely and wordlessly, as if that particular time were the last time ever. And on other nights he would lie by her side, her head resting on his shoulder and his arm about her, while he told her the names of the different constellations and where to look for them in the black night sky. He smiled at her more often and even told her about other trips like this that he had taken, although he minimized the risks.

"You make it all sound like a—an amusing game!"

"Hide and seek? I've played that one, too, but always for real. Are you still worrying?"

She shook her head, lying bravely but not, she suspected, too convincingly. She was spared by the thought that he

might decide to send her away, and to distract him she began to kiss him, caressing his hard, scarred body with her
fingertips until she heard his breathing quicken; and then,
with a quick, supple movement that took him by surprise,
she twisted herself around, her hair brushing his thighs
while her mouth found him. It was strangely satisfying to
feel him jerk as if her mouth had burned him, to feel the
power that she could wield. *Jane* would never dream of doing this! Oh, she would make him need her and crave her
just as much as she wanted him.

"And where did you learn *that?*" His voice sounded harsh,
but his breathing was still ragged, and Marisa smiled in the
darkness, nuzzling her lips against his face.

"From you. You do that to me, and I wanted to find out
what it was like. You tasted of me."

"Oh, God!" he said feelingly and kissed her violently to
keep her from saying any more.

That was the night before they crossed the Trinity River,
stopping there for two days to water their horses and scout
out the country that lay ahead.

"Going to be a long, hard haul until we reach the Brazos
River country," Trudeau warned Marisa. He gave her one
of his half-mocking, half-malicious smiles. "Better learn to
watch your water and cook over buffalo-chip fires. You
won't find any wood on these prairie lands."

He threw a sly, appreciative look at her bare, sunburned
legs before he rode off, leaving Marisa frowning slightly.
She wished Trudeau had been one of those who had gotten
himself a woman at the Comanche camp. And of late, since
her boys' clothes had worn out, she was forced to wear skirts
—kilted up to permit her to ride astride. The long buffalo
grass could cut as sharp as knives, and her legs were scratch-
ed and bleeding from ankle to knee.

"Well, I'm not going to lend you a pair of *my* breeches!"
Dominic exploded when she tentatively broached the subject. She had interrupted him at his map-making, and he
was irritable, his finger rubbing at the stubble of the beard
he was growing. "And that's final!" he warned her when she
opened her mouth to protest. "You couldn't get into them
anyhow, I won't let you cut them up."

"You're a selfish, inconsiderate—ooh!"

She whirled about and left him in a rage but later she followed Lalie's advice and bribed one of the Comanche women into fashioning a pair of fringed leather leggings for her, very much like the high-topped moccasins of the men.

Trudeau gave a chortle of laughter and told her she looked like a cross between a Mexican peasant and a squaw.

Her eyes flashing she looked challengingly at Dominic, but preoccupied, he only shrugged and told her she looked fine—and what in hell did it matter how she looked out *here,* anyway? For a moment she was tempted to make the childishly vindictive gesture of tearing her blouse open to the waist, asking him sarcastically if *that* didn't matter, either. But he had already ridden off ahead, leaving her to stare after him thoughtfully, and trying to negate with anger the knife-thrust of fear in her heart.

Was something wrong? Was he growing indifferent to her, or was there something else on his mind?

Chapter Fifty-three

The days and nights ran into each other, disappearing down the tunnel of time. Marisa learned the feel and the smell and tasted the dust of the enormous emptiness of the rolling grasslands. Five more days until they reached the Brazos River, and now, she began to see for the first time the enormous herds of wild horses known as mustangs. Perhaps the excitement that now prevailed among the rest might have infected her, too—if it hadn't been for Dominic.

Something was eating at him. He wouldn't tell her what it was, and she couldn't ask him. Oh, he still came to lie beside her at night, but when he did it was usually very late; and unless she made some obvious movement to show she wasn't asleep, he'd lie on his back, looking up at the stars, keeping his thoughts inside himself. The last few nights she didn't stir at all; instead she watched him covertly from behind the dark screen of her eyelashes. She learned that he could lie very still, like an Indian, and that he did nothing but look at the damn stars, as if the same sky he had already seen over and over again held some new fascination for him. If she didn't move, he made no attempt to touch her. If she tossed about restlessly or let him see she was watching him, he would usually take her in his arms and make love to her. But it wasn't the same as it had been in the weeks before when he had talked to her as if he had suddenly discovered she was a thinking human being and had even teased her, smiling down into her face, his eyes crinkling at the corners.

'What have I done?' she asked herself at first. And then, despising the craven, all-too-female question, she asked, 'What's wrong with him?' But he wouldn't tell her, and

577

their conversation, if there was any, was confined to trivialities.

She watched him drawing maps sometimes, squinting through the portable sextant she already hated. And there were times when he reined his horse up beside her, pointing out this or that, explaining how the place named Painted Spring had gotten its name, for instance, or the methods the Indians used to break wild horses.

At such times, with the sun warm against her shoulders and his eyes on her, she would tell herself that it was all in her imagination, that there was nothing the matter. But then she would spend half a night waiting for him, and when he finally came, dropping silently down on his makeshift bed, he seemed content with his own company. And all the uncertainties in her mind would rise up again like a million gnats, torturing her with unanswered questions.

They reached the Brazos River at last, finding a country very different from the grasslands that afforded no sustenance. Here there were elk and deer and buffalo, as well as timber for cooking and building: elm, pecan, stunted oaks, and blackjack. And the rich grass and numerous streams of the bottomlands attracted not only the game they needed for food but the wild horses as well.

A site for the camp was selected on the banks of a small tributary of the Brazos—the Rio Blanco, which formed a kind of fork with the Brazos itself on one of the maps that Dominic had drawn up. They built a timbered fort here, only partially roofed, and enormous horse corrals for the mustangs they would capture. And while the building was in progress, the women erected tepees, so that theirs looked almost like an Indian camp, if seen from a distance.

All this activity took considerable time and effort—an excuse for him to plead tiredness at night?—Marisa had begun to wonder bitterly. And one night, when the position of the stars told her it was very late, she rose deliberately and went to look for him.

He was sitting by the solitary fire that still burned, his head bent, copying some of his maps. In spite of the quietness of her approach on bare feet, he sensed her presence and looked up, frowning.

"If that's what keeps you up so late every night, why didn't you ask me to help? I have always been good at drawing?" She came and knelt by him giving him no chance to avoid her this time.

"And have you aid and abet me in spying against your own people?" His voice was sarcastic. "Go back to bed, Marisa."

"I'm not a child to be ordered about! Why must you make copies of your maps?"

"Why must you persist in asking me questions?" He sighed and sat back, stretching his legs. "Christ, what time is it? We start the hunting tomorrow."

"Do you? But then, I'm not a tame mare, to be fobbed off by a sugar cube. *Why*, Dominic?"

Suddenly, he leaned forward, lifting her hair from the back of her neck to imprint a light kiss there. "There are some things you're better off not knowing." His voice sounded muffled. "Marisa, I'm not used to answering to anyone. I've always done what I felt I had to do."

She shivered under the touch of his lips, but her back remained obstinately stiff. "I'm well aware of *that!*" she answered him bitterly. "But have you thought that I might feel the same way, too?"

He lifted his head to look at her, his hands still in her hair, and she rushed on recklessly, "I won't ask you any more questions, if you don't want me to. But there's no reason . . . Whatever you're doing, let me help you!"

"Copying forbidden maps of Spanish territory?"

"I don't care!"

"Traitress!" he said, but his voice was gentle, and this time he put his kiss against her half-open mouth, stilling whatever else she was about to say.

He put his maps away and carried her off to her rumpled blankets, but to her frustration, he had still told her nothing. And did not, even in the days that followed, while she almost bit her tongue in the effort to keep silent.

In any case, Dominic had no more time to spend mapping; he and the rest of the men were all busy trapping wild horses. They would "cut out" a certain herd, or part of it, and follow it, riding in relays of about ten men at a time, keeping the animals moving constantly until they were weak and half-crazy with the need for sleep and food and water. And in this state the horses were easily driven into the huge pens they had erected against the river banks where they were kept to be lassoed and "choked-down"—broken in slow, cruel stages to the feel of a hackamore or bridle and then a saddle.

It all took time, and, God, she should have been glad of more time! But Dominic was always busy now and too tired during the nights he was with her to do anything more than fall into an exhausted sleep. And she could not stand to see how the free, wild creatures were tamed into servitude. So she spent much of this time alone or talking to Lalie, who felt the same way as she did.

Lalie had become her friend and confidante and advisor, and it came as a shock one morning when Lalie told her, tears streaming down her face, that she and Paulus would be leaving them.

"It's our chance to be free and to own some land of our own. You understand, don't you? It's about ten acres of land, not too far from Nacogdoches, and a house, too, that some Spanish man ran away from because the Comanche Indians kept raiding his place. But they took kind of a shine to Paulus, you know, and he smoked their pipe with them, so they'll let us stay there. And now we got papers that say we're Spanish citizens—"

How? Marisa looked into Lalie's face and guessed, without having to be told. Dominic. Those four whole days he had been away riding after a herd of mustangs, he said. He had friends in Nacogdoches from other times—he had confided that much in her, at least. But if he had traveled as far as Nacogdoches, why had he taken the risk, and why hadn't he told her? She couldn't spoil Lalie's happiness by showing any signs of the turmoil that raged inside her. And so she hugged her friend and forced a smile as she wished her well. And hated Dominic all over again, mentally swearing at him.

The hate she had tried to build up slipped away into weakness when she faced him again. The white scar stood out on his face against his sun-browned skin and the beard he had grown again. And he looked so tired, as if he'd ridden for days and nights without sleep. No matter what he did or had done, she loved him. And at least he continued to keep her with him; she didn't care about anything as long as he did.

If he had expected a burst of fireworks from her, she disappointed him.

"Why didn't you tell me?"

"I couldn't be certain it would work out. I'd made Paulus a promise a long time ago, and he was the first one I told."

"But you took a crazy, irresponsible risk, going to Nacogdoches!"

"This beard makes me look different." He had the effrontery to grin at her. "And I do have friends there. I couldn't tell you because I didn't want to disappoint anybody in case things didn't turn out the way I hoped they would."

"Will it really be all right for them? Will they be safe?"

"As safe as anyone can be in this part of the country. But Paulus knows the risks, and he was willing to take them."

"And me—are you giving me the same choice?"

This time she wouldn't let him evade her, and this time at least, he didn't try, putting his fingers under her chin to tilt her face up to his.

"You're risking enough being here with me. Do you want to go back to safety?"

Wordlessly, she shook her head, and wordlessly, he possessed her mouth, stopping all her questions with the answer his body gave her.

It was enough, for that particular night. But there was the next night and the one after that, and the long, hot days in between when Marisa began to feel she was cut off from human communication and missed Lalie who had always been there when she needed someone to talk to.

She was living in a sun-scorched, time-stilled vacuum. The captain's woman, to whom he came on the nights when he wasn't busy chasing horses or making maps. And yet, it was by her choice that she remained here—or was it? Had he really been offering her an alternative or merely testing her reaction? She couldn't bear to leave him, yet could hardly bear the pain of staying with him, knowing the impermanence of their relationship. She felt herself growing soured and bitter; and sometimes, when the ripples shattered her reflection in the stream where she went to bathe, she thought she saw her image in the future—gaunt-cheeked and hollow-eyed, like the Spanish woman who had been the Comanche chief's third wife.

Held captive by a memory. How many more weeks had she left? They had over three hundred wild horses in the pens by now, and the men spent most of their time break-ing them. Just as she had been broken and gentled without her realizing it. Now she was a willing prisoner, loving her jailer. When would he turn executioner and let the axe fall, severing them forever?

Already the men had started to talk jubilantly about going home, and were planning what they would do with the money they would earn. The woman they had brought along were only borrowed or cheaply bought—soon to be forgot-ten once they had safely crossed the border of the United States.

"Know what I'm going to do? Buy me the biggest damn jug of whisky there is!"

"Me, I'm going to buy me some land and build the house my old woman said I'd never build."

"I'm goin' to have me a turn at all the fancy women I can find and keep one for my own in her own little apartment in New Orleans. Hey, Trudeau, what about you?"

Sitting back in the shadows, wrapped up in her own thoughts, Marisa thought she felt the man's eyes brush over her half-bare shoulders.

"Me? Why, I guess I'll do the same. Find me a woman. Only she won't be any fancy woman. Going to get me a piece of land in the place they used to call Acadia. And find the kind of woman who'll help me build a house and raise kids and be happy doing just that."

Inevitably, the question came. "What *you* going to do, captain? You got plans, too, like the rest of us?" It was Tru-deau who asked it. *Why?* So that she would be sure to hear his answer?

But Dominic was noncommittal, shoulders shrugging. "I'm going to spend whatever money I make. That's what money's for, isn't it?"

Soon after that, he rose and left the firelit circle and the talk of places and people. They all had something to return to—only *she* did not. And yet, even while she despised herself for it, Marisa followed him. If he expected questions from her, he wasn't going to get them. Let him remember her, at least, as still being possessed of some pride and spirit.

They walked together and yet apart, not touching, in the star-flecked darkness that lay beyond the man-made light of the fires. And here, close to the river where the huge horse pens had been built, she could hear the ceaseless, restless motions and protesting sounds of the captive wild horses. The poor creatures! How much worse captivity must be to those who had been free all of their lives!

They walked away from the corrals and along the riverbank, and the men who were appointed to stand guard called out low-voiced greetings. Soon they were away from even the distant glow of their campfires; and there was only the starlight and the patches of inky blackness under the trees and the scuttling noises as shy wild animals, scenting their approach, ran away. Dominic walked fast; or perhaps she only thought so because his long strides covered almost twice the distance that hers did. And yet, when she stumbled over a root once, he stopped in mid-stride, his hand shooting out to steady her.

Marisa felt the hard grip of his fingers just under her elbow; and over the sound of her own quick breathing she became aware of another sound, a soft, high sighing that was almost like singing.

"The wind's come up. That's all you're hearing. It makes that sound sometimes, through the rigging of a ship or when it comes driving up through the long prairie grass and ends up quarreling with the trees that won't bend before it."

It was seldom that the Irish part of him surfaced, but she could hear it now in his voice, and she remembered vaguely that someone—she couldn't recall who—had told her once, "All the Irish have a blackness in their souls—a mixture of fierceness and sadness and stubbornness. . . ." Had it been Dominic himself?

They were both still now, listening to the night sounds; and after a while, as if he couldn't help himself, he turned and drew her into his arms. In the darkness his lips moved over her face, closing her eyes gently before they sought her mouth and, finding it, captured it with kisses that were as wild and all-consuming as the wind itself.

He had not meant to touch her, much less to lose his senses in kissing her; he sensed the new, total response in her that still surprised him when he remembered how things had been between them. He had left the fires and the talk for many of the same reasons she had herself, but he had not expected her to follow him, nor to keep up with him silently. He had told himself earlier that they would have to do some serious talking. He would have to make her see things in their proper perspective. He would warn her. . . .

But now with her lips parting softly under his, all the warning signals his mind put up were directed against him and his own emotions. When he held her in his arms, he did not want to let her go. And yet, they had both known at the outset that she was to be returned to her uncle's care while *he* would go back to building a future for himself. It wasn't as if either of them were inexperienced; after all they had always contrived to do very well during the times they had been apart and on their own. And for too long now, he had never permitted himself to get too close to another human being, particularly a woman.

He should never have let himself feel sorry for her in the first place. And in the second, having been burned once, he should have never allowed himself to get involved with her again. Marisa, too, would be better off without *him*—these were some of the things he had meant to make her realize. But when she pressed herself even closer to him in a completely abandoned fashion, her lashes lying like dark butterfly wings against the pale gold curve of her cheek, how could he think of anything else but taking her and possessing her and feeling that she was his for one more time, one more night, one more day. . . .

As it turned out, there were no more days, and very little time, although neither of them knew it then.

The Comanches—a small raiding party returning from a foray across the Rio Grande and all the way into Mexico—came before dawn, in the light of a late-rising half-moon. There were, Marisa noticed, about twenty warriors—at least three of whom she recognized. Two of the men, who had young, recently married wives, had brought their women along; and there was also an unmarried, wild-spirited Comanche girl who had ridden along with them to follow the young man of her choice. For the rest, there was the usual miserable, motley collection of captives, five of them women who looked half-dead from shock, misuse, and exhaustion.

It was all Marisa could do not to run to them and offer them some kind of comfort—food, water, even kind words. But she was kept from it both by Dominic's harsh, snapped-out warning and her own hardly gained self-control. There was nothing she could do that would not make matters worse than they were for those poor creatures.

"What will happen to them?" she asked the Comanche woman who had made her leggings for her. The woman, who had learned some Spanish at a mission school, shrugged her plump shoulders.

"Who know? Maybe they stay captive. Maybe, if lucky, some warrior take for second or third wife. Some captives, they trade back to their people—the black-robes or the soldiers of the presidios." The woman gave a malicious, gap-toothed grin. "They rape first, many times! Sometimes beat up plenty, to make the Spanish pay more."

Marisa felt sick, her stomach knotting with revulsion. But she persisted, perhaps to keep her eyes from wandering back to the women and silent, terrified children.

"The little ones, the children. What will they do with them?"

"Only bring the strong ones—boy children. If they truly strong and learn fast, they lucky. Become adopted, maybe grow up to be warriors, too. Nermenuh!" This last, she had learned was the name the Comanches gave to themselves. It meant "the People."

So the children, if they survived, would be the luckiest. Children forgot quickly. No doubt in a few years they would become just as cruel and bloodthirsty as their captors; they would forget their real birth and background and think of themselves only as Comanches.

And Dominic. Had *he?* . . . He had lived with the Comanches, and he was familiar with Indian customs. As a boy, he had been adopted into one of the mighty Iroquois tribes. "A savage," that old woman in Cornwall had called him. Was he still so very far removed from that? Her eyes looked for him instinctively and found him, his bearded profile turned away from her as he engaged in earnest conversation with the Comanche war chief who had led the little band. She noticed that Trudeau, sitting beside him, wore an unusually sour expression. Occasionally he interrupted, using sign language. And they had gone back to drawing their eternal maps in the dirt.

"What? . . ."

The Comanche woman shrugged, but her eyes had gone opaque.

"Too far away to hear man-talk. But it look like maybe we move soon. I see sign language that mean Spanish soldiers. And now, I think, big argument begin. See? With our men. Nermenuh, they don't care."

Leaving Trudeau conversing in sign language with two of the younger Comanche warriors and translating the signs in an angry, low voice to the men of the camp who crowded around him, Dominic and the arrogant-looking war chief with his frightening buffalo-horned headdress had risen and walked apart from the others, still talking.

The woman shot Marisa a strange, speculative look. "When two chiefs talk, they make bargain. Maybe for horses."

It was only some hours later that Marisa learned the bargaining had been over *her.*

PART FIVE

∾∾

The Anger and the Passion

Chapter Fifty-four

He tried to explain it to her, but she was past the point where words helped or explanations held any meaning. For all the dispassionate tone he used at first when he tried to make her see "reason," her stubbornness and her fury incited him into an answering rage until Marisa thought her shoulders would break under the hardness of his grip.

"For God's sake! Don't you understand what I've been telling you? There's a large and heavily armed Spanish force marching in this direction. Whether we stay to fight them or run, I don't want you around cluttering up things."

"You said you brought me along as a hostage. What about that? If they're Spanish—"

"Do you think they'll stop to ask who you are if it comes to shooting? There's always a chance they wouldn't give a damn." His voice became brutal. "I thought I needed you, but we have our horses now, and I can't take you back with me where I'm going. Whichever way we decide, you'd only be in the way now. I'll only be doing ahead of time what I intended to do in the first place. Return you to your people. Why don't you use your head and realize you're going to be better off this way?"

Her shoulders hurt, and her head hurt. Every breath she drew seemed to rasp through her lungs with a separate agony.

"I'd be better off as an Indian captive? As a—slave again? Is that why you brought me here, to make sure I suffered more?"

"You know damn well that's not why." His voice roughened, slashing at her like a dull-edged blade, exacting every bitter second of extra torment. "But you knew, too, what would happen in the end. I tried not to lie to you, menina."

589

How dare he call her by the name that recalled far too much of the past? His eyes were like silver daggers cutting out her heart until she could almost have screamed out aloud.

Her voice, when it finally emerged from her aching, contracting throat, was no more than a whisper.

"You tried—I remember that—once before. What was the message you sent me then? 'The game is over.' Isn't that right? You played it well, Dominic. But then, you always did. I—why didn't you just—send me away at the very beginning? Why did you have to pretend—"

"Marisa!" She imagined for one suspended instant that he was about to take her into his arms. Had it been real, that note of torment she thought she heard in his voice when he cried out her name, or only something she thought she heard because she wanted to?

Dominic had more experience at hiding his feelings than she had; and his hands suddenly dropped from her arms so that the two of them were facing each other with nothing but space between them. He put her own secret, frightened thoughts into words when he said harshly, "There's no point in going back to the past—not for either of us. And since you won't listen to reason, I'm going to have to tell you how things are going to be. If we're going to make a stand here and fight—or make a run for it—you're a distraction I can't afford. Do you understand?"

"No!" She flung the word back at him, and then, not wanting to look at him any longer or meet the cold, closed look that had dropped over his face like a mask, she turned and tried to escape him.

But his hand caught her, spinning her around.

"Not yet. There's more I have to tell you, whether you like it or not!"

"I don't want to hear any more excuses! I'm in your way. You've —*sold* me—"

"I haven't sold you. Damn you for not listening! But you'll be sold back to the Spaniards. You might as well resign yourself to that."

"*Resign* myself! . . ."

"It won't be the first time, will it?" The studied cruelty of his words made her gasp; and then, dealing her shock

upon shock, he continued in the same measured voice,
"There's only one little problem. A tradition among the
Comanche tribe is that they never return a female captive
who has not been raped first by a member of their tribe."

The pupils of her eyes seemed to enlarge. Hardly believing what she had heard him say and not wanting to believe
what she read in his face, Marisa shook her head silently.

"No!" Had she breathed the word or only thought it?
She did not want to listen to any more. This was not reason
but lunacy—another bad dream, to cap all the others.

"They use this to taunt the Spaniards with. Marisa, I have
no more time left to explain. But I have spoken to Standing
Antelope who is a powerful war chief and will be a powerful
protector. Once it is done, you will be safe among them.
You will not be touched or hurt again—he's given me his
word. You'll be a captive in name only. He has promised to
take you into his lodge and treat you as a guest or as one of
his daughters until the time comes. He'll take you to San
Antonio—you have friends there, don't you? People who
know you—"

She tugged her arm from his grasp and stumbled backward, feeling the rising wind blow her hair against her face,
stinging her eyes.

"Do I know *you*? Did I ever? You're giving me to a chief
named Standing Antelope who will rape me first and then
treat me as a daughter. Wouldn't it be simpler all around if
you just killed me instead? I think I would prefer it—or shall
I make it easier for you and do it myself?"

She made a sudden wild dive for the knife he always
carried at his belt, but he captured her wrists before she got
close and held her as a squirming, sobbing prisoner.

"You don't understand." His voice was taut and as
strained as her own nerves. "I was adopted into this particular Comanche band some years ago. Do you think I want
anyone else to have you? If anyone hurts you, it's going to
be me."

Her mind flew back to another time—a voice with an Irish
lilt taunting her contemptuously before he took her, stamp-
ing her thigh with his seal first.

"Don't!" Her own scream seemed to pierce her eardrums,

echoing and echoing in her mind. And a hawk screeched overhead, wings outspread against the sky.

"Dominic—please! Not like this. Not like this!"

She felt and heard her clothing rip; and she was aware of the murmur of voices—and of eyes watching. Her first impulse, when he had carried her here into the Comanche camp, set a short distance from their own, had been to lie still pretending she was dead already and couldn't know what was happening to her.

But then he struck her across the face, forcing her back to awareness.

"Fight me—or is this the way you always react to rape?"

After that she used her nails and her knees and her teeth. But all the while she had the timeless feeling that all this had happened before and was happening again because it was meant to.

He struck her again, muttering, "You wildcat! How many men will it take to tame you?" And finally, when she had become exhausted by her own struggles, like one of the wild horses they broke, he mounted her, his hands holding her arms spread out and immobilized and his mouth choking off her screams of anger and humiliation.

His forcible entry into her body brought her nothing but pain. Dry and unprepared, she might almost have been a virgin again, and if she didn't bleed, he hurt her just as much as he had that first time.

It was over quickly—once he had her positioned and pinioned. Marisa's head was spinning, and her limbs felt like lead.

"If anyone hurts you, it's going to be me," he had said. And although he'd done precisely as he'd threatened, afterwards he wrapped her half-nude, trembling body in the shirt he had been wearing. If the whole Comanche tribe had raped her next, she would not have been capable of protesting or caring.

But nothing like that happened. The Comanche women, notoriously cruel to captives, stared at her a trifle curiously at first but seemed to accept her as one of themselves, especially after she had dressed herself in the beautifully ornamented buckskin garments that had been presented to her only a few weeks ago. No, she could tell herself bitterly a few hours later, "tolerated" would perhaps be a better word to describe her rather ambiguous positon among them. A captive-guest, a temporary "daughter," until it became time for bargaining. But she had horses of her own, which gave her some position among the Nermenuh, who prized horses over their women. Her bride-price, if she had been a Comanche woman herself. Beautiful animals. And the one she rode was a brown-gold stallion, a mount she knew Dominic had tamed and gentled for his own. But Oro was hers now—he who had been wild and running free across the prairies and ruling his own timid mares only two months ago.

What did it mean? Did she want to think? It was easier to accept her fate and try to make the best of it as she had done so many times before. For all intents and purposes, she was Standing Antelope's woman now. Since he had not brought his own wife with him, she would prepare his meals and skin and cure any game he took along the way. What she did not know already, the other women would teach her. Wasn't it time she bowed down to fate instead of trying to circumvent it? She should never have begun to hope. . . .

"I don't need you any longer—you'd only be in the way—why don't you use your head and realize you'll be better off back with your own people?"

Each remembered word was like a hammer blow in her head. If only she could strike out every other memory! But it was impossible, no matter how tired she became. Had it only been her imagination or had he really whispered, just before the horror had finally ended:

"Oh, love—I meant not to hurt you again. . . ."

His voice had seemed to hold as much torment as her own mind and body did. But had he really said that? Why, oh God, why, so suddenly, when she hadn't had time to become prepared?

She had time now. Time enough, as the days and nights seemed to slide by her and she wasn't being kept busy, to think back and divide her life into so many segments. The postulant, the gypsy, the unwilling bride, the butterfly. . . .

but what did it all matter in the end? All along, she had been a prisoner of fate—or *kismet* as the Moslems had called it. Did that mean that her future was already preset and predecided? Thinking that, how could she bear to go on living? With nothing. No hope, no . . .

Standing Antelope knew a smattering of Spanish, and she had learned some sign language. She cornered him at a moment when he had entered his hastily erected tepee to get some sleep. Her continuing stubbornness at first angered him, and then, when she wouldn't flinch from his clenched, raised fist, she confused him. He was not used to women who acted like this one; at times she was meek and mild and obedient, and he almost regretted having given his word that she would be returned to the Spanish, for she would make a good wife for him, thinking secretly of persuading her to stay with the People as one of his wives, and then suddenly, she turned into a shrew.

She questioned—she dared to *demand* answers! And yet she was clever enough to weep, also, and to promise that she would not be any more trouble once she had been told the truth.

Truly, this was a woman with *puha*—magic—standing Antelope reflected ruefully. Already, her Comanche name was "Woman of the White Buffalo"; and since there were no other witnesses when she began to nag and question him, he gave her the answers that she sought and hoped that she would settle down afterwards.

Half in sign language and half in Spanish, he told her grudgingly of the reasons why he had allowed his small war party to be saddled with her. Being what he was, he boasted first, relating his brave exploits and their success. She appeared properly impressed; and so he did not feel his manhood threatened by telling her the rest.

The Spanish did not dare risk offending the Nermenuh —the People. That was why they were able to go boldly up to the presidios to trade furs and captives. But on this occasion the Spaniards who flattered themselves by calling themselves masters of this land had been unduly agitated by rumors of trespassing Americanos who were spies and the forefront of a threatened invasion. They had picked up this information from an Americano trader in Nacogdoches and from rumors they had heard from contacts in Louisiana. Nevertheless, they had been warned. And their soldiers were even now converging on the fork of the Brazos River and the Rio Blanco.

Danger? He looked at her with disdainful surprise. Of course, there was always danger, making life eventful and giving warriors a chance to prove themselves. But, he said boastfully, *she* was safe enough! But women were distracting when it came to a fight. It was for that reason that he, Standing Antelope, left his wives behind when he went raiding across the border.

So now she had some of her answers at least. What good did they do her? Dominic had sent her away from him. To safety—or oblivion? Which was it?

"I don't need you any longer. . . ."

But before he said that, he had tried to explain, and she hadn't wanted to listen. '*He's* the one who's in danger,' Marisa's mind told her when she was capable of intelligent thought again. She remembered her forebodings, her angry, warning words to him that had been snatched away by the hot wind of desire springing up when he put his hands on her. Now, seen in a different prespective, her mind made the rediscovery that he hadn't been entirely indifferent to her after all. Had she been deliberately blind or only frightened to admit the truth? During the past few weeks they had gone beyond mere desire and wanting. They had laughed together and talked together, watching the ageless stars fall from sight overhead to be replaced by the rising sun. There had been times when they had both been content merely to *sleep* together, not needing any more at the moment but the warmth of each other's bodies. Why had she forgotten that part of their newly burgeoning relationship? Why had he tried to make her forget?

Marisa asked Standing Antelope, "What do you think they will do?" And he shrugged his powerful, muscular shoulders. It was clear that he eyed her doubtfully now, unsure of her reactions.

"They will hold a council to decide. There are the horses, and the many moons that must have passed while they first captured and then tamed them. The horses *you* were given were among the best. *I* would not give up the fruit of my sweat and my efforts to run away like a woman."

"But if they stay?" she persisted, torturing herself with her own questions, and the Indian gave her a look that mingled surprise and contempt.

"Do you know nothing of men? If they stay they will fight to defend what they have gained. They have weapons and ammunition, and the Spanish are not that many."

'Not that many. . . .' And they would be prepared, thank God! But why had Dominic wanted her out of the way? Why didn't they take the horses they already had and head back across the border? Why did there continue to be such a sense of fear and foreboding in her mind, like a leaden weight she carried with her constantly?

'I hate him for sending me away and for the manner of it. But at least I know now why he did.'

Her thoughts brought her no comfort and the days of traveling no respite. Marisa lost count even of time which the Comanches counted by the changing of the moon. Her mind, like an hourglass, merely registered its passing.

There was the time after they arrived at the Comanche camp, the time spent hunting buffalo again, and finally, the journey back. Back to what she did not know—nor care by now. Whatever happened, let it be over with quickly!

The Comanches usually did their trading further to the west, in Santa Fe or Taos. But when they approached San Antonio, the strongest mission fortress in the Southwest, straddling El Camino Real—the King's Highway—the Spaniards came out to greet the horse-barbarians for whom they had gained such a grudging respect.

With the winter coming on, they would willingly trade for buffalo hides. But captives? Poor, unfortunate Indian peasants from Mexico? They might excite the pity of the priests, but after all. . . .

Standing Antelope was good at bargaining. He only threw out hints at first, to excite the curiosity of the Spaniards. He would consider the price offered for their buffalo hides. And the captives. If the Spaniards did not care for the fate of their own people, they could be sold into slavery elsewhere. Yes, even the niece of one of the most powerful of the black-robes, a woman who had hair like the gold the Spaniards sought so avidly.

An old mission Indian acted as translator, and as Standing Antelope began to stalk away arrogantly, he called him back.

"This female captive you mentioned—they would like to see her. How did you come by her?"

"An Americano traded her to me. But she's too willful to make a good Comanche squaw. However, if you don't want her, we could sell her elsewhere. Women can be broken as easily as horses—"

"Wait a moment! The capitan would like to see this female of whom you speak."

When they brought her forward, Standing Antelope twisted his fingers in her tangled gold hair, drawing her head back so that the Spaniards could see her face clearly. Marisa's glazed, golden eyes were suddenly staring into a face she recognized; and it was clear from his startled, shocked expression that Capitan Higuera remembered her, too.

"Dios mio!" He swore under his breath and then made a gallant effort to control himself. "How did this happen? Señora, are you . . ." His words dragged to a stumbling halt as he took in her bedraggled, sunburned appearance, remembering, Marisa supposed with the part of her mind that was still functioning, all the tales he had heard about the Comanches and the manner in which they treated their women captives.

While the bargaining went on, Marisa had time to feel sorry for the poor young man so obviously taken aback and at a disadvantage.

Standing Antelope got a good price for her and for the rest of the miserable captives he had brought along. But surprisingly, when he released her, he let her keep the golden stallion Dominic had named Oro.

Chapter Fifty-five

On this occasion, the quiet retreat of the Carmelite nunnery brought Marisa no peace at all. She had grown too independent, and the good nuns could not control her. Moreover, to their barely hidden dismay, she displayed no signs of shock or fearfulness or shrinking; in fact, she had none of the symptoms that a young woman in her position, who had been through what she must have had to endure, would be expected to feel.

She insisted on being allowed to ride her horse—and astride at that. And Capitan Higuera was forced to assign some of his men to ride with her when he could not do so himself. And to the further unhappiness of the unworldly sisters in whose charge she nominally was, she *would* speak to the awkwardly placed young captain alone and unchaperoned.

Her uncle, the monsignor, was in Mexico City. Although word had been sent to him at once, who could tell how long it would take to reach him or how long it would take him to get here after that? In the meantime, there was no controlling the young woman who had changed so much since her last sojourn here.

But if the good prioress felt at her wits end, so did Marisa herself who had also to cope with the knowledge that Capitan Higuera had fallen in love with her. The poor young man! He saw her as a tragic figure—a kind of martyr—and not as she really was. But having learned at last about loving and the hurt it could too easily inflict, Marisa made sure he suffered from no illusions that she might ever return his regard. All the same, he was someone to talk to; and, because of his position, he would know if—if. . . .

There were times she almost had to bite her tongue to

keep from asking the frightening questions that filled her
mind. "A large force of heavily armed Spanish soldiers headed
this way. . . ." Had it been true or only an excuse to be rid
of her? But if it had been true, she could not give away
their position. The capitan had questioned her and the nuns
had urged her to confess, but through it all she had continued to shake her head stubbornly, pretending that the hor-
rors she had undergone had made her lose her memory.
She had been traded to the Indians by some men who had
abducted her. On purpose, the only name she said she could
remember was John Murrell. Anything else she did not want
to think of. After a time they left her alone, the nuns hoping prayerfully that her uncle would arrive soon to take his
wayward niece off their hands.

What had happened back there at the camp on the Rio
Blanco?

The question haunted all her hours, waking and sleeping.
Once, waking up drenched in sweat from a particularly ugly
nightmare, Marisa found her way, stumbling, to the small
chapel where she tried to pray. 'If he's alive—oh, God, only
keep him alive, and I won't care even if he has to go back
to Jane Byron. I won't ask anything for myself.' But she was
trying to bargain and realized it, and after a while, with the
silence in chapel growing oppressive, and without finding
any of the answers she sought, Marisa went back to her small,
uncomfortable pallet in the cell which had been allotted to
her.

"You have circles under your eyes as if you do not sleep
well," Fernando Higuera commented diffidently the next
day when they were out riding. "If you are not comfortable,
if there is anything you need—"

She made an effort at cheerfulness, her hand stroking her
restive stallion's arched neck.

"I'm used to worse discomfort, truly!" And then, catching
his look, she went on swiftly, "But why talk about me? You
never speak about yourself. I'm sure you must lead a very
exciting life here on the frontier. What with the Indians and
other perils! I remember hearing, when I was in Louisiana,
that the Americanos have their eyes on this part of the world
as well, now that they have gained so much. Is that true?

What with all these rumors of impending revolution in Mexico itself—it must be very dangerous, the life of a soldier!"

She despised herself, especially when he rose to the bait, his shoulders straightening.

"Oh, it's dangerous all right, but *you* have nothing to fear here, believe me! And as for all the rumors—I sincerely believe that's all they are! Merely some peasants and Indios protesting. They don't know when they're well off!"

"And you don't think we're in danger of an invasion, either?"

"Invasion? Bah! The Americanos are too busy quarreling among themselves, I understand. Occasionally there are some of them who venture too far into our territory looking for personal gain—furs, wild horses. We call them filibusteros, and believe me, we don't tolerate their presence here for too long! We try to make an example of them, to discourage others who might follow. Why, only a month and a half ago—" He broke off, leaning forward solicitously. "Is there something wrong? You should not stay out under this sun for too long; it can give you a fever. Perhaps we should turn back now."

Her hands shook and her knees shook, and it was all she could do to control her restive mount who was longing for a gallop.

"No! That is—I'm all right of course. And I'm used to the sun. Please go on. I was fascinated by what you were saying."

He flushed, both with flattery and embarrassment.

"I didn't mean to make you nervous. I only wanted to explain that we *are* alert at all times. Fortunately, we have our informants on both sides of the border who warn us—"

Why wouldn't he get to the point? Clenching her teeth, Marisa nevertheless managed to force a smile. "You must know by now that I don't become nervous easily! But you were saying that just a month and a half ago? . . ."

"Oh, it was nothing important. Just an example I meant to give you of our vigilance. A group of Americano adventurers —thieves or spies—thought to evade us! But our soldiers caught up with them in the end; although some of them escaped with the horses they had captured, the others, who tried to fight us off were taken. They surrendered, I understand, after their leader's death." The veneer of civilization falling away, Higuera grinned savagely. "Colonel Arteaga, who personally commanded our troops, had his head cut off and sent back to Natchitoches, as an example to others. The rest of them will be either imprisoned for life or executed —one in each town along the way. As a matter of fact. . . ."

Marisa did not hear what else he started to say for her horse bolted, feeling, perhaps, the sudden looseness of the reins she always held so firmly or perhaps sensing some of the emotions of shock and turmoil that suddenly churned within her. For some moments, she just let the stallion carry her, not caring if she were thrown and ended up with a broken neck.

'No—no, no! Someone else. He's speaking of someone else—'

Wind against her face, sand stinging her wet cheeks, she remembered how the Comanche squaws mutilated themselves, chopping off their hair and gashing themselves with knives when they heard of the death of a husband, father, or brother. Dominic was none of those things to her—or all of them? He couldn't be dead—it was a mistake!

"Colonel Arteaga, who personally commanded our troops. . . ." Pedro, filled with hate and resentment. She would kill him if it was the last thing she did. Kill him—kill him!

Somehow, Oro had slowed into a trot after his wild gallop. Poor animal, had he thought to find freedom again? She had lost her reins and was clinging to his mane, her tears mingling with the sweat that streamed off his quivering golden hide. Oro—the golden one. "I'm going to name him after you, menina," Dominic had teased her. "You're both wild and frightened, but I think he's going to be easier to tame than you are!"

He was *not* dead! And with all the darkness of her passionate Spanish blood, Marisa whispered over and over again, her face buried against the wild stallion's mane, "I'll kill him. I swear it for both of us, Oro. I'm going to kill him!"

She was still whispering it, over and over, when the frantic young captain caught up with her—his hat lost, his face pale.

Forgetting himself entirely, he called her by her name.

"Marisa! Dios, but I thought. . . . You are safe now—are you listening to me? And if you want this animal destroyed. . . ."

She raised fierce, tear-drenched eyes to his, causing him to draw back the hand he extended.

"Destroyed? Don't you dare touch my horse! It wasn't his fault; he's still half-wild, you see. Like—like me!"

"But I thought—" He didn't know what to think, seeing her state. "You were saying—"

"I don't know what I was saying! I was thinking of someone else." She drew in a long, shuddering breath and sat up straight. "I'm sorry to cause you so much trouble. Perhaps we should return now."

Her face was still streaked with dust and tears, but she made no attempt to wipe it. And Capitan Higuera did not know what to think.

He was even less capable of coherent thought when she knocked softly at the door of his hot, miserable little room late that night, gliding in past the eyes of the astonished man who opened it and ignoring the surprised, lascivious gaze of the soldiers outside.

Caught without his shirt, a flush rose under his sun-browned skin, and his first impulse was to slam the door shut as quickly as he could. God! Was he dreaming this? What was she doing here, compromising herself and him? But without volition his eyes were taking her in, from her bare feet and loose golden hair to the thin cotton skirt and even thinner blouse or *camisa* she wore—the coarse weave of the material making it plain she wore no shift underneath.

He was speechless as she quite calmly walked over to a small brazier he had lit for warmth. Holding her small, cold hands over it, she said over shoulder, "I hope you don't mind my coming here unnanounced? But you're the only friend I have, and I wanted to talk to you."

Snatching for his shirt, he was trying clumsily to slide his arms into the sleeves when she turned to face him.

"It's so warm in here—why do you bother? Do you think I have not seen a half-dressed man before?"

"I—you—you shouldn't talk like that! And it's not proper

603

that you should be here. I won't be able to stop my men
from gossiping."

"Do you think I'm afraid of gossip? Wherever I've been I've
been talked about." And then, dropping her eyes, "Do I
make you nervous? I had hoped not. You're the only person
I can talk to around here, you see. Please don't send me
away."

He groaned aloud, fingers stopping their fumbling with
shirt buttons.

"The devil take me! You don't know—you don't realize
what you are saying! Your uncle—the good sisters—"

"But my uncle is so far away! And the sisters are all in
their beds sleeping soundly, I think. I could not sleep." She
raised her head, looking back boldly into his eyes as she
whispered softly, "I am not used to sleeping alone."

He repeated in an agonized voice, "You don't know what
you are saying! I—why did you come here? I am not made
of steel, you know, and if I don't take you back quickly—"

"Back? Back to what? I am so lonely and that little room
cuts off my breath. I thought—I thought you might help me
to—to find him. You said his name today, and it was such a
shock! The man who deceived me and called me his *novia*
before he—let me be sold into slavery! If my uncle was
here, *he* would know what to do, *he* would help me. But
he is not, and I cannot tell the nuns what I have told you.
Help me find him, and I will do—whatever you want me
to." Her voice had dropped into a whisper, and having begun
to go to her, Fernando Higuera stopped in mid-stride, his
hands clenching and unclenching at his sides as he tried to
control his own feelings and his desire to take her in his
arms and crush her against his body. He tried to shut his
mind to the pictures that suddenly flamed his imagination.
Had the Indios had to force her? Had she been willing?
Why not take what she offered him freely?

"Madre de Dios!" he swore out loud. All this—for another
man! Colonel Arteaga. Now that he thought of it, he remembered that she had left San Antonio with the colonel
before. Remembered his feeling of regret. But what had
she meant by the rest of it? The colonel would not have . . .

She must have read his mind. "Don't you believe me? His

cousin, my stepmother, wanted the plantation my father left to me in Louisiana. Perhaps he didn't know exactly what she planned when she—tried to get rid of me. But I must know—and that's why I must find him! Please—say you'll help me?"

Like a man bemused or bewitched, he reached out and took her in his arms, smelling the freshly-washed fragrance of her hair and body.

"Perdición! You love him so much that you'd even do—this for him? Offer yourself to me?"

She leaned against him, allowing his fingers to slide under her blouse, caressing her back and breasts. He thought he heard her breath catch in her throat.

"I love him enough to dare anything." It was the barest whisper. A minute later he bent her head back under the force of his hungry, searching kisses.

What he did not know was that it was not of Pedro Arteaga she was speaking.

Chapter Fifty-six

They had drawn lots to see who would go and who would stay. Only Dominic and Trudeau stayed aloof from the drawing.

"We'll keep them off!" Trudeau had said jubilantly. "Man, we have enough guns and ammunition to stave off an army, and you know the Spaniards are ill-armed! We'll fight them off and then slip away after dark some night. And by that time the others will be safely across the border with the horses. Think I'm going to let myself be cheated of all the money we're going to make after all the time and effort we've put into this expedition?" He looked at Dominic, who was silent and grim-lipped. "What's the matter, mon ami? Are you still thinking about her? That was some exhibition you put on, I tell you! And she's the kind of woman a man cannot put out of his mind too easily, hein? Well, like you said, she's better off, and safer, where she is now. And you can always find her afterwards, eh?"

"Trudeau—shut up! Or I'll save the Spaniards the chance to kill you!"

"Oh, I do not think so, capitaine! You need me—oui? And besides, I promised the little one I'd look after you. She's something, eh? Wish I'd met a woman like her long ago instead of that bitch I made my wife!"

Not wanting to listen, Dominic walked away, going to stand at one of the slits they had left in the walls of their improvised fort for just such an eventuality.

He looked out and saw the dying sunlight reflected off water, turning it to gold. Marisa. Golden skin, golden eyes. Panther eyes, he had called her once during one of their many fights. Did she understand, even now, why he had

sent her away? Probably not—and for the best. *Her* best.
There had been too much unsaid between them—too much
to regret now that it was too late. Strange, how having her
and knowing her had managed to wipe away the memory of
every other woman he'd had until there was only her, his
wild gypsy wench, taken without thinking or planning,
embedding herself under his skin like a splinter that went
too deep to be gotten rid of. Why was he here, being fool-
ishly, hopelessly heroic, when he might just as well have
participated in the draw, trusting in his luck and his instinct
for survival? If there was nowhere else to go, he could have
gone back to becoming a Comanche again, with her as his
squaw. But he'd had to be noble. . . .

Thinking of her made him blind when he should have
been watchful. The first explosion of firing took them by
surprise, with all the shock of an earthquake.

"Jesus God! They've a cannon out there!"

"Bastards!"

From then on there was no more time for thinking. Dominic felt himself slammed back against the earthen floor, realizing with a surprised shock that he had taken a bullet in the
shoulder.

There was no pain yet, only the warm trickling of blood
as he stumbled back onto his feet.

There was a cessation of firing as the Spaniards who ringed
them called for surrender.

"We want your leader to come outside! Surrender and
you'll live. Don't, and we'll blow you all to bits!"

Negating the reasonableness of their offer, there was another burst of cannon fire blowing a hole in one side of their
log fort. Flying splinters cut Dominic's forehead, making the
blood trickle down into his eyes, half-blinding him.

"We ain't got a chance in hell!" Who'd said that? It didn't
matter because he had realized that for himself. No chance—
at least not against a couple of small cannon.

"The rest of you stay here and cover me. I'm going out
there." If the Spaniards were looking for blood, it was his.
Let them have it! His rifle was loaded, and when he went
out, blind or not, he would point it in the direction of that

voice he had heard and fire. And the hell with what happened next!

"Where the hell do you think you're going?"

Trudeau's voice sounded scratchy with fury.

"Get out of my way. And stop shooting. At least until I've gone out there."

"You're going to show those bastards the white flag?"

"You want to sit here and get blown to bits? Listen, if they have me, maybe they'll let the rest of you off with a warning."

"What you want to be, a bloody martyr? Son of a bitch—look at you, bleeding all over. Listen, I'm taking over as leader, you hear me, capitaine? Gave the little girl a promise—"

"Trudeau, get out of my way!"

He didn't see the pistol butt that came up to hit him, knocking him backward. With his last remaining shreds of consciousness, he heard Trudeau's voice from somewhere above him.

"If anyone is going to be a goddamn bloody hero, it's going to be me, you hear?"

And the last thing he remembered, before blackness engulfed him, was a volley of shots.

*   *   *   *   *

Don Pedro was enjoying himself. Ever since he had received the coded message from his old friend, General James Wilkinson, he had been preparing himself for just such a triumph—and revenge. Now—now at last! . . . He didn't care that all but a stubborn twelve of the American *filibusteros* had escaped taking their captured horses with them. What mattered was that he had the rest; and most important of all their leader, his old enemy.

"You're dead. At least as far as anyone in *your* country is concerned. A head, half-decomposed with the eyes pecked out by buzzards, is not easy to identify, is it? So your fiancée mourns for you and wears black, and the Americanos across the river mutter angrily and threaten revenge, but they will do nothing, as usual, because you were trespassing—you had no right to be here. And now, you do not exist—for *them*,

609

at least. Do you understand that? For them. But for you, it will take some time. You will die in the end, publicly executed as an example to others like yourself. But before then, you will suffer a lot. And you will write and sign a full confession."

His head ached. Hammer blows pounding against his temples. And his shoulder wound had begun to throb with worse agony.

"Do you understand! Do you understand? . . ."

The words came at him from all directions, it seemed, until he couldn't avoid them and had to open his eyes and his mind to what had happened and what was happening.

"I took pains to keep you alive—you are not going to die yet. And not as easily as you might have anticipated. The other man, your friend, died in your place."

Other man. Trudeau? Crazy, irresponsible Trudeau! Dominic tried to move and couldn't.

"Did you know that the Inquisition came this far? The holy friars were anxious to convert—and question. Unfortunately for them, their victims were mostly Indios who expected torture and remained stoic. But will *you*, I wonder?"

He didn't know where he was. Some presidio or some mission, where the instruments of the Spanish Inquisition were still carefully preserved. He was strapped to a wooden wheel, his ankles manacled to the floor, his arms stretched above his head.

"Another half turn," Pedro Arteaga ordered carelessly; and with the creaking sound came the unendurable sensation of his body being pulled apart, stretched beyond the limits of human endurance. His throat muscles knotted and convulsed as he tried to keep back the groan of agony that escaped nevertheless. There was a feeling of heat all over his skin as drops of blood erupted from torn, strained capillaries.

"A whole, complete confession. Written in your own hand and signed by you. A sentence of death—but isn't death better than this?"

"No!"

He hadn't realized he had that much breath left in his

body— the word seemed to force itself out in spite of himself.

"I had hoped you'd say that," Pedro Arteaga said softly. Turning his head painfully, Dominic saw the long-bladed knife that was turning red-hot in the coals of a brazier.

Arteaga held the knife hilt in his gloved hand, drawing the red-hot blade against Dominic's taut, shrinking skin very slowly. Over and over. In between there were the periods when he left the blade in the coals to grow red-hot again. And then he held it against the festering wound in Dominic's shoulder—to cauterize it, he murmured with mock concern.

It took less than fifteen minutes. Then, sick to his stomach and sick at himself, Dominic professed himself willing to sign anything. He was a survivor, not a martyr, he told himself bitterly. And what the hell difference did it make if he was going to die anyway? He had the impression that Pedro was disappointed and that Pedro didn't want to hear some of what he had to say.

"You bastard—you're lying!" Pedro shouted angrily. "Inez wouldn't . . . You took her off yourself because you wanted her! And then you sold her to the Comanches. I want you to write that down, too, exactly what you did with her!"

He did that, too; by now it didn't matter. By now Marisa would be safe with her uncle. Beyond that—he tried to detach his mind from his body, as he had done before, in the past.

Trudeau was dead in his place. Damn Trudeau for taking the easy way out! At least, he had died instantly and cleanly, while the rest of them. . . .

The rest of them weren't dead yet. And while they were all beaten and bloody and badly off, at least they still had some time left. Escape. Gritting his teeth against shock waves of pure agony that came every time he moved his body, Dominic fixed his mind on that thought.

They were manacled hand and foot and lying on the cold stone floor of what must have once been a storeroom of some kind.

Dominic heard a low, hoarse whisper and turned his head, even that much movement bringing him pain.

"Captain. Them bastards. . . . Think we got a chance?"

Ethan Stewart was the youngest of them all, a tall bright-eyed boy who always moved with a man's swagger. He was eighteen, barely that, and his voice shook slightly. "Why don't they shoot us an' get it over with? Think I could take that better than—"

"Hanging's just as final as shooting," Dominic said with deliberate bluntness. "But as long as you're alive there's always a chance at escape. It's going to be a long march to Saltillo, and they could get careless along the way. If you see your chance, take it." To himself, he asked, 'And run where? . . .'

After some days had passed, he had closed his mind to thought—concentrating only on putting one foot in front of the other.

"Keep walking, Americanos! You will soon know every inch of our country, eh? Isn't that what you came here for? March!" And march they did, not being given any choice. It was that or be dragged along in the wake of one of the baggage wagons. Their leg shackles were removed every morning and put back at night; the shackles on their wrists, with short lengths of chain connecting them, remained. Symbolically perhaps, for the Spanish were capable of grim humor, each of the prisoners was forced to wear a rope noose about his neck.

Mostly they were fed some kind of mush made from ground corn; occasionally they were given beans with perhaps a few bits of tough dried meat thrown in for extra flavor. And water was rationed. Herded and driven like cattle, they reacted like animals whenever they crossed a stream or a river—running for the water and immersing themselves in it, gasping and choking, until their captors, laughing, prodded them forward.

They were exhibited in the marketplace of every small village they passed through as if they had been strange wild beasts. Everywhere people crowded around to stare. The women, for the most part, were kinder than the men. Their eyes held pity, and occasionally one of them would slip past the soldiers to offer water or fresh fruit to the unfortunate Americanos who would have to die soon.

"Are you enjoying your walk down the El Camino Real?"
Pedro Arteaga laughed down from his horse. It was hard
to recall that they had once been friends, before a woman
and politics had come between them.

"Not especially. But that wasn't your intention, was it?"
Pedro's dark eyes locked with Dominic Challenger's gaze,
smoky and smoldering despite his pain and fatigue. He had
made him sign a confession, but the damned, arrogant bastard
wasn't broken yet. And this was the same man who had
tried to avoid becoming the lover of the queen of Spain, taking her because he had to and leaving her as if she had been
nothing more than a passing trollop who had flung herself
at him. And there was Marisa—what had really happened between them? Where had she ended up?

"It is my intention that you should suffer as much as you
possibly can before they hang you—and even that will be
very slow and painful, I assure you! It is time an example
was made of people like you. Spies—filibusteros! But before
then, you will have time to regret that you were not killed
before."

He'd had time to regret that already: feeling the red-hot
caress of a knife blade against his skin and smelling the
ghastly odor of burning flesh and blood; and still later, when
he had watched them hang the boy, Ethan Stewart, because
he had broken his ankle stepping in a pothole and could
not walk any longer. But he had seen worse and experienced
worse in Ireland. And in that jail cell in England and on His
Majesty's ships later, he had learned to count the minutes
and survive.

Saving his breath, feeling it burn in his lungs, Dominic
said nothing else. His feet bled and were blistered, but he
continued, doggedly, to walk. When did reason and thinking
drop away and mere survival, for as long as possible, become
uppermost? Keep walking—keep moving. His mind instructed him in that much at least; and Pedro Arteaga's gloat-
ing voice, continuing to attack his dulling senses from time to
time, had no more power to affect him.

"Señor Colonel! A message from San Antonio!"
There was a pause in the marching, while Pedro scowlingly
perused the dispatch that had been handed to him. He swore,

not quite under his breath. "Maledición! The governor has waked up, it seems. We are to take our prisoners and ourselves back to San Antonio for a formal trial, before we go on to Saltillo."

They had almost reached the Rio Grande and now turned back. The road to San Antonio was like another river, a river of dust and sand kicked up by the hoofs of the horses ridden by the Spanish soldiers and thrown back by the cumbersome wheels of their baggage wagons.

The most powerful mission-presidio in the southwest, San Antonio was already ancient—its brick and adobe buildings weathered to a mellow pinkish-brown by the sun and the ceaseless winds.

Through their grilled windows and from their balconies, the women peered to get a closer look at the Americano prisoners who would soon kneel in silence to receive their sentence of death.

The setting sun turned everything blood-red—the sky to the west, the buildings, and even the dusty streets themselves.

"If we don't get a good look today, we'll see them tomorrow, in the plaza. . . ."

Marisa stayed behind the wall of the convent, cynically aware that the nuns were praying for her and hoping she had changed. But if they knew! The soldiers did, although they only whispered among themselves. She was Capitan Higuera's woman and, of late, Governor Elguizabal's sometime mistress as well. At least their capitan was a young and virile man, but the governor was old, and with an ailing, complaining wife into the bargain. But who could blame him? Old or not, he was a man!

Marisa soaked in a copper half-bath of tepid water, her hair in damp curls pinned atop her head. And closed her mind to everything but her momentary comfort. She didn't want to see those poor, miserable prisoners. How many of them might she know—or would recognize *her*? Easier to fix her thoughts upon Pedro Arteaga—Colonel Arteaga—whom she would meet tonight at dinner in the governor's house. He wouldn't be forewarned; she was sure enough of her men to be certain of that much, at least. And *she* would pretend to know nothing. Fernando would glower angrily, no doubt; and the governor, being much older and wiser, would merely lift his shoulders and shrug. But she would flirt with Pedro —tease him—taunt him—lead him on. And then—then there was the little bone-handled knife she always carried with her. He would taste its kiss when he sought to taste hers. And then she would cut her own wrists—she had it all planned.

Kill! Oh, this was the darkest part of her blood, pushing her in the direction she had cold-bloodedly decided to take. Spanish-Moorish, Gypsy, African voodoo woman. If she had been an Aztec priestess, she would have watched his heart being cut out of his still-living body and thrown her head back in laughter!

Rising from the bath to dry herself, she was all pagan, a golden statue, perfectly formed. She did not need to see herself in a mirror, which in any case the nuns would not have allowed. She had seen herself mirrored in the eyes of too many men before.

"You are like Diana, the goddess of the hunt," Napoleon had whispered to her. And to Kamil she had been a boy-woman. Only Dominic, her hate-love, had taken her for what she was. Gypsy wench, cabin boy, woman—woman! To Fernando she was a dream that he could not quite believe even when he held her in his arms. To the governor, she was a memory of his virile youth and an illusion. But for Pedro Arteaga, once her novio, she would be death.

"Where are you going? It's late. You are surely not going out?" Sister Vera scolded ineffectually.

Marisa had worn a high-waisted white muslin gown cut shockingly low in front; and she carefully pinned up her hair so that it was caught up high at the crown of her head, to fall in artless curls about her face and neck.

"I've been invited to dinner with the governor. It would be rude to refuse."

"But my child—that gown! The way you look!"

"I shall be wearing a shawl. So. Do I look more respectable now?"

"Oh, I wish the monsignor would come!" Sister Vera

started wringing her hands helplessly. If Marisa had been an Indian peasant, she would have ordered her whipped for the good of her soul. But she was a high-born Spanish lady and an archbishop's niece. What could one do, except pray?

~~~~~~

Chapter Fifty-seven

~~~~~~

Pedro Arteaga, sitting slumped rather sullenly in his chair, a glass of wine held to his lips, suddenly went as stiff as a ramrod.

Madre de Dios—no! It couldn't be! But it was no mistake or illusion—not with the governor himself introducing her in his dry, old-fashioned, formal manner.

"La Doña Maria Antonia Catalina de Castellanos y Gallardo—although of course," he added with an unexpected return to humanity, "we all call her Doña Marisa."

Pedro found himself rising automatically, like every other man present. In spite of the simplicity of her dress and manners she carried with her the air of a princess.

He noticed that she inclined her head coldly in his direction—but she sat next to that imbecilic Capitan Higuera and smiled at him. What in hell was she doing here? How? . . .

The dinner party dragged on as formally as if they had been in Spain itself, and Pedro could hardly keep his seat. How? . . . Why? . . .

Fortunately, the thin-lipped woman seated beside him, a sister-in-law of the governor, seemed glad to enlighten him.

"That young woman! You know her?"

"Only slightly," he stammered, hardly able to take his eyes off her all the while.

"Well! I suppose you're fortunate then—or immune. She's turned this town upside down since she arrived here. Can you believe it, she was *bought* from those wild Comanche Indios? One wouldn't think it from the airs she puts on, though!" The woman sniffed. "That poor Capitan Higuera hasn't been himself since she turned her wiles on *him*—and as for my brother-in-law, who is a *married* man—well! I'm

617

sure I don't want to offend anyone. And you know her, I take it?"

Her avid curiosity was obvious, and it was all Pedro could do to keep his tone nonchalant.

"I used to know the señorita—some months ago. But I had no idea—"

"You didn't? I don't suppose . . . After all, living with those filthy Indios must *harden* one! If only the monsignor was here! But as it is—I do not mean to criticize, of course, but—"

He understood, of course. Very clearly, as he was meant to. And in spite of all the poison that was poured into his ear, he could not take his eyes from her.

Marisa. Flirting with that bumbling Capitan Higuera and looking up now and then to catch the governor's eye when his emaciated, ugly wife wasn't aware of it. Bitch! Whore for any man who was available! And yet he kept watching her, and once or twice her golden eyes met his with an unfathomable look before she looked away.

She had been playing games with him. He discovered that after the last course of what seemed to be an interminable meal had been cleared away, and they all stood up.

It was clear that even now, she had not become used to conforming.

"Must I retire with the ladies? Here is Pedro whom I haven't seen for *months,* not since his cousin, who was my stepmother, you know, stole my father's plantation in Louisiana from me. And—oh, but I don't mean to *embarrass* anyone! Perhaps Pedro didn't know, after all. Did you, Pedro? And how *is* Doña Inez?"

Her high, clear voice stopped everyone in their tracks, although, tactfully, they pretended not to hear. And Pedro could have wrung her neck, although he schooled his face to remain stolid.

"Believe me, I *didn't* know!" He knew his voice sounded grating and couldn't help it. "And Inez is—dead." He was watching her narrowly, and her eyes blinked once but remained unchanged—the glazed, yellow stare of a predatory cat, ready to pounce.

"How sad! You must tell me about it. . . ."

How she had changed! Her eyes did not drop from his, and her slim body, held erect, stood before him unflinchingly. It was *he* who wanted to flinch, but his pride held him there, glaring back at her.

The governor himself came to Marisa, squeezing her arm in an outwardly paternal fashion that deceived no one.

"My dear! You mustn't be too hard on our gallant colonel who has recently risked his life to free our frontiers of the Americano menace! I'm sure there has been some misunderstanding between you. Colonel Arteaga, isn't that so? If you want to talk alone, you may use my study—but mind," his voice suddenly becoming heavily playful, "you mustn't take too long! I can't have the ladies whispering maliciously among themselves, you know! We are going to dance and be gay—and I want you both to join us. Soon." His eyes hardened as they looked at Pedro who inclined his head respectfully.

Impatiently, obviously knowing her way around the governor's mansion, Marisa led the way to his study, whirling around after Pedro had closed the door.

"Well? You were going to give me your excuses, señor!"

She walked with quick, short steps to the fireplace, warming herself before the small fire that burned there. Her voice was still high—whether from anger, excitement, or tension he couldn't tell.

"Don't you have anything to say? They say you are a hero. Surely you're not afraid of me? I am waiting to hear you tell me that you knew nothing of what your precious cousin was planning. She's dead, did you say? How did it happen? Don't expect me to say I'm sorry because I'm not!' She gave a short, harsh laugh as she turned to face him, the firelight behind her making an aureole of her hair. "She told me, you know, that I should have agreed to marry you—before she sold me—as a slave. Did you know about *that?*"

"No! I swear it. You drove me mad with your teasing and your cheating, but I didn't know that!"

He took a step towards her and stopped, warned by the tension in her body.

"Marisa," he said heavily, "there was a rebellion of the slaves of Congracia. Perhaps you know that already. Several

619

of them escaped. Some of them died. But they burned the house. And Inez died a week later when her horse threw her—she broke her neck. The slaves say it was because of some kind of curse that old voodoo woman who died in the fire put on her. Everything was burned, do you understand? Papers, everything!"

"But in Louisiana I'd still be considered a slave, wouldn't I? *Gens de couleur*. What do you feel about that, Pedro? Don't you consider yourself fortunate that you didn't marry me, after all?"

"I would have married you, no matter what, if it hadn't been for that—that damned bastard Americano, who—"

"Your *friend!* Or don't you remember that time in Spain?"

"I remember also that time in France! And afterwards, in Natchez when you made a fool and a bitch of yourself! But I swore that I would have my turn, do you remember that? Por Dios, revenge can be very sweet!"

She walked away from the fire and came very close to him —so close that he could smell the perfume she was wearing.

"Hero! You killed him, didn't you? So brave—"

"One would think," he said harshly, hearing her breathing in the silent room, "that you continued to have some affection for this spy—this Americano criminal who took you and used you and sold you to the Indios when he had tired of you! The same man who had a rich fiancée who will wear black for a while until she is tired of mourning for him! Do you mourn, too?"

She slipped away from him like a wraith, away from the treacherous firelight.

"Do you think I'm the kind of woman who would mourn for any man? And do you imagine I care what you think? As you said a few moments ago, what can be sweeter than revenge? An eye for an eye. You know all about it, don't you?"

By God, she sounded different—she *was* different! And no wonder. No doubt she had experienced enough, since he had seen her last, to turn her into what she was now. His mind put the word there, and he said it aloud.

"Puta!"

She laughed. It was a high, tinkling sound, like the sound of breaking glass.

"Does that shock you, Pedro? Or—does it intrigue you? Would you still want to marry me—now?"

"No. Not now. But I would like to have you. And since you agree with me that vengeance is sweet, why, perhaps I can arrange for that, too, in return for your—er—gratitude."

"What do you mean?"

He laughed, suddenly sure of himself.

"Tomorrow—in the plaza. You should be there for the trial. And afterwards, if you can tear yourself away from the governor and your besotted little capitan, I might show you what you've been missing. You'll realize by then that I'm not quite the fool you take me for!"

She had the look of being poised for something as she stood there, her eyes wide and her shoulders and arms gleaming like pale, polished gold in the firelight. For flight maybe? Or because she was considering what he had told her? His hot, slitted eyes seemed to burn into her as for just an instant, the two of them formed a tableau in the suddenly quiet room.

'I will have her. I should have taken her by force a long time ago and made her submit. . . .' He was imagining her, suddenly, as a slave on the auction block—half-naked, pawed about by any man who had a fancy to buy her. And damn his dear dead cousin for not telling him! But now he would take her and master her and . . . Was that what she was waiting for at this very moment?

He was not aware that his triumphantly thrown out words had acted like a glass of water flung in her face. That she had come here with him not to flirt with him but to kill him.

Pedro took a step towards her, and at the same instant there was a tapping at the door, and the governor's querulous voice was calling that they had had quite enough time together, and that they must come out and join the rest of his guests.

Before Pedro could move, Marisa had whirled around to open the door. Through the frustrated hammering of the blood in his temples he heard her say in the high, brittle voice she seemed to have adopted, "I was just coming! You haven't forgotten, have you, señor, that you promised to dance with me?"

Mollified, Governor Elguizabal could be heard chuckling as he murmured in a much softer voice that he had not forgotten—*anything,* including her promise to him.

Pedro Arteaga, fuming, could only watch as she put her fingers on the old fool's arm and walked away, without so much as a backward turn of her head. It was *he* it seemed, who had been forgotten by them both!

For the remainder of the evening, Pedro's eyes stayed fixed on her. His eyes were dark and smoldering, holding a promise—a silent menace. Marisa tried to shut out his gaze, out of her consciousness, even as she must set aside in the recesses of her mind, Pedro's startling words, to be brought out and examined more closely later when she was alone. For now, she must laugh and dance and flirt as if she had no other thought in her mind but gaiety and pleasure.

Don't think, don't think! But was it possible? Oh, God— was it? How long since she had last prayed?

The evening was color and lamplight and guitar music and wine. There was the smell of cigar smoke and fires for the governor believed in lighting fires every night, and outside the faint scent of jasmine and gardenia. A quarter-moon was already disappearing behind the housetops.

She was leaning up against a wall. There were hands on her shoulders, shaking her. For a moment she had no idea whose hands they were.

"Are you feeling all right? You had too much wine. What got into you this evening? You made all the old women frown and whisper among themselves about you, that you are—" Fernando Higuera's voice halted, choked with his own emotions. "Dios! Was it all because of *him?* The colonel who. . . . Well, it doesn't matter, for you can have him back again if you want him, didn't you see for yourself? Is he still what you want? Is he?" And then, despairingly, "Why do you do what you do? If I only understood that—"

Surprising him, she reached up her hand and touched his young, earnest face with a kind of sad affection. "Oh, but Fernando—you are so young! I do what I do for hate—or for love. The difference is really very small, you see!"

"I am older than you are!" he cried out. Taking her in his arms, he said in a tone of desperate desire, "Why won't you forget about all this? Marry me, become my wife, and I swear I will make you happy! My pay's not much, I know, but I will get promoted soon, and maybe I can ask for a transfer somewhere else—to Mexico City, perhaps. You would be more at home there. I beg you, forget the past! *I* don't care about it—about anything you've done!"

"But *I* cannot forget! And you don't know, you don't know what I might be capable of, to—to find what I am looking for." Her words came out as a whisper, and she could feel her head swimming as she pressed her fingers, in an unconscious gesture, against her temples. "Fernando, please don't —don't press me any more tonight! I don't feel well. Yes, I know I drank far too much wine! But now I have to think— I—"

"Forget him! He does not look the kind of man who would be kind. I promise you that I will look after you—yes, and I will not make any more demands on you tonight. I will even take you back to your room if you want to go. Don't you know that I would do anything for you?"

"Anything?"

"Yes! Have I not said so? Marisa—"

Her pallor alarmed him, but her eyes had suddenly taken on a kind of wild brilliance, and now her fingers clutched at his shoulders.

"Can I trust you? To—to do something for me, something that is very important to me—only a *little* thing—without asking me questions?"

Dumbstruck, he found himself listening to her, his mind whirling with the very questions he had promised not to ask.

"The—the Americano prisoners. I know that I cannot go to see them, but *you* can, can't you? Curiosity—surely they won't be surprised, and they might even be glad of the chance to boast, the soldados who took them! Please! I'll keep him busy until I see you come back in. And after that— after that I will ask that *you* and only you escort me back to my room. I'll come to yours later, if you want me to—I know my way by now, don't I? I have to be prepared, I have to *know!*"

"But I—"

"I know you don't understand! But if you will only do this one little thing for me—for the sake of my peace of mind, my sanity! Please? And I *will* explain later. I promise you I will! I—"

Staring down into her taut, upturned face, her eyes burning in it like tiny flames, he had to disengage her clinging hands.

"I have already told you I would do anything for you. But this! You have not even told me what you want me to find out for you. What are you looking for? Who? I do not not know if I will be allowed to talk to them—"

"That's not necessary! Only tell me, tell me if there is, among them, a man with grey eyes, very light, like—like silver. And he has—had—a scar on his right temple. . . ."

Marisa went back into the overheated, overcrowded room, fanning herself. And almost immediately, Pedro was standing in front of her.

"You have not danced with me all evening." The glitter in his dark eyes belied the politeness of his words. "But you're so popular with the men, I suppose I must congratulate myself on finding you alone! These musicians are just starting to learn to play a waltz—you are accomplished at it, as I recall. Shall we show them?"

Without waiting for her answer, he put his arm around her waist and grasped her cold hand in his. She was aware that the heads of all the other women present had turned to watch them; and that Pedro held her far too closely, his head bent so that his lips might almost have brushed the curls at her temples.

"Please! Not so fast! I already feel quite giddy!"

"Then why don't you fall into my arms? And what happened to your devoted little captain? I saw you two sneak off into the garden together!"

"We—quarreled. Over you, if you must know it! But he *is* quite devoted, of course, and he'll be back after his temper has cooled off, to see me home."

"Home? And where is that? Do you have a little house of your own?"

"I have a room in the convent. And the nuns let me in and

out. Why do you look so disappointed? What did you expect?"

His arm seemed to crush her against him so that she gasped for breath.

"A convent! But then, as I recall, you make a habit of running away from convents. And you've tried to elude me for too long. I want you—"

"You make it only too obvious!" she whispered angrily. "Please, señor!"

"Señor? I think it is time we were not so formal! You know that I am going to have you, and I'm tired of evasions and excuses! You are neither a virgin nor inexperienced, and you've played with me long enough!"

"Do you mean to rape me right here in front of them all?" And seeing his glowering look she forced herself to laugh teasingly, even though she felt her ribs were crushed. "You forget—Pedro—that you promised me something in exchange for my—gratitude. Isn't that the way you put it?"

His head reared back in an ugly fashion, reminding her of a snake about to strike.

"Revenge, both yours and mine, was what I promised. And you shall have it, you little whore!"

She merely smiled sweetly up at him, and if the corners of her mouth trembled with the effort she was making, he was too incensed to notice.

"But a whore always makes sure of her payment first. *You* should know that, Colonel Arteaga!"

"Tonight!" He whispered angrily, fiercely.

"No. Only when *I* am ready. You had better understand that at the outset. My body is my own, to give to whom I please and when I please!"

"And *I* tell you—!"

She put both her hands up and pushed them against his chest.

"Oh—enough! I vow I am quite dizzy and exhausted! Governor—"

He had, perforce, to release her, and she went straight up to the governor himself, who had been watching them with a quizzical smile.

"Sir, won't you rescue me? I swear I cannot dance another

step! And the colonel insists on arguing with me. We always did, didn't we, Pedro? He thinks I am too bold and too familiar with everyone—but I am not, am I?" She pouted, putting her hand on the older man's sleeve. "When my uncle gets here, he will probably put me in a nunnery for good, so why shouldn't I enjoy myself first? Don't you agree? And besides—" she turned and gave a smiling glance into Pedro's black, carefully controlled face—"you gentlemen must want to talk business. Although I must admit I'm quite dying of curiosity myself. What will you do with those Americanos you caught?"

There. It was out in the open. Let Pedro say what he would! She looked from one to the other of them, her eyes deliberately, beguilingly wide with what seemed to be innocent inquiry.

On the surface she seemed merely a silly, pretty woman, all brittle sophistication and too much chatter. But her shell was fragile and growing more so by the minute. She couldn't bear much more! Where was Fernando? If she didn't escape soon, to be alone with her thoughts and her questions. . . .

"My dear!" Governor Elguizabal was saying, patting her hand in a benevolent, almost fatherly fashion. "You don't want to hear of such unpleasant subjects, do you? A pity—but they must be made an example of."

"We have signed confessions from all of them—there is no question of their guilt." This was Pedro, and he was looking at her, a slight, unpleasant smile curling his lips like a sneer. "And although I'm sure you are softhearted like most women, you should understand that there is more than deliberate trespassing into our territory and thievery involved. One of them, at least—a stubborn devil who was not so stubborn in the end—has confessed to worse crimes. Spying. You know how greedily the United States government looks in this direction? And even more than that." Now his eyes caught and held hers, and he had the satisfaction of seeing her bite her lip. He dropped his voice, and the ugly purr in it, reminding her too much of Inez, was for her alone. "There are certain crimes, against our women, especially, that no Spaniard worthy of his blood can tolerate! At the trial, though, I'm sure his Excellency here will—take pains to protect the fair name of the *innocent!*"

"Now look here—Arteaga—" Marisa had gone as white as a sheet, and the governor put his arm about her waist protectively as he looked from one to the other of them. "What is this? Hardly a conversation for a drawing room and for female ears, is it? And," he added querulously, "you did not tell me about these confessions. Don't you think I should know everything before those rascals stand their trial? My dear, are you quite well? You should not have danced so energetically perhaps; this heat—"

"My apologies." Pedro's voice was smooth. "To you, excellency, and to Doña Marisa. My blunt speech is, I'm afraid, the result of too much soldiering and too few hours spent in the company of women as lovely as the señorita. Can I not make amends by taking you home? Or outside for a breath of fresh air?"

"You're very kind—and especially you, dear sir!" She forced herself to smile into the governor's concerned face. "But I see that my escort has returned. Capitan Higuera has been *so* kind! He'll take me back to the good sisters who I'm sure will be waiting up for me. If you'll please be kind and excuse me?"

Outside, her farewells made, her thanks prettily said to the cold faces of the governor's ailing wife and skinny magpie of a sister-in-law, Marisa was thankful to have Captain Higuera's arm supporting her.

She insisted upon walking, and the small escort of trusted soldiers followed at a discreet distance behind, winking slyly at each other.

She leaned against him as if she could hardly stand.

"Oh—oh, it was terrible, So hot, and I felt so—so. . . . Why didn't you come sooner? I was on the point of fainting. This cold air feels so good."

She was postponing the moment of his telling her what he had gone to find out, and they both knew it.

He broke grimly into her gasping chatter. "He is among them—the man you wanted me to look for. They all looked very much alike, those poor wretches with their shaggy hair and beards. But they keep him apart from the rest. Ever since he created a diversion that helped one of them escape while they were crossing the Angelina River."

"Oh!" Her breath escaped in what might have been a sigh or a sob, and he shook her fiercely, to release some of the tension that was in him.

"Listen! I don't know why you had to know this. You made me promise not to ask you. But I might as well tell you this, in case you've got any more schemes cooked up in your pretty little head: there is no question of escape! And especially not for *him*. They have him chained so heavily he can hardly move—even if he could! The guards told me that Colonel Arteaga took special pleasure in meting out his punishment himself, and—"

She stumbled and fell against him; unmindful of the staring soldados behind, he lifted her suddenly limp body in his arms, carrying her the few yards that remained before they came to the gate of the convent, set in a high adobe wall.

≈≈≈

Chapter Fifty-eight

≈≈≈

Marisa did not remember afterwards how she got to her room. Two of the nuns must have carried her, she supposed. She fell across her narrow pallet like a broken doll, and Sister Maria Beatriz, grumbling under her breath, undressed her, slipping a voluminous cotton nightshift over her head before forcing some drink that was bitter and hot between her clenched teeth.

"Drink—drink! It will make you sleep—and perhaps cure the effects of the liquor I smell on your breath! Poor wayward child. When will you learn?"

The good nun knelt by her bedside and prayed for her soul, but Marisa knew nothing after that. She had begun to dream fitfully, tossing about in her bed.

Pedro was raping her, tearing off her garments one by one, very slowly, until she was naked. And Dominic was watching. She screamed out to him, begging him to help her, but he only stood there, a cold, harsh expression on his face. And then she realized, suddenly, that he was standing on a gallows with a noose about his neck.

"Help me, help me!" she screamed. But he shook his head, and then she saw the executioner come up behind him, holding an axe and grinning, and the executioner had Pedro's face, too.

"If anyone else is going to hurt you, menina, it's going to be me," he said to her softly, and she struggled frantically, trying to explain, while Pedro did terrible things to her body; the gallows was suddenly a scaffold, with the executioner raising his axe, still grinning. . . .

"Dominic—Dominic!"

She sat bolt upright, sweat streaming down her body in

629

rivulets from her scalp into her eyes, almost blinding her. Her mouth was still open, and the sound of her own screams echoed in her ears, reverberating off the walls.

Sister Maria Beatriz came running, her brown habit rustling with every step she took.

"Child, child! Whatever is the matter now? All these late nights, riding out in the sun, drinking and carousing—no wonder you have bad dreams!" Her voice was severe, but her eyes showed some concern; and when Marisa began to weep, sobbing desperately, the older woman came to her, clucking disapprovingly.

"Now, now! It was only a dream—and no wonder! If you'll come with me to the chapel, you'll feel better. I'll send for Father Juan to hear your confession. Don't you think it's time? You cannot hold everything inside yourself; we have been praying for you—"

Marisa swung her legs off the bed, feeling dizzy and sick as she did so.

"I cannot—not now—not yet!" She was still sobbing, the words almost incoherent. "I'm going to be sick—I don't want you to watch, sister. Sister, I'm sorry!"

Sister Maria Beatriz, for all that she looked frail, was made of sterner stuff. She held the girl's head, smoothing the hair away from her forehead and face and murmuring under her breath.

"Go away, indeed! What nonsense! There, there. You'll feel better now. If you would only listen—never mind! Come back to bed—lie down. And you had better make your confession before it's too late, my child! Whatever will the monsignor say? That we have not been taking good care of you, that's what. And we haven't." She wiped Marisa's face with a napkin dipped in cold water. "You had better be married quickly, child. Not that I am experienced in such matters myself, but I can remember when—" The sister's lips closed tightly all of a sudden as if she had almost admitted too much, but Marisa was hardly listening. Her eyes were like those of a trapped animal as they roamed around the room.

"What time is it? Where are my clothes? I must go out!"

"Out? When you are unwell. You cannot think of it! It's past noon, and it is the hour of the siesta. There's no one about except for those poor wretches on exhibition in the plaza. But you won't want to see such things—lie down and rest. Listen to reason for once!"

'Save yourself the pain—don't go out in the plaza tomorrow!' Fernando's hoarsely whispered words in her ear. 'I don't know what this man means to you, but you are better off not seeing.'

When had she ever listened to the advice that people gave her?

She began to dress, pulling on her clothes frantically, and when Sister Maria Beatriz, meaning well, locked the door of her cell, she put her face against the narrow windows and began to scream until they all came running, surrounding her with their kind, stern faces and rounded, questioning eyes.

"You cannot keep me a prisoner! I'll tell the governor himself. I'll tell my uncle when he comes that you locked me up and starved me! Or would you prefer that I should kill myself? I'll beat my head against this stone wall—I'll tear my own flesh to ribbons or cut my wrists! Will you pray for your own souls, then?"

"I think she has become demented!" one of the sisters murmured softly, crossing herself, but the prioress intervened, shaking her head.

"Child, don't you realize we are only concerned for *you?* Where must you go so urgently? We can send a message—"

"I do not think it would reach—the person I have to see. I have to go myself." Marisa tried to calm herself, but it was no use.

"But who is this person? Where must you go? At this time—"

They scattered before her like brown sparrows when she showed them her knife.

"Try to stop me and I'll use this—on myself! I'm going to the plaza. You can follow me if you like. And you should, perhaps! What good does it do for you to hide behind these walls praying? Do you know what you are praying for or for whom? Have you any idea of the misery and suffering out *there?* Or do you care? It's safer to hide away from reality and pray, isn't it? Not for me! I'm going outside these walls and I'm going, if you must know, to find my man—my hus-

band—the father of the son I bore him two years ago and of
the child I'm carrying inside me now—or didn't Sister Maria
Beatriz tell you?"

Dressed in a skirt and a blouse, barefoot, she ran past them,
and this time they made no movement to stop her. The poor
sisters, shocked and stunned, did not seem capable of moving at all.

She unbolted the wooden gate and tugged it open herself, letting it slam shut behind her with a final sound. And
then she ran—through almost deserted streets of red dust—
past shuttered houses where their inhabitants enjoyed the
drowsy time of siesta.

There was a scattered crowd in the plaza, at least, some of
them standing around staring or jeering while small boys
darted about picking up clods of earth to fling while they
laughed shrilly and called out taunts.

Marisa brushed through them, and they moved aside grumbling, staring at her curiously. Some of them recognized her
—it didn't matter. She was past caring.

At the outermost fringes of the crowd she stopped to
draw breath, and perhaps to prepare herself. Up until now
she hadn't known and hadn't wanted to wonder what she
might see. A scaffold, like the one in her dream? A gibbet
with bodies hanging from it?

She saw a makeshift cage, with wooden bars, built onto the
wide bed of an open wagon. And through her sweat-blurred
eyes, she saw kneeling men, a pitiful few, with ropes knotted
around their necks as if to prepare them for the gallows.
Grinning soldiers, standing at casual ease, ringed them loosely,
exchanging comments with the crowd.

They were exhibited like animals—caged—and the cage
had been placed next to the fountain where the water kept
up its cool, constant splashing. A further refined torture,
no doubt! And these people all watched! *They* are the animals! Marisa thought, and her eyes moved quickly, from one
beard-shadowed, gaunt face to another. Dominic. Which one
of them? . . .

"They keep him separated from the others," she remembered Fernando Higuera's painful words and finally saw him,
and the breath caught in her throat.

The others were manacled by the wrists to the top of the improvised cage and faced outward. *He* faced the fountain itself, and the rope around his neck was fastened to the stout wooden pole that was notched in the bend of his elbows, running behind his back, his wrists fastened to its ends so that he would be forced to kneel erect, his head up, or strangle to death.

She made a strangled sound in her throat as she ran forward. One of the soldiers, his waterskin raised to his mouth, stared in astonishment as she snatched it from him, calling him a beast and a pig as she did.

"Now see here, muchacha!" He put a rough hand on her shoulder, and she spat at him, "Don't you dare touch me! Do you know who I am? Ask the governor if you don't!"

A friendly, anonymous voice from the crowd called, "It's true, soldado! In spite of those clothes, she's Governor El-guizabal's little ward and the niece of our cardinal archbishop —ask Capitan Higuera!"

All the other soldiers had come to attention, starting to converge on her, but her clipped, precise Castilian Spanish held them at bay.

"Are you Pedro Arteaga's brave soldiers? My goodness, you are real heroes, aren't you? And worse animals than the Indios you pretend to chase and are so afraid of! Is this what you draw your pay for—to stand guard over these prisoners who could not move even if they tried?" Now she looked towards the foot-shuffling crowd, and her voice was just as contemptuous. "And you. Is this all you can find to do of an afternoon? Stand around and bait these poor men who cannot defend themselves? Will you admit to this when you go to church on Sunday and make your confessions? Christians! Can you call yourselves that? You are worse than the ancient Romans who laughed when they threw Christians to the wild beasts! Is this what you think of as an afternoon's amusement? You ought to be ashamed!"

She whirled about, brushing the stunned soldier's hand from her arm.

"I'll answer to the governor himself. And you will, too, if you try to stop me! Brutes! Don't you have any feelings?

You are worse than the Indios you all talk about and are so
scared of!"

Even the dust felt hot under her bare toes. She saw
cracked lips and sun-scorched faces, lines of pain showing
on all of them. And they were bare from the waist up; and
the ragged breeches they wore revealed more than they hid.
All of them bore signs of mistreatment and near-starvation,
but Dominic. . . .

There was not an inch of his flesh that was not either
burned or bloody, and she could not help crying out loud
when she stopped before him, holding the waterskin to his
mouth and watching the precious liquid trickle down.

"Dominic! . . ."

His eyes opened at the sound of her voice but didn't seem
able to focus. His face had the grey look of a dying man, and
she wanted to scream out loud, but only a whisper escaped
her.

"Dominic—*please!*"

She poured water onto her shaking hands and put them
against his face and cracked, parched lips. And suddenly his
eyes found hers, recognizing her at last. They looked the
color of lead, and they were as dull. She started to reach out
through the bars to touch him, but his muscles flinched instinctively, and she drew back, holding the waterskin up and
letting its precious contents trickle past his lips.

They moved, and his throat seemed to convulse with the
effort of speaking.

"Go—away!" He saw tears spilling from her eyes, and his
face contorted.

"Oh, God—Marisa—please! Not here! Not like this! I'm
not—" And then his body seemed to stiffen against itself,
and he whispered, "Why won't you go? Gloat, if you came
to—but go, after that!"

One of the soldiers came up angrily, snatching the waterskin from her grasp as he raised his arm in a threatening
gesture.

"Hey, what is this? Don't you know you're not supposed
to communicate with these prisoners? I ought to . . ."

Marisa's already exacerbated emotions made her turn on

the man like a spitting cat, her eyes still gleaming with tears.

"You oaf! Ought to what? Hit me? Shoot me? Go ahead. It's easier to beat women and bound men than it is to fight Indios, isn't it? Well, go ahead if you dare!"

Embarrassed and made even angrier by her taunting defiance, he made a rough attempt to shove her back into the crowd, but she kicked him in the shins with her bare foot, following that up by clawing at his face.

"You!" Goaded beyond endurance by her unjustified attack and the laughter of the crowd, the soldier had a good mind to throw her into the fountain and give her a good wetting down. With a bellow of pain and rage; he grabbed at her wrists and he dropped them just as suddenly when he heard the crisp command.

"Soldado, you will release the señorita immediately!" Stumbling backward, Marisa looked up into Fernando Higuera's set, strained face.

"Fernando! Please—"

He spoke to her formally. "Doña Marisa. If you will come with me, please. I have brought a horse for you." He snapped an order to one of the men who had accompanied him. "Help the señorita to mount and be quick about it. The rest of you—go back to your duties, do you understand?"

"No!" Marisa said stubbornly. "I won't—I can't leave now! How can you stand by and let such a thing happen? The hot sun—and they are without water. Are you all barbarians? It's inhuman!"

She had never seen him look at her with such fury or heard him speak to her so harshly.

"Get on that horse! Or was it your intention to make an even worse spectacle of yourself—and of *them?*" Her eyes widened, and he said to her in a lower, harder voice, "Por Dios! If you care for this man, if you are truly capable of such an emotion, don't you understand what you have done to *him?* Would you take away from him all he has left of his pride and his manhood? I warned you to stay away last night, remember? And I thought you'd have enough sense to understand what I meant! So now that you've accomplished enough damage for one afternoon—"

635

"That's enough!" she whispered and without another word, let the soldier help her up on her own golden stallion, trying to close her mind and her eyes to the faces that were turned towards them, to the silent, caged animals—no, prisoners, a fine distinction that!—and especially to one of them. . . .

"Give them some water. It might keep them alive for the gallows." Was that really Fernando's voice? So firm and sure of himself.

"But the colonel gave orders—"

"*I* am the captain in charge of this presidio, soldados. And I have given you an order. See that it's carried out!"

One of the soldiers on guard nudged the other and muttered, "Didn't I tell you? That's the capitan's woman. And the governor's plaything, too. You should have been more respectful, amigo!" The laughter that followed relieved their feelings of embarrassment.

Marisa felt numbed by shock and pain. What good had her defiance done, her desire to *do* something?

"Go away!" Dominic had whispered. "Marisa, please! Not here, not like this." And then Fernando had opened her eyes, making her want to die.

At least the feel of her horse moving restively, tossing his head impatiently, was familiar. After they had ridden out of the plaza, she forced herself to lift her head. And Fernando's eyes were on her, more pained than angry now.

"Why did you do it?"

She shook her head. "I don't know! I had to do—something, I suppose! I couldn't just let—and I won't let it be! Perhaps I should not have gone down into the plaza today, but I saw him! At least I saw him! And I won't let them kill him! No. I'll do anything I have to—"

"So that is the real reason why you came to me that night! And visited the governor. And now, will you offer youself to Colonel Arteaga as well? Do you really imagine that you can prevent what must happen and will happen by doing so? Marisa!"

"I'll do anything I have to do!" she whispered, and his face looked gaunt with anguish for a moment before it closed against her.

"I see," he said in the same formal, stilted voice he had used earlier. Then, "The sisters have been very worried about you. If they had not sent a message to me—"

"Thank you. Fernando, forgive me!" There was blood on her lip where she had bitten into it. And the traces of tears sheening her face. "I did not mean to—I didn't *know*—"

"You lied to me! Which one of them do you really want? Or does it make a difference?"

She flinched from the bitterness in his voice.

"I thought that he—that Dominic—was *dead!* Don't you understand? That Pedro had killed him! And the only reason I asked about *him* and where he was, was because I meant to kill him. I almost did so last night before he started hinting. . . . You see, I am telling you the truth now, all of it! If you—"

"I cannot save him for you! It is for *you* to understand this, for a change. But in spite of everything, I continue to —to love you, you little bitch! I think you have been hurt enough. Or at any rate, I cannot bear to see you suffer!"

"Then help me!" She began to weep helplessly.

"I am taking you to the governor." His voice was still harsh for all that it held a tremor in it. "What happens after that is up to you."

Chapter Fifty-nine

"But, my dear little girl, why didn't you tell me all this before?" The governor's voice was kind enough, for all that she had disturbed his afternoon siesta and sent his wife off into one of her sick tantrums. He put his hand on the shoulder of the sobbing girl who sat huddled up in one of his padded leather chairs and then took it away quickly, to resume his pacing about the room. A kindhearted man, he could not bear to meet her pleading, tear-swollen eyes. But what did she expect him to do?

He continued to talk as he paced, trying to forestall any further entreaties on her part. She must see reason—accept the cold logic of facts as they were.

"If you had told me! Yes, yes," he added hastily, "I realize, of course that you had heard he was dead! But even last night—you little minx!" With a forced attempt at lightness, he said, "You led me to believe all along that it was Colonel Arteaga you were interested in! And by the way, I must warn you that the accusations you have made against him—although I realize your state of mind, of course—are a serious matter! You should not repeat them to other people who might not understand! Nor must you talk so wildly of murdering him! My dear, young ladies of your birth and breeding simply do not run around carrying knives! Try to understand—"

She interrupted him, her fingers tightly clenched on the arms of the chair. "How can you expect me to understand anything, and especially what you call Spanish *justice*, when everything I've told you is *true*? I found out that Dominic saved me from—from the horrible, degraded existence that might have been my fate if Doña Inez's plans had not gone

639

astray! And he only came to New Spain because of *me*, don't you see that? If that nasty, treacherous General Wilkinson had not forced him into this expedition as a price for giving him the money with which to free me—"

"My dear, you are distraught! I understand that this man was engaged to be married to a very rich young lady at the time and had every intention of going back to marry her! Surely you're letting your imagination run away with you? General Wilkinson has always been a friend to Spain—and after all," he added cunningly, "this Americano did sign a confession in which he admitted to everything quite willingly, including the callous way in which he abandoned you to those Comanche devils."

"Willingly?" She cried wildly, half starting up from the chair. "You must have seen the marks on his body! Under such torture, don't you think any man would have signed anything that was put before him? What would *you* have done in his place?"

For the first time the governor showed himself to be obviously ruffled although he tried to keep his patient, paternalistic air. "But I am not in his place. I am not a spy and have never been! And as for his condition, Colonel Arteaga was merely meting out some discipline after he had helped one of his fellow prisoners escape! I'll admit that he might have got a trifle carried away, but that's beside the point. Don't you see there's nothing I can do now? Their trial was held this morning, and I, myself, sentenced them to death. And I might add that this man on whose behalf you plead so vehemently admitted that he had signed his confession willingly—that it was all true! What do you expect me to do now? If I had known earlier what you have only told me now, I might have made some attempt to commute *his* sentence to life imprisonment, but even that would have been difficult. I have a duty to perform, you know! As it is, the matter is quite out of my hands. They are to be taken to Saltillo, and from there to Chihuahua where they will be executed. Please, try to keep calm. . . ."

He saw that she had turned faint from shock and clumsily tried to soothe her.

"Look here. I promise to send a doctor to him tonight!

And there will be no more public exhibitions as long as they are here. They were to be marched off tomorrow, but I will insist to Colonel Arteaga that they be kept here in San Antonio until they are fit to stand the journey—"

"You'll try to—to keep him alive so that he can be hanged in the end?" she whispered bitterly, each word a gasp between her heaving sobs. "Do you think he'll thank me for it? And yet, I cannot bear for him to die! What am I to do? Isn't there something—someone else I can go to who—?" She flung herself out of the chair and at the governor's feet, much to his embarrassment. "Please! You've always been so kind to me, and I have . . . Isn't there some higher authority I can turn to? The queen of Spain herself? I met her once." She remembered the occasion of their meeting and burst into renewed weeping, quite unable to talk any further.

Elguizabal touched her bright, damp hair unwillingly, not able to help himself; he remembered how warm and affectionate she had proved to be on the two or three occasions when he had taken her to bed. Damn it—he *was* fond of her! She was a pretty, winning little creature, and it was a shame to see her suffer such obvious agony involved in such a hopeless passion. He would have liked to comfort her in the age-old way, but of course it wasn't possible. Not now and certainly not here, with his skinny sister-in-law probably lurking outside the door listening avidly to every word they exchanged.

"The queen of Spain is too far away, my little dove! There is the viceroy, of course, but he is in Mexico City, and for you to get there would mean months of traveling—far too long! Not that I think he would do anything, either. For you have to understand that with our borders menaced on all sides by greedy, land-hungry men, we dare not show trespassers any mercy!"

"Can you not at least keep him here until I go to Mexico and return?"

He sighed heavily, continuing to stroke her hair. "My dear, I cannot! I am only the governor of this small province. And *he* is Colonel Arteaga's prisoner, already under sentence. But while he is here, I'll do whatever I can. Come, there's no use in continuing to cry! You'll get over it, after a while.

641

There is that young capitan who is madly in love with you, and you are still very young! When you thought this man was dead, you seemed to become resigned to the fact now, weren't you? Go back to the convent, and try to rest. Think of your child. Perhaps we can make arrangements to have him brought here to you, eh? For all that you say and think about General Wilkinson, he has always been most helpful and obliging. I'm sure he'll be so in this case. So you see? You have something to look forward to. And soon you'll become resigned and forget this unpleasant time in your life!"

Forget, forget, it was impossible! The governor squeezed her arm and cupped her breasts in a quick, furtive gesture, and passively, she let him, realizing that in his way he was being as kind and obliging as he could. A doctor, food and water. And no more ugly, public displays in the plaza. But oh, God, there had to be *something!* Something else she could do to stave off the impossible.

"There's no hope," Govenor Elguizabal had told her gently, but she wouldn't admit it. There was, there was! She remembered meeting the viceroy, remembered his kindness towards her. If only she could reach him—send a message to him at least! The nuns were praying for her; they had told her so, and they were very kind, very patient. But what good did that do when what she needed was a miracle? She had even tried praying herself, but the words wouldn't come. 'As long as he's alive, alive,' but the thought of death hung over her like a pall, and she could hardly breathe—nor did she want to.

Marisa had been lying rigidly on her back, her eyes staring at the ceiling. She continued as she was when Sister Maria Beatriz came into her room. The small lamp, still lighted, shone on glazed golden eyes that looked sightless.

"Doña Marisa—child—" The nun's voice whispered like the sound of her rope-soled sandals on the straw matting.

"There's no need to keep a watch on me. They took away my knife so I can't kill myself or anyone else. I don't want to eat, and I find I have forgotten how to pray. Why won't you leave me alone?"

"There is a man waiting in the parlor, he called to see you. The prioress tried to tell him you were asleep. After all it *is* past seven o'clock! But he was insistent. A Colonel Arteaga. He said you would want to talk with him if you knew why he was here."

Pedro?

"Colonel Arteaga has given me his solemn word that he knew nothing of the scheme his cousin was hatching up. In fact he told me he had been betrothed to you once, by your father's wish, and hoped to marry you, even afterwards. My dear, you do him an injustice! He is most concerned and unhappy for you." The governor's words. And although she knew better—*why* had Pedro come here? To—offer her something? And dear God, could she disdain even a straw of hope held out to her? No matter what she had to do. . . .

She did not bother to dress except for slipping a pair of sandals, such as the nuns wore, on her feet and throwing a shawl about the crumpled blouse and skirt she had worn that afternoon. At Sister Maria Beatriz's insistence, she ran a comb through her tangled hair but let it remain hanging loosely about her shoulders. What did he want? What had he come for?

Resplendently dressed in a newly laundered and pressed uniform, his high-topped boots gleaming, Pedro Arteaga bowed formally as he took Marisa's limply offered hand and pressed it to his lips.

"I could not wait to come to you! My dearest heart, why did you not confide in me? That act you put on last night! But when I heard what happened this afternoon, and the governor told me of your visit to him, how you humbled your pride to plead with him—"

Marisa heard the door close softly behind the prioress, and she snatched her hand away from his.

"There is no more need for your polite pretense now, señor! If you will tell me why you are here?"

He looked at her reproachfully, but there was a fire behind the dark gleam of his eyes that did not deceive her and made her shiver.

"How could you? I understand now why you acted as if you hated me, but, again, how was I to know? I did what I did out of the desire to avenge *you* and out of a sense of jealousy of course; I must be honest enough to admit that!

After all, I've always treated you like a gentleman, even you will admit that? If you had told me there was a child involved and that was why you acted as you did—could you not have trusted me to understand? And now I gather that you are in similar circumstances? Ah, dulce amor! No wonder you were in such pain!"

"Pedro—stop! Only tell me, why are you here?"

"You look like a little cornered doe, with those big, tear-filled eyes of yours!" he said softly. "I wonder if you would ever cry so for me? You cried for the governor, I understand. He was very much upset and unhappy. But since I understand you better now, I am here of my own accord, to offer you—" He paused deliberately so that she was forced to whisper, between clenched jaws: "To offer me—what?"

"Why, an honorable solution, of course. An answer to all of your problems—what did you think? Amends for all that my cousin tried to do to you. Poor Inez!" He shook his head seeming sorrowful. "She was always so greedy and so grasping! How many times have I warned her about it? And she overstepped herself. If *I* had been there, none of the unpleasantness would have happened, but you drove me away with your coldness, did you know that?"

"Get to the point, please! What are you trying to say?"

"Why, I thought it must be clear to you by now. I am offering you marriage, of course. The governor knows and approves. He has already dispatched a messenger to General Wilkinson, and to some of our—er—friends in Natchitoches. Your son, about whose future I know you must be very worried, will be on his way here within a month. The child you are carrying—you *are* with child again?—will at least be legitimate. We will be quite a family, won't we?" He showed his teeth in a smile, and she backed away from him.

"No! Have you gone crazy? You told me last night that—"

"But that was last night, my treasure. Before I knew all of the facts! Do you think I could leave you to face all the ugly scandal alone? And your son will need a man to protect him. Anything could happen on this wild frontier, as you very well know! Indian raids, accidents. Surely you can see the risks? With me as your husband, we could go back to

Louisiana after my tour of duty is over and rebuild Congracia. Our children will grow up there. . . ."

She kept shaking her head, not wanting to understand what he was saying—the veiled threats under his smooth words.

"You can't want me. Not after—do you forget what I am? A slave—a *femme du couleur*—"

"What nonsense! Did you believe any of that? That old woman was crazy and so was Inez! Why, I can testify to the fact that your poor father was so sick with fever that he would have signed any piece of paper she held out to him! I've made my own inquiries, and General Wilkinson, too, was most helpful. It's true your father sired a child by his favorite slave mistress who was your mother's half sister, by the way! But there was no exchange of children. The child was a girl also, but it died on a ship traveling to Martinique. After that the woman became devoted to you, seeing in you a substitute for her own lost child, I suppose! And I understand you both took after your father, so—"

"It *could* be true, though! How can you know? The woman you say was my mother never came to see me, but Delphine did! She—"

"And I tell you that those people will accept my word! And the word of the witnesses I can find. Just as they accepted what Inez told them, remember? They will accept you again when you are married to me, just as they accepted you and invited you to their fine houses in Natchez. That fact alone will make them come around! Inez was an unfaithful wife, greedy for an inheritance that was not hers. An old story, si?" He stepped forward and grasped her by the shoulders, bringing his dark face close to hers. "I am offering you a future—and a name of some respectability. I was your own father's choice of a husband for you. Think of that and of the future of your children, if your own does not matter to you!"

Marisa felt buffeted and set upon from all directions. What was she to do? How was she to answer him? There were the implicit threats he had made, and the more explicit threat of the present, and Dominic, who would die. . . .

Hadn't she told herself earlier that she would do anything

at all to save him? She said faintly, turning her face away: "There is one other thing. There is—"

"Would you bargain with me now, like a whore?" His voice was biting with anger.

"You called me that before, and I will admit to it. Does that change your mind? And no matter what you say, and what threats you make, you will never have me unless you set him free. There is always my uncle, you know, who has the ear of the viceroy. *He,* at least, will believe what I shall tell him."

"Will that matter when it's too late? Listen to me, Marisa. There is a doctor with him now, and he will be fed and watered and I will curb my impulses while we are here, but *that* will only be for a few more days! Do you realize what I could do to him along the long road to Mexico with no one to stop me? What he has suffered up until now will be nothing, I promise you, to what I will do after we have left here! He won't live to hang, it's true, but he will have enough time to wish he had!"

She gave an involuntary whimper of pain and terror, and he laughed softly, still holding her shoulders in an iron grip.

"Are you strong enough to carry that on your conscience, too? Well, I will go one step further as proof of how much I want you and that is as far as I will go! Marry me tonight —yes, with the governor's connivance it can be arranged!— and I will take you to see him. And you will tell him what you have done, of your own accord—it will be that way, I think. Remind him of the child. You will do that, too; it's little enough to ask, isn't it, compared to what *I* will do? For I swear to you that if you do all these things of your own will and volition, I will contrive to let him escape. It will be only after we are in Mexico, and he will have to run his own risks with the Indios there. But he will go free, and I will not lay a hand on him after we leave here. Well—is it a bargain?"

of all to save harm? She had hardly realized yet that every
now form time to time, Pedro...
...Would you finanlly with me, She said, a knowl... was
... was filling with anger.

Chapter Sixty

The priest who married them had a nervous stutter that made a mockery of the hurried, almost stealthy, ceremony. And the governor, beaming paternally and kissing her soundly afterwards, gave her away. How different, this, from the other ceremony she remembered! But it was best *not* to remember.

She had made her confession, perjuring herself by naming Pedro as the father of the child she was carrying; because of the circumstances, the priest said solemnly, the banns could be waived.

The governor insisted on toasting their health and happiness with wine. One glassful, hastily swallowed, hit her empty stomach like a jolt, making her even more dazed than she was already. She drank another glass of wine hoping that it would send her to oblivion, dulling all her emotions. Instead, she was sick on the way to the prison and had to submit to Pedro's impatient, careless ministrations. She was still weak but unfortunately clearheaded when they arrived there.

The soldiers who were on guard hastily stood at attention. Marisa recognized one of them, at least, from that afternoon. Was it possible that so much had happened in so short a space of time?

"Come along!" Pedro seemed impatient now, as eager to get everything over with as she was herself.

Barred cells, set into thick adobe walls. Moaning noises coming out of the dark to snatch at her nerves. A flight of steps leading down, with Pedro holding a pitch-pine torch aloft. And finally, a small, cold cell, underground. And Pedro,

647

with mock solicitousness was warning her to avoid the round hole set in the floor, with a six-inch wall around it.

"Be careful, my love. It's a well. Sometimes, we lower particularly recalcitrant prisoners into it by placing a wooden bar across the top, to which their wrists are suspended. Not a very pleasant way to pass a night, but then, what would you have? They are not nearly so stubborn when they are hauled out in the morning, I assure you." He stuck the flaring torch into a wall sconce, and when he turned back to her, Marisa, shivering, could see the white flash of his teeth.

"Do you not agree with me, amigo? Tonight, at least, I see you have been made really comfortable. I have brought my wife, who is naturally softhearted, here to make sure of it herself. And it was she who persuaded the governor to be so kind; she is very persuasive when she wants to be, isn't that so?" His voice suddenly cracked against her nerve ends like a whip. "Tell him, my love! No more secrets between the three of us, remember? You can go up closer—he can't hurt you. And tell him in your own words."

She had to force herself to look at him even if it was only to reassure herself that he was still alive. He was lying on his back on an indescribably filthy heap of straw, his torso swathed in bandages, his arms drawn back over his head and manacled to an iron ring set in the wall. His eyes were open looking at her, but there was no emotion in them at all.

"Dominic," she whispered, and he still stared back at her, eyes like stormy skies. He made it easier for her to recite what she had to. Just as she had rehearsed it in her mind during the preceding hours.

"Pedro and I were married tonight—just a few hours ago, as a matter of fact. And—we shall be going back to Louisiana to live, in about six months from now. Pedro has promised to connive at your escape, but you must give us your word that you—will not return there to—interfere with us. You can always—go back to Europe, can't you? And I will have —General Wilkinson is sending Christian here to me, and he will be—safe and happy, as long as—" Her voice choked off in spite of herself, and Pedro finished for her, putting his arm possessively about her shoulders, his fingers on her breast.

"As long as you stay out of our lives, my wife meant to say. I hope you understand? I am being generous in this instance, but I think you have found out I can be—otherwise, too, eh? I am willing to accept your bastards as my own as long as their mother is my faithful, obedient wife and you remain dead. Do you understand? You don't answer. I hope for your sake and hers that you do!"

"Pedro, that's enough. I cannot bear any more—"

"Can you not, my love? But since your erstwhile lover appears to have been struck dumb, I think I will have to show him how things are between us. We are married now, and I have already waited for too long."

She turned her face dumbly toward him, hardly understanding what he meant and met his smile—and his eyes. His arm tightened around her shrinking shoulders, not allowing her to pull away.

"You are used to copulating under all kinds of conditions, are you not, my sweet? Out in the open, in Comanche tents, in Captain Higuera's wretched little room with his men standing outside to keep guard? It shouldn't matter to you if we consummate our marriage here—with a witness to prove that it was done? Don't pretend to be modest. If it's comfort you're thinking of, I will put my cloak down on the floor for you to lie upon. And *he* has seen you naked before!"

Now at last, as if something had snapped inside her, she began to fight against him in earnest.

"No, Pedro—no! You promised—you never said—"

"I never said I would not do it this way, did I? You'll submit to this whim of mine, my little wife, just as you'll submit to all my whims in the future! I want you to remember the first time I take you!"

The torchlight flickered as if in some way a draft had found its way into this damp, airless place, and it sent shadows leaping grotesquely against the walls: hers, as Marisa tried to escape him, fighting as if it were for her life; and Pedro's as he sent her staggering backward with a blow against the side of her face, and then followed with a leap, catching the front of her gown with his fingers and ripping it all the way down the front.

He pinned her flailing arms behind her the next instant,

staring down into her face as if they had been quite alone.

"You are my wife, now, Doña Maria Antonia Catalina, and I will take you when and where I please. And after I have done so tonight—here—you will never again lie with another man for I will kill you if you do. I'll have no more of other men's leavings fathered upon me!"

"And if you do this to me, here and now, Pedro Arteaga, I swear you will have to take me by force every single time until I find the chance to kill you—or you do it first to me!"

He grinned, pushing her backward with her arm still painfully twisted behind her. "But first we will do this thing tonight. For your benefit and *his*. And afterwards—"

Despairingly, she began to scream—for what or why she did not know, except that she could not, would not, stand this further violation of her body. And she tried to struggle and squirm from his grasp, but she was tired and too weak, and *he* was used to dealing with recalcitrant prisoners. He flung her down on the cold earth floor, the force of the fall partly stunning her. With one hand grasping her wrists, he ripped off what was left of her clothes, putting his knee between her thighs.

"And now we will finish this, and you will learn who you belong to," he said between his teeth.

Marisa screamed again, and leaning down, he struck her across the face drawing blood from her lips. The sounds of her own screams seemed to bounce off the walls, ringing in her ears.

Pedro's hand groped between her thighs before he began to loosen his clothing, smiling all the while lips drawn back from his teeth.

"And now—"

"And now, señor, you will take your hands off her and stand up and fight me instead. *Now*, or I will be forced to run you through with my sword."

"What is this, Capitan Higuera? Have you forgotten yourself? Are you serious in challenging me to a duel over my own wife? I would think carefully if I were you! After all, we both happen to know what she is—"

Pedro had risen, nevertheless, releasing the crushing pressure of his hand about her wrists and his body over hers.

Marisa sat up with a cry, realizing even as her fingers clutched at shreds of cloth that there was nothing left of her clothing for her to cover herself with.

She saw Fernando, his face shadowed and grim, standing on the bottom step, his sword already drawn; and she saw Pedro straighten, standing above her, his hand going down to his belt.

"Whatever she is, I will not stand by and let you abuse her—colonel. So, if you please, you will defend yourself." He walked steadily, and Pedro backed off, but he sounded contemptuous all the same.

"Are you insane, capitan? Do you remember who you are and who I am? I was merely going to teach my wife a well-deserved lesson, in the presence of her ex-lover. Your gallantry is ill-conceived and senseless! Or did you wish to take my place on her body? Is that it?" He laughed. "Too bad. But I am a more experienced duelist than you; and I'm afraid, little capitan, that you have overstepped your limits this time!"

"We'll see about that." Fernando Higuera's voice was hoarse but determined; and recovering some of her wits, Marisa rolled out of the way.

'Be careful—he has a pistol!' Had her mind only registered the words or did she actually cry them aloud? Or was it possible that it was Dominic's voice she really heard?

She had no time to think on it for everything that followed seemed to run together.

Pedro—stepping backward again as he drew a pistol from his belt. Fernando—standing frozen with the torchlight glittering off his blade while Pedro laughed, cocking his pistol. Tableau—and then movement, blurred through the moisture in her eyes. Dominic had doubled up his legs, ankle manacled to ankle, and caught Pedro behind the knees, sending him off balance. Pedro suddenly staggered forward, the pistol exploding harmlessly as he tried to keep his balance, his steps as grotesque as those of a clumsy ballet dancer.

The well! He stepped across it almost into Fernando's drawn sword, and then, trying to regain his balance, stepped back—and into nothingness; his scream echoed and rechoed before it was cut off, with a splashing, gurgling noise.

"My God! I've heard it is without a bottom, that well—"

She wasn't listening. Mindless of her nakedness, Marisa scrambled to her feet and ran to where Dominic lay, still panting.

"Dominic—Dominic!"

His eyes, glittering like steel, acknowledged her presence for the first time since Pedro had brought her down here. She reached her hands out to him, but his voice, husky and tired and bitter, stopped her movement in mid-motion.

"Don't! Will you make it worse! Your husband is dead. Go away with your lover and mourn him!" He closed his eyes against her bruised, shocked face as if he could not bear to look at her any longer. "Why did you have to come to the plaza this afternoon? Why couldn't you let me be? There is some dignity in dying, at least; but no, you had to sell your body for food and water and a damned doctor to keep me alive long enough to kick at the end of a rope! Christ, isn't this enough?"

"You don't understand! Pedro threatened—he said that—"

"Must I hear it? Do you think I enjoyed lying here helpless watching the two of them fight over you like two dogs over a bitch? You belong to the victor now, and he's waiting. Why don't you go with him?"

She was aware of Fernando standing above her and of other voices as men came clattering down the steps. Fernando threw his cloak over her naked shoulders and said roughly "Marisa, come away now, you must!"

And Dominic kept his face stubbornly turned away, his eyes still shut.

In spite of that, knowing he was not able to stop her, she leaned down and put her lips against his tightly closed mouth.

"Whatever I have done, it's because I love you. I won't let you die—do you hear me? I'll do anything—"

"Then go away. Oh, for God's sake, must I beg you? I want nothing more from you except your permission to die, at least, in peace. Marisa." His voice had dropped to a strained whisper, and his eyes opened long enough to catch hers again. "Go back to your life and leave me to what's left of mine. At least leave me with some shreds of my pride remaining!"

Fernando drew her roughly and firmly to her feet, keeping his cloak wrapped tightly about her. Vaguely, she heard him making some explanations to the soldiers who now crowded around, their eyes avid, some of them peering down the well and muttering among themselves. "Dios! What an end! How did it happen? And the woman—his wife—"

"Some of you will go with us. I'll make my explanations to the governor himself, you understand? And you will keep your mouths shut!"

"But capitan—"

"The governor himself will tell you what he wishes you to know."

"We'll never find the body unless it floats to the top," someone said with grim foreboding, and Marisa shuddered, feeling Fernando's arms tighten around her shoulders. Torn shreds of her gown lay everywhere for everyone to draw their own conclusions. But did it matter? Let them think what they pleased. She felt herself fall into a kind of daze in which her mind repeated his name over and over. 'Dominic—Dominic!' But he didn't want her. He wanted her gone. He—

Suddenly, she was out in the starlight, the cold air biting into her naked flesh. Fernando held her tightly, and his arms were warm. Was it true that she could forget quickly? Was she really the kind of woman who could go from one man's arms to another's without regret or compunction? Dominic thought so. He didn't want anything from her, he despised her, and yet, no matter what she did with her body, her mind was still shackled to his.

Starlit nights, like this. Dominic's arm under her head, holding her closely while he told her the names of the constellations and how they could be a guide if she was ever lost. And she was lost now and had lost him, too—if she had ever had him.

"Marisa, must I beg you?" he had said.

Pedro was unimportant. Pedro was gone like a nightmare. She felt nothing. Was that how Dominic felt? Nothing—

emptiness—mind like a bowl from which everything had been spilled.

She began to babble compulsively, wanting to keep it that way.

"Fernando, how did you—"

"I followed you. Do you think I could bear to let you out of my sight? And then I heard you scream. Hush now. You have only to tell the truth. I'll take the consequences."

Back went her mind, like a pendulum. "But—but what will happen now, to him?"

"Nothing has changed! You must face that! You really love him, don't you? But it's too late, Marisa—and even *he* understands that. So must you."

Everything came back to her in a rush, and she began to shake and cry helplessly in his arms.

"I only married Pedro because—because he promised—"

"Don't talk about it! Do you think I want to hear? You care nothing for a man's pride, do you, Marisa?"

"Pride—pride!" It was like a needle jabbed into her, forcing emotion back. "Is *that* what is most important to a man? And what about me? What about my pride and *my* feelings? Are they not important only because I happen to be a woman? Don't I count as a person? Doesn't it count what I want? I—for myself! I'm tired of being raped, of being protected and shunted off to safety for my own good! Oh, damn all men and their superior ways! From now on I'll stand on my own two feet and fight for what I want—any way I have to. With my body and my wits, and—and any other weapons I can think of to use! Why not? In your man's world, what other choice do you leave a woman who possesses a mind? Well, I'm going to use it—"

"Marisa!"

"I'm sorry if you do not like to hear the truth, Fernando. I'm grateful to you for what you did for me tonight. I'm not very strong physically as you saw, and if *you* wanted to take me by force now, I couldn't stop you. But it doesn't matter. If I have to endure it, what's one more rape? You'll never rape my mind, not you or—or Dominic—and all your talk of masculine pride cannot conquer me. While there's life in me and breath in me I'll be myself and belong to myself, no matter how many times I might have to lend out my body. Do you understand? Look at me—*see* me, Fernando!"

In the very doorway of the governor's house, she let his cloak slip from around her body and stood there unashamed and defiant while he mechanically gathered it up and put it about her again; he was confused and didn't really know what she meant.

"You're hysterical. I don't think you know what you are saying! Please try to calm yourself!"

"But I *am* calm. And I am sane and in the possession of my own mind—for the first time in my life, I think. I am glad Pedro is dead, and I am glad Dominic killed him. And, yes, I will tell the governor that. And no, I don't care any more for his stupid pride, any more than I care for yours or my own! You men can fight your stupid, senseless wars with each other; I'll fight my own battles for what I want—and in my own way!"

The door opened, and the governor stood there with a dressing gown thrown over his nightshirt; his sister-in-law was peering from behind a crack in the door down the hallway to his rear.

"What is the meaning—" And then recognizing her and seeing her condition, his jaw dropped. "Marisa! That is—señora—"

"You will please not call me by that name? I am not sure that my marriage to Pedro was legal especially since I have already borne a child to Dominic Challenger and am expecting another. And if it was—I am a widow. Pedro took me down in that dungeon in your prison and tried to rape me there. And then Fernando came to save me and distracted him. And Dominic—"

"This is all very interesting," said a calm, dry voice she remembered so well. "But I think we should find a more private place for the rest of your disclosure, my niece. And perhaps some clothes to cover yourself with? The cloak is hardly adequate in spite of the capitan's efforts."

The cloak dropped away completely as she ran towards him, uncaring.

"Uncle! Monsignor!" Her face, turned up to his, had

grown suddenly bright with hope. "You'll help me! You'll understand!"

"We would all do better, I think, if we were not distracted by your—er—condition, my child. You are not Eve, and this is not the Garden of Eden, you know!"

Chapter Sixty-one

His prison itself had been changed, and his condition—but not the fact of his imprisonment itself. There was food and water without rationing now, and the Spanish doctor came and went, frowning and shaking his head without saying much beyond giving certain orders. And having been close enough to death, to the point where the thought only held a feeling of welcome release instead of fear, Dominic Challenger found it hard to find himself still actually living and becoming daily more aware. Life had been forced upon him —but only so that he could look forward to dying.

He was still in a cell by himself, but at least it had a window—small and barred, set high in the thick adobe wall. There was a chain still attached to one of his ankles, but at least it was long enough to offer him enough freedom to walk about. From the day when he felt strong enough to stand up, he had walked, and he noticed after a while, with grim fatalism, that the stone floor had actually become slightly worn down in places by a previous occupant or occupants of this cell who must have walked just so, in the same patterns, back and forth, over and over. Waiting.

The young Spanish capitan he remembered vaguely and unwillingly came back to see him. He was admitted to the cell and stood stiffly just inside the heavy, barred door.

"I have come to tell you that—"

His voice was formal and stilted. Only his eyes were human.

Dominic leaned with his back against the wall, listening, with no expression at all and hardly any emotion.

"The monsignor, who returned—the viceroy. . . . In any case, the men who were with you are to be pardoned and allowed to return to the United States. It is hoped that they will discourage any others from following your unfortunate example, señor. In your case, however—" Dominic saw the young capitan's eyes waver and refuse to meet his; heard the jerky, staccato voice hesitate. Had Captain Higuera, of all people, been sent here to tell him as a penance? Well, he would not make it easy for him—why should he? Marisa's lover, who had come to save her from Pedro, while *he*—

To cut off his own thoughts, Dominic said evenly, "And in my case?"

Higuera's face looked wooden, and he cleared his throat. "You are not to be pardoned, nor will you be allowed to go back with the others. In fact, and you might as well know this, you were removed, while you were unconscious, to —another prison. The men who were with you were told that you—did not survive. And they believe this. In fact," he went on in a rush of quickly spoken words, "they were overheard talking together after they had been told, and I understand they decided that, in order to spare your—er— fiancée any further pain of mind, they would not mention your having survived the fighting."

"So now I do not exist?" Bitterness escaped him at last, mixed with frustrated anger. "My God! Why go to all the trouble of keeping me alive! Why didn't you just—" He bit off his words and managed a shrug, his voice more controlled this time. "Am I allowed to know what they intend to do with me? Or is it supposed to come as a surprise this time?"

The underlying sarcasm in his tone made Higuera flush darkly, but he maintained his wooden look. "You will be informed," he said shortly. "But not until after the other Americans have gone. And until then, you will be kept here, incommunicado. *I* will come to see you again from time to time, of course."

Why had he put that slight emphasis on the word? Or had he meant anything by it at all? Frowning, not moving, Dominic remained gazing at the door long after it had closed behind the capitan.

He had plenty of time in which to think, and to weigh and wonder unwillingly about every word Higuera had uttered. And time in which to pace from one end of the cell to the other as far as the chain would allow him to go, his feet following, quite naturally, the path that others had followed before him. Time itself had become meaningless, merely a succession of days and nights, glimpsed through the small window.

Dominic had been in prisons before as he reminded himself grimly, and this one was better than most. But was there ever a man shut up in one who did not wonder when he would be leaving it and for what?

The food was adequate, and they allowed him plenty of water. He ate when he was hungry and slept when he was tired and walked about the rest of the time merely to make himself tired enough so that he could sleep again. Was this how those unfortunates who had been cast into secret dungeons in the Bastille, in the days before the Revolution, had felt? After a while, there should come a sense of detachment, of no longer caring. In spite of Higuera's promise, he saw no one but the heavy-mustached guard who brought him food and water, always carrying a rifle and motioning him to stand back against the wall before he entered. The man never spoke a word, eying him as if he had been a dangerous animal, and Dominic was stubborn enough not to give way to the impulse to speak or ask him questions, either.

And yet, each time he heard the big key turn in its rusty lock and the door open, his nerves jumped. He raged at himself afterwards. Fool! Did he actually expect her to come? He was relieved that she didn't, that at last she seemed to have found enough sense to take him at his word. He didn't want to see her again, there would be no point in it, and, he admitted this much, it would be too painful. Marisa. Her golden ghost stayed with him no matter how hard he used his intellect to fight her off; she followed him into sleep most nights. He held her, wet and shivering and dressed as a cabin boy, against his body, feeling the frightened beating of her heart. He danced with her, smelling her perfume and catching the winking of jewels in her ears and around her slim throat. He lay with her, crushing her resistance when she fought against him like a wildcat, and enjoying her much, much more when she did not—when she returned his kisses fiercely and yielded her body to his without pretense or evasion.

Marisa! Oh, God, when had he begun to love her? At the very beginning, the night when they had been married and he'd run off with her, or later? When he'd known he had to send her away with the Comanches? From the first time— when had he not wanted her? The trouble was, he was not used to loving a woman. It was an emotion he was almost ashamed and frightened to admit feeling.

And after having sent her away from him, he hadn't wanted to find out that she'd been selling her body to one man and then another for revenge or in a mistaken attempt to save *him*. She had willingly thrown away her pride, and he had clung to his—and all for what?

He hoped the mysterious monsignor, her uncle, would take her away with him. Who knew better than he that she deserved something better? No, he did not want her to come, not now. The monsignor, no doubt, would be a practical man. And perhaps Capitan Higuera would be kind.

"Kamil was kind to me. He—he loved me!" Why must he keep remembering? Even Philip Sinclair, in his weak fashion, had been kind. And he had not.

He had been trying to sleep. Swearing aloud, Dominic dragged himself to his feet and began to pace again. Back and forth, covering over and over the short distance that was allowed to him. Damn! Why wouldn't they come for him? Why couldn't it be over with soon?

Captured between bars for a few minutes, the moon shone coldly into his cell and gave him no answer at all.

Even if she came, he would have to send her away. He was a man who had too long cheated death and was tired of the game. A man with nothing, a dead man who did not exist in the minds of all those who had known him. And Marisa was alive and was life. She would, and could, forget, in spite of all the passion in her body and in her voice when she had said, "Whatever I have done, it's because I love you. . . ." It was the first time she had said so. And she had met with rejection.

Why didn't they come? Or was he to be left here forever? The cell was dark, and Dominic had almost fallen asleep when Capitan Higuera came, preceded by a flaring torch held upright by the guard who always attended to him.

"I was told to ask," the capitan said in his stiff voice, "whether you would come with me willingly and without resistance. In which case I shall have the fetters struck off you. If not, I shall be forced to take you with a gag in your mouth. Either way, you are going from here, and I will have a pistol held against your side all the while."

"Told to ask—by whom?" The sleepiness disappearing from them, Dominic Challenger's eyes looked like silver shields, shutting off all emotion or reaction as he came to his feet easily, looking from one man to the other with one eyebrow raised as if such a summons did not matter to him in the least.

Fernando Higuera found himself hating this man as well as resenting his attitude, even while he managed to control the strain in his voice.

"The monsignor. And the viceroy himself, who came here with him. But I have not had *your* answer yet, señor."

"Am I really left with a choice? To tell the truth, these chains have grown burdensome, like my incarceration here in this little room. Did you need my word that I would not try to escape, nor cry out for help? I'm sure your pistol will see to that!"

They sat beside each other on the seat of a rough, open wagon, with the taciturn guard sitting behind, the muzzle of his rifle touching between Dominic's shoulder blades as a reminder. The capitan was obviously unhappy over this errand he had been sent to perform; but for himself, Dominic was too occupied with breathing in deep gulps of the cool, fresh night air and watching the stars which seemed pasted to the sky overhead, to care.

To be under the open sky again, breathing fresh air, was enough for the moment. Soon enough, he would find out what the monsignor wanted with him.

It became darker when they left buildings and lamp light behind them; and yet, somehow, the thought of escape at all costs seemed to have left him. The monsignor. A Richelieu or a Mazarin born out of his time, perhaps. As a man, what would he be like?

661

The journey to wherever they were going must have covered several miles although it seemed all too short. Halfway, the mustached guard who had hardly seemed human before, passed up a wineskin, still without a word, and still holding the rifle steadily. Dominic took it with a murmured "gracias," letting some of the warm, strong liquid pour down his throat. Higuera, he noticed, said nothing at all; but he drove the horses to move faster, swearing at them under his breath.

The wind was gone before faint lights loomed up before them—soon multiplied and intensified by torches held by vaqueros and uniformed soldiers. There were wagons all around telling of recent arrivals—or hasty departure.

"The monsignor is in the sala. He has been waiting."

The rifle still at his back, Dominic walked past the lights and the impassive, incurious faces and found himself in a room that was surprisingly small and austerely furnished. The man who turned around at his entrance seemed just as austere and not at all as he had imagined. A tall, spare man dressed in a plain black habit, like a Jesuit monk, a silver cross winking on his chest. Only his blue eyes, set deeply under blond eyebrows, showed a resemblance to his brother Don Andres.

The rifle was no longer at his back, and the door closed behind him. Without the chains he had grown used to, Dominic felt strangely clumsy. What was he supposed to do? Fall on his knees and kiss his ring?

And then, from a corner of the room where he had not noticed her, Marisa flew at him, barefoot, the marks of tears still streaking her face.

"Dominic—Dominic!"

She fell against him like a small invasion, and his arms, still unused to freedom, seemed to go around her of their own accord. He forgot about her uncle, smelling the sweetness of her hair and rediscovering the sweetness of her body pressed against his. He was either drunk with wine or dreaming again, but it didn't seem to matter as she turned her mouth up to his.

EPILOGUE

❧

All the Answers

Chapter Sixty-two

On a dark night, inflamed with love's desires,
oh sweet happiness, I went forth unnoticed, when
my house was already asleep . . .

She whispered to him, not caring if it was sacrilegious, the
spiritual songs of San Juan de la Cruz.

I know very well that the fountain spurts and flows,
though it is night. This eternal and secret fountain—I
know very well its hiding place, though it is night.
Its source I do not know, perhaps none there is . . . but
I know all take its beginning from it, though it is night.
I know there can be nothing so beautiful . . . though it
is night.

Marisa felt his arms go about her, his breath warm against
her cheek as he asked, slightly amused, "Is *that* what you
were taught when you were learning to become a nun?"

She shook her head. "It was what I enjoyed most, while I
tried. It sounded so beautiful, even then, but now I think
I understand. Dominic?" Her eyes searched for his shadowed
face in the darkness, catching only the star-flame faintly reflected in his eyes.

"What is it now? No more poems, love. It's night, and
you're beautiful, and I'm hungry for you—I think I always
will be."

"And I for you," she whispered, feeling his muscles tense
under her hands before his lips searched for hers and found
them.

And then, only then, at times when reality and dreams merged and she was held closely in his arms, could she bear to think of the weeks and months past. The torture of time and hours crawling by like scorpions over her skin when she thought she could not endure, could not, and did, all the same.

The Americans left, to go back home, and then she had waited, fighting and screaming against her uncle's inexorable kindness and patience until at last, already feeling the movements of her second child inside her, she saw her first clinging to the hand of his nurse and foster mother, who would not leave him. Selma-Bab—she couldn't think of her any differently.

And the woman herself saying constrainedly, "And where are we going from here? The poor child's worn out with traveling and with everything so new and different!"

It was the monsignor, Marisa's uncle who had answered her, his voice gentle and yet firm. "To California. I have business there, if you can call it so. And I have obtained from the viceroy the deed to a large land grant made out in the name of my niece and her husband."

"Husband?" It would take more than that to quiet the militant New England soul of the woman, but she had grown quieter and less prickly when she found out what he meant.

"You have created quite a problem, theologically," the monsignor had murmured to Marisa in his dry voice. "When I obtained an annulment, I had not known there was a child of your union. And now, with another one on the way—" He'd sighed, steepling his fingers. "I will marry you again, to make sure. And find out, in the meantime, if I can annul an annulment! *This* time, however, you are both certain of what you want?"

This time, it seemed, they both were; and on the long journey overland, the monsignor made it a point to tactfully leave them alone.

Through Marisa, Dominic found himself a Spanish citizen; and if his pride had started to balk at the idea in the beginning, the reality of having her and being able to hold her in his arms again kept him silent on the subject. It seemed that even Paulus and Lalie were to join them—being uneasy where they were.

They would all start out anew in a new, raw land with the ocean on one side and the mountains on the other. A challenge. All the more so because Marisa's second child, another boy, was born there before there was time to erect more than the roughest kind of shelter, a brush and adobe hut such as the Indians might have put up.

This time too, Selma was with her, holding her hands and wiping the sweat from her writhing body. It brought the two women, so different, closer together.

When it was over though, it was Dominic who gently sponged her perspiring body and lay beside her, watching her hold her newly born child to her breast.

"If I had known how much you had to suffer to give birth to a child, I might not have lain with you, love." He lifted the now-long heavy masses of her tangled hair and kissed her very gently on the temple, where a pulse beat.

"And if you had not," she whispered, "I would not have known this peace inside me."

Peggy was laid to rest at last as were the devils that had ridden him for so long as he felt her fingers mesh with his and her head come to rest against his shoulder.

The monsignor had already gone on to the Mission San José. Through a gap in the carelessly erected roof, the moon that had already seen so much shone through on both of them, giving them her own kind of absolution—and promise.

It is shocking. It is intimate.
It is the one novel her millions
of readers dare not miss . . .

THE
CROWD
PLEASERS
ROSEMARY
ROGERS

"It's sweet/savage cinema verite
every page of the way."
Publishers Weekly

CPL 1-79